KT-366-878

Santa Montefiore

The BUTTERFLY BOX

SIMON & SCHUSTER

London · New York · Sydney · Toronto · New Delhi

First published in Great Britain by Hodder & Stoughton, 2002

First published in Great Britain by Simon & Schuster UK Ltd, 2014

This paperback edition published 2020

Copyright © Santa Montefiore, 2002

The right of Santa Montefiore to be identified as author of this work has been
asserted in accordance with the Copyright, Designs and Patents Act, 1988.

With thanks to Gibran National Committee for granting their
permission to quote from Kahil Gibran's *The Prophet*

1 3 5 7 9 10 8 6 4 2

Simon & Schuster UK Ltd
1st Floor
222 Gray's Inn Road
London WC1X 8HB

Simon & Schuster Australia, Sydney
Simon & Schuster India, New Delhi

www.simonandschuster.co.uk
www.simonandschuster.com.au
www.simonandschuster.co.in

A CIP catalogue record for this book is available from the British Library

Paperback ISBN: 978-1-4711-9645-4
eBook ISBN: 978-1-4711-3211-7

This book is a work of fiction.
Names, characters, places and incidents are either a
product of the author's imagination or are used fictitiously.
Any resemblance to actual people living or dead,
events or locales is entirely coincidental.

Printed and bound by CPI Group (UK) Ltd, Croydon, CR0 4YY

MIX
Paper from
responsible sources
FSC® C020471

Praise for
Santa Montefiore

'Nobody does epic romance like Santa Montefiore. Everything she writes, she writes from the heart'
JOJO MOYES

'Santa Montefiore at her best – an enchanting read overflowing with deliciously poignant moments'
DINAH JEFFERIES

'One of our personal favourites … sweeping stories of love and families spanning continents and decades'
THE TIMES

'Santa Montefiore is the new Rosamunde Pilcher'
DAILY MAIL

'I have a tenderness for sweeping and epic romantic sagas set around huge houses and aristocratic families, and Santa Montefiore hits the spot for me like few other writers'
SARRA MANNING

'A superb storyteller of love and death in romantic places in fascinating times'
VOGUE

'Anyone who likes Joanne Harris or Mary Wesley will love Montefiore'
MAIL ON SUNDAY

'A gripping romance … it is as believable as the writing is beautiful'
DAILY TELEGRAPH

Born in England in 1970, Santa Montefiore grew up in Hampshire. She is married to writer Simon Sebag Montefiore. They live with their two children, Lily and Sasha, in London.

Visit Santa at www.santamontefiore.co.uk and sign up for her newsletter.

Also by Santa Montefiore

The Affair
The Italian Matchmaker
The French Gardener
Sea of Lost Love
The Gypsy Madonna
Last Voyage of the Valentina
The Swallow and the Hummingbird
The Forget-Me-Not Sonata
Meet Me Under the Ombu Tree
The House by the Sea
The Summer House
Secrets of the Lighthouse
The Beekeeper's Daughter
The Temptation of Gracie
The Secret Hours
Here and Now

The Deverill Chronicles

Songs of Love and War
Daughters of Castle Deverill
The Last Secret of the Deverills

To my parents

Love gives naught but itself and takes naught but from itself.
Love possesses not nor would it be possessed;
For love is sufficient unto love.

Kahlil Gibran, The Prophet

PART ONE

Chapter 1

Viña del Mar, Chile, Summer 1982

Federica opened her eyes onto a different world. It was hot, but not humid for the sea breeze carried with it a cool undercurrent from where it had dallied among the waves of the cold Pacific Ocean. Her room was slowly coming to life in the pale morning light that spilled in through the gap in the curtains, casting mellow shafts onto the floor and walls, swallowing up the remains of the night, exposing the regimental line of sleeping dolls. The constant barking of Señora Baraca's dog at the end of the street had left the animal with little more than a raw husk, but he still continued to bark as he always did. Some day he'd lose his voice altogether, she thought, which wouldn't be a bad thing; at least he wouldn't keep the neighbours awake. She had once tried to feed him a biscuit on her way to school but her mother had said he was probably riddled with all sorts of diseases. 'Best not to touch him, you don't know where he's been,' she had advised, pulling her six-year-old daughter away by the hand. But that was the problem; he had never been anywhere. Federica breathed in the sweet scent of the orange trees that floated up on the air and she could almost taste the fruit that hung heavily like lustrous packages on a Christmas tree. She kicked off the sheet that covered her and knelt on the end of her bed, leaning out through the curtains onto a world that wasn't the same as the one the sun had set on the day before. With the rising of the new sun a quiver ran through her skinny body, causing a broad smile to spread across her pale face. Today her father was coming home after many months travelling.

Ramon Campione was a giant of a man. Not only in stature – at well over six foot he was tall for a Chilean and tall for an Italian, which was where his family originated from – but in his gigantic imagination, which, like the galaxy itself, seemed never-ending and full of surprises. His adventures took him to the far corners of the earth where he was inspired by everything different and everything beautiful. He travelled, wrote and travelled some more. His family barely knew him. He was never around long enough for them to find the person behind the writing and the magical photographs he took. In the mind of his daughter he was more powerful than God. She had once told Padre Amadeo that Jesus was nothing compared to her father who could do so much more than turn water into wine. 'My papa can fly,' she had said proudly. Her mother had smiled apologetically to the priest and rolled her eyes, explaining to him quietly that Ramon had tried out a new contraption in Switzerland for flying off the mountain on skis. Padre Amadeo had nodded in understanding but later shook his head and worried that the child would only get hurt when her father toppled, as he surely would some day, off the tall pedestal she had so blindly placed him upon. She should focus such devotion on God not man, he thought piously.

Federica longed for it to be time to get up, but it was still early. The sky was as pale and still as a large, luminous lagoon and only the barking dog and the clamour of birds resounded against the quiet stirring of dawn. From her bedroom she could see the ocean disappearing into the grey mists on the horizon as if the heavens were drinking it up. Her mother often took them to Caleta Abarca beach, as they didn't have a swimming pool to cool off in, although the sea was almost too cold for bathing. Sometimes they would drive to the small seaside village of Cachagua, about an hour up the coast, to stay with her grandparents who owned a pretty thatched summerhouse there surrounded by tall palms and acacia trees. Federica loved the sea. Her father had once said that she loved the sea because she was born under the sign of Cancer whose symbol was a crab. She didn't much like crabs though.

After a long while she heard footsteps on the stairs then the high-pitched voice of her younger brother Enrique, nick-named Hal after Shakespeare's 'Prince Henry'. That had been Ramon's idea – although his wife was English she had no interest in literature or history unless it was about her.

'Darling, you're dressed already!' Helena gasped in surprise as Federica jumped across the landing and into Hal's bedroom where she was dressing him.

'Papa's coming home today!' she sang, unable to remain still even for a moment.

'Yes, he is,' replied Helena, taking a deep breath to restrain the resentment she felt towards her absent husband. 'Keep your feet still, Hal darling, I can't put your shoes on if you keep moving.'

'Will he be here before lunch?' asked Federica, automatically helping her mother by opening the curtains, allowing the warm sunshine to flood into the dim room with the enthusiasm that belongs only to the morning.

'He'll be here sometime before noon, his flight gets in at ten,' she replied patiently. 'There, sweetie, you look very handsome,' she added, smoothing back Hal's black hair with a soft brush. He shook his head in protest and squealed before wriggling off the bed and running out onto the landing.

'I put on my best dress for him,' said Federica, following her mother down the stairs with buoyant footsteps.

'So I see,' she replied.

'I'm going to help Lidia cook lunch today. We're making Papa's favourite dish.'

'What's that then?'

'*Pastel de choclo* and we're making him *merengon de lúcuma* as a welcome home cake,' said Federica, flicking her straight blonde hair off her shoulders so that it fell thickly down her back. She had pushed it off her forehead with a hair-band, which along with her small stature made her appear younger than her six years.

'Papa's coming home today,' said Federica to Hal as she helped her mother lay the table.

'Will he bring me a present?' asked Hal, who at four years of age remembered his father only for the presents he gave.

'Of course he will, sweetie. He always brings you presents,' said Helena, placing a cup of cold milk in front of him. 'Anyway, it's Christmas so you'll be getting loads of presents.' Federica supervised Hal while he dipped his spoon into the tin of powdered chocolate and dropped it into his milk. She then grabbed the cloth from the sink to mop up the chocolate that hadn't quite made it to the cup.

'Fede, the croissants are ready, I can smell them beginning to burn,' said Helena, lighting a cigarette. She looked anxiously at the clock on the wall and bit her lower lip. She knew she should take the children to the airport to pick him up as other mothers would. But she couldn't face it. The awkward drive from Santiago airport to the coast, all the while making conversation as if everything was positively rosy. No, it would be much better to see him at home, the house was big, more space for them to lose each other in. How silly, she thought bitterly, they had lost each other a long time ago somewhere in the vast distances they had placed between themselves. Somewhere in the faraway lands and imaginary characters that seemed so much more important to

Ramon than the people in his life who were real and who needed him. She had tried. She had really tried. But now she was empty inside and tired of being neglected.

Federica buttered a croissant and sipped her iced chocolate, chattering away to her brother with an excitement that made her voice rise in tone, irritating the raw nerves of her mother who stood by the window blowing smoke against the glass. Once they had been in love, but even hate was an expression of love, just a different face. Now Helena no longer hated him, that alone would have been a good enough reason to stay. But she felt indifference and it frightened her. Nothing could grow out of that. It was a barren emotion, as barren as the face of the moon.

Helena had made a life for herself in Chile because she had believed, as did her daughter later, that Ramon was God. He was certainly the most glamorous, handsome man Polperro had ever seen. Then his article had appeared in *National Geographic* with photographs of all the old smugglers' caves and crumbling castles Helena had shown him, and yet somehow the photographs were suffused with a light that didn't belong to Nature. There was something mystical about them that she couldn't put her finger on. Every word he wrote sung out to her and stayed with her long after she had turned the last page. Now she recognized the magic as love, for it had followed them for the first six years, converting even the most mundane things, like filling the car up with petrol, into a magical experience. Their lovemaking had pertained to another plain far above the physical and she had believed that the power was within him and in him alone. Only after it had gone did she realize that the connection had been cut – like electricity, their 'magic' had been caused by the two of them and ceased the minute one of them felt disenchanted by it. Once it had gone it was gone for ever. That kind of sorcery is of high energy but low life span. At first they had travelled together, to the far corners of China, to the arid deserts of Egypt and the wet lakes of Sweden. When she became pregnant with Federica they returned to settle in Chile. Their 'magic' had followed them there too where the white powder coast and pastoral simplicity had enchanted her. But now it echoed with the emptiness she felt within her own being because the love that had filled it had drained away. There was no reason to stay. She was tired of pretending. She was tired of pretending to herself. She longed for the drizzly, verdant hills of her youth and her longing made her hand shake. She lit another cigarette and once more eyed the clock.

Federica cleared away her breakfast, humming to herself and skipping around the kitchen as she did so. Hal played with his train in the nursery. Helena remained by the window.

'Mama!' shouted Hal. 'My train is broken, it's not working.' Helena picked up her packet of cigarettes and strode out of the kitchen, leaving Federica to finish clearing up. Once the table was wiped and the crockery washed up she put on her cooking apron and waited for Lidia to arrive.

When Lidia bustled through the gate she saw Federica's small eager face pressed up against the glass, smiling broadly at her.

'*Hola*, Señorita,' she said breathlessly as she entered the hall. 'You're ready early.'

'I've even cleared away the breakfast,' replied Federica in Spanish. Although her mother spoke excellent Spanish they had always spoken English as a family, even when her father was home.

'Well, you *are* a good girl,' Lidia wheezed, following the child into the kitchen. 'Ah, you angel. You've done all the work,' she said, casting her dark eyes over the mixing bowls and spoons already laid out on the table.

'I want it all to be perfect for Papa,' she said, her cheeks aflame. She could barely contain her impatience and suppressed her desire to run by skipping instead of walking. That way the nervous feeling in her stomach was indulged a little but not too much. Lidia struggled into her pink overalls then washed her swollen brown hands. She suggested Federica do the same.

'You must always wash your hands before cooking, you don't know where they've been,' she said.

'Like Señora Baraca's dog,' giggled Federica.

'*Pobrecito*,' Lidia sighed, tilting her round head to one side and pulling a thin, sympathetic smile. 'He's tied up all day in that small garden, it's no wonder he barks from dawn till dusk.'

'Doesn't she take him out at all?' Federica asked, running her hands under the tap.

'Oh yes, she takes him out occasionally, but she's old,' Lidia replied, 'and we old people don't have as much energy for things like that.'

'You're not old, Lidia,' said Federica kindly.

'Not old, just fat,' said Helena in English, walking into the kitchen with Hal's toy engine. 'She'd have much more energy if she didn't eat so much. Imagine carrying that bulk around all day, no wonder she wheezes all the time.'

'*Buenos días, Señora*,' said Lidia, who didn't understand English.

'Good morning, Lidia. I need a knife to mend this blasted train,' said Helena in Spanish, not even bothering to force a smile, however small. She was too anxious and impatient to think of anyone else but herself.

'I wouldn't worry about that, Don Ramon will be home soon and he can fix it. That's men's work,' said Lidia cheerfully.

'Thank you, Lidia, that's very helpful. Fede, pass me a knife,' she said edgily. Federica handed her the knife and watched her walk out again.

'Oh, it's so exciting that your Papa is coming home,' enthused Lidia, embracing Federica fondly. 'I'll bet you didn't sleep a wink.'

'Not a wink,' she replied, looking up at the clock. 'He'll be here soon,' she said and Lidia noticed that her small hands trembled when she began to cut the butter up into pieces.

'Careful you don't cut yourself,' she said gently. 'You don't want your Papa to come back to a daughter with only seven fingers.' She laughed, then wheezed and coughed.

Helena, who was usually very deft at mending things, broke the engine. Hal started to cry. Helena pulled him into her arms and managed to cheer him up by promising him another engine, a bigger, better one. 'Anyway, this engine was old and tatty. What use is an engine like that? The train looks much better without his engine,' she said and thought how much she'd like to be a carriage on her own without an engine. She lit another cigarette. The doors to the garden were open, inviting in the gentle sea breeze that smelt of oranges and ozone. It was too hot to be sitting in suburbia, they should be down on the beach, she thought in frustration. She wiped her sweating brow with her hand then looked at her watch. Her throat constricted. His plane would have landed.

Federica and Lidia buzzed about the kitchen like a couple of bees in a flowerbed. Federica loved to be included and followed Lidia's instructions with great enthusiasm. She felt like a grown-up and Lidia treated her as one. They chatted about Lidia's back pain and her stomach cramps and her husband's verruca, which was giving him a lot of trouble. 'I'm afraid of putting my feet where he's put his,' she explained, 'so I wear a pair of socks even in the shower.'

'I would too,' Federica agreed, not sure what a verruca was.

'You're sensible like me,' Lidia replied, smiling down at the skinny child who had a manner well beyond her years. Lidia thought she was far too grown-up for a child of almost seven but one only had to look at her mother to understand why. Helena gave her so much responsibility, too much probably, that the child would be quite capable of running the entire household without her.

When Helena entered the kitchen the smell of *pastel de choclo* swelled her senses and her stomach churned with hunger and tension combined. Federica was drying up while Lidia washed the utensils and mixing bowls. Helena managed to grab the remains of the cream before Lidia's podgy hands pulled it into the soapy water. She scraped her finger around the bottom of the bowl and brought it up to her pale lips. 'Well done you, sweetie,' she said, impressed. She smiled at her daughter and stroked her hand down her shiny blonde hair. 'You're a very good cook.' Federica smiled, accustomed to her mother's changeable nature. One minute she was irritable, the next minute she was agreeable, not like her father who was always cheerful and carefree. Helena's praise delighted Federica as it always did and her spirits soared until she seemed to grow an inch taller.

'She's not only a good cook, Señora, but she's a good housekeeper, too,' said Lidia fondly, the large black mole on her chin quivering as her face creased into a wide smile. 'She cleaned up all the breakfast by herself,' she added in a mildly accusing tone, for Señora Helena always left everything to her daughter.

'I know,' Helena replied. 'What I would do without her, I can't imagine,' she said nonchalantly, flicking her cigarette ash into the bin and leaving the room. She walked upstairs. She was weary. Her heart weighed her down so that even the stairs were an effort to climb. She walked along the cool white corridor, her bare feet padding over the wooden floorboards, her hand too disenchanted even to deadhead the pots of pale orchids as she passed. In her bedroom the white linen curtains played about with the silk breeze as if they were trying to open all by themselves. Irritably she pulled them apart and looked out across the sea. It lay tremulous and iridescent, beckoning her to sail away with it to another place. The horizon promised her freedom and a new life.

'Mama, shall I help you tidy your room?' Federica asked quietly. Helena turned around and looked at the small, earnest face of her daughter.

'I suppose you want to tidy it up for Papa?' she replied, grabbing an ashtray and stubbing her cigarette into it.

'Well, I've picked some flowers . . .' she said sheepishly.

Helena's heart lurched. She pitied her daughter for the love she felt for her father in spite of the long absences that should have made her hate him. But no, she loved him unconditionally and the more he went away the happier she was to see him when he returned, running into his arms like a grateful lover. She longed to tell her the truth and shatter her illusions, out of spite because she wished she still shared those illusions. She found the world of children so blissfully simplistic and she envied her.

'All right, Fede. You tidy it up for Papa, he'll love the flowers, I'm sure,' she said tightly. 'Just ignore me,' she added, wandering into the bathroom and closing the door behind her. Federica heard her switch on the shower and the water pound against the enamel bath. She then made the bed, scenting the sheets with fresh lavender like her grandmother had shown her and placed a small blue vase of honeysuckle on her father's bedside table. She folded her mother's clothes and placed them in the old oak cupboard, rearranging the mess that she found there until all the shelves resembled a well-organized shop. She opened the windows as wide as they could go so that the scents of the garden and the sea would spirit away the dirty smell of her mother's smoke. Then she sat at her dressing table and picked up an old photograph of her father that grinned out at her from behind the glass of an ornate silver frame. He was very good looking with glossy black hair, swarthy skin, shiny brown eyes that were honest and intelligent and a large mouth that smiled the crooked smile of a man with an irreverent sense of humour and easy charm. She ran her thumb across the glass and caught her pensive expression in the mirror. In her reflection she saw only her mother. The pale blonde hair, the pale blue eyes, the pale pink lips, the pale skin – she wished she had inherited her father's dark Italian looks. He was so handsome and no doubt Hal would be handsome just like him. But Federica was used to getting a lot of attention because of her flowing white hair. All the other girls in her class were dark like Hal. People stared at her when she went into Valparaíso with her mother and Señora Escobar, who ran the sandwich shop on the square, called her 'La Angelita' (the little angel) because she couldn't believe that a human being could have such pale hair. Helena's best friend, Lola Miguens, had tried to copy her by dying her black hair blonde with peroxide, but had lost her nerve half way through so now she walked around with hair the colour of their terracotta roof, which Federica thought looked very ugly. Her mother didn't bother to look after herself like Chilean women who always had long manicured nails, perfect lipstick and immaculate clothes. Helena bustled about with her hair scrunched carelessly up onto the top of her head and she usually had a cigarette hanging out of her mouth. Federica thought she was beautiful when she made an effort and judging by old photographs she was once very beautiful indeed. But recently she had let herself go. Federica hoped she would make an effort for her father.

Helena stepped out of the bathroom followed by a puff of steam. Her face was pink and her eyes sparkled from the moisture. Federica lay on the white damask bedspread and watched her mother dress and prepare herself for her husband's return. Helena could smell the lavender and the ripe scent of oranges and refrained from lighting another cigarette. She felt guilty. Federica was so excited she quivered like a horse in the starting gate while *she* awaited Ramon's return with trepidation and the secret knowledge that any moment now she'd gather together her courage and leave him for good. As she painted her face she watched her daughter in the mirror while she didn't know that she was being watched. She stared out of the window across the sea as if her father was arriving by boat and not by car. Her profile was childish and yet her expression was that of a grown woman. The anxious expectation in her frown and on her trembling lips betrayed too much awareness for a child her age. She worshipped her father with the devotion of a dog, whereas Hal worshipped his mother whom, Helena felt, was more deserving of his love.

When Helena was ready, in a pair of tight white trousers and T-shirt, her hair scrunched up on her head, still damp and knotted, she sat on the bed beside her daughter and ran a damp hand down her face.

'You look lovely, sweetie. You really do,' she said and kissed her innocent brow affectionately.

'He'll be here soon, won't he?' said Federica softly.

'Any minute,' Helena replied, masking the tremor in her voice with a deftness that came from years of practice. She got up abruptly and hurried down the stairs. She couldn't smoke in the bedroom, not after Federica had prepared it so lovingly, but she was in desperate need of a cigarette. Just as she reached the bottom, her espadrilles landing on the cold stone tiles of the hallway, the front door swung open and Ramon filled the entrance like a large black wolf. Helena gasped and felt her stomach lurch. They stared at each other, wordlessly assessing the frigid estrangement that still grew up between them whenever they found themselves together in the same room.

'Fede, Papa's here!' Helena shouted, but as impassive as her features were her voice croaked with repressed emotion. Ramon's dark brown eyes pulled away from the stony countenance of his wife in search of his daughter whom he heard squeal with delight from the landing before the soft patter of her small feet scurried across the floorboards and skipped down the stairs two at a time. She jumped past her mother and into her father's sturdy embrace. She wrapped her thin arms around his bristly neck, nuzzling her face into his throat and inhaling the heavy, spicy scent that made him different from everyone else in the world. He kissed her warm cheek, lifting her off the ground and laughing so loudly she felt the vibration shake against her body like an earthquake.

'So you missed me!' he said, swinging her around until she had to wrap her legs about his waist to stop herself from falling.

'Yes, Papa!' she laughed, clinging on as her happiness almost choked her.

At that moment Hal ran into the hall, took one look at his father and burst into tears. Helena, grateful for the distraction, ran to him and picked him up in her arms, kissing his wet cheek. 'It's Papa, Hal darling, he's come home,' she said, trying to boost her voice with a bit of enthusiasm but her tone was dead and Hal sensed it and cried again. Ramon put his daughter down and walked over to where his son was weeping in his mother's arms.

'Halcito, it's Papa,' he said, smiling into the child's frightened face with his large, generous mouth. Hal buried his head in Helena's neck and wriggled closer against her.

'I'm sorry, Ramon,' she said flatly, sensing his disappointment but secretly taking pleasure from the child's rejection. She wanted to tell him that he couldn't expect his children to love him when he took no part in their lives, but she saw Federica's love set her cheeks aflame and the admiration shine in her pale, trusting eyes and knew that it wasn't entirely true. Nevertheless, he didn't deserve his daughter's love.

'I've got a present for you, Hal,' he said, walking back to his bag and unzipping it. 'And I've got one for you too, Fede,' he added as his daughter placed an affectionate hand on his back as he rummaged around for his gifts. 'Ah, this is for you, Hal,' he said, walking over to the little boy whose eyes opened wide at the brightly painted wooden train that his father waved in front of him. He forgot his fear and held his hands out. 'There, I thought you'd like that.'

'I broke his engine today,' said Helena, making an effort for the sake of the children. 'That couldn't have come at a better time, could it, Hal?'

'Good,' Ramon replied, retreating to his case.

'Now where's yours, Fede? I've got you a very special present,' he said, looking up at her expectant face. He felt her hand on his back again. It was so typical of Federica who always had to have some sort of physical contact to feel close. His hands burrowed deep into the bag that was filled not with clothes but with notepads, camera equipment and souvenirs from faraway countries. Finally his fingers felt the rough surface of tissue paper. He pulled it out, taking care not to knock it against the hard metal of his equipment. 'Here,' he said, pressing it into her trembling hands.

'Thank you, Papa,' she breathed, unwrapping it carefully. Hal had run off into the nursery to play with his new train. Helena lit a cigarette and smoked it nervously, leaning back against the banisters.

'So how are you?' he asked without approaching her.

'Fine, you know, nothing's changed,' she replied coldly.

'Good,' he said.

Helena sighed wearily. 'We have to talk, Ramon.'

'Not now.'

'Of course.'

'Later.'

Federica unwrapped the paper to discover a roughly carved wooden box. It wasn't pretty. It wasn't even charming. She felt the tears prick the backs of her eyes and her throat constrict with disappointment. Not because she wanted a nicer present, she wasn't materialistic or spoilt, but because Hal's present had been so much more beautiful than hers. She understood his presents as a reflection of his love. He couldn't love her very much if he hadn't even bothered to find her a pretty gift.

'Thank you, Papa,' she choked, swallowing back her tears in shame. 'It's very nice.' But she didn't have the strength to rebel against her emotions. The excitement had been too much, now the disappointment threw her into a sudden low and the tears welled and spilled out over her hot cheeks.

'*Fede, mi amor*,' he said, pulling her into his arms and kissing her wet face.

'It's nice,' she said, trying to sound grateful and not wishing to offend him.

'Open it,' he whispered into her ear. She hesitated. 'Go on, *amorcita*, open it.' She opened it with a shaking hand. The little box might have been plain on the outside, ugly even, but inside it was the most beautiful thing she had ever seen, and what's more it played the strangest, most alluring tune she had ever heard.

Chapter 2

Federica stared into the box in awe. The entire interior was covered with neatly cut stones of every colour that shimmered as if each little gem contained a small heart of light all its very own. There was not one patch of wood, not even a minute piece, that lay exposed between the mesmerizing crystals. From within, the box appeared to be made solely out of jewels and not out of wood at all, like the core of a crystallized piece of rock. On the floor of the box trembled the delicate wings of a butterfly that varied in colour from a dark ink blue against her body to the palest of aquamarines and finally amber. So delicate were they that Federica placed a finger onto the surface in order to convince herself that they were really stones and not drops of glittering water from some enchanted pool. A strange, iridescent light caused the butterfly to shudder as if about to extend her wings and fly away. Federica moved the box about slowly to see where the light was coming from and at once she was taken by the magical movement of the butterfly who, as she tilted the box, seemed to change from blues to pinks, reds and oranges. She caught her breath and put the box straight again. The butterfly returned to her cool sea tones before changing once more into fire as Federica tilted the box again.

'It's beautiful,' she sniffed without taking her eyes off the sparkling treasure chest.

'Beauty isn't always on the outside, Fede,' he said softly, hugging her. He looked up at his wife who still stood stiffly against the banisters, blowing smoke into the air like a dragon. She sighed impatiently and shook her head before walking out of the hall into the corridor, the smoke floating eerily behind her like a phantom. She wanted to tell him that he couldn't buy his daughter's love with presents all the time. But regretfully she knew he didn't have to buy it at all; he already had it for free.

Ramon stood up and tore his eyes away from the trail of smoke, which, along with the ill feeling, was all that remained of his wife. He looked down at the radiant face of his daughter, oblivious to the tension that caused the atmosphere to quiver with the invisible force of disappointment. He ran a hand over his unshaven face and down his dirty black hair that was long and reached his shoulders. It was hot. He needed air and he needed a swim. He had looked forward to returning home, built it up in his mind, romanticized it. But now he was home he wanted to leave again. Home was always a rosier place in the mirages of his mind. It was better to leave it there.

'Come, Fede,' he said. 'Let's go down to the beach, just you and me. Bring the box with you.' Federica jumped to her feet, clasped her treasure against her thin chest and, taking his hand, she followed him out through the front door.

'What about Mama and Hal?' she said, delirious with happiness that she had been chosen to go with him and she alone.

'Hal's happy with his train and Mama's with him. Besides, I want to tell you how I found your box. There's a very sad legend attached to it and I know how you like stories.'

'I love your stories,' she replied, skipping along to keep up with his lengthy strides.

Helena watched helplessly as her husband left the house, taking with him the overbearing weight of his presence and suddenly she felt cheated, as if the pressure that had built up inside her chest had been for nothing. The house felt still and somehow bigger than when his powerful body had dwarfed it and she bit her lip in frustration. 'How dare he leave us,' she thought bitterly, 'why can't he just stick around for once?'

The midday sun was scorching in spite of the sea breeze that cooled it off around the edges. They walked down the street, passing Señora Baraca's dog who pulled on his leash and let out a frenzied round of barks when he saw them. Federica told her father how the dog barked all the time because he wanted to run about and wasn't able to in his small garden.

'Well, let's take him out then,' said Ramon.

'Really? Can we?' she replied in excitement. She watched with pride as her father rang the bell. They waited in the shade of an almond tree. The sound of children playing in the street resounded through the air, their laughter like the song of sea birds on the beaches. Federica didn't wish to be with them. She wished only that her father would stay this time and never go away again.

'*Sí?*' came a voice from behind the door. It was deep and guttural, muffled by the phlegm that caught in her throat.

'Señora Baraca. It's Ramon Campione,' he said with the assertiveness that pertained to everything he did. Federica pulled herself up, copying her father who always walked tall.

'Ramon Campione, indeed,' she replied, venturing out of the house like a timid crow. She was old and bent and wore a black dress of mourning even though her husband had died more than ten years before. 'I thought you were the other side of the world,' she croaked.

'I'm home now,' he replied, softening his voice a little so as not to frighten her. Federica held tightly on to his hand.

'My daughter would very much like to take your dog for a walk on the beach. Perhaps we could do you the favour of exercising him.'

The old woman chewed on her gums for a moment. 'Well, I know you, so you won't be stealing him,' she replied. 'Perhaps you could shut him up for me. If I don't go insane with grief, I'll go insane with the barking.'

'We'll do our best for you,' he said and smiled courteously. 'Won't we, Fede?' Federica cowered behind him and lowered her eyes shyly. Señora Baraca's knotted fingers fumbled clumsily with the lead, the hairs on her chin illuminated like cobwebs by the sun. Finally she opened the gate and handed the dog to Ramon. The dog stopped barking and began to jump about, puffing and snorting with the enthusiasm of a freed prisoner.

'His name is Rasta,' she said, hands on hips. 'My son gave him to me before he disappeared for good. That's all I have left. I'd rather have my son, he made much less noise.'

'We'll bring Rasta back before lunchtime,' Ramon assured her.

'As you wish, Don Ramon,' she replied, blinking into the sunlight with the discomfort of a creature grown accustomed to the darkness of her melancholy.

Ramon and Federica strode down the hill towards the sea, half running to keep up with Rasta who jumped and skipped in front of them, straining at his leash, thirsting to sniff every gateway and post, every patch of grass or tree, cocking his leg indiscriminately everywhere the scent of another animal lingered. He was pathetically happy. Federica's heart floated with joy as she watched the skinny black mongrel experience freedom for the first time in perhaps many months. She looked up at her father and her cheeks burned with admiration. There was nothing he couldn't do.

They crossed the road that ran alongside the coast, then made their way down the paved steps to Caleta Abarca beach. One or two people walked up and down, a child played with a small dog, throwing a ball into the sea for it to chase. Federica took off her sandals and felt the soft sand, like Lidia's flour, between her pink toes. Ramon changed into his bathing shorts, leaving his clothes and leather moccasins in a heap for Federica to look after while he went and washed himself off in the cold waters of the Pacific. She watched him jog towards the sea, followed eagerly by Rasta. He was strong and hairy, with the powerful physique of a man capable of climbing mountains, yet he walked and moved with surprising grace. Ramon Campione's imagination was as deep and mysterious as the sea, full of shipwrecks and sunken continents. Federica had grown up on his stories and somehow those stories had made his absences less acute. When she looked back on her short life she saw only the long rides through her father's fertile mind. Those were the adventures she remembered, not the many months of drought. She watched him splash about with Rasta in the glittering water. The light caught the tips of the waves and the silk of his hair and if she hadn't known better she would have thought he were a playful seal. She placed the box on her lap and ran her hand over the rough wooden surface. She wondered to whom it had once belonged. A shudder of anticipation careered up her spine at the thought of another magical story. She opened the box to the ringing of little bells and marvelled once again at the glittering gems that caused the butterfly's wings to quiver.

Finally, Ramon's wet body sat down next to her on the hot sand to dry off in the sun. Rasta, unwilling to stop enjoying his liberty even for a moment, galloped up and down the beach, playing tag with the sea. Ramon was pleased his daughter liked the box. She deserved it. After all, Helena was right, he wasn't a good father. Good fathers gave their children their time. He couldn't be that sort of father. It wasn't in his nature. He was a wanderer, a nomad. His mother used to tell him that children give according to what parents put in. Well, he must have done something right, for Federica loved him and her love showed all over her face. He cast his eyes out over the blue horizon and wondered how long he'd last on this shore before the itchiness in his feet got the better of him and the winds of new adventures blew outside his window to lure him away.

'Tell me the legend, Papa,' said Federica. Ramon lifted his daughter between his legs so that he sat behind her with his arms around her body and his rough cheek against hers. They both looked into the mosaic of crystals and listened to the light clatter of tiny bells.

'This box once belonged to a beautiful Inca princess,' he began. Federica gasped in delight. She loved his stories and nestled in closer, for she knew this one would be special. She kept the box open on the folds of her yellow dress, running her hands over the stones and turning it from side to side to watch the colours mysteriously change as if by magic. 'The Inca Princess was called Topahuay and lived in a palace on the hillside village of Pisac in Peru. The Incas were an ancient Indian civilization who worshipped the sun, Inti, and paid homage to their Emperor, the ruling Inca. Beneath the Emperor were the nobility, the "Capac Incas", the true descendants of the founding Inca, Manco Capac. Topahuay was a member of one of these ruling houses called *panacas*. She had smooth brown skin, a round open face, sharp green eyes and long black hair that she tied into a plait that fell down her back, almost to the ground. She was admired by everyone and all the young men of the nobility longed to marry her. But Topahuay was secretly in love with a man of lowly birth, a member of the *yanakuna*, a domestic class who served the *panacas*. A marriage between these two such distinct classes was unthinkable. But Topahuay and Wanchuko, which was his name, loved each other so fiercely that they defied the laws of their land and saw each other in secret. Sometimes Topahuay would disguise herself as a woman from the *yanakuna* and they would walk the streets unnoticed, hold hands away from the suspicious eyes of her relatives and even kiss when no one was looking. Now, Topahuay was only thirteen years old. You may think that is very young for a girl to be thinking of marriage, but in those days thirteen was the beginning of womanhood and her parents were scouring their society for a worthy husband for her. Topahuay felt trapped in a world of strict social codes with no escape. She knew in her heart that she would have to marry a nobleman and relinquish Wanchuko for ever. So Wanchuko decided to make her a box that was so unremarkable she would be able to take it with her wherever she went without attracting suspicion, but which contained a secret message within that only she would ever see, to remind her of his love. So he set about making a plain wooden box. He made it so plain that it was almost ugly.

Once the box was made he searched the hills and caves for the most beautiful stones he could find. Some were precious, some were simply crystals, others were rare gems he found at the bottom of the lake of such exquisite blues and greens that he believed them to have been made out of the water itself. Once he had gathered all his stones together he locked himself in his small room from dawn to dusk where he chiselled and carved, setting each stone carefully into the wood. Then he fashioned a much smaller box, which contained a special mechanism he invented so that when the larger box was opened a strange music, like the tinkling of tiny bells, resounded within. Legend has it that the box was a magical box, made with the very force of his love that was not of this world. It was due to that higher vibration that the stones were set in place, as if by enchantment. You see, he didn't use a type of glue, as others would have, instead the stones are held together by each other, like a magnificent mosaic. If you were to take one stone out they would all fall away and the picture would be lost for ever. So you see, it must have been made with magic. There is no other explanation. On the bottom of the box he designed a butterfly to symbolize Topahuay's entrapment and her beauty. When he gave it to her she cried large silver tears and said that she wished she had wings like a butterfly so that she could fly away with him. What Wanchuko didn't know was that the symbolism of the butterfly would go beyond entrapment and beauty. Butterflies only live for a day. Topahuay's life would be cut short, just like the butterfly's, at the height of her magnificence.

The Inca Empire was also at the height of its powers. It was the largest and most potent empire that South America had ever known. But it was all to go drastically wrong.

The Spanish arrived to conquer Peru in one of the bloodiest episodes in the history of the empire. It was then, when all hope had drained away and the blood of thousands of Incas ran in rivers down the hills into the valleys that they sacrificed their most beautiful and cherished Topahuay to their god of war, in the desperate hope that he would save them. Clasping the box to her breast she was dressed in exquisitely woven wools, her hair plaited and beaded with one hundred shining crystals. Upon her head was placed a large fan of white feathers to carry her into the next world and frighten the demons along the way. Wanchuko was unable to save her. He could only watch, helpless and heartbroken, as she was led up the small mountain path together with an entourage of high priests and dignitaries. As she passed him her large green eyes gazed upon him with such intense love that a light ignited about her head, a light not of this world. His lips trembled and his outstretched hand grabbed her woollen cloak in an effort to save her. But it was no good, the entourage passed him and continued up into the mists of the mountain. Up to the bridge that joined this world to the next, a bridge that Topahuay would have to cross alone. He was too angry to cry, too afraid to run after her. He stood petrified, waiting, wanting it to be over. When he unclenched his hand he saw a brightly woven piece of wool sitting in his shaking palm. A moment later he heard a short, piercing scream. He turned his eyes to the mountain where the scream echoed momentarily off the jagged peaks before disappearing into the wind. When he looked down at his hand the piece of wool had transformed itself into a resplendent butterfly. He watched, aghast, as she stood quivering in his palm for a brief second as if stunned by her own metamorphosis. Then she lifted her fragile wings and flew away. Topahuay had become a butterfly after all and her spirit was free.'

Federica was so moved a tear trailed slowly down her shining cheek, dropping off her lip onto her chin and finally into the box where it seeped into the crystals. 'How did you get the box, Papa?' she whispered, as if the sound of her voice would shatter the tenderness of the moment.

I found it in a village called Puca Pucara. Topahuay's family had managed to salvage it before she was buried on the mountainside. They brought it down to their village where they kept it for a while until the Spanish came with their weapons and their slaughter. It was then that Topahuay's mother gave it to Wanchuko, for she had always known what her daughter's secret heart contained, and told him to leave Peru until it was safe to return. So Wanchuko left as he had been told only to return many decades later as an old man. He had never married for he had vowed in his heart to love only Topahuay. He had wandered the world alone, thinking only of her. In dreams, when he was awake as much as when he was asleep, her open face and smiling eyes would come to him and comfort him through his lonely life. When he returned to Pisac he recognized no one. His family had been slaughtered along with Topahuay's; in death there were no social divides. They had all died together, emperors and servants alike. On the brink of despair he climbed up the same path that Topahuay had walked that fateful day, all those years ago. At the top, to his surprise, he saw a little old woman sitting on the grass, looking out across the kingdom of mountain peaks. She was quite alone. When he approached her he recognized her as Topahuay's sister, Topaquin. Time had warped her skin and shrunken her bones, just like his. But he knew her and when he came closer, she too recognized him and invited him to join her. There they talked about Topahuay, her short, tragic life and the Spanish armies of destruction who had stamped out their culture and way of life for ever. Wanchuko gave Topaquin the box, telling her that the spirit of Topahuay danced in the light of the crystals and sang with the music of the tiny bells. Then he lay back on the spot where Topahuay's life had been so cruelly taken from her and died. He, too, crossed the bridge that joins this life to the next. But, he wasn't alone, for Topahuay was with him and her love was there to guide him so no evil could touch him.

The box was taken to Puca Pucara and remained there for all that time, handed down from one generation to another. The strange thing is that an old woman gave it to me. She said that it has special powers. She said that I needed it more than she did. So, she wrapped it up and handed it to me. It must be priceless, Fede, like you. So you treasure it, for it was made with love and must be cherished with love.'

'I'll cherish it for ever, Papa. Thank you,' she replied, overwhelmed with gratitude and so moved by the story that her lips seemed to lose their colour and turn pale.

Ramon glanced at his watch while his daughter sat transfixed, stroking the butterfly with an unsteady hand. 'We should go home for lunch,' he whispered into her ear, stroking the soft skin of her white neck with tender fingers. 'Where's Rasta?' he chuckled, casting his eyes up and down the beach. He stood up and stretched before putting his clothes back on again. Federica followed his lead reluctantly. She closed the box and got to her feet. She straightened out the creases in her pretty yellow dress and called for Rasta. Still full of energy he appeared wet and sandy with a ball in his mouth.

'Here, Rasta,' she said, patting her thighs. He trotted up to her and dropped the ball on the ground. She shook her head. Some poor person would probably want that ball back, she thought, picking it up with a finger and thumb so as not to dirty her hands. She looked around but saw no one. 'What shall I do with this ball, Papa?' she asked.

'Oh, I think he can keep it. Poor old Rasta. He doesn't have anything else to play with and I can't see anyone looking for it,' he replied, slipping his feet into his moccasins. Federica threw the ball up the beach. Rasta scurried after it. 'Come on, let's go,' he said, taking her hand and leading her back up the steps.

'That was such a beautiful story, Papa.'

'I knew you'd like it.'

'I love it. I love the box. I'll treasure it for ever. It will be my most treasured possession,' she said, clutching it against her chest again.

★

Ramon was pensive as they walked up the hill towards home. He had a dark premonition that Helena had given up. There was a distant look in her eyes that hadn't been there before. A resignation of sorts. The feisty expression was no longer set into her features, as if she'd grown tired of battle and wanted out. He sighed deeply. Federica was still far away in Pisac with Topahuay and Wanchuko and walked up the hill beside him in silence.

They returned Rasta to Señora Baraca who was grateful that he no longer barked, but panted heavily and wagged his thin tail with pleasure. She said that Federica could take him out whenever she wanted. 'As he hasn't bitten you, he must like you,' she said without smiling, chewing on her gums.

Federica followed her father up the street. 'Mama says I shouldn't touch him. She says we don't know where he's been,' she said to her father.

'We do now,' he replied, smiling down at her. 'Still, I'd do as she says and wash your hands before lunch.'

'I cooked your favourite lunch with Lidia,' she said proudly.

He grinned, his gleaming teeth whiter against his dark skin. '*Pastel de choclo*,' he said and she nodded. 'I don't deserve you.'

'Oh yes you do. You're the best father in the whole world,' she replied happily, hugging her magical box and gripping his hand so tightly that he knew she meant it.

Chapter 3

Federica followed her father across the midday shadows of the leafy acacia trees, through their front gate and up the path towards the front door. Just before they reached it Lidia appeared, scarlet-faced and anxious.

'Don Ramon! Señora Helena is waiting to have lunch. She told me to go and find you,' she puffed, her heavy bosom heaving with exertion.

Ramon strode up to her, disarming her with his wide smile. 'Well, Lidia, you won't have to now as we're back. I hear there's *pastel de choclo* for lunch,' he said, walking on past her into the hall.

'*Sí*, Don Ramon. Federica cooked it all by herself,' she said, closing the door behind her and following them into the kitchen.

'Smells delicious,' he said, inhaling the warm aroma of onions. 'Don't forget to wash your hands, Fede,' he added, running his under the tap. Federica's eyes sparkled with happiness and she smiled without restraint. After washing her hands she rushed into the sitting room to tell her mother about the legend of the box.

'Mama!' she cried, skipping up the corridor. 'Mama.'

Helena emerged cross-faced and weary, carrying Hal in her arms.

'Where have you been, Fede?' she asked, running her hand down the child's windswept hair. 'Hal's dying of hunger.'

'We went to the beach. We took Señora Baraca's dog, Rasta. You know he doesn't bark any more, he just wanted to be let out to run around. Poor thing. Then Papa swam and I looked after his clothes. Rasta swam, too. Then Papa told me the legend.'

'What legend?' Helena asked, humouring her daughter as she ushered her into the dining room.

'About Topahuay and Wachuko. The Inca princess. This box was made for her.'

'Really. How lovely,' said Helena, patiently. She looked up at her husband as he walked into the room, filling it with his presence and the tense atmosphere that had once more returned to the house. They locked eyes for a moment like two strangers curiously looking each other over for the first time. Helena averted her eyes first.

'I want to sit next to Papa,' Federica announced happily, pulling out a chair and patting the placemat possessively.

'You can sit wherever you like, sweetie,' said Helena, dropping Hal gently into his chair. 'I hope you washed your hands,' she added, remembering the dog.

'Oh yes. Señora Baraca looks like a witch,' Federica laughed.

'She does, actually,' Ramon agreed, chuckling, attempting to lighten the atmosphere.

'Well, I hope she didn't cast a spell on you,' said Helena, making an effort for the sake of the children. Her throat was tight and her chest constricted under the pressure of having to perform. She longed to talk to Ramon on his own. She needed to release the burden of her thoughts. She needed to resolve the situation. They couldn't go on like this. It wasn't fair on either of them.

'Oh no. She was very grateful we had walked her dog for her,' said Federica.

'I want to see the dog,' Hal whined, wriggling in his chair with impatience. Lidia entered with the steaming *pastel de choclo*.

'Fede made this for you this morning,' said Helena, sitting down at the other end of the table from her husband.

'So I'm told. You're very good to me, Fede,' he said truthfully.

'She certainly is,' said Helena dryly. She would like to have added that he was wholly undeserving of her affection, but she restrained the impulse with a gulp of water from her glass. 'She worked all morning, didn't you, Fede?'

'Papa hasn't seen his room yet,' she added and a bashful smile tickled her face.

'What have you done to my room, you naughty monkey?'

'You'll have to see for yourself,' she said.

'Fede picked flowers this morning,' said Hal disloyally. 'Didn't you, Fede?'

'Mama!' protested Federica in frustration.

'Have you enjoyed your train, Hal?' Ramon asked in an effort to distract the child from giving anything else away.

'It's brightly coloured and goes very fast,' he said, making 'chuga chuga chuga chuga' train noises. Lidia placed a hot plate of food in front of him. 'I don't like sweet corn,' he grumbled, sitting back in his chair and folding his arms in front of him.

'Yes, he does,' said Federica. 'He's just pretending because I made it.'

'No, I'm not.'

'You are.'

'Not.'

'Are.'

'All right you two. Enough of this,' said Ramon firmly. 'Hal, eat your corn or you go to your room without lunch or your train.' Hal scowled at his sister, his brown eyes darkening with resentment.

★

Ramon and Helena's conversation revolved around the children. If the children went silent, which they often did after an argument, they would be forced to talk to each other, which neither wanted to do, not with that false politeness, like a couple of actors in a badly written play. Ramon let Federica tell her mother the story of the Inca princess, only interrupting her when she turned to him for help over some detail that she had forgotten. Ramon was surprised at how much she had managed to remember. Helena listened, turning to answer her son once or twice when he whined 'Mama' just to get attention. Federica was used to being interrupted by her brother, she was also used to her mother indulging him by saying 'What is it, my love?' in a slow, patient voice. She didn't mind. One often tolerates things purely out of habit.

'Darling, what a delightful story. And the box is now yours. You are a very lucky little girl,' said Helena. She didn't add 'and I hope you'll look after it', as other mothers would, because she knew Federica was more responsible about things like that than she was herself.

'I thought we could drive up to Cachagua for a couple of weeks,' Ramon suggested casually as if everything were normal, as if he hadn't noticed the change in Helena's countenance. 'Spend Christmas with my parents. They'd love to see you and the children.'

'Oh, yes please, Mama!' squealed Federica in delight. She loved staying with her grandparents. They had a cosy, thatched house overlooking the sea. Helena wished he hadn't brought it up in front of the children. They needed to talk first. He hadn't consulted her. Now if she said they couldn't go, she'd disappoint them. She couldn't bear to disappoint them. Hal gazed up at her with hopeful brown eyes.

'Yes! Yes!' he cried, knocking his fork on the table. He also loved staying with his grandparents. They bought him ice creams and took him for pony rides up the beach.

His grandfather read him stories and carried him about on his shoulders.

'Okay, we'll go to Cachagua,' she conceded weakly. 'Ramon, I need to talk to you after lunch. Please don't disappear off with Fede again.' She tried to sound casual so as not to alarm the children. She knew in her mind what she wanted to say to him and feared that her thoughts might seep through her words and betray her.

'I won't,' he replied, frowning at her. There was something final in the tone of her voice and he didn't like it. Women always had to tie everything up with bows. Everything had to be worked out. Helena was like that. She was incapable of just going along with things and seeing how they turned out. She had to make decisions and formalize them.

After the first course, for which Ramon thanked his daughter by kissing her pale forehead fondly, she skipped out with Lidia to put the final touches on the welcome home *merengon de lúcuma*. While she was out Helena and Ramon talked to Hal, anything rather than talk to each other. Hal began to show off with all the attention and started singing a song he'd learnt at school about a donkey. Both parents watched him, anything rather than watch each other. Finally, the door opened and in walked Federica holding a white meringue cake with a single candle flickering on top. Hal sang Happy Birthday. Ramon and Helena both laughed and for a moment the strain in Helena's neck and chest lifted and she was able to breathe properly.

Federica placed the cake in front of her father and watched as he blew out the candle. Hal clapped together his small hands and giggled as the candle caught alight again as if by magic. Ramon pretended to be surprised and blew at it again. Both children laughed at the joke, certain that their father was truly baffled by the inextinguishable flame. Finally, he dipped his fingers in his water glass and pinched the wick. The flame was smothered and smoked away in protest. 'Welcome home!' he read out loud Federica's curly girlish handwriting, written with brown icing sugar onto the white frothy cream that resembled a choppy sea. 'Thank you, Fede,' he said, pulling her into his arms and kissing her cheek. Federica stayed on his lap while he cut it. Hal waved his teaspoon at the cake, catching a bit of meringue on the end, which he then hastily put into his mouth before anyone could tell him not to. Helena pretended she hadn't noticed. She was too tired to use the little energy she had left for her talk with Ramon on her mischievous child.

After lunch Federica reluctantly joined Hal in the garden while her parents went upstairs to talk. She wondered what they needed to talk about and resented her mother for dragging her father away. She carried the box into the garden and, sitting under the shade of the orange trees, she opened it and reflected on the story her father had told her.

'Can I see your box?' Hal asked, sitting down beside her.

'Yes, if you're careful.'

'I'll be careful,' he said, taking it from her. 'Wow!' he enthused. 'It's very pretty.'

'Yes, it is. It used to belong to an Inca princess.'

'What's an Inca?' he asked.

'The Inca were a race of people who lived in Peru,' she replied.

'What happened to the princess?' he asked.

'Didn't you listen to my story at the table?' she said, smiling down at him indulgently.

'I want to hear it again,' he said. 'Please.'

'Okay. I'll tell you again,' she agreed. 'But you must listen and be quiet or I won't tell you.'

'I'll be quiet,' he said and yawned sleepily. It was very hot, even in the shade. The low hum of bees in the flowerbeds and the distant roar of the sea were a soothing backdrop to the languid hours of siesta time. Federica placed her arm around Hal's body and let him rest his head against her.

'Once upon a time in deepest Peru,' she began and Hal closed his eyes and looked into a strange new world.

Ramon followed his wife upstairs. Neither spoke. He watched her walk down the corridor with her shoulders stooped and her head hung. As he approached his room the scent of lavender reached his nostrils and reminded him of his mother's house in Cachagua. As if sensing his thoughts Helena told him that Federica had prepared his sheets with fresh lavender from the garden.

The room was breezy and clean and smelt also of oranges and roses. He cast his eye around the place they had shared for the best part of seven years of their twelve-year marriage, but he didn't feel he belonged there. In spite of Federica's flowers and loving preparation it was his wife's room and the coldness of her demeanour told him that he was no longer welcome.

He placed his suitcase on the floor and sat on the edge of the bed. Helena walked over to the window and looked out across the sea.

'So, what do you want to talk about?' he asked, but he knew the answer.

'Us,' she replied flatly.

'What about us?'

'Well, it's just not the same, is it?'

'No.'

'I'm tired of pretending to the children that everything's fine. It's not fine. I'm not happy. It's all very well for you, travelling the world like a gypsy, writing your books of stories.

But I'm the one trapped here in this house without you. Without any support. I've brought these two children up almost single-handedly,' she said and felt the strain in her neck rise to clamp her head in its vice.

'But you always knew that was my life. You didn't have any expectations. You said so yourself. You gave me freedom because you understood that I couldn't survive without it,' he said, shaking his head and frowning.

'I know. But I didn't know how it was really going to be. In the beginning we travelled together. It was a dream. I loved it and I loved you. But now . . .' Her voice trailed off.

'Now?' he ventured sadly.

'Now I don't love you any more.' She turned to face him. Noticing the hurt cloud his face she added quickly, 'Love has to be nurtured, not left to rot with neglect, Ramon. I loved you once, but now I don't know you any more. I wouldn't recognize love if it slapped me in the face. All I know is that I'm tired of being alone and you always leave me alone, for months on end. You always will,' she said and the tears cascaded down her cheeks, one after the other, until they formed two thin streams of misery.

'So what do you want to do?' he asked.

She walked timidly over to him and perched next to him on the bed. 'If you were afraid of losing me, Ramon, you'd stay and write here. You'd change for me. But you won't, will you?' He thought about it for a moment, but his silence answered her question. 'Do you love me, Ramon?' she ventured.

His shiny conker eyes looked at her forlornly. 'Yes, I do, in my own way, Helena. I still love you. But I don't love you enough to change for you. If I stayed here with you and the children I'd shrivel. I'd dry out like a plant in the desert. Don't you see that? I don't want to lose you, or the children, but I can't change,' he said, shaking his head. 'I arrive home and the first thing I think about is when I can get going again. I'm sorry.'

They both sat in silence. Helena cried with the relief of having given vent to her feelings. She felt the heaviness lift and the tension ease on her temples. Ramon sat wondering what she was going to do. He didn't want to lose her. She was his safety net. He liked to have a home to come back to. Even if he rarely used it, he still liked it to be there. He loved his children. But he wasn't used to the day-to-day routine of children. He wasn't a family man.

'So what happens now?' he said after a while.

'I want to go home,' she replied, standing up again and walking over to the window.

'You mean to England?'

'Yes.'

'But that's the other side of the world,' he protested.

'Why should you care? You're always the other side of the world and you always will be. What difference does it make where we are? You'll always be on another continent.'

'But the children?'

'They'll go to school in England. We'll go and live in Cornwall with my parents.' Then she rushed to his side and knelt on the floor at his feet. 'Please, Ramon. Please let me take them home. I can't bear it here any more. Not the way it is now. Without you there's no point, don't you see? I don't belong here like you do. I would have belonged, I had planned to, but now I want to go home.'

'What will you tell them?'

'I'll tell them that we're going home. That you'll come and see us, the same as you always have. We'll just live in a different country. They're young, they'll accept it,' she said firmly. She looked at him imploringly. 'Please, Ramon.'

'Do you want a divorce?' he asked impassively.

'No,' she replied quickly. 'No, not divorce.'

'Just a separation then?'

'Yes.'

'Then what?'

'Then nothing. I just want out,' she said and hung her head.

His premonition had been right. She was leaving him. She needed his permission to take the children out of the country and he would give it to her. How could he deny her that? Their children were more hers than his if one judged it by the amount of time they both spent with them. She was right, what did it matter where they were, he was always thousands of miles away.

'All right, you can take the children back to England,' he conceded sorrowfully. 'But first I want to take them to see my parents in Cachagua. I want to give them a family Christmas, so they'll always remember me like that.'

'Ramon,' she whispered, for her voice had gone hoarse with emotion, 'you will come and see us, won't you?' She searched his eyes, afraid that by cutting herself off from him he would no longer make the effort to be a part of their children's lives.

'Of course,' he replied, shaking his shaggy head.

'The children will miss you terribly. You can't desert them, Ramon. They need you.'

'I know.'

'Don't punish them for my actions. This is between us as adults, not them.'

'I know.'

'Fede loves you, so does Hal. I couldn't live with myself if you deserted them because of me.' She sat up abruptly. 'I won't go if leaving you means depriving my children of their father. I will sacrifice my own happiness for theirs,' she said and began to sob.

Ramon was confused. He ran his hand down her blonde hair. 'I won't desert them, Helena,' he said.

She looked up at him with glassy eyes. 'Thank you.'

Suddenly his mouth was on hers. Without understanding their actions their bodies rebelled against the cold detachment of their minds. They clawed off their clothes like thirsty animals scraping at the ground for water. Helena felt the sharp bristle of his chin against hers and the soft wetness of his lips and gums. For the months he had been away she had only dreamed of making love to other men. She had had opportunities but she had rejected every one for the simple reason that she was the wife of someone else, if only in name. Now she abandoned herself to the touch of a man, even though she felt nothing for him now but gratitude. In these intense moments of intimacy they could have been mistaken for believing their love to have been re-ignited. But Helena knew that sexual pleasure alone was a false love, as illusory as a mirage. She closed her eyes, blocking out the sad reality of her situation and allowed herself to take pleasure as his hands stroked the curves of her body as if exploring them for the first time.

It had been many months since they had last united in this way. They had both forgotten what the other's body was like. As if she had no control over her impulses, her fingers followed the ridge of his spine and caressed the hair on his shoulders like they used to do when they had been driven by love. She ran her tongue over his skin and it tasted of the sea mingled with the scent of man. When he kissed her, his mouth on her mouth, his face only inches away from hers, she opened her eyes to find his were closed. She wondered whom he was dreaming of and whether he too had had opportunities on his travels. She didn't want to know. Then he was inside her, awakening her dormant desire that had endured many months of hibernation and she thought no more about the other women he might have had. They both forgot the other as they moved like one writhing beast, oblivious to the low groans that escaped from their throats and the delirious sighs that vibrated deep within their bellies. When they lay sweaty and exhausted, the heady scent of their skin mingling with the sweet fragrance of lavender and rose, they both stared up at the ceiling and wondered why they had allowed themselves to get carried away.

Helena was too embarrassed to look at him and covered her steaming body with the bedspread in shame. A ridiculous action after he had tasted it so intimately. She fumbled in the bedside table drawer for a cigarette. Finding one she lit it with a trembling hand and inhaled impatiently. How strange it is, she thought, that we can be as close as two people possibly can be then suddenly, in the space of a second, lie here side by side but thousands of miles apart. She looked over at him and he turned to face her.

'That was nice,' he said.

'Yes, it was,' she replied tightly.

'Don't regret it, Helena. It's okay to indulge in the pleasures of the flesh, even if you feel nothing but physical desire.'

She inhaled again. 'I don't regret it,' she said. She didn't know whether she did or didn't. Had she really made love without love? She waved the thought away with the smoke. It no longer mattered. She was going home.

Chapter 4

Ramon watched his wife dress in the dim light of the bedroom. Neither spoke. The smell of cigarettes masked the lavender Federica had pressed into the linen and the garden flowers she had so lovingly picked and placed on his bedside table in the shiny blue vase. The messy bed was all that was left of their passion. He wondered if there was anything left of their love. Then he heard Federica's soft voice singing in the garden and he realized that his children were the physical expressions of a love they had once happily given to each other, and he shuddered at the thought of being without them.

Helena's body was still firm and slim with that translucent pallor that had first attracted him to her twelve years before. She was now thirty years old, too young to be on her own without the attentions of a loving man to nurture her. When he had found her on those cold Cornish beaches she had been young and ready to sacrifice everything just so that she could be near him. They had travelled the world together, united by his thirst for adventure and her desire to be loved. It had worked until domesticity drove them apart. He watched her brush her long blonde hair and pin it onto the top of her head. He preferred it when she wore it down her back. Once it had reached her waist. Once he had threaded it with jasmine. She had been beautiful then. Now she looked tired and her disenchantment drained her face of colour so that her pallor, once so alluring, no longer glowed but lay stagnant like a diminishing waterhole in the dry season. If he didn't let her go there'd be nothing of her left.

She caught him watching her in the mirror but she didn't smile like she once would have done.

'When do you want to go to Cachagua?' she asked.

'Tomorrow. I'll call my parents, tell them we're coming.'

'What will you tell them?'

'About us?'

'Yes.'

He sighed and sat up. 'I don't know yet.'

'They'll think I'm heartless. They'll blame me,' she said and her voice quivered.

'No they won't. They know me better than you think.'

'I feel guilty,' she said and stared at her reflection.

'You've made your decision,' he said impassively and got to his feet.

Helena wanted him to beg her to stay. She had hoped he would fall to his knees and promise to change like other men would. But Ramon wasn't like other men. He was unique. It had been his uniqueness that she had fallen in love with. He was so self-sufficient he didn't need anyone. He just needed the air to breathe, his sight to take in all the wondrous places he travelled to and a pen to write it all down. He hadn't needed her love but she had given it to him, desiring nothing in return except his acceptance. But it is human nature to always want more than one has. Once she had won his love she wanted his freedom too. But he had been unwilling to relinquish it. He still was. He had been as difficult as a cloud to pin down, she should have known he would never change, that there would come a time when she would be alone, for the world possessed his soul and she hadn't the strength to fight for it any more. But she still wanted him to fight for her. How could he still love her but refuse to fight for her? He made her feel worthless.

Helena stepped out into the garden, squinting in the white glare of the sunshine, to find Hal asleep in the shade of an orange tree while Federica sang to herself on the swing. She knew Federica would be broken-hearted leaving Viña, but her parents' separation would hurt her so much more. Helena watched her swinging in the sun, ignorant of the dark undercurrent that swelled beneath her perfect day. When she saw her mother standing in the doorway she leapt off the swing, picked up her magic box from the grass and ran towards her.

'Have you finished talking to Papa now?' she asked.

'Yes, I have, sweetie. We're going to Cachagua tomorrow,' she replied, knowing how happy that would make her.

Federica grinned. 'I told Hal the story of the Inca princess. He's asleep now.' She laughed. Hal lay on his back, his arms and legs spread in blissful abandon, his chest gently rising and falling in the afternoon heat.

'Well, let's not wake him,' Helena said, watching her child with tenderness. Hal was so like his father. He had Ramon's dark hair and conker eyes without that maddening glint of self-sufficiency. Federica was happier on her own but Hal needed constant attention. He was the part of Ramon she had loved and been allowed to hold on to. Hal needed her and loved her unconditionally.

Federica skipped into the house to find her father in the sitting room, talking on the telephone in Spanish. She walked up to him with her box and perched on the armrest, waiting for him to finish so that she could talk to him. She listened to the conversation and realized he was talking to her grandmother. 'Tell Abuelita about my box,' she said excitedly.

'No, you tell her,' he said, handing her the receiver.

'Abuelita, Papa's bought me a box that once belonged to an Inca princess . . . yes, a real princess . . . I will, I'll tell you tomorrow . . . so am I . . . a big kiss to you, *yo tambin te quiero*,' she said and blew a kiss down the telephone, which made her father chuckle as he took back the receiver.

'We'll see you in time for lunch, then,' he said, before hanging up. 'Right, Fede, what shall we do now?'

'I don't know,' she replied and grinned, for she knew her father always had something planned.

'Let's go into town and buy your grandmother a present, shall we?'

'And buy a juice,' she added.

'A juice and a *palta* sandwich,' he said, getting up. 'Go and tell your mother we'll be back in time for tea.'

Mariana Campione put down the receiver and shouted to her husband Ignacio who was lying in the hammock on the terrace reading, round glasses perched on the bridge of his aquiline nose and his panama hat pulled down over his bushy eyebrows – an indication that he did not wish to be disturbed.

'Nacho, Ramon's back and he's coming to visit with the family tomorrow,' she said in delight. Ignacio did not move, except to turn the page. Mariana, a full-bodied, large-boned woman with silver-grey hair and a kind open face, walked out through the French doors to where her husband was lying in the shade of an acacia tree. '*Mi amor*, did you hear me? Ramon's home. They're coming to visit tomorrow,' she repeated, her cheeks stung with joy.

'I heard you, woman,' he said without looking up from his book.

'Nacho, you don't deserve to have grandchildren,' she said, but she smiled and shook her head.

'He disappears for months without so much as a letter, what sort of a man does that to his family? I've told you before, Helena will lose patience with him eventually. I lost my patience with him years ago and I'm not married to him,' he said firmly, then glanced at his wife over his book to see her reaction.

'Don't be silly,' she chided gently, 'Helena is a good wife and mother. She's loyal to Ramon. I'm not saying he's right to desert her like that all the time, but she's an old-fashioned woman. She understands him. I'm thrilled they're coming to stay.' Her large face creased into a tender smile.

'How long are they staying for?' he asked, still looking at her.

'I don't know. He didn't say.'

'Still, I suppose we should be grateful,' he said sarcastically. 'Out of our eight children Ramon's the one we see the least so when he shows up it's more of an event.'

'Now you're being petulant.'

'For the love of God, Mariana, he's a forty-year-old man, or thereabouts, it's high time he grew up and took some responsibility before he loses everything. If that long-suffering wife of his leaves him he'll only have himself to blame, and I'll be on her side one hundred per cent.'

Mariana laughed and retreated into the cool interior of the house. She had listened to his argument enough times to know it by heart. Ramon was just a free spirit, she understood him like Helena did, she thought, wandering into the kitchen to inform their young maid, Estella, about the change in numbers. He was so talented it would be very wrong to tie him down and stifle such precious creativity. She read and re-read all his books and articles and felt immense pride when people told her how much they too enjoyed his writing. He was celebrated in Chile and he had earned every bit of the respect he was given. 'I know I'm his mother,' she said to her husband, 'but he really does write most beautifully.'

Estella had awoken from her siesta and was already chopping the vegetables for dinner when Mariana entered the kitchen. As in most Chilean households of the well-to-do, the kitchen was part of the maid's quarters, along with her bedroom and bathroom, which were situated at the back of the house, hidden behind thick perennial bushes and bougainvillea trees. Estella was new. After Consuelo, their maid for twenty years, had died the previous summer they had been very fortunate to have found Estella, through friends who had a summer house in Zapallar, the neighbouring village. Mariana had liked her immediately. Whereas Consuelo had become too old to clean properly and too sour to cook with any enthusiasm, Estella had set to work immediately, polishing, sweeping, scrubbing and airing with an energy bestowed on her by her youth and with a smile that bubbled up from her sweet nature and desire to please. She was courteous, discreet and a quick learner, which was vital, for Ignacio was impatient and pedantic.

'Estella, my son Ramon is arriving tomorrow at lunchtime with his wife and two small children, please make sure that the blue spare room is made up for them and the room next door, I know how my son likes his space. The children can share, it's more fun that way.'

'*Sí*, Señora Mariana,' she replied obediently, trying to conceal her excitement. She had heard an enormous amount about Ramon Campione, seen his picture in the papers many times and even read a few of his articles. The poetry of his descriptions had stirred her heart and she had longed to meet him from the moment she had realized who her new employers were. She enjoyed wandering about the house, gazing at the photographs scattered over tables and mantelpieces. He was so handsome and romantic-looking, with his long black hair, acute brown eyes and generous mouth that seemed too large for his face but at the same time utterly captivating. She had spent long moments polishing the glass that protected his face from the dust. Now she was going to meet him, she could barely contain herself.

'Scent the linen with lavender and I want fresh flowers in all three bedrooms. Don't forget the flowers. Federica appreciates nature. She's a sweet girl. Clean towels, fresh drinking water and fruit,' said Mariana, not forgetting a single detail.

'How long will they be staying, Señora Mariana?' Estella asked, trying to control the tremor in her voice lest it betray her.

Mariana shrugged. 'I don't know, Estella. Ten days, maybe more. I'm going to try to persuade them to stay for New Year, although it'll be hard pinning my son down. Ramon takes every day as it comes, he never makes plans,' she said proudly. 'One minute he's here and you think he's here to stay then suddenly he'll get up and leave, just like that. Then we don't see or hear from him for months. That's the way God made him so I don't complain.'

'*Sí*, Señora Mariana,' said Estella.

'My grandchildren love *manjar blanco*, please make sure there is enough in the house, I'd hate to disappoint them,' she added before leaving the room.

Estella sighed with pleasure. She set about preparing the rooms at once. She swept through the children's room like a tornado, making up the beds with real Irish linen sheets, sweeping the wooden floorboards and dusting the surfaces. The marital room she arranged with more care, scenting the linen with lavender and opening the shutters to the fresh sea air and sound of chattering birds hopping about in the eucalyptus trees. When she opened the door to Ramon's room she breathed in deeply before making the bed slowly and tenderly, smoothing her elegant brown fingers over the pillow to flatten any wrinkles. She imagined him lying there, gazing up at her, beckoning her to join him. Then she lay on the bed and closed her eyes, breathing in the heady scent of tuberose she had set in a vase on the dresser. She smiled as she thought that perhaps tomorrow his head would lie where hers was lying now and he would never know how close they'd been.

She hoped he'd stay for a long time.

★

Ignacio put down his book and rolled out of the hammock. He felt sleepy and lethargic. The evening was cool, the shadows lengthening, the tide edging its way up the shore like a nightly predator. He stood on the terrace, leaning against the railings, looking out over the smooth surface of the sea that sighed hypnotically. He felt uneasy. His weathered face crinkled anxiously as he tried to discover the root of his ill-ease. The light had ripened to a warm orange as the sun hovered behind the horizon about to dawn on another shore. Perhaps it was the natural melancholia of sunset that had brought on this feeling, he thought hopefully. But he knew it had more to do with his son than with nature. He sensed things weren't as they should be.

Mariana wandered out to join him with his nightly glass of whisky and water. 'Here,' she said, handing it to him. 'You're very quiet this evening,' she added, smiling at him.

'I'm sleepy,' he replied, sipping from the glass.

'You've been reading too much.'

'Yes.'

'It can make one subdued, all that reading,' she said kindly, patting him on his weather-beaten brown arm.

'Yes,' he repeated.

'Still, you'll have Ramon and Helena to entertain you tomorrow, and those adorable children.'

'I know,' he agreed, nodding solemnly.

'He's given Fede a box that once belonged to an Inca princess, or so she tells me,' she said, watching the sun flood the sea with liquid gold.

'That sounds like one of Ramon's stories.'

'Yes, it does, doesn't it?' she chuckled. 'Typical Ramon, his imagination never ceases to amaze me.'

'An Inca princess, indeed.'

'Fede believes it.'

'Of course she does, Mariana, she worships her father,' he said, shaking his head. 'She worships him and he just abandons her. It's too bad.'

'Oh, Nacho, really. Is this what your silence is about? Ramon's lifestyle? It's really none of our business. If it works for them it shouldn't concern you or me.'

'But *does* it work for them?' he said, looking at her steadily. 'I don't know that it does. I feel something in my bones.'

'They're old bones, Nacho, I'm surprised they still feel anything at all.' She smiled.

'They're old bones, woman, but they're as sensitive as they always have been. Will you walk with me up the beach?' he asked suddenly, draining his glass.

Mariana looked surprised. 'Now?'

'Of course. We old people have to strike while we're still able to. Tomorrow may be our last.'

'What nonsense, *mi amor*, you really are very miserable to be with sometimes. But, yes, I'll walk with you up the beach. We can take our shoes off and get our feet wet, hold hands like we used to.'

'I'd like that very much,' he said, removing his panama hat and kissing her soft cheek.

'You old romantic,' she said and laughed at their foolishness. They were too old to play these games.

Ramon tucked Federica into bed. He noticed the box was on the table beside her.

'I'm frightened the box might not be here when I wake up,' she said suddenly, her smooth face creasing with anxiety.

'Don't worry, Fede, it will be here when you wake up. No one's going to take it while you're asleep, I promise.'

'It's the most beautiful thing I've ever had, I don't want to be without it, ever.'

'You won't be,' he reassured her, kissing her forehead. 'Have you noticed Señora Baraca's dog isn't barking tonight?'

'He's happy and tired, like me,' she said, smiling up at her father.

'He's exhausted.'

'What about tomorrow, can we take him out before we go to Cachagua?'

'Of course we can,' he said, touching her cheek with the tips of his fingers. 'We can take him up the beach again.'

'I feel sorry for Señora Baraca,' she said.

'Why?'

'Because she's so sad.'

'She chooses to be sad, Fede.'

'Does she?'

'Yes. Everyone has a choice, they can either be happy or sad.'

'But Mama told me her husband died,' she protested.

'Mama's right. But her husband died over ten years ago, before you were born. Now that's a long time ago.'

'But Wachuko was sad for his whole life.'

'Yes he was. But he didn't have to be. Sometimes it's better to move on rather than dwell on the past,' he said. 'One should learn things from the past and then let them go.'

'What should Señora Baraca have learnt from her past?' Federica asked, yawning.

'That she should spend more time looking after her dog than mourning her dead husband, don't you think?' he laughed.

'Yes,' she said and closed her eyes. Ramon watched her as she drifted off into the world of princesses and magic butterflies. Her long lashes caught the light that entered from the corridor, giving her a celestial beauty. Her face was long and noble, generous and honest. He felt his throat tighten with emotion at the thought of leaving her and while it didn't weaken his resolve it just made it a little harder to accept. He bent down and kissed her forehead again, feeling her velvet skin against his dry lips. He smelt the fragrance of her soap and the clean scent of her hair. He wanted to wrap her up in his arms and protect her from the harsh reality of a world that would only disappoint her.

Before he went to bed he crept into Hal's room to watch him as he slept. He didn't feel so close to his son. The child was only four and barely knew him. He was more attached to his mother and gave his father little attention. Hal didn't need him like Federica did. He watched the little boy suck on his thumb and cuddle his toy rabbit as he slept. Hal looked as if he embodied the qualities of an angel, as though he had been dropped into bed by God himself. His skin was flawless, his expression serene and contented. Ramon ran his rough hand over the boy's hair. Hal stirred and changed position but he didn't wake up. Ramon left as quietly as he had come.

The bed was cold in spite of the warm night. Helena slept curled up at one side, almost falling off the edge in her effort to avoid him. Ramon lay on his back staring up at the icy moonlight that crept across the ceiling. Neither recalled the fevered interlude of the afternoon. They didn't want to. Helena wished it hadn't happened and flushed with shame when she thought of it. So she pretended it simply hadn't happened. She felt him next to her, not because he moved, he didn't, but because the atmosphere was so heavy it was as if a third person occupied the space between them. She felt afraid to move or make a sound so she breathed shallow breaths and lay as rigid as a corpse. When sleep finally overcame them it was tortured and fragile. Helena dreamed of arriving in Cornwall but not being able to find Polperro. Ramon dreamed of standing on the beach while Federica drowned out to sea. He did nothing to save her.

Chapter 5

When Federica awoke she was disappointed to see the sea mist swirling dense and grey outside her window, obscuring the morning sunshine and silencing the birds. It was chilly and damp. Her mother always told her that the sea mist was sucked into the coast by the heat in Santiago. If it was really hot in the capital, Viña was misty. Federica hated the mist. It was depressing. Then she forgot all about the dreary skies and pulled her butterfly box onto her lap. She opened it, moved it about, ran her fingers over the stones, pleased that the light was still there causing the iridescent wings to shudder and tremble. That was how her mother found her, absorbed in Ramon's magic world of make-believe, somewhere amongst the mountains of Peru.

Helena had barely slept at all. Or at least she felt she hadn't slept. Her head was heavy and pressured. She had taken pain-killers and hoped they'd be quick to take effect. She padded into Federica's room in her dressing gown, followed by Hal who was already dressed and playing with his new train. When Federica saw her, pale faced and grey around the eyes, she noticed immediately and asked if she was all right.

'I'm fine, thank you, sweetie,' Helena replied, forcing a thin smile. But her eyes didn't smile. They remained dull and expressionless. Federica frowned and closed the lid of the box.

'You don't look very well, Mama. Shall I make you breakfast? Where's Papa?' she asked, jumping off the bed.

'Papa's still asleep, so best not to wake him. Why don't you put on your dressing gown and we can make breakfast together?' she suggested, patting Hal on his shiny head as he passed her making train noises. Federica scrambled into her dressing gown and wondered whether her father would remember his promise to take her to the beach with Rasta. She hoped he'd wake up and not spend all morning in bed, as he was apt to do. She skipped lightly down the stairs, through the hall and into the kitchen. Hal sat on the floor running his engine over the terracotta tiles, under the table and chairs, talking to himself and still making the noises of a train.

Federica helped her mother lay up for breakfast in the dining room. When her father was at home they stopped eating in the kitchen, which was an English habit of Helena's that she had never dropped, and ate like Chileans in the dining room. Lidia would arrive at ten to clean the house and cook the lunch. Ramon rarely went into the kitchen. He had grown up with staff, unlike Helena, whose family kitchen had been the very heart of her home.

Ramon awoke to find himself alone in the strange bed. It took a moment for him to remember where he was and for the heavy feeling of his wife's unhappiness to find him again. He cast his eyes to the window where the curtains danced with the cold breeze that came in off the Pacific bringing with it the damp sea mist. He didn't want to get up. The atmosphere in the room was stiflingly oppressive. He wanted to cover his head with the sheets and imagine he was far away on the clouds, above the mist and the misery that hung dense upon the walls of the house like slime. He lay there with a sinking feeling in his chest, suppressing the impulse to get up, pack his bag and leave.

Then he heard the gentle footsteps of his daughter. The sinking feeling turned to one of guilt and he peeped out over the sheets.

'Are you awake, Papa?' she asked. He saw her expectant face advance, her large blue eyes blinking at him hopefully. She treaded softly so as not to wake him if he was still sleeping. She moved slowly like a shy deer uncertain whether the animal in the bed was friend or foe. Ramon pulled the sheet down so that she could see he wasn't sleeping. Her face lit up and she smiled broadly. 'I've made you breakfast, Papa,' she said and her cheeks shone proudly. 'Can we go down to the beach, even though it's misty?'

'We can go to the beach right now,' he said, brightening up at the idea of getting out of the house. 'We'll take Rasta with us. You'd like that, wouldn't you? Then we'll head off to Cachagua.'

'Mama says it'll be sunny by the time we get to Cachagua,' she said, jumping from one foot to the other impatiently.

While Ramon was in the bathroom Federica skipped around the room, opening the curtains and making the bed. She was used to looking after her mother, but looking after her father gave her more pleasure. It was a novelty. Ramon ate his breakfast for Federica's sake. Hal had finished his and was playing quietly by himself in the nursery. His interest in his train far exceeded his interest in his father, whom he looked upon with suspicion because he sensed the strained atmosphere as all small children do. Helena sat at the table sipping a cup of black coffee. Ramon noticed her eyes were red and her face sapped of colour. He smiled at her politely, but she didn't smile back until Federica bounced in with hot croissants. Only then did she sit up and make an effort to act as if everything were normal.

After breakfast Ramon once again took Federica by the hand and led her down the road to the beach, the other hand holding onto Rasta's leash. Federica no longer cared whether it was sunny or misty. She was with her father, just the two of them. She felt special and cherished and she hugged the butterfly box tightly against her chest. They took off their shoes, Ramon's large brown explorer's feet made Federica's small pink ones look even smaller and more vulnerable. Together they walked up the beach, letting the sea catch their toes and cover them with foam. Ramon told her stories of the places he'd visited and the people he'd met and Federica listened transfixed, begging for another one until they were on the road to Cachagua, driving through the mist up the coast.

As they left the town behind them the road ascended into the pastoral charm of the countryside. They passed small villages of brightly painted houses with crude corrugated tin roofs and glassless windows into dark interiors. Open fruit stalls spilled out into the road and mangy horses and carts ambled up the sandy tracks driven by weathered Chileans in ponchos. Skinny dogs sniffed the dry ground for something to eat and grubby-faced children played with sticks and faded cans of Coca-Cola, their large black eyes staring at the car with curiosity as it sped by. The road was dusty, with the odd precarious hole here and there. They stopped after a while for a break and a drink. The mist was beginning to lift and the sun push through. The shade of the slender acacia trees darkened as the light intensified behind them, fighting its way through the fog. Federica sat drinking a large glass of lemon soda while Ramon chewed on an *empanada*. The dark Chilean children sat in a huddle against the bleached wall of the shack, watching Federica and Helena with wide eyes, whispering behind their hands, longing to creep up and touch their white angel hair to see what it was made of.

Helena and Ramon each felt much better being out of the house, away from the place that represented nothing but unhappiness for Helena and disappointment for Ramon. With the emergence of the sun they began to smile at each other and abandon themselves to the cheerful chatter of their children. The strain in Helena's eyes lifted and the colour returned to her cheeks. Ramon hoped that perhaps she might change her mind. A couple of weeks away would do her good.

Mariana and Ignacio took breakfast in the dining room as the sea mist made it too unpleasant to eat outside on the terrace. When Estella entered with the coffee and toast, in her clean blue uniform with her raven hair shining and loose down her back like a glossy pony, Mariana noticed there was something different about her and mentioned it to her husband.

'Looks the same to me,' he said, raising his eyes above his glasses to see her better. 'The same to me,' he repeated, returning to the large puzzle he was busy putting together.

Mariana watched her pour the coffee. She definitely looked different. It wasn't the hair, because she often let it down. It was something about her face. She was wearing more make-up. Her cheeks were pink and her eyes shone like wet pebbles. She smelt of soap and roses and her skin glowed due to the oil she had rubbed into it. Mariana smiled and wondered why she had made such an effort.

'I think she's got a "friend" in Cachagua,' she said to Ignacio, who wasn't remotely interested in the private life of his maid. 'Yes, she must have a suitor, Nacho. Now I wonder who that could be?' she said thoughtfully and rubbed her chin with her sensible brown fingers. Estella noticed Mariana watching her with a knowing look on her face and blushed. She smiled back nervously and turned away, fearful that Señora Mariana might guess the reason behind her blushes.

By midday the sky was a majestic blue, the last of the mist burnt off by the fierce heat of the December sun. Mariana sat in the shade on the terrace, listening for the sound of the car, quietly doing her embroidery while Ignacio wrote letters inside. She had been to check the bedrooms and bathrooms and came away very pleased with their new maid who had carried out her every command, forgetting nothing. She liked the fact that the girl had initiative. She went that little bit further without being asked. Mariana swept her soft grey eyes over the dark wooden terrace, at the pots of plants and tall palm trees that gave it respite from the sun and noticed they had all been watered. Now she hadn't asked Estella to do that, she had taken it upon herself without waiting to be asked. That was initiative, she thought to herself contentedly.

As the car descended the sandy road into Cachagua, Federica rolled down the window and poked her head out. Cachagua was the most charming of seaside villages. A low wooden fence, partly obscured by rich green ferns and palms, surrounded each thatched house. Sometimes the only visible proof that a house lay concealed behind such an abundance of nature was the tall water tower that rose up to catch the rain. It was an oasis of trees – palms, acacias and eucalyptus. Their sweet scents mingled with the salt of the ocean and the bushes of jasmine buzzed with the contentment of bees. The sandy track weaved its way through the *pueblo* down to the long golden beach and navy sea. Ignacio and Mariana's house was the nicest house in the village. Obscured behind frothy trees it resembled a log cabin on stilts with a large terrace overhanging rocks at the water's edge. Inside it was sparsely decorated with brightly woven rugs and deep crimson sofas. Mariana had always had beautiful taste and Ignacio hated clutter. He had been known to throw his hands impatiently across surfaces that he felt were too busy, knocking everything onto the floor. He had a violent temper, which only

Mariana could assuage with her calm, soothing voice and gentle manner, always detecting it early by the sudden swelling of his ears.

As the car drove through the gates into the sandy driveway, Ramon beeped the horn. Mariana's heart jumped in her chest, more out of surprise than delight, for she had drifted off and forgotten to listen out for their arrival. She called to her husband and, getting up slowly – age didn't allow her to leap to her feet as she used to do as a young woman – she made her way through the house to greet them.

Estella's hands were clammy with nerves. She leant back against the kitchen sink and smoothed down her pale blue uniform. She heard the excited voices of the children, the bubbling laughter of Señora Mariana as she hugged and kissed their eager faces, then the deep, gravelly voice of Don Ignacio. She strained her ears to find the voice of Ramon Campione but the low chatter of adult voices made his unrecognizable. She didn't even know what he sounded like.

Federica skipped onto the terrace holding her box out for her grandmother to admire. Helena gently told her to be patient, Abuelita would have all the time in the world to look at it later, once she had had a chance to talk to Papa. Federica retreated obediently to the hammock, where she curled up like a dog and watched as her grandparents chatted to her parents. Hal sat on Helena's knee with his train, which he rolled up and down the table. After a while Federica grew tired of waiting and opened the box to gaze into her secret world of make-believe.

'How long will you be staying?' Ignacio asked bluntly, noticing the impatience in his son's eyes. Ramon shrugged and glanced warily over at the hammock. Federica was no longer listening.

'I don't know,' he replied.

'You will stay for Christmas, won't you?' Mariana said. 'Surely you weren't going to leave again before Christmas?' she added, appalled at the thought.

'Of course not,' Helena said and smiled tightly.

'Then why don't you stay here until New Year? I don't know who's coming yet, probably Felipe and Maria Lucia and Ricardo and Antonella. No one tells me anything, you just all turn up when you feel like it,' she said, pretending to complain but smiling happily. Ramon looked at Helena, but their art of silent communication had been lost long ago with their intimacy.

'We'd love to,' Helena replied, thinking of the children and the extra week they would have with their father. They could return to England after New Year. A new year and a new start, she thought and sighed heavily. Mariana noticed the strain between them and her buoyancy subsided a little. She glanced at her husband who could feel her thoughts even without looking at her.

'Good,' he said and nodded gravely.

At that moment, just when an uncomfortable silence was about to slip into their conversation, Estella appeared on the terrace with a tray of *pisco sour*. She kept her eyes focused on where she was walking for fear of stumbling and making a fool of herself. Ramon leapt to his feet to relieve her of it.

'Careful, it's heavy,' he said, taking the tray.

She looked up at him from beneath her thick dark lashes and replied in a soft chocolate voice, 'Thank you, Don Ramon.'

He smiled down at her and she felt her stomach lurch and her cheeks burn. She lowered her eyes again. Her face was so smooth, so innocent and generous that Ramon's immediate impulse was to study it some more, but he could feel his parents and wife watching them. Regretfully he tore his eyes away, turned and placed the tray on the table. When he glanced behind him the maid had disappeared into the house leaving only a faint smell of roses.

Ramon poured the traditional Chilean drink of lemons and *pisco* and handed them around. Once he had sat back down he noticed the maid appear once again with two cups of orange juice for the children.

'Estella's new,' said Mariana quietly. 'She's wonderful. Do you remember Consuelo?' she asked. Ramon nodded absent-mindedly, with half an eye on the ripe young woman who padded tidily across the terrace. 'Well, dear old Consuelo died last summer. I was at my wits' end, wasn't I, Nacho? I didn't know where to look.'

'So how did you find her?' Helena asked, glad the conversation had begun to flow again.

'Well, the Mendozas, who have a summer house in Zapallar, found her for us. She's the niece of their maid Esperanza. The one with the bad squint,' she said, then added as an after-thought, 'poor old Esperanza.'

'So you're happy with Estella?' Helena asked, wiping the hair off her son's forehead and kissing his soft skin tenderly.

'Very. She's efficient and hard working and gives us no trouble at all.'

'Not like Lidia then,' Helena laughed. 'She's always got something wrong with her. If it isn't her back it's her front, her foot or her ankles that swell in the heat. She can barely walk around the house, let alone tidy it up. Dear old Federica does everything.'

'Surely not!' Ignacio exclaimed, appalled.

'Well, she likes it,' said Helena quickly.

'She seems to,' Ramon added in her defence. 'Helena's a good mother, Papa,' he added, glancing at his wife in the hope of winning a smile. She remained tight-lipped as if she hadn't heard him.

'Of course she is,' said Mariana. 'Fede, come here and show me your lovely box,' she called to her granddaughter, who rolled out of the hammock and walked hastily over to her.

'I want to see it too,' said Ignacio, pulling the child onto his lap.

Federica placed the box on the table. 'This once belonged to an Inca princess,' she said gravely. She then paused for effect before slowly lifting the lid. To her delight her grandfather caught his breath and dragged the box closer to get a better look. He pushed his glasses up his nose and peered inside.

'*Por Dios*, Ramon, where did you find this treasure? It must be worth a fortune?'

'I was given it in Peru,' he replied. Federica shivered with pride.

'In Peru, eh?' he mused. Then he ran his fingers over the stones.

'It's a magic box, Abuelito,' said Federica.

'I can see that,' said Ignacio. 'Here, woman, have a look at this. It's extraordinary.' He pushed it across the table to Mariana. Helena felt guilty that she hadn't paid it more attention.

'My dear, it's beautiful,' she said admiringly.

'If you move the box about the wings move. Look!' said Federica, pulling the box back and holding it up, tilting it from side to side. They all stared into it in amazement.

'My dear, you are absolutely right,' said Mariana, shaking her head in disbelief. 'I've never seen anything like it.'

'Papa, can I tell them the story?' Ramon nodded and Federica, her large blue eyes shining excitedly, began to tell them the legend of the butterfly box. They all listened quietly as Federica recounted what her father had told her.

Without being seen Estella stood behind the French doors watching Ramon's raffish face smiling at his daughter with great tenderness. He was more handsome than he was in photographs and had a charisma that filled the house and overwhelmed her. She stood in the shadows, as still as a marble statue, and left her eyes to gaze upon him while her mind drifted into the realm of fantasy.

After dinner, when the children had gone to bed, Ignacio and Ramon took their drinks onto the beach and walked in the foam of the surf as Ignacio had done the night before with his wife. The sky was bright and tremulous, the sea lit up by the phosphorescent moon that hung weightless above them. At first they talked about trivialities, about Ramon's latest book and his latest adventures. Finally his father drained his glass and stood in front of Ramon.

'What's going on, son?' he asked bluntly.

Ramon fell silent for a moment. He didn't really know. 'She's leaving me, Papa,' he said.

Ignacio stopped walking. 'She's leaving you?' he repeated incredulously.

'Yes.'

'Why?'

'She doesn't love me any more.'

'What a load of rubbish!' he growled. 'She's crying out for attention, any fool can see that. What else?' he demanded.

Ramon shuffled in the sand, making piles with his toes. 'I'm not there for her.'

'I see.'

'She wants me to change.'

'Why can't you?'

'I can't.'

'You're too selfish,' said his father grimly.

'Yes. I'm too selfish.'

'What about the children?' Ramon shrugged his shoulders. 'You love them, don't you?'

'Yes, I do, but—'

'But! There are no "buts" when it comes to children, son. They need you.'

'I know. But I can't be what they want.'

'Why not?'

'Because I just can't be a family man, Papa. I'm not cut out for it. The minute I come home I want to leave again. I get this claustrophobic feeling in the pit of my stomach. I need to be on the move. I need to be free. I can't be tied down.' He choked.

'Grow up, Ramon, for God's sake,' he said impatiently. Ramon stiffened. He felt like a little boy again being chastised by his father. They stood in silence, staring at each other through the twilight. Finally, they began to walk back up the beach towards the house, each alone with his thoughts. There was nothing more to say. Ramon couldn't begin to explain the claustrophobia he felt and Ignacio knew his advice was unwelcome.

Helena was relieved when Ramon suggested he sleep in the next-door room. She smiled at him gratefully. He didn't tell her about the conversation he had had with his father. She wasn't his ally any more. They were strangers. Polite, distant, mistrustful.

Ramon slipped into bed. He could smell lavender and tuberose and thought of Estella. He thought of her hands making the bed and placing the flowers in the vase. There was no point suppressing his desires as he would have done in the old days, before adultery had become a way of life. In those early days he had desired no one but his wife. She had loved him like he believed no one else could love him. He'd close his eyes and still be with her; later he'd close his eyes to be with someone else, anyone else. Now he closed his eyes and thought of Estella. Her timid expression, fearful yet brazen somehow. Her trembling lips that begged to be kissed and her glowing skin that failed to cover the longing that lit her up inside like a fire. He wondered where her bedroom was and whether she'd be surprised to find him standing in her doorway. He almost climbed out of bed to find her, but he cautioned himself against such recklessness. It was all very well when he was on his travels, alone with his secrets. But here in his parents' house was incorrect. He sighed and rolled over onto his back. The breeze was cool, slipping in through the gaps in the shutters, but he still felt hot and restless, his loins wracked with desire.

Then he did something completely crazy. He got up and walked down to the beach. In the silvery light he slipped out of his towel and walked naked into the sea. The cold water stunned his senses and he gasped for breath. He swam out until his feet no longer felt the bottom and his body was so cold it no longer felt desire. There he lay on his back, steadying himself with his outstretched arms, paddling gently with his hands. He gazed up into the inky sky and wondered what lay beyond the stars. He drifted on the current until he felt the humiliation of his father's unkind words no more. In the silence of his watery bed he no longer cared about anything. His mind was numb and his heart cold and unfeeling. When he finally pulled himself up he saw that he had drifted much further out than he had meant to. Frantically he swam back to shore, his mind clattering with the many stories he had heard as a child of men being swept out to sea and drowned. When he was able to stand his heart quietened and he waded back towards the beach, grateful to be alive.

Estella stood on the terrace anxiously watching the beach for Don Ramon who had disappeared into the sea. She had been unable to sleep knowing that he was sleeping under the same roof. Her body trembled with a yearning she could scarcely control. So she had walked out onto the terrace to breathe the air and clear her head. It was then that she had seen him wander up the sand, drop his towel and wade naked into the sea. She had had to hold onto the balcony to stop herself from following and declaring her feelings to him. But then minutes had passed and he hadn't returned. She knew of people who had drowned in these cold waters and her stomach had churned with the thought that he might join them.

To her intense relief she spotted his dark figure wading out of the water. He was alive. He was safe. She could breathe again. Hidden by the darkness she watched him pick up his towel and roughly dry himself. Then he began to make his way back towards the house with the towel casually draped around his neck. She stepped back against the wall as he neared her. She couldn't help but watch as he strode towards her, ignorant of her curious eyes that feverishly consumed his naked body. Once he had disappeared she collapsed onto the wooden floor and put her head in her hands. She was going mad. What would he think?

When Ramon once more slipped between the sheets he felt cool and less disturbed. He closed his eyes and listened as his heartbeat slowed down and his breathing became heavy with sleep.

Estella retreated to her room as agitated as before, where she lay on her bed, tormented with frenzied thoughts of him.

Chapter 6

The following morning Ramon awoke to the sounds of the children playing outside. He lay staring at the shutters, at the lucid shafts of light that streamed in through the gaps in the wood, searching him out. He thought of Estella and the thought of her made him climb out of bed with enthusiasm. He opened the shutters. He could hear Federica's excited voice on the terrace and the calm, indulgent tones of his mother. He pulled on a pair of shorts and a shirt and walked barefooted into the sunny corridor. Noticing that the rest of the family were outside he stole into the kitchen hoping to find Estella. He was disappointed. The kitchen was still and gloomy. She had been there for the bread was out on the table and the vegetables in neat piles on the sideboard. He could smell the fragrance of roses mixed with something that belonged only to her. Like an animal he sniffed the air. He waited but she did not appear. Frustrated, he walked into the sitting room, following her scent that got increasingly stronger until he knew she was somewhere close. His heartbeat quickened with the excitement of the chase.

'*Buenos días*, Don Ramon,' came a voice from behind him. He turned to find her crouched down changing the record. He noticed her exposed thigh and the neat curve of her ankle. He wanted to reach out and touch her.

'*Buenos días*, Estella,' he replied and he saw that her cheeks stung crimson at the mention of her name. He smiled down at her until the pressure of his gaze caused her to turn away. With a shaking hand she placed the needle on the rotating disc of the gramophone. Cat Stevens resounded through the room. 'Do you dance, Estella?' he asked. She stood up and looked embarrassed.

'No, Señor,' she replied, blinking at him nervously from under her long lashes.

'I love to dance,' he said, swaying to the music and the lightness in his heart that compelled him to move. Estella smiled. When she smiled her whole face came alive, he thought. Her teeth were gleaming and white against the milk chocolate colour of her skin. Her silky black hair was pulled off her face into a thick plait that fell down her back. With an unsteady hand she curled a piece that had come astray behind her small ear. He watched her every move and she felt his eyes upon her and blushed. 'Do you like it here?' he asked, attempting to engage her in conversation.

'*Sí*, Don Ramon.'

'My mother tells me you do a very good job.'

'Thank you,' she said and smiled again.

He was suddenly disarmed by the charm of her radiant face. 'You look beautiful when you smile,' he said impulsively. She recognized the longing in his voice and shuddered because she knew she was unable to hide the longing in hers.

'*Gracias*, Don Ramon,' she said hoarsely, lowering her fevered eyes that burnt when she blinked.

'Did you put the lavender in my room, and the flowers?'

'*Sí, Señor*,' she replied breathlessly, suffocated by his proximity. He was so close she could smell him.

'They're lovely. Thank you.' He watched her hover, not knowing whether to leave or stay, knowing she should scuttle back to the kitchen but unable to tear herself away. She licked her dry lips with her tongue. He stepped closer. She caught her breath and with startled eyes watched him watching her.

'You find me attractive, don't you?' he said softly, smelling the sweat that seeped through the pale cotton of her uniform.

'I do find you attractive, Don Ramon,' she whispered and swallowed hard.

'I want to kiss you, Estella. I want to kiss you very much,' he said, inching closer towards her. The chatter from the terrace faded with the roar of the sea. It was only him and Estella and the doleful melody of Cat Stevens that sang out 'Oh baby baby it's a wild world' on the gravelly record behind them.

'Papa, shall we go down to the beach soon?' said Federica, skipping into the sitting room, pleased to find her father up and dressed. Ramon stiffened. Estella's shoulders tensed and she turned with the grace of a panther and slipped back to the cool sanctuary of the kitchen where she leant against the table and fanned herself with her cookbook. Her heart jumped about like a frightened bird and her legs shook as if she were walking on them for the first time. She felt the sweat trickle down her back and between her breasts. She was excited that he desired her too, yet afraid because she knew she shouldn't sleep with a married man whose wife and children were in the same house. She knew she could lose her job. She also knew that he just lusted after her, wanted nothing more than to make love to her then cast her aside and return to his marital bed. But she didn't care. One night, she prayed, God give me one night and I'll never misbehave again. She couldn't help herself. She was powerless to resist. She bent over the table and began to chop up the vegetables to calm her agitated nerves.

Ramon followed his daughter reluctantly out onto the terrace and sat down at the table, glad to be able to hide the excitement that strained against his shorts. He poured himself some coffee and buttered a piece of toast. Helena was sitting at the other end of the terrace with his mother and Hal. She looked happier and more relaxed but Ramon didn't notice, all he saw was Estella and all he could think about was how he was going to engineer it so that he could make love to her.

Federica sat on the chair next to his with her legs swinging in the air impatiently. She placed the box on the table in front of her and opened and closed it, turned it around and tilted it but Ramon was too distracted to give her the attention she wanted.

'Good morning, son,' said Ignacio, emerging with his panama hat placed firmly on his head, in a pair of loose ivory trousers and a short-sleeved, sky-blue shirt. 'I thought we could go and have lunch in Zapallar today then drive on to Papudo. I know someone around here who wants to ride on the ponies,' he said and chuckled as Federica leapt down from her chair and ran up to him.

'Yes please!' she cried, throwing her arms around his waist. Ignacio patted her white hair and took off his hat to fan himself. It was hot and the air was sticky with the scent of the eucalyptus trees.

'That's a lovely idea, Nacho,' said Mariana. 'The children would love that. You'd like an ice cream, wouldn't you, Hal?' she said to Hal who was playing with the box of toys Mariana always kept in the house for her grandchildren. Hal nodded before once again busying himself with his game.

'I'm going to take Fede down to the beach,' said Ramon, who had no intention of going to Zapallar for lunch. He was going to spend the afternoon making love to Estella.

'I'll come with you, Ramon,' said Mariana. 'I could do with a walk. Will you be all right here, Helena?' she asked.

Helena smiled and nodded. 'I'll be fine with Hal, thank you,' she replied. She hoped Ramon would tell his parents of their plans, because she didn't think she had the courage to tell them herself. She watched them disappear back into the house. She had slept well and woken in a good humour. Mariana and Ignacio's house was serene and cool, away from the tension that seemed to cling to the walls back in Viña. Here she felt liberated. They had separate rooms and she had her own space. Ramon was diluted with his parents. He didn't seem so big and oppressive with them as he did when he was alone with her. She lay back in her chair and thought of Polperro.

Ramon and Mariana wandered down the beach while Federica skipped and jumped, playing tag with the waves that rushed up onto the beach. It was too early for people to start filling up the sand with their towels and their oiled bodies, so they had the beach to themselves.

'I'm so pleased you've come back, Ramon,' said Mariana happily. She had taken off her sandals to reveal her painted red toenails that ate into the sand as she walked. 'We do miss you when you're away. I know you and understand you,' she said sadly, 'so I'm not complaining. You do give us such pleasure.'

'Mama,' he said, taking her hand. 'You give me pleasure too. I don't know why I can't stick around for long, something inside me just tells me to keep moving.'

'I know. It's your creativity, *mi amor*,' she said as if that excused everything.

'I wish I were married to someone like you,' he sighed.

'Helena understands you more than you think. It's good for you both to get away together. She looked very strained yesterday, but the colour has come back to her cheeks today. She seems much happier.'

'Does she?' he asked. He had barely noticed her.

'Yes, she does. You know she needs a bit of time to get to know you again each time you come back. You have to be patient and not expect too much.'

'Yes,' he said. He was glad his father hadn't shared their conversation with her. He knew he should tell her the truth himself. That Helena was leaving him, leaving Chile, leaving to start again on a distant shore. But he knew it would break his mother's heart to tell her that she wouldn't watch her grandchildren grow up and he couldn't bear to upset her. She was so happy to see them, now wasn't the moment. So he just smiled down at her.

'Mama, do you mind if I don't come to Zapallar with you all. I'm weary. I'd really appreciate some time alone. I know you understand me better than anyone. I want some quiet time without the children,' he said carefully, knowing how to get around his mother from years of practice.

Mariana concealed her disappointment. 'Well, seeing as you're spending so much time with us I'll let you off,' she said and chuckled.

'Four weeks,' he said.

'Is it really that long until New Year?' she asked in amazement. 'No, it must be less, *mi amor*, we're already in December.'

'Well, just under.'

'What have you got the children for Christmas?'

'I don't know,' he replied truthfully. He and Helena had been so preoccupied with their own troubles they had completely forgotten about Christmas.

'You gave Fede that stunning box. I think she's so happy with that she won't expect anything else,' said Mariana, remembering the staggering beauty of that strange object.

'Oh, Helena has bought them trunkloads of gifts. In that department they are certainly not lacking,' he chuckled.

'How lucky they are. We'll have a lovely Christmas, you'll see,' she said, squeezing his hand.

★

Federica was disappointed her father wasn't joining them for lunch in Zapallar and swallowed back her tears. Helena suffered a confusing mixture of emotions. On one hand she was relieved and looked forward to some time without the unsettling weight of his presence, but on the other hand she was drawn to him like a reckless fly about the head of a bull. She felt compelled to be near him if only to provoke a reaction. Ignacio commented dryly that he had already had three months on his own, but after their conversation the night before he understood that his son wanted time, not on his own, but away from his wife and that saddened him. He hoped they would wake up and realize their marriage was worth saving.

Ramon watched the car disappear up the sandy track and waved at Federica who waved forlornly back with her small, pale hand.

It was very hot. The midday sun pounded against the earth with its full force. He wiped his sweaty brow with his sleeve then headed back into the house. He went straight into the kitchen in search of Estella, but she wasn't there. So he walked hastily onto the terrace, his heart pounding against his chest in anticipation, but she wasn't there either. His eyes scanned the sitting room with impatience. He didn't want to lose a moment. Finally he strode down the corridor towards his room. He heard the rustle of linen and the low hum of her voice as she sang happily to herself.

When he appeared at the door of his room Estella sprung around in fright. No one had told her that Don Ramon wasn't going to Zapallar with the rest of the family. She remained startled, blinking at him with uncertainty. 'Don Ramon, you scared me,' she said and her voice was breathless. She placed her hand about her neck as if attempting to loosen the clamp that had taken hold of it.

'I'm sorry, I didn't mean to sneak up on you. I didn't know you were here,' he lied.

'I can do your room later,' she said, dropping the sheet and walking around the bed towards him with the intention of leaving.

'Yes, you can do it later,' he replied, stopping her from going by grabbing her upper arm. She gasped. He then placed both hands on her arms and pushed her up against the wall. Her breasts heaved expectantly. He noticed a bead of sweat cling to the soft skin that formed the valley between them. He placed his finger there and lifted it off her body.

'Are you nervous?' he said, his dark eyes studying her anxious face.

'You're married,' she replied foolishly.

'Only in name, Estella. Only in name,' he said regretfully. Then he lowered his lips and brushed them softly across hers. She swallowed to release the tension that made her throat ache and closed her eyes. He kissed the moist skin of her neck, running his tongue up towards her ear. It tasted salty and smelt of roses. His hands found the bottom of her uniform and crept up inside it, his fingers tracing the soft curve of her thighs and hips. She caught her breath. Overwhelmed by the force of his charisma she felt her body go limp and surrender to a will far greater than hers. Moments such as these were the stuff of dreams and she was determined to steal her pleasure because tomorrow it might be gone. The bristle of his chin on her neck distracted her momentarily so that when his mouth fell on hers she realized his fingers were playing with the edge of her panties and caressing the damp skin of her upper thighs. When his tongue began to explore the smooth interior of her mouth she lost herself completely. His fingers pulled her panties aside and found the core of her longing where she ached to be touched. They remained pressed against the wall, their breathing heavy and in unison, their hot bodies bathed in each other's sweat. His fingers felt the velvet of her most tender places and he enjoyed watching her eyelids flutter like butterflies as she abandoned herself to his caresses.

He laid her on the bed and lifted her dress over her head to reveal even brown skin and generous breasts. He had seen her body in his fevered dreams; it didn't disappoint him in reality. He gently slipped off her underwear and gazed upon her bare sensuality with appreciation. She opened her eyes and looked up at him dazed with pleasure, her eyelids heavy and half closed. She was no longer shy or ashamed. She lay wantonly, waiting for him to do with her whatever he wished. He scrambled out of his shirt and shorts and stood before her, showing her the full glory of his naked body. She allowed her eyes to linger on it admiringly. Her face was aflame and her lips stung crimson from his kisses. She was beautiful and her beauty lifted him out of the misery of his marriage and he bathed in it and forgot himself.

When they lay entwined on the half-made bed, illuminated by the shimmering sunlight that crept in through the shutters Estella had closed to keep the room cool, Ramon felt the satisfied aching of his loins and the slowing thud of his heartbeat. He looked down at her burning face and long ebony hair that spread out across his chest in a glossy fan. She noticed him looking at her and smiled contentedly. He ran his hand up and down her naked back, his fingers playing with the bumps on her spine absent-mindedly. Most women he wanted to get rid of the minute he was finished with them, but there was something warm about Estella. He wanted her to stay.

'You're very nice to lie on,' he said at last.

Estella felt drunk with love. 'Thank you, Don Ramon,' she replied, wanting the afternoon to last for ever. She could hear his heartbeat in his large chest and feel his hair against her face. He was soft and warm to lie on too. She wanted to tell him but in spite of their physical closeness she knew they were oceans apart by the very nature of their places in the world and cautioned herself against speaking out of turn.

Federica rode the little pony up and down the beach. Helena even let her trot by herself while she led Hal's pony by the reins. Papudo was a pretty fishing village overlooking the sea, nestled at the foot of hazy blue mountains. Mariana bought them ice creams while Ignacio sat in the shade of the eucalyptus trees drinking coffee and guarding Federica's precious butterfly box while he played Solitaire. Helena had enjoyed lunch in Zapallar, the children had enchanted them all with their innocent conversation and laughter and she had barely thought about Ramon.

Federica hadn't stopped thinking about Ramon. She missed him. She had wanted him to watch her riding and remembered how he had once built her the prettiest castle in the sand decorated with white petals and shells. When they piled back into the car to drive home for tea she felt her spirits rise with the thought of seeing him again.

Ramon made love to Estella for the second time. She was a delicious feast and there were parts of her he hadn't yet tasted. Once he had satisfied his lust and his curiosity he pulled her laughing and protesting into the shower where they reluctantly allowed the water to wash away all traces of their adultery. It was only when he towelled himself dry that he looked at his watch. It was late afternoon. They would be back any minute. He told Estella to go and change her uniform that was creased and stained with sweat. She panicked when she saw the state of the room and thought of all the chores left undone that might expose her. But Ramon wandered out onto the terrace where he sat in the sunshine, picked up his father's book and began to read with a contented expression softening his rugged face.

Estella ran into her room where she hastily tied her hair in a plait, changed her uniform and patted her skin with cologne. She then set about making up the rooms without further delay. She hadn't time to dwell on the sweetness of the afternoon, the languor of their lovemaking or the passion that had made everything else seem unimportant and dispensable. When she heard the voices of the children as the door in the hallway was thrown open she gasped because they would be expecting tea and she hadn't even begun to make it.

'Papa, I rode a pony all by myself!' Federica cried, rushing to her father's side. He was in a good humour and pulled her onto his knee.

'All by yourself, you clever monkey,' he exclaimed and chuckled, kissing her hot cheek.

'Hal rode too, but Mama had to lead him, he's still too small to ride by himself. Abuelito looked after my box. He guarded it all afternoon,' she said proudly, placing it on the table.

'I hope you don't forget it one of these days,' he said.

'Papa! I will *never* lose this box,' she replied, astounded that he would even, for one minute, think she could mislay her most important possession.

'Fede rode all by herself,' said Mariana, fanning herself as she wandered slowly onto the terrace.

'You look exhausted, Mama.' He smiled fondly at her.

'I am, Ramon. It's been hot and tiring. But it was lovely. We missed you, *mi amor*.' She sank into an easy chair.

'Well, it's been very quiet here,' he said, yawning. 'I've done nothing all afternoon but read Papa's book. It's rather good.'

'*Me alegro*.' She sighed. 'I'm glad you had a nice time.'

'How about you and me go for a swim this evening before bedtime?' suggested Ramon to Federica, suddenly wanting to make up for not having joined her for lunch.

'Yes please, Papa,' she enthused. 'Abuelito can look after my box again,' she said and watched him come out into the sunshine in his crooked panama hat. 'Can't you, Abuelito?'

'What's that, Fede?' he replied, opening his eyes wide, pretending to look startled. Federica giggled; she loved it when her grandfather pulled faces.

'You can look after my box while I'm swimming with Papa in the sea,' she said.

'Careful the crocodiles don't eat you,' he said humorously.

'There are no crocodiles in the sea, silly!' she laughed.

Estella emerged with a heavy tray of tea, cake and biscuits. Ramon helped her unload it onto the table. Their eyes met and there passed between them the silent bond of complicity. She looked the same as she had that morning except the corners of her mouth curled up with satisfaction in spite of her efforts to dissemble.

'I think Estella has a lover in the village,' Mariana commented once the maid had retreated back into the house.

'*Dios*, Mariana, what does it matter?' said Ignacio, slicing the cake.

'Oh, it doesn't matter, Nacho, I'm just rather curious as to who it is,' she replied, taking a cup and saucer and handing it to Helena who emerged with Hal from the dark sitting room.

'What makes you think she's got a lover, Mama?' Ramon asked, amused.

'Because she glows. It's a woman thing. I can sense it in her step and in her eyes.'

'You perceptive old devil,' he laughed. Helena sat down next to Federica and lit a cigarette. The sight of her husband made her feel uneasy.

'I might be old, *mi amor*, but I'm not a devil,' Mariana replied, her pale grey eyes smiling at her son affectionately.

'So what if she has a lover,' said Ignacio, shrugging his shoulders.

'Who's got a lover?' Helena asked, handing Hal a piece of cake.

'Estella.'

'I agree,' she replied. 'It's a woman thing, as Mariana says. It's in her eyes.'

Ramon laughed heartily. 'Good girl. No wonder she looks well. She looks satisfied,' he said with pride.

'Well, if he's compromised her I hope he marries her. Some men aren't as honourable as they should be,' said Mariana sternly. 'Poor girl, I hope she knows what she's doing.'

Ramon chewed on the cake. 'Good, isn't it, Fede?' he said, smiling down at her. She grinned up at him and nodded. Mariana watched her granddaughter and noticed that she never took her eyes off her father. She loved her mother too. Helena was a good mother. But there was a very special bond between Ramon and his daughter. She was saddened that he had to rush off and leave her all the time. She watched the child's adoring face and felt pity for her.

Chapter 7

The next few weeks were hot and languorous. Mariana took time to enjoy her small grandchildren and give Helena a break from domesticity. She noticed that her daughter-in-law was often tense and unhappy, usually when she was with her husband, for then she smoked twice as many cigarettes as usual. She also noticed, however, that she was constantly watching him. When she spoke it was for his benefit and when he didn't react she would go silent as if intent on forcing a reaction. At times Ramon barely acknowledged her presence. But Mariana refused to believe that their marriage was disintegrating and put it down to the natural estrangement bred during their long months apart.

Federica and Hal played on the beach, dipped in the cold sea and entertained themselves drawing pictures and showing them to their proud grandparents and parents who applauded them and loved them, making them feel cherished and secure.

Ignacio watched his son with increasing gloom. He disguised his pessimism behind the face of a clown that he put on for his grandchildren to play the fool. But inside he knew that unless his son settled down and looked after his family properly, Helena really would leave him. He wondered whether that would mean she would leave Chile altogether. It would break their hearts if she took her precious children to England. They would grow up on another shore, with other grandparents and forget their Chilean family. It would be all Ramon's fault. He was selfish and irresponsible. That marriage had been doomed right from the start.

Ramon's liaisons with Estella were snatched whenever they were able to steal some time alone together. She would creep into his room in the middle of the night when moonlight bathed the bed in silver and the scents of jasmine and eucalyptus rose up on the heat to wrap them in their heady perfume. They would make love in the secrecy of the small hours when the rest of the house were far away in their private worlds of dreams. At first Estella had captured Ramon's curiosity and desire; she never even hoped to capture his heart. But little by little, in those magic moments when they lay together separated only by their skin, Ramon felt a strange power within her that ensnared him and refused to let him go. He missed her when he played the husband and father during the day and longed for the languid nights when she would appear to love him again. He saw her face whenever he closed his eyes and felt her presence long before she entered the room. Her unique scent of roses clung to his nostrils and reminded him of their passion and their tenderness and he longed to carry her away with him.

Christmas came and went. His two brothers, Felipe and Ricardo, joined them with their wives and children, so that Federica and Hal had their small cousins to play with and the house disintegrated into a large playroom with toys scattered over the floors and laughter echoing through the rooms. It was only after they had left that Ramon and Helena sat down with Mariana and Ignacio to inform them of their plans.

'We're separating,' Ramon announced flatly, staring at the floor so that he didn't have to suffer his mother's disappointment. There followed a heavy pause during which Mariana's eyes welled with tears and Ignacio rubbed his chin trying to think of something to say. Helena had lit a cigarette and smoked it nervously, hoping that they wouldn't see her as the villain of the plot.

Finally, Ignacio spoke. 'When are you going to tell the children?' he asked.

'Do you have to tell the children?' Mariana choked, wiping her eyes. 'They'll be so hurt, especially Federica. Can't you just go on the way you are? You barely see each other as it is.'

'Helena wants to take them back to England,' said Ramon accusingly. Helena stiffened.

'To England?' Mariana gasped. She felt winded, as if someone had punched her in the stomach. She tried to breathe regularly but her breaths were short and shallow.

'I feared the worst,' said Ignacio.

'All the way to England?' Mariana repeated sadly, dropping her shoulders in defeat. 'We won't see them grow up,' she whispered.

'I can't go on like this,' Helena stammered, apologetically. 'I want to start again.'

'But why England, it's so far away?' said Mariana helplessly.

'Only to you. To me it's home. To me Chile is the other side of the world. We'll come and visit and you can come and see us. Ramon will, won't you, Ramon? You said you would,' she replied quickly.

'Yes, I will.'

'You can't desert your children, son. You spend half your life in faraway places, England won't be much out of your way,' said Ignacio gruffly.

'I don't want to hurt the children. But I'm unhappy and they feel it,' Helena explained weakly. 'Ramon isn't at home to be a proper husband and help me raise them, I can't do it on my own. I've had enough of this kind of life.'

'But doesn't it worry you how the children are going to take it? Especially Fede, she's so sensitive. She'll be devastated. I just have to watch her gazing up at her father with that adoring face to know that this will break her little heart,' Mariana sobbed, taking Ignacio's hand for support.

Helena felt wounded; Federica loved her mother too. 'I know. I've thought about that. But they're young. I can't live my life for my children. I have to think about me too,' said Helena, taking a long drag with a shaking hand. She wanted to add 'because no one else is going to'.

'Ramon, can't you try? Can't you stick around at least for a few months and give it another try?' Ignacio suggested. But he knew his powers of persuasion weren't as strong as they once might have been.

'No,' Ramon replied emphatically, shaking his head. 'It won't work. Helena and I no longer love each other. If we stay together we'll end up hating each other.'

Helena swallowed hard and blinked back her emotion. He had said earlier that he loved her.

'So this is it, then?' said Mariana sadly, lowering her head.

'This is it,' Helena replied, sighing heavily.

'So when will you go?' Ignacio asked bleakly.

Ramon looked at Helena. Helena shrugged and shook her head. 'I don't know yet. I suppose it will take a while to pack up our things. I'll have to tell my parents. We'll have to tell the children. I suppose we'll leave as soon as we're able to,' she replied, then began to bite her nails with impatience. She wanted to leave right away.

'Divorce will not be easy,' said Mariana, thinking of the Catholic Church that prohibited it.

'I know,' Ramon replied. 'We don't want a divorce. We don't want to marry anyone else. We just want to be free of each other.'

'And I want to go home,' said Helena, surprised that she and Ramon were at last agreeing on something.

Ramon thought of Estella and wished he could take her away with him. Helena thought of the shores of Polperro and felt herself getting nearer.

'When are you going to break it to those dear little children?' Mariana asked coldly. She thought their actions wholly selfish. 'Think very carefully before you do it,' she warned. 'You'll hurt them beyond repair. I hope you know what you're doing.'

'We'll tell them tomorrow, before we go back to Viña,' said Helena resolutely, watching her husband warily. How far did she have to push him? she thought, his heart must be made of stone. Mariana pulled herself up from her chair and retreated sadly into the house. She suddenly looked old.

'At least they'll have their grandparents around to comfort them,' Ramon said with bitterness, looking at his wife accusingly.

'This isn't my fault, Ramon,' she said in exasperation. 'You're the one who is refusing to change.'

'It's no one person's fault, Helena,' Ignacio interrupted. 'It's the fault of the both of you. But if that is what you want it's the way it has to be. It's life and life isn't always a bed of roses.' Ramon wished it were a bed of Estella's roses. 'Tell them tomorrow and be kind,' he added, but he knew there was no gentle way to tell children that their parents no longer loved each other.

Helena was too emotional to sleep. She sat outside beneath the stars, devouring one cigarette after another, watching the smoke waft into the air on the breeze before being swallowed up by the night. She was deeply saddened and anxious about telling her beloved children, but she knew it couldn't be avoided. It would have been crueller to pretend nothing was wrong. They'd suspect something in the end, or at least Federica would. She imagined her daughter's innocent face and felt a stab of guilt penetrate her heart. She dropped her head into her hands and wept. She tried to convince herself that it would all be okay once they were settled in Polperro. They would be gathered up by her parents, whom Federica had met a few times and Hal only once. They would love England and make new friends. She thanked God she had always spoken English to them, at least that was one obstacle they wouldn't have to overcome.

It must have been about one in the morning when she treaded softly down the corridor towards the room where her children were quietly sleeping. She crept in and watched their still bodies in the dim moonlight. They slept unaware of the earthquake that was going to shatter their lives on the morrow. She ran her white hand down Hal's brown face and kissed him on his cheek. He stirred and smiled but didn't wake up. Then she tiptoed over to where Federica slept, her magical butterfly box on her bedside table where she could guard it, even in her sleep. She picked up the box and studied it without opening it for she didn't want to wake them with the music. Her heart lurched when she recalled Federica's happy face gazing up at her father in gratitude, holding his gift against her chest, treasuring it as much because it was from him as for the box itself. Suddenly she was overcome with remorse. She couldn't do it to them. She couldn't tell them. She couldn't deprive them of their father. As much as she needed to leave for herself she suddenly felt unable to use her children as innocent pawns in her battle with Ramon. She would have to think of another strategy, another plan.

Weeping she ran down the corridor to Ramon's room. She wanted to tell him she had thought again. That she had realized she wasn't able to tear their children away from everything that was familiar to them. Gasping for breath, the tears blurring her vision, she stood trembling outside his bedroom door, afraid to go in. She placed her hand on the doorknob, about to turn it, when she heard voices. Surprised, she held her breath and listened. Appalled, she recoiled. He was making love to someone. She recognized his sighs immediately and the slow rustle of sheets. When the low, contented laughter of a woman resounded off the walls she felt her stomach churn with fury. She wanted to storm in and expose them. But she was afraid of Ramon, she always had been. Pressing her ear to the door she strained to recognize the voice of the woman. She heard whispering and more laughter. It revolted her that he could be making love to another woman under the same roof as his children. Then it all fell into place. The woman could only be Estella. She then remembered their conversation about Estella and her lover and recalled the look of pride that had inexplicably swept across his conceited face. No wonder he had been so pleased with himself. She could scarcely restrain her anger and her disappointment. She had been ready to sacrifice her happiness. It was plain that he wasn't ready to sacrifice his – not even for his own children. She stepped back and, blinking away tears of pain and self-pity, she walked defeated up the corridor to her room.

The following morning Helena awoke early. It wasn't surprising she had slept badly, a shallow sleep tormented by disturbing dreams brought on by anxiety. She had tossed in her sheets, struggling with the implications of her husband's infidelity. She had been so close to changing her mind, but now nothing could alter it. Not even repentance. The carefree chatter of birds and the timid dawn light nudged her back to consciousness and she was relieved the night was over. She showered and dressed before lighting a cigarette to give her courage. She was going to talk to Ramon.

She opened the shutters and blew the smoke out into the fresh morning air. The sea was pale and smooth, gently caressing the shore with the rhythmic motion of the tide. It reminded her of Polperro although the sea was very different in Cornwall. There the waves came crashing into the land. They used to throw themselves against it as children and surf onto the beach, which was dense like clay and good for building castles. The smells were different too. The salty ozone, the damp and the coarse sand full of crabs and rock pools lined with prickly urchins. Her heart lurched for her home and hardened her resolve. She stubbed her half-smoked cigarette into the ashtray and taking a deep breath walked purposefully towards the door.

She hesitated outside his room. The voices were now silent and she could feel the contented sleep of satisfied lovers seeping through the gap below the door. Recalling the horror of her discovery she turned the doorknob and marched in. Ramon was lying on his back. Estella was curled up against him with her head on his chest. His hand was flopped over her long black hair that lay loose and wanton down her back. They were naked except for the sheet, which did little to cover them. Helena stood with her arms folded in front of her, her mouth little more than a thin line of bitterness. Ramon felt her presence in his dreams and opened his eyes. He didn't move, but stared at her as if trying to focus, not sure whether he was still in the realm of fantasy. He blinked. Helena stood staring back at him in disgust. He then realized that blinking wasn't going to send her away or wake him up because he was already awake. He nudged Estella who writhed in that pleasurable state of half-sleep. He nudged her again, this time more urgently. She opened her eyes in alarm to find Helena smouldering at the end of the bed. She gasped in horror, leapt off the mattress with a cry and hastily gathering her clothes, ran from the room, sobbing in shame. Ramon put his hands behind his head and glared at her.

'What do you think you're doing, Helena?' he said, as if she were guilty of intruding.

She shook her head in disbelief. 'What do you mean, what am *I* doing?' she snapped in fury. 'You're fornicating with the maid under the same roof as your wife and children. Don't you have any respect?'

'Calm down, Helena,' he said in a patronizing tone. 'We both know our marriage is little more than a shoddy bit of paper. You're the one who wants to end it. I don't. I don't want to tear our family apart, you do. What does it matter to you whether I sleep with the maid or anyone else?' He sat up.

'It doesn't matter to me whom you choose to fornicate with, Ramon. But I would have thought you'd have some human decency left. Your children are in the room down the corridor. What if Fede had had a nightmare and come looking for you?' she reasoned, her eyes livid with exasperation.

'She didn't,' he said flatly.

'Thank God.'

'Look, it's your decision to leave me and take them to England,' he said, raising his voice.

'Only because you don't want us any more,' she replied, almost shouting at him in frustration. 'You said so yourself, the minute you arrive home you long to leave again. How do you think that makes us feel? We're not a family any more and you know it.' She wanted him to protest that they could be, that he wanted to try to make it work, but he just narrowed his empty black eyes and stared back at her.

'Okay. We've already discussed this,' he said and yawned. 'We'll tell the children today as planned and you can leave as soon as you're ready. I won't stop you.'

'No, you won't, because it doesn't suit you to stop me. I'm giving you your freedom. All of it,' she said. 'Now you won't have to come home ever again.'

In the brief pause that followed, while they both simmered at each other with loathing, the deep, heartbroken sobs of Federica trickled under the door. Helena gasped. Ramon went pale. 'Oh my God,' he murmured, standing up and scrambling into his trousers as he rushed towards the door. They both opened it at the same time to find their daughter in a crumpled, shivering heap on the floor. She had heard everything. Estella had run past her bedroom sobbing, waking her up and sending her to her mother's room in a panic, only to find her mother wasn't there. She reached her father's room in time to hear them shatter everything she had grown up to believe in.

'Fede, sweetie,' said Helena, crouching down and gathering her into her arms. 'It's all right. Papa and I were just having a silly argument.'

'We didn't mean everything we said,' Ramon added, trying to take her from her mother's embrace.

'Leave us alone, please, Ramon,' said Helena in a voice of raw steel. Ramon pulled away, surprised by the force of her tone. He watched helplessly as his wife lifted Federica into her arms and carried her down the corridor to her room. Once inside she closed the door, shutting him out. He suddenly felt a tremendous wave of loneliness. He walked back into his room and sat down on the bed. He didn't know what to do with himself. His chest burned with guilt and remorse. He hung his head in his hands and wept.

Helena sat on the bed with her sobbing daughter clinging to her in despair. She wrapped her arms around her and gently rocked her, kissing her fevered brow and running her hands down her long hair in an effort to soothe her. It broke her heart to see her suffer so and she felt the resentment towards her husband rise in her stomach like bile.

'It's all right, Fede. Papa loves you very very much,' she said. 'We both love you very much.'

'Papa doesn't want us any more.' The child sobbed. 'If he wanted us he wouldn't go away all the time.' Helena wanted to shoot her husband for the pain he caused his children. They were innocent victims of an adult world which they were too young to understand.

'Papa does want us. At least he wants you and Hal. He loves the two of you so much. That's why we're both so unhappy. Because we want you and Hal, but we don't want each other.'

'Don't you love Papa any more?'

'It's not that simple, sweetie,' she said, trying to lessen the blow. 'Papa travels so much, it's his work and he has to do it. It's not because he doesn't want to be with us. You know all those wonderful stories he tells you?' Federica nodded. 'Well, he wouldn't have those colourful tales to tell you if he didn't go to wonderful places around the world. He comes back full of fantastic adventures to tell you, and of course the magic box he found you. If he didn't love you he wouldn't have given you that box. He wouldn't spend so much time with you. So don't doubt his love, sweetie. Mama and Papa just don't want to be together any more. But that's nothing to do with you and Hal. This is to do with us, and only us. Do you understand?' Federica nodded. 'Now we're going on an adventure. You, me and Hal,' she said, trying to make it sound exciting.

'To England,' said Federica gloomily.

Helena winced at the proof that she had heard their entire conversation. 'Yes, to England,' she said. 'Now you'll love England. We're going to a beautiful town by the sea. There are lovely big seagulls that fly over the beaches. The rocks are full of crabs and shrimps. You can go fishing with Grandpa and Granny will take you to the fair. There are ruined castles to explore and new friends waiting to know you.'

'But will I ever see Abuelito and Abuelita again?' she asked forlornly.

'Of course you will. And Papa will come and see us just like he always has done. Except we'll have a different house and no one will speak Spanish. We'll live with Grandpa and Granny, so you'll see them all the time.'

'Can I take the butterfly box with me?'

'Of course you can, sweetie. You can take anything you like.'

'I won't see Rasta any more,' she said in panic. 'Who will walk him?'

'Someone will walk him. Don't you worry.'

'He'll start barking again.'

'Maybe we can buy you your own dog. Would you like that?' Helena suggested, desperate to make it up to her child.

Federica sat up and wiped her nose with her hand. Her eyes opened very wide with a tremor of excitement. 'Can I have a dog of my very own?' she asked. Suddenly England didn't sound so bad.

'Yes. You can have a dog all of your very own,' Helena said, relieved that Federica was smiling again.

'When are we going to England?' she asked.

'As soon as we have packed everything up at home.'

'Can I go and tell Abuelita that I'm going to have my own dog,' she said, slipping off her mother's knee.

'I'll come with you. Let's get you dressed first and wake up Hal.'

When Ramon walked out onto the terrace, Helena was at the breakfast table with Federica, Hal and his parents. His eyes darted from one to the other anticipating his wife to have told them everything. Federica watched him warily over her cup of chocolate milk. Hal chattered away as if nothing had happened. Ramon sat down next to his mother and waited for someone to speak.

'Fede tells me she's going to get a dog of her very own when she gets to England,' said Mariana and although she smiled her eyes showed their strain. She only had to imagine them leaving for her vision to cloud with misery.

'Really, Fede? That's wonderful,' he said sheepishly. 'What are you going to call it?'

'Rasta,' she said but she didn't smile. Ramon felt his heart ache.

'Why can't I have a dog?' Hal whined, looking up at his mother.

'You can enjoy Rasta too,' she said wearily, trying to sound happy when all she wanted to do was hide away and cry.

'I want a rabbit,' he said. 'Are there rabbits in England?'

'If you get a rabbit, Rasta might eat him, Hal,' Federica said not unkindly.

'Lidia doesn't like dogs, so Fede will have to leave Rasta in England when we come back,' he said, taking his mug in both hands and gulping down his iced chocolate.

Ramon and Helena caught eyes where they both remained for a long moment, staring at each other helplessly. Helena hadn't had the courage to tell Hal that they wouldn't ever be coming back.

When Estella appeared on the terrace, pale and ashamed, Ramon realized that Helena hadn't told anyone about his adultery, for Mariana commented on her appearance with the same curiosity she had shown earlier.

'Oh dear. I think Estella's had a fight with her lover. She doesn't look very happy,' she said, sipping her coffee.

'She'll get over it,' said Ignacio with indifference.

'Yes, she will,' Helena agreed without looking at her husband. 'Some men are not worth the tears,' she added caustically.

Estella returned to the kitchen and once more burst into tears of shame and self-pity. She recalled Señora Helena's face, twisted with fury, as she stood as still as an icon of the Virgin Mary at the end of the bed. Don Ramon would never speak to her again. It had been heavenly but now God would surely punish her. She had only asked for a night and she had been given so much more. But it wasn't enough. She loved him. She knew she shouldn't. He wasn't from her world and the class divides were as wide as they were severe. But her heart was ignorant of the boundaries and yearned for him still.

After breakfast Helena tried to encourage Federica to play with Hal, but all she wanted to do was curl up on her mother's lap and suck her thumb, which she had stopped doing a long time ago. Helena wanted to talk to Mariana. She had only managed to tell her that Federica had been told as gently as possible that she was going to live in England. Federica had then rushed in and told her grandparents that she was going to be given a dog.

Ramon offered to take Federica down to the beach for a swim, but she held her magic box to her chest and curled up closer against her mother. Ramon felt crestfallen. Ignacio went with him instead and they talked man to man. As Helena had only informed them that Federica had been told, Ramon didn't enlighten his father on any further details. He didn't want to be cast in a bad light. His parents didn't need to know any more. He thought of Estella, pictured her bowed head and the hurt in her eyes and longed to go to her.

Federica helped her mother pack their clothes while Hal made a nuisance of himself unpacking everything they put into the cases. Federica chose to carry her box herself, she didn't want to lose it among all their clothes and Christmas presents. Ramon hurriedly searched the kitchen for Estella. He knew he didn't have much time before they had to leave

and he didn't want to be caught again. He wandered around
the house pretending to search for his camera. He found her
finally in her room, weeping on her bed into the cotton and
lace *pañuelo* her grandmother had made her. When he stood
in the doorway she sniffed and told him to leave. But Ramon
knew better than to believe that was what she wanted. He sat
down next to her and cupped her tear-stained face in his
rough hands.

'I'm not leaving you,' he said. 'I'll come back for you, I
promise.'

She looked at him, startled. Her trusting brown eyes gazed
up at him in bewilderment. 'But I will have to leave,' she
stammered.

'Why? Helena didn't tell my parents. They think you've
had a fight with your lover,' he said. 'Helena is going to
England with the children. I'll come back for you.' It seemed
so simple, so easy.

She threw her arms around him in gratitude. 'Thank you,
Don Ramon,' she said and sobbed into his neck.

'For God's sake, call me Ramon.' He laughed. 'I think
we're intimate enough now to be rid of those silly
formalities.'

'Ramon,' she breathed. She liked the sound of that and
said it again. 'Ramon.'

He touched her feverish face with the palm of his hand and
pressed his lips to hers, breathing in her scent and tasting the
salt of her tears.

'Wait for me, Estella. I will come back. I promise.' He
stood up and left her crying once more into her *pañuelo*.

But her tears were no longer of grief but of hope.

Mariana and Ignacio hugged the children with sadness, unsure
of whether they'd ever see them again. They embraced their
daughter-in-law, repressing the resentment they both felt,

wishing her a safe journey to England. Mariana secretly blamed her for the breakdown of the marriage in spite of her reasoning that told her Ramon was more to blame. It felt unnatural to begrudge her son and she had to begrudge someone. She kissed Ramon with a love that was unconditional and wilfully blind. Ignacio wasn't so blinkered. He had predicted this would happen for some time. Now it had he was deeply saddened but realistic. He hugged Ramon and wished them both well. 'Don't let them drift away, Ramon. They need you,' was all he said before his son climbed into the car and the subdued family disappeared up the track. With sad old eyes Ignacio and Mariana watched until all that was left was the dust the tyres had kicked up and the sorrow that weighed heavily in their hearts.

Estella moved away from the window, afraid of being seen, and retreated into the kitchen. She sat down to chop the vegetables and wait, as he had instructed.

Federica sat in the back of the car in silence. She wanted to cry but she knew she had to be strong for her mother. Crying would only make both her parents sad. So she swallowed hard and strained her neck to prevent the tears. She looked across at her brother who was oblivious to the sudden change that was about to rock their lives. She remembered every word of her parents' fight and wondered whether it was true that her father didn't want her any more. In spite of her brave efforts a fat tear trickled down her cheek. Hastily she wiped it away before anyone spotted it. She opened her box and tried desperately to find in its magic her father's love.

Chapter 8

The next few days were suspended in a surreal limbo. While Helena packed up the things that were precious to her and her children, Ramon took Hal and Federica for long walks up the beach with Rasta and into Calle Valparaíso for *palta* sandwiches and juice. Everything seemed normal. Beneath the surface, however, things were far from normal.

The night they returned Federica awoke crying. When her mother rushed to her she discovered that her daughter had wet her bed. She pulled her child into her arms, kissing her damp cheeks, reassuring her that it was okay; even grown-ups wet their beds occasionally. Federica didn't understand what had happened and buried her face in her mother's bosom in shame. But Helena understood only too well and longed for life to settle down in Polperro. She would have taken Federica to her bed had Hal not already occupied the space between Ramon and herself, the space usually left for indifference and self-pity. He had shuffled into his parents' room crying, having had a nightmare. But Helena knew that his nightmare was nothing more than a symptom, like Federica's incontinence, of the stress their marriage breakdown was causing them. They only had themselves to blame.

When Ramon slept he dreamed of Estella. When he was awake he fantasized about her. It was only because of Estella that he was able to get through the traumatic few days that ensued. Long days of packing up the house, organizing estate agents to put it up for sale, travel agents to arrange Helena and the children's trip to England. He longed to be on the road again, free from the turbulence Helena had invited into their lives. He'd buy an apartment in Santiago, somewhere to have as a base. Somewhere for him alone, without the constraints of domesticity, where he could come and go without explanation. He arranged to wire money to England, enough for them all to live well. Helena should have been grateful, his offer was generous, more than generous, but she only felt bitterness. Like his gifts, Ramon found it easy to buy people's affection, as long as he didn't have to invest his time, or himself. She accepted because she had to, for the sake of the children, but she would have preferred to have thrown it back in his face.

Federica curled into a ball. The light from the street lamp scattered her room with an orange glow. The light used to be reassuring. It used to make her feel secure. But not any more. She pulled her knees up to her chest and sucked her thumb. She had gone to the bathroom at last twice in ten minutes. Not that she needed to go, but because she was afraid of wetting her bed again. Her father had kissed her goodnight. He had even told her a story. One of his adventures. She had listened, seated on his knee as usual. But when he had kissed her goodnight she had found herself wanting more. A longer kiss, a longer hug. When he had left the room she felt deprived, as if he hadn't loved her enough. She no longer felt secure and cherished. She felt needy. She longed for her mother to embrace her and hold her against her body. She lay awake in bed devising plans to justify going into their room in the middle of the night. A nightmare was Hal's excuse, she had to think of something different. So she pretended to be ill. Her mother had been sympathetic and allowed her to sleep in their bed on the second night, but on the third Hal had had another nightmare so she was swiftly taken back to her room where she cried herself to sleep. She was frightened about going to England. She didn't want to leave Viña del Mar, or Chile or Abuelito and Abuelita. She didn't want things to change. Most of all she wanted Mama and Papa to be friends again. But as much as they put on a show, she knew they no longer liked one another. She had heard everything.

Finally the day of their departure arrived. With solemn faces they watched as Ramon loaded up the car with their cases. Federica couldn't stop herself crying. She didn't want to leave her father. She didn't know when she would see him again. In Viña she had been happy to wait, after all it was his home, he was bound to come back at some stage. He always had. But now her new home wouldn't be his home.

He picked her up in his strong arms and held her tightly, kissing her face. 'Papa loves you, Fede. Papa loves you so much. Just remember that, *mi amor*. Papa will always love you, even if he's not with you. When the sun shines and you feel that heat on your body, that's Papa's love. You understand?' Federica nodded, too distressed to speak. She didn't want him to let her go. But he had to. They had a flight to catch and the taxi was waiting to take them to Santiago. Helena had thought it less traumatic for the children if Ramon said goodbye to them at the house and didn't accompany them to the airport. He picked up his son, who didn't really understand what was going on, and kissed his plump face. 'Papa loves you too, Hal. Be good for Mama, won't you,' he choked, closing his eyes, burying his face in the child's glossy black hair.

Federica clutched the box against her and waved at her father who stood forlornly in the road, waving back with an unsteady smile, like a clumsy giant. She turned to look out of the back of the car and waved until they had turned the corner and he had gone. Then she sat slouched against the window, watching the houses pass by, numb with sadness. She felt as if her insides had been scooped out, leaving a gaping hole that only her father could fill. She worried all the way to the airport about Rasta. She worried that no one would walk him and that he'd start to bark again out of sheer boredom and misery. It was only when they were on the plane that she stopped crying. She had never been in a plane before and it fascinated and excited her. She took her mother's hand as they careered up the runway. Helena smiled down at her lovingly and squeezed her hand.

When the lights were turned out and Hal and Federica lay sleeping in their chairs, Helena reflected on the past few days, relieved that they were over. She would put Chile behind her, Ramon too. She'd start a new life in England. She felt drained of energy, depleted of emotion. She replayed the telephone conversation she had had with her mother and found the tears welling in her somnolent eyes. She had been so busy playing the glad game for the children she hadn't allowed herself the luxury of crying. Now they were asleep she wept silently, relieving the strain in her neck and jaw. The thought of her mother's voice made her stomach flutter with longing. She had heard her father in the background and suddenly she had wanted more than anything in the world to run to them, as she had done as a child, and let them soothe her with their gentle words and reassuring presence. They had been saddened to hear that Helena had decided to leave her husband, but glad that they were coming home.

Jake and Polly Trebeka had watched helplessly as their daughter had married and gone to live on the other side of the world. They had both liked Ramon in spite of the vast difference in culture that had prevented them from understanding him. They were never given the time to get to know him properly. Both would have preferred a gentle Cornishman for their daughter. But Helena had been consumed by him almost from the minute she met him. The first indication of his feelings for her and off she had gone to follow him wherever he chose to go, like an adoring shadow. Of course, Polly knew all about their troubles and blamed Ramon entirely for the disintegration of their marriage. She had had her reservations right from the start. He was from a different world, a wanderer and it was all very well while they floated about just the two of them, but there would come a point when Helena would want a family. Ramon had always been selfish. The world revolved for him alone and she doubted he'd ever change his ways for anyone. Well, now it had imploded. Jake and Polly were distraught but realistic. Helena was still young, only thirty years old. There was plenty of time to find a nice, kind Cornishman to look after her as she deserved to be looked after. Ramon was an unfortunate error; but he was now in the past.

Polly immediately set about preparing for their arrival. She spent hours deliberating whether Hal and Federica would like to share or whether they'd prefer to have their own rooms. The house was large. There was space enough for everyone. Finally, after having discussed it with her husband she decided to give them their own, each with twin beds, so that if they felt lonely they could share. She aired Helena's old bedroom, still with the clothes and trinkets she had left behind packed neatly in the cupboards. She had never cleared them out. She hadn't had to. As far as she was concerned that room had always belonged to Helena.

Chapter 9

Ramon walked up the beach and experienced for the first time in his life the hollow pangs of bereavement. It was evening and he was alone. He hadn't even been able to take Rasta for a walk, for without Federica there didn't seem much point. So he had walked past the dog's small prison looking the other way and ignoring the animal's excited breath and husky barking. His heart ached with remorse and self-loathing and yet he didn't consider changing his ways as Helena had asked him to. He hadn't even offered to try. He wallowed in his misery, enhanced by the natural melancholy of the dying day. He turned his weary eyes to the sea and tried to imagine their new home in England. He remembered Polperro and the first time he had seen Helena. He imagined it the way it was then.

He sat on the sand and rested his elbows on his knees looking out over the choppy Pacific Ocean that stretched out before him, untamed and free. He had been like the sea then, going wherever the tide of his imagination took him. Those were the days when he was young and adventurous and blessed with immortality. Or so he had thought. He could do anything he wanted. So he had travelled, sometimes sleeping under the stars, other times boarding with strangers generous enough to take him in. He had been born into a world of privilege and yet money had never meant a great deal to him.

As long as he was on the move he was happy. At first he had written poems, which a friend of his father's, who owned a small publishing firm in Santiago, had published for him. It had been immensely exciting seeing his work in print for the first time, with his name in big letters, positioned in the bookshop window for all to see. But he didn't care too much for fame either, he was happier wandering the world unnoticed. Then he had written a collection of short stories, inspired by his adventures and embroidered with his fantasies. After that he was no longer an unknown in Chile; he began to be recognized. His book sold in bookshops all over the country. His picture appeared in *El Mercurio* and *La Estrella* and alongside the articles he wrote for various magazines such as *Geo Chile*. His desire to be creative was insatiable, nothing could pin him down. He'd stay in Chile long enough to see his family and then he'd be gone again, as if he were afraid his own shadow might catch up with him.

When he first met Helena he was writing a piece for *National Geographic* about the historic sights of Cornwall. He had been inspired to write the story having met a weathered old seaman who had grown up in St Ives before joining the Navy and finally ending up in Valparaíso. He had woven a compelling tale of the land of King Arthur and Ramon had been struck with the urge to go to see it for himself. He hadn't been disappointed. The villages and towns were stuck in the past as if the modern world had not yet discovered them. The houses were whitewashed and built into the rich green hills that fell sharply into the sea. The bays were solitary coves haunted by the ghosts of smugglers and shipwrecks. The roads were little more than narrow, winding lanes lined with tall hedgerows scattered with cow-parsley and long grasses. He had been enchanted. But if it hadn't been for Helena he would only have scratched at the surface.

Helena Trebeka had been sitting on the quayside in Polperro when Ramon had first seen her. She was slim, carefree, with long wavy hair of such a pale blonde that he was immediately struck by it. He sat down to watch her, making mental notes in order to put her into one of his stories. He imagined she was the granddaughter of a smuggler. A girl with a wild nature and rebellious inclination to do exactly as she pleased; he wasn't far wrong. She caught him staring at her and stared back in defiance. Not wanting to offend her he walked over and placed himself next to her so that their legs dangled over the edge together.

'You're very beautiful, like a mermaid,' he mused, smiling at her. She was caught off guard. Englishmen were never that poetic or daring and most of the men she knew were afraid of her.

'Well, I'm sorry to disappoint you, I have legs not fins,' she said and smiled back vivaciously.

'So I see. Much more practical, I should imagine.'

'Where are you from?' she asked. He spoke with a heavy accent and his black hair and brown skin were new to her, as were the leather moccasins he wore on his feet.

'I'm from Chile,' he replied.

'Where's that?' she asked, unimpressed.

'In South America.'

'Oh.'

'There is a world outside Polperro, you know,' he teased.

'I know,' she said tartly, not wanting him to think her provincial. 'So what are you doing here in my little town?' she asked, unable to curtail her curiosity.

'I'm writing an article about Cornwall for a magazine,' he said.

'Do you like it?'

'What, Cornwall?'

'Yes.'

'So far, I like it very much.'

'Where have you been?' she asked, smiling, for she knew he wouldn't have been to the secret places that weren't to be found in guidebooks. So he listed the towns he'd visited and some of the history he'd picked up.

'You know, my grandfather was a smuggler,' she said proudly.

'A smuggler.' He laughed, congratulating himself on his acute powers of perception.

'A smuggler,' she repeated.

'What did he smuggle?'

'Brandy and tobacco, that sort of thing. They used to cart it by the wagon-load to Bodmin Moor where they would hide it. They'd sell it for a fortune in London.'

'Really?'

'Yes. Now that's the sort of thing you should be writing in your article. Everyone's bored of King Arthur. Why not write something original?'

'Well, I—'

'I could show you all the secret coves and bays and Dad could fill you in on the details,' she said impulsively. Ramon thought that sounded like a good idea. At least if the smuggling story didn't work he'd have some time to get to know this intriguing character who was presenting him with a tempting challenge. She wasn't like other girls he'd met. She was outspoken and confident.

'Okay. I'd like that,' he replied, surprised at her forwardness that contradicted sharply her almost angelic looks.

Jake and Polly Trebeka were appalled when Helena skipped in for lunch to tell them that she had made a new friend, a writer from somewhere in South America, whom she was going to show around all the old smuggling sights.

'You can't go picking up strangers, Helena. You don't know anything about him,' said Jake sternly, carefully hingeing the miniature wooden door on the model boat he was making.

'He could be a murderer,' Polly added wryly, as if murderers were commonplace. She took a steaming vegetable lasagne out of the Aga and placed it on the table. 'Where the devil is that brother of yours? Toby!' she shouted. 'Toby!'

'Mum, he's not a murderer,' Helena protested.

'Well, you'll only find out when it's too late.' She chuckled heartily, wiping her hands on her woollen skirt. Polly was a large woman, not fat, but big-boned and strong. She thought diets were frivolous and spending time in front of the mirror a wasteful indulgence of the very vain. Like a magnificent galleon she dwarfed her husband who trailed behind her like a crude sailing boat. Not that Jake was slight; he might have been small in stature but he could knock the breath out of any man who caused him offence. They looked an odd couple but they were immensely fond of each other and agreed on everything as much out of habit as out of a united opinion. Jake owned a thriving joinery business and Polly ran the house, raised the children and the beds of flowers that blossomed every spring. They were comfortable but not rich. 'What do I need a lot of money for?' Jake would say. 'I can't take it with me when I die, can I?'

Toby descended the stairs, the loud thumping noise of his feet on the wood shaking the entire building. 'What's for lunch, Mum?' he asked, smelling the heavy aroma of his mother's celebrated cooking.

'Vegetable lasagne,' she said briskly, placing a water jug on the table.

'My favourite,' he enthused. Jake had always said that Toby must have holes in the soles of his feet because he had an amazing capacity for food but never gained weight. He was slim and lithe like a rubber plant, with the gypsy black hair of his father and the good humour of his mother. When it came to food he had an appetite that far exceeded both theirs combined.

'Jake, can't you finish that after lunch?' said Polly impatiently. 'Why we need another model boat is beyond me.' She sighed, casting her eyes over the rows of models that cluttered up her surfaces like the shelves of a toyshop.

'What if I bring him here to meet you, then you can judge for yourselves?' Helena persisted.

'Bring who here?' Toby asked, dishing himself a large portion of lasagne.

'Helena's met a man in Polperro who wants her to show him all the old smuggling sights for an article he's writing,' said Jake.

'Oh yes?' Toby exclaimed. 'That's a good one.'

'No, he really is writing an article,' Helena insisted.

'Why, did you see it?' said Toby.

She pulled a face at him. 'Of course not, stupid. He hasn't written it yet.'

'All right, all right. Enough you two,' said Polly as if she were talking to a couple of rowdy dogs. 'Tell him to come here for tea, then we can meet him for ourselves.' Helena smiled triumphantly.

'How old is he, Helena?' Jake asked seriously, pulling out a chair and joining them at the table. He dug his fork into the lasagne.

'Mid to late twenties,' she replied and shrugged because she didn't really know. He was bristly and hairy, well built and confident. He could have been anything between twenty-five and forty.

'And he's travelling alone?' he said, chewing on his food. 'Polly, this lasagne is really very good,' he added as his wife sat down and helped herself to what was left.

'Looks like it,' said Helena.

'At eighteen you might think you're a woman, but when I was your age I had to have a chaperone,' said Polly.

'As if you needed a chaperone, Mum, you could flatten the strongest of men with one wave of your big hand,' Toby chuckled irreverently.

Ramon met Helena as planned on the harbour wall. She was embarrassed to tell him that she had to introduce him to her parents before they'd allow her to go anywhere with him.

'My mother thinks you're a murderer,' she said and sighed.

'Well, you can never be too sure.'

'You come from a strange country, how are we to know, you might be a cannibal.' She laughed.

'Well, if I were I think you'd be pretty tasty.'

She smiled coyly but didn't lower her eyes or blush. She looked at him with her steady blue eyes, assessing him. 'You think so,' she replied loftily. He nodded and grinned at her. Her arrogance amused him although he was sure it wasn't meant to. 'Well then, I think you'd better come and meet my parents. We live just outside Polperro so you can either travel as I do by bike or walk.'

'I'll find a bike,' he said. 'We can go together.'

They cycled up the hill out of Polperro, leaving the sleepy harbour and whitewashed houses that were stacked up the banks of the hill like dolls' houses. It was a clear summer day, the seagulls floating on the salty breeze and the bees humming in the cow-parsley. As they cycled together Ramon told her about Chile and his book of tales. When he told her he was a well-known writer, she didn't believe him, retorting that she had never heard of him. 'Well, if you come to Chile you'll hear about me,' he said.

'Now, why would I want to go to Chile?' she replied.

'Because it's beautiful and a girl like you should see the world,' he said truthfully.

'I'll see the world one day. I'm only eighteen, you know.'
'You have plenty of time.'

'And lots of more important places to see first,' she said.
Ramon laughed and shook his head. He was suddenly overcome with the urge to kiss her, but he bicycled on. There
would be time enough for that later.

Helena's house was a pretty white building crawling with
an abundance of clematis that climbed up the walls and onto
the grey tiled roof above like the tentacles of a floral octopus.
Ramon noticed a family of pigeons hopping about by the
chimney, watching him from their lofty height with shiny
black eyes. 'Well, it ain't much but it's home,' she said,
dismounting and throwing her bike against the wall. 'Let's get
this over with,' she added, winking at him mischievously.

Polly Trebeka was not as Ramon had expected. She had
pale hair like her daughter which was streaked with a silver
grey and tied into a rough bun which left curly wisps floating about her neck. Her face was completely free of makeup.
She seemed the sort of woman who never bothered with
creams yet her skin was soft and youthful and her smile that
of a young girl. When he was introduced to Jake Trebeka he
saw where Helena's pale blue eyes came from. They were
almost the colour of aquamarines. In Jake they were more
evident due to his swarthy skin and jet-black hair. He looked
like a strange gypsy with the eyes of a hawk. Helena had
inherited their best features and was more refined than both
of them.

Toby had taken special care to be present for this meeting.
He had noticed the excitement burn in his sister's cheeks
when she spoke about this man and was curious to see what
it was about him that made him different from all the other
young men in Polperro who fell in love with her.

'Please sit down, Mr . . .' said Jake politely, looking to his
daughter to introduce them. Helena, of course, didn't know

his name. Toby caught her eye and grinned. She shot him a look to tell him to behave himself before turning back to her parents.

'Campione, Ramon Campione,' said Ramon and sat down on the sofa. His presence was somehow too big for the small sitting room. Helena was undeterred by the amount of sofa he took up with his long arms and legs and sat down next to him.

'I'm Jake Trebeka and this is my wife Polly and Toby, our son. It's a pleasure to meet you. My daughter tells me you're a writer,' he said.

Ramon nodded. 'Yes, I've written a couple of books of poetry and some short stories,' he said and his heavy Spanish accent sounded out of place in such an English home.

'But you're not here for a book,' said Polly, putting down the tray of tea. She noticed Ramon's long glossy hair which she thought could have done with a good cut and the mahogany colour of his intelligent eyes. He was so totally foreign. She had never spoken to a foreigner before.

'No, Señora, I'm writing an article for *National Geographic*,' he said.

Polly's eyes widened and she looked at her daughter in exasperation. 'Why didn't you tell us he was writing for *National Geographic*, Helena?' she said, placing her large hands on her round hips. 'I love that magazine, so does Toby, don't you dear?' she enthused, feeling more comfortable now she was able to place him in a familiar box.

'We love it,' Jake agreed, impressed. 'What's the article on besides smuggling?'

'Well, it's meant to be on the land of King Arthur,' Ramon explained. 'But Helena suggested the smuggling idea. I haven't passed it by the editor, though.'

'Oh, the land of King Arthur. What a magical idea,' enthused Polly.

'No it's not, Mum, it's unoriginal,' said Helena bluntly.

'Helena's right, it's very unoriginal,' Toby agreed, grinning at his sister.

'That all depends on how it's written,' said Ramon, his shiny brown eyes smiling at Helena playfully.

'Well, I said I'd show him the haunts and you, Dad, could fill him in on the history,' said Helena breezily, smiling back at Ramon.

'I'd be happy to help,' said Jake. 'The *National Geographic*, eh. Now that's a prestigious magazine. Do you take the photographs as well?'

'Everything,' said Ramon. Polly nodded in admiration.

'So you see, he's not a murderer, is he?' said Helena. Polly glared at her. Jake laughed. Toby nearly choked on his tea.

'I hope not,' he chuckled. 'Be sure to show him Crag Creek,' he added.

Helena beamed triumphantly. 'I'll show him everything,' she said.

Helena and Ramon spent the following ten days cycling around the coast. She showed him places he would never have found without her help. She'd prepare picnics for them, which they'd eat on the beaches, chatting with the familiarity of two people who have known each other for a good many years. They talked to people in pubs and fishing boats, explored caves and creeks and swam in the sea. Ramon had wanted to kiss her from the first moment he had endured the arrogance of her conversation. His chance came after a couple of days when they were picnicking quietly on a remote beach. Helena had only packed one piece of her mother's chocolate cake. Ramon suggested she halve it. Helena refused and placed the whole piece into her mouth at once, giggling triumphantly.

'Well I'll just have to go and get it then,' he said. Helena tried to stand up, silently protesting with her hands for her mouth was too full to speak. But Ramon was too quick for her. He lay on top of her and pinned her onto the sand with his hands. She glared at him with ice-cold eyes that a moment before had been warm and inviting. But to his amusement she couldn't refuse him verbally, so he placed his mouth onto hers with his Latin ardour and kissed her chocolate lips. Then he devoured the curve in her neck and the rise of her collar-bone. Finally she swallowed hard and was able to speak.

'Ramon! What are you doing?' she protested.

'Shut up, I've heard all I want to hear from you for the moment. Now, relax and let me kiss you, I've been longing to from the first moment I saw you in Polperro,' he said and placed his lips on hers again to silence her. She relaxed as he had instructed and closed her eyes, aware only of his warm mouth and the light feeling in her stomach.

Ramon left Polperro after two weeks. He kissed Helena goodbye on the quay where they had first met. She was too proud to show her sorrow so she smiled at him as if she didn't care. Only afterwards did she cry into the spongy bosom of her mother. 'I think I love him, Mum,' she sobbed. Polly wrapped her arms around her and told her that if he loved her he'd come back for her. If he didn't then she wasn't to waste any more of her time on him. 'Summer romances are lovely things in themselves, dear, sometimes they're best left as they are.'

But Ramon hadn't forgotten about Helena. He had tried to. He had written up his article and sent it off to his editor. Then he had gone to his parents' house in Cachagua where he had moped around like a lovesick schoolboy, sat on the beach watching the sea with a heavy heart, thinking of Polperro and the mermaid he had left there. He tried every-thing to forget her. He slept with a few girls he picked up, but that only made his ardour stronger. He wrote poems about her and a short story about the daughter of a Cornish smuggler. His parents were delighted. He had never been in love before and they had almost despaired of his cold heart and lonely wanderings. So Mariana had talked to him, told him to follow his feelings instead of fighting them. 'They're not going to go away, Ramon,' she had said. 'Enjoy them and indulge them. That's what love is for. You're lucky to feel like that, some people go through life and never experience it.' So Ramon had called his editor and asked to add one small paragraph.

'What's that then?' his editor asked curiously. He liked the article very much, but they wanted to run it immediately. 'I hope it's not long, I won't have space,' he said.

'No, it's not long. I'll dictate it to you.'

'All right. Go ahead.'

'The most beautiful and magical place of all is Helena Beach in Polperro, a small cove of silver white sand with a pale blue sea of such translucence that she lures you into the depths of her mysteries until your heart is captured and your soul enslaved. I left knowing that I would never be the same again and that I would be hers for ever. It is only a question of time before I go back to give myself to her, body and soul.'

'Quite a beach, Ramon,' said the editor dryly. 'I shouldn't allow it to go in, but as it's you.' Then he added with a smile, 'I just hope none of our readers try to find it, they might be disappointed!'

When Helena received the copy of *National Geographic* she knew it was from Ramon, although there was no note attached. She tore open the paper and leafed through the pages with a trembling hand. Then she sat at the kitchen table and read his article. She wept at the photographs, taken together, and the way he wrote which was uniquely poetical and touched her heart. When her eyes found the paragraph about 'Helena Beach' they were so misted she could barely read it. Blinking away her tears she had to read it again in case she had read too much into it. Then she smiled because she knew that he loved her and that he'd come back for her. He had been worth waiting for after all.

Ramon sat on the beach, thinking of Polperro, thinking of his wife and children sitting on the quay in the harbour and his heart lurched for them. He thought of the way he first felt about Helena and the way he now felt about Estella. Love, he sniffed, what's the use? It always goes sour in the end, he thought bleakly. How could he love Estella when he hadn't even been capable of loving his wife properly? It was better not to love at all.

Later when he returned to the house he had made up his mind. He would leave immediately and forget about Estella. He should have forgotten about Helena all those years ago, at least he wasn't about to make the same mistake twice.

Opening his maps he cast his eye to India and nodded. India, that's as good a place as any.

Chapter 10

England

Toby Trebeka had stayed the night in London in order to be close to Heathrow airport for his sister's arrival the following morning. He had volunteered to go. He didn't like to think of her having to take a train or a bus down to Cornwall, especially not in her fragile state of mind. His parents had told him she had decided to leave Ramon. He was saddened. She had been so happy at the beginning. Wasn't everyone? He felt sorry for the children, torn between two people like that, feeling themselves to blame for their parents' failure to love one another. It always affected children more than people realized. Still, he thought, one can't live one's life entirely for one's children. Not that he'd ever have that problem.

Toby had always been different from the other boys growing up in Polperro. In spite of being of an athletic build he hadn't enjoyed sport, except for fishing, which the other boys thought incredibly dull and antisocial, especially because he always threw back the fish he had caught. He refused to eat meat – 'anything with a mother or a face' he explained. But Toby had sailed off in his father's small boat to look at the fish in spite of their mockery. He used to sit out there in the rough sea for hours on end with only the seagulls for company and the sound of his own voice humming the bad love songs he listened to on the wireless. He was handsome with pale luminous skin and sensitive eyes that cried easily, usually at things other people wouldn't have even flinched at, like the sight of a shimmering shoal of fish beneath the surface of the sea or a lone crab running for cover beneath a rock. It was only his cheery nature and sharp wit that prevented him from being bullied at school and because he was so much brighter than the other boys. He earned their respect by humour and by his readiness to laugh at himself. He collected insects, which he kept in large glass containers with all the luxuries they could possibly need from foliage to food, and spent hours nurturing and studying them. He read books on trees and animals and subscribed to the *National Geographic*. He knew he was different. His mother had told him to 'make a feature' of his differences. So he hadn't tried to like football or rugby, he hadn't tried to like smoking and sitting in pubs discussing girls. For that matter he hadn't tried to like girls either – well, not in the way the other boys expected him to 'like' them.

When he was about fifteen and the only boy in the class never to have kissed a girl he forced little Joanna Black up against the wall and kissed her in front of everyone just to prove that he could. He had hated himself for it. Not only because he had hurt Joanna Black and sent her running into the classroom sobbing with the force of a woman robbed of her virginity, but because he hadn't liked it. It hadn't felt right. The boys patted him on his back with admiration. Joanna Black was one of the prettiest girls in the school. But the hot rush of pride to his head had been quickly replaced by a burning shame that tugged at his conscience. Joanna Black never spoke to him again. Even when he saw her in the grocery shop years later, she still stuck her nose up and stalked out without so much as a glance. He had tried to apologize, but it felt silly apologizing for something that had happened so long ago.

In the sixties, when Toby was a teenager, he had more 'girlfriends' than any other boy in Polperro. Girls adored him. He was funny, enjoyed gossip and intrigue, treated them with respect and was never nervous with them or too shy to say what he thought. He was attractive in an endearing way with those lucid eyes that assured them he understood them better than other boys. His large smile was honest and his kind face approachable. They all loved him and yet he never loved them in the way they longed for him to love them.

The sea was an escape for Toby when he wanted to avoid the boys in the pub discussing girls and how far they'd got. He would sail out into the salty mists where he could be himself, where he didn't have to conform to anything. He remembered his mother's advice, but he couldn't make a feature out of homosexuality without offending the entire town. He had known he was gay from a very early age, but homosexuality was vehemently outlawed by their sheltered society and Polperro was too small to hide in. So, in 1967, at the age of eighteen, he chose to leave Polperro and look for work in London. His parents hadn't understood why he needed to go off and work in London, there was plenty of work locally for an intelligent young man like Toby. His father wanted him to work with him making windows and doorframes but Toby couldn't explain that he winced at the very idea of cutting magnificent trees into little pieces. He couldn't explain so he didn't. He just packed his bags and left. His mother was devastated, his father angry. 'You sweat blood to bring them up and then the ungrateful sods leave without so much as a thank you,' he growled. By that time Helena was travelling the world with Ramon. Jake and Polly found themselves more alone than when they had first married, because they knew what it was like to have the house filled with the laughter of their children. Now all they had left were echoes, which were louder than the silence had been in those pre-children days.

It had taken years for Toby to find a job. Not because he wasn't employable – he had left school at eighteen with good grades – but because he couldn't find something that he enjoyed doing. As he explained to his parents, 'If I'm going to be working for the rest of my life it had better be something I love or it's not worth living.' They couldn't help but agree with him, which is why they were confused by his decision to leave Polperro. There were no fishing boats in London, no wide-open sea for him to lose himself in. Toby had tried working in the City but only lasted three weeks. He brushed off his hasty departure with a cheery smile stating simply that he wasn't cut out for the City. He tried his hand at everything from selling to marketing to designing kitchens. But he soon grew disheartened and behind the smile he presented to his friends as each new failure defeated him lay the frightened soul of a man confused and alienated. He didn't belong in London, or the City, or the offices of Mayfair. He didn't belong in the world of married couples and children either. He knew where his world lay, but it might as well have been at the foot of the rainbow for he was too afraid to find it. He longed for his home, for the sea and for the security of that fishing boat hidden in the impenetrable ocean mists. Then one night in a bar he met a flaxen young man called Julian Fable who changed his life for ever. They both had too much to drink, Toby to drown his misery, Julian to give him courage. When they left the bar Julian turned to Toby and, taking his forlorn face in his hands, he kissed him. Suddenly Toby felt an enormous release, as if the shadow he had been was at last covered with a skin that felt comfortable to live in. Finally in 1973, at the age of twenty-four, he returned to Polperro with Julian, complete and contented. They bought a cottage outside Polperro where Julian built a dark room for his photography and Toby bought a boat, which he christened '*The Helena*' and started up his own business taking tourists for rides around the coast, and at last he settled down. He had found himself.

For the first few years no one thought it was in the least bit strange that Toby Trebeka was living with another man. But when people began to notice that they never dated nor chased girls, gossip and rumour started to rise like the sea mists until it became overwhelming and impossible to ignore. Toby had been happily going about his own business, never interfering with anyone else's. It deeply saddened him that he should have to explain himself to anyone. But he was left no choice. He arrived one evening at his parents' house for dinner. They were curious as to why he should invite himself for dinner in the middle of the week and an uneasy feeling invaded their home. Jake and Polly had both suspected he might be gay, but as long as it wasn't discussed or flaunted in front of them they ignored it. Pretended it wasn't there. Like hiding a stain in the carpet with a potted plant, they were happy to leave it unattended in spite of the friends and neighbours who talked about it behind their backs.

'How is everything?' Jake asked warily while Polly stirred the vegetable soup with a firm hand.

'Fine, thanks, Dad,' said Toby, swallowing down a gulp of wine to give him courage.

'So all's well then,' said Polly from beside the Aga, her tight smile betraying her anxiety.

'Look, Mum, Dad. I'm gay,' Toby said bluntly. He had the same direct approach as his sister yet it still managed to take both parents by surprise. He sighed heavily and let the wine feel for him. Jake knocked back his brandy. Polly stirred the soup with vigour. For a while no one spoke. Left alone with their thoughts the silence isolated them from each other. Only Toby's heart soared weightless in his chest, more buoyant than ever.

'So Julian's your . . .'

'Lover, Dad. Julian's my lover, my friend. I don't expect you to understand, just to accept that this is the way I choose to live. I don't want people gossiping about me behind your backs. You have a right to know,' he replied, looking at his father steadily.

'I've always taught you to be independent,' Polly began, approaching the table.

'To make a feature of our differences,' said Toby wryly.

'To make a feature of your differences,' she said and chuckled. 'Well, I'm proud of you. It takes a lot of courage to go against the tide.'

'I think I've been swimming against the tide all my life,' Toby mused, smiling sadly.

'Well, I'll swim with you, Toby dear,' said Polly, bending down to kiss him.

He put his arms around her thick waist. 'This means a lot to me, Mum,' he choked.

'I know,' she replied, patting him on the back. 'I know.'

Jake accepted it as his son had asked him to, but he never spoke about Julian or wished to see him or entertain him in his house again. Toby was mortified that suddenly a wall had been erected between them. His father had liked Julian before, but now, out of sheer prejudice, he saw him as a threat and decided to go against his initial judgement and turn against him. However, Polperro was a small village and they simply couldn't avoid each other. When they did eventually meet one hazy Saturday morning on the quay, while Julian moored Toby's boat, *The Helena*, and Jake walked past on his way to his own boat, they nodded politely, but that was as far as it went. Jake had acknowledged him without venturing further than his good manners pushed him. Toby was pragmatic. At least he had told them, there were no secrets to pull him down. The only road ahead was up.

★

Federica and Hal arrived at Heathrow airport dazed and exhausted. The flight had been long, stopping in Buenos Aires, Rio, Dakar, and finally Heathrow. Their world had been reduced to the small interior of the aeroplane for what had felt like an eternity. They had played games with the pencils and paper the air hostesses had given them and slept as much as they were able to, using their mother as a cushion and comforter combined. But they were restless hours punctuated by frustrating stops and once the novelty of flying had worn off they had both wept weary tears. Helena had tried to keep them distracted and she had even asked Federica to tell her the story of her box again just to use up a few more empty minutes with something.

Finally Toby's long, smiling face loomed into focus, as he waved at them madly when they walked slowly out through customs. Neither Hal nor Federica recognized him. But Helena ran into his arms, the sobs spilling out of her lungs as the pressure of having to be strong for her children burst with relief. She rejoiced at the familiar feel of his body and the familiar scent of his skin. She was home. The nightmare was over.

'I'm your Uncle Toby,' said Toby, bending down and shaking Hal's hand, which was immediately swallowed up by his long fingers. Hal clung onto his mother's legs and looked at the strange man with suspicious eyes. Federica extended her hand and said 'hello' politely but without smiling. 'You are even prettier than your mother described you,' he said, taking Federica's hand and shaking it gently. Then noticing her box he added, 'What's that you're carrying?'

Federica clutched it in her hand possessively. 'Papa gave it to me. It's a magic box,' she replied quietly.

'I bet it is. You'll need a magic box in Polperro.' He chuckled.

'Why?'

'Because there are magic caves and mysterious creeks and haunted beaches,' he said and watched her tired eyes flicker momentarily with interest.

'Really?' she exclaimed and her mouth lengthened into a thin smile.

'Really. I'm very pleased you've brought your box,' he said, then stood up. 'You must be exhausted, Helena. Let's get you to the car immediately, the children can sleep on the back seat.'

Toby pushed the trolley laden with their cases, while Helena walked holding her two children by the hand. When they got to the car, Toby loaded the luggage into the back and then settled the children on the rear seat, which he had prepared with pillows and rugs. It was a long seven-hour drive to Polperro. 'I can't believe you've put all this together for the children,' said Helena gratefully. 'They'll sleep like kings in there.'

'It's an arduous drive. Poor lambs, they look shattered and bewildered,' said Toby, shutting the door. Federica closed her eyes and leant her aching head against the pillow. She had no time to reflect on her situation for sleep overcame her, numbing her senses like a drug.

'Oh Toby. I can't tell you what I've been through. I've left Ramon and broken my children's hearts all because I couldn't cope any more,' said Helena, the tears glistening in her blood-shot eyes.

'Don't blame yourself, Helena, it's life. They'll cope. Don't worry. It's happened to tons of children before them and they've survived,' he said, patting her on her arm. 'Now do get in or you'll catch a cold. I don't imagine you thought of bringing coats,' he said, looking at her shivering in her sweater and slacks.

She shook her head bleakly. 'Of course not, it's midsummer in Chile,' she said, thinking suddenly of Ramon and wondering what he was doing.

'When the children are asleep you can tell me all about it,' he said, climbing into the car.

Helena watched the grey cloud hang low in the sky like a shroud and yet it didn't make her feel depressed as bad weather often did, but gave her a contented feeling of reassurance. It was all so familiar and so comfortable. As they drove towards the motorway she cast her eyes about her at the naked trees with their branches stiff from the cold and the sleek black rooks that pecked at the winter fields. She remembered England like this and smiled inside.

'It's good to have you back, Helena,' Toby said, glancing in the mirror to check the children were asleep. 'Poor darlings, they're shattered. Look.' Helena turned her head around wearily. Hal and Federica were asleep curled up against each other like a couple of puppies. She thought of Ramon and wondered whether he was missing them or whether he had simply deleted their memories and moved on. More countries, more books, no commitments.

She sighed. 'It's been a while since I last talked to you. How's Julian?' she asked, staring at the moving ground in front of them, blinking away her fatigue.

'Julian's doing well. He spends a lot of time in London on assignments. He's getting lots of work and becoming rather successful. He'll be keeping me in my old age,' he chuckled.

'Lucky old you!'

'Not really. Dad's the same.'

'That doesn't surprise me. He's a man's man. Proud with it. He probably blames himself,' she said.

'It undermines his own masculinity.'

'He'll come round one day, don't expect miracles. There are far more important things to get upset about. You haven't killed anyone.'

'No, not yet.' He smiled. 'But it's been two years since I told him and he still hasn't spoken to Julian. When Julian first arrived in Polperro he was only too happy to embrace him into the family as my friend. He was charmed by him. How narrow-minded can a person be to ostracize someone because of their sexuality, which is a private matter anyway? Especially as he liked Julian very much as a person.'

'That hurts, doesn't it?' said Helena, noticing his white knuckles grip the steering wheel in frustration.

'Yes, only because we've always been so close. It's not the same now. You'll see.'

'He just pretends Julian doesn't exist?'

'Yes.'

'How does Julian feel?' she asked, trying to take an interest but all she could think about was her own pain.

'He's so laid back, he doesn't care. He's far too interested in his photography to worry about whether Dad likes him or not. Anyhow, he's thirty-five years old, he's seen it all before and it doesn't faze him. I mind for me, that's all.'

'Dad probably feels you've been led astray by an old pervert.' She watched Toby's mouth twist into a reluctant smile.

'Hardly old, Helena.'

'Seven years older than you. To Dad you're still a baby.'

'Well, this baby knows what he wants.'

'Then that's fine. To hell with Dad. Who cares! As long as you're happy. You have to think of yourself, you know, and not live your life for other people,' she said, considering her own situation and the two heartbroken children who slept innocently on the back seat.

'We both have to think of ourselves, Helena. No one else is going to,' he replied gravely then fell silent and watched the grey road stretch bleakly out in front of them.

Helena and Toby had always shared all their secrets. Even though he was younger than his sister by two years he had always been more mature than other boys his age. That's what comes of keeping secrets, it wears one out and makes one furtive, Helena reflected. She had known Toby was gay long before he had decided to tell his parents. She had always known he wasn't interested in girls, that he was happier with his books on worms and beetles than going to nightclubs. It wasn't that he was frightened of women, he wasn't. He adored his sister, admired his mother and had lots of good girl friends. Toby just wanted their friendship; the idea of physical contact was as alien to him as football. When Helena's friend Annabel Hazel fell in love with him, crying hopeless tears of unrequited love onto her shoulder, Helena began to wonder whether Toby might be gay. He never dated anyone. He could hardly marry one of his unfortunate beetles. Helena was usually too distracted by her own desires to have the time to notice anyone else's, but Toby's sexuality intrigued her and wrenched her out of herself. She watched him closely. It was in the Chilean summer of 1972, that Toby had flown out to spend a few weeks with his sister who had settled happily into married life with Ramon.

Helena was distressed to see that Toby had grown fat with misery and taut with anxiety. He was suppressing his feelings and choking on his efforts. He was unemployed and unhappy and his usually buoyant smile could barely manage to float. They walked up and down the beach and talked as they had never talked before. Toby spoke of his difficulty in finding a job in London, how the fumes of the cars made him sick and the noise made him nervous. 'I just don't feel me any more,' he explained hoarsely.

'Well, you're not going to get a boyfriend by being miserable,' Helena said nonchalantly. Toby stared at her, his face at once pink and white and his eyes full of terror. 'It's okay to be gay, you know,' she continued and smiled at him in understanding. 'You're still my darling Toby.' Toby sat down on the sand and put his head into his fumbling hands and sobbed as he hadn't done since his dog, Jessie, had been run over that hideous winter morning fifteen years before. Helena sat next to him and placed her arms around him. 'You're fat because you're not happy, you're not happy because you're confused. You always have been. That's why you went to London because you couldn't cope with your secret in Polperro. I don't blame you.' She laughed. 'That town is way too small for you. But you know, it's where you belong and it's where you'll be happy.'

'I know.' He sniffed. 'I want to go home. I hate London. But,' he sighed heavily as if the weight of his secret was being released through his breath. 'I want to be loved like everyone else.'

'And you will be. There are lots of gay people all over London, all over the world. You only have to have the courage to find them.' Toby turned and looked at his sister with shiny blue eyes that resembled a clear sky after a heavy rainfall.

'How come you knew?' he asked.

'Because I know you. Because I care,' she said. 'I've known for a long time. Ever since you rebuffed Annabel Hazel. I began to think about it then. You never dated anyone, you were more interested in those wretched insects of yours. I thought there was something strange about that. No one else did, mind you, because you had always been eccentric. But no one was as close to you as I was.'

'Still are,' he said and smiled with a gratitude that made her eyes water with emotion.

'So,' she said, blinking happily, 'if we're going to get you a boyfriend we've got to get you looking good. You're far too fat!' Toby laughed bashfully. 'The diet starts today, and you're staying more than a month. Ramon and I aren't travelling again until March and I'm not sending you back to London until you're ready, understand?' He nodded. 'Love is the best thing in the world. I want you to have the sort of love I have,' she added.

'For the first time ever I feel it's possible,' Toby replied, taking her hand and squeezing it. Suddenly he felt lighter and more positive. As they walked back up the road to Cerro Castillo where Ramon and Helena had a beautiful house overlooking the sea, Toby felt as if he was seeing the world for the first time in many years. He wanted to take a boat out and lie under the sun, rocking gently on the waves, gazing out onto the horizon that suddenly held so many promises he wanted to run to it and embrace it.

Toby looked across at Helena who now lay sleeping against the seat belt, her troubled eyes shut to the turmoil of the last month, dreaming of better times no doubt. Her breathing was slow and deep as if even in sleep she recognized the familiar air of her home country. How life has its ups and downs, he thought, at least after a down one can only go up. He glanced at the children in the mirror and noticed the gentle stirring of their bodies as they left the comfort of their secret worlds to open their eyes onto unfamiliar countryside. He wished it were spring, then England wouldn't look so bleak.

Federica sat up and blinked out of the window at the passing fields, scattered white with a thin covering of frost.

'Are we nearly there?' she asked.

'Not quite, Fede,' he replied jovially. 'Tell me about your magic box?' he asked, watching her open and close it absent-mindedly.

She sighed and her face lengthened sadly. 'All right,' she said, recalling her father's secure embrace and inwardly wincing because with that memory invaded the less pleasant one of the conversation she had overheard in Cachagua. But as she began to tell him the story of the Inca princess the colour returned to her cheeks and her spirits lifted. By the time they stopped for lunch in a quaint village pub she no longer felt sad but intrigued. Intrigued by all that was new about her.

Chapter 11

When they turned the corner into the narrow lane that wound its way down to the house where Toby and Helena had grown up, Helena felt her heart turn over. She rolled down the window to smell the familiar scents of her childhood. But it was January and the air was frosted so she smelt nothing. This did not dampen her enthusiasm. As they drove through the gates and onto the gravel the white house rose into view like a steady old friend, exactly as it always had been, pretty in spite of the winter that left its walls naked and exposed.

On hearing the car, Jake and Polly, who had spent the previous hour pacing the rooms in agitation, hurried out of the front door to welcome the weary travellers home. Polly noticed immediately that her daughter was thin and gaunt but she was surprised at how well the children looked. Federica ran into her arms and embraced her in excitement.

'You have your own room, Fede, and I've even made you chocolate crispies for tea because I remember how much you liked them when I made them for you in Chile,' said Polly, hugging the skinny child who held on to her waist like an orphaned monkey. Hal clung to his mother's legs and begged to be picked up.

'Hal, sweetie, you're too big to be carried. You're four and not a small four either,' Helena laughed, kissing her father with emotion. 'God, it's good to be home. I feel better already.'

'Do come in out of the cold. It's warm in the kitchen, let's all go and talk in there,' Polly suggested, ushering Federica in with her capable big hands.

'Well driven, Toby,' said Jake, patting his son stiffly on his back. 'It was very good of you to pick them up.'

'No trouble at all, Dad,' he replied, grateful for his father's praise. He didn't get much of it these days.

Polly laid the table with a chipped teapot that Toby had once dropped and an odd collection of mugs she had acquired over the years. She then loaded up a tray with chocolate crispies, biscuits, cake and Marmite sandwiches. Unlike other Chilean children Hal and Federica had grown up on Marmite which Polly had sent out regularly to Viña along with the Mary Quant makeup Helena couldn't do without. Polly looked at her daughter with worry. She was still good looking but her radiance had faded like a dried flower. Neglect had sucked the juice out of her and left her dehydrated. Polly wanted to wring Ramon's neck, but she was careful to wait until she was alone with Helena before she talked about her errant husband. The children warmed up in front of the Aga, eating their way through the tea like hungry locusts. They settled in quickly and Hal overcame his shyness when he saw the chocolate cake.

'It's so wonderful to be home again. It's just like the old days. Nothing's changed,' said Helena, surveying the room in one swift glance while she lit a cigarette and inhaled slowly, savouring the first rush of nicotine. Her mother had barely aged in the last few years. She was an agile sixty-year-old with plump honey skin that seemed too lubricious to dry into lines and the shining eyes of someone blessed with a strong constitution and good health. If it hadn't been for her greying hair that she twisted into an untidy bun and the matronly clothes she wore, she wouldn't have looked a day older than fifty. Her father's hair was now a dignified silver which softened his craggy features and made him look less like the swarthy smuggler he had resembled when it had been black. He still said little but observed everything. When he did speak everyone listened.

'It's lovely to have you back,' Polly enthused, her ruddy cheeks hot from the excitement of seeing her child and grandchildren again. 'I've got the perfect friends for Federica and Hal,' she added happily. 'Do you remember the Applebys?'

Helena looked at Toby. 'What, that mad family who live at Pickthistle Manor?' she replied, smiling at her brother because as children they had always tried to engage old Nuno Appleby in conversation whenever they saw him because he was Polperro's most entertaining eccentric. He had been in his early sixties then, walking on the balls of his feet with a very straight back, nodding his tortoise-shaped head at people as he passed them as if he were mayor. He had been born in Cornwall and yet, because he had spent much of his youth in Italy studying art, he spoke with a pseudo-Italian accent and had changed his name from Nigel to Nuno. He lived in Pickthistle Manor with his daughter Ingrid, an avid bird watcher, and her writer husband Inigo and their five wild children.

'Well, they're not mad, dear, original perhaps, but not mad,' Polly replied.

'Original!' Jake chuckled, grinning a lopsided smile that revealed one crooked wolf's tooth. 'And I usually count on Polly to say it like it is.' He laughed.

'Ingrid and Inigo have five children,' said Polly, ignoring her husband. 'Let me see, there must be one or two compatible with Fede and Hal.' She squinted her pale blue eyes as she tried to remember them.

'Well,' interrupted Toby, 'Sam must be about fifteen, so

he's no good.' He recalled the rather arrogant boy who rarely spoke to anyone and always had his nose buried in a biographical dictionary.

'Goodness no, I'm talking about Molly and Hester,' said Polly.

'Ah yes. Molly must be about nine and Hester seven,' said Toby. 'Perfect playmates. They both go to the local school so it could work very well.'

'That would be nice for Fede,' said Helena, watching her children who now laughed happily, playing with the presents Ramon had given them.

'Lucien and Joey are little, Hal's age more or less,' Polly added. 'I think we should invite them over for tea sometime soon.'

'I remember Ingrid,' Helena laughed, 'just as crazy about animals as you, Toby. If there was a wounded creature within five miles she'd find it, box it and nurture it back to health in her airing cupboard.'

'Well, if they weren't wounded they pretended to be, that airing cupboard was like the Ritz,' Toby chuckled. 'Do you remember those flea-ridden hedgehogs she kept in the scullery?'

'And the goose who was so vicious they couldn't use their kitchen for a week until its leg had recovered. *You* can hardly talk with all your insects installed in five-star incubators,' Helena added, grinning at her brother.

'She still spends most of the day on the cliff painting seagulls,' said Polly. 'She paints beautifully.' She sighed in admiration. 'Mind you it's all at the expense of those dear children who live like gypsies.'

'Rather grand gypsies, Polly,' Jake interjected wryly.

'Yes, grand gypsies, but they run wild. Ingrid's so vague and Inigo spends all day locked in his study writing or tearing through the house grumbling about everything. Best to stay out of his way I always think. Still, they are charming children even though there's not an ounce of discipline to share between them.'

'Do you think they're the right sort of children for mine?' Helena asked anxiously, flicking her ash into the bin.

'Of course they are. Federica could do with a little freedom,' said Polly, remembering how Federica wasn't allowed out of her front garden without the supervision of a maid or her mother. Police patrolled the streets and the military enforced the curfew. Viña del Mar was carefree enough but a suburb was no place to bring up children. 'The countryside will do them the world of good,' she added, taking joy from the idea of them playing on the beaches and running through the fields with their new friends. Federica was still a child although she seemed like a young woman in a child's body. Polly thought it was high time she was allowed to enjoy her childhood, or at least the few years she had left.

When Federica was tucked up in her new bed she lay on her side and stared at the butterfly box that sat on her bedside table. It was so dark that she had asked her mother to keep the door open onto the landing so that the light could flood in and dilute the night that seemed all consuming in this unfamiliar country. She looked at her box and took courage from it, a little piece of home in a strange land, a little bit of her father to cling onto until he arrived to love her properly.

Helena had allowed Hal to share her bed for the first night. She didn't realize at the time but she needed him as much as he needed her and he would consequently share her bed for the next six months, until Polly finally intervened and tactfully suggested that perhaps it wasn't healthy for a young boy to be so dependent on his mother. But that first night had been important for both of them. Helena clung to his warm body hoping to reassure him and assuage her guilt at having torn him away from his father and home. She knew her children were young enough to cope with the trauma of uprooting, she knew they'd make friends and one day almost forget they had ever lived in Chile. Certainly for Hal, Chile would pale into a murky memory whereas for Federica it would be harder. She thought of Molly and Hester Appleby and her hope rested with them. She resolved to introduce them as soon as possible. Federica hadn't had many friends in Chile, she was by nature more of a loner, probably due to having had three years as an only child. She closed her heavy eyes and let sleep wash over her, drowning all the unpleasantness of the past and leaving her to dream about the wonderful new life that was opening up to them. But every now and then Ramon's imposing will would invade her thoughts and claim her once again while she was powerless to fight him.

'Poor Helena,' Polly sighed, pulling the covers above her matronly breasts. 'She's done the right thing though. I hated thinking of her out there in Chile without anyone to watch out for her. Now she has us, we'll take care of her.'

'Don't let her get you running around for her, Polly. You know what she's like,' said Jake, climbing into bed.

'Helena needs us.'

'Yes she does. But go easy or you'll end up her slave just like the old days,' he said, rolling over and turning off the light.

'She's different now. She's been through a hard time and she needs our support,' she insisted.

'Don't say I didn't warn you,' he mumbled before sighing heavily, indicating that he was too tired to talk any more.

Molly and Hester Appleby were intrigued by the thin, trembling girl who stood shyly before them. Their mother had invited her mother to tea telling them that Fede, pronounced Fayday, had just arrived in England and had no friends. They were to make her feel welcome. In typical Ingrid style she threw the children together and told them to run off and play while she caught up with the girl's mother.

'Fede's a funny name,' said Molly, narrowing her green eyes suspiciously.

'It's short for Federica,' Federica replied hoarsely.

'That's funny too,' said Molly.

'My father's from Chile,' she said, then noticed the two girls' faces staring blankly back at her. 'That's in South America,' she explained. They both understood South America from the map which their nanny had painted on the nursery wall and nodded.

'Is your Daddy black?' Hester asked.

'No,' Federica replied, shocked. 'He's got black hair though,' she added and smiled as she thought of him.

'Our Daddy has black moods,' said Molly and laughed. 'We'll show you around if you like.'

Federica nodded.

Federica borrowed a pair of Wellington boots and a coat that was much too big for her and followed them out into the winter garden. Their house was a large white manor with tall sash windows and a wide terrace, descending onto the lawn by way of an imperial set of large stone steps. The ground was hard and glittered with crisp white frost that Federica had never seen before. She had seen snow, because her father had taken them skiing a few times in the Andes resort of La Parva, but she had never seen frost. They wandered down the lawn towards the lake that lay flat and icy at the bottom of the garden. 'Let's ice skate,' Molly suggested, padding carefully onto the lake. Federica followed her, wincing as she took her first faltering steps over the slippery surface.

'Careful you don't fall,' said Molly.

Federica didn't want to go on the ice. She was frightened it might break. But she watched miserably as the two unfriendly girls skated their way into the middle of the lake and knew that if she wanted them to be her friends she would have to follow. Reluctantly she stood unsteadily on the shiny surface. Relieved that it felt sturdy and secure she skated stiffly after them. 'Come on, Fede!' Molly shouted, smiling at her. 'Well done!'

'Bet you never did this in Chile,' said Hester. She was right. Federica nodded.

'Isn't this fun? I'd like to skate properly with proper skates,' said Molly. 'I wish Daddy would buy me a pair, then I could twirl around.' She demonstrated a shaky twirl. Hester tried to copy her but fell on her bottom. They laughed and Federica laughed too, feeling the first thrill of camaraderie. She practised a few turns which resulted in her falling onto the ice as well.

'Like this,' Molly instructed, taking large steps and lifting one leg into the air. Hester and Federica copied her, giggling at their hopeless efforts.

'Look, there's Sam!' Hester shouted, waving to her brother who descended the lawn towards them.

'Get off the ice!' he shouted. 'It isn't safe.'

'Spoilsport,' said Molly under her breath. 'Come on,' she sighed, skating off towards him.

Suddenly there came a deep cracking noise, like the awakening groan of a monster from the deep. Molly roared with laughter, Hester screamed in alarm and Federica, some way behind them, began to run in her effort to get off the ice. She didn't realize that one shouldn't run on ice. The groan got louder and more threatening. She ran faster but her feet started to falter. Suddenly they slipped up from under her and she landed on her chest winding herself, knocking her chin against the surface with a terrifying crunch. When she tried to get up she saw blood on the ice and cried out in terror. As she raised herself onto her knees, barely able to breathe because of her fall, it gave way and she slid into the freezing water of the lake. Panic seized her around her throat so that her cry was nothing more than a pathetic whisper. She tried to grab onto the ice that surrounded her but it crumbled in her hands like icing on a cake. Her coat was too big and restricted her movements. She tried to kick with her legs but she felt nothing but the cold. She began to sink and squealed in fright as the water reached up to her neck.

'You're all right,' came a calm voice. She raised her bloodshot eyes to see the pale face of Sam Appleby looking down at her from where he was lying above her on the ice. He grabbed her arms. 'It's all right, I've got you,' he said, locking his eyes into hers to reassure her. 'Now, I'm going to pull you up so when I say "go", start kicking with your feet,' he instructed.

'I can't feel them,' she sobbed.

'Yes you can. Now GO!' Federica began to kick furiously as Sam slowly pulled her out of her black hole. The ice creaked ominously again, but Sam continued to pull and Federica continued to kick as her very life depended on it. 'Good girl,' he kept saying to encourage her. Finally she lay on the ice like a heavy wet seal, panting and whimpering with shock. 'Now we're going to slide along, okay? We're not going to walk, you understand?' She nodded, her teeth chattering as much out of fear as out of cold. Sam put his arm around her and together they wriggled their way towards the grass. Her body was so numb she could barely move it. It seemed an age before they touched the solid ground. Once on the land Sam wasted no time in lifting Federica into his arms, striding urgently up the garden to the house with Molly and Hester following behind like a couple of breathless geese.

The girls rushed into the sitting room to tell their mother and Helena while Sam stalked up the stairs shouting for Bea, the children's nanny, who was in the nursery supervising

Lucien, Joey and Hal. When she saw the sobbing child in Sam's arms she gasped in horror and led them into Molly's bedroom. 'What happened?' she cried as Sam put the child down.

'Molly again. Stupid girl!' he exclaimed hotly. 'That child could have died. Get her out of those clothes at once before she catches pneumonia,' he instructed before leaving the room. Helena and Ingrid rushed up the stairs and into the bedroom where Federica, naked and shivering, fell into her mother's arms and sobbed all over again.

'Did you think you were going to die?' said Molly later, when Federica was warming up in front of the sitting room fire, dressed in Hester's clothes, toasting marshmallows in the hot flames for tea.

'Yes, I really did.'

'You were so brave, crawling over the ice like that,' said Hester in admiration. 'Was that the first time you had been ice skating?'

'Yes. I don't think I'll be going again for some time,' she replied and laughed.

Molly handed her another marshmallow. 'These are good, aren't they? You really deserve them. I'm so sorry,' she said and smiled sheepishly, curling her auburn hair behind her ear.

'That's okay. You couldn't have known that the ice would break,' said Federica kindly.

'So lucky that Sam was there,' said Hester.

'Big brothers have some uses,' Molly laughed. 'He is a bit of a hero though,' she conceded.

'He was very brave. He saved my life,' said Federica, chewing on her sticky marshmallow and feeling light in the head with the thought of Sam carrying her into the house. 'How old is he?'

'Fifteen,' said Molly. 'I'm nine and Hester's seven like you. Mummy had two miscarriages in between Sam and me otherwise we'd be seven.'

'I'd like to be seven,' said Hester.

'Well, we're six now,' said Molly, grinning at Federica.

'Oh, yes, so we are,' Hester agreed happily. 'Better show you around the house then,' she added, looking at her sister for approval.

Molly nodded. 'Grab a piece of cake and I'll introduce you to Marmaduke,' she said.

'Who's Marmaduke?'

'The skunk Mummy rescued last week, he lives in the cupboard in the attic because sometimes he makes such a smell he has to have the whole floor to himself.'

Helena watched the girls disappear through the sitting room door and felt a tremendous wave of gratitude, not only towards Sam who had saved Federica's life, but to the girls for liking her and embracing her so readily. 'Your girls are very kind,' she said to Ingrid who sat smoking out of an elegant lilac cigarette holder and wearing the most extraordinary patchwork coat that looked like a quilt. Her hair cascaded over her shoulders in wild, auburn curls and around her neck hung a large gold monocle that she put to her eye every now and then to see better. Helena had never noticed before but one eye was blue and the other green.

'Molly's rather like Sam, they both think they're better than everyone else, because they're clever,' said Ingrid. 'Hester's sweet and not very bright. She's a good painter like me.'

'I owe Sam a huge debt of gratitude. If he hadn't been there I dread to think what might have happened.'

'Oh, she would have died, for sure,' said Ingrid, flicking the lighter to light Helena's cigarette. 'Molly always has to go one step too far.' She sighed. 'I'm sorry about Ramon.'

'So am I,' said Helena, inhaling the nicotine with an unsteady hand.

'It'll take a while, but you will recover,' said Ingrid, noticing the cigarette shaking in Helena's hand. 'You know, I
remember when you ran off with Ramon. You were so
young. I must be a good ten years older than you. I remember thinking how incredibly romantic it was. He was dark
and foreign and you were pale and English. There was something wonderfully exotic about it. Mind you, I did worry for
you, out there the other side of the world. It's not like going
to live in Leicester, is it?' She laughed, revealing crooked
white teeth. When Inigo had courted her all those years ago
he had told her she resembled a beautiful portrait hung
crooked on the wall. She liked things to be imperfect, there
was nothing duller than perfection.

'Well, it was exotic and wonderful at the time. It just went
sour. Sad for the children, but I have to admit I feel different
already,' said Helena.

'Children need stability – one parent can give them that.
Really, two is an extravagance,' Ingrid replied, playing with
one of the fat curls that bounced around her neck. 'I've
brought the children up single handed, almost. Inigo's children are his books. I only wish people would buy them.
They're frightfully dull though. I can't get beyond the first
page. Philosophy has never been an interest of mine. I prefer
things one can touch.'

'Like animals?' Helena suggested.

'Quite.'

At that moment old Nuno shuffled in on the balls of his
feet.

'Ah, two delightful virgins to greet,' he said in a heavy
Italian accent and bowed theatrically.

'Pa, you remember Helena Trebeka, don't you?' said
Ingrid.

'Why, of course, Helen of Troy was not more fair. "Sweet
Helen, make me immortal with a kiss!" It is a pleasure to see

you,' he said, bowing again. Ingrid frowned. 'Marlowe,' he added, raising his feathery eyebrow at her in disapproval. 'Young Samuel would know that one.'

'Helena's left Chile to live here again,' said Ingrid, ignoring him.

'Far too chilly in Chile I should imagine.'

'Where the heart is concerned, at least,' Ingrid laughed. 'Would you like some tea, Pa?'

'I'd like something much stronger than tea, *cara*. Ignore me, I'm not really here,' he said, shuffling behind the sofa towards the drinks cabinet.

'You're not easy to ignore, Pa.'

'I hear young Samuel is to be knighted for bravery. He is now Sir Samuel Appleby and I shall bestow on him the Order of the Skate to remind us all of his *coraggio*.'

'I'm so grateful to him,' said Helena, wishing Toby were there to laugh with her at the Polperro eccentric.

'I think he has won the fair maiden's heart, like in tales of yore,' said Nuno, raising his bushy eyebrows suggestively.

'Well, that wouldn't surprise me,' said Helena. 'I'm in love with him too.'

'Hearts have been won by lesser feats that that,' he said, picking up his glass and wandering out of the room.

'He came, he drank, he commented, he left,' Ingrid sighed, flicking her ash into a Herend dish.

'And he's married off my daughter, I'd say that's a good day's work done, wouldn't you?' They both laughed and poured more tea.

When the time came for Federica to leave with her mother and Hal, she wished she could stay for ever. Molly and Hester had introduced her to Marmaduke who gave off such a vicious smell it sent the three of them running down the corridor holding their noses, giggling profusely. She had met the fox cub who lived in the airing cupboard and the jackdaw who perched on Ingrid's kitchen chair and drank tea like the rest of the family. A strange pig, which Federica thought looked more like a miniature brown cow, snuffled about the house as if he were the family dog and answered to the name of Pebbles. He even ate from a dog bowl in the scullery along with Pushkin, the Bernese mountain dog, who managed to clear a whole tabletop with one swish of his white-tipped tail. Federica was enchanted.

But at six years of age Federica was now in love with the gallant hero who had saved her from an icy grave at the bottom of the lake. When he appeared in the hallway to find out whether she was okay she was suddenly overcome with shyness and her words came out as mere husks with no substance. 'You look better,' he smirked, running his eyes over the awkward child who blushed up at him gratefully. 'Your lips were blue. Mine go blue sometimes because I put the wrong end of my fountain pen in my mouth.' He laughed.

'I cannot thank you enough, Sam,' said Helena. Sam was tall, almost six foot, and looked down his nose at her loftily.

'My pleasure, I would say any time, but to be honest it was a bit cold, so I'd rather not plunge in again, at least not for a while,' he replied and laughed again.

Helena ushered Federica and Hal to the car. Federica climbed into the back seat and watched as Sam waved good-bye on the steps with his sisters who broke into a run and chased the car down the drive.

'Charming people, aren't they?' said Helena.

'I really like them,' Federica agreed. 'Can we come back soon?'

'You'll be going to school with the girls, Fede, so you'll see them all the time.'

'Good,' she replied and gazed dreamily out of the window.

Chapter 12

Cachagua

It had been four months, four days and four hours since Estella had last kissed Ramon Campione in her small, breezy room in Cachagua. She had waited for him to return as he had promised, but she hadn't heard anything, she hadn't even received a letter. Yet she waited as he had asked her to, as she had reassured him she would. She now sat on the beach, the soft autumn light receding into evening, flooding the horizon with an amber luminosity that poured melancholy into her heart. She placed her hand on her belly and felt the growing child within: Ramon's child. She smiled sadly to herself as she remembered those tender moments when they had been one, free from the social distinctions that separated them. Love has no boundaries, she thought optimistically, then wondered whether he had changed his mind. Whether he had realized their affair had been nothing more than a summer romance by the sea, as unreal as the fantasies he wrote about. She had found his books in his parents' bookshelves and taken them to her room where she had read every one. They were magical, surreal and compelling. Poetic stories of love, friendship and adventure set against the exotic landscapes of countries she had never even heard of. She had recognized his voice in each word as if he were some place near, whispering to her, loving her. She longed for him to come back. She longed to tell him about the life they had created together. God had given them a child and God didn't make mistakes.

Estella's future was uncertain. For the last few months she had been able to hide her secret. She had even managed to hide the sickness that had awoken her every morning and sent her running to the bathroom with the bile rising in her throat. Yet she hadn't minded, she had taken pleasure from it because everything from Ramon was a gift, so she cherished it. However, now her belly was beginning to swell and she found she tired easily which made her slow to complete her tasks. Señora Mariana watched her with narrowed eyes, in fact, Estella suspected she probably already knew. Señora Mariana had a sharp intuition about such things. If she could just get through the next few weeks, then Don Ignacio and Señora Mariana would return to their home in Santiago until the following summer. At least the next six months would be secure. If they discovered her condition before they left she feared she would have to leave her job and return in disgrace to her parents in Zapallar. They would be mortified because no man would want to marry her in that condition. What man could want another man's child? Her mother had always told her that any man worth his salt would want to marry a virgin. She was lost for sure. But as bleak as her future appeared she still believed that Ramon would return. He had not only promised, he had fervently promised as if he couldn't live without her, and she had agreed to wait because she loved him and believed he loved and needed her too. Yes, she thought, I know he'll come to find me.

She wandered back up the beach towards the house and remembered that time she had watched him from the shadows as he walked naked towards her. She had desired him then and she desired him now. Yet she didn't dream about making love to him but about lying next to him with his protective arms around her, his proud hand on her belly. She dreamed about him as the father of her child. When she entered the house Señora Mariana was waiting for her in the hallway.

'We need to have a talk, Estella,' she said, leading her into the sitting room. Estella knew she had been discovered and the beads of sweat collected on her brow. It was all over, for sure, she thought, and her chest constricted with panic.

'I have taken the opportunity to talk to you tonight as my husband is not here. Woman to woman,' said Mariana, smiling kindly at the trembling girl who perched on the edge of the sofa in discomfort.

'Sí, Señora Mariana,' she replied obediently.

'You are pregnant, are you not?' she asked, her grey eyes resting on Estella's swollen stomach. She noticed the girl lower her eyes in shame and a large tear roll down her beautiful face. 'I'm not angry with you, Estella.' Estella shook her head in despair. 'Surely this young man you've been seeing will marry you?'

'I don't know, Señora Mariana, he has gone,' she stammered.

'Wherever has he gone to?'

'I don't know, Señora Mariana. He's just gone.'

'Might he come back?' she asked gently, observing the girl's obvious distress and feeling her heart sag with pity.

'He promised he would. I believe him.'

'Well, that's all we can do, can't we? If you believe him then so do I,' she said and smiled sympathetically. 'We must find someone to replace you while you have your baby. Don Ignacio and I will be leaving for Santiago in a few days and won't be returning until October. That will be near the time when you have your child, I imagine. Please don't cry, dear, we'll muddle through. If he promised to come back I'm sure he will. You're too beautiful to leave in this condition,' she said, patting Estella's shaking hand.

'You were right, Nacho, she's pregnant,' said Mariana later when her husband returned for dinner.

Ignacio rolled his eyes and nodded. 'So I was right,' he said.

'Sadly, yes,' she replied and sighed heavily. 'What should we do?'

'Who's the father?'

'She didn't say.'

'Did you ask?'

'Well,' she shrugged, 'I tried to.'

'The point is will he marry her?'

'Of course not, he's scarpered, hasn't he?' she said crossly, folding her arms in front of her. 'It's really not fair.'

'It's the way it works in their world,' he said, dismissing her class as a group of uncultivated savages.

'It shouldn't be. She's so beautiful and charming, what sort of a man would do that to her then run off?'

'It happens all the time in their world. There's no honour among thieves.'

'Really, Nacho, they're not all like that.'

'No?' he challenged. 'I'll bet you they are. In their world women are victims. That's the way it is. She's no different. She'll have her baby, go back to her family in Zapallar and eke out a living somehow.'

'Nacho!' Mariana exclaimed in horror. 'You're not going to fire her?'

'What do you want me to do?' He shrugged.

'She can work for us *and* look after her baby,' she suggested calmly.

'We're not running a charitable organization here,' he retorted firmly. Mariana noticed his ears go red, usually a sign that he was on the verge of losing his temper.

'I can't bear her to lose her livelihood as well as her fiancé. We can't be so heartless, Nacho. *Mi amor*, let's not talk about it any more, we have five or six months to think about it.'

He nodded gruffly and watched her walk out onto the terrace. The problem with people, he thought to himself, is that they take no responsibility for their actions. Ramon is just as bad as Estella's lover, he concluded, he brings shame on his own class.

Ramon had slept with several women since he had left Chile and yet he still couldn't erase the sweet memory of Estella that dogged his mind and refused to give him any peace. On top of that he felt guilty. He had told her to wait for him. He knew she would. The right thing would be to write and put her out of her misery and yet he couldn't. He didn't want to lose her. He wanted to keep the door open in case he woke up one of these mornings with the urge to go back to her. Sometimes he woke with a gnawing longing that racked his loins as well as his conscience and yet he managed, every time, to persuade himself that he couldn't love her the way she wanted to be loved, the way all women wanted to be loved. Just like Helena. He couldn't be there for her. He couldn't be there for anyone.

Ramon sat on the old rickety train that cut through the arid western Indian desert on its way to Bikaner. The sun blazed down upon the roof of the train, cooking up a sweltering heat inside that smelt of sweat and the intoxicating aroma of spices that clung to his nostrils and made his throat dry. The compartment was crowded with the dusky brown faces of men in turbans of saffron and fuchsia, their dark-eyed children watching him with innocent curiosity and giggling behind grubby hands. They knew he was a foreigner in spite of his homespun kurta pyjamas and chappals. When he had entered at Jodhpur he noticed the women arrange their veils in front of their aquiline faces with an almost ethereal move- ment of their long bejewelled fingers to ensure their modesty. Their timid eyes were at once lowered behind their veils like exotic birds in mist. After a while they forgot he was there, watching them with the scrupulous gaze of a voracious story- teller and they chattered away among themselves in a language he didn't understand. He loved Indian women. He was enchanted by their delicate femininity and their virtue, the graceful way they moved behind their glittering saris, bright flowers against so dry a desert. He didn't prey on these women, they were paragons of virtue, but he found the mysterious theatre of their world too compelling a spectacle to tear his eyes away from them. He felt that if he made too abrupt a movement they would fly off to settle in the green leaves of one of those banyan trees that miraculously survived in such barren terrain.

The dust entered through the windows like thin smoke and settled wherever it could. A bony old Indian sat cross- legged in the corner under a scarlet turban and unloaded his tiffin box, arranging the aromatic food and utensils around him with the ritual of a priest. He had taken up two seats in spite of the weary passengers who crowded the corridors for lack of places. A small child watched the man arrange his food, dribbling with hunger and hopeful that if he stared hard enough the man might offer him a bite.

Suddenly the train screeched to a frantic halt. Ramon looked out of the window through the horizontal bars. The compartment erupted out of its somnambulant state into confused chatter as the passengers left the train to see why it had stopped. Ramon watched them all spill out onto the desert like ants. Soon the heat grew too intense for him to stay inside without being fried alive and he too joined them to choke in the dust under the sun. As he descended he noticed a beautiful European woman move through the crowd with the gracelessness of a mule walking through a herd of elegant sambar. Just like Helena, he thought to himself and guessed she must be British. She was striding impatiently towards the throng that had gathered around the railway track. Her face was pinched with irritation and yet she still managed to look down her nose with a haughtiness more at home in the days of the Raj. She wore a pair of white trousers and knee-high riding boots, revealing long legs and a shapely bottom.

He grinned to himself and strode up to her. 'Do you want some water?' he asked in English. She blinked at him from under her hat that resembled a pith helmet.

'Thank you,' she sighed, taking the bottle from him. After gulping down a large swig she exploded into complaints. 'What the bloody hell has happened? The train was late leaving and now we'll be late arriving. Nothing goes when it says it will in this country.'

Ramon laughed. 'This is India,' he said, looking her up and down.

She narrowed her pale blue eyes and scrutinized him back. He could have been Indian but his accent gave it away.

'Angela Tomlinson,' she said, extending her hand and looking at him steadily.

'Ramon Campione,' he replied, taking it.

'Spanish?'

'Chilean.'

'More exotic. I'm afraid I'm from England,' she said, smiling at him. 'That's not very exotic.'

'Only to the British,' he said. She laughed and wiped her freckled face with a firm hand. 'I think England's very exotic.'

'Well, you must be the only one. Aren't I lucky to have found you!' she chuckled.

'I imagine it's an animal on the line, or a person,' he said, squinting into the sun but he couldn't see past the multitude of Indians clamouring to see for themselves what had fallen onto the track.

'How horrid. Will it take long?' she asked, screwing up her nose in distaste.

'Why are you in so much of a hurry?'

'I'm meant to be in Bikaner already. Meetings, you know. I'm boringly punctual, I'm afraid. Hate to keep people waiting.'

'What's your business?'

'Hotels. I'm a consultant. We're constructing a new hotel, the one I'm to stay in will be much less glamorous I should imagine.'

'But infinitely more charming,' he said, imagining the kind of monstrosity her company was constructing.

She smirked flirtatiously. 'What takes you to Bikaner?'

'The tides,' he replied. She looked at him, impressed.

'That's all?'

'That's all.'

They stood chatting for a while, during which time a dead cow was dragged off the track and laid out on the sand for the flies and birds to peck at. Slowly the weary passengers wandered back to the train and into the throbbing heat of the carriages. Ramon followed Angela into her first class carriage and the train lurched back into motion once again. First class wasn't all that different from the crowded carriage he had been travelling in before, the aroma of spices and wafts of dust invaded the compartment, which was also overcrowded with chattering Indians and desperately hot. Angela sat beside the window allowing the wind to cool her down. She closed her eyes and let it wash over her. She reminded Ramon in a strange way of Helena and he found himself wondering about her and his children. He was so far away it was difficult to imagine them in England, settling into Polperro, forgetting that he ever existed. But Angela possessed the same graceless-ness as Helena, that very same directness that belonged only to the British and he found himself, in spite of his efforts, missing her.

Angela had arrived too late for her meeting. 'God, I'll be hung, drawn and quartered,' she complained, fiddling with her watch in agitation.

'You're not going to change the time by playing with it,' said Ramon, ushering her past the throbbing crowd of people and into a taxi, where a wizened old man sat at the wheel of a dusty car embellished with tinsel, carrying on his shoulder a small grey monkey who played with the swinging pack of plastic gods that hung from the mirror.

'I know. It's just so unlike me,' she whined.

'Look, this is India. They'll know the train was late – nothing runs on time. You can have your meeting tomorrow. One of the many reasons I could never work for anyone else is because I couldn't hack someone controlling the way I spend my time,' he said.

'Lucky old you,' she exclaimed.

'Why don't you branch off on your own?' he suggested.

'I'd be far too lazy and irresponsible.'

'Sometimes it's fun to be irresponsible.'

'Yes.' She sighed and caught him looking at her intensely. 'I suppose you're going to invite me out for a drink now?'

'If you like.'

'I think I need one.'

'Good.'

'Let's go to my "infinitely more charming" hotel,' she said and laughed.

'Good idea. I hadn't thought about accommodation.'

'Just going with the tides.'

'Exactly.'

'Well, darling, you've been washed up on my shore,' she said and placed her hand on his. 'Lucky me.'

Making love to Angela only reminded Ramon of his wife and of Estella. Her English accent made his stomach lurch with the memories of his last few days with Helena and consequently turned his thoughts to his children, yet the scent of her body and the taste of her skin only encouraged him to miss Estella by virtue of the fact that Estella tasted infinitely sweeter. It was a disappointment. He may as well have been a horse for she rode him furiously with the stamina of a professional jockey. When she was satisfied she had flopped onto the bed and fallen asleep like a man. He looked across at her pale blotchy skin and knotted hair and knew that he couldn't spend another minute in her bed. He got up, dressed and left without so much as a goodbye note.

He walked out into the sultry night air. The dawn was already seeping gold into the cracks in the sky and the monkeys were skipping on the rooftops, chasing one other across the shadows. He felt melancholic. Bad love always made him morose and he craved the poetic love of Estella. Sitting under the vast desert sky he pulled out of his rucksack the pen and paper he had stolen from Angela's hotel room and began to write to Federica. He wrote with the intention of it being read by Helena. He missed her, which was strange, as that feeling had been covered in dust for many years due to lack of use. He had never missed her before. But he missed the idea of her. She was no longer there for him. He felt he couldn't just 'rock up' like he used to. He missed Federica's adoring face. He even missed Hal whom he had never really bonded with. His base camp had gone. Now he had nowhere to go home to. Not even in his dreams.

He wrote a story for Federica about a mysterious girl who

followed him about on his travels. 'She must be an angel,' he explained, 'for her hair is long and flowing and the colour of clouds at sunrise. She's beautiful, not only on the outside but on the inside, which is the most important and the most rare. I first saw her in a dream. My longing for her was so great that when I awoke she was sitting on the end of my bed, watching me with pale, luminous eyes filled with affection. And so she has accompanied me everywhere. Up the Himalayan mountains where yaks roam the snowy peaks down to the huge lakes of Kashmir where large exotic birds feast on flying fish, catching them in the air and carrying them off into the sky. She enjoys all the wonders of the world just like me. She makes me very happy. Now I realize, of course, after many days and nights travelling in her company, that she isn't real at all, but imaginary. I realized only after I had tried to touch her and my arms went right through her, rather like a ghost. But she isn't a ghost because I know she really lives in Polperro with her mother and brother Hal. So I don't try to touch her any more, I just watch her and smile. She smiles back and that to me is the most miraculous part of all.'

Chapter 13

Polperro

'How's Federica getting on at school these days? Better?' asked Ingrid who was bent over her easel painting a portrait of Sam reading on the lawn. 'Blast!' she exclaimed hotly. 'I'm so much better at painting birds.'

'Fine,' Molly replied absentmindedly, concentrating on the daisy chain she was making.

'Oh, I am pleased. It can't be easy moving to a new country and having to make friends all over again.'

'She was very quiet at first, but Hester says she's happier now. She's more Hester's friend,' said Molly, who was a couple of years older and bored by their childish games.

'The summer term is always much more fun anyway,' said Ingrid, sitting back on her stool and exchanging her paintbrush for her cigarette that smoked in its elegant lilac holder on the table beside her. 'Sam darling, don't move a muscle,' she instructed, putting the monocle to her eye and studying her painting in detail.

'Mum, I haven't moved for the last hour, why would I want to move now?' said Sam, who was lying on his front reading Maupassant's *Bel Ami*, unamused at being disturbed. Ingrid grinned at him from under the wide brim of her sunhat.

'It's a precaution, darling. I don't want you to ruin my picture.'

'Is it any good?'

'Quite. But it would be better if you were a seagull or a hawk.'

'Sorry,' he replied and the beginning of a smile tickled the corners of his petulant mouth.

'Federica fancies Sam,' said Molly, putting down her daisy chain and patting Pushkin who lay panting beside her in the heat.

'She's got very good taste,' said Ingrid, lifting her eyes over the easel and smiling at her son with pride.

'What do you think, Sam?'

'I simply don't think, Molly,' said Sam, irritated.

'You seem to think about everything else,' she said.

'Perhaps, but I don't think about Federica Campione.'

'Darling, she's a very sweet girl,' Ingrid interrupted.

'Exactly. A girl,' said Sam. 'If I fancied anyone she would be a woman, not a girl.'

At that moment Hester skipped out onto the lawn followed by Pebbles the Vietnamese pig and cradling a snuffling hedgehog in her arms. 'I think Prickles is better now,' she announced. 'He can walk again.'

'Thank Heaven for that. Have you fed him?' Ingrid asked, momentarily looking up from her work.

'Yes. He drank all his milk. He's still covered in fleas, though. Nuno says you shouldn't have brought him into the house, he says he's been scratching ever since.'

'Your grandfather's very impressionable. If you hadn't told him about the fleas he wouldn't be scratching.'

'Fede's coming for tea,' said Hester.

'Good.'

'Her mother lets her bicycle now.'

'About time too. She's somewhat overprotective. Mind you,' said Ingrid thoughtfully, her paintbrush poised, 'after what that poor child has been through it's hardly surprising.'

'What has she been through?' Hester asked innocently.

'Well, she's had to leave her home and start again in a new place,' said Ingrid.

'She hasn't seen her father since she left Chile,' said Molly, plucking another daisy from the overgrown lawn. 'I don't believe she's even received a letter from him. I bet he's really horrid.'

'You can't call someone horrid when you don't know them, Molly. Anyway, I don't think he's intentionally horrid, just selfish and irresponsible.'

'Poor Fede,' Hester sighed. 'She talks about her father all the time.'

'I bet he doesn't think about her ever, or her mother. Have they divorced?' Molly asked dispassionately.

'Goodness no!' replied her mother, licking the end of her paintbrush. 'They've just separated. I'm sure they'll get back together in the end. I imagine it was hard for Helena living out there. It's not England you know.'

'Helena will probably fall in love with someone else,' said Molly, relishing the idea of a scandal.

'You've been reading too many romantic novels, darling,' Ingrid laughed, shaking her head at her daughter with the same indulgence that had allowed all her children to behave exactly as they pleased all their lives.

'Hester,' said Molly. 'Is or isn't it true that Fede fancies Sam?'

'Leave it, Molly,' said Sam, without looking up from his book. 'Mum, if they don't shut up I'm going to read in the orchard.'

Ingrid sighed. 'Girls.'

'Yes, it's true. Ever since he rescued her from the ice,' Hester replied, unable to resist her elder sister.

'Girls, Sam is trying to read. I'm sure he's very flattered that Federica has taken a shine to him, but really, he's fifteen years old and has much more important things to think about than the infatuations of a six-year-old child.'

'He should be grateful anyone fancies him at all,' added Molly, who always liked to have the last word. Sam ignored her and turned the page.

'What glorious sunshine!' exclaimed Nuno trotting out onto the lawn. '"As night is withdrawn from these sweet-springing meads and bursting boughs of May,"' he said, surveying the tranquil scene before him.

'Robert Bridges, "*Nightingales*",' said Sam casually, turning another page of his book.

'Quite right, dear boy,' said Nuno, nodding his approval with the slow inclination of his head as if he were on the stage.

'You must be thinking of Italy, Nuno, weather in this country is usually foul whatever the month,' said Molly sulkily.

'Oh dear! Moody Molly is like a *grande nuvola* obscuring the sun. I simply cannot tolerate the whining of a capricious child.' He sniffed. Molly rolled her eyes and smirked at Hester. 'Don't think I don't see the silent communication between you and your accomplice,' he added, glaring at them in mock anger. 'You'll both be shot at dawn. Now, Ingrid, let's see your *opera d'arte*.' He leant over his daughter's shoulder and peered at the canvas with great self-importance. 'Not bad, our Italian masters might not celebrate your achievements with a glass of Chateau Lafitte in Heaven but neither would they recoil in horror,' he said slowly in the clipped Italian accent that he had cultivated over so many years he was now unable to speak without it. 'There is no mistaking that it is Sam, my dear, only which end is his head and which end are his feet?'

'Oh for goodness' sake, Pa, go and scratch somewhere else,' Ingrid sighed, inhaling her cigarette once again in a gesture of dismissal.

'On that not so pretty subject I might add that animals with fleas are not hygienic to have in the house. I am being driven mad by scratching and no amount of bathing will relieve me. The hedge pig has to go.'

'Hester, you'll have to let Prickles go,' she sighed.

'What an unimaginative name for a pet,' said Nuno disapprovingly, straightening himself up. 'With a name like that he's not worthy of being invited into the house in any case.'

Federica was fast becoming a regular visitor to the Applebys' rambling manor. At least her name was Italian so she was immediately embraced by Nuno who remarked that with a name like that she was not only ensured great beauty and charm but also a touch of mischief which, he added imperiously, was as vital as a dash of Tabasco to the most enticing spaghetti napoli.

Hester was thrilled to have found a new friend. She had always trailed behind her elder sister, Molly, who bossed her around because she was older and cleverer then dismissed her when she found better company at school. Federica made Hester feel important. She cycled eagerly up the lane to see her almost every day and gratefully allowed her to take the lead. They indulged in childish games without the inhibitions that crept in when Molly was around. They clambered down the cliffs to the hidden bays and coves where they would find caves to hide in and share secrets. The sea was different in England, dark and murky, filled with seaweed and smelling strongly of salt and ozone. But Hester showed Federica how to love it, how to build castles in the thick sand and how to find shrimps and crabs in the many rock pools that collected during the high tides. They built a raft for the lake, fashioned fishing rods out of sticks and toasted marshmallows on the fires they were only allowed to build if supervised by an adult. As winter thawed into spring and the days lengthened and warmed, their friendship blossomed with the apple trees.

Sam had O levels to take at school. He didn't do much work. He didn't need to. He was by far the cleverest boy in the school and looked on most of the other children as either slow or just plain stupid. He rarely read the books he was supposed to, preferring to read nineteenth-century French authors such as Zola, Dumas and Balzac that his grandfather Nuno gave him. He still managed, somehow, to come top of every class, even maths, which he didn't consider himself very good at. With sandy blond hair, large intelligent grey eyes and a smile that curled up at the corners, he was charismatic and arrogant. He knew he was different from everyone else.

So Federica fancied him. He had smiled to himself in amusement and then forgotten all about it. Most girls fancied him. What other boys failed to realize was that girls liked boys who excelled. Whether they excelled on the games field or in the classroom, it didn't matter. Girls wanted boys who were commanding and confident. Boys who shone.

Sam shone. He didn't enjoy football or rugby – he hated group activities. He was good at tennis but only played singles. Doubles bored him. He liked to run around and get as exhausted as possible. He bored easily of girls, too. He wasn't unkind. In fact, when he liked a girl he was romantic, phoning them and writing to them. His intentions were always good. But rather like a new book, once he had read it he moved on to the next.

His mother told him that his behaviour was only natural in a young man of his age. 'Sow your wild oats, darling,' she said, 'one day when they're tamed oats you'll be glad that you did.' Nuno said that women weren't worth wasting his time on and gave him more books to read. "'Alas! The love of women! It is known to be a lovely and a fearful thing,'" he said, to which Sam dutifully replied, 'Byron, "*Don Juan*".' His father, on the odd occasion that he emerged out of his philosophy books, advised him to go for the more mature woman, as there was nothing more unattractive than a man who didn't understand the complexities of the female body; an older woman would teach him the art of good love.

So Sam was determined to find an older woman. The girls he knew were far too young to hope for anything more than a kiss. A kiss was fine, up to a point. He had now reached that point. The point where his loins ached with a longing that was beginning to distract him from his schoolwork and drag his mind off his much-beloved nineteenth-century French literature. He found himself thinking about sex at the most inopportune moments, like in a car or on a train, usually when he wasn't alone to indulge in his private fantasies. If he didn't find a woman soon he'd go out of his mind with frustration.

Federica had spent the morning with her Uncle Toby and his friend Julian in his boat, *The Helena*. The sea was as calm as a lake allowing them to sail for miles with the help of a firm but warm southerly wind that sent the boat slicing through the surface like the fin of a shark. Federica liked her uncle very much. He had taken her to his cottage and shown her his collection of insects. He had explained to her how ants built their hills and how hard they worked, like a little army of very disciplined soldiers, carrying pieces of food, sometimes twice their size, back to their nest. They had hidden in bushes at night to watch the foxes and badgers and he had built her a tree house in his parents' garden so that she could wait for the rabbits to steal into the kitchen garden and nibble on Polly's cabbages. In April when they had found an abandoned baby blackbird who had most probably fallen out of its nest they had immediately driven up to the Applebys' manor to give it to Ingrid to nurse back to health. Toby and Federica had visited every day to check on its progress. Federica had been too shy to visit on her own, especially as she was afraid she might find herself alone with Sam and not know what to say. He wasn't in the least bit interested in her. Why would he be? She was a child. But she couldn't stop thinking of him. The bird had been promptly christened Blackie, another unoriginal name for Nuno to complain about, and no amount of coaxing would encourage it to fly away. 'Life's much too good!' said Nuno as little Blackie perched on a coffee cup in the sitting room and ate breadcrumbs out of an adoring Hester's hand. After that Hester had insisted Federica visit every day. She had been reluctant at first, but soon her desire to belong far exceeded her awkwardness and she found herself cycling up the lane daily for afternoon tea.

Hester had supported Federica during her first term at school like an overprotective nanny. Having been a shy child herself the teachers were surprised at how much she had grown in confidence in one term. Thanks to Hester, who included her in everything, Federica had made friends for the first time in her life. In Chile she had always preferred to be on her own. She had been happy that way. Now things were different. She needed Hester and to her delight Hester needed her too. But nothing could replace her father, not even Uncle Toby.

When Federica returned home from sailing she found her mother crying on the sofa in the sitting room. 'Mama, what's happened?' she asked, her heart at once filling with dread that something might have happened to Hal or her grandparents.

'It's a letter from your father,' Helena sniffed, handing her daughter the tear-stained piece of paper. 'Sorry I opened it, sweetie, I thought it was addressed to me.'

She lied. She had been unable to resist. She hadn't heard from Ramon since they had left in January. When she recognized his handwriting she hadn't wasted a moment, but tore it open in a sudden fit of rage and longing. It was written from India on hotel writing paper and had taken a month to reach them. He had written such an enchanting story for Federica that the tears had welled in her eyes until they had spilled over, running down her face in a stream of jealousy and resentment.

'I hate Ramon for what he has made me become,' she explained to her mother later that evening when Federica had gone to bed. 'I'm jealous of my daughter because he wrote to her and not to me. He loves her. In his hopeless way he loves her. Then I resent him for maltreating her. For writing this letter which will only bring her hope. He's not coming back. It's over, for all of us. For Federica too. But this letter will only make it worse. He raises her hopes only to dash them later. He's always been like that, impulsive. Suddenly gripped by remorse or homesickness or God knows what, he writes this epistle of love, but he'll have forgotten all about it by now. That's what sickens me. He's so damned irresponsible. If only he'd come clean and tell her to forget him then she wouldn't be constantly on the brink of having her heart broken. I can't bear it for her. He doesn't even write a message to me, not even a few words at the bottom. Or Hal, it's as if we don't exist. He's Hal's father too.'

Federica read the letter while her heart inflated like a happy balloon, filling her chest with excitement. Surely this must mean that he will be coming to visit soon, she thought, biting her lip to contain the impulse to scream with joy. Then she ran into her grandfather's study to find where India was on the map. It wasn't too far from England. Not that far at all, she deduced, turning the globe around to find Chile. Chile was the other side of the world. But India was close. Close enough for him to stop and visit on his way back to Santiago. She read the letter several times before placing it in the butterfly box that sat on her bedside table. As she listened to the light clatter of tiny bells she was comforted by the certainty that he loved her and was thinking about her. That letter made up for the four months of silence during which she had almost given up hope that he remembered her at all.

'I received a letter from Papa today,' Federica told Hester as they sat on the raft in the middle of the lake. 'He'll be visiting us soon.'

'That's nice, what did he say?'

'He wrote me a story. He writes wonderful stories,' she said, her cheeks burning with pleasure.

'Is that his job?'

'Yes. He writes books. He once wrote about Polperro for the *National Geographic*. That's how he met Mama.'

'Really, how romantic.'

'It was. He wrote a secret message in the article that only she would understand. She realized then that he loved her.'

'Molly says your parents are divorced,' said Hester suddenly before she had time to stop herself. Federica gasped in horror and her face stung crimson.

'Divorced? No, that's not true. Who told her that?' she asked tearfully.

'I imagine she made it up,' said Hester quickly.

'Well, it's not true. They aren't divorced. Papa's coming to visit soon. Tell her that. If they were divorced he wouldn't write me such a nice letter, would he?'

'Of course not. Molly makes up loads of things,' Hester said, wishing she hadn't mentioned it for Federica's face was now grey and agonized. They sat in silence while Hester was tortured with regret and Federica with uncertainty.

'If I tell you a secret, will you promise to keep it for ever?' said Federica quietly, blinking sadly across at her friend.

'For ever. You can trust me. You know you can,' said Hester, wishing to make it up to her.

'Don't tell anyone about this. Anyone at all.'

'I won't, I promise.'

'Not Molly.'

'Especially not Molly,' said Hester firmly.

'Well, we were in Cachagua, staying with my grandparents. I overheard my parents arguing,' she began hesitantly.

'What about?'

'Mama was accusing Papa of not caring about us, that's why he spent so much time in other countries. I didn't tell you before, but Papa always travelled a lot. We rarely saw him. He'd suddenly turn up out of the blue after a few months. Sometimes one month, sometimes more. He'd never say when he was coming home, he'd just arrive. She said that their marriage was only a bit of paper and that she was giving him his freedom. She said he'd never have to come home again.' Federica's chin wobbled with despair.

'But he's written you this letter,' said Hester, shuffling up to her friend and placing a comforting arm around her shoulders.

'I know. He wouldn't have written it if he wasn't coming back, would he?'

'Of course not. If he didn't want to see you again he wouldn't have written at all, would he?'

Federica shook her head. 'No, he wouldn't have written,' she agreed.

'So there's nothing to be sad about. In fact there's everything to be happy about. He'll be coming to visit soon. Maybe very soon.'

'If they were divorced, I'd know about it, wouldn't I?'

'Yes. They would have told you.'

'Mama said that we'd live in England and Papa would come and see us just like he always has done.'

'Well then, that's the truth,' Hester conceded. Federica wiped her tears with a hanky that she pulled out of her pocket. The only person Hester knew who carried a hanky in their pocket was Nuno. 'You know, my mother says that people often say things they don't mean when they fight.' She added, 'My father says terrible things, but we don't really worry about them because when he's angry he's a different person. I think your parents were different people when they fought. I doubt they meant it.'

'Me too,' Federica agreed, feeling a lot better.

'Why don't we ask Sam to light a fire for us, then we can toast some marshmallows?' Hester suggested happily.

Federica blinked across at her friend with gratitude then focused her thoughts on Sam. At once she forgot about her father and the conversation she had overheard in Cachagua. Paddling furiously, they made their way across the glassy lake to the long reeds and bulrushes.

Sam was not happy to be distracted from his book. They found him lying on the sofa in the sitting room, eating a packet of salt and vinegar crisps and listening to David Bowie. He told them to go and find someone else.

'But there is no one else, Sam,' Hester said.

'What about Bea?'

'It's Saturday, silly,' she replied.

'Well, she's here because I heard her,' said Sam, taking another handful of crisps.

'Well, if she won't do it, then will you?'

'I'll jump that when I get to it. Just go and call her,' he instructed. Hester walked out into the hall and shouted for Bea. Federica followed sheepishly behind her not wanting to be left in the room with Sam. While Hester called for Bea,

Federica watched Sam through the crack in the door. He was
so handsome she wished she were fifteen too, then he would
notice her.

When Bea trotted down the stairs she looked completely
different to the scruffy nanny who had helped Federica out of
her clothes that winter day when she had fallen through the
ice. She was dressed to go out in a very tight black dress with
high stiletto shoes and a froth of wild blonde curls that
bounced as she walked. Her face was painted like a doll with
thick black eyelashes and shiny red lipstick. 'What do you
want, Hester?' she asked, leaning over the banisters. 'I'm
about to go out.'

'We wanted you to light a fire for us,' said Hester.

'Well, I can hardly do it dressed like this, can I?' she replied
and smiled sympathetically.

'Sam won't do it.'

'Why not?'

'Because he's reading.'

'For goodness' sake, he's been reading all day. Where is
he?'

'In the sitting room,' said Hester, watching as Bea tottered
passed them to confront Sam.

Sam sighed and raised his eyes above his book with impatience. When he saw Bea towering over him with her long
naked legs strapped into shiny black stilettos he put the book
down and sat up in amazement. 'Sam, can't you tear yourself
away from your book for five minutes and light the girls a
fire?' she said, but Sam wasn't listening. He was watching her
scarlet lips and imagining what they could do for him.

'Sorry?' he stammered, shaking his head in order to shatter
the image he had conjured up.

'I said, please can you light the girls a fire?' Bea repeated
impatiently.

'Yes, of course,' he replied beneficently.

Bea straightened up. That was easy, she thought to herself in surprise. Usually it was impossible to get Sam to do anything he didn't want to do. 'Thank you, Sam,' she said, self-consciously pulling her skirt down her thighs as Sam's eyes crept up it.

'My pleasure, Bea,' he replied, regaining his composure. 'You look very nice tonight, where are you going?'

'To the pub with friends,' she replied unsteadily.

'Well, you'll outshine them all,' he mused appreciatively.

'Thank you.'

'Make sure you're escorted, I wouldn't trust any man to keep his hands to himself with a dress like that,' he said and smirked at her. Her face flushed.

'Really, Sam,' she muttered, pulling it down again. 'Is it too short?'

'Not too short, Bea. In fact, it's too long,' he replied, imagining what she would look like without a dress on at all.

'You're too young to make comments like that.' She laughed and walked out of the room with faltering steps. 'There you go, girls, Sam will light your fire,' she said.

Sam overheard and chuckled to himself. Given half the chance he'd light *her* fire.

Chapter 14

It was late when Bea crept across the shadows and into her bedroom. She didn't want to wake the children by turning on the light on the landing so she let the moonlight guide her. She had drunk too much wine and flirted too much with the strange men in the pub. It didn't matter, weekends were for having fun. After all, the rest of the week she was tied to the nursery and all girls needed to let their hair down every now and then. She closed the door quietly and slipped out of her heels, kicking them across the room.

'Ouch!' came a voice in the corner as one of the flying shoes met with flesh. Bea caught her breath and stood as rigid as a dog that has just smelt danger. With a trembling hand she felt across the wall for the light switch. 'Don't turn on the light,' continued the voice, now so close she could feel his breath on her neck.

'Sam!' she gasped in relief. 'What are you doing in here?'

'I had a nightmare,' he said and she could detect a grin sweep across his face.

'Go back to bed,' she stammered, trying to blink herself back to sobriety. Sam ran a finger up her neck. She shrugged him off. 'For God's sake, Sam. What are you doing?'

'Don't pretend you don't know,' he whispered.

'You're a child,' she protested.

'Well, teach me then.'

'I can't,' she said and giggled at the absurdity of their conversation.

'Why not?'

'Because I'll get the sack.'

'No you won't.'

'I will.'

'Who'll tell?'

'I don't know that you can be trusted,' she replied coyly.

'So it's not that you don't want to then?' he said and placed his lips on the soft flesh where her neck met her shoulders. She shivered with a pleasure she wished she had more strength to resist.

'You're a boy,' she repeated weakly.

He took her hand and placed it on his trousers. 'Is this the behaviour of a boy?' he asked.

She felt the solid evidence of his desire and giggled again, more out of nervousness than merriment. 'I suppose not.' She chuckled.

'I'm ready for you,' he breathed into her ear.

Bea couldn't help but find the situation amusing. She suppressed her laughter. 'I'll bet you don't know what to do with it,' she said, gently squeezing it with her hand.

'I'd like you to show me,' he said. Suddenly Bea felt like a temptress and she liked the sense of power it gave her. The wine had made her reckless, dulled her reasoning so that tomorrow seemed another lifetime and tonight a magical limbo in which anything was possible. She turned and allowed him to kiss her. As his wet mouth descended onto hers she forgot that he was a fifteen-year-old boy, the son of her employers. He kissed like a man. It was only when they fell onto her bed that she was jolted back to reality. He was hard and energetic and yet he was ignorant of the complex labyrinth of the female body. After the initial kiss she lifted his fumbling hand off her breast and resolved to teach him how to make love like a man.

The following morning Bea was thankful it was Sunday so that she could spend the entire morning in bed. Before Sam had returned to his room in the early hours he had boasted that he could have gone on all night and probably all weekend. She had believed him. He was a quick learner and like any child with a new toy had been reluctant to put it away and go to bed. She smiled to herself in that pleasant heavy-eyed limbo between consciousness and unconsciousness and recalled with pride her eager student who by five o'clock in the morning had mastered the art of a soft touch, a slow kiss but not quite managed the patient restraint. That would come, she thought to herself, with maturity. Then she panicked as she remembered he was only fifteen years old and she sunk deeper beneath the blankets.

She was awoken a short time later by a sensual licking of the spaces between her toes. She writhed in her sleep as a warm sensation crept up her legs and into her belly. When the feeling of a wet mouth on her thigh became too intense to be imaginary she managed to open her eyes and peer down her body. 'Sam. Not now,' she protested and rolled over.

But he persisted. 'You can't send me away, I know how you like it. You can't resist me,' he said, running his hand over her naked leg.

'Just watch me,' she replied, pulling the pillow over her head. But Sam was right. She was defenceless. He knew her vulnerable places and how to stimulate them. She was powerless against the responses of her body in spite of her mind that cried out for more sleep. She allowed him to coax her onto her back where she feigned reluctance as he practised the lessons of the night before.

★

Sam could think of nothing but sex. Seducing Bea had had the opposite effect to the one he had hoped for. Instead of toning down his lust it had only intensified it. He was now less able to concentrate on his studies than before and spent most of the day gazing out of the classroom window imagining what he was going to do to Bea when he next saw her. The fact that it was illicit made the whole affair irresistible. He enjoyed sitting across the breakfast table having sneaked out of her bed only a few minutes before, talking to her with his usual indifference, relishing the fact that no one knew of their nocturnal adventures.

He took her wherever possible whenever they found themselves alone. Behind the pool house, in the barn, beneath the apple trees in the orchard, down on the beach or in the hidden caves that still echoed with the urgent whispers of long-dead smugglers. Bea worked hard in the day looking after Lucien and Joey, who needed constant supervision and entertainment, then serviced their elder brother through the night. She was exhausted but she couldn't refuse him. He gave her too much pleasure.

Sam didn't boast about it at school. He didn't need to. He had changed and the other boys sensed it and admired him for it. Ingrid was too vague to notice her weary nanny or the self-satisfied expression on the face of her eldest son. Inigo rarely left his study and the girls were too preoccupied with their childish games to pay attention to their little brothers' nanny. They considered themselves too grown-up for a nanny.

'Come down to the orchard with me,' Sam suggested, running a finger up the inside of Bea's forearm.

'I can't. I should listen out for the boys in case they need me,' she replied, withdrawing her arm.

'They've never needed you before. They're asleep,' he retorted, smelling the sweat on her body and feeling once again the ache in his groin.

'It's not safe. Anyone could discover us.'

'Don't be silly. Mum's on the cliff painting, Dad's in his study where he always is, the girls are at Federica's house and Nuno, well, who cares about Nuno.' He chuckled.

'I don't want this to get out of hand,' she said, trying to sound sensible. 'You're just a boy.'

'You've made me into a man,' he teased.

'I shouldn't have done.'

'Well, nothing can stop me now. I desire you.'

'You desire anything in a skirt and I'm the closest thing available,' she replied.

'That's not true, Bea. I like you. I really do,' he said, trying to sweet talk her into the orchard.

'Sure.'

'I do. Look,' he said, taking her hand and putting it on his trousers.

Bea sighed and smiled at him fondly. 'There's more to relationships than him,' she said, shaking her head and retracting her hand.

'Don't pretend you don't want him. You taught him how to satisfy you. Now he can't get enough of you. Doesn't that make you feel desired?'

'Yes,' she conceded. 'But I have to keep reminding myself that you're only fifteen.'

'Almost sixteen, actually.'

'It doesn't matter. Sometimes you're so adult you could be any one of my friends. But you're not.'

'Does it matter?' he asked. Bea wanted to tell him that she was falling in love with him, that she lay awake at night pondering on the ten-year age difference and trying to figure out how a real relationship might work. But she knew in her heart that he wanted her only for sex and that he didn't love her. He wasn't even in love with her. He'd grow up and be off, breaking hearts all over the country, she thought wistfully. She gazed into his shallow grey eyes that had yet to deepen with the experiences of life and onto his mop of sandy hair that fell over his trouble-free forehead. His grin was mischievous with the charm of a monkey and yet his gaze was lofty, as if he knew he was cleverer and more beautiful than everyone else.

She sighed and ran a hand down his cheek. 'I may as well enjoy you while I can,' she conceded, smiling at him thoughtfully. He returned her smile with a twinkle in his eye as he followed her down the stairs and out into the garden.

It was evening. The scent of hay lingered in the cool air as the dew stitched her diamonds into the freshly mown lawn and surrounding flowerbeds. The sky was pale and receding as the sun was chased away by an impatient moon. The distant roar of the ocean and the sad cry of seagulls faded into the background as Sam opened the gate into the walled orchard and pulled Bea into his arms to kiss her. She had no time to savour the melancholy of the twilight or taste the scent of ripe apples, for at once Sam was pressed up against her, his mouth on her neck and her shoulders and then on her breasts that he released from her brassiere with one swift movement of his fingers.

He liked her breasts. They were large and soft like the marshmallows Molly and Hester were always toasting over fires. Pale, pink and pert, they were always enthusiastic, always responsive. He knew how to run his tongue around them. She liked it gentle. She barely liked to feel anything at all except a rapid teasing sensation that she had told him sent the blood rushing straight to her belly. She was large and curvaceous, all woman, every bit of her, and he enjoyed exploring again and again those female places that never ceased to fascinate him. She released him from his trousers to find he was as alert and impatient as ever. Falling to her knees she took him in her mouth with the enthusiasm of a woman desperate to do anything to keep her man. It was at that moment that Nuno trotted up from the other end of the orchard on the balls of his feet. Neither Sam nor Bea noticed him for his footsteps were light and his amusement such that he didn't want to disturb the sensual scene being played out before him.

Sam stood with his eyelids fluttering with pleasure, his mouth open, his jaw loose. Nuno thought he looked quite beautiful, like a golden youth from mythical times, a young Adonis or Hercules. He turned discreetly to face the rose bed while his grandson reached the *moment critique*, he didn't want to ruin the boy's pleasure. He felt immensely proud that his grandson had discovered the joys of the flesh. About time too, he thought, it must have been the influence of Zola's *Nana* that stirred his budding sensuality.

Sam gave a moan and then a long, satisfied sigh. Bea giggled and got to her feet. Then Nuno turned around and coughed, loudly. '"The only way to get rid of a temptation is to yield to it,"' he said, then raised his thick grey eyebrows at Sam.

'Oscar Wilde,' said Sam dutifully.

'*Molto bene, caro.* Now you have yielded perhaps Miss Osborne had better return to the nursery.'

Bea nodded numbly and ran through the gate without so much as a parting glance. Her face burned so red it throbbed. She was mortified. She wanted to die of embarrassment. But Nuno was greatly amused.

'Come with me, young Samuel. I think I have to adapt your reading list,' he said, wandering out of the gate that Bea had left swinging on its hinges.

Once in his library Nuno stood before the dusty bookshelves, running his hand over the spines of his beloved books. 'These give me much pleasure, Samuel. My admiration for women was shattered when I discovered they were not as perfect as the ancient Greek sculptures I studied as a boy.'

'How come?' Sam asked, throwing himself into his grandfather's leather sofa.

'I only made love to your grandmother once.'

'Really? You must have been fertile, Nuno.' He chuckled.

'Indeed I was, as luck, or the Gods, would have it. No, my dear boy, when I discovered women had pubic hair they toppled for ever from the heavenly pedestal I had so innocently placed them upon.'

Sam laughed. 'All because of pubic hair? You can't have believed women to be literally like those sculptures?' he said in amazement.

His grandfather pulled out a couple of books and lovingly stroked their covers. 'Indeed I did, Samuel. They were never quite the same after that.'

'Poor Grandma.'

'She was devoted to me. Devoted. You'll learn that the pleasures of the flesh, the entwining of loins, the stimulation of the genitalia,' he said, clipping his words for emphasis, 'are nothing more than illusions, dear boy. False love. You lose yourself in them momentarily, then they are gone and you are left lusting after the next fleeting pleasure. You can chase it all your life, but you can never hold onto it. No, dear boy, love is something more profound. That is how your grandmother loved me. Not like an animal but like a divine being. Yes, a divine being. *Ecco*,' he said, handing Sam the books.

Sam took them and eyed them suspiciously. 'Casanova's *Memoirs* and Oscar Wilde's *The Picture of Dorian Gray*,' he read.

'The first will teach you about the joys of the flesh, the second will teach you not to abuse them,' said Nuno wisely.

'Thank you,' said Sam, getting up.

'Sexual pleasure can be a weapon as well as a wand, young Samuel. Use it well.'

'You won't tell Mum, will you?' Sam said, hovering by the door, shuffling his feet.

'It's your business, dear boy, but might I suggest you keep your loving to the dark hours when there is no chance of someone walking in on you.' He turned back to his books.

'"Love ceases to be a pleasure when it ceases to be a secret,"' replied Sam, grinning smugly.

'Aphra Behn, *The Lover's Watch*,' said Nuno pompously, without turning around. 'It is still a secret from the rest of the household, dear boy. Enjoy it,' he added, and smiled proudly because he had taught his grandson to appreciate literature.

Helena stood at her bedroom window and watched Federica playing in the garden with Hester and Molly. She was glad that Federica had settled into their new home. Her first term at school had been a great success. Hester had taken Federica under her wing and made her feel part of their family, which was what Federica needed, a large, loud family to take her mind off her absent father. When the term had finished they had spent many long afternoons on the beach, building sand-castles, picnicking on the cliff, exploring caves and listening to Jake's old smuggling stories. Uncle Toby had taken her out in his boat with Julian and taught her how to fish, except that Toby always threw them back into the water again. He hated to hurt any living creature. Federica had developed a crush on Sam Appleby, which didn't surprise Helena at all, Sam was a very beautiful young man. At least that took her mind off her father. All to the good, she thought. But what of her?

Helena was tied to the house, looking after Hal. She had been mortified to read the letter Ramon had sent to Federica. She found she missed him in spite of her efforts and caught herself more than once recalling that strange moment in Viña when their impulses had overcome their reasoning and they had made love. She had then remembered discovering him in bed with Estella and felt that nauseating anger all over again, as if it had been yesterday. She had hoped that she would have left all her memories of Ramon in Chile, along with the sentimental nonsense collected during their first happy years together. But it was harder to let him go than she had predicted. He clung to her thoughts in order to torment her. As much as she tried to shake him off she was plagued by images of him. She wondered where he was, whether he ever thought about her, whether he would turn up one of these days and tell her that he had made a mistake, that he would fight for her after all, that he would make an effort to change. How could he love her and not fight for her? She couldn't understand him.

Then there were the children. She couldn't comprehend that someone could love their children and yet care so little for them. He had written once but he hadn't visited. It was now August. She often heard Federica listening to her butterfly box, miles away, riding on the mesmerising waves of her father's stories as if that would bring her closer to him. Suddenly she was overcome with the possibility that something ill might have happened to him. She hadn't considered that as a reason for his silence, she had been too busy blaming him for neglecting them. Defeated by guilt and remorse she pulled herself away from the window, lit a cigarette and dialled his parents' number in Santiago.

'*Hola*,' responded the maid in a distant voice. Helena tried to ignore the lengthy delay and asked to speak to Mariana. She waited with a constricted heart as Mariana came to the telephone.

'It's me, Helena,' she said, trying to sound buoyant.

'Helena. How nice to hear from you,' Mariana replied, her tone at once betraying her resentment. She had thought so often of her grandchildren, wondering how they were and whether they were happy in their new home. She had minded very much that they hadn't written. She had waited for their letters with growing impatience and disappointment. But she didn't want to reveal her feelings to Helena in case she put the telephone down and shut them out for ever.

'I haven't heard from Ramon since I left. Is he all right?' Helena asked quickly, but she could tell from her mother-in-law's voice that nothing dramatic had happened.

'Hasn't he called you?' said Mariana in surprise.

'No. He wrote to Fede,' she said weakly, trying not to get emotional. She wasn't meant to care any more.

'Is that all?'

'Yes.'

'Well, he's now back in Chile. He's bought an apartment here in Santiago. He's got a new book coming out next March, it's getting quite a lot of attention.'

'I see.'

'How are the children?'

'They're happy here. Of course they miss you both. They're enormously fond of you and Nacho. So am I,' she said, inhaling the cigarette held with a trembling hand. Suddenly she felt a stomach-wrenching homesickness that took her by surprise.

'Are you happy?' Mariana asked, sensing her daughter-in-law's distress across the wire.

Helena paused. She wanted to say that she was happy, but she didn't know whether she was or not. She only knew that for some strange reason she missed Ramon and needed to hear from him. 'Yes,' she replied impassively.

'I am pleased,' said Mariana, not convinced.

'It's just taking a while to get used to living here again,' she said. 'I'm lonely,' she added to her amazement, then wondered where the devil that had come from.

'You'll settle in. It's a big thing starting all over again in a new country. Sometimes the grass is greener on the other side until you discover that your problems follow you wherever you go.'

'Yes,' Helena replied automatically. Suddenly she realized that Mariana was right. Her problems had followed her to Polperro. She was still lonely. Still dissatisfied. She had believed that coming home would change everything, that she would be able to return to her childhood, to that idyllic state before responsibility and domesticity had changed her.

'You don't often know what you have until you have lost it,' Mariana added gravely. 'What shall I tell Ramon?' She still hoped they might see sense and realize that what they had was worth holding on to.

'Tell him that his children miss him. Tell him to call or write or, better still, to come and visit,' she said, unable to prevent the bitterness from seeping into her words. 'Tell him not to desert them because they need him.'

'And what about you, *mi amor*?'

'Nothing. I'm calling for the sake of the children,' she retorted flatly.

'*Bueno*. I'll tell him,' she replied. 'Please send the children all our love, we miss them terribly. Perhaps they could write, we would love to hear from them.'

'Of course. I'm so sorry. My mind has been elsewhere,' said Helena guiltily and made a mental note to get the children to paint pictures of their new home for them.

When Helena put the telephone down she sunk into an armchair and watched the shadows edge their way into the room and into her head, where they grew, casting doubt into her mind. Had she perhaps been too hasty? She tormented herself with memories of Chile. Having despised it she now longed for it. She thought of her friends, the sunshine, the beach, the smell of the orange trees in the garden, the sound of children playing in the street, the barking of Señora Baraca's dog. She remembered the days when Ramon would return home to her outstretched arms, carrying her straight up to their bedroom where they would lie for hours discovering each other again after long weeks of separation. Those had been happy times. He had even managed to satisfy her when she had hated him. Such was the power of his nature. She had been eaten up with bitterness because she had been unable to possess it, to tame it. Here she was now, the other side of the world, still longing to possess him. She didn't dare ask herself whether she might have brought her children to England in order to get him to react, because he hadn't reacted in the way that she had hoped he would. He had let her go. So now what?

When she turned out Federica's light she told her that she had spoken to Abuelita, that she had sent her love and that she wanted her to paint her a picture of her new home. At first Federica had been pleased. She closed her eyes and imagined the picture she would draw and the letter she would write. But then she felt her heart lurch with longing. She remembered her grandmother's gentle face, the summer house in Cachagua that she loved so much, the navy sea and the soft sand so unlike the sand in England. She remembered her grandfather in his panama hat, the horse ride on Papudo beach and Rasta. Then she recalled her mother's promise of a puppy and she began to cry. Not because she hadn't been given a puppy but because the promise had been made to distract her from the argument she had overheard. 'Now you won't have to come home ever again.' Her mother's words echoed about her head until it throbbed with pain. Finally, when she could no longer bear her desolation she opened the butterfly box on her bedside table and allowed her mind to drift into the secret world of her father's stories. The pain began to subside as she floated across the Andes Mountains, chased lions in Africa and sailed high above the plains of Argentina in a hot air balloon. As she drifted off to sleep she felt the sun on her face and the heat on her body and basked in her father's love.

Chapter 15

Santiago, Chile

When Mariana told Ramon that she had spoken to Helena, he felt his stomach churn with guilt. He had only written once and he hadn't telephoned, even though he could well afford the expense of the call. He knew he should have. The only explanation he could give was that he had been busy travelling. Too busy finishing his book. In reality he had deliberately lost himself in India. He had rented a shack on the beach and written his novel. He had tried to forget Helena and the children. He had tried to forget Estella. He had succeeded in the former because things didn't feel very different. He was used to being alone on his travels so as far as that was concerned nothing much had changed. But Estella was a different matter altogether. He missed her all the time.

In spite of his apparent neglect his conscience was alerted to the misery he might be causing her. He had told her to wait and he had no doubt that she *was* waiting for him, dutifully, in the kitchen, chopping vegetables, floating through the house leaving the warm scent of roses as she went about her chores. He didn't want to telephone her or write to her, he didn't know what to say. He couldn't say what she wanted to hear, because he knew he could never commit to anyone ever again. He had hurt Helena and the children and he didn't want to do the same to Estella. Perhaps he would return in the summer and make love to her again.

When he considered the possibility of Estella falling in love with someone else the jealousy rose in his stomach like an uncontrollable demon to take possession of his mind and torment him to the point where he nearly packed his few belongings and returned to Cachagua to claim her. But then his reasoning had assuaged him. She loved him and a woman in love was as faithful as a dog. So he spent unsatisfactory nights loving strangers, imagining they were Estella, no longer possessed by the demon but looking forward to returning in the summer to find her again.

When he returned to Chile at the end of August he went directly to Santiago where he moved into his new apartment in the barrio of Las Condes. But it didn't feel like home. In fact, he longed for Viña and he longed for his family. He was bereft without them. Suddenly, after having spent months on his own in India, he was no longer comfortable with himself. He wasn't used to a solitary existence in Chile and it just didn't feel right. So he partially moved into his parents' colonial house in Avenida el Bosque. His mother was delighted to see more of him and took over the domestic side of his life like an adoring wife. His father was less enthusiastic.

'He's got a wife, woman. He's too old to need his mother,' he growled one evening when he came home to find the sitting room carelessly cluttered with Ramon's camera equipment, piles of prints and other belongings.

'Nacho, *mi amor*, he's going through a painful time. He's lonely on his own,' she protested, following him into his study.

'Well, why doesn't he ask Helena to come back? It's very simple. But if you're always there for him he won't make the effort.'

'He doesn't know what he wants,' she said, her voice dripping with pity.

'He wants the bread and the cake, Mariana. I don't know where we went wrong, but for some reason he is unable to commit to anything.' He shook his head dismissively. 'He didn't want Helena to leave him, but he wasn't prepared to change his ways for her or ask her to stay. He would have liked everything to tick on as always like a familiar although somewhat tiresome clock. I don't blame her for leaving him, though I suspect she had hoped she might force his hand.'

'What do you mean?' Mariana asked slowly, sitting down on the worn armchair that Ignacio used for reading in the evenings after dinner.

'I think she hoped that by leaving him he might be forced to change in order to keep her. I hoped he might make the effort. But he's an avoider. He let it happen and then disappeared for months to pretend it hadn't. That's why he's come home to live with us, because he misses them now he's back in Chile.'

'I wouldn't have believed you had I not had that strange call. I think Helena misses him too.' She recalled Helena's strained tone of voice and now recognized it as an unspoken cry for help.

'I bet she does.'

'Do you think she regrets leaving?'

'The grass is always greener.'

'Perhaps not as green as she had hoped.'

'Perhaps not.'

'We have to force him to question what he has done. Something's got to jolt sense into him. He hasn't quite grasped the seriousness of it all. He just can't treat people in this way. Someone's got to teach him the value of life.'

'You're right,' she said, lowering her eyes. 'What do you want me to do, Nacho? Turn him away?'

'That would be the best thing. He's not going to miss his wife if you're buzzing around him looking after him.' He noticed the dejected expression in his wife's grey eyes. He sighed and shook his head again. 'I'm not going to insist that you do it. How can I? You're his mother.'

'I want what's best for him,' she said and pulled a thin smile.

'Then tell him he can't move back in with us.'

Mariana laughed bitterly. 'Oh no, Nacho, I'm not going to tell him. It's your idea so you tell him.' She left the room.

Ramon arrived on time for dinner. Ignacio rolled his eyes at his wife as if silently to indicate his exasperation at his son's ever-increasing presence in their house. Mariana pretended she hadn't noticed and poured Ramon a glass of whisky on the rocks. 'There you are, Ramon, have you had a busy day?' she asked kindly. But Ignacio spoke before Ramon had time to.

'Have you decided what you're going to do about Helena, son?' Ignacio sank into an easy chair opposite Ramon who managed to take up most of the sofa with his long legs and arms. Ramon sipped at his whisky as if playing for time. Ever since childhood he had been unable to avoid his father's questions and he still felt pathetically weak every time he answered them, like an obedient schoolboy.

'I think my next trip will be to England, Papa,' he said, trying not to give too much away.

'When will you go?' he persisted.

'Oh I don't know, perhaps in a couple of months,' he replied vaguely.

'A couple of months? Why can't you go sooner?'

'Ramon is very busy with his work,' Mariana interrupted in her son's defence.

'I'm not asking you, woman,' said Ignacio firmly. 'Ramon is old enough to answer his own questions. For God's sake, you're forty years old.'

'Forty-one,' said Ramon and grinned at his mother.

'Exactly. You're a man. You should have settled down by now, not be wandering the globe like a gypsy.'

Ramon wanted to tell his father to mind his own business, but then he remembered that he was virtually living in their house so he had a right to know his plans. 'I'd like to spend some time in Cachagua, start a few projects. The weather's getting nicer now . . .'

'You can take the house,' Ignacio said breezily. 'It's yours when you want it,' he added, avoiding the confused expression that had alighted across Mariana's face.

'But there's no one to look after him,' Mariana protested, still frowning.

'What about Estella?' Ramon asked quickly. He then checked himself to avoid showing too much. He knew his father well enough to know that the slightest change in the tone of his voice would be noticed and analysed.

'Oh poor, dear Estella,' Mariana sighed, dropping her shoulders. 'That dear child, she was such a sweet girl. No one looked after the house like she did. I don't know what we'll do without her.' She looked at Ignacio accusingly. Ramon's eyes darted from his mother to his father, aware that his heart had plummeted to his stomach, leaving only a throbbing anxiety in its place.

'It had to be done, woman. She can't look after us and a baby at the same time,' he replied, shrugging off her accusations. 'Ramon, she's pregnant.'

'Pregnant?' Ramon repeated slowly.

'Pregnant,' said Mariana. 'Poor child. You know that young man she was seeing last summer in Cachagua?' Ramon nodded gravely. 'Well, the fool got her pregnant then ran off.'

'It happens all the time, Mariana,' Ignacio argued wearily.

'But I liked her. She didn't deserve to be treated like that. She was a good girl, not one of those women of easy virtue that hang about the port in Valparaíso. She was too trusting. I'd wring that boy's neck if I ever got the chance.'

'So where is she now?' Ramon asked, feeling sick in the stomach and dizzy in the head. He drained his glass and swallowed uncomfortably.

'Ignacio sent her back to Zapallar,' said Mariana in a clipped voice.

'I said she could come back when she's had the baby. Perhaps her mother can look after it during the day when she works,' Ignacio said with forced patience.

'I know, but she was so upset. You know, Ramon, she believed he'd come back. He told her he would and she believed him. I didn't want to shatter her hopes so I just agreed with her. But as far as I know there's no sign of him. *Dios mio*, the indignity of it all.' She sighed again.

'Did she tell you the man's name?' Ramon asked carefully.

'No, she wouldn't say. She was too ashamed, no doubt.'

'Enough, woman, my head is spinning,' Ignacio said with irritation. 'Ramon can have the house. If he wants a maid he can look for one.'

'Temporary, of course, Estella may come back and I'd like to leave the job open for her,' Mariana repeated anxiously.

'That's fine by me,' said Ignacio. 'When do you want to go?'

'Tomorrow morning,' Ramon replied automatically. His mind was whirring like the internal machinations of a clock. 'I'll just go and wash my hands before dinner.' When he looked at himself in the mirror he noticed his features had completely drained of colour leaving his complexion grey and sallow. He rubbed his cheeks with his fingers in order to encourage the blood to return, but it was useless, his shock showed all over his face.

'Why are you giving him the house?' Mariana asked her husband while Ramon was out of the room. 'I thought you were going to tell him not to live with us any more.'

'Because time alone at the summer house might just remind him of his wife and children. He may find his senses out there on the coast. I don't know. I'm clutching at straws, woman, but maybe the sea and the sunshine will remind him of the good times he shared with Helena, before it all went wrong.'

Mariana placed an affectionate hand on her husband's arm and smiled at him reassuringly. 'We suffer almost more than he does,' she said, remembering Federica and Hal with sadness.

'For sure we suffer more than him. That's the trouble, he doesn't suffer at all,' said Ignacio. 'Quiet now, I can hear him coming.'

When Ramon returned to the sitting room his parents were already standing up and moving slowly into the dining room. Mariana looked at him and smiled sympathetically. Ignacio was less tactful. 'Are you all right, son, you look pale?'

'No, I'm fine,' Ramon replied flatly.

'Look, I understand this has not been an easy time for you. I just think you've been avoiding the issue.'

'I haven't, Papa, I think about Helena and the children all the time,' he lied.

'Then why don't you go and see them? What are you afraid of?'

'I'm not afraid. Helena needs time on her own,' he began.

'For God's sake, son, that's the problem, she's been on her own far too long,' Ignacio interrupted edgily.

'She needs time to settle into Polperro. The last thing she needs is me whipping her up again.'

'Then write to the children, call them from time to time, be a father, Ramon. Don't avoid your responsibility.'

'I think of that dear little Federica and how much she loves you, *mi amor*. Your father is right. You mustn't neglect them,' Mariana said, touching her son's forearm and patting it fondly.

★

When Ramon set off the next morning for Cachagua, Helena, Federica and Hal could not have been further from his mind. All he could think about was Estella. He had spent a tormented night fighting off the demons of guilt and remorse that had flown about his bed, pinching him and pulling him, making sleep an impossibility. He had fought them off by trying to focus on the new book he was going to write, but Estella had kept surfacing to the top of his mind like a rosebud in a pond that refused to sink.

At first he had tried to convince himself that the child wasn't his, but that was useless wishful thinking. There was no mistaking that the child was his, it couldn't have been anyone else's, not only because of the timing which confirmed the summer conception, but because he knew Estella. She wasn't the type to sleep around. That in itself made him wince. He had seduced her and then abandoned her. That would have been bad enough, but he had abandoned her with child. Even he was repulsed by his own conduct. He had longed for morning, but every time he had looked at his clock it was always only a few minutes on from the previous time. He would have gone there and then had it not been for the curfew that prohibited anyone from leaving their houses between two and six a.m. Finally, when dawn had torn apart the night's sky and the light had poured in, he had grabbed his bag, clambered into the car and set off. It was six in the morning.

It was only when he caught sight of himself in the rear mirror that he realized he hadn't shaved or washed his face. He looked like a tramp with long knotted black hair, a dark shadow across his face and weary, bloodshot eyes. He would normally have stopped along the way, had a cup of coffee or a lemon soda, then he could have splashed his face with water and wet his hair, but he didn't have time. He didn't want to leave Estella alone for another minute. He pressed his foot on the accelerator pushing the limit as far as he could go without risking being caught by the police for speeding. When he arrived finally at Zapallar he hurriedly parked the car and strode out into the bright morning sunshine.

He didn't know where to look. He didn't even know Estella's last name to ask, and anyhow he didn't want the entire village to know about it. He would surely be recognized by someone. He wandered up the beach hoping that perhaps she might be there, that perhaps he might pass her on her way to buy the bread or simply taking a stroll. But there was no sign of anyone. An early spring was beginning to inject the surrounding trees and bushes with a new vitality and the air was distinctly warmer. He half expected to smell her scent of roses and follow it until he found her. But that was the kind of romantic notion he might have written into one of his novels, it wasn't real life. After walking up and down the beach for a while he realized that he would simply have to ask someone. He'd have to describe her and risk the whole village knowing about it. There was no other way. He was desperate.

When he saw an old man sitting on a bench gazing out to sea he suppressed his embarrassment and approached him. 'Good morning, Señor. I'm looking for a young woman called Estella. She's heavily pregnant, long black hair, down to her waist, about so high,' he said, indicating her height with his hand. The man eyed him bleakly through tiny black eyes that watered and blinked at him dispassionately. He leant with brown leathery hands on a knobbly wooden stick and chewed on his gums for he had no teeth to grind. 'She lives with her parents, must be about twenty or so. She used to work in Cachagua. She's very beautiful,' he continued, then sighed in disappointment. 'You'd recognize this description if you knew her,' he added, turning away. The man continued to chew without muttering a word. Then something prompted Ramon to add that she smelt of roses and suddenly life returned to the old man and he began to mumble something about her scent reminding him of his mother's funeral.

'They buried her in a grave full of rose petals,' he said wistfully. 'They said it would soothe her in the event of her waking up and not knowing where she was.' He turned and cast his eyes over to where Ramon was standing hopefully in the shade of a eucalyptus tree. 'Your Estella lives up the road, about half a kilometre, on the hill overlooking the sea. You'll recognize the house because it's yellow,' he said, nodding to himself. 'Whenever I go to the cemetery I can still smell them. One day I'll go there and never come back.'

'One day we'll all go there and never come back,' Ramon said to the old man's astonishment. He didn't think the young man was still there. He waited for Ramon to go before he continued his solitary conversation about the dead.

Ramon walked up the hill with hasty strides. It was still early. A light mist smudged the edges where the sea joined the sky so that they merged into one shimmering blue horizon. As he looked about him for the yellow house he remembered those lazy days the summer before when he had loved Estella without distraction, without guilt, without remorse and without this terrible fear of entrapment.

When he saw the house he stood on the dusty track and watched. It was still and shaded beneath the budding trees that were beginning to reveal the almost phosphorescent green of their new leaves. The house was a small bungalow with about two or three rooms. It was neatly kept with a little garden that looked well tended and cared for. He could hear a dog barking in the distance and the staccato voice of a mother berating her child that sent a ripple of commotion through the sleepy village. He continued to watch but still nothing moved. Finally impatience led him to her door where he stood anxiously and knocked. He heard a light rustle of movement come from within. For a moment he panicked that he might have got the wrong house, but then he smelt the heavy scent of roses waft through the open window and he knew she was there and his heart inflated in his chest.

When Estella opened the door and saw Ramon towering over her like a wolf, blocking out the light, her face went white before the blood was pumped urgently around her arteries in an effort to revive her. She would have cried out but she had no voice, it was lost along with her reasoning. She blinked and then blinked again. When she was sure that it was indeed Ramon who stood in front of her and not some apparition inspired by the herbs her mother gave her for her pregnancy, she threw her arms about his neck and allowed him to sweep her off her feet and carry her into the cool interior of the house.

He laid her gently on her small bed and gazed down at her adoring face that glowed with happiness. 'I knew you'd come back,' she sighed, running a soft hand over the rough bristle on his face. Falling into her beautiful features he was suddenly filled with confusion and wondered what had possessed him to leave her. What had possessed him to fear her? As he kissed her grateful lips he believed he would never leave her again. He breathed in her unique smell and tasted the salt on her skin. Then he placed a hand under her white cotton nightdress and over the swell of her naked belly.

'This is my child,' he said and was certain he felt a life stir within. Estella smiled the smile unique to expectant mothers, tender yet proud and fiercely protective.

'If he is a boy we shall call him Ramon,' she said.

'And if it's a girl, Estellita,' he replied and buried his face in her neck.

'So you are not angry?' she asked, looking up at him timidly.

'No, I'm very happy,' he said truthfully, surprised by his own reaction. 'I'm sorry I—'

'Don't be sorry, my love,' she said, placing her finger across his lips to silence him. 'You've returned as I knew you would and I'm contented.'

He kissed her finger and then the palm of her hand, up her arm and finally on her heavy swollen breasts. 'I want to see you naked,' he said suddenly, overwhelmed by the sensuality of her fulsome body. He unbuttoned her nightdress with trembling hands and pulled it over her head, then he sat back to admire her.

Estella lay proudly before him watching his eyes as they traced the voluptuous curves of her new body. She was like a shiny, plump seal. Her skin was glossy and smooth and glowed with an internal ripeness that lit her up from within. He wanted to lose himself in her and yet didn't dare for fear of hurting her or his child. So he kissed her shoulders and her breasts, her belly down to her feet. 'I want to take you away from here, Estella,' he said, kissing her lips again.

'I don't want to leave Zapallar, Ramon. Not until after the baby is born.'

'Then at least come and live with me in Cachagua, then we can think about what to do.'

'What about your parents?' she asked with a shudder.

'They won't be coming up until October. It'll be just you and me.'

Estella didn't need to be persuaded, she had already envisaged every possibility over the last six months. It was what she wanted. 'Just you and me,' she said, smiling with pleasure.

Chapter 16

Estella had grown strong over the last six months, ever since she had been fired by Don Ignacio. She had returned to her parents in Zapallar and told them about the dark bear of a man who had stolen her heart and left a part of him growing inside her womb. Her mother had wept copious tears. Her father had thumped his fist against the wall leaving a large hole in the plaster that still remained months later as they didn't have the time or money for repairs. He had vowed that if he ever laid eyes on the scoundrel he would personally cut off his penis with a carving knife. 'If he can't trust himself to use it properly, he shouldn't have it at all,' he bellowed, nursing his swollen hand. Estella had tried to convince them that he would come back to her. She told them he had promised and she believed him. But they gazed at her with wise eyes that had seen almost everything during the rough course of their long lives and shook their heads in despair.

Pablo and Maria Rega were almost too old to have a daughter of twenty-two. They had married young and tried for many years to have a child. But after her fragile womb rejected seven babies they had given up hope of ever having a family. More tears, more fist-bashing until finally they had resigned themselves, too weary to fight any more. Pablo had thrown himself into his work caring for the cemetery that overlooked the sea, talking to the unknown unfortunates who lay in the earth beneath his feet about his longing and his regret. 'They can't help me,' he told his wife, 'but they're good listeners.' Maria continued to work in the grand house of Don Carlos Olivos and his wife Señora Pilar, cleaning and cooking from dawn till dusk. She had always helped herself to food from his fridge, but when she had finally resigned herself to the fact that she simply wasn't made for producing children she had eaten to dull the pain and to fill the hours she would have spent thinking about her brood. When she was young they had called her 'Spaghetti' because she had been as thin and as fragile as a strand of pasta. But when she started eating she couldn't stop. Her misery clung to her body in the form of thick rolls of fat until she was so large she could barely climb the big staircase in Don Carlos's house without wheezing and holding onto the banisters for support. Pablo liked her better that way. He would mount her and lose himself in the rolling plains of her body. There was more of her to love.

Then one morning Maria had just managed to reach the top of the staircase after a long climb, during which she had had to pause on every other step in order to catch her breath, when she had fainted onto the floor, only to be discovered by Don Carlos's mistress, Serenidad, furtively leaving his bedroom on tiptoe. Serenidad would have liked to ignore the woman who lay on the wooden floorboards like a heaving ox, but her conscience overcame her revulsion and she called for her lover, fanning Maria with the wad of notes Don Carlos had given her to pay off her debts. So embarrassed was Don Carlos at having been discovered with his mistress that he sent Maria immediately to the private hospital in Valparaíso where she was informed by a kindly doctor that she was in labour. Don Carlos's chauffeur drove Pablo into Valparaíso to join his wife. They held hands as Maria pushed, but she didn't feel any pain or any discomfort. Their baby slid out of her body like a newborn seal, with silky brown skin, shiny black hair and the correct number of little fingers and little toes. Maria and Pablo were too in awe of the miracle to cry. They watched their child as if she were the first child ever to have been born into the world. 'She shall be called Estella,' said Maria with reverence, 'because she is a star loaned to us from the heavens.'

Maria lost weight. It didn't happen gradually, but within the short space of a month. She was never again the 'Spaghetti' of her youth, but Pablo liked her that way. Now he had two people to love.

Pablo had always found it difficult to communicate, even to his wife. So he talked to his subterranean dead – an ever-increasing audience – with a fluency that evaded him when he spoke to the living. He patted his favourite tombstone that marked the grave of Osvaldo Garcia Segundo who died in 1896 from a single shot in the head delivered by the man whose wife had meant to run away with him. The wife had killed herself afterwards, with the same gun. But her husband had refused to have her buried anywhere near her lover and threw her body into the sea. Pablo wondered whether Osvaldo Garcia Segundo could see her from where he was, high up there on the cliff. He hoped so. That story had always touched him. He now unburdened his worries about his daughter and the man who had not only stolen her heart but her future in one short, useless affair, because he felt that Osvaldo would understand.

'She'll never marry now, you know,' he said, tapping his fingers on the gravestone. 'Not now. Who'll have her? She's pretty enough, but her belly will put them all off. Who'd want another man's child? She believes this young man will come back, but you know that's not the way life is. I don't know who's been feeding her these romantic ideas but they'll come to no good. Mark my words. No good at all. I don't know what to do. Maria has flooded the house with her tears and I put my fist through the wall. What's going to become of us?' he sighed, remembering his little girl as a child and the pleasure she gave them. 'You give them everything you have, your possessions, you earnings, your love, your dreams and what do you get in return? Nothing but ingratitude,' he continued, staring out across the sea. 'Ingratitude.'

Estella had grown strong. She had temporarily sunk into despair after being dismissed from her job. But then she had pulled herself up by focusing on the two important things in her life – Ramon and her child. While she still believed he would come back for her she had the will-power to put her job behind her and think only of the future. She hadn't listened to the ranting of her parents. She had waited as Don Ramon had asked her to and all the while she waited she had considered her dreams, like a pharmacist weighing out medicine. Don Ramon would return, of that she had no doubt, but what would become of her? He was still married. She wouldn't want to go and live in the city; she had no desire for a glamorous life. She had no desire to see the world, either. She didn't want to tie him to a life that wouldn't suit him. She simply wanted to breathe the same air as him, make love to the distant roar of the ocean and bring up their child with love. She had longed for him to come back so that she could tell him she didn't want any more of him than that.

She had worked out his reservations from the conversations she had overheard between Don Ignacio and Señora Mariana as they discussed their 'irresponsible' son. Señora Mariana had been forgiving, explaining to her husband that Ramon was a free spirit, a being blessed with an unquenchable creativity. That explained why he couldn't stay in one place for very long, why he was incapable of being a proper husband and father to his wife and children. Don Ignacio's ears had throbbed with blood and he had sent his fist crashing onto the table, stating cuttingly that it was about time Ramon grew up and stopped behaving like a spoilt, petulant and selfish child. 'The world will continue to revolve without him setting it in motion with the burning soles of his feet, woman,' he had growled, 'but Helena and those children will be much the worse off without him.' Estella had vowed not to be like Helena. She would give him his freedom in return for his love.

Estella left Zapallar with Ramon, leaving a note for her parents telling them that her lover had returned as she always knew he would. Ramon had had no desire to meet them and Estella hadn't insisted; she worried that her father might carry out his threat. So they had returned to the summer house in Cachagua where the memories of their affair echoed off the walls to remind them of the way it was then, when they had made love in the dark hours, claiming the night for themselves, enjoying each other without a thought for the future. Now they had a future they had to wrench themselves out of the present and decide what they were going to do with it.

They walked up the beach. The sun had set leaving the coast cold and blustery. They held hands and reminisced about the summer before.

'I watched you swim that night you couldn't sleep,' said Estella, smiling. 'I couldn't sleep either, so I watched you from the shadows.'

'You did?'

'Yes, I watched you walk naked up the beach. I wanted you so much, I didn't know what to do with myself,' she said huskily.

'What are we going to do with you now?' he asked and his voice betrayed his uncertainty.

Estella sighed. 'I've spent the last six months preparing speeches for you. I planned what I would say when you came back, but I haven't told you any of it yet,' she said, looking down at her bare feet as they sunk into the fine sand.

'I think I know what you want to say,' Ramon said, squeezing her hand.

'I don't think you do.'

'All women want the same things,' he said, as if it were an accusation.

'So what do all women want?'

'They want security. They want marriage, children and security,' he replied bleakly.

'You're not wrong. That's what I always wanted for myself. But then I met you and you're not like other men. So that's not what I want.'

'What do you want?' he asked in surprise.

Estella stopped walking and stood opposite him, looking at him steadily through the dusk. She put her hands in the pockets of her wool cardigan and shuffled her feet in preparation of giving the speech she had practised. 'I want your love and your protection,' she began. 'I want it for myself and for our child. I want him to know his father and to grow up with his love and guidance. But I don't want to chain you to a home. Travel the world and write your stories, but promise to come home to us every now and then. I will store up your kisses in my heart but once they run low you must come back to fill it up again. I don't want to find it empty.' She smiled at him as if she understood him better than he understood himself.

Ramon didn't know what to say. He had expected her to beg him to stay with her and not go away, as Helena had when Federica was born. But Estella blinked at him with confidence. He knew she meant it.

Pulling her into his arms, he kissed her temples and her cheekbone, breathing in her rose scent and feeling closer to her than ever before. He searched about the pit of his stomach for that familiar feeling of claustrophobia yet it was nowhere to be found. Estella was prepared to love him enough to give him his freedom. But neither had prepared themselves for the wrath of Pablo Rega.

Pablo and Maria had returned home at dusk to discover Estella's neatly written note.

He's come back for me like I promised you he would. Please don't be angry. I'll come back soon.

Pablo would have thumped his fist carelessly against the wall had it not been for his wife who threw herself between him and the hole he had left the previous time, begging him to calm himself and think rationally.

'It's a blessing he came for her,' she insisted, rubbing her hands together in anguish. 'No one else would have her.'

'How respectable can he be?' he argued furiously. 'He didn't even bother to ask for her hand in marriage.'

'Marriage?' stammered Maria.

'Of course. He can't plant his seed in her womb and not marry her.'

'Perhaps that's why he didn't want to meet us. Maybe he has no intention of marrying her.'

'He'll marry her. By God he'll marry her or I'll damn him to Hell!'

'Where are you going?' Maria cried, watching helplessly as her husband stalked out of the house.

'To find them,' he replied, climbing into his rusty truck and disappearing down the hill, leaving a thin cloud of dust behind him.

Pablo Rega didn't know where to start searching, he knew he just had to look or he'd go out of his mind with madness. He drove down the coast towards Cachagua. The sun hung low in the sky like a glowing peach, causing the ripples on the sea to glimmer with a warm pink light. He thought of his daughter and the miracle of her birth. He wasn't going to let some irresponsible ruffian ruin it all now. Not after they had sweated blood to raise her. As he neared the village of Cachagua he decided to ask at the house of her former employers, Don Ignacio and Señora Campione. He had no idea where to find her and their house was as good a place as any to start.

He drove down the sandy track into the village that sat in the quiet evening light, apparently deserted except for a three-legged mongrel that sniffed the ground hungrily. When he saw a car parked in the driveway of Don Ignacio's house his heart leapt in his chest – at least someone was home. If Estella needed help of any kind he was certain she would run to Señora Mariana whom she liked very much. He looked at his reflection in the mirror, licked his hand and smoothed it over his thin hair in an effort to make himself look respectable. Then he jumped out of the truck and dusted down his shirt and trousers. He did up the buttons as far as his chest, leaving the remaining few loose to expose the silver medallion of the Virgin Mary that he always hung about his neck for luck, and to protect him against the odd evil soul who cursed him in the cemetery. Then he inhaled deeply, remembering afterwards to hold his stomach in and his shoulders up, and made his way towards the front door.

He hesitated a moment before ringing the bell. The tall acacia trees towered over him like sentinels. The house was as big as a fortress. Suddenly he felt humbled and embarrassed that he had come at all. Besides, he wouldn't know what to say. The living muted him. He was about to turn and leave when he heard voices coming from the other side of the house. He stood and listened. There was no mistaking that the laughter was Estella's. She had a very distinctive laugh, like the bubbling of a merry river. Pablo loved that laugh more than any other sound on earth and he felt a suffocating fury grip his throat again. He clenched his fists and ground his teeth like a bull about to be taken on by the bullfighter. He rang the bell.

The laughter ceased immediately, dissolving into urgent whispers and the light patter of feet. Pablo rang the bell again. Then he waited completely still as if conserving all his energy for his fight. The door opened after a long pause and Don Ramon Campione stood in the doorway.

'Can I help you?' he asked politely. Pablo searched for the right words but he had never been very good at expressing himself in syllables to living people so he simply pulled his arm back and sent his fist crashing into the proud jaw of his adversary, sending the larger man reeling back into the house where he fell to the floor and glared up at Pablo Rega in astonishment.

'*Hijo de puta!*' he exclaimed, taking his hand away from his wound and examining the blood. 'What the hell was that for?' But he knew.

'Papa!' Estella cried. 'What have you done?' she gasped in horror when she saw Ramon stagger to his feet, his face dripping with blood.

'How dare you steal my little girl?' Pablo stammered angrily, his fist poised to hit him again.

'He didn't steal me, Papa, I came willingly. Didn't you get my note?' she interrupted in exasperation, bravely placing herself between her father and her lover. 'Enough, Papa,' she ordered. 'You've done enough!'

'Marry her, Señor!' Pablo pointed a threatening finger at Ramon, who looked down at the squat little man with impatience.

'There's the slight problem of me being married already,' said Ramon flippantly.

Pablo's face swelled crimson and his lips began to tremble. 'So what are you going to do?' he asked hoarsely, shaking his head incredulously.

'Papa, please come in and we can discuss this calmly,' said Estella, taking her father by the arm and leading him into the house. Ramon watched them walk through the hall and sitting room and out onto the terrace. He noticed how her confidence had grown with the baby and he admired her for it. He remembered the shy little girl he had seduced and smiled in spite of his throbbing jaw.

Pablo slumped into a chair and looked up at his daughter with weary resignation. Estella sat opposite him, placing her hands on her large belly. Ramon stood by the door with his arms folded in front of him. He let Estella do all the talking; he had no desire to sweet talk the old man. As far as Ramon was concerned, his affair with Estella had nothing to do with anyone else but them.

'Papa, I love Ramon. He is the father of my baby and I want to be with him. I don't care about marriage. Ramon will buy us a house in Cachagua and make sure we are looked after. This is what I want,' she said calmly.

'Your grandmother would turn in her grave,' he muttered, gazing at his daughter with watering eyes.

'Then she'll have to turn, Papa,' Estella replied resolutely.

'You're committing adultery. God will punish you,' he said, instinctively touching his silver medallion of the Virgin Mary. 'He'll punish you both.'

'God will understand,' said Ramon, who hated the way the church kept everyone in line by filling their hearts with fear.

'You are a godless man, Don Ramon.'

'Far from it, Señor, I am a believer. I just don't blindly believe the garbage I'm told by weak mortals who call themselves priests and claim to be in constant dialogue with God. They are no more holy than I.'

'Papa, Ramon is a good man.'

'He's lucky he's not a dead man,' Pablo replied, getting up. 'Go on then, live in sin. I don't know you any more.'

'Papa, please!' Estella begged tearfully, throwing her arms about him. 'Please don't turn your back on me.'

'As long as you're with this selfish, godless man, I don't want to see you,' he said sadly. Estella followed him out to his truck. She tried to persuade him to give Ramon a chance, but Pablo refused to listen. 'After all we've done for you,' he said, turning the key in the ignition.

'Papa, please don't leave like this,' she sobbed.

But he drove up the road without so much as a glance in his rear mirror.

Estella gave birth to a baby boy in the same hospital in Valparaíso that she had been born in twenty-two years before. Ramon was as proud as any new father and held the tiny creature in his big hands, declaring that he be named Ramon. He placed his lips on his mottled forehead and kissed his son. 'Ramon Campione,' he said and smiled at Estella. 'We don't need marriage when we have Ramoncito to bind us together.'

Estella missed her mother dreadfully. The birth had been painful without her herbs and soothing words. She longed to contact her but she was afraid of their rejection. Her father's harsh words had inflicted a deep wound that had left her feeling isolated and more dependent on Ramon than ever. A month after the birth they had moved into a pretty beach house that Ramon had bought just outside Zapallar so that she could be near her parents and the friends she had grown up with. He reassured her that her father would forgive her in time.

'Time heals everything,' he said knowingly. 'Even my father might forgive me one day for letting Helena go.'

★

At the end of October Ignacio and Mariana had moved to their house in Cachagua for the duration of the summer. Mariana had hired a new maid called Gertrude, a sour old woman who had nothing pleasant to say about anyone and complained constantly about the state of her health. Ignacio liked her because she was so disagreeable he didn't have to make the effort to be nice to her. In fact, she responded better to his cantankerous nature than she did to Mariana who tried to mollify her with kind words and smiles. Gertrude never smiled. When Mariana had foolishly mentioned Estella, Gertrude took it upon herself to inform her that there was a rumour that Estella had given birth to a monkey as a direct result of her getting pregnant outside wedlock. 'That's what happens to those who disobey God's commandments,' she crowed gleefully.

It never occurred to Ignacio and Mariana that their son might be the father.

'I miss Estella,' Mariana said to her husband.

'Yes,' he replied, laying out the pieces of a monumental puzzle on top of the card table in the sitting room.

'How could Gertrude be so unkind? A monkey indeed.' She sighed despairingly. 'Where do these people hear such rubbish?'

'It's folklore, woman,' Ignacio replied, adjusting his glasses.

'Well, any intelligent human being must know it's untrue.'

'You believe in God, don't you?'

'Yes.'

'But you have no proof.'

'Nacho!'

'It's just an example, woman.'

'On a completely different level.'

'As you wish,' he replied, hoping she'd leave him alone to concentrate on his puzzle.

'You know, I might find out where Estella lives and go and visit her. You know, just to make sure she's all right.'

'*Como quieras, mujer*,' he said impatiently. Mariana shook her head and left him to his puzzle. 'The minutiae of my wife's world never cease to amaze me,' he sighed once she had gone, and sat down to commence his task.

Ramon watched his son sleeping in his cradle. The baby didn't move, didn't even twitch. Once again he panicked that his son might be dead. He bent into the cot to listen for his breathing. When he heard nothing he put his face to the baby's in order to feel his breath on his cheek.

'*Mi amor*, you're not worrying again? Ramoncito is alive and well,' Estella whispered, placing the clean washing on the chest of drawers.

'I just had to be sure.' He grinned at her bashfully.

'You've forgotten what it was like,' she chuckled, planting a tender kiss on his cheek.

'Yes, I have.'

'Go and see them,' she said suddenly.

'What?'

'Go and visit your children, Ramon,' she said.

'Why?'

'Because they need you.'

'I can't.'

'Yes you can. If you left me and started a family with another woman I would like to think that you would still be a good father to Ramoncito.'

'I'm not going to leave you, Estella,' he said firmly.

'That's not what I mean. Those children need you to be a father. Whatever went wrong between you and Helena has nothing to do with them. If you don't go, they'll blame themselves. They must miss you. I look at Ramoncito, he's so vulnerable and so innocent. He needs us both.'

'I'll go sometime,' he said casually.

★

Estella was the first woman he had ever been with who didn't beg him to stay. He was surprised that she had suggested he go. Suddenly he worried that she was growing tired of him. She was twenty years younger than he. Perhaps she longed for a man of her own age. Then he reassured himself that she couldn't possibly want anyone else. He was the father of her child. She had also promised him that she would never complain if he left as long as he came back from time to time. The irony was that now he didn't want to go anywhere. He could write at their beach house, take long walks in the sunshine, swim in the sea, make love in the afternoon and enjoy watching his baby grow each day. He found that his poems came easily. He didn't have to find the words in faraway places, they were right there in their beach house. Estella read them and when she understood them she wept. She never asked when he was leaving and she never again suggested he go. But her words had settled into his conscience and grown. He knew she was right. He knew he should go and see his children. But he always put it off until tomorrow. Tomorrow was a long way away.

Chapter 17

Polperro

Federica bicycled down to the post office with Hester to post the picture she had painted for her grandmother. It was of her new house and her new friends Molly and Hester. She had included Sam, painting him in bigger than everyone else, even bigger than her mother and grandparents. Hester had admired it. 'You should be a painter like Mummy,' she had said. 'But Mummy can't draw people, they all end up looking like birds.'

'Oh, I think she's rather good.'

'Well, when you know Mummy better you won't be too shy to say what you really think.' She had laughed. Federica also had a letter to post to her father. She hadn't told her mother and as she didn't know her father's new address she had popped the letter into the envelope addressed to her grandmother. She knew Abuelita would pass it on. She had told him that she missed him and that she thought of him every day when she woke up and every night before she went to bed, because those were the times she reserved for her butterfly box. She told him that he was right, the box was magical, because when she opened it her mind automatically drifted off to faraway places where she rode on clouds, fished pink fish out of silver rivers and ate delicious fruit unlike any fruit she had ever seen before. Then she asked him to come and see them because she was growing up fast and if he didn't come soon he wouldn't recognize her. Satisfied that he would surely come, she had sealed the envelope with a wish.

Federica had spent almost the entire summer with the Applebys, leaving her mother to concentrate her attention on Hal. Polly cooked, cleaned and cared for Helena as if she were a child again. Nothing was too much for her to ask. Jake just rolled his eyes as he watched his wife run around after their daughter as if the last ten years had been but a blink. Polly insisted that she was only doing what any other mother would do for her child. Jake couldn't disagree; he didn't know what other mothers would do but he only had to look at Helena running around after Hal to know that there was at least a certain amount of truth in his wife's excuses.

Hal could do no wrong, if only in the eyes of his mother. He had his father's glossy black hair and dark, heavy eyes into which Helena would fall and disappear for hours. During those periods there was very little anyone could do to get her attention. She would laugh at all the quaint things he said, play whatever games he suggested and praise him even when he hadn't done anything worth praising. At four years of age Helena felt he was the brightest, most charming child she had ever seen. Well beyond his years. She refused, however, to acknowledge his moods that swung from absolute affection to blind fury and loathing, for no apparent reason. When Hal swelled with rage not even Helena could reach him. Somehow she found excuses for these tantrums and if anyone mentioned them she turned on them with all her defences. Federica knew instinctively when to leave her mother and Hal alone together and play on her own. Her mother didn't love her less, she understood that, Hal just needed her more than she did. After all Hal didn't have any friends like Molly and Hester. Lucien and Joey included him at their tea parties, but

Hal wasn't an honorary member of the Appleby family like she was. He was too little.

Federica wanted to join Hester for Christmas, but Helena insisted she stay at home with her own family. 'You're not an Appleby, you're a Campione,' she said, much to Federica's disappointment because she was beginning to feel more like an Appleby every day. Ingrid began to decorate the manor in October. Instead of tinsel she made garlands of flowers made out of crêpe paper, which she hung up the banisters and around the cornices in the hall and sitting room. The tree was hung with large goose eggs that she painted in festive colours and lit with a conventional string of Christmas tree lights. On the top she made a nest for Blackie to sit in. To Federica's surprise Blackie was delighted with her new bed. None of the Applebys were in the least bit surprised, for when it came to animals Ingrid had the touch of Saint Francis. But the most surprising of all was Nuno. Apparently every Christmas Nuno made the pudding. It was a ceremonial affair, which was taken very seriously indeed. The entire kitchen had to be cleared for a day. No one except Sam was allowed in so the rest of the family had to have lunch at the pub while Nuno floated about the kitchen in a state of rapture. Even Inigo was dragged out of his philosophy books and his black mood and forced to join in the fun at The Bear and Ball. Nuno believed himself to be a phenomenal cook.

'It's not so much about the right quantity of ingredients, dear boy, but the way the pot is stirred,' he told Sam.

'I don't see the point in cooking,' Sam replied. 'It takes much too long to prepare and is much too brief to eat.'

'"Kissing don't last. Cookery do!"' said Nuno in his clipped Italian accent.

'That one's lost on me,' Sam admitted in irritation, after having thought about it for a while.

Nuno widened his glittering eyes and tapped his wooden spoon on the butcher's table. 'Come come, dear boy, think.'

'Sorry, Nuno. I can't,' he replied, defeated.

'Meredith Middleton.'

'Of course. "Speech is the small change of silence,"' Sam sighed, shaking his head. 'That was an easy one.'

'It's always the easy ones that get us, Samuel. And we're always got in the end.'

For Federica Christmas with her grandparents was going to be very dull in comparison to the Applebys'. Polly and Helena decorated the house with conventional streamers and the tree with tinsel and shiny baubles. Federica would have joined in had she not preferred to help Hester make presents for all the animals. Jake thought Christmas highly overrated and began to build a new model ship, leaving glue and pieces of wood all over the house, much to Polly's chagrin. Helena found her daughter's daily jaunts up the lane excessive and decided that Hal and Federica were going to paint pictures for their grandparents' presents and set them to work at the kitchen table. 'I want the most beautiful paintings you can do, and if it doesn't take at least a week you're obviously not doing it properly,' she said, directing her comments at Federica. Federica's heart sank. She set about her task with little enthusiasm, wondering at every moment what Hester was doing up at Pickthistle Manor.

Toby had told his parents that he was going to spend Christmas with Julian's family in Shropshire. They were hurt. No less hurt than they had been the Christmas before or the Christmas before that. But Toby wanted them to be sorry. As long as his father refused to have Julian in the house he would make him suffer by staying away too.

Helena was furious and confronted her father about it. 'He's my brother and I won't stand by and watch you treat him in this way. He's not a leper, you know, he just happens to be in love with a boy. What's the big deal?' she said angrily.

But Jake didn't want to discuss it with his daughter. He wasn't able to speak about his son's homosexuality to anyone, not even to his wife. He was too ashamed. Helena didn't give up. She spoke about Julian at every opportunity. 'I went up to Toby's today with Hal. Really, Julian is so sweet with him. I left them together while Toby and I went for a walk. He couldn't have been in safer hands. I'd trust him with my life,' she would say, but Jake would ignore her and either leave the room or bury his nose further into the bowels of his model ships. But Helena was determined their family shouldn't be wrenched apart because of some old-fashioned, irrational, misguided prejudice. She didn't know how she'd do it but she was confident she could rectify the situation given time. In the meantime she was saddened. Christmas would be deeply lacking without Toby.

By the time Christmas arrived a thick covering of snow had transformed Polperro into an ice kingdom. The sky was pale and timid, the sun no more than a resplendent haze that hung low in the eastern sky. The trees had retreated into themselves, leaving only their frozen shells to fend off the bitter wind and in spite of their naked branches a few rooks and the odd robin braved the cold and sought shelter there. Federica and Hal were enchanted by the snow. They awoke early and pressed their noses against the frosted windows to marvel at the white garden that lay silently in the emerging dawn light. They had been so excited by the snow that neither had noticed the fat stockings which lay full of presents at the end of their beds.

Scrambling into Helena's bed Hal and Federica excitedly tore open the tissue paper on each carefully wrapped present. 'How come Father Christmas found us in England?' Federica asked her mother, squealing in delight as she pulled out a brand new paint box.

'He's very clever,' she replied, watching as Federica folded each bit of wrapping paper neatly in a pile while Hal threw his on the floor for someone else to pick up later.

'I hope he found Papa in Santiago,' said Federica, remembering how both parents used to get stockings too. 'I wish he were here,' she said wistfully, turning one of her gifts over in her hand thoughtfully. She wanted him to see her opening her presents although she knew no present would ever beat the butterfly box he had given her. 'Where's yours, Mama?' she asked, noticing that Helena didn't have anything to open.

'Father Christmas left it outside your bedroom by mistake,' said Polly, entering in her dressing gown and slippers with her greying hair long and wild about her shoulders. She handed her daughter the stocking.

'Thank you, Mum.' She smiled at her mother, making space for her on the edge of the bed.

Polly sat down and touched her daughter's cheek with her large hand. 'Don't thank me, thank Father Christmas,' she said and winked.

Federica ate her breakfast in silence. She had loved her presents, especially the Snoopy dog that came with lots of different outfits so that she could change him for each new occasion. Her grandmother had put little gifts on their places at breakfast and her grandfather had turned the Christmas tree lights on making the house look festive. She loved the snow and longed to run outside and play in it. But nothing could make up for the absence of her father. She tried not to think about him, she wasn't meant to be sad on Christmas Day and she didn't want to spoil it for her mother by sulking, but in spite of her smiles she missed him so much she wanted to cry.

Helena noticed her shiny eyes and knew immediately what was wrong. 'Why don't you and Hal finish breakfast now and go and play outside. You can build a snowman if you like,' she suggested kindly, hoping that the snow might distract her. But nothing could.

Federica didn't want to go to church even though she knew the Applebys would be there. She didn't feel like it. She didn't feel like watching all the other children with their fathers, looking at her and wondering why she didn't have one too. She wanted to hide. But her mother wouldn't let her and told her that she had to go to church to thank God for all the wonderful things He had given her during the year and to thank Him for giving the world baby Jesus. On the way to church she thought about what her mother had said. God had given her lots of wonderful things, Hester, for example, and she liked Polperro. But she couldn't help but feel deeply let down. If God could give her Hester why couldn't He give her back her father? She resolved to ask Him in her prayers.

The church was said to be so old that it was listed in the Domesday Book. Toby had taken Federica there when she had first arrived in Polperro to show her the grave of Old Hatty Browne, the witch burnt by the villagers for sorcery in 1508. Toby added darkly that on very clear nights she was often spotted in the yard picking herbs for her potions, with which she would minister to the dead. Federica had been enchanted and wanted to know more, so they had sat among the daffodils and talked until sundown.

The church itself was small and quaint with a sloping roof and rickety porch, surrounded by snow-capped graves and a low brick wall to keep the dogs out. For some inexplicable reason there was nothing they liked better than to cock their legs on the gravestones. Nuno said it was due to the pungent scent of the deceased that rendered the earth irresistible to them but Inigo lamented their lack of respect and said that they enjoyed 'pissing on the deceased because they couldn't piss on the living'. The nave and balcony only managed to seat about fifty people but due to the unlikely charisma of the Reverend

Boyble there was rarely a spare seat in the place. Helena had brought her children up in the Catholic faith, because Ramon was Catholic. But now she was back in England and on her own she had reverted to the Protestant faith with which she had been raised. It gave her a sense of belonging.

Everyone was dressed in their best coats and hats. Federica had squeezed into an old tweed coat of her mother's that Polly had kept sealed in a large white box with tissue paper. She didn't like it because it was scratchy and a little too small, but Helena thought she looked very smart and refused to let her take it off. Consequently she tugged at the collar throughout the service. The church smelt of pine tree and perfume, mingled with the waxy scent of the candles. Old Mrs Hammond played the organ with faltering precision, her shrivelled face pressed up against the hymn book because she was too proud to admit she needed glasses. A murmur passed through the congregation when the Appleby family entered and took their places at the front of the church. Nuno trotted in first on the balls of his feet with his tortoise nose in the air and a devout expression frozen onto his face. 'Girls, you're not a pair of pious penguins. Hold your hands together in front of you like vestal virgins,' he hissed to Molly and Hester whose shoulders hunched up and shuddered as they tried their best to suppress their giggles. Hester caught Federica's eye as she passed and winked at her. Federica forced a thin smile in return but she didn't feel like smiling. Ingrid swept by dressed in a velvet turban and long green velvet coat that reached to the ground and trailed along behind her as if she were an ageing bride. She greeted everyone with a gracious nod of her noble head but she didn't see any of their faces because her eyes had misted over with the beauty of the music. Inigo shuffled down in a mangy brown duffel coat and felt hat pulled low over his ill-tempered face followed by Sam, who was already bored, Bea in a short skirt, Lucien and Joey.

Once the Applebys had settled into their seats the Reverend Boyble sprung into the centre of the nave like a jolly frog. His bulbous brown eyes swept cheerfully over the attentive faces of his congregation and he smiled a very wide, charming smile. 'Welcome,' he enthused in a surprisingly high, thin voice. 'Welcome everyone. Today is a very special day because it is Jesus' birthday.'

Sam yawned, opening his mouth wide like a hippo. The Reverend Boyble noticed his yawn and chuckled. 'I see some of you would prefer to be in bed on this glorious morning, or perhaps you're tired of opening all those presents. I thank you for making the effort to come.' Sam sat up stiffly and tried to prevent his face from flushing by focusing on the crucifix that hung above the altar.

'Effort, hmmm . . .' murmured Reverend Boyble thoughtfully, rubbing his thumbs over the surface of his prayer book. 'Effort is a virtuous thing. It's all too easy to allow laziness to lead us down the path of evil. I wonder whether you all know the story of the two frogs in the milk bowl.' He cast his eyes about the faces that stared back at him expectantly. 'They were stuck and couldn't get out. It would have been quite easy for the stronger frog to have stepped on the weaker frog, thereby ensuring him a swift leg-up to safety. But the stronger frog didn't go for the easy option. Instead he continued to kick and kick together with the weaker frog in an enormous effort to throw himself up the side of the bowl. Well, his efforts were rewarded. They kicked so hard and for so long that the milk turned to butter, thereby allowing them to simply hop out with no trouble at all. That is effort, my good people. It brings its own rewards.' A murmur of admiration rippled through the congregation. 'Today is Jesus' birthday, so let us celebrate with the first carol on your service sheet, "Away in a Manger."'

Federica knew some carols because they had sung them at school in Chile, although the words had been in Spanish.

It had been an age since she had last spoken Spanish, she thought unhappily, and she attempted to sing along quietly the way she had been taught in Viña. Suddenly all the homesickness and longing she had suffered silently for so long rebelled against her failing will and clawed their way into her throat, causing her eyes to water in discomfort and her chin to tremble. In her mind's eye she saw scenes of her past opening up to her like a vision of a lost world. Her heart stalled when she saw the dark face of her father emerge in all its magnificence and as much as she tried to hold back the tears they cascaded down her cheeks because she searched his eyes for love but found only indifference. At once she felt desperately empty and sad. All those wasted hours believing he'd come and visit. How naïve she had been. He had obviously forgotten about them because it was Christmas and he had never missed a Christmas, ever. She knew now that he would never come and her spirits sunk lower than they had ever sunk. Helena placed a hand on her shoulder, sensing her daughter's distress. She too missed Chile and in a strange way, Ramon. But she was more practised at hiding her melancholy and sang more heartily than ever.

During the sermon Reverend Boyble spoke about the meaning of Christmas with great enthusiasm. 'Christmas is a time for love and forgiveness,' he preached. Federica listened to him but she felt no love or forgiveness, just an aching wound that refused to heal. As the full enormity of her father's rejection reached her understanding, her vision misted until the candles glowed like small suns and Reverend Boyble was reduced to a black blur, his voice no more than a low hum in the distance. She felt the heat prickle on her skin as she made one last effort to suppress a sob, but her chest was too small to withstand such a violent tirade. Abruptly she stood up and shuffled blindly past her grandparents who looked at each other in bewilderment. She then ran up the aisle, pushed open the heavy oak door and burst out into the snow where she was finally able to let herself go and howl into the icy air.

Holding her stomach she bent over and cried at the injustice of the world. She loathed Christmas and she loathed England. Suddenly she felt a heavy hand on her back. She stopped crying and straightened up. Wiping her face with her glove she lifted her eyes to find the dark eyes of her father staring into hers with love and remorse. She swallowed hard and blinked.

'Papa?' she croaked, catching her breath in her throat with surprise.

'Fede. I'm sorry.' He drew her kicking and screaming into his arms.

'I hate you, I hate you!' she sobbed, as he held her in a firm bear hug, burying his face into her hot neck, whispering words of tenderness and encouragement. As she felt herself enveloped in the familiar smell of his body she closed her eyes and stopped fighting, giving in to the security of his embrace, conquered by her love for him. Finally he crouched down and held her by her narrow shoulders.

'I missed you,' he said emphatically, searching her expression for submission. He wished he had missed her much sooner. 'I got your letter,' he added, grinning at her sheepishly.

'Is that why you came?'

'No. I was always going to come and see you. I've just been very busy. But your letter made me realize that I couldn't leave it any longer.'

'I'm glad you're here,' she said and smiled timidly.

'There, that's better.' He wiped her face with his thumbs. 'You have so much to tell me. You've been living an adventure. I want to hear everything. Do you like England?'

'Sort of. I have a best friend called Hester.' She sniffed, cheering up.

'What about that dog Mama was going to buy you?' he asked.
'She hasn't yet.'

Ramon rolled his eyes. 'Oh dear. Do you want one, as a Christmas present?'

'No thank you. You're my Christmas present and I couldn't ask for anything else.'

Ramon had forgotten how much he loved his daughter. It had been too easy to forget. But now, as he held her against him again, his heart reeled with tenderness.

Suddenly the door opened with a low groan and out walked Helena. When she saw Federica in the embrace of a strange man she was about to object. But then she recognized the wide shoulders and the strong back and felt her head swim with uncertainty. When he turned around to face her she stood blinking at him with her jaw open, not knowing what to say and fighting the impulse to slap him around the face and slate him for not having come months ago.

'Helena.' He said and smiled at her.

Helena stared back at him, her face pale in the blue winter light, her lips quivering, anxiously trying to find the words. 'Ramon,' she replied in confusion. Then added clumsily, 'What are you doing here?'

'As there was no one at the house I presumed you'd be at church,' he replied casually, as if he dropped in all the time.

'Yes, we are at church,' she retorted stiffly, finding her wits again. 'We're at church. Now if you'd kindly let Fede go we'd like to finish the service,' she said tightly, taking Federica by the arm.

'I'm not leaving him,' Federica hissed, grabbing onto his hand.

'Fede, he'll be here when we come out.'

'I'm not leaving him,' Federica repeated before dissolving into tears again.

'It looks like I'm going to have to join you,' said Ramon with a smirk, squeezing his daughter's hand.

Helena pursed her lips together and let out a long-suffering sigh. 'There's very little room,' she argued, not wanting to incite the curiosity of the congregation by walking back up the aisle with Ramon.

'I'll find somewhere,' he said, shrugging his big shoulders.

'As you wish,' Helena conceded, reluctantly opening the door.

Ramon followed her into the church, which he dwarfed with the sheer scale of his charisma. As they walked down the aisle Helena felt innumerable pairs of inquisitive eyes settle on her husband, eager to know who the strange, dark foreigner was. But Federica placed a proprietorial hand in his so that no one would be in any doubt that he was her father.

Jake and Polly's eyes widened with surprise when Helena asked them to move up to make space for Ramon. They sat staring at him with their mouths agape like floundering fish. Fortunately Reverend Boyble was still merrily giving his sermon about the meaning of Christmas so they didn't have the opportunity to ask questions or voice their shock. Federica grinned up at her father and held his warm hand in both of hers to prevent him from getting away. Hal squeezed closer to his mother, sensing her uneasiness and feeling fear but not understanding why. Helena wished she hadn't been so unfriendly, but she was in shock, what did he expect? He could have let her know. A letter or a telephone call would have been nice. She sat scowling into her prayer book trying to draw some peace from the words written on its pages, anything rather than look at him. She struggled with her pride, which longed for him to see her happy and settled and regret letting her go, and her heart, which suffered the weight of her memories and yearned for him still. Ramon sat back and glanced at the unfamiliar faces around him. Then he settled his gaze on his daughter whose tear-stained face glowed with love and pride. He was happy he had come.

Chapter 18

Once the service was over the church turned into a parochial cocktail party as the village wished each other a very happy Christmas. Ramon shook hands with Jake and kissed Polly on her stiff cheek as if he had seen them the week before. He lifted a reluctant, wriggling Hal into his arms and kissed his face before handing him back to Helena.

'Does it surprise you that he doesn't recognize you?' she hissed.

Ramon lowered his eyes and shook his head. 'I'm sorry. I didn't mean to leave it this long,' he replied, ashamed.

'You never do,' she retorted bitterly.

Federica took him by the hand and led him through the throng of strange people to meet the Applebys.

'This is my father,' she said proudly to Ingrid who extended her hand graciously.

'It's a great pleasure to meet you. Fede has told us so much about you,' she said and smiled broadly.

'You must be Hester's mother,' he said.

Ingrid's face expressed her surprise. 'Why, yes I am,' she replied, wondering how he had worked that one out.

'Fede's lucky to have a best friend in Hester,' he said. Federica squeezed his hand because he knew nothing about Hester except what she had told him outside.

Ingrid placed her monocle in her eye to study him in more detail. He was devastatingly handsome with the remote, mysterious eyes of a wolf. She also found his accent most charming; his was genuine, Nuno's was not.

'Come with me, I'd like to introduce you to the rest of my family,' she said, gesticulating to her father and husband who stood talking to each other because they found the after-church chitchat with the village superficial and tiresome. Both longed to be back at the manor with their books. 'Pa, Inigo, it gives me great pleasure to introduce Ramon Campione,' she said and smiled broadly. 'Isn't he quite the most handsome thing Polperro has ever seen?'

Ramon chuckled to hide his discomfort but Federica's grin increased until it was in danger of swallowing up her entire face.

'Really, darling, you shouldn't judge people by their appearance. I apologize for my wife,' said Inigo, shaking Ramon firmly by the hand.

'"It is only shallow people who do not judge by appearances,"' said Nuno, bowing to Ramon.

'Ah, you're an admirer of Oscar Wilde,' he replied, bowing back.

Nuno's eyes flickered their approval. 'So are you. Now I hold you in great esteem. When can you come to lunch? I would like to show you my library,' said Nuno, turning to his daughter and raising an eyebrow. 'I could tell young Federica comes from a learned family.'

'Ramon is a famous writer,' said Ingrid, who knew all about him from Helena. 'He's highly regarded in Chile.'

'I understand you have taken my daughter under your wing,' said Ramon. 'I'm very grateful to you.'

Ingrid patted Federica on her head as though she were a rather well behaved dog. 'It's a pleasure. My daughters adore her. My father is right, Ramon, you must come for lunch. How long are you staying?' she asked, hoping he was going to stay for a long time. She liked nothing more than colourful people.

'I don't know yet.'

'Divine! I love a man who takes every day as it comes. Much the best way to go through life. It lasts longer that way,' she said and laughed. Then she leaned in closer to him and whispered, 'We have invited the vicar to lunch today, so I think we had best be heading back to Pickthistle Manor. You will come to lunch, won't you?' she added. 'Tomorrow?'

'Of course. It would be a pleasure,' he replied with a courteous inclination of his head.

'Good. Tomorrow it is then. Bring Helena and the children. It's always a delight to see your wife.'

Helena was furious. 'You want to go around presenting as a family?' she raged. 'How dare you show up here and take everything over.'

'I'm not taking anything over. I came to see my children. Isn't that what you wanted?'

'You sweep in without a single apology for not writing, not calling, not being there when your children need you.'

'I'm here now,' he replied.

'You're here now, but gone tomorrow. I had given up on you. It was easier to give up. Now you're back I don't know where I am any more.' She folded her arms in front of her obstinately.

Ramon shrugged his shoulders and sighed. There was simply no point in arguing with her. He watched her rigid features; the bitter line of her mouth, the pinched skin and frozen eyes and remembered why he had let her go. 'What more can I say? I'm sorry,' he ventured in an attempt to alter her expression.

Her lips twitched as she pondered her next move. 'I don't want Fede to hear us arguing again,' she said. 'Let's go for a walk and discuss this calmly.'

They walked up the lane, through a mossy wooden gate and into the field and woods beyond. Helena lit a cigarette and blew the smoke into the icy air where it floated on the cold like fog. Ramon was dismayed to find that Helena hadn't changed at all in the months that they had been apart. She was just as unhappy as ever. She hadn't even bothered to wash her hair for church. He was disappointed. He sensed a strange feeling of *déjà vu* along with those familiar contractions in his gut, that summoned him away.

'So how long will you be staying?' she asked as they walked up the field, their boots scrunching into the melting snow.

'I don't know yet,' Ramon replied, struggling against the impulse to return as quickly as possible to the serene and untroubled home Estella had forged for him.

'Nothing's changed, has it?' she sighed. 'Well, I'll tell you how long you'll stay, a week, perhaps ten days, then we'll begin to bore you and you'll be off again.'

'You and the children never bored me,' said Ramon seriously.

'No?' she retorted grimly. 'Well, that's what it felt like.'

'Look, Helena. I'm sorry I didn't call. I wanted to surprise you,' he said, placing his large hand on her shoulder. She shrugged it off. 'Fede was pleased to see me,' he added and smiled a small, pensive smile.

'Of course she was. But you haven't been around for the past eleven months wiping her tears. Not a day has gone by when she hasn't thought that perhaps, just maybe, today will be the day Papa turns up. What sort of a childhood is that, Ramon? If you just wrote regularly, kept in touch, let her know your plans then she wouldn't live in such an uncertain world. It makes her very insecure, you know, and I suffer with her.' Her voice dripped with bitterness.

'I'll try,' he conceded.

'And what about Hal?' she continued. 'It's as if he doesn't exist. You write to Fede but not to him. He's your son and he needs you just as much as Fede does. More so, because he's never experienced your affection like she has.'

'You're right,' he said simply. 'You're right about everything. I haven't come here to fight with you.'

Helena blinked in surprise and kept her eyes fixed on the snow-laden trees in front of them. She hadn't expected him to be so compliant.

They walked up the path until they came to the high cliffs which cut straight down to the sea. Helena led him to a small iron bench where she often came to sit alone and gaze out over the waters. There, the view that stretched out before her into the mists of infinity would take her soul back to the sweet days of her past before acrimony had seeped in to sour it. Now she sat down and surveyed the frosty sky and icy clouds with the man whose love had once been as intense as the sun. Once more the horizon dragged her spirits out of the shadows of her unhappiness and she remembered how it had been then. She felt her heart thaw in the midst of such splendour, in the midst of such vivid memories. She burrowed in her coat pocket for her cigarettes and lighter. With a shaking hand she lit one. She felt Ramon's overbearing presence and the desire to cry. How did it all go so dreadfully wrong?

'So, how are your parents?' she asked after a while, placing a hand on her aching temple.

'Well. They're in Cachagua.'

'I miss Cachagua,' she said quietly, almost as if she were talking to herself. She didn't look at him but continued to stare out over her memories. 'I miss the heat, the sea, the smells. I never thought I would miss it, but I do.'

'That's the trouble with loving two countries, you always want to be in the one you're not in. It gives one too much choice,' he said. 'Sometimes it's better not to have the choice.'

'Your life must be very hard indeed, you have the whole world to choose from,' she said and chuckled resentfully.

'You have two, sometimes that's harder.'

'Oh, I'm very happy here. Very, very happy,' she said, but Ramon was not convinced and neither was she.

'Have you got one of your headaches?' he asked, noticing her massaging her temple with her hand.

'Yes, but I'm fine, they come and go,' she replied dismissively.

'Come here,' he said, moving her so that her back was facing him. She tried to object but he silenced her with his assertiveness and placed his hands on her head and started massaging her.

'Really, Ramon. I'm fine,' she argued weakly as the sensation of his touch caused her skin to prickle with nostalgia.

'You're not fine. But I'm going to make you fine,' he said and laughed.

She resented his cheerfulness and wondered why everything was always so straightforward for him.

Ramon's fingers working into her skull were too pleasurable to resist so she ceased to fight and leant back against them, taking in a long, deep breath. As she relaxed her head his hands moved down to her shoulders, moving beneath her coat and sweater to her skin.

'Tell me how the children have been?' he asked and she told him about Federica's infatuation with the Applebys, her crush on Sam and her progress at school.

'She adores the Applebys,' she said. 'She never had many friends at school in Viña, but they've become like a second family to her. It's done wonders for her confidence.'

'That's good.'

'Oh, it's wonderful. At first England frightened her. It was so cold and grey, not like the blue skies of Chile. It's good we moved to the sea though, at least that's familiar.'

Then she told him about Hal and her shoulders eased up and her throat loosened until she began to laugh without bitterness or resentment.

'At least they are happy here,' he said.

'They seem to be.' She closed her eyes to the luxurious feeling of his fingers sending the blood back into her dried-out muscles.

'But what about you?' he asked.

'Oh, Ramon. I'm fine.'

'I'm asking you as a friend, not as your husband.'

'You're still my husband,' she said throatily and smiled, recalling a lost age when their shared happiness had eclipsed the impending unhappiness that would overwhelm them.

'Okay, so I'm asking you as your husband.'

'I don't know,' she replied, shaking her head.

'What do you do all day?'

'I look after Hal.'

'What do you do for you?'

'For me?'

'For you,' he repeated.

She thought about it for a while. She didn't know what she did for her. She sometimes accompanied Federica up to the Applebys for tea, or took Hal to the beach. She visited Toby and Julian, chatted to her mother. But she couldn't think of anything she did purely for her own pleasure.

'I don't know, Ramon. I can't think of anything,' she said bleakly and felt her throat constrict again with emotion. 'The children give me enormous pleasure.'

'Of course they do. But that's domesticity. I mean an indulgence. A selfish pleasure which you don't share with anyone.'

Helena considered his question – Ramon was a master of self-indulgence and she of sacrifice, that's why it had all gone so wrong.

'Everyone needs time to themselves,' he continued. 'A long bubble bath, a trip to the hairdresser, I don't know what makes you happy.'

'Well, I've lost touch with myself,' she sighed, 'because I don't know either.'

'Perhaps you should start thinking about you. I give you enough money?' he asked.

'You give me more than enough money.'

'Well, go and spend it, for God's sake. I don't know what you girls do, but buy a new dress, go to a beautician, enjoy yourself. Don't chain yourself to the nursery; you're not a domestic. If you need a domestic, hire one. If you need a house of your own, buy one. I don't care but you have misery written all over your face and it's not very attractive.'

Helena was stunned. She couldn't remember the last time they had talked so frankly. She couldn't remember the last time he had thought about her and her happiness. She felt her stomach stagger with the recollection of what it had been like when they had been friends. They had talked without pause, about everything and anything, laughed at the smallest things and communicated without words across the lines of love. She wondered when their conversation had dried up and why. She dared not turn around because she knew if she looked into his eyes she would close up again with uncertainty, so she kept her eyes shut in an effort to extend the moment.

'I moved the children to England for me, but ironically they are the ones who enjoy it. Not me. I wonder, I don't know, I wonder . . .' She hesitated.

'What?' he asked quietly.

'I wonder, oh God, Ramon, I can hardly say it.'

'Say it. You'll feel a hell of a lot better if you do.'

'Have I made a huge mistake?'

Ramon stopped massaging her shoulders. She sat up and turned to face him. He looked at her with dark, impenetrable eyes and she felt herself slowly closing up again with inhibition and shame.

'Have you made a mistake?' he asked seriously, thinking of Estella and hoping she wasn't suddenly going to change her mind.

'I don't know whether I've made a mistake leaving Chile. I miss it. Perhaps it's nothing more than nostalgia,' she added dismissively.

'Perhaps,' he agreed thoughtfully.

'I don't know.'

'I think you need to give it a chance here,' he said. 'You need to throw yourself into it like Fede has.'

'It's much easier for children. They just get on with things and don't brood.'

'Look,' he said. 'It was your choice, Helena. I never asked you to leave. I didn't want you to. But I understood why you did and I support your choice. I think you are encountering the same problems here as the ones you faced in Chile. You're a mother on her own who's dedicated her life to her children. I think you'll find if you dedicate some of that time to you your feelings might change. You're young, you're good-looking.' She blushed and turned her face away. 'You need to find a hobby, something that takes you out of yourself and out of the home.'

'Perhaps you're right,' she said, feeling happier. 'You know, we haven't talked like this for years.'

'I know. We were too busy resenting each other, we now know where we both stand.'

She looked at his diffident profile as he stared out across the sea. Then lowered her eyes. 'Yes,' she said sadly. 'We do.'

★

Federica was so happy to have her father back that she was unable to sleep. Her parents slept in different bedrooms, but she didn't mind. She was grateful that he was there at all. Jake and Polly accepted his sudden arrival once they saw how he and Helena got on much better than they had predicted. There were no fights, no tantrums, no bitter comments, no tears. Helena washed her hair, applied makeup and even bought herself some new outfits in town. They disappeared every day as a family. They went for walks along the beach with the children, explored ruined castles and hidden caves. In fact, they did all the things that they had done ten years before when they had first met. The only difference was that they didn't kiss and they didn't laugh quite as much. But Helena was less resentful and Ramon more attentive to her needs. She no longer felt numb inside but regained her awareness. Her indifference had, after all, been nothing more than a rebellion of the senses, a stagnation of the heart. As her anger dissolved she discovered she cared. While they retraced the paths of their courtship she began to find the man she had fallen in love with behind those dense eyes and her spirit stirred for him again.

Ingrid was enchanted by the swarthy foreigner who had suddenly appeared in their midst. He had come for lunch on Boxing Day with Helena and the children and entertained her with stories which he recounted in his thick accent and foreign intonation. She wished she spoke Spanish because she would have bought every book he'd ever written. But he charmed her none the less with stories he invented off the top of his head and tales of his adventures that he embellished with his rich imagination until he had captivated the attention of the whole table, even the lofty Sam who was usually bored by the men his mother suddenly 'took shines to'.

★

The weeks that ensued were punctuated with invitations to Pickthistle Manor. Helena felt herself swelling with pride as Ramon dazzled everyone with his presence and his uniqueness. The atmosphere was charged with a rare energy when he was present and no one felt it more than his wife.

'Why you're the other side of the world from this delightful young man is beyond me,' Nuno said to Helena one day over lunch.

'Oh, Nuno, it's not that simple. You don't have to live with him,' she laughed.

'No one else will have me besides Ingrid so it's not an option,' he replied, looking down at her loftily with intelligent blue eyes. 'Sometimes one realizes what one has lost when it is too late. I hope, my dear, that you won't suffer the same fate.'

'He's here for the children, not for me,' she said coolly. But she looked across the table at Ramon's animated face and wished he had come for her. She wished he could just bury his pride and beg her to come back to him. She wished he could change for her. But her heart sank because she knew the true nature of the man. He was like the wind and he always would be – he'd never know where he was going to blow next.

'Ramon's the same as ever, Nuno, when he's with you, you feel there's no one in the world more special to him than you. Take Federica, for example.' They both looked over at the small child who clung onto every word her father said. Everything she did was for his benefit; her laughter, her jokes, her stories, her comments, her smiles. She worshipped him. 'Federica believes he loves her more than anyone else in the whole world. Right now he does. I really believe that. He's full of remorse that he didn't come earlier, that he never wrote or called. He's mortified. Wracked with guilt. But then he'll be off soon and we won't hear from him for months, perhaps years. Because with Ramon, out of sight is out of mind, I'm afraid.'

'Love is understanding someone's faults and loving them in spite of them,' said Nuno philosophically.

'Is that a quote?' she chuckled.

'No. It's mine, but unfortunately not terribly original. None the less, it's true.'

'Ramon and I spent years trying to understand each other until we gave up trying.'

'It's never too late to try again.'

'I don't know. I think we've always misunderstood one another.'

'"To be great is to be misunderstood,"' Nuno quoted. 'Ralph Waldo Emerson. A very perceptive man.'

'So I see.'

'He also said another very acute thing, my dear.'

'What is that?'

Nuno leant over to her and whispered in her ear. '"We are always getting ready to live, but never living."'

Helena thought about that all through lunch and throughout the afternoon. Indeed, for some reason she was unable to think of anything else.

'Fede?' said Hal, brushing his teeth over the basin.

'Yes?'

'Do you think Papa is going to stay?'

Federica hung his wet towel over the radiator. 'I don't know,' she replied, not wishing to voice her hope in case she raise her brother's unnecessarily.

'Maybe he'll take us back to Viña,' he added, spitting into the running water.

'I don't think he'll take us back to Viña, Hal,' she replied carefully.

'Why not?'

'Because we live here now.'

'I would rather live in Viña,' he said decisively.

'But you love it here with Granny and Grandpa,' she insisted.

'I miss Abuelito.' He pulled a sad face.

'So do I, Hal.'

'Grandpa doesn't carry me on his shoulders or swing me around by the arms,' he complained.

'I know.'

'Or take me riding.'

'He's very busy.'

'I want to go back to Viña. I think Abuelito misses me.'

'I'm sure he does. I'm sure they both do,' she said wistfully. 'It's bedtime now, Hal. Shall I read you a story?'

'Where's Mama?' he asked, padding out of the bathroom in his bare feet.

'At Joey and Lucien's house.'

'She's always up there.'

'I know. She likes the Applebys.'

'I don't.'

'Yes, you do.'

'No, I don't.'

'You always play with Joey.'

'I don't like Joey.'

Federica sighed in anticipation of a row. 'Come on. I'll read you a story,' she cajoled brightly.

'I want Mama to read me a story,' he insisted. 'I won't go to bed until she does.'

'What about Granny then?'

'I want Mama,' he whined and folded his arms in front of him stubbornly.

'All right,' she sighed. 'Get into bed and wait until Mama comes back, she shouldn't be long.' But Federica knew that by the time she returned they'd both be asleep.

★

It was late when Federica heard the wheels of the car scrunch on the gravel in the driveway outside her window. The light penetrated her bedroom for a moment before she was once more plunged into darkness as the engine was switched off. She listened for their voices as her parents hurried in out of the cold. They were laughing, but she couldn't make out what they were saying. She hadn't heard her mother sound so happy in a long time. She sat up in bed and strained her ears for some indication that her father might stay, but she only heard muffled voices that revealed nothing except a growing friendliness between them.

'I really enjoyed tonight,' said Helena, climbing the stairs. Federica cowered in the darkness, watching as her mother came into view through the crack in the door.

'Me too,' Ramon agreed, following closely behind her.

Helena hesitated outside Federica's room. 'I'm glad you like the Applebys,' she said softly so as not to waken her children.

'Nuno's an original,' he chuckled. 'As for Inigo.'

'You're the only one I know who gets Inigo's point. He barely talks to anyone, shuts himself up in his study all the time. It must be exasperating for Ingrid.'

'I have to admit I find him fascinating.'

'I can't imagine what you talk about.'

'Everything.'

'Really?'

'He's learned and wise. You just have to penetrate his disappointment.'

'Disappointment?' She frowned.

'He doesn't have Nuno's ability to rise above the world.'

'Like Ingrid.'

'Exactly. He spends his days pondering life and dwelling only on the negative. If we look hard enough we can find ugliness in anything. The trick is not to look for it.'

'I don't know what you're talking about,' she said lamely and chuckled to hide her ignorance. 'Thank you for making such an effort with Hal these last few days.'

'He's a sweet boy,' Ramon replied.

'He is, but you never knew him. It's important for him to feel your affection. I know Federica's more interesting to you. She's older and more outwardly loving. But Hal loves you too, he just doesn't understand it.'

'It's been good for me to see them.' He nodded then yawned.

'It's been good for us, too,' she said and looked at him steadily.

He caught her eyes and smiled ruefully. 'It has,' he agreed in such a low voice, that Federica hardly heard him.

'I'm glad you came.'

'Me too.'

They both hovered awkwardly before Ramon walked on up the corridor. 'Goodnight, Helena.'

'Sleep well, Ramon.' She watched him go with tenderness. Then she too disappeared out of sight.

Federica felt a shudder of anticipation cause her skin to shiver as if it were cold. But she felt very hot and very excited. She squeezed her eyes closed and hoped that what she had just witnessed was the beginning of a new love affair between her parents. She was sure then that her father would stay.

Helena lay in bed and thought of Ramon. She then thought about what Nuno had said. 'We are always getting ready to live, but never living.' She repeated it again and again in her head, pondering on the meaning and how it applied to her. Nuno was so right. Ramon was living. He didn't bother about preparation; he just rushed off to live as much as he could, whereas she was always preparing to live. Ramon was like a large bird. For him there were no frontiers, he just flew where he wanted, when he wanted. She envied his spontaneity yet resented his lack of responsibility. He didn't answer to anyone, not even the pleas of his children. Much less the entreaties of his wife. But, he was certainly living. Ralph Waldo Emerson would have approved of Ramon.

She lay in solitude and yet, tonight, her solitude felt heavier and more uncomfortable than ever before. She stared up into the blackness and remembered those early days with Ramon when she had curled up in the warm reassurance of his embrace and slept without doubts. She felt his presence in the house because it was as dense as smoke and hot like fire. She was powerless to ignore it and unwilling to fight it any longer. She remembered Ralph Waldo Emerson and climbed out of bed.

She slipped into her dressing gown, opened her bedroom door and crept down the corridor towards Ramon's room. She didn't hesitate outside his door as she had done that terrible night the previous January, but opened it quietly and walked into the darkness. 'Ramon,' she whispered. He stirred beneath his bedclothes. 'Ramon,' she repeated. He stirred again. She felt her way to the bed and prodded him. 'Ramon.'

He woke up. 'Helena?' he mumbled. 'Are you all right?'

'I'm cold,' she said, because she couldn't think of anything better to say. Her body was trembling all over, surprised by the impetuosity that had suddenly overcome it. 'Can I get in?'

Ramon shuffled to make room for her. She climbed in beside him and pulled the covers about her. 'What do you want, Helena?' he asked. But she ignored the impatient tone of his voice and persisted.

'I want you to stay,' she said.

He sighed and pulled her against his warm body, wrapping his arms around her and breathing into her hair. 'I can't.'

'Why can't you?'

'Because my home is Chile.'

Santa Montefiore

'Can't you just stay for longer? You can write here. You don't have to be in Chile. The joy about your work is that you can take it anywhere.'

He sighed again. 'I can't change,' he said flatly.

'Why can't you, Ramon? Because you don't want to?'

'Because I can't.'

'But we've become friends again. We haven't enjoyed each other like this for years. We're getting to know each other again. No, let me finish,' she said when he tried to interrupt her. 'I thought I didn't care about you any more, let alone love you. I felt this dead indifference and it scared me. I thought there was nothing left of our relationship. So I came home. I thought it was the only option. But I was wrong. I see that now and I pray that it isn't too late. We can make it work, I really believe we can.'

'But we'll face the same problems we have always faced. It doesn't matter where we are, our problems will follow us.'

'I need you,' she said, then swallowed because she heard the desperation in her voice and it frightened her.

'You don't need me, Helena. You need a life.'

'But you didn't want me to go, are you saying now you don't want me back?'

'I'm not saying anything at all. I'm just saying that we both need this time apart.'

'Then you don't want me at all,' she said with resignation, ashamed that she had declared herself so carelessly.

'I want you, Helena,' he said and kissed her forehead. 'I would make love to you now, happily. I have always enjoyed you.'

'Then why don't you?'

'Because I'm not going to stay.'

'Because you don't desire me any more?' she said, defeated.

'Because the holes in our marriage are still there, Helena.'

'The holes were made by me. I was confused. I was hurt. I felt dejected.'

'You were right. You were dejected. Nothing's changed. Nothing's changed at all.'

'You said you loved me then,' she choked.

'And I do, but not in the way that you want to be loved. You want a man who can love you every day. I'll be gone soon and then you'll be left alone to feel dejected. I can't help that.'

'Then there really is no chance?'

'Of what?'

'Of trying again?' she said, and her voice trailed off in humiliation.

Ramon stroked her hair and lay staring up into the darkness. He thought of Estella and the confident way that she loved him. There was something very needy about Helena and he felt that old, familiar sense of claustrophobia suffocate him once again. He still loved her. But he couldn't change her and as long as she enveloped him with her needy love he couldn't love her in the way that she longed to be loved. He felt the wind of change blow outside his window and knew that it was time to leave.

The following morning Ramon came down to breakfast with his bags packed.

'You're leaving?' said Helena tightly. Her headache had returned and she was filled with shame. She wished she could rewind the tape and erase the previous night. She could barely look into his eyes. When she did they were once more dark and impenetrable. She had gone too far and ruined everything.

'I'm leaving,' he replied, then sat down next to Federica.

'You're leaving?' she stammered. 'Now?' She watched her father's grim face nod at her sadly. Had she dreamed the night before when they had talked on the landing with such affection? She was certain they were falling in love again. How could it all have gone so wrong in one night? She didn't understand.

'Don't be sad, *mi amor*.' He touched her forlorn face. 'I want you to write to me and tell me how you're getting on and what you're doing. Don't miss out a single detail.' He wiped a tear off her cheek with his thumb. 'You be good and don't cry, because I'll be back very soon to see you.'

But Federica's face crumpled into misery and she threw her arms around his neck and sobbed. 'I don't want you to go,' she choked. 'Please don't go.'

'I can't stay for ever, *mi amor*. I'll be back, I promise,' he reassured her. 'Remember to write to me,' he added and kissed her wet face.

When he gathered Hal into his arms the child squirmed and cried out for his mother. Helena soothed him with gentle words and gathered him up, where he clung to her like a frightened monkey. Ramon didn't pursue it. There was nothing more to say. He kissed Helena's stony face, then he was gone leaving a feeling of emptiness in their hearts and a terrible sense of loss. Helena wondered when he'd come back. She had a premonition that it wouldn't be for many years.

Federica ran upstairs and slammed her bedroom door behind her. She threw herself onto her Snoopy duvet and cried. How could he rush off like that with no warning? She had invested all her hopes in him. She was sure he was going to stay. Besides, he had enjoyed it in Polperro. They had had fun. He liked the Applebys but most of all he had appeared to like her mother again. They had become friends. What went wrong? When she had tired of crying she pulled the butterfly box onto her knee and opened the lid. She stared down into the glimmering crystals and watched the butterfly extend her wings, changing from reds to blues as if in sympathy. In the mesmerizing shades of the ancient stones she hid from her unhappiness and the sudden sense of rejection that gripped her heart with cold claws. Slowly she lost herself in her memories that seemed to resonate in each tiny gem. She saw her grandparents on their balcony in Cachagua and Rasta running up Caleta Abarca beach. She saw the house where she used to live and then the wide open sea, she smelt the lavender and felt the sun on her face. Dizzy with the invasion of so many recollections she closed her eyes and drifted on her father's love.

Chapter 19

Cachagua

It was just before Christmas that Mariana finally made the effort to visit Estella. A Christmas visit of goodwill. She would take her a silver necklace that she had bought in Santiago as a present. After all, it hadn't been her idea to sack her. In fact, Mariana had done everything in her power to persuade Ignacio to keep her on. She had liked her and she was the first maid she had ever had who did the jobs without being asked and used her initiative without being prompted. Estella had been far too intelligent to reduce her talents to cooking and cleaning but she seemed to enjoy it.

Mariana had been forced to ask the ill-tempered Gertrude to find out where Estella was now living. She was unable to discover her whereabouts on her own, especially now that rumour had it that Estella was no longer living with her parents. Gertrude had been quick to point that out. She had added with glee that according to her cousin who lived in the same village as Pablo and Maria Rega, not even they knew where their daughter's house was.

So Mariana had driven herself to Estella's beach house, following the directions that Gertrude had given her. The old woman had offered to accompany her but Mariana had graciously declined her offer with a shudder. She could barely spend more than five minutes in the maid's company in her own home, let alone in the claustrophobic interior of a car. The thought of it made Mariana's mouth curl downwards with distaste. Not only was Gertrude insolent but she also had a strange tendency to smell strongly of aniseed. Mariana was old fashioned and liked the parameters between employer and employee to be clearly defined. Gertrude hurled herself against those parameters without thinking and always caused offence. Ignacio dealt with her firmly by shouting at her to 'know her place', to which Gertrude responded with a scowl but also a reconfirmed sense of duty and commitment to her job.

When Mariana first saw Estella's beach house she was immediately impressed by the size and quality and curious how a woman in her position could afford such luxury. It was built into the bank overlooking the sea and had the good fortune of being the only house for some distance. It was painted white with an American-style veranda and large green shutters to keep the interior cool in the summer-time. The roof was thatched and the walls supported an abundance of sky-blue plumbago which had managed to weave its way over the veranda where it hung down and fluttered in the wind like butterflies. Mariana had never suspected Estella's errant lover to be rich. She had assumed he came from the same world as she did. She had been wrong.

The door was open and she could hear Estella singing inside and the cheerful gurgles of a baby. Mariana recalled Gertrude's vicious comment about the monkey and smiled with satisfaction. That was most certainly not the noise of a monkey. She hesitated a moment before calling for Estella because she noticed evidence of the presence of a man. A man's shirt hung on the back of the chair on the veranda and a pair of moccasins were placed by the door. Well, she thought, if he's here I may as well meet him too. So she called out 'Estella' and waited.

Estella recognized the voice immediately and she stood rooted to the ground, stunned with panic. Ramon was in England yet all his belongings were scattered over the house. In the brief moment between Mariana's call ánd Estella's thin reply she tried to remember what items of Ramon's were where and which would give him away. Finally she laid Ramoncito in his cradle and walked up the corridor to the door where Mariana was inching her way in, curious to cast her eyes about the house.

'Señora Mariana, what a surprise,' said Estella firmly, attempting to hide the tremor in her voice. 'Let's talk outside, it's very hot in here,' she said, ushering her former employer out onto the veranda. Mariana was disappointed. She had wanted to see the house. But her good manners prevented her from requesting a tour.

'I'm sorry I came unannounced. Are you alone?' she asked.

Estella noticed her eyes rest on the pair of shoes by the door. 'Yes, I'm alone,' she replied casually. 'Please, sit down and make yourself comfortable.' She gesticulated to the chair with the shirt hanging off it. Estella removed the incriminating item and placed it inside the front door along with the shoes. Mariana noticed everything and wondered why she was so embarrassed. Then it suddenly occurred to her that perhaps the man sharing her house was not the father of her child.

'I see you are quite happy,' said Mariana tactfully. 'You have a beautiful house.'

'Thank you, Señora Mariana.'

Mariana noticed how nervous the girl was and concluded that it was only natural after Ignacio had so brutally asked her to leave his employment. 'I'm so sorry about your job,' said Mariana, desperately trying to put the girl at her ease. 'Ignacio can be very insensitive. He doesn't mean to. It's his way. But not everyone understands him like I do. Are you being taken care of?' It was a clumsy question but Mariana couldn't resist. Estella stiffened and her eyes lowered as if she were ashamed to look at Mariana directly.

'I am very content,' she replied simply.

'You have a little baby now. A boy?' Estella nodded and she smiled without restraint. 'He's obviously giving you a lot of pleasure. I adored every one of my eight children and grandchildren,' she sighed. 'Grandchildren give me the same pleasure all over again.' Then she thought momentarily of Federica and Hal and her eyes misted. 'What is he called?' she asked, deliberately forgetting her own melancholy.

Estella's cheeks burnt with guilt. She could tell the truth and risk suspicion or she could lie. She raised her eyes to Mariana's and decided that lying was without doubt the only option.

'I have not decided yet,' she said, looking steadily at the other woman in an effort not to appear shifty.

Mariana was surprised. 'You haven't decided yet?'

'No.'

'Well, you must call him something!'

'I call him Angelito. My little angel,' she said quickly.

Mariana smiled. 'Angel. That's a nice name,' she said, but her intuition told her that something wasn't quite right.

'I'm glad things turned out well for you. Last summer I was very worried.'

'Me too.'

'But you have a lovely house, a little boy and' – she hesitated but then threw aside her reservations and continued without inhibition – 'you have a man to take care of you.' She watched as Estella's face burned again and her eyes shone awkwardly. 'Don't worry, my dear, I'm not prying,' she reassured her quickly, thinking of Gertrude and wishing that she hadn't gone so far. 'I don't need to know who he is, it just makes me happy that you're happy. I am very fond of you, Estella, and it gave me much grief to see you suffering. You're a good girl and you didn't deserve to be treated with such callousness. There are plenty of girls who deserve that sort of treatment, but not you, you're a cut above them. I wanted to tell you that if you ever need anything to come and see me. I'll always try to help you in any way that I can. A reference perhaps or advice. I'm here to talk to if ever you need some-one who's detached from your family. An outsider. I would only be too happy.'

She watched Estella's face relax and the colour drain away again as her embarrassment was replaced with gratitude. 'You're very kind, Señora Mariana. A girl like me is very lucky to have a protector like yourself. I'm very privileged and I thank you,' she said, wondering how Mariana would feel if she knew they were Ramon's shoes in the doorway and Ramon's shirt that had hung over the back of the chair. Estella doubted she would offer her protection if she knew her son was committing adultery with a lowly maid.

Mariana rose to leave. She swallowed her curiosity and restrained herself from asking to see inside the house. But before she left she felt it wasn't unreasonable to ask for one thing. 'Estella, I would dearly love to see Angelito,' she said.

Estella went pale. 'Angelito,' she repeated.

'Yes. If it's not too much bother. He's obviously a good baby as he hasn't made a squeak.'

'He is a good baby. But he might be asleep,' said Estella, trying to make excuses.

'Then I can come and take a peek. I won't wake him,' she insisted.

Estella had no choice. If Mariana came into the house she would no doubt recognize her son's belongings. 'No, I'll go and get him and bring him out here,' she replied quickly, retreating into the house. Mariana thought her behaviour most strange. If her child had really been a monkey she would have reacted in the same way. For a brief moment Mariana wondered whether there was perhaps something wrong with the child. If the child was in some way deformed it was quite wrong of her to insist on seeing it. But before she had time to tell Estella not to worry, the young woman appeared out of the shadows carrying a small bundle in her arms. Mariana felt an itchy heat crawl about the skin on her neck and prepared herself for the worst.

Estella hoped that Mariana wouldn't recognize her son in Ramoncito's conker eyes and languid smile. But when she saw the baby blinking up at her sweetly Mariana's face opened like a flower and a wide, genuine smile swept across it expressing her delight.

'He is quite the most beautiful baby, Estella. Can I hold him?' she enthused, pressing her hands against her cheeks in wonder. 'Adorable, completely adorable,' she sighed, taking the child from his mother and pressing him against her bosom. Estella smiled too, relieved that grandmother hadn't recognized grandson and she was able to breathe again.

Mariana sat back down in her chair while the baby smiled happily up at his grandmother. Estella brought out a tray of iced lemon and the two women sat under the plumbago and talked about the baby. 'He is so like you, Estella. Such a pretty baby. Look at his long eyelashes and dark eyes. He'll be breaking hearts all over Chile. Won't you, Angelito?' she clucked, gently rocking him.

'He's a good baby. He rarely cries,' said Estella proudly.

'I bet he eats well, too.'

'He does. He's growing so quickly.'

'I can see.'

'I love being a mother. I have a purpose in my life now. I feel needed,' said Estella thoughtfully.

'Motherhood is a wonderful thing. It changes your life for ever. Suddenly there's this little person who needs you more than anyone else in the world. He's from your own body. Imagine that bond, how strong it is. He's a part of you and even when he's grown up and gone he's still connected to you, because you made him, gave birth to him and suckled him.'

'You're so right,' agreed Estella and she told Mariana about how she felt when he was growing inside her.

The two women began to talk as equals about the duties of a mother, the joys and the sorrows that were the two sides of the privilege of motherhood.

'We feel their pain and their pleasure. We can't help it. It's our lot,' said Mariana, remembering Ramon and the break-up of his marriage. 'But they are individuals and have to make their own choices. We can only advise and be there when things go wrong. But I would never change any of it for a second. Motherhood is the most wonderful gift of life, and I'm very fortunate to be a woman,' she said and smiled at Estella.

'Me too,' Estella replied, smiling back.

When Mariana finally got up to leave the midday sun was high in the sky. She looked at her watch and realized that she had been there for well over an hour and a half. 'Goodness me, look at the time!' she exclaimed, handing the child back to his mother. 'Angelito must be hungry.'

'He's always hungry. I think he's going to be a big boy,' she said, kissing his forehead tenderly.

'Thank you for letting me see him,' said Mariana grate-fully. 'He really is very dear.'

'It was a pleasure,' Estella replied. 'Thank you for coming.'

Mariana was no more than ten steps from the house, reflecting on the delightful baby Angel, when she put her hand in her pocket and felt the silver necklace she had bought for Estella. She sighed in frustration at her own forgetfulness and turned back. Estella had disappeared inside, leaving only the wings of the plumbago flowers to flutter about the walls of the beach house in the cool sea breeze. Mariana stood once again in the frame of the door, uncertain whether to knock or walk straight in. She smiled with tenderness as she heard the excited tones of Estella playing with her child.

'Ramoncito, my little angel. Ramoncito,' she laughed as the baby squeaked and gurgled back.

Mariana's smile slowly slipped off her face. She held her breath as the blood drained from her head to her feet, fixing her to the ground when all she wanted to do was run away as fast as her old legs could carry her. When Estella repeated his name Mariana was left in no doubt that she had heard correctly and arrived at the right conclusion. With great effort she turned as quickly and as quietly as she could and hastily made her way back to the car, her temples throbbing with the sudden sporadic appearance of thousands of unpleasant images.

Once inside she sat behind the wheel with her heart thumping like a maddened bat inside her breathless chest, as if she had just witnessed a murder. With a trembling hand she turned the key in the ignition. It was only when she was on the open road that she began to breathe again. The father of Estella's child was none other than her own son, Ramon. There was no doubt about it. It all made complete sense. The camera in her mind had at once been turned into focus and she could see clearly the events of the summer before. Estella's lover had been Ramon. He had seduced her, impregnated her then left her. That sort of callous, irresponsible behaviour was not limited to the lower classes, as Ignacio had maintained, but to their own flesh and blood. Mariana was repelled by the thought of adultery. They were clearly living together; Estella couldn't afford a house like that. Now she understood the girl's reluctance to show her the baby and her unease. Ramon's possessions littered the house. Mariana thought of Helena and her children and suddenly felt consumed with resentment and regret. When her old eyes welled with unhappiness she was forced to pull the car up on the side of the road and give way to her tears. She couldn't understand Ramon. But she loved him and tried desperately to justify his actions. She blamed Helena for driving him into Estella's arms and Estella for being too beautiful for him to resist. But her arguments paled in the light of her reasoning, which told her Ramon was guilty. He was a victim of his own selfishness. He wilfully sacrificed everything he loved for a vacuous freedom, which would inevitably leave him lonely and full of regret. He would leave Estella too.

By the time Mariana returned home she had decided not to tell Ignacio. She had also decided to look out for Estella. The girl didn't know it yet, but she would need support.

Mariana knew her son better than anyone.

PART TWO

Chapter 20

Federica bicycled up the hill, her breaths staggered and short as she sobbed and pedalled, barely able to see the road for the tears in her eyes. The warm May sunshine had tempted the trees and bushes into blossom and bud, the unlikely snowfalls in April were now over for good. But Federica didn't care for the beauty of nature. She didn't even notice the armies of bluebells in the woods or the sweet smell of fertility as the ground woke up from her winter sleep. Her heart felt as if someone had wrenched it from her chest, beaten it about, then carelessly put it back again.

The ride up the lane to Pickthistle Manor seemed much longer than normal. Her face was red and sweaty from exertion and her eyes swollen like two baked apples. When she cycled into the driveway she was greeted by Trotsky, the rather arrogant Great Dane that Inigo had given Ingrid to console her after the death of her favourite dog, Pushkin. Trotsky was honey-brown with skin like velvet and the intelligent face of a Cambridge scholar, his eyes surrounded by dark circles which gave the impression that he was wearing little round glasses, much to everyone's amusement. Hence the name Trotsky, which he lived up to with great pride and dignity. Federica patted him absentmindedly as she passed.

He sensed her distress and bounded after her with long, leisurely strides.

She threw down her bicycle on the gravel then rushed inside shouting for Hester. She held her breath and listened for a reply, but none came. Only the sound of Inigo's classical music escaped under his study door and floated through the house. She didn't want to disturb Inigo who was obviously working so she wandered through the rooms hoping to find one of the girls. She was mortified to discover that the house was completely empty except for Sam who sat at the kitchen table eating a large peanut-butter sandwich, reading the Saturday papers. When he saw her standing awkwardly in the doorway he put down his paper and asked her what was wrong.

'I'm looking for Hester,' she said quietly, wiping her face with her hands and hoping he wouldn't notice she was crying. She took a deep breath and forced a smile.

But Sam wasn't fooled. 'The girls have gone shopping with Mum and the boys are having a picnic tea on the beach,' he said, then smiled sympathetically.

'Oh,' said Federica, not knowing what else to say. She had always felt suffocated when alone with Sam. He was too handsome to look at, too clever to talk to and much too grown up to be interested in her. So she began to back away through the door, mumbling that she'd find Hester later.

'Why don't you have a peanut-butter sandwich?' he asked, holding up the jar. 'They're extremely good. Mum calls this type of food "comfort food" and you look as though you need some of that.'

'No, really, I'm not hungry,' she stammered, embarrassed by her own incompetence.

'I know. But you're unhappy,' he said and smiled again. 'At least have some to make you feel better.' He pulled out a couple of slices of bread and began to prepare a sandwich for her. She had no choice. She walked up to the table and sat down on the chair that he had pulled out for her. 'I'm afraid I can't resist a weeping woman,' he said. Federica laughed as the tears blurred her vision again. A month off thirteen she could hardly be considered a woman, not even by a long stretch of the imagination. She lowered her eyes and took a timid bite of her sandwich. 'You know,' Sam continued, 'women's tears are their secret weapon. I know I'm not alone. Most men go weak at the sight of them, or they don't know how to handle them so they leave themselves vulnerable to every sort of manipulation. They'll do anything to bring a smile to the lady's face. What can I do to bring a smile to your face?'

'There's nothing you can do. I'll be fine,' she replied, staring down at her sandwich, anything rather than look at him.

'Well, there's nothing worse than sitting about inside on a sunny day like this feeling miserable. Why don't you join me for a walk? The bluebells will cheer you up and by the time we get back the girls will probably have returned. How does that sound?'

'You must have better things to do,' she said, not wanting to be a bore.

'Now you're sounding like Eeyore. Try and be more like Pooh, or Tigger. Actually,' he said, grinning at her, 'you're more like Piglet.'

'Is that meant to be a compliment?'

'Definitely. Piglet is a fine fellow. So how about a stroll in the hundred acre wood?'

Federica rarely saw Sam. He had left school and travelled for a year before taking up his scholarship at Cambridge. The long holidays were usually spent travelling, weekends up in London at parties. When he came home he'd only stay for a couple of days, locked in Nuno's library or in heavy discussion with his father. Federica would bicycle up the drive, her heart in a state of quivering expectation, hoping that his green and white Deux Chevaux would be parked outside the house indicating that he was at home. When the space on the gravel was empty she'd still keep her ears open and hope that perhaps during the course of her visit he might very well turn up and surprise them all. But he rarely did.

During the previous seven years Federica's crush on Sam had neither waned nor tempered. If anything it had grown more intense, teased by the fact that she so rarely saw him. She knew he was too old, she knew he would never look at her as anything other than his little sister's friend, but still she fantasized about him. Molly and Hester knew of her crush. The whole family did and they all found it charming, even Sam, whose ego wasn't immune to the blushes of a twelve-year-old child. But no one ever spoke of it in front of Federica. She was shy and ill-equipped for their type of humour.

It was warm. The bluebells flooded the ground like a violet river, drowning the disintegrating winter foliage beneath them, shimmering in the breeze and heralding the return of spring. Sam pulled off his sweater, tying it about his waist and walking in his shirtsleeves, leaving the cuffs undone to flap carelessly about his hands. Trotsky trotted along behind them, sniffing the bushes and cocking his leg everywhere because the scent of spring excited him. 'I do love this time of year. The smells are rich, the trees in bud. Just look at that green, it's unreal, isn't it?' he said, pulling a piece of blossom off a tree and smelling it.

'It's beautiful,' she replied, following him up the path that wound its way through the trees.

'I remember when you first moved here,' he said.

'Me too. I nearly died in the lake.'

'Not a very auspicious start,' he chuckled.

'It's got better, though,' she replied. It *had* got better, but now it had all gone wrong.

'Do you miss Chile?' he asked, slowing down for her to catch up as the path widened to allow them both to walk side by side.

'I miss my father,' she said truthfully, swallowing a sob. 'Chile is little more than a faded memory. If I think of Chile I think of my father.'

Sam pulled a sympathetic smile. He was very aware that she never spoke about her father. Nuno had condemned him as heartless, Inigo irresponsible. Only Ingrid took Ramon's side and believed there was more to it than the superficial actuality of a father deserting his family.

When Ramon had left Polperro seven years before, everyone had remained electrified by his sudden visit. Federica had talked proudly about him at every opportunity, clearly expecting him to return every once in a while to see her, perhaps one day coming to stay for good. She had written to him. Long letters in her childish hand, signed with love and sealed with hope. He had written poems for her and a novel which he had dedicated 'to my daughter' about a little girl called Topahuay who lived in Peru but which none of the Applebys understood except for Nuno who had a basic knowledge of Spanish because of his ability to speak Italian. Then the letters had begun to arrive with less frequency until they had almost dried up altogether. There was no surprise visit, no telephone call. Federica kept his letters in the butterfly box, which she hid under her bed. Without knowing why she began to shroud Ramon in secrecy. She stopped talking about him. She showed no one her butterfly box. She possessively protected his memory in the silent halls of her mind where she alone could visit him. The only person she allowed into these halls was Hester. And Hester loyally kept all

Federica's secrets. She even managed to keep them from Molly who had attempted to force them out of her sister with both manipulation and force. But Hester had never given in and took great pride in her loyalty.

As the years passed Federica's shame grew. Everyone else had a father. The other schoolchildren wondered why Federica didn't have one and whispered about it behind her back. Deep in her subconscious she couldn't help but wonder whether she had done something wrong, for he couldn't love her. If he loved her he would want to see her. If he loved her he'd miss her like she missed him. She remembered his words about Señora Baraca because she remembered everything he had ever said to her. 'Sometimes it's better to move on, rather than dwell on the past. One should learn things from the past and then let them go.' He had chosen to stay away, would he prefer them to let him go?

'I liked your father very much,' said Sam carefully. He watched her mouth twist with misery and her eyes glisten again with tears. 'I'm sorry, I shouldn't have brought him up. It must be very painful for you,' he apologized, touching her arm.

'I miss him, that's all,' she sniffed.

'Of course you do,' he agreed, pushing his glasses up the bridge of his nose, a gesture he often did when he felt awkward.

'Sometimes it's fine. Then all of a sudden, for no reason, I think of him and feel sad.'

'That's only natural.'

'I know. Is Mama having a serious boyfriend natural too?' she asked and a large tear wobbled on her upper lip before dropping into the bluebells.

Sam stopped walking and instinctively drew the sobbing child into his arms. 'So this is what it's all about,' he said, hugging her. She nodded but her throat was too strained to speak. 'It was always going to happen, Fede. Look, let's sit down and talk about this,' he suggested, patting her gently on the back before releasing her.

They sat in the sun among the bluebells, Federica cross-legged and Sam with his long legs stretched out in front of him leaning back against the trunk of a tree. Federica couldn't believe that only a moment ago she had been in his arms. To her shame her tears ceased immediately and she blinked across at him, her cheeks aflame.

'She's had boyfriends before, but Arthur wants to marry her,' she said in despair.

'What's this Arthur like?'

'He's all right, I suppose. He's not very interesting. In fact, I think he's very dull. He's quite fat and has no hair, but he laughs at all Mama's jokes and tells her how wonderful she is all the time.'

'What does he do?'

'He's a wine merchant. An old wine merchant. He must be at least fifty. Mama says he's very clever and has a very good job. He's reliable, dependable and nice. Yes, that's the word, nice. Nice, nice, nice.'

'But he's not your father,' said Sam.

'No,' she croaked, 'he's not Papa and he never will be.'

'I thought your parents were still married?'

'They are.'

'Then your mother would have to get a divorce in order to marry this boring Arthur person,' said Sam.

'Yes, she would.'

'Well, that would take ages.'

'Yes.'

'Has your mother agreed to marry him?'

'No, she hasn't yet. I just overheard them talking.'

'What did she say when he asked her?'

'Well, Arthur goes, "You're a delicate flower in need of protecting,"' said Federica in a low voice. Sam laughed at her impersonation. Federica's mouth curled into a small smile. 'Then Mama said, "I wish I were as beautiful as a flower." To which Arthur replied, "With a little watering you'll blossom into one. Marry me, Helena."' Federica grimaced, blinking away tears that now seemed out of place amid the humour of her recital. 'I nearly threw up. Mama might be many things but she is certainly no flower. What would Papa think?'

Sam was chuckling. He had never bothered to talk to Federica before, he had always thought her rather dull and quiet, but he was seeing a side to her that he never knew she had. He didn't blame his sisters at all for liking her.

'It's clear that she's enjoying the attentions of a kind man. You don't know the dynamics of your parents' relationship. As your father was away all the time your mother must have felt neglected. Dull Arthur obviously makes her feel attractive. She's enjoying the attention,' said Sam, believing he had summed up the entire situation in a couple of sentences. He took off his glasses and began to clean them on his shirt.

'But if she marries him we'll have to move away from Polperro,' said Federica in panic.

'Ah, now that is a problem,' he agreed.

Federica's face lengthened again in gloom. 'I couldn't bear to move away. I love it here,' she said huskily.

'I know Molly and Hester wouldn't want you to move away either.'

'What can I do?'

'You can't do anything. But if I were you,' he said loftily, 'I would talk to your mother and ask her what she intends to do.'

'But I can't admit that I was eavesdropping.'

'Why not? I eavesdrop all the time. There's nothing wrong with it. If people don't want to be heard they should make sure no one can hear them. It was their fault. Arthur's not only dull but obviously stupid too,' he said. Sam had little tolerance for stupid people.

'I suppose I could talk to her.'

'Of course you could.'

'But she's only interested in talking about Hal. I don't think I'd make the slightest bit of difference.'

'Oh dear,' said Sam, nodding his head. 'Some mothers adore their sons to the exclusion of the rest of the family.'

'Not in your family.'

'No. Mum has always been far too vague to adore any of us too much. She's not really on the planet, you know. She always looks rather surprised that she had any of us at all. I think if someone told her the stork brought us into the world she'd believe it. She has no memory of childbirth at all. We still manage to amaze her.'

'Your family is the nicest I've ever met. I wish mine was like yours,' she said wistfully.

'One's own problems always seem so much greater than anyone else's because you never see past the veneer of other people's families. Believe me, each family hides skeletons in its cupboards. I'm sure you'd be surprised by some of ours,' he said and laughed.

But Federica didn't believe him. She doubted they even knew what a skeleton looked like.

'I imagine it's only natural that Mama should want to marry again,' said Federica, picking a bluebell and turning it around between her fingers.

'Everyone needs someone,' said Sam.

'Not Papa. He doesn't need anyone at all.'

'You never really talk about your father. Is that because you're ashamed of him?'

Federica wouldn't normally have answered such a personal question but she felt safe with Sam. 'Yes,' she replied, breaking the bluebell into small pieces. 'I wish we were a normal family like everyone else's. Like yours. When I was smaller, in Chile, Papa used to take me down to the beach or into Viña to eat *palta* sandwiches in the sunshine. We'd go and stay with my grandparents in Cachagua. It was lovely then. Although he didn't come home very often, when he did it was like Heaven and I always knew when he left that he'd come back. His clothes were in the cupboards, his books in the sitting room. There was evidence of his presence everywhere. Now there's nothing. It's as if he's died – worse, because if he was dead everyone would make an effort to remember him. But no one talks about him at all. You see, in Viña everyone knew of Ramon Campione. He was well-known in Chile. He was a famous writer, a poet, and everyone thought he was very clever and gifted. I was so proud of him. Here no one's ever heard of him. If it weren't for his letters I'd wonder whether I'd made the whole thing up.'

'Oh, Fede,' he sighed. 'I'm so sorry. It's hideous for you. Because you never show your feelings or talk about him we just assumed you were all right. But, how can you be? It's monstrous of him to desert you like that.'

'Is it really that easy to forget?'

'He forgets because he's probably plagued with guilt when he remembers. In that sense it's the easy option, total avoidance.'

'I've always put him on a pedestal,' she exclaimed, pulling a thin smile.

'No one's infallible, Fede. Not even Ramon.'

'But seven years is worse than careless,' she argued.

'Has it really been so long?' Sam asked, feeling very sorry for her. She reminded him of one of his mother's broken animals.

'Yes. He used to write all the time. I haven't had a letter from him for about six months. I still write to him, but not as much as I used to. I'm frightened I'll forget him. I don't want him to turn up one day and not recognize him.' Her voice thinned again as her throat constricted with sadness. She opened her eyes very wide in an attempt to force her tears back. 'I should be angry with him. But I'm not. I just want him to come home.'

'Can't you talk to your mother about this?' he asked, shuffling over to sit beside her so he could place an arm around her.

'I could. But Mama's very fragile. She hates Papa so I can't mention his name in the house. Hal doesn't even remember him. Arthur's become more of a father to Hal than Papa ever was. But he'll never be a father to me, never,' she sobbed and the tears finally rebelled and spilled out over her cheeks.

Sam tried to comfort her by squeezing her around the shoulders and giving her the best advice he could think of. 'Talk to your mother. The most worrying thing is the doubt. You don't know if she's said "yes" to boring Arthur and you don't know what that means for you if she has said "yes". You need to find out. She might have no intention of moving away from Polperro.'

Federica nodded her head and sniffed. 'I'll ask her.'

'Good. You must let me know what she says.'

'I will.'

'You can come and talk to me any time, you know,' he said. 'Hester's all very well, but sometimes a grown-up is better. Especially if you can't talk to your mother. Everyone needs someone to talk to.'

'Who do you talk to?'

'Nuno or Dad. Mostly Nuno, I suppose.'

'Isn't he a bit mad?' said Federica.

Sam smiled at her. 'Eccentric, but not mad. In fact, he's the cleverest man I've ever met. He taught me more than I would have ever learnt at school. He's far too wise for his own good.'

'I wish I were wise.'

'You will be one day. But no one can teach you wisdom, they can teach you knowledge and warn you so that you avoid the mistakes they made. But on the whole you need to live to acquire wisdom. "'Tis held that sorrow makes us wise" – Lord Alfred Tennyson.'

'Then I must be quite wise by now,' she said and grinned at him with self-pity.

'Don't put your happiness in other people's hands.'

'What do you mean?'

'Don't rely on other people to make you happy or you're sure to be unhappy always. People will inevitably disappoint you,' he said. 'On that positive note, let's head back to the house. I bet Hester's back by now with a whole new wardrobe to show you,' he chuckled, pushing himself up from the ground. 'Feel any better?'

She nodded. 'Thank you,' she said, full of gratitude. Finally Sam had noticed her. She felt a lightness of being in spite of her heaviness of heart.

He patted her between her shoulder blades. 'Come on. And that means you too, Trotsky,' he said to the dog, who had slept through their entire conversation. He got to his feet and stretched before trotting on down the path they had made through the bluebells. The clamour of birds filled the trees, punctuated occasionally by the sharp cough of a pheasant. The sunlight bathed the woods in a resplendent mist and Federica felt she was walking through an earthly paradise. She watched Sam, tall and straight, lead the way and knew that she could never leave Polperro because the Applebys were her family and she simply couldn't be without them.

Chapter 21

When Helena watched Ramon walk out seven years before she knew she had driven him away. She had admitted regret, opening herself up to be wounded once again by Ramon's indifference. She thought he had changed. But she knew in her heart that he would never, ever change. He had always been far too selfish to think of anyone but himself. So she had swallowed her humiliation and let him go, quietly resolving to get on with her life in Polperro in spite of him.

Helena might have believed she had cleansed herself of her husband's presence, but unknown to her his words had penetrated her subconscious where they had taken root and grown. She began to make some space in her life for herself and her own needs. She relied more on her mother to help her with Hal – Federica didn't need much looking after: she was responsible and self-sufficient. She looked after herself and her mother too. So Helena didn't worry about Federica, she worried about Hal.

Hal was dependent and needy and as self-centred as his mother. He was also extremely moody, up one moment, down the next, floundering in a pool of his own dissatisfaction. Polly was delighted to be needed again and threw herself into the roles of mother and grandmother with relish. Jake just pushed his nose further into his miniature boats and tried to ignore the rest of the household, who moved around in barely contained longing to satisfy the demands of his daughter and grandson.

So, Helena had moved on. She went out on dates. She even slept with a few of the men she dated and almost managed to convince herself that she liked it. But none of them made love to her like Ramon and as much as she knew she was no longer really married and free to see whoever she chose, she was still wracked with guilt afterwards. It wasn't until she met Arthur Cooke that everything changed.

Polly noticed that Arthur was different from the others because Helena cut her hair, painted her nails, bought a new wardrobe and began to take pride in her appearance. A light skip crept into her walk and she held her shoulders back and head up as she had always done as a teenager. Suddenly she began to look her age, thirty-seven, rather than the old woman who had surreptitiously slipped beneath her bitter skin.

Arthur Cooke was forty-nine years old, divorced, with three children who were all in their early twenties. He prided himself in his ability to sustain a good relationship with his wife, who had married again, and children who didn't seem to resent him for the break-up of their family. When Helena had first met him, at an eye-wateringly boring drinks party given by one of her dates, she had thought he looked like an egg. A smiling egg. He wasn't tall, didn't have much hair, didn't dress particularly well and had nothing physically that would have attracted her to him. But Helena was too busy assessing what he didn't have to notice what he did have. She found that out later.

Arthur was kind, witty, energetic, enthusiastic and generous. When she found herself talking to him because there simply wasn't anyone better to talk to, she discovered sharp brown eyes that noticed everything, a smile that reached across the whole of his jovial face and a contagious laugh that bubbled up from his belly. When he touched her hand his was soft and gentle, when he spoke his voice was full of understanding and when he listened she realized that he did so without distraction as if she were the most fascinating woman he had ever met. By the end of the evening she had talked to no one else and had completely ignored the man she had arrived with. Arthur invited her to join him for a drink and she left her floundering date without an explanation, knowing that she wouldn't care if she never saw him again.

They went to a quiet bar that overlooked the bay and sat in candlelight listening to the schmaltzy music that accompanied the soporific rhythm of the tide and talked for hours. By the time Arthur dropped her off at her home he knew everything about Ramon, Federica and Hal. She had allowed him to strip her soul layer by layer with the help of various glasses of wine until she stood naked before him, lonely and unhappy. He had then helped her dress it again with compliments and words of encouragement and compassion. When she awoke the following morning she looked in the mirror and saw a haggard old woman staring back at her in surprise. She had never noticed her before. Shocked, she left her mother to look after the children and disappeared into town for half the day to discard Ramon's wife and emerge as someone different. When Helena returned looking rejuvenated, her mother told her that a man called Arthur had telephoned. She smiled in a way that Polly hadn't seen her smile for a long, long time.

Arthur made her feel good about herself. He seemed to understand her and her needs. He held her hand when it began to shake and taught her how to breathe deeply from the pit of her stomach when she felt nervous. He rang her all the time for no reason at all, simply to hear her voice and to make sure that she was okay. He made her feel protected. He made her laugh with the inhibition that had characterized those first heavenly years with Ramon, with a loose throat and an aching stomach. He made her feel that nothing really mattered and she suddenly realized why Ingrid was always happy, because she dwelt in a vague, carefree world that hovered above the preoccupations of more earthly people. She would never be like Ingrid, but she was now able at least to see her world and aspire towards it.

As much as Arthur had endeared himself to her she was terrified of taking the relationship into a physical dimension. Sex with Ramon had been otherworldly. No one could compete with that. Certainly not Arthur. He wasn't a physical man. He didn't play sport, was flat-footed and unfit. He loved good food, good wine and good company, but she couldn't imagine him in bed and she feared sex would ruin the relationship beyond repair. So she rebuffed his advances when he tried to kiss her. But Arthur's sharp brown eyes had noticed everything. He wasn't the sort of man to dither and brood. If he had something to say he simply said it.

'Helena,' he said one winter evening as they drained their wine glasses beside the boisterous fire in his sitting room.

'Yes, Arthur,' she replied nervously, fearing that he was going to ask her to stay the night.

'Your hand is shaking again. Give me your wine glass,' he said. She handed it to him and smiled hesitantly. 'Close your eyes,' he said, taking her hand in his. 'Now, take a deep breath, right from the bottom of your lungs. That's right. Now let it out. Let out all that fear and all that uncertainty. Well done. Now let's do it again.' He instructed her to repeat the exercise three times. 'Now you should feel better,' he said, but she didn't. 'This time I want you to close your eyes and let me kiss you.'

'No, Arthur . . .' she protested.

'You want me to, but you're afraid. You've slept with men since your husband but none of them managed to satisfy you.

You're afraid I will disappoint you. I can assure you I won't,' he said. So Helena reluctantly closed her eyes and hoped the wine would dull her senses. She felt his mouth brush hers, but it could have been the warmth of the flames that flickered in the fireplace. A moment later she felt it again, followed by that familiar tingle in her belly, stirring with the memory of Ramon's touch. She wanted to open her eyes but she kept them firmly shut for fear of seeing Arthur's earnest face close to hers and losing her nerve. Then she felt his lips sink onto her anxious mouth. Surprisingly it felt quite nice. Then his hand was in the small of her back. A firm, supporting hand confidently pulling her towards him as his lips opened and he kissed her with tenderness. In spite of her fears, her senses rebelled against her reasoning and she became aware only of the screaming of her nerves as they cried out for him to caress her and love her.

Arthur took her by the hand upstairs to the bedroom. Then he proceeded to make love to every inch of her body with the enthusiasm and attentiveness of a man whose only purpose is to give pleasure because in so doing does he derive his own pleasure. Helena abandoned herself to his devotion without feeling guilty or undeserving. Then once she was convinced of his prowess he made love to her again with humour until they both rolled about on the bed laughing uncontrollably.

There was no comparing him with Ramon because he was so entirely different. Arthur's sexual proficiency was his trump card. It was so totally unexpected. Once Helena had discovered it, she could not get enough of it. With Arthur she felt feminine again and very much alive. She was no longer getting ready to live but living, and Ramon's sour-tasting memory sweetened into the recesses of her mind until it no longer plagued her or hounded her. Arthur occupied her present and there simply wasn't time to look back on the past.

Until Arthur asked her to marry him and suddenly Ramon reappeared in her thoughts.

She told him that she would think about it. But she had to consider the feelings of her children. She knew Federica didn't like Arthur, in spite of his persistent attempts to befriend her. She answered his questions in monosyllables with a long, scowling face. But the worst was the sad, dejected look in her eyes which Helena was unable to ignore. Hal liked Arthur. But he wanted his mother to himself. As long as she gave Hal enough of her time and attention he would accept Arthur without complaint. If she considered her own happiness she knew that she couldn't do without Arthur. But she was still married to Ramon and something inside her remained reluctant to give him up.

When Federica slipped into her mother's bedroom after having returned from Pickthistle Manor, Helena was getting changed. Arthur was coming for dinner. Federica lay on the bed and watched her mother dry her hair in front of the mirror. She recalled those days in Chile when she didn't bother with her hair and scrunched it up onto the top of her head. Now she spent hours in front of the glass gelling it, teasing it with brushes and combs. She looked radiant again. She looked happy. Federica knew she should be happy too, but she couldn't be. Arthur had made her mother no less selfish, in fact he indulged her on every level allowing her to be the centre of his world. She rarely asked him about himself. She noticed it more when her mother was on the telephone. Me me me, thought Federica gloomily.

'How do I look?' Helena asked, pinching her cheeks.

'Beautiful, Mama,' Federica replied truthfully.

'Try to be nice to Arthur, Fede. He's doing his best to become your friend.'

'He can be my friend,' said Federica, her heart beating with adrenaline in preparation of the next sentence, 'but not my father.' She blinked in surprise at her own courage.

Helena turned around slowly and stared at her daughter, her smile falling off her face, leaving a serious line in the place of her mouth. 'Did you overhear us this afternoon?' she asked.

Federica nodded. She remembered what Sam had told her and tried not to feel guilty.

'You had no right to listen to my conversation,' she said crossly, reaching for the packet of cigarettes.

'I couldn't help it. You were both talking so loudly, I hadn't meant to hear,' Federica explained. Helena placed a cigarette between her pink lips and lit it. Federica winced as she blew the smoke into the room. The smell made her nauseous.

'I hardly need explain to you then what he said,' she snapped sarcastically.

'He asked you to marry him,' said Federica, but her voice was more of a croak.

Helena softened. 'Look, sweetie. He'll never be your father. He doesn't want to be. He has three children of his own already. He just wants to be your friend.'

'He wants to be your husband. But you're still married to Papa.'

'Only in name. A divorce can be arranged very easily,' she said carelessly, for Federica's eyes dimmed with unhappiness. As long as her parents were still married there was hope. 'Your father and I haven't been together now for a long, long time. You can't possibly be hoping for a reconciliation, can you, Fede?'

Federica's lower lip trembled. She shook her head, but in her heart she wanted nothing more than a reconciliation. 'Are you going to say yes?' she asked hoarsely.

'I'm thinking about it.' Helena turned back to the mirror.

'What does Hal think?'

'He wants me to be happy,' she replied in an almost accusing tone as if she were about to add 'unlike you'.

'I want you to be happy too,' said Federica, feeling guilty.

'Then let me do what's best for me. I've sacrificed everything for you children. You're almost thirteen now. Soon you'll be a woman. Aren't I allowed some happiness too?'

Federica nodded her head. 'If you marry him, will we have to leave Polperro?' she asked.

'We might have to,' Helena said, stubbing out her cigarette. 'Arthur's job is in town.'

'Then I don't want you to marry him,' she cried, suddenly overwhelmed by the force of her emotions and unable to control them.

'Now, Fede—' began Helena impatiently.

'No. I won't go. I won't!' she snapped, quite uncharacteristically.

'We won't go far. You can still see the Applebys as much as you want to.'

'I want to stay here with Granny and Grandpa,' she sobbed.

'We'll talk about this later when you're calm,' Helena said, pinching her lips together with forced patience.

'I won't go. I won't go,' she repeated.

Helena was confused by her daughter's outburst. She was usually so quiet and accommodating. 'All right, calm down, sweetie,' she said wearily, sitting down next to her and putting an arm around her. 'I haven't agreed to marry Arthur, and I am still married to your father, so let's not get too overexcited about all of this. Dry your tears and come downstairs, Arthur will be here in a minute and I don't want him to see you upset. He'd be mortified and he's such a kind man.'

Polly and Jake liked Arthur very much because he had lifted their daughter out of her dark pit and made her smile again. They noticed Federica's tear-stained face at the dinner table and the short replies she mumbled to him when he tried to talk to her. They understood her but hoped she would grow to like

Arthur because Helena's happiness was their main concern. Federica felt as if she was being swallowed up into a big grey cloud where no one could see her or hear her cries for help.

That night she wrote an urgent letter to her father telling him that her mother wanted to marry a 'horrid, ugly man called Arthur' who was going to take them all away from Polperro to some nasty town. She added that if she was taken away from all she loved she would kill herself. When she sealed the letter she was sure that he would come as quickly as he could to rescue her from the impending doom. Then she lay in bed, the room illuminated by the clear spring moon, and opened the butterfly box. She listened to the clatter of bells and watched the butterfly flutter her wings in the phosphorescent light, giving her a strange, unearthly beauty. She thought of her father and wondered what he was doing and whether he ever thought of her. Falling into the spell of the box she closed her eyes and once more joined him on the familiar beaches of Chile, where the sun was warm and the sand like Lidia's flour between their toes. She concentrated on his stories as if her very life depended on it and slowly she retreated into the secret halls of her mind where no one but her father could reach her.

The following day Helena left Federica alone in the house while she went to church with her mother and the eleven-year-old Hal. 'She needs some time on her own,' she explained to her mother as they wandered up the lane.

'She's having trouble accepting Arthur, isn't she?' said Polly, patting Hal on the head. 'Not like this little monkey.'

Hal looked up at her and grinned smugly. If he had had a tail he would have wagged it.

'I suppose it's understandable, but Ramon and I haven't been together for years, you would have thought she'd be used to it by now,' Helena sighed.

'Well, every child is different and she always had a very close relationship with her father.'

'She's just got to get over it and move on. I had to, Hal had to. I love Arthur and I won't give him up. Not for anyone,' insisted Helena melodramatically.

'I like Arthur,' Hal said, knowing that would make his mother happy.

'I know you do, and Arthur likes you,' said Helena happily.

'Doesn't Arthur like Fede?' he asked.

'He does like her and he's trying very hard to make her like him. But Fede's being very stubborn. Poor Arthur.'

'Poor Arthur,' Hal agreed. 'I hope we see a lot of him. He makes you happy, Mama, and that's all that I care about.'

Helena was touched. 'You're so sweet, Hal. What would I have done without you?' she said.

'Not a lot,' Hal laughed, pushing his thick black hair out of his eyes. 'If you don't mind me saying, Papa's a real moron to have given you up and Arthur's a very lucky man.'

Helena sat through the entire service thinking about Arthur and debating his proposal. She hadn't told her mother about it as she wanted to have time to think about it first before everyone else had their say. She felt cherished and protected with Arthur. He carried all her worries and fears. Ramon had thought only of himself, her needs had always been second to his. With Arthur she came first, in everything. His life now revolved around her happiness and he did whatever was necessary in order to see her content. When the Reverend Boyble spoke about the virtue of unselfishness and putting others before oneself Helena thought of Arthur and smiled with satisfaction, as if she deserved praise for his good qualities. She tried not to think of Ramon. There was no point, he had gone and he wasn't coming back. She had made her choice. He had made his. He didn't want her back. She pictured Arthur's gentle face and persuaded herself that she didn't want Ramon back. But still she doubted and by the end of the service her mind was no clearer than it had been before. She didn't know what to do. Divorce was so final.

Federica met Hester in their cave hidden within the cliffs, where seagulls swooped down and built their nests and where the tide swept in every night to wash away their secrets. They sat in the cool shade of the rock and Federica told her all about Arthur. 'If I have to leave Polperro, I'll die,' Federica said firmly.

'You can't leave Polperro! Does that mean you'll go to a different school?' Hester asked anxiously.

'Everything,' Federica sighed miserably. 'Everything will change. I just don't know what to do.'

'You have to refuse to go. She can't make you. How can she?' suggested Hester naïvely. 'Just dig in your heels and refuse.'

'I don't want to live in a town.'

'I'd hate to live in a town.'

'I don't want to live with Arthur, he's dull. He's fat, sweaty and dull, I can't see what Mama sees in him. Papa's so handsome.'

'Your father is the most handsome man I have ever met. Mummy quite fancied him, you know,' Hester giggled.

'Did she?'

'Yes, so did Molly and I.'

'You all have extremely good taste,' said Federica proudly. 'You know, I wrote to him.'

'Did you?'

'Yes, I told him about Arthur and that Mama wants to marry him. I also said that if they marry and take me away from Polperro, I'll kill myself.'

Hester gasped. 'Oh my God! He'll come over for sure.'

'I think so too. He'll get us all out of this mess, you'll see. He'll never let this happen.'

Federica returned home at lunchtime to find Arthur's car parked outside on the gravel. She rolled her eyes and pinched her mouth into a thin line of resolve before walking into the hall to face him. He was sitting on the sofa in the living room talking to Hal and Jake while Polly prepared the lunch in the kitchen with Helena.

'Ah, Federica,' said Arthur as she walked into the room. 'Just the person. I've got something for you.' He chuckled amiably, pushing himself onto his feet. Federica noticed the sweat collect on his brow and begin to drip down the side of his face. She watched him disappear into the little room that Jake reserved for the drinks cupboard. She looked at her grandfather and raised an eyebrow quizzically, but he just grinned back at her. Arthur then reappeared carrying a large cardboard box, which looked quite heavy for he struggled with it, but he managed to smile as he carefully placed the box on the floor in front of Federica.

'What on earth is it?' she asked, staring at it.

'Open it,' said Arthur.

'Go on, Fede,' said Hal. 'I know what it is,' he added, 'and I know you'll like it.'

Federica opened the box. To her delight and amazement she saw two shiny eyes staring up at her forlornly.

'A dog!' she cried. 'A real dog!' She threw her hands into the box and gathered the fat little puppy into her arms where she covered his white fur with affectionate kisses.

'You have to read the collar,' said Hal, joining her on the sofa and cuddling the puppy too.

'Rasta,' read Federica, holding the silver disc in her fingers. She suddenly felt a rushing sensation in her head as she remembered Señora Baraca's dog and the promise her mother had made her in Cachagua. 'Thank you,' she said sheepishly, feeling slightly guilty that she had been so unkind to Arthur. 'Is he really mine?' she asked.

'He's really yours,' said Arthur, smiling with relief. He caught Jake's eye and nodded. They had all been right, a puppy would do the trick. Rasta wagged his little tail with such excitement he almost took off like a helicopter. But Federica kept him firmly in her arms, letting him lick her face and sniff her skin. She thought of Trotsky and looked forward to introducing them. They were sure to become firm friends. Ingrid would love him too and so would Sam. She decided to take him up to Pickthistle Manor straight after lunch to show him off.

Helena and Polly heard the squeals of delight and rushed into the room to find both Hal and Federica lying on the floor with the dog. 'Ah, he's very sweet,' said Polly, winking at Arthur. 'Aren't you a lucky girl, Fede.'

'He's half Labrador, half something else, but Arthur and I haven't exactly worked out what that something else is,' Helena said. Federica watched her mother join Arthur on the sofa. She noticed he took her hand and squeezed it. He obviously thought he had won her over with his gift, but he was wrong. She grinned deviously to herself. Papa was about to return and change everything.

Chapter 22

'Look at the camera, sweetheart. There, you're gorgeous. Gorgeous. That's right, a bit more chest, too much, too much. That's better, now eyes to camera. Simmer, sweetheart, simmer. Good.' Julian clicked the camera in a series of staccato snaps at the laminated young woman who reclined on the divan like a glossy jungle cat. Her eyes were green and swept upwards with heavy lids that fanned her face with long, black lashes. She was beautiful, confident and alluring. So much, so young. She was only eighteen.

Julian had met Lucia Sarafina in a London club and listened to her dreams of becoming a famous singer. 'I have the looks and the body, it's just a question of training the voice,' she had said coolly in a thick Italian accent. Julian, who appreciated the aesthetics of a good-looking woman, had invited her to the cottage he shared with Toby to take her publicity shots. She had agreed immediately, seizing the chance to make use of yet another bedazzled man, seduced by her beauty. She watched him with the steadiness of a preying panther, wearing only a pair of faded denims and sandals, his body firm and tanned. She was sure he was ripe to be converted to the world of the heterosexual.

It was a humid day. A froth of purple clouds advanced slowly in over the horizon promising an afternoon of thunder and rain. But while the light remained in such a tenuous limbo, suspended between sunshine and thunder, Julian hurried to photograph her before it was lost in the impending storm.

Lucia wore a simple white dress that dropped low over the cleavage of her breasts and rose high on the leg to expose her brazen thighs. With every pose she arranged herself to her best advantage and gazed into the camera with the self-confidence of a professional model.

'You can relax now, I'm going to change the film, then perhaps we can take you under the blossom tree or something,' he said, turning around to get a new film out of his bag. 'Do you want a drink?' he asked, ripping open the silver paper that wrapped the film.

'I don't think I can go anywhere dressed like this,' she said and laughed smoothly.

'Why not?' he asked, turning to face her. She smiled at him and raised her eyebrows suggestively, tossing her dress onto the grass with a sly grin.

'What if your boyfriend comes back, I might give him a fright?' she said, running a hand down her naked body. Julian was surprised but not shocked. He had been in the business for long enough to have experienced almost every kind of come-on. In fact, he was tired of fighting them off. Beautiful women found it hard to believe that he didn't desire them in spite of his open homosexuality. They were all sure they could convert him and deeply offended when they discovered that they couldn't. Julian clicked the film into the camera and wound it on as if he hadn't noticed her.

'Right then, sweetheart,' he said in a brisk tone. 'Let's have you somewhere else, that divan's getting tedious.' He cast his eye about the garden. 'A chair under that blossom tree. You'll look like a forest nymph, very alluring,' he said, disappearing into the house. Lucia sighed heavily but not in surrender. She was very sure of her charms.

Julian placed the chair under the pink and white blossom and moved his tripod and camera into position. Lucia glided over naked and turned the chair around so that the back was facing the camera, then she silkily placed herself astride it, resting her head on her folded arms, staring unblinking at Julian.

'Now, sweetheart, I really don't think this is a good idea. You're a singer not a porn star,' he said, focusing.

'This one's for you,' she said and smiled graciously, expecting him to be grateful.

He wasn't. 'I'm afraid it'll go into a file and be forgotten. What did you say your boyfriend was called? Let's do it for him,' said Julian, changing to Polaroid.

'He's called Torquil.'

'Well, this one's for Torquil,' he said, replacing the Polaroid with film.

'He'll be very amused,' she said, sitting up straight and smirking at him. 'We can give him the Polaroid as a present when he comes to pick me up later.'

'If that's what you want,' he replied, tearing open the Polaroid and taking a look at the image. 'Very nice, Lucia. *Playboy* would kill for it. Perhaps you should think of changing your career path – it's less effort and you seem to be a natural.'

'Oh, I couldn't pose like this for just anyone,' she said thickly, looking up at him with doe eyes.

'You could have fooled me,' he replied, clicking again. 'Now sultry, I don't want you smiling. Smoulder, look alluring, cross even. That's better. There, head up a bit, yes, higher, now a little to one side, less, there, eyes to camera, flash them at me. Good.' And he clicked a whole roll.

'Now, how about you put your clothes back on and we do some more publicity shots,' he said, changing the roll.

'I'm bored of posing and anyhow, I like to be naked. Don't you?'

'Sometimes, but not when I'm working.'

'I'm not working now, I'm playing.'

'Well, let's have some tea then.' He began to pack up his equipment. He looked up at the sky and noticed the storm was almost upon them. 'We definitely got the best of the day,' he said, folding up his tripod.

'Oh no, the best of the day is still to come,' she said, getting up from the chair and walking towards him.

Julian sighed wearily. 'Actually, Lucia, it really isn't.'

'Yes, it is,' she said firmly, stopping in front of him and running a long nail down between his pectoral muscles. 'You look after yourself, don't you?'

Julian grabbed her hand with his and removed it from his body. 'Lucia, I'm gay. I like boys and you're a girl. It's very simple,' he said seriously.

'Come on. Don't tell me you don't think about it occasionally?' she said and pouted.

Julian was repelled. 'Not at all,' he replied.

She then placed a hand on the front of his trousers. 'I can feel you desire me.'

'Then you have less experience than I thought, because I'm far from aroused,' he said brutally.

At least she had the decency to blush. 'You're afraid Torquil might turn up. I can assure you he won't. It's too early. I said I'd be here all afternoon.'

'Let's go in and have some tea,' he suggested again, moving past her.

Suddenly the clouds were upon them and a clap of thunder sent a shuddering vibration across the earth, drenching them both in the rainfall that ensued. Giggling, Lucia ran for cover into the house, followed closely by Julian. Once inside the dark interior she fell upon him, kissing him and undoing his trousers.

'Excuse me, I hope I'm not interrupting anything,' said Toby, standing stiffly in the doorway. He had watched them run in out of the rain and although his stomach lurched, he knew Julian fended off over-enthusiastic girls all the time, it was part of the job.

Lucia pulled herself away and wiped her wet face with the back of her hand. 'You must be Toby,' she said. 'Are you convertible too? We could have a threesome.'

'Sorry, no takers,' said Toby coolly, 'but I'll put the kettle on so you don't catch a chill.'

'I don't have anything to wear. My dress will be soaked,' she said, leaning back against the wall and grinning at Julian. 'Saved by the rain, cameraman.' She giggled.

'I'll lend you a shirt,' he said with a sigh. 'Toby, I'll have a coffee, a strong one please. Come on, Lucia.'

While Julian was upstairs with Lucia, Toby stood by the kettle and tried to suppress the jealousy that sunk into his belly, dragging with it the good mood with which he had arrived. He stared at his reflection in the silver surface of the kettle but as much as he despised the expression on his face there was very little he could do to remove it.

Just then the front door opened and in ran Federica, short of breath from cycling and carrying in her arms a fluffy white puppy. 'My God!' he exclaimed. 'Whose is that?'

'It's mine, Uncle Toby,' she cried, placing him carefully on the kitchen tiles.

'He's adorable.'

'Isn't he?'

'What's he called?'

'Rasta,' she said. 'Because I knew a Rasta in Chile. Look, it even says his name on his collar.'

Toby bent down and stroked his soft fur. 'Cuddly little thing,' he mused. 'I suppose you're going to let it sleep in your bed with you.'

'If Mama lets me.'

'That's a difficult one,' he said, knowing how strict Helena could be.

'No it isn't. She wants me to like her boring boyfriend and he gave me the dog. So I suspect she'll let me do anything I want.'

'Ah.' Toby nodded, standing up. 'Arthur.'

'Do you like him?'

'Of course I do,' he replied diplomatically.

'Do you think they should marry?' she asked.

'Do you know something I don't?'

'No. Just, what if?'

'Well, I don't think Helena is ready to marry again,' he replied, taking a few mugs down from the cupboard and pouring the boiled water into the teapot.

'I think she is. They're always together holding hands and kissing. I think he's ugly. Papa is so handsome.'

'Beauty isn't everything, Fede. He's a kind, gentle person and he wants to look after your mother. I think that's much more important than beauty.'

'I don't like him,' she said, sitting on floor and pulling the puppy into her lap.

'That's only natural. If he wasn't in love with your mother you'd probably like him very much.'

'I don't want to leave Polperro,' she said seriously.

'Why on earth would you ever leave Polperro?'

'Because if Mama marries him I'll have to go and live in town with them.'

'Oh. Well, that's another "what if".'

'But I won't go,' she insisted.

'You can live with us instead. I'm never going to leave Polperro,' he said casually, without hearing the turning cogs of her mind or noticing the seed that he had sown there.

'Do you mean that?' she asked in amazement.

'Do I mean what?' he said, spooning out the tea bags from the pot.

'That I can live with you if Mama marries Arthur?'

'Oh that. Yes, darling, you can live with me and Julian. Most certainly.'

When Lucia returned to the kitchen dressed only in a large shirt of Julian's she barely noticed the pale child with luminous skin and long white hair sitting on the floor playing with a puppy. Julian introduced them but Lucia wasn't interested in children and didn't like dogs because they were too hairy and smelt. So she forced a brief smile as she stepped over them on her way to the mug of steaming tea Toby had made for her. She leant against the railing of the Aga to keep warm and sipped her tea.

'Where's that Polaroid, Jules, I want to show Toby,' she giggled, crossing her naked legs to keep warm.

'I don't know where I put it,' said Julian weakly.

'Yes you do. Go on, don't be a spoilsport. I look my best.'

'Beauty's in the eye of the beholder, Lucia, and I've seen you look better,' he replied, digging about in his bag. Finally he pulled out the photograph and handed it to her. She looked at it and smiled proudly.

'Torquil's going to love this. Can you blow one up for me, really big? Then I'll give it to him for his birthday,' she said, showing it to Toby.

Toby smiled to hide his disgust. 'I'm afraid the only pussy I'm interested in is the four-legged variety,' he said cuttingly.

Lucia swallowed her tea to hide her indignation then offered to show the shy little girl who sat quietly on the floor in order 'to teach her a few things'.

Federica blinked up at her uncle in confusion but neither Julian nor Toby thought Lucia's joke very funny and wished her boyfriend would hurry up and come and collect her.

When Torquil finally arrived, the engine of his Porsche sending the nesting pigeons and swallows into the air in panic, he strode confidently into the house without knocking. 'Ah, there you are, Lucia,' he said when he found them in the kitchen. He ignored Julian and Toby, passing them over with a superior grimace and looked his girlfriend up and down suspiciously. 'Where are your clothes?' he asked. She handed him the photograph and watched as his cheeks drained into his neck, turning it red with fury.

'What the hell is this all about? I thought you were doing publicity shots, not porn,' he snapped, pushing his dark hair off his beautiful face.

'This one was a special one for you,' she said, kissing him.

'If the photographer wasn't gay I'd kill you,' he said without smiling.

'Oh, he's gay. Quite gay,' she said. 'Aren't you, Julian?'

Julian recoiled. He wanted them both out of his house at once. 'I'll send you the shots once I've developed them. It'll take a few days,' he said, ignoring her. Ignoring both of them. They were two of the most self-satisfied people he had ever met.

'Right then, let's not hang around. We've got to be in London by seven for the premiere of *Crazy Hearts*, and you, sweetness, take hours to get ready.'

'That very much depends on what she wears, I should imagine,' Toby said, grinning at Julian.

'Come on,' Torquil repeated, deliberately overlooking Toby and ushering Lucia out of the kitchen.

Federica watched them go. He had been quite handsome, she thought, and wondered why men like him fell in love with nasty girls like Lucia. She hadn't even bothered to pat Rasta.

'I'll give you back your shirt sometime, I won't forget,' Lucia called from the hall.

'Don't bother,' Julian shouted, relieved that they were leaving. 'You can keep it.'

Once again the motor sent every bird and animal hurrying for cover. When it had gone the silence was almost audible. Julian and Toby sighed heavily. 'Thank God they're gone,' said Julian, putting his arms around Toby and hugging him. 'That's not what it looked like,' he added apologetically.

'I know,' said Toby. 'And I know you.'

'Good.' He breathed heavily and rested his head on Toby's shoulder. 'Where's that strong coffee?'

'Wouldn't you prefer whisky?'

'You're right. Much better. I need a week off after that. What hideous human beings. I hope they don't breed.'

'They shouldn't be allowed to.'

'The tragedy is that they do,' said Julian.

'Ours is that we don't,' Toby laughed, patting his friend on the back.

'When I come and live here, can I bring Rasta?' asked Federica, who was still sitting quietly on the floor.

Toby and Julian both turned to look at her together.

'Good God, I forgot you were there,' said Toby in surprise.

'Of course you can bring Rasta,' said Julian, then he looked at Toby. 'When's she moving in?'

Chapter 23

Just when Helena thought she would never be able to make up her mind whether or not to marry Arthur, she received a telephone call that decided her future for her.

'Helena, it's Ramon, I'm in London.'

Helena's stomach turned over at the sound of his granular voice, a voice that held within it the resonance of too many memories. She floundered, not knowing what to say, wanting to be furious but not having had the time to rouse her fury.

'Helena?' He repeated into the silence.

'What do you want?' she asked coldly, playing for time.

'I want to see my children,' he replied.

'You can't,' she said simply, fumbling for her cigarettes, remembering Arthur's advice to breathe deeply when she was nervous, but it was all she could do to breathe at all. She was not going to allow him to revive Federica's distress; she was just beginning to get over him.

'Helena, you can't prevent me from seeing my own children,' he replied. 'I received a letter from Fede. She needs me.'

'Like a hole in the head, Ramon,' she said sarcastically, placing the cigarette in her mouth and lighting it unsteadily.

'You're angry.'

'Of course I'm angry, Ramon. I haven't seen you for seven years,' she snapped, blowing the smoke out into the mouthpiece. 'Bloody hell, Ramon! Who do you think you are?'

'Calm down,' he said, then inhaled deeply. His tone was irritating.

'For God's sake. You're a useless father. I'm surprised Fede hasn't forgotten about you. She damn well should have. My brother's been more of a father to her than you ever were. You can't come back here after seven years and expect us all to embrace you. You chose to rush off again and you chose not to come back. If you're regretting it, too bad.'

'So, who's Arthur?' he asked.

She dragged heavily on her cigarette. 'My fiancé,' she replied smugly.

'That's what Fede feared.'

'So that's why you've come is it? Fede's knight in shining armour, what a joke.'

'I'm coming down whether you like it or not,' he said.

'Fine, but I won't let you near the children.'

'If you want to deprive your own children of their father, that's up to you, but I'm coming anyway.' He put the telephone down.

Ramon put his bag into the back of the black Mercedes and asked the driver to take him to Polperro. Then he sat in the back and brooded. It had been too easy to let them slip away. How the years had passed without him noticing the relentless passage of time. He had been too happy with Estella and Ramoncito to throw his thoughts across the ocean. Helena and the children had been like nagging stones in his shoe. He was always aware that they were there yet never got around to doing anything about them.

Estella loved him unconditionally like a child, tenderly like a mother and unpossessively like a friend. With her he didn't feel the need to leave all the time, on the contrary, he travelled with speed looking forward to the day when he would be embraced in her warm arms again. Sometimes, when he was far away, alone with his thoughts, he would wake to the smell of roses and believe that she had come to relieve the increasing monotony of his solitary wanderings. Other times he would hear the whisper of the sea or the laughter of a stream and have to pause a moment to recall Estella's honey voice and her joy. As Estella's gentle features supplanted those of Helena, Federica and Hal, he found himself forgetting that they had ever existed. How easy it was to forget.

Mariana wrote to her grandchildren with enforced regularity in order that she didn't forget. Helena sent her photographs when she remembered and Mariana dutifully enlarged them, framed them, and gazed at them with determination, fearful that if she didn't remind herself to look at them at least once a day she might wake up one morning to find that she hadn't thought about them in years. In her mind's eye they were still the little children they had been that last summer in Cachagua, in spite of the photographs that captured their growing up and their growing away. Her other grandchildren visited regularly. She now had twenty-four, making it all the more difficult to remember the two she had loved the most.

Mariana hadn't told Ignacio about her visit to Estella's beach house. She knew his ears would go red with fury. He'd not only be angry but disappointed and she didn't know whether his heart would be able to contain the excess of emotion without breaking. But she was unable to forget about her grandchild. She spent long evenings wandering up and down the beach, gazing out to sea, wondering what to do. She was certain that Estella would dry up with neglect, that Ramon would spend more and more time travelling, leaving his son to grow up fatherless just like Hal and Federica. When she had returned to Cachagua the morning she had visited Estella, she had been so angry with Ramon for his carelessness that she had sent Gertrude home and spent the rest of the day furiously polishing all the floors and furniture in the house. When she was through she had collapsed onto the bed and woken up at lunchtime the following day much to Ignacio's surprise as well as her own, for he had been unable to wake her. Anxious evenings on the beach had ensued where she bit all her nails down to the quick and lost so much weight she had to buy herself a whole new wardrobe when she returned to Santiago. Ignacio believed she was suffering from missing Helena and the children and did his best to comfort her. But she couldn't be comforted.

Finally, at the end of January she had returned to Estella's beach house, pale-faced and grim, not knowing what she was going to say, only that she had to say something. Estella noticed at once Mariana's distress and burst into tears on the veranda.

'Is it Ramon?' she choked impulsively, staggering towards her, her eyes at once welling with despair. 'Is he all right?'

Mariana was so moved by Estella's tears that she embraced her. 'Ramon is fine, Estella. It is you and my grandchild I'm worried about,' she said, releasing her.

Estella stared at her with glassy eyes. 'I'm sorry,' she whispered. 'I forgot myself.'

'I knew already,' Mariana replied kindly.

'You'd better come in then.'

Mariana was no longer curious about the house or surprised by its size. She recognized Ramon's typewriter on the desk and the first pages of a manuscript piled neatly beside it. Ramon had never been tidy, nor had Helena, but Estella kept the place as immaculate as she had kept Mariana's house. Estella showed her into the sitting room, which was light and spacious with pale Venetian blinds drawn half way down the French doors to keep the room cool. She admired the elegance of Estella's taste. The floor was covered with brightly woven rugs from India, she had filled the room with large pots of geraniums and fairy roses and the bookshelf was a library of European writers, philosophers and biographers. Mariana noticed that Ramon had taken the most exquisite pictures of Estella and their son and placed them in silver frames on every surface. Wherever her eye rested she was able to follow her son's travels around the world – a Brazilian balanganda in silver to induce fertility, a Greek icon of Saint Francis from a monk on Mount Athos and an African spear from a tribe he had befriended deep in the African jungle. Together Ramon and Estella had made a warm home for themselves.

Estella sat opposite, staring at Mariana with limpid eyes.

'I'm not here to chastise you, Estella,' she said, following her instincts, feeling her way. 'I worry for you, that's all.'

'How did you find out?' Estella asked boldly.

'At Christmas when I visited you, I left forgetting to give you the gift I had brought, so I turned back.'

'Oh,' said Estella, nodding sadly.

'I heard you call your child Ramoncito, then it all made sense.'

'Yes.'

Mariana got up and walked over to where Estella sat uncomfortably on the edge of the sofa. She sat down next to her and looked at her with understanding. 'I'm a woman too, I know what it is like to love a man. I love Ignacio. He's difficult to say the least. But I love him in spite of his sometimes irksome nature. I know Ramon well enough to realize that it was he who seduced you. I don't blame you. I pity you. I've watched his marriage disintegrate. Helena couldn't cope with his wanderings. Can you?'

Estella's face glowed like a rosy apple and she smiled the smile of a woman contented with her lot. 'I love Ramon. He loves me. That is all that I ask. I don't want to imprison him in the home. I just want his love. I'm happy, Señora. Happier than I've ever been.'

'I believe you,' she said, touching the young woman's arm. 'But, what do your parents think? He's still married to Helena.'

The spring drained away from Estella's face and it acquired an autumnal sadness. 'They have disowned me,' she stated simply, flatly, as if she had built an inner barrier of indifference in order to prevent herself from hurting any more.

'I'm so sorry,' said Mariana. 'If there's anything I can do.'

'No, no,' Estella replied. 'There's nothing anyone can do.'

'Have they seen your child?'

'No.'

'If they were to see him . . .'

'They won't come anywhere near the house.'

'Do they know who the father is?'

'They do, and they don't care. My father wants Ramon to marry me . . .'

'I see.'

'I'm happy. They should be happy that I'm happy, but I bring disgrace on the family,' she said and her eyes glistened against her will.

'Why don't you show them Ramoncito? Their hearts will soften, I promise you. He's so adorable. He's a little angel. Can I see him again?'

Estella showed Mariana into the little room where Ramoncito was quietly sleeping in the cool shadows. She ran a finger down his soft cheek and felt the emotion gather in her throat and in her eyes that stung with tears. 'Take Ramoncito to see them,' she said.

'Shall I tell Ramon that you came?'

'No,' Mariana replied firmly. 'It will be our secret. He will let me know in his own time. But if there is anything I can ever do for you, please don't feel too afraid to call me. You know where I am. I won't impose on you any more.'

Estella touched Mariana's hand and smiled. 'I want you to come. I want Ramoncito to know his grandmother,' she said and her lips trembled.

Mariana was too touched to reply. She nodded her head, swallowed hard and blinked away her gratitude.

The following evening Estella braced herself for the most difficult task of her life. She wrapped Ramoncito in a woollen shawl, packed enough food and clothes for a week and laid him on her parents' doorstep with a note which said, simply, '*I need your love.*' Then she turned and walked away. As she reached the bend in the road she almost repented and ran back to reclaim him, but she remembered Mariana's words and continued up the track with a heart of lead but a mind hardened with resolve. After a suffocating couple of hours, during which time anxiety clawed at her conscience like a crow trying to scratch his way out, she could bear it no longer and hurried back along the coast to where her parents' house nestled against the hillside.

Ramoncito was no longer on the doorstep. Terrified that he might have been taken by a stray dog or a thief she crept up to the window of the house, holding her breath so as not to give herself away. At first, when she looked through the glass she saw nothing but an empty room. Then just when an inner sob began to choke her, Maria wandered into the room with the baby safely wrapped in her solid arms. She was smiling broadly and the tears were falling over her old cheeks in rivers of joy.

Pablo Rega sat on the grass next to his friend, Osvaldo Garcia Segundo, and began to talk, as he always did, with poetry and candour.

'My old heart has softened, Osvaldo. *Sí*, Señor, it has. Maria returned home to find Estella's bastard on the doorstep. She had just left him there. Just like that. With a note. As if we'd be in any doubt as to who the child belonged to.' He chuckled and shook his head, playing with the Virgin pendant that clung to his chest. 'He's very small, I was frightened to touch him until Maria placed him in my arms – for the love of God, Maria, I said, if I drop him the devil will take him. But she just laughed and cried again. His smile is mine, so Maria tells me, God bless the poor lamb if he resembles me. A lot of good that'll do him! You'd be right to ask what I did. I should have sent him back to his mother. But Maria wouldn't hear of it. There she was with the baby in her arms, loving it as if it were her own, tears of joy running down her face. I'd be a monster to send him back. I'm not a monster, just a tired old man with little to live for but life. Ramoncito is another life, another transient life to suffer and die on this earth. What the devil is it all for? You know, Osvaldo, *sí*, Señor, you do. If you could speak from beyond the grave you'd probably give me a few pointers. Perhaps my old ears are too blocked with earthly concerns to hear you.'

Now Ramon sat in the car and watched the city trail off into verdant English countryside. He thought of Ramoncito, now six years old, almost the age Federica had been when he had waved her goodbye that hot January morning all those years ago. He looked back over the years and recalled how Ramoncito had healed the relationships between him and his mother, Estella and her parents. Pablo Rega was still suspicious of him, though. He had developed a habit of nervously playing with the pendant around his neck in the same way that one would hold up a cross when faced with a vampire, but at least he loved his grandson and embraced his daughter as before. His own father was ignorant of the child who walked around, not more than four miles from his summer house, with his own blood pumping through his veins and his own genes set to father a whole new generation some day. But Mariana had insisted he shouldn't be told. It was their secret, between the three of them.

'The right moment will come,' she had told Ramon, 'but let me tell him in my own good time.' Six years had gone by and she still hadn't told him. Ramon wondered whether she ever would.

Helena sent the children up to Toby's cottage. 'Ramon's appeared. I don't want him to see them,' she told her brother over the telephone.

'What? Ramon's in England?'

'Yes.'

'My God,' Toby exclaimed, sitting down. 'After all this time, what's he suddenly turned up for?'

'To see the children, so he says.'

'Just like that, out of the blue?'

'I don't want him to see the children,' she repeated anxiously.

'Is that wise?' he asked uneasily. 'He is their father, after all.'

'Only biologically. I won't let him come back and upset them. Fede's getting on with things now. She's happy. The last thing she needs is Ramon appearing and promising her the world.'

'Well, you're right about that,' he agreed.

'I know I am.'

'How will you get rid of him?' Toby asked, envisaging Ramon staking out the house until their return.

'Don't worry, I will.'

'I don't think Arthur's much of a match for Ramon.'

'I wasn't thinking of Arthur. I can get rid of him myself. Kill him with kindness,' she said and laughed nervously.

'You've got to be cool, Helena, and strong,' he suggested encouragingly. 'Don't flare up and don't let him walk all over you. You're an independent woman now. You don't need him. You've got on very well without him. Show him how you've changed. You're not the woman he used to know, all right?'

Helena nodded to herself. 'You're right. If I show weakness he'll use it against me.'

'Exactly. You're a force to be reckoned with. Pummel him into submission, he's only human after all.'

Once she'd sent the children up to Toby's house on their bicycles she bathed and dressed, trying to convince herself that the makeup and grooming was simply to show Ramon how she'd changed. But she knew the truth and it angered her that she still felt the need to impress him.

She waited in the garden, on the bench under the cherry tree where Polly usually sat surveying her borders and flowerbeds. As a child Helena had watched her plant that tree. How quickly it had grown. Rather like her children. She, too, marvelled at the rapid passing of time. Chile seemed like another life. A life shrouded in shadow because she had become frightened of looking back on it, frightened of missing it. She had made her choice so she had started another chapter, closing the old one for ever. When she heard the sound of wheels on gravel her heart accelerated, pumping the blood through her veins at an uncomfortable speed. Once again her past surfaced to torment her. She stood up shakily, resisting the urge to smoke and walked with forced calmness towards the garden gate.

Ramon hardly recognized Helena. She had cut her hair short. It was paler, thicker, and her skin had recovered that lucid quality he had found so enchanting the first time he met her. Her pale eyes shone with health and she smiled serenely.

He had expected her to demand that he leave, but she greeted him with the affability of an old friend, catching him off guard and throwing all his plans awry. Helena noticed he was lost for words and growing in confidence she invited him to join her in the garden for a drink.

'You look well,' he said when they were both seated under the cherry tree with glasses of Polly's homemade elderflower juice. Helena thanked him and looked at his lined face and long greying hair. He resembled an ageing lion. He was still awesome and compelling. He was still king of the jungle, just not her jungle any more. His hesitation exposed his weakness and sensing it immediately she grabbed the opportunity to take control. To her amazement she was no longer afraid of him.

'You look well too. Older,' she said with a malicious smile, 'but still handsome.'

'Thank you,' he said and frowned. 'I'm sorry it's been so long.'

'That's an understatement,' she laughed, but she was careful not to reveal undertones of bitterness. 'You're not cut out for fatherhood, Ramon. But don't torment yourself. We've done very nicely without you. In fact, I should thank you. You liberated us from the rut we had dug for ourselves in Chile. We're very happy here,' she said and looked at him steadily.

He noticed she wasn't smoking and her hand wasn't shaking. He felt uncomfortable. 'I've been a hopeless father,' he conceded. 'But I love them.'

'In your own way, I'm sure you do. They love you too. They love the memory of you. But they've survived without you.'

'I see,' he said in a tone that sounded more like a deep groan. He leant forward and rested his elbows on his knees. 'Fede doesn't want you to marry Arthur.'

'I know,' she said. 'She doesn't want anyone to replace you.'

'She wrote asking me to prevent it.'

'How will you do that?' she asked and smiled with confidence, as if she regarded his sudden peacekeeping mission as a source of amusement.

'I don't know. I came to talk to you, that's all,' he said, sitting back and looking at her with solicitous eyes. He drained his glass.

'Look, I'm tremendously fond of Arthur. He's good to me. He's always there for me. You never were, Ramon. But I don't blame you. I chose you and I chose to leave you. It's that simple. Now I want to marry Arthur and Fede will just have to live with it.'

'She doesn't want to leave Polperro,' he said.

'I know but we can't always have what we want.'

'Hasn't she been uprooted enough?'

'You're one to talk,' she retorted curtly, restraining her anger. 'If it wasn't for you we wouldn't have uprooted in the first place.'

'If I remember, I didn't want you to leave.'

'But you refused to change. I had no choice.' Helena's cheeks stung crimson betraying for a moment her inner fury. She turned her face away and poured more juice, aware that if she showed the smallest sign of vulnerability, he would pounce and she'd be lost.

'Do you love this Arthur?' he asked.

'I'm very fond of him,' she replied.

'That's not what I asked.'

'Don't tell me you don't have some poor, neglected woman tucked away somewhere in Chile,' she replied defensively, avoiding answering his question.

He smirked and nodded. 'Yes, I do.'

Helena was stunned by his honest reply in spite of the fact that she knew he would have found someone in the seven years that they had been apart, it was inevitable. She wanted to ask what she was like, whether she was patient and submissive, whether she minded his long absences like she had. But she resisted the temptation.

'Well, you know what it's like then. When you care for someone,' she replied, swallowing her disappointment while outwardly smiling at her husband.

Ramon watched her impenetrable coolness and wondered whether Arthur had given her the confidence to be so self-assured. She had been like that when he had first fallen in love with her. Had he really worn her down like a beautiful rug?

'So, do you want a divorce?' he asked, biting the inside of his cheeks apprehensively.

'Yes,' she replied, ignoring the small voice inside her head, which begged her to hold onto him.

'Then you shall have it.'

She nodded stiffly. 'Thank you.'

'What will you do about Fede?'

'Why do you care?' she snapped in exasperation, suddenly letting slip her carefully cultivated composure. 'You neglect her for seven years then suddenly turn up because of a letter she wrote you? You have no right to even ask how she is, or Hal. They are nothing to you now. They don't belong to you. If you cared you would have been there when Fede fell off her bike, when she was teased at school because she was the only child without a father, or . . . or . . . when Hal awoke with nightmares or the normal doubts that children suffer from. But you weren't. You know you weren't. Why don't you go back to your woman in Chile and forget about us? You've had no problem forgetting us for the last seven years. For God's sake, Ramon,' she exclaimed, raising her voice until it quivered with anger and hurt. 'You've let us all down badly. Very badly. I want you to go.'

Ramon didn't want to leave her. She had changed. Gone was the neurotic, stifling woman who clung to him like ivy, refusing to allow him space to breathe. Helena had grown into a woman who knew her mind and had the strength of character to execute her wishes. He knew Arthur was behind it and he was curious to see for himself the man who had succeeded where he had failed. But Helena looked at him steadily with eyes of stone. Her argument was strong and he knew he was unable to manipulate her like he had always done in the past. She no longer feared him.

Reluctantly he got to his feet. 'So this is it then?'

'This is it,' she confirmed, standing up.

'We'll communicate through our lawyers.'

'Right.'

'I don't think I can go on for ever without seeing my children.'

'Give me time,' she conceded, suddenly feeling saddened by the finality of their decision to divorce. 'I want to marry Arthur. If Fede thinks you're back I'll have one hell of a battle on my hands. You've waited seven years, another year won't make any difference, at least not to Fede.'

Ramon lowered his eyes. 'You really want to marry him?' he asked, wondering why he cared.

'Yes,' she replied, maintaining her composure with a great deal of effort.

'Well, good luck.'

'Thank you.' Ramon leant over and kissed her on the cheek. Helena withdrew quickly, afraid that he might linger there too long, afraid that she might not be able to resist him. Then he turned and left. She sank back onto the bench and waited for the sound of the car to disappear out of the driveway. Then she placed her head in her hands and cried.

★

Federica cycled down the lane. She had left Hal with Toby and Julian who both agreed that he was too tired to bicycle all the way home after such a heavy tea. They would drive him back later. Federica was delighted – at least on her own she could go as fast as she liked without worrying that a car might appear from around the corner and frighten her brother. She took her feet off the pedals and freewheeled down the road. With the sun on her back and the spring wind raking through her hair she felt exhilarated.

Suddenly a shiny black Mercedes roared around the bend, sending her hands straight onto the brakes in a panicked attempt to control the bike and avoid crashing into the car. With her heart suspended between beats she felt the hot rush of air as it passed dangerously close by, then heard the screech of tyres as it pulled up in the middle of the road behind her. She drew her bike to a shaky stop by dragging her shoes along the tarmac. Then she positioned her unsteady feet on the ground and turned around. The sun was so bright she had to put her hand over her eyes to shield them from the dazzling glare. She watched the car, but no one got out. She squinted her eyes in an effort to make out who was inside, but the reflection on the glass prevented her from seeing in. She remained motionless, wondering what was going through the driver's mind that inhibited him from descending and apologizing to her for nearly claiming her life. She was visibly shaken, for her whole body trembled, but still no one appeared. Then to Federica's bewilderment, the car started up again and left just as suddenly as it had come, restoring the lane to its previous tranquillity as if nothing had happened.

Only the black marks on the tarmac betrayed the stranger's indecision.

Chapter 24

Autumn 1990

Federica insisted she was too old to be a bridesmaid at her mother's wedding.

'You're fourteen,' said Helena simply, 'and anyway, you're small for your age.' Once again Federica walked out of the room, out of the house and off onto the cliffs, followed loyally by Rasta, who was now a fully grown Labrador with enormous paws and a large black spot on his nose which baffled everyone.

Helena sighed wearily and decided that Hal would have to be a single page – at twelve years old he wasn't very enthusiastic but agreed because of a hidden mechanism in his make-up that made it impossible for him to deny his mother anything.

After Ramon's brief visit Helena had resolved to marry Arthur. It had taken eighteen months for the divorce to come through. Helena had disintegrated into tears at the sight of the physical proof that her marriage to Ramon was over. She had held the piece of paper in her hands and wondered whether marriage to Arthur was really what she wanted after all. But then she had forced herself to remember how unhappy marriage to Ramon had been and how kind Arthur was and she had filed the document away and continued with her plans in her own stubborn way, refusing to listen to her heart that beat inaudibly for Ramon.

During that time Helena had fought almost daily with her daughter who still believed her father would appear to save her from the dreaded Arthur.

'Arthur will never be my father,' she had shouted at her mother in one of her many fits of hysterics. 'And I will never move away from Polperro. Papa's so handsome, what do you see in Arthur?'

Helena ignored her, hoping that she'd get used to Arthur in time. She didn't.

Federica had taken to walking high on the cliffs, watching the surf crash violently against the rocks below and the mesmerizing rise and fall of the cold ocean which, like a beast, seemed to mirror her own inner fury. Rasta would sit with her, the wind drawing his ears back against his sandy neck, cowering against her for warmth, detecting her pain and sympathizing in his own unspoken way.

Federica couldn't understand why her father hadn't written. She had begged him to help and he had ignored her. She felt gutted inside. Within her head she was screaming for compassion but no one heard her. Occasionally her despair boiled over and she fought with her mother, but Helena never bothered to search beneath the outward expression of a grief than ran much deeper than she imagined. No one did. Federica confided in Hester, but Hester was only a child, like she was, and unable to do more than listen and sympathize. She had a father so how could she?

Federica would like to have talked to Sam, but Sam wasn't often at the manor and when he was she found the words dried up in her mouth and she was unable to communicate with him in anything other than empty smiles. She knew he saw through her smiles, he was smart enough to recognize her unhappiness and he often placed an affectionate arm around her for no apparent reason, or asked her how she was in a compassionate tone of voice. Hester told her that she had heard him confess to her mother that he had a soft spot for her, which only made Federica more self-conscious and less able to speak to him. But she was secretly delighted and sensed they shared a special bond, forged that day in the bluebells. He no longer ignored her. Even though she was still very much a child, he had noticed her. She felt herself so in love she was unable to concentrate on anything else. Only her mother's impending wedding distracted her from her ardour.

The day of Helena's wedding arrived and Federica awoke with the unavoidable sense of doom that had dogged her for the last few months. She looked out onto an October morning. The sky was watery, shimmering through the golden leaves and silky dew that seemed to cling to everything like tears. She cast her eye over the place that had become her home and loved it all the more because she knew she was leaving it.

'Oh, to be a grown up,' she thought miserably, 'then at least I could make my own decisions.' But she was fourteen years old and still had to obey her mother. Moodily she ate her breakfast while her mother paced up and down the house in a pre-wedding panic having lost her shoes, then her mascara and finally the dress itself, which she had forgotten hung in her mother's cupboard because it was less damp. Much to Federica's annoyance she found herself clearing up after her mother, pouring her endless glasses of wine and standing by like an unwilling assistant receiving bouquets of flowers, wedding presents and answering the telephone. Polly sat with her daughter in her bedroom while the stylist did her hair and makeup, trying to prevent her from drinking too much and keeping the atmosphere light.

Hal lay on the bed playing with a computer game oblivious to the chaos that raged around him.

Federica sulked the entire way through her mother's wedding; it was all she could do not to cry. When she thought things simply couldn't get any worse, Sam sauntered into the church with a new girlfriend hanging decoratively on his arm. The girl was tall, with long dark hair and long legs striding confidently out from under a very short pink skirt. Federica wanted to crawl under the nearest tombstone and die.

The ceremony was one of blessing in the village church, given by the excitable Reverend Boyble who'd had his robes dry-cleaned especially for the occasion and his shoes polished with such enthusiasm that they shone out from under his skirts like a couple of silver fish.

Jake had refused to attend because Helena had refused to exclude Julian. Polly had told him to 'grow up'. 'Really, Jake, you're being very childish,' she said as she left him brooding in the kitchen among his toy boats. 'This silly feud has been going on long enough! Honestly, one would think you'd put it to one side in order to give your own daughter away at her wedding.'

Toby was best man and stood apprehensively at the end of the aisle with Arthur, whose brow was studded with jewels of sweat and his buttonhole wilted due to the heat exuding from his thick body. Toby winked at Federica who managed to pull a weak smile in spite of her misery. He wasn't sure he didn't agree with his niece, Arthur was a poor choice of husband. He cast his eyes over Arthur's side of the congregation and decided that if he were to squint he would see little more than a monotonous grey blur. Federica stared at her scarlet shoes and wished she could tap them together three times and disappear back to Chile.

At the moment the bride was due to arrive an expectant silence subdued the chitter-chatter of the congregation.

The Reverend Boyble strode importantly up the nave, his shoes silencing the last of the whispers with their metallic tap-tapping as he took great care not to slip. Everyone turned their eyes to the door. But when it flew open there was no sign of the bride, just Molly and Hester who scuttled down the aisle with their hands pressed firmly over their mouths in an attempt to stifle their laughter.

'Shit,' Sam hissed to his girlfriend, rolling his eyes. 'They've been at my spliffs again, God damn it.' Indeed, Molly had learned how to roll her own and knew where her brother hid his grass. Ingrid caught Sam's eye and frowned, cocking her head to one side, but he shrugged his shoulders, denying responsibility. Hester waved at Federica who looked back gloomily, but Hester was too high to notice her misery.

When Helena finally arrived, dressed in a stunningly embroidered ivory dress, a sigh of admiration swept through the congregation, followed immediately by a gasp. Leading her up the aisle was none other than Nuno.

'Good God!' Ingrid exclaimed. 'What's Pa doing?'

Inigo's scowl softened and the corners of his mouth turned up with pleasure. 'Now that is splendid. Splendid,' he said, rubbing his hands together.

'Whatever do you mean, darling?' Ingrid replied, nudging him with her elbow.

'Well, it's the blind leading the blind.' He chuckled.

'Helena's not blind.'

'She must be to marry that turnip,' he said and laughed quietly.

'Well, I suppose you're right,' Ingrid agreed. 'Quite a compromise after having been married to the gorgeous Ramon,' she added, remembering that handsome Latin who had given them all so much pleasure before leaving as quickly as he had come.

'Where's Grandpa?' Federica hissed to her grandmother, temporarily emerging out of her dark cave of self-pity. Polly shrugged and glanced over at Toby who blinked helplessly back.

'Oh dear,' Polly sighed sadly. 'Jake didn't make it. I am sorry.'

Helena had waited ten minutes outside the church for her father to arrive. She had known there was a good chance he wouldn't come and she had been prepared to walk down the aisle alone with Hal. She wasn't angry, just saddened. If his own daughter's wedding couldn't soften his prejudice she wondered what on earth could. When Reverend Boyble had started playing nervously with his prayer book and twitching at the corners of his mouth, Helena knew she couldn't hold the service up any longer. Even though it was her wedding. Julian, who was taking the photographs, had snapped one last shot of the agitated bride before creeping silently into the church. Helena had nodded to Reverend Boyble to commence and winked at Hal, who smiled back proudly in his sailor suit.

Then suddenly Nuno's clipped syllables had stopped her at the door. 'My dear, who's going to give you away?' he asked, trotting up the path as if he were out on a Sunday stroll.

'Nuno,' she replied, turning around.

'I'm tardy, I'm afraid,' he said, checking the gold watch that hung on a chain about his waist.

'I suppose you're going to tell me that "punctuality is the thief of time",' she laughed.

'No, my dear, age is the thief of time, it steals one's faculties in their entirety, including one's ability to remember important events such as your wedding. I only remembered because I had tied a knot in my handkerchief, but then it took me a good fifteen minutes to work out why I had put the knot there in the first place. You see, dear girl, age steals everything.'

'Well, you had better slip in then,' she suggested, standing aside for him, noticing Reverend Boyble's chubby fingers tapping with impatience on his prayer book.

'God will wait, good man,' Nuno said with a sniff.

The fingers ceased to tap and Reverend Boyble remained for once speechless with his mouth agape.

'Actually, Nuno,' said Helena, with the glint of an idea shining in her eye. 'Would you do me a favour.'

Helena once more suffered doubt as she walked on Nuno's arm towards the man who would in a matter of minutes be her husband. She made a great effort to rid her thoughts of Ramon and pushed aside any uncertainty with a will of iron. She fixed her eyes on Arthur and remembered his kindness and his adoration and her mind cleared. 'I deserve you,' she thought to herself as his clammy hand found hers and he smiled merrily across at her. His eyes told her that she looked beautiful and she returned his smile wholeheartedly.

As Nuno tripped to his seat beside his daughter he heard the muffled squeals of Molly and Hester who jiggled up and down like two clockwork mice in the row behind. 'High on life,' said Ingrid vaguely, shaking her head.

'So that's what they're rolling nowadays, is it?' he replied, sitting down.

'Really, Pa. They're just children,' she replied, opening the order of service.

'No, my dear, they're *your* children and if they continue to screech like a couple of pigs in a farmyard, I would like you to send them out,' he sniffed, lifting his chin up piously and turning his attention to the marriage ceremony.

★

The service was long due to the over-exuberance of the Reverend Boyble who loved to hear the sound of his own voice, inspired by God, echo about the stone walls of his church. It was better than singing hymns in the bathroom. Every eye was on him, thirsting for his words to inspire them up the narrow path to God. Marriages were his favourite services and he liked to make them last as long as possible not only for himself but for the happy couple and their friends who had gathered together to hear him. So taken was he by the wit and intelligence of his sermon, he failed to notice the eyes of his congregation droop with boredom and the sound of impatient fingers rustle through the order of service, wondering how long it was going to last.

Finally everyone emerged dazed from the church except for Arthur who strode out like a triumphant gladiator.

'My darling wife,' he said, kissing her on her pale cheek. 'My dear, darling wife. Now we belong together for always.'

'Yes,' she replied, swallowing the ugly knot of doubt that had found its way into her throat. 'For ever,' she repeated, not wanting to think too hard about what that meant.

After smiling for Julian they climbed into a horse-drawn carriage and slowly made their way back to the house for the reception. The warm autumnal light set the sky aflame as the evening closed in and the sun began to sink low over the western horizon.

'You are so beautiful, Helena,' Arthur said, taking her hand. 'I am the luckiest man alive.'

Helena squeezed his hand, suddenly overcome by the splendour of the dying day and the affection that blazed in her new husband's eyes. 'I'm lucky to have you,' she replied truthfully, looking into his gentle features that promised her a life of indulgence and love. 'I'm going to give up smoking as a tribute to you and to announce the beginning of a new life. I really am very lucky that you want to take me on.'

'No, my darling. The luck is all mine and something I won't forget even for a moment.' He bent his head and kissed her. She closed her eyes and breathed in the security of his scent. That calmed her nerves and reminded her of all the reasons she had chosen him.

As the guests arrived gasping for sustenance, Polly rushed about the tent they had erected in the garden with trays of scones and sandwiches while Toby saw to it that everyone had a glass of champagne. Hester and Molly found Federica sitting alone in her bedroom.

'We've been looking for you for hours,' said Hester, joining her on her bed.

'Are you all right?' Molly asked. 'You look miserable.'

'I don't want to leave Polperro,' she sniffed unhappily.

'We don't want you to leave Polperro either,' said Hester.

'I don't like Arthur,' she said, crossing her arms in front of her. 'He's now my stepfather. Yuck.'

'He's not that bad,' said Molly helpfully.

'But he's not Papa.'

'No, he certainly isn't Ramon,' Molly agreed, giggling at Hester. 'But no one's as handsome as your father.'

'He didn't come,' said Federica, lowering her eyes. 'I was certain he would.'

'Perhaps he didn't get your letter,' said Hester, putting an arm around her friend.

'Perhaps.'

'I know a way to cheer you up,' said Molly, grinning at her sister and putting her hand in her pocket.

'What a good idea,' Hester gasped, smacking her hand across her mouth and blinking at Federica guiltily.

'What is it?' Federica asked.

'One of Sam's special cigarettes. We didn't finish it.' Hester giggled nervously. 'No one's going to find us here, are they?'

'Hester, it's called a spliff, and no, no one's going to find us here,' said Molly, flicking her lighter. 'I take it this is your first?' she added, nodding at Federica, who nodded back anxiously. 'Okay, so you smoke it like a cigarette,' she said.

'I've never smoked a cigarette.'

'Well then, you'll learn something new today,' said Molly, puffing on the spliff, setting it alight. 'Open the window, Hester.' Hester opened it wide, and the light sound of music wafted up above the low hum of voices.

'They sound like they're having a good time,' Hester laughed.

'Not as good as us,' said Molly, handing Federica the spliff. 'Now, breathe in deeply, hold it in a few seconds then let it out. And for God's sake let's not have any of that silly coughing business, it's so immature.'

Federica was determined not to cough. She put the spliff to her mouth and breathed in as deeply as she could. The two sisters watched in amusement as her face flushed purple while she dutifully held her breath.

'Well done,' said Molly, taking the spliff from her and handing it to Hester.

Federica exhaled frantically and gasped for breath.

'How does it feel?' Molly asked.

'Okay,' said Federica, who didn't feel anything at all.

'Have another go,' said Molly, taking a drag before handing it back to her.

After a few minutes Molly and Hester were laughing like a couple of hyenas while Federica cried without being able to stop.

'I love Sam,' she began. 'I really do. I can't help it. But he'll never look at me. I'm too young and ugly. Not like that model he's brought with him today. I suppose that's his girlfriend?' she asked.

Hester and Molly laughed even louder. 'You can't be in love with Sam, he's such a dork!' said Molly. 'Anyway, he's only interested in one thing. They all are.'

'And that's not poetry,' Hester smirked.

'Hester, that's so clever.'

'Really?'

'Yes, you've just said something very funny.'

'Well, is she his girlfriend?' Federica sobbed.

'For the moment, but of course he'll change her next week. He has a new one every week, you know. Sam's weekly fix,' said Molly. 'I'm not interested in men who only want sex. I want a man with a good mind.'

'Sam has a good mind.'

'Yes, he does, Fede, but it's firmly installed in the end of his willy at the moment,' said Molly, and she and Hester collapsed with laughter.

Federica sobbed even harder.

Finally, Molly realized that the spliff had only made Federica worse and instructed Hester to run off and find Toby or Julian fearing that she might kill herself with despair.

'Don't worry, Fede, you'll go off Sam in the end. You don't want someone that much older than you. Good God, he'll be twenty-nine years old when you're twenty. And anyway, you don't want to be Federica Appleby, do you?'

Federica was just on the point of replying that she wanted nothing more than to be Federica Appleby when the door opened and in walked Toby and Julian, out of breath and anxious.

'Okay, girls. Why don't you leave us alone with Fede and go back to the party,' said Julian, waving his hand to clear the smoke.

'You can chuck away the rest of that spliff,' said Toby crossly, shaking his head. 'You're too young to be experimenting with those.'

Molly and Hester scuttled out of the room. Molly had no intention of throwing away her precious spliff, they were hard to come by, especially as Sam hid them in different places all the time.

Toby sat beside Federica and drew her into his arms while Julian sat on the chair opposite. 'This is a horrid day for you,' Toby said, kissing her wet face. 'But it'll be over soon . . .'

'And I'll be leaving Polperro.'

'Ah,' said Toby, raising his eyebrows at Julian. 'I quite forgot about that. Julian, will you stay with Fede while I nip down for a second. There's something I need to do.' Julian took his place next to Federica and put an arm around her.

'I'm in love with someone who doesn't love me,' she said, blinking up at Julian in misery.

'How could he not love you?' Julian said gently. 'Who is he and I'll kill him?'

'Sam Appleby.' Federica sniffed.

'Ah, yes, he is very attractive,' he agreed. 'He's clever. I like clever men. He's also a sensualist. You have very good taste.'

'But I'm too young,' she complained.

'Not at all,' said Julian. 'You are at the moment. You're what? Fourteen and he's twenty-two or twenty-three? The sort of women he chooses at the moment are much older than you and prepared to sleep with him. That's what he wants. All men are the same. If I were you, I'd put him on ice like a good champagne and save him up until later.'

'But I can't wait that long,' she protested.

'Of course you can. If you really want someone you'll wait for him for ever. I'd wait for Toby for ever.'

'You're lucky you've got Toby,' she said. 'I've got no one.'

'You've got us and we'll take care of you,' he said, squeezing her.

'I just feel I don't matter. Mama has Arthur and Hal has Mama. Papa no longer writes to me, he might just as well be dead,' she said. 'Arthur will never be a father to me. Never. I'd rather die.'

'He doesn't want to be your father,' said Julian. 'He already has children of his own. He just wants to be a husband to your mother. You can't blame him for that. She's very beautiful and not an easy woman either. Arthur deserves a medal.'

'Perhaps.'

'And she deserves a bit of happiness, don't you think?'

'Yes,' she replied and sighed in resignation.

'It's sad when marriages break up, it's sad for the parents and sad for the children. But you have to move on and make the best of it,' he said. 'You never know, perhaps in time you can go out and see your father yourself. When you're older you won't need permission from anyone. You can just go. So hang in there for now.'

When Toby returned, his face glowing with pleasure, Julian knew he had good news. Federica looked up at him hopefully wondering what his two-minute disappearance had managed to achieve. He sat down opposite her and held her hands. 'I've struck a bargain with your mother. She's in a good mood today, it was the perfect time to approach her.'

'What about?' Federica asked, not daring to imagine.

'Well,' he replied, smiling. 'If you like you can stay on at the same school and live with me and Julian during the week, as long as you return to your mother and Arthur on weekends.'

Federica gasped in disbelief. 'She means it?' she exclaimed, wiping her face with her sleeve.

'She does.'

'And Rasta?'

'And Rasta. I suppose we can cope with the two of you.' He laughed.

'Oh, thank you, Uncle Toby,' she said in excitement, throwing her arms about his neck. 'I can't believe it.'

'It'll be like weekly boarding,' said Julian.

'You can give me photography lessons,' she said happily, 'and I'll bake you cakes and look after you. You won't know what's hit you. I'm very tidy and organized and an extremely good cook. I won't be any trouble,' she added, unable to contain her delight.

'Cakes for photography lessons, that sounds good to me,' said Julian, nodding his approval at Toby.

'Can I move in today?'

'As soon as your mother's safely off on her honeymoon, and on one condition,' said Toby.

'What's that?' she asked apprehensively.

'That you be nice to Arthur.'

'Oh, all right,' she conceded and added mischivously. 'I won't call him an old fart any more.'

Jake sat in his study and smouldered like a freshly stoked piece of coal. He would like to have been at his daughter's wedding, but she had made her choice. She wasn't prepared to sacrifice her brother's lover for her own father. He was deeply hurt. But Helena had always been troublesome. Ever since she was a child she had managed to have everyone running around her. She was stubborn too and always got what she wanted – well, nearly always. He pitied Arthur and wondered whether he had the endurance to satisfy her whims. He knew she still craved Ramon. She never said so, but he could tell. She had brooded over the divorce papers, not wanting to sign them yet knowing she had to, because divorce had been her choice. Like leaving him in the first place. Her choices and she had to live with them. The problem with Helena, he thought, was that she was used to forcing people's hands by pushing them to the edge until they had no choice but to give in to her will. She had probably hoped Ramon would refuse to let her go, then refuse to divorce her. But he was stronger than she was.

She had met her match, and lost. Arthur was a safe bet. No match there at all. Maybe after all those battles she wanted a quiet life. Don't we all, he thought miserably, picking up a miniature wooden barrel to stick onto the pirates' boat he was making.

Chapter 25

The following year was a happy one for Federica and a miserable one for Jake. While Federica lived in contentment with her Uncle Toby and Julian, baking cakes, learning how to take photographs and cycling up to Pickthistle Manor as she always had done, Jake withdrew further into the bowels of his miniature boats, disgusted that his daughter had allowed Federica to live with homosexuals at such an impressionable age. Polly tried to discuss it with him, but he wouldn't be drawn on the subject.

'It's not right,' he would say at his kindest and 'It's disgusting!' at his most vitriolic.

But it was all part of Helena's plan and typical of her pattern of manipulation. She would force his hand in the end, she was sure of it.

Polly sent Helena photographs of Jake at previous weddings so that she could superimpose him into her album, but Helena only laughed and sent them back.

'Really, Mum, I thought Dad was the eccentric in the family, not you,' she said. But Polly minded much more than she let on. She also missed having her daughter and grandchildren about the house and spent hours devising excuses to drive up the lane to Toby's cottage to see Federica.

'You know, Federica's very happy, Jake,' Polly said, one afternoon after she had watched her return from a boat trip with Toby and Julian in *The Helena*.

Her cheeks were ruddy from the wind and they were all laughing. Toby carried the picnic basket full of empty dishes that Federica had made and Julian had taken photographs. Rasta trotted along behind them, fat from sharing their vegetarian pies and weary from the games on the beach. 'You know, they all looked so well. They could have been any normal family,' she continued, not caring whether or not he was listening. She wanted to share her joy and was damned if his prejudice was going to stop her. He continued gluing the small pieces of wood and sticking them together with total concentration. 'Toby's like a father to Federica. I think it was the best thing Helena ever did sending her to live with them. She's grown up so much, too. She's a young lady now and so capable. She cooks for them and looks after them like a little mother. I'm so proud of her. So proud! Julian has taught her photography. She's got quite an eye, you know. Yes, she really has. He's framed some of them and put them up on the wall. It's done her self-esteem the world of good. That's what she needed, a father. Now she has two.' She eyed her husband warily but he continued to focus on his project as if he hadn't heard her.

When Hester approached her mother with the idea of a sixteenth-birthday party Ingrid immediately called Helena and suggested she share it with Federica. 'Kill two birds with one stone,' she said, knowing she wasn't capable of organizing the party by herself.

'What sort of party are you thinking of?' Helena asked, wondering whether Ingrid knew the first thing about sixteen-year-old children and the bedlam they would make of her home.

'Oh, something pretty. A nice tent,' she said vaguely.

Helena smiled at Ingrid's blissful detachment. 'What are they going to eat?'

'Oh, a buffet, I should imagine. I'll get a company to do it,' she said breezily.

'How many people?'

'How many friends do they have?' Ingrid replied distract-edly, her mind already focusing on the milky evening sky and the perfection of the lake that had now become home to flocks of nesting birds.

'Why don't we get together with the girls and discuss it,' she said, aware that Ingrid's attention was waning.

'Darling, what a good idea. Why don't you come for tea tomorrow with Federica.' Then as an after-thought she added, 'Do bring Hal, Joey and Lucien will be here and I know they would love to see him. We don't see Hal so much these days.'

Hal was very fond of Arthur. He remembered his father only rarely when the fog in his memory subsided enough for him to see him clearly. A vague impression of a man with the rough, weathered look of a wolf and the imperious nature of a king. As a child Ramon had frightened him but now he was older he only feared him in his dreams. Arthur, however, made him feel special. He took time with him, encouraged him and never belittled him. Arthur's love for Helena was all-consuming, but never too much to come between her and her son. He understood their closeness and was touched by it. He tried to be a good father to Hal and was rewarded with the boy's trust and affection. Helena had expected Hal to be jealous of her relationship with Arthur, it would have been only natural, but to her surprise Hal responded to him in a way he had never responded to his own father.

Only Federica kept a candle lit for Ramon.

Helena watched as Arthur slowly endeared himself to everyone in Polperro. Having started off as a comic figure to be laughed at, he gained the respect of the whole town by the sheer geniality of his nature. He always smiled, always took the time to talk to people and never tired of listening to their problems, offering sound advice with honesty, never gossiping about what they told him. He was a man who could be trusted. Even Ingrid grew fond of him as he won her affection through his surprising knowledge of birds and love of animals. He helped Hester rescue hedgehogs and praised Inigo's flourishing wine cellar. Nuno nicknamed him 'Arturo', which everyone found very amusing and adopted at once. Only Federica continued to call him Arthur out of sheer spite. Helena was infuriated by her daughter's unwillingness to embrace her new stepfather. She felt she was most undeserving of a party.

'"Party-spirit, which at best is but the madness of many for the gain of a few,"' said Nuno, pouring Helena a cup of tea. He raised his thick eyebrows at her, which had aged as he had and resembled two white waves on the sea.

Helena shook her head. 'Sorry, Nuno, beaten again,' she said, smiling at him indulgently.

'Ah, for the sharp wit of young Samuel, were he here he'd get that one in a blink.' He sighed, putting down the pot. 'Alexander Pope, my dear,' he said. '"Woman's at best a contradiction still,"' he added with a smirk, 'that's him too.'

'All right, Pa, enough showing off, my head is spinning,' Ingrid complained, sipping her tea. 'I've noticed you no longer smoke, Helena,' she said, observing that she no longer trembled either. 'Arturio must be doing you the world of good.'

'He is. I'm very happy. Though there are times when I crave just one cigarette,' she replied truthfully. 'He is extremely indulgent, though. I'm very lucky.'

'How nice. I wish Inigo were. The only trace of him I see these days is his black mood seeping under his study door like gravy. I wonder, are all philosophers so miserable?'

'My dear, they are pondering the great mysteries of life which cannot be proven. That must, surely, be demoralizing,' said Nuno wisely.

'But really, he should philosophize about himself, there is no greater mystery,' she replied.

'But even more demoralizing,' Nuno added.

'Well, let's not get distracted,' said Helena. 'Where are the girls, we should start discussing their party?'

'Of course,' Ingrid replied, lighting a cigarette. 'The party. I can't think of anything nicer than having a jolly bunch of young people to dinner in a tent. How romantic, a tent in the garden! Just like your wedding, Helena. Shame Molly's too young to wed otherwise we could have made more use of it.'

The date was set for a Saturday in July, midway between Federica's birthday, which was in June, and Hester's, which fell in August. They planned a large tent on the lawn overlooking the lake because Ingrid wanted the young people to enjoy the magnificent water at sunset. When Helena offered to pay half Ingrid waved her hand dismissively. 'Goodness no,' she replied, flapping her cigarette in the air. 'It's the least Inigo can do and besides, he'll pay not to attend.' She laughed mischievously.

Helena dreaded to think what the whole event was going to cost, the girls had far too many ideas. They wanted a hundred and fifty friends, caterers, disco, dance floor and lots of alcohol. Ingrid had suggested a fruit punch but Nuno insisted that they all drink wine. 'If you treat them like children they'll behave like children,' he said. 'Give them wine and they'll carry themselves with the sophistication of young Parisian aristocrats.'

Helena didn't think it would make the slightest bit of difference: drunk Parisian aristocrats were probably much the same as drunk Cornish schoolchildren. Nuno and Ingrid were in for a nasty surprise.

★

The evening of the party was typical of English summer weather. It had rained most of the day on and off, flooding Polperro with exuberant sunshine only to withdraw it a moment later and plunge it into shadow. Federica packed her night bag and Toby dropped her off at Pickthistle Manor in the afternoon.

'I can't bear it if it rains the whole way through the party,' she wailed. 'Ingrid's made such an effort making the garden nice.'

'Don't be under any illusions, sweetheart,' Toby said with a smile. 'No one's going to give a monkey about the garden, they're all going to be far too busy looking at each other.'

'Still, not much fun if it rains.'

'I disagree, things go much better when everything's thrown into chaos. If I were you, I'd hope for rain.'

As they approached the house Federica's stomach lurched and then shuddered. Sam's green and white Deux Chevaux was parked in the driveway.

Since her mother's wedding the year before, Federica had barely seen Sam. He had long since left Cambridge and on Nuno's advice had lived and worked in Rome for a year before returning to a job in finance in London. Nuno was furious that he wasted his 'brilliant mind' on a career that anyone with half a brain cell could do, but Sam reassured him that it would only be temporary; he wanted to see how the City worked. Federica had longed for his car to be parked in the drive, but now it was there, she panicked once again that she wouldn't know what to say when she saw him. She wished she were older, taller, prettier and more confident.

'Toby, Sam's at home,' she said in a thin voice.

'Good. It's about time he saw you blossoming into a beautiful young woman,' he replied, drawing up outside the house.

'I'm scared.'

'Of course you are, and that's what makes it so exciting. If you weren't scared you wouldn't be you, and you're lovely.' He glanced across at her earnest profile and hoped Sam had grown up too.

'But you would think that, you're my uncle.' She laughed.

'I'm also a man,' he said, touching her cheek. 'And I think you're beautiful. So go in there and be you. He won't know what's hit him.'

Federica kissed her uncle fondly before stepping unsteadily out of the car. Toby watched her walk inside and thought she looked like a blushing apple on a tree, she was still green, but with the right nurture she would make a very fine apple indeed.

Federica opened the door just as the sky parted again, pounding the ground with arrows of water. 'Bloody hell!' Hester complained, rushing up to her. 'Thank God you're here. Look at the weather!'

'It'll be lovely, darling,' said Ingrid, floating through the hall with a pot of orchids. 'These will brighten the tent up.'

'Mum thinks we're giving a gala for young debutantes. She hasn't a clue,' hissed Hester, grinning mischievously. 'The bore is Sam and his friend Ben are going to police it tonight.'

'What do you mean?' Federica asked, going pink at the mention of his name.

'Well, check up on us. Make sure nothing naughty is going on in the bushes.' She laughed.

'If this weather continues no one will go anywhere near the bushes,' said Federica, her heart basking in the sunny anticipation of Sam's presence.

When Federica and Hester walked across the sitting room and out through the French doors into the tent, Sam waved at her and then said to Ben, 'She's a dark little horse, that one.'

'What, her?' asked Ben, lying like a spider across the sofa.

'Yes. Fed-er-ica,' he said, clipping each syllable in the name as Nuno did.

'She's jailbait, mate,' Ben laughed.

'She is for now. But mark my words, when she's older she'll be gorgeous. I've been watching her. She's different from everyone else, there's something unfathomable about her and I like it. Give her a few more years and she'll have matured into a beautiful young woman.'

'So why wait?'

'For God's sake, Ben. I'm not into deflowering children.' Sam was appalled.

'Isn't this her sixteenth birthday party?'

'Yes, it is,' he replied.

'Well, she's ripe for the picking then. Better get her before anyone else does. Will you introduce me, I'd like to take a closer look.'

Ben followed Sam across the tent, which Ingrid had filled with large pots of orchids in spite of the florist who was busy decorating it with her own creations. Gazing out onto the garden Hester and Federica stood with their arms crossed gloomily in front of them, watching the downpour while frantic caterers bustled about erecting tables and chairs. Dodging the lighting men and the rehearsing band of musicians, Sam and Ben made their way over to join them.

'Hello Fede.' Federica turned around and felt the heat prickling her neck and chest as Sam sauntered up to her. The more she concentrated on not blushing the hotter her face became. She smiled, trying to act naturally and lowered her eyes. 'This is Ben,' Sam said. Ben extended his hand and studied her face through narrowed eyes.

'The policemen,' she said with a smile.

'The policemen,' said Sam, putting his hands in the pockets of his trousers. 'At least that was the only way we could get ourselves invited.'

'We don't need policemen,' Hester said sulkily.

'That's what you think,' Sam laughed. 'You might be pleased to have me and Ben muscling in when all those drunken boys are fighting over you.'

'I wish,' she replied. 'Look at it,' she said, putting her hand out and feeling the drops.

'I like the rain. It's romantic,' Sam said. Federica avoided making eye contact with him, but in spite of her efforts she could feel his stare on her face like the heat of the sun. She wondered why he was suddenly so interested and wished he'd leave before his proximity suffocated her.

'Well I don't,' Hester complained. 'Of all the days, why does it have to rain today? The place will be a mud bath.'

'You can all get naked and mud wrestle,' chuckled Ben, looking at his friend for approval. Hester giggled. Sam changed the subject.

'How's it going living with your uncle?' he asked Federica. He remembered their conversation in the bluebells and how upset she had been at the prospect of leaving Polperro.

'Fine, thank you,' she replied, managing to look at him briefly before finding the intimacy of his eyes too much to bear and pulling away. She felt foolish, as if her tongue were too big for her mouth. She wished she could find something intelligent to say. 'Julian's giving me photography lessons,' she said, filling the silence that seemed embarrassingly large and vacuous.

'I bet you're quite good now,' he replied. 'You should be with a teacher like Julian.'

'She is. I've seen some of her pictures,' Hester said loyally. Sam raised his eyebrows with interest.

'Not that good,' interjected Federica bashfully. 'Not yet.'

'A career as a photographer would be very appealing,' Sam said, nodding his head ponderously. 'You can take it anywhere, and you'll always be your own boss. There's a lot to be said for freedom, I can tell you.'

'I know. But I've got a long way to go before I get to that stage.'

'It goes very fast,' Sam said, reflecting on how the past year had slipped by almost unnoticed and how much it had changed her.

'I hope so,' Federica replied, noticing to her bewilderment the intense expression on his face as he looked at her. She was thankful when Hester suggested they start getting ready for their party.

'We haven't got time to stand here chatting to a couple of old men,' she said, dragging Federica away by the arm. Federica was only too pleased to go.

'I never wished her a happy birthday,' Sam said, watching them disappear into the sitting room.

'You can do it later when you're pulling her and some groping adolescent out of the bushes.'

'Shut up, Ben,' Sam snapped irritably. 'Sometimes you're more of a child than they are.'

Federica enjoyed a hot bath in the company of Trotsky who took it upon himself to keep vigil as none of the doors in Pickthistle Manor had locks. He lay there in the steam panting with his noble head resting on his paws and his pink tongue hanging out. Once more Federica's mind found Sam within the secrecy of its halls. She closed her eyes and imagined a world where everything she said was witty and clever, where she never blushed or stammered, where she always looked ravishing. Sam loved her in that world. He loved her passionately. He kissed her with tenderness and urgency, barely able to let her out of his sight even for a moment. His affection was all consuming. In his arms she felt secure and cherished, safe from the doubts and worries that silently plagued her in the real world.

She was dragged out of those pleasant halls by the loud, impatient yawn of Trotsky who had jumped to his feet and was waiting by the door wanting to be let out. Federica found Hester in front of the mirror in her bedroom. She had already dried her hair and Molly was applying mascara with the steady hand of a professional makeup artist. 'I'll do you after Hester,' she said.

Federica shuffled in her towel. 'I don't know. I've never put makeup on before,' she said, screwing up her nose.

'Well, tonight is your birthday party and you're going to look wonderful. Hurry and put your dress on,' she said bossily, standing back from her sister to admire her creation. 'Hester, you look beautiful,' she said, brushing on blusher with brisk strokes.

When Hester and Federica appeared in the tent in their dresses, their hair and makeup gave them the cool sophistication of much older girls. Molly stood proudly behind them like a nanny, pushing them forward so they could be admired. Ingrid clasped her hands together and exclaimed that they both looked like princesses. Helena realized that her daughter was growing up and felt a stab of sadness at her passing childhood. She wore a pale blue strapless dress that matched her aquamarine eyes and Molly had pinned her pale hair up onto the top of her head. She looked innocent yet remote, unlike other children of her age who were either far too knowing for their own good or much too infantile. She had acquired an ethereal quality in the last year, but Helena was certain she wasn't aware of her own allure; she was too insecure.

'You both look lovely,' she said, tucking a stray piece of white air behind Federica's ear. 'Lovely,' she said wistfully. She wished Ramon were there to see her. He'd be so proud. She shook off her regret and pulled a thin smile. 'Toby will pick you up in the morning. You look wonderful, Fede, a young woman now.'

'*Che belle donne!*' Nuno declared, trotting into the tent dressed in white tie.

'Pa, what on earth are you wearing?' Ingrid exclaimed, looking him up and down in puzzlement. 'It's *black* tie.'

'*Cara mia*, I live my own dress code,' he said with a sigh. 'It is my granddaughter's ball and I owe it to her to look my best.'

'Are you sure you want to come to my party, Nuno?' Hester laughed. 'You look like a penguin.'

'I'm flattered, truly,' he said with a bow. 'It's an honour to be in the company of two beautiful princesses. Let us celebrate with a glass of champagne!'

Federica was disappointed Sam hadn't come down. She felt pretty and wanted him to see her. While she drank endless toasts with Ingrid, Nuno and her mother she kept a keen eye on the French doors, her heart quivering in anticipation of his arrival. But he never appeared. Finally she asked Hester, 'Where are the policemen?'

'Watching telly, I suspect,' she said to Federica's disappointment. 'They'll appear when things get going.'

Things got going pretty fast. The guests arrived and proceeded to finish almost the entire supply of alcohol before sitting down to dinner. The buffet was served early to compensate but no one moved towards the food until Trotsky was seen at one of the tables like a canine vacuum cleaner, polishing off the sausages with one inhalation. Once Hester had dragged the dog out into the garden, the guests fell upon the dishes in fear of losing it all to the other animals who wandered in and out as if they owned the place. Federica sat next to two boys she didn't know who talked most of the evening across her about cricket and O levels. Too shy to assert herself she just sat back and listened submissively, watching Molly near by who managed to have the attention of her entire table and smoked a long thin cigarette with great panache. Federica felt conspicuous and foolish by comparison.

Federica danced with a couple of boys, but she was too self-conscious to enjoy it. She noticed they looked over her shoulders, probably hoping for more interesting girls to dance with. She watched one of Molly's friends in a black lace dress move with the lithe sophistication of a professional dancer and wished she had such self-assurance and grace. Finally, when she was about to retreat to a lone chair somewhere in the corner of the tent, preferably underneath a large orchid, her dance partner suddenly swelled green in the face, like mouldy yoghurt, and grabbing Federica by the hand dragged her outside into the night.

'I think I'm going to be sick,' he groaned as the alcohol caused his stomach to heave.

'What do you need *me* for?' she asked in bewilderment, as her heels sunk into Ingrid's sodden lawn.

'I don't want to die alone,' he replied, pulling her into the night.

'I don't think it's that bad, is it?' she asked, hoping he'd make a miraculous recovery and take her back to the party. She shivered with cold as the drizzle dusted her face and shoulders.

'It's very bad,' he replied before throwing his head into a bush and vomiting loudly. Federica winced as he covered Ingrid's beautiful roses with bile and minced sausages. She stepped back in alarm and put her hand over her mouth in disgust. Suddenly the drizzle turned to rain that fell thick and heavy, pounding onto her silk dress and seeping through to her skin. She cowered her head, not knowing whether to leave him in the flowerbed and run for cover or stay with him. When she heard her name echo across the garden she turned her attention away from the grunting bush in relief. It was Sam.

'Federica!' he shouted. Federica strained her eyes to see Sam running towards her through the deluge. 'Federica. Are you all right?' he asked, jogging up to her. His white shirt was so wet it stuck to his skin like paper revealing beneath it the colour of his flesh. His blond hair was dripping over his face, but his smile was broad as if he enjoyed the drama the rain brought with it.

'What?' she stammered, blinking at him in confusion.

'Hester said you'd been dragged away by a drunkard,' he said, catching his breath. Federica pointed into the bush. 'Good God!' he exclaimed, putting a hand over his nose. 'Let's get out of here. He'll sober up by himself,' he declared, taking her by the hand and leading her off in the opposite direction of the tent.

'Where are we going?' she shouted as she hurried to keep up with him in her fragile heels.

'Far away from that dreadful party,' he replied in disgust. 'You haven't been enjoying it, I've been watching you.' Federica's belly shuddered with pleasure at the thought of him watching her, at the thought of him noticing her. She was grateful that the night hid her burning cheeks as well as her running mascara. When he opened the door to the barn they crept into the darkness. She heard him shuffle about with the latch and smelt the scent of warm hay and cut grass. Seconds later he flicked his lighter and lit a candle.

'I've never been in here before,' she said, casting her eyes about her curiously.

'I come in here all the time. Especially at night because there's a family of wild ducks who live here. That's why I don't use the light. It'll scare them away. I keep a candle so I can observe them.'

'A family of ducks. Are you serious?' she said.

'Come,' he whispered, taking her by the hand. 'I'll show you.'

Sam led her slowly over the floor that was covered in golden sticks of straw, which caught the light and glittered. The barn was used for storing grain and hay for the animals and logs for the house fires. The sound of rain rattled on the roof, but inside it was warm and dry. Without making any noise they climbed onto the bales, crouched down and peered over to where the family of ducks sat comfortably in a warm bed of feathers. The ducklings were all asleep, oblivious to the strange creatures who watched them quietly, while the mother, cautious yet fearless, sat unmoving with her black eyes open and alert. Sam grinned at Federica who smiled back in delight. Neither spoke, they just watched without allowing the sound of syllables to ruin the moment.

When Sam leant over and kissed her, Federica was taken completely by surprise. His hand held her by the back of her neck and his lips kissed her stunned lips before drawing away and looking into her face for her reaction. She looked petrified.

'Didn't you like it?' he asked softly. Federica tried to speak but the words didn't form as she had hoped. 'Would you like me to kiss you again?' She nodded mutely, overwhelmed by the closeness of his body. He placed his mouth on hers again, tracing her lips with his, feeling her skin without tasting it. She sat rigidly, too afraid to move, unsure of what to do. As if sensing her discomfort he pulled away and stroked his fingers through her hair that was wet from the rain and hanging over her face.

'Is this the first time?' he asked.

'Yes,' she replied hoarsely.

Sam smiled with tenderness. 'The first time is always a bit frightening. I remember mine,' he said. 'It's worse for a boy because you're supposed to know what you're doing.'

'How did you know what to do?' she asked in an attempt to make conversation but all she could think about was the sensation of his lips on hers and the fearful anticipation of him doing it again.

'Instinct,' he said simply, taking off his glasses. Then he looked at her with an intensity that made her heart lurch and ran his hand down the slope of her neck. 'Look, close your eyes. Don't be shy. Listen to your senses not your mind that's whirring around asking what's going on. Kissing is meant to be pleasurable not uncomfortable. Just relax and concentrate on what your body's feeling. Don't let yourself get distracted by your fears. I'm not judging you, just enjoying you.' Federica giggled nervously. 'Close your eyes, go on,' he insisted. Federica giggled again, then closed her eyes expectantly. Her stomach flinched as she felt his lips on her skin, kissing her jawbone, the muscle below the ear, her temples and her eyes. As much as she tried to detach her mind, she couldn't allow herself to bask in the pleasure of her senses as he had suggested for fear of letting go and looking foolish. She could smell the spice of his aftershave mixed with the natural male scent of his body and she wanted to pinch herself to make sure it was really happening. Then, just when she thought her mind would ruin so magic a moment, his lips fell onto her mouth again, opened and ceased the frenetic racing of her thoughts. She tasted the wine on his tongue and felt his rough chin against hers. Aware only of the sensual aching of her limbs she responded instinctively. He wrapped his arms around her body and drew her against him. There in the flickering candlelight of the barn her whole being stirred with the flowering of spring.

Chapter 26

Helena returned home to find a note on the kitchen table from Arthur.

Gone to the cinema with Hal, see you later. Love Arturo.

She opened the fridge, took out a can of Coca-Cola and a plate of cold meat and sat down to eat alone. She glanced at the clock on the wall and wondered how Federica was doing at the party. She had been too distracted with her new husband and son to notice the ripening of her daughter. In the past year Federica had quietly begun to metamorphose, emerging from her chrysalis as a lucid young woman, with deep melancholic eyes and the shy smile of a child uncomfortable with the shedding of her girlhood. On one hand she was capable, sensible and independent, yet Helena recognized in her a growing neediness and insecurity because those were the traits she had inherited from her. She ate her meat with little enthusiasm. The resplendent image of Federica in her party dress cast a shadow of regret over her heart that she was unable to shake off. She tried not to think of Ramon, but his image surfaced in her thoughts like a buoy on the sea. There he floated, unwilling to leave. His coal-black eyes bore into her inquiringly and she could almost hear him asking her if she was happy.

She wasn't as happy as she had expected to be. Arthur was good to her and she was deeply fond of him. He was a saint, putting up with her changing moods and impatience with the kindly smile of a doting father. He was everything that Ramon was not. He was unselfish, tolerant, non-judgemental, yet he lacked the charisma, the passion and the drama of Ramon. With Arthur she still yearned for something more. She wished he were better looking, thinner, less clumsy. The jolly bounce in his stride irritated her and she longed for him to hold himself back rather than rushing up to people like an over-enthusiastic Labrador. His ebullience grated. She was afraid to dwell too long on the first few years of her marriage with Ramon because nothing in the world could compete with that all-consuming joy and sense of fulfilment. In Federica she saw the reflection of the girl she had once been. Flawless, like a piece of virgin paper waiting for someone to paint it with love. She thought of her own sheet of paper and what life had imprinted upon it, so many colours, but she didn't have the courage to look deep enough to notice that most of the ugly colours were of her own making.

When Toby arrived at Pickthistle Manor the following morning to collect Federica, he found her radiant face smiling out at him from Hester's bedroom window. She ran down the stairs and threw herself into his arms. 'It was the best party ever!' she enthused, barely able to disguise the smile of a satisfied woman. She had intended to keep her midnight kisses with Sam a secret but once she was alone in the car with her uncle the words came spilling out as if she had no control over them. 'He took me into a barn and kissed me. It was so romantic,' she sighed, fanning her face with the AA manual. 'It was raining outside, but warm inside with the smell of hay. He lit a candle and showed me a nest of sleeping ducks. He was so sweet. We talked all night. He was so understanding and kind, not like those awful oafs I danced with. Sam rescued me like he did that day in the lake. I can't imagine what he sees in me, though.'

Toby smiled a little nervously. He didn't imagine someone of Sam's age would want a long-term relationship with a girl of Federica's, and he knew what she would be hoping for.

'I know what he sees in you, Fede. You're a beautiful young woman. It doesn't surprise me at all that he thinks you're wonderful.'

'What will happen now?' she asked.

Toby sighed and stared ahead of him.

'Don't expect too much, sweetheart,' he said, not wanting to dampen her excitement nor allow it to fly to fanciful heights.

'What do you mean?'

'He's a lot older than you. Just don't expect too much, then if he wants to be with you it will be a bonus.'

'Oh, all right.' She smiled happily, rolling down the window. 'I'll see him up at the manor anyway. Hester's asked me up for tea this afternoon.'

'Good,' said Toby.

'Don't worry, I'll bicycle. The exercise will make me glow.'

'You're glowing already,' Toby chuckled.

Arthur, Helena and Hal came over for a barbeque lunch to hear how the party had gone. The rain had cleansed the sky during the night and it now shone with renewed brightness and clarity. Federica managed to tell her mother and stepfather enough about the party to satisfy their curiosity, without mentioning her tryst with Sam. Toby winked at her and grinned mischievously, silently promising to keep her secret. Arthur, Hal and Julian played croquet on the lawn while Helena sat in the shade drinking Pimms. Federica was too distracted to notice the strain that had become ingrained in her mother's features and skipped off for a walk with Rasta. Toby was never too distracted to notice his sister's moods and joined her at the table. 'Fede's happy,' he said.

'Yes, she is,' Helena replied flatly. 'It's all thanks to you and Julian. I think it's done her good living with a couple of men.'

'She still misses her father though,' he said, pouring himself a cup of coffee. 'I sometimes catch her playing with that butterfly box of hers. You know she keeps all his letters in there.'

'I know. Tragic, isn't it?' said Helena bitterly.

'It's only natural.'

'It's not natural to leave your family for years though, is it?'

'No, it's not.'

'It's not natural for a child to live with her uncle either. Not when her mother is just down the road.'

'Is that why you're depressed?' he asked sympathetically.

'Oh, I don't know.' She sighed. 'I feel I've cocked up. I tore them away from their father, their country, their grandparents. I married again, someone Federica doesn't like. So I let her live somewhere else so that she can be near her friends. Is that natural?'

Toby touched her hand that rested on the table beside her glass. 'Dad ignores Julian and refuses to give his own daughter away at her wedding because he can't face his son's lover. He sacrifices his relationship with his son because of his sexual persuasion – that's not natural either,' he said and smiled with empathy. 'It doesn't matter what's natural and what isn't. It's all a matter of opinion anyway. If Federica's happy with us, it's natural. If Hal is happy with you and Arthur, that's natural too. Fede and Hal see each other enough. They feel like brother and sister. Imagine, some people send their children away to boarding school for years. Is that natural?'

'I suppose you're right,' she conceded gratefully.

'But that's not what's bothering you,' he ventured quietly, glancing across the lawn at Arthur who had just hit his red ball through the hoop and was flapping his arms about in delight, like a fat penguin.

Helena laughed cynically. 'You know me too well,' she said.

'I know.'

'At times like this I wish I hadn't given up smoking.' She sighed, filling her glass. 'I'm content, Toby. Arthur's good to me. He looks after me. Does everything for me. He's the opposite of Ramon who was a selfish shit.'

'But you still love that selfish shit,' said Toby.

'I wouldn't use the word "love",' she interjected quickly, lowering her eyes that burned when she blinked.

'But Arthur doesn't do it for you.'

'Arthur,' she sighed in resignation. 'Arthur isn't enough.' Toby looked at his sister pensively. She shook her head. 'But I'm stuck. That's it. I've made my choice. Look how much Hal adores him. They've really bonded, it's lovely.'

'Helena, we all have to compromise in life. You're unlikely to get the qualities you like in Ramon and those you like in Arthur rolled into one man. It just won't happen.'

'But I didn't want to leave Ramon in the first place,' she whispered, looking at her brother steadily.

'What do you mean?' he asked slowly, hoping he had misheard her.

'I didn't think he'd let me go.' Her eyes glistened with tears.

'God, Helena,' he gasped, shaking his head.

'Once I'd started I couldn't back out. I had to go the whole way. Then . . .' She hesitated as if barely able to divulge the depravity of her secret.

'Then what?'

'Then, I married Arthur because the idea of it infuriated Ramon. I could see it in his eyes. I was hurting him and it felt good.' She drained her glass. 'Am I evil?'

'Not evil, Helena, but very misguided.'

'Don't tell anyone,' she said firmly.

'I won't,' he promised. 'But by God you've got yourself into one hell of a mess.'

She nodded bleakly. 'And there's no one to tidy it up for me,' she said, and pulled a thin smile.

Federica returned from her walk and went straight to her room where she lay down on the bed and closed her eyes. She mentally replayed the scenes of the night before, rewinding them over and over again, enjoying his kisses and caresses as if for the first time. They had sat in the trembling light of the candle and talked until the music from the party had ceased to reverberate through the rain and the sound of cars and departing guests had faded into the night. Federica had sat in his arms and allowed him into the secret halls of her mind. She had told him about the butterfly box, the story of Topahuay and her father's letters, which she re-read whenever she felt sad. With Sam she had found forgotten memories hidden behind the clutter of her present life, such as the time she had found a dead fish on the beach in Viña and her father had taught her about death. He had picked up a shell and sitting down with her on the sand he had explained that when a creature dies it sheds shells, its fins, its body and floats up into the sky to be with God. He had then made a pendant out of the shell and hung it about her neck. 'You see the shell isn't important, it's the spirit within that matters and cannot be destroyed,' he had said, but it was only later when she was older that she understood what he meant.

Sam listened intently to her, stroking her hair, amused by

some of her stories, moved by others. 'You're very special, Fede,' he said wistfully, kissing her temple.

'What do you mean by "special"?'

'Well, you're just different. I think you've lived more than other girls of your age. '"Experience maketh man",' he quoted, 'and you've experienced more than most women twice your age. I can see it in those big sad eyes of yours.' He laughed, kissing her temple again. 'You need someone to look after you.'

Federica snuggled up against his body and felt for the first time in many years the same sensation of security that she had felt in the arms of her father. 'I wish I was older,' she sighed. 'Independent, not having to go to school.'

'You haven't got long now.'

'You're lucky, you're in London. You'll never have to do anything you don't want to ever again.'

'That's not true. We always have to do things we don't want to do. I'd rather live here in Polperro for a start.'

'Really?'

'Yes, I'm not a Londoner at all. But I'm not ready to "bow out" yet.'

'What's your dream?' she asked curiously.

'A cottage overlooking the sea, dogs, a pig perhaps, a family, an extensive library and a long list of bestsellers behind me.'

She laughed. 'A pig?'

'Absolutely, a cottage isn't complete without a pig.' He chuckled. 'What's yours then?'

'I'd like to take photographs and travel the world,' she declared, then added, 'and I'd like to return some day to Cachagua. I don't know why, but I miss my grandparents' house more than I miss my own.'

'I'm sure one day you will.'

'I'd also like to live in London, be very rich and famous like my father.'

'Well, you'll probably succeed there too,' he said. 'Or you'll achieve your dreams and realize that they were empty vessels all along.'

'"You can teach people knowledge, but wisdom, dear boy, has to be learned through experience,"' said Federica in Nuno's clipped Italian accent.

Sam laughed. 'So you do listen to what old Nuno has to say,' he exclaimed in admiration.

'I can't help it, he repeats everything so many times his sayings get ingrained.'

'And a good thing too. You won't ever meet anyone wiser than him.'

Federica lay on her bed and smiled as she recalled their conversation. She had sat in his arms until her clothes had dried and the gentle light of dawn seeped in through the cracks in the barn, like mist announcing the beginning of day. They had talked like old friends and she had discarded her inhibitions with each caress and her fears with each kiss. When she had crept into Hester's room she had been unable to sleep. All she could do was think of Sam. She had always known in her heart that Sam was meant for her.

Toby and Julian were sitting outside on the terrace reading the papers and commenting on the issues of the day when Federica skipped downstairs, ready to bicycle up to Pickthistle Manor. The house was now quiet as Helena had left with Arthur and Hal to have tea with her parents. Toby put the paper down and scrutinized her.

'Well?' she asked. 'Do I look all right?'

He nodded thoughtfully. 'You look pretty good to me,' he said smiling, removing the square-shaped glasses that gave him the look of a seventies singer-songwriter.

'Well, actually, I'm not so sure you don't look as if you've made too much effort,' said Julian, rubbing his chin.

'Really?' she asked, looking down at her jeans and pumps.

'Darling, she looks wonderful,' Toby insisted.

But Julian shook his head. 'No, no,' he muttered. 'Put on your trainers instead of those pumps, I think that's what it is. You don't want to look like you're trying.'

Federica ran off upstairs, appearing two minutes later in a pair of white gym shoes.

'Darling, you're right,' said Toby, impressed.

'I'm not a photographer for nothing,' Julian replied, tapping his cheekbone with his finger and raising his eyebrows. 'You have to have a good eye.'

'Sweetheart, you look very cool,' said Toby. 'Have fun and behave. Remember, he's much older than you.'

'Be firm and say "no",' Julian added. 'Whatever he asks of you, say "no".' Federica rolled her eyes and laughed.

'It'll make him keener,' said Toby.

'Little bastard, putting his dirty paws on our Federica,' Julian muttered, grinning at her.

'I want to hear you say it, sweetheart,' said Toby. Federica giggled, wandering off.

'Go on!' Julian shouted after her. 'It's the most important word in a woman's vocabulary.'

'NO!' she retorted, turning the corner.

Toby shrugged at Julian. They were both thinking the same thing. They'd be there for her when it all ended badly.

Federica cycled up the winding lanes lined with cow-parsley and buttercups, humming to herself with gusto. When she turned the corner into the drive the first thing she noticed was the space left by the absence of Sam's car. She stopped humming and a frown replaced the smoothness of her brow. She leant the bike against the wall of the house and ran in.

During the summer months when the weather was good Ingrid liked all the doors to be open so that the scents of the garden and the roses that covered the walls of the house would fill the rooms with the fertile fragrances of nature. It also allowed the various animals rescued by Hester to come and go freely without having to ask to be let out. The swallows that always nested in the porch year after year dived in through the open windows and the odd brave mouse crept into the kitchen to satisfy his greed in the dog bowls. Federica walked through the rooms to the lawn where the tent was being dismantled by an army of tanned men in baseball caps and khaki shorts. She found Hester and Molly lying on the grass still in their dressing gowns, drinking cups of coffee.

'Hi, Fede,' said Hester wearily, peering at her over her dark glasses.

'We can't be bothered to get dressed,' said Molly. 'We're knackered.'

'It was a wonderful party, though,' Fede said, casting her eye about for Sam.

'Great party,' said Hester. 'Come and join us.' Federica sat down on the grass and played with the daisies distractedly.

'You look sickeningly well for someone who was up all night,' said Molly, looking her up and down.

'Whom did you disappear with for so long? I didn't even hear you come to bed,' said Hester, rubbing her red eyes.

'No one very exciting, I'm afraid,' Federica muttered, doing her best to dissemble.

'Like hell. You're blushing,' Molly said sharply.

'Did he kiss you?'

'No, no. We just talked,' she insisted lamely.

'Talked?' Molly scoffed. 'People don't "talk" at parties, they snog.'

'Well, I'm afraid we talked.'

'What about?' Hester asked, screwing up her nose.

'He talked about himself,' said Federica casually. 'Actually he was sick in the bushes, which wasn't very nice. Then it started to pour with rain so we ran into the barn and sat in there out of the rain. I listened to him until about four in the morning.'

'Poor old you. You missed your own party,' said Hester. 'Was he very boring?'

'Dreadfully,' Federica replied.

Molly looked at her suspiciously. 'Don't be so gullible, Hester,' she said, grinning at Federica. 'I don't believe you for a moment.'

'Molly, she won't have kissed someone just after they were sick.'

'Perhaps he wasn't sick,' said Molly, raising an eyebrow.

'Look, it really doesn't matter,' said Federica. 'What about you?'

Hester giggled. 'I snogged two people,' she said. 'But Nuno caught me the second time and insisted on dancing with me. You know he's a wonderful dancer, you'd be surprised.'

'He hasn't surfaced today, must be hung over,' Molly laughed. 'Mum's on the beach painting, she thought it was a lovely party even though her orchids were all trampled on and Joe Hornish drove his bike across the lawn in the rain leaving marks all over it. Dad's livid and says he'll pay not to have a party next time.'

'And the policemen?' Federica dared to ask, lowering her face to hide her eyes lest they give her away.

'Oh, Sam's gone back to London with Ben,' Hester said.

'Oh,' said Federica, forcing a smile.

'I think he's had enough of drunk sixteen-year-olds to last him a lifetime,' said Molly.

Federica's mind flooded with gloom. Her cheeks flushed with disappointment as she felt once again that clawing sense of rejection. He hadn't even waited to say goodbye. Did the night before mean nothing to him at all? When she had stayed long enough to leave without causing suspicion she rode her bicycle home through copious tears and aching sobs that opened up the old wound her father had made all those years ago. When she arrived back at the cottage she ran up to her room and flung herself on her bed in despair. She had truly believed he loved her, as she had believed her father had loved her too. She opened the butterfly box and recalled with shame how she had allowed him to share her deepest secrets, invited him into her private world, only to discover that he wasn't really very interested. It was a painful awakening.

When Toby arrived back from the sea he saw Federica's bicycle carelessly thrown onto the gravel and sensed that something was wrong. He ran upstairs to find her crying over the letters from her father. Gathering her into his arms he didn't need to ask what had happened. He knew. It was exactly as he had feared.

'Everyone I get close to runs away,' she whispered, wiping her tears on her uncle's jersey.

'That's not true,' he insisted. 'We'll always be here for you.'

'He's just like Papa. Why do they have to leave without a word? I feel so worthless.'

'They don't deserve you, Fede. You're so much better than they are.'

'But I love Sam,' she wailed.

'Darling girl, you're so young and your love is so innocent.'

'No it isn't. I truly love him.'

'He's young too, Fede. What could you expect? He'll want a relationship one day, but right now he's enjoying his freedom. Sweetheart, you're still at school.'

She looked up at him with swollen eyes. 'But I don't want anyone else but him,' she explained. 'There's no one in the world like Sam.'

'I know,' he soothed. 'You just have to be patient. You've both got a lot of growing up to do. It was highly irresponsible of him to raise your hopes. He must know how you feel.'

'He's so sweet and kind,' she said. 'He would never hurt me on purpose.'

'Of course he wouldn't. You just have different expectations, that's all. I just hate to see you hurt, I'd like to box his ears.'

'I wouldn't let you.' She smiled sadly.

'You're going to be okay, Fede,' he said, and squeezed her affectionately.

But at that moment she didn't think her heart would ever recover.

That evening Federica walked along the cliff-tops with Rasta. Her recollections of the night before had now been soiled. She felt nothing but resentment and self-pity. Everywhere she looked she saw Sam; in the pink clouds that caught the sunset to the waves that washed over the rocks in their eternal battle to wear them down. The familiar feeling of emptiness gnawed at her heart, reminding her of the unhappy times in her life when her love had been thrown back at her. She feared she might never have the courage to love again. Sitting on the grass she pulled Rasta against her and buried her face in his damp fur. Then she threw her wishes into the sea and watched them sink.

Chapter 27

Sam drove up the motorway while Ben snored and dribbled in the passenger seat. He listened to the radio for a while but soon found his mind wandering back through the night until he found himself in the barn with Federica and he was awash with guilt. What had he been thinking of? A few hours of self-indulgence was hardly worth the hurt that was sure to follow. He felt like a monster. That is why he had insisted they leave straight after breakfast. He didn't have the courage to tell her to her face that it had been nice, but that's all it was: a kiss in the hay. He wasn't cruel or callous. He was extremely fond of her. She had grown into a surprisingly beautiful and captivating young woman, but like a peach on the brink of ripening, he had picked her too soon. Her innocence had been too tempting to resist, and he couldn't bear the idea of someone else spoiling her. Any of those oafs at the party could have lured her into a drunken brawl in the bushes, a hurried grope in the dark, a slobbery kiss for no other reason than to boast about it later to his friends. He had seen her run out into the garden with precisely the sort of ruffian he was afraid of and had pursued her with the intention of escorting her back to the tent. His intentions had been good, even if he hadn't had the strength of character to follow them through.

What happened after that was shameful. He was nine years her senior with enough experience to know what a first kiss can do to a girl like Federica. But there in the golden light of the candle, enveloped in the sweet smells of nature, she had looked at him with such adoration and such longing that he had found the seat of his own longing momentarily disturbed. Surprised by his sudden response to a girl he had known since childhood, he was at once disarmed and unprepared. His impulses responded to his instincts and before he had time to listen to the muffled voice of his reasoning he had kissed her. At first she had been awkward and afraid, fighting her own inner battles in an effort to overcome her shyness. But then she had finally surrendered to the new sensations that stirred her loins. Charmed by her innocence he had enjoyed caressing away her fears and watching her conquered by her senses. A kiss is never again so sweet as that first time – that first small awakening and his heart heaved with remorse.

He watched the sun burn away the morning mists and settle into a splendid summer's day, causing the freshly washed countryside to glitter about him. He switched off the radio and glanced across at his friend whose body was recovering in sleep from the alcohol and debauchery of the night before. Sam was happy to be left alone with his thoughts, however much they tormented him. He had listened to Ben's crowing enough. It made him feel even more ashamed; was he no better than him? He firmly reassured himself that he was better than Ben. While Ben was kissing and groping his way around the tent, he had enjoyed a tender moment with a dear friend. Yes, a dear friend. It had been sweet and touching and anyhow, it wasn't just about the kiss. They had talked until dawn, about anything and everything, and were truly fond of each other. But she was too young. It was as simple as that. So why couldn't he do the decent thing and tell her?

Sam struggled with his conscience all the way up to London. Stopping en route for petrol he bought the papers and a packet of chocolate raisins and woke up his friend.

He was ready to talk. He needed distracting. 'So,' he said, climbing back into the car and starting it up. 'Are you feeling any better?'

'I'm feeling like shit,' Ben replied, and yawned. 'But it was worth it. Still, I'm looking forward to getting back to the big smoke. I've had enough frigid babes for the time being. There's only so much fun to be had in kindergarten. Know what I mean? I'm ready for the university of life!' He chortled, plunging his hand into the packet of chocolate raisins.

Sam rolled his eyes and switched on the radio. 'Quite,' he agreed flatly. 'The university of life.'

Sam quickly forgot his guilty qualms about Federica as he lost himself in his London life. He travelled to the City every morning by tube, put as little effort into his work as possible, then returned home in the evenings to go out with his friends. Every now and then he would pick up a girl, make love before supper then see her off before bedtime. The thought of waking up to a stray in his bed repelled him. He needed sex like he needed to eat, but once the meal was over the sight of the dirty plate was most unattractive. He never remembered their names and rarely their faces, yet his appetite never waned. Tenderness was an emotion he had left in the barn, along with the family of ducks and the smoking candle. No one managed to stir his heart or unsettle his emotions, which remained cool and aloof and seemingly impenetrable.

In the autumn, when he finally returned home to Polperro, he hid in Nuno's study discussing Balzac's *Cousin Bette*, afraid that Federica might cycle up to see Hester and look at him with those large, sad eyes of hers, and fill him once again with remorse. He wanted to tell Nuno but was too ashamed to mention it. So he skulked about the house filling it with his icy presence.

'Goodness me, Sam,' Molly sighed, 'you're a miserable sight this weekend. What's the matter?'

'Absolutely nothing,' he replied flatly.

'You could have fooled me,' she sniffed, watching him warily. 'Girl trouble, I can tell,' she added with a grin.

'I don't encounter trouble in that department,' he replied loftily.

'Well, why don't you take Trotsky out for a walk or something, you've got that horrid London colour'.

'What's Hester up to?' he asked casually.

'I don't know,' she shrugged, 'but I'm going to watch a video.'

'Which one are you going to see?'

'"An Affair to Remember",' she said happily, opening the box.

'Not that old chestnut again.' He laughed.

'I adore it. Men just aren't made that way any more.'

'Cary Grant's far too smooth for you, Mol, I thought you preferred them rough.'

'Only as a compromise,' she retorted. 'If a Cary Grant swept me off my feet I'd never look at another bricklayer again!'

Sam chuckled and wandered out of the room whistling for Trotsky.

It was windy up on the cliffs, but it felt good to have the sea breeze on his face. At least out of the house he could avoid bumping into Federica. He swung his arms as he walked, wrapped in Nuno's sheepskin coat, patting the dog every now and then as he rushed back and forth sniffing the dormant earth for sleeping rabbits. He reflected on his work, which he loathed, and the City, which he also loathed, and fantasized about making a home in Polperro one day. London was all very well for a while, but his heart lay in the countryside and his soul belonged to the sea, not to the dusty streets of a sterile town. He looked out over the choppy waves and breathed in the salt, filling up his lungs with memories of his childhood. What he wanted to do more than anything was to write.

Nuno was more than encouraging. He told him firmly that he was wasting his unique creativity in some impersonal bank, doing a job more suited to a halfwit. 'You have imagination, dear boy, and talent, it gives me great pain to see it in restless hibernation.' He was right, of course. But there was something holding him back. Talent was all very well if one knew where to channel it. But Sam didn't know what to write about.

With that gloomy thought, he lifted his eyes. He noticed two small figures in the distance, slowly making their way towards him. Suddenly gripped with panic he was about to turn and walk the other way when one of them waved. She persisted until he responded with an unenthusiastic flap of his hand. It was Hester and Federica and there was no avoiding them.

As they came closer his heart raced with apprehension. He would rather ignore her but that would be unkind. He would have to try to act as if nothing had happened. He hoped she hadn't told Hester.

'Hi, Sam,' his sister shouted through the wind. Rasta bounded up with exuberance and began to frolic about with Trotsky. That enabled Sam to divert his attention to the dogs, calling them and patting them, crouching down on his haunches to cuddle the Labrador.

'Hi, Sam,' said Federica.

He raised his eyes reluctantly and forced a weak smile. Her face was red from exertion and her eyes sparkled from the cold. She was obviously making an effort to dissemble as well. He welcomed her sophistication and his gloom lifted.

'How are you, Federica?' he asked, standing up and look-ing down at her earnest face.

'Fine thanks,' she replied, putting her hands in her pockets and shuffling her feet to keep warm.

'Cold, isn't it?' he said.

'It's flipping freezing out here,' Hester complained. 'But it's good for the skin,' she added. 'It'll make us glow.'

'You're both glowing rather nicely already.' He chuckled.

'Good,' she enthused. 'Told you, Fede.' Federica smiled shyly but said nothing.

'How's school?' he asked her, but Hester interrupted and answered for her friend.

'We're being made to study so hard my brain's gone on strike.' She giggled.

'"Knowledge is power",' Sam quoted, glancing at Federica who was watching the dogs.

'Knowledge is boring,' Hester moaned. 'Anyway, it's better to keep walking. Do you want to join us?' she asked. Federica looked at him hopefully and he heard himself saying that he'd love to.

'The dogs are happier together,' Hester said. 'I defy you to part them, look they're having such fun!'

They watched Rasta and Trotsky race after a slim hare, who zigzagged across a field as if making a mockery of their stumbling efforts to catch him. They all laughed when the dogs returned with their tongues hanging out and their heavy tails wagging to conceal their embarrassment.

'These two spend far too much time on sofas,' Sam exclaimed.

Federica grinned. 'And too much time with their mouths full of biscuits I should imagine,' she said.

'I don't think they'd know what to do if they managed to catch it,' said Hester, patting Trotsky who nudged his face against her hip. 'Still, he's wanting praise for the effort.'

'They can certainly have that,' Sam laughed, stroking Rasta's sleek back as he passed. It was a fleeting moment when Federica's hand brushed Sam's as she too reached out to touch her dog, but it felt like an age. They both withdrew with speed, each pretending that they hadn't noticed, when in fact their skin burned from the contact.

Federica could barely look at Sam after that, her cheeks stung more from awkwardness than from the cold and she was afraid he might notice. She thrust her scalded hand into her pocket where it tingled with a strange pleasure. She took care not to walk too close in case their bodies jostled together by mistake and kept her eyes fixed in front of her. She was relieved that Hester was talkative because she dominated the conversation, chatting about everything but noticing nothing. Sam tried to include Federica but her words were swallowed up by the enthusiasm of her friend who answered for her, seemingly out of habit. As they reached the house he was beginning to find his sister's dominance tiresome. Federica had barely said a word. He was disappointed. He was surprised to find that he was even more disappointed when she said she had to go.

'But don't you want any tea?' he asked, hovering by the front door while Hester struggled out of her boots in the porch.

Federica shook her head. 'I have to get back to Toby's, Mama's coming to pick me up at four,' she explained.

'Oh, I forgot, you spend weekends with your mother, don't you?'

'Yes,' she replied. 'Most weekends.'

'Well, why don't I drive you back?' he suggested to his own amazement.

'Really, I'm happy to cycle,' she protested.

'It's cold and anyhow, it's getting dark,' he argued, looking out at the evening sky that balanced unsteadily between afternoon and dusk. 'Rasta can sit in the back and I'll put your bike in the boot. Simple!'

'See you at school, Fede,' said Hester to her friend before disappearing into the hall and closing the door behind her.

Federica had no choice. Rasta was already sitting in the back of Sam's Deux Chevaux, steaming up the windows with his hot breath.

Federica climbed into the front seat and waited for Sam to finish securing the bike. She rubbed her hands together nervously. Catching sight of her mottled face and wispy hair in the wing mirror, she did her best to tidy herself up while he wasn't looking. She listened for his footsteps but all she could hear was the rhythmic panting of her dog behind her.

Sam closed the boot as far as it could go then walked around the car to the door. He had no idea what he was going to talk to her about, or why he had suggested he take her in the first place. She seemed to have a knack of undermining his better judgement. He climbed in and closed the door with a slam. 'I bet Rasta doesn't often travel first class,' he joked, lightening the atmosphere.

Federica chuckled. 'He's usually a foot soldier,' she replied. 'I just hope you haven't raised his standards too high or he'll never want to travel any other way.'

'Well, we won't give him any extras then,' he said. 'That's no whisky and no duty free.' They both laughed while Rasta panted in the back.

The car left the drive and bounced down the lane. The evening sky was suddenly transformed into an almost fluorescent flamingo pink as the sun began to set, catching her parting rays on the feathery clouds as she bade farewell to the day. They both looked out on it with wonder.

'It's beautiful,' Federica sighed dreamily.

'It's as if Nature sometimes feels she needs to protest her supremacy and show us all how powerful she can be,' said Sam, slowing down the car.

'It's always so fleeting.'

'I know, a golden moment and then it's gone. But that's what makes it so magical. Sometimes things are more special *because* they're transient.'

'A rare glimpse of Heaven,' she said, unwittingly recalling their stolen kisses in the barn. She lowered her eyes and felt the heat on her face.

'Look how it's washed all the fields with orange,' he exclaimed, drawing the car into the side of the lane. 'I have a sudden desire to walk in it, come on.'

Federica followed him out into the field. Without speaking they strode up the hill to walk in the rare golden light. 'Your face is now orange,' he laughed, looking down at his golden fingers.

'So is yours. Talk about glowing!'

'Let's go to the top. We'll be able to see the effect it has on the sea.' Then he allowed his impulses to once more take control. He took her cold hand in his and led her up to the summit. She felt her heart inflate like a hot air balloon and literally lift her feet off the ground. She was unable to contain the smile which alighted across her entire face. When they arrived at the top they were able to appreciate the full scale of Nature's magnificence. The sea was oddly calm, stretching out to the horizon beneath a canopy of gold.

Neither spoke. They just stood in the tender light and watched the heavenly display take place about them. It was as spellbinding as it was transitory. Once the sun disappeared behind them to entertain another shore they were suddenly plunged into shadow. With the shadow came the drop in temperature. Federica shivered.

'Cold?' he asked, squeezing her hand.

She nodded. 'But it was worth it,' she said, dazed with happiness.

'It certainly was. You don't often get to see a sky like that. I'm glad I shared it with you.' He looked at her with affection.

She caught her breath and gazed at him in bewilderment. His warmth was unexpected. In the aching silence of the last few months she had longed to hear such words. She had dreamed that she would find herself once more alone with him, but as the months had rolled on she had doubted such a moment would ever come again. Now she looked into his face, trying to read his intentions in his features. But he only grinned back at her, giving nothing away.

'Come, you'll be late for your mother and I'll be in terrible trouble,' he said at last, dropping her hand and thrusting his into the pockets of his coat to keep warm. Disappointed she followed him down the hill to the car.

It was only when they got back to the lane that Federica realized they had completely forgotten Rasta. 'I don't believe it!' she wailed. 'Poor darling Rasta. He must have been going out of his mind with frustration watching us up there on the hill.'

'I'm so sorry,' said Sam, shaking his head. 'I was so distracted by the sunset he completely slipped my mind.'

'And mine.'

'Do you think he'll forgive us?' he said and grinned at her.

Federica smiled back. 'I think he will if you promise you won't ever forget him again,' she replied, climbing in. Rasta's tail wagged as much as it was able in such a confined space and he dribbled all the way down the back of the seat in his excitement to see them again.

'I think I'll pay for it,' Sam said, looking at the dog's slobber as it ran in a healthy stream down the leather.

'Oh dear, you're going to wish you had taken him,' she laughed.

'I'm afraid, Rasta, that this was a moment for me and your mother *only*,' he said, starting the engine. 'You can come next time.'

Federica's spirits lifted at the thought that there might be another time. He may not have kissed her but he had certainly made her feel that she was special. That he cared. When he dropped her off at her uncle's house he leant over and kissed her softly on her cheek. She was sure he lingered there longer than was normal.

'See you soon,' he said, pulling away.

'Thanks, Sam, I really enjoyed that,' she replied seriously. 'So did Rasta,' she added for fear of sounding too sentimental.

'So did I,' he agreed. He helped her with her bicycle while she opened the door for Rasta, who leapt out and immediately cocked his leg on the steaming tyre. They both laughed and Sam rolled his eyes. 'How much longer do I have to go on paying for my negligence?' he joked.

Federica shrugged.

'You take care now,' he said before climbing back into the car.

Federica watched him go and waved until he turned out of the driveway and disappeared down the lane.

PART THREE

Chapter 28

London, Autumn 1994

'Life would be ever so simple for all of us if robbers walked into the shop in black and white striped prison outfits with sacks of stolen goods slung over their backs,' said Nigel Dalby, the security officer, who sat on the desk with one foot perched up on a chair and two sharp blue eyes skipping eagerly from one face to the other. He spoke with a strong Yorkshire accent and had a head that was too small for the rest of his body, like an urban sloth. Federica noticed that although he spoke to eight new members of staff his eyes kept homing back to her. 'But they don't stand out like that, do they? And they don't have big signs on their foreheads saying "I'm a robber" either.' He laughed at his joke and slapped his thigh. Federica's eyes were drawn to the clearly defined bulge that strained against his tight trousers. Embarrassed that her attention had somehow drifted there she focused on his face and tried to concentrate on the lecture.

'They look like you and me. In a minute I'm going to show you a video of real-life shoplifters so that you can see how clever they are. You all have eyes – I'm asking you to use them. You must always be on guard. In a shop like this thousands of pounds are stolen every year by crafty shoplifters.' He clicked his tongue and pointed two fingers into his eyes. 'Use them. Be vigilant. Now, on the telephones you'll see three buttons: code A, B and C. Code A is only to be pressed if the situation is threatening. Say, for example, a man with a gun walks in and threatens you personally or your customers – this call goes directly to the police station and they can guarantee to be with us in about two minutes. Code B must be pressed if someone looks suspicious, then I'll come down the stairs and subtly follow them about the store. Code C is for assistance, a difficult customer, that sort of thing.' He licked his lips with a dry tongue and looked at Federica. 'Any questions?'

One of the boys put up his hand after a scuffle of encouragement from a friend. 'What does someone suspicious look like?' he asked, trying not to smirk.

Nigel nodded seriously. 'Good question, Simon. I'd say a man looks suspicious if he's wearing a baseball cap, unshaven, sloppily dressed, foreign.'

Federica glanced at her colleagues to see if they were as appalled as she was. They didn't seem to be.

'And in women?' asked Simon, showing off in front of the girls who smiled behind fringes of long shiny hair.

Nigel sniffed impatiently, anxious not to be made a fool of. 'God gave you good brains, that's why we've hired you. Think about it.' He clicked his tongue again and switched on the video.

Federica tried to watch the television but found her eyes drifting back to Nigel Dalby, whose long white fingers fidgeted with the remote control.

After the lecture Federica returned to the gift department on the ground floor and into a dense mist of Tiffany perfume. 'How did it go, m'darling?' asked Harriet, one of the girls who had worked on the shop floor for a couple of years. She was tall and buxom with a penchant for bright clothes and glittering jewellery. 'I'm afraid Nigel tends to love the sound of his own voice, I can see he had you in there for over an hour. Probably fancies you. He's a bit of a ladies man,' she added and laughed loudly, flicking her chestnut curls over her lime-green shoulders and pearl necklace.

'I can't imagine he has much success with the ladies,' Federica replied. 'He's only compelling because he's so odd to look at.'

'Darling girl, you'd be surprised. Though he's not Torquil Jensen, is he?' she said thickly, pursing together her cherry lips.

'Who's Torquil Jensen?' Federica asked.

'Of course, you wouldn't know who Torquil is.' Harriet's eyes shone with admiration. 'Torquil is the most gorgeous man you're ever likely to meet,' she whispered confidentially. 'He's the nephew of Mr Jensen, the old codger who owns the store, and does a terrific amount of shopping in here.'

'Have I met Mr Jensen?'

'Darling girl, you'd know if you had!' she exclaimed, playing with the pearls about her mottled neck. 'He walks around with a vast entourage of hangers-on and advisers and never talks to anyone. He communicates with his staff through his side-kicks. A little slug of a man, his nephew is a genetic miracle! The old boy rarely comes into the store. I think he sends Torquil in to spy for him. Do watch out, though, the telephones are all bugged. Mr Jensen is a control freak.'

'Really?' Federica gasped, appalled.

'Good God, yes. Don't make any personal calls, m'darling. It's not worth it. They'll sack you immediately. A few months ago Greta had a sweet, sweet girl working as her assistant. Sadly, one personal call and she was out. No explanation given. I think the staff room is bugged too, so no jokes about Mr Jensen, or the Ice Maiden for that matter.'

'The Ice Maiden?'

'Greta.' She sniffed and screwed up her nose.

'What's she like?'

Harriet fumbled with the large silk bow about her neck, pulling it loose and tying it up again.

'A horror, m'darling, an absolute horror,' she stated emphatically.

'Oh.'

'She's from Sweden and if you ask me she's never fully defrosted. But don't worry, she's cold with everyone. She says what she thinks and doesn't bother about the delivery. Torquil once took her out for a few weeks and she swanked about as if she owned the place and started referring to Mr Jensen as William. A definite no-no, believe me. Of course, it didn't last and now Torquil barely acknowledges her. My advice to you is just obey quietly and don't pick a fight with her. Just do what she says and stay out of her way. You're lucky you're so junior. She won't bother with you.' Federica smiled with relief. 'Except you are very pretty. That could be a problem.'

'Is Mr Jensen married?'

'No, bachelor. Shame with all that money. Neither's Torquil. But he always has a girlfriend in tow. You know he drives a Porsche and lives in The Little Boltons. Now, that's a grand address. My father lost all his money in Lloyds. Bloody shame, now I have to look out for a rich hubby. And to think I was once an heiress. Where do you live?'

'In Pimlico with a couple of girlfriends,' Federica replied.

'Pimlico's lovely. Pretty white stucco houses. I like that. They look much grander than they are,' she said.

No sooner had they finished talking when Greta glided down the stairs behind them. She was slim with shiny blonde hair pulled back into a chignon at the nape of her elegant neck. She wore a navy Chanel suit with gold buttons and matching navy shoes. She was much older than Federica had expected, at least forty, and although she was tall and slim she had the thin-lipped, brittle face of a deeply unhappy woman.

She strode up to Federica and looked down at her imperiously with frosty blue eyes. 'I'm sorry I haven't had the chance to meet you yet. Welcome to St John & Smithe.' She smiled only on the surface of her face, a fleeting gesture in order to be polite. 'Rule number one is that you don't stand around talking all day. There are customers to be served and it is very rude to talk to each other and ignore them. Harriet should know better.' She spoke with a slight accent, clipping her words with an icy formality. Harriet began to apologize but Greta cut her off with a snort. 'Ya, ya, she's new so it's okay,' she said briskly. As she walked off through the department to her office Harriet rolled her eyes at Federica and winked.

'Don't look so worried, m'darling, the rest of the group are real muckers,' she said, then looked at her watch. 'Good God, time for a ciggie break, see you in fifteen!'

Federica had moved to London at the end of the summer of 1994. She was eighteen years old. Inigo had bought Molly and Hester a flat to share in Belgrave Road, and they had insisted Federica come and live with them for a very low rent, as there was space for another bed in Hester's room. Molly was studying history at London University and Hester was at Saint Martin's School of Art, following in the footsteps of her mother.

Federica hadn't considered further education. She wanted to be a photographer like Julian and her father, but Helena had shuddered at the thought of her daughter leading the same nomadic life as Ramon and encouraged her to try other avenues.

'You must earn some money first and that can only be done with a proper job,' she had said. 'Once you can support yourself you can do what you like.'

Federica rarely saw Sam except in her dreams. Dreams that punctuated the long days and filled her nights with restlessness and longing. The rare times that they did meet, down at his home in Polperro or occasionally at the flat in London, he smiled at her with fondness and asked her about herself. But the promise of something more than friendship dissolved like that flamingo pink sky and left her floundering in shadow, wondering why he no longer cared. Living with Molly and Hester only fanned her infatuation and reminded her at every step of the young man who had first won her heart on the iced lake over ten years before. Occasionally he rang to speak to his sisters. If Federica answered the telephone she controlled the tremor in her voice with a will of steel and conversed as friends do, but lived off his every word until the next call as lovers do. As much as she tried to persuade herself that there was no point loving Sam and living off memories which he once shared but had most probably now forgotten, she could not control her heart. There was no one in the world like Sam.

For the first time in her life Federica experienced what it was like to be independent and she relished it. At the end of September she received her first pay cheque; seven hundred pounds. Harriet took her shopping in Knightsbridge and she spent nearly all of it on new clothes, arguing with her friend who wanted her in the same bright colours that she wore. In each shop mirror Federica assessed whether or not Sam would approve of her choice, then found herself wondering whether he ever thought of her at all. But she didn't give up – perhaps she was still too young, perhaps he was waiting for her – perhaps . . . When she appeared at work the following day she looked quite the Londoner in a short grey skirt and high-heeled shoes with her face prettily made up with mascara and face powder that Harriet had insisted she buy.

Greta sniffed jealously at her and told her not to overdo the smiling. 'You're not an advert for toothpaste, Federica, and you look much too keen, you'll frighten the customers away.'

Federica blushed to the roots of her white hair and lowered her eyes in humiliation.

'That's better,' said Greta. Then in a bid to keep her off the shop floor and hidden away she sent her down to the basement to tidy up the stockroom. 'I want it so orderly and clean I could eat my breakfast in there,' she added, stalking back into her office.

In spite of Greta's occasional rudeness Federica loved her job. She enjoyed the security it gave her and the money it paid. She laughed with Harriet and the young people who worked in the other departments swiftly became an almost extended family. The majority of the customers were pleasant and the odd male customer asked her out. But Harriet advised her not to mix business with pleasure and so she declined their offers graciously, flattered that they noticed her. But the number of hopeful men who lingered about the gift department grew as Federica's confidence grew. Exasperated, Greta banished her to the stockroom as much as possible but still they persisted.

One cold November morning Federica and Harriet were standing by the counter when a fat old gypsy shuffled in out of the winter mist, carrying a large number of grubby Tesco bags filled with what looked like more paper bags.

'This is a job for Nigel,' Federica whispered gleefully, pressing the code B button on the telephone.

Harriet giggled, 'He's going to love this one, m'darling.' She snorted. 'This woman lives on the streets and comes in here once in a while to use the bathroom.'

'How disgusting,' said Federica, screwing up her nose in repulsion.

'You think that's disgusting, she washes her bottom in the basin,' she added. 'The secret is not to tell anyone and hope that Greta uses it immediately after her.'

'Damn! Too late now,' Federica hissed, watching Nigel bound down the stairs with a predatory grimace staining his face pink. Nigel blinked three times at Federica who cast her eyes across to the gypsy who was bustling her way down the corridor that led to the Ladies' Room. Nigel deftly dodged a couple of elderly customers but didn't manage to get to the gypsy before she squeezed into the small room and locked the door behind her. Nigel pounded his fists upon the door, exclaiming loudly, 'This is the police, please will you come out of the toilet.'

To which the gypsy replied, 'Fuck off, I'm a lady!' just as Torquil Jensen strode into the store.

Greta immediately sprung out from her office and strode up to Federica. 'I have told you two countless times not to stand and gossip on the shop floor. Federica, go down to the stockroom and sort out the recent delivery of photograph frames,' she ordered.

'But there are hundreds,' Harriet protested on Federica's behalf.

'Do not talk back to me. I am your boss and I am giving Federica an order. If she doesn't have the courage to complain to me herself she might as well find another job, because I have no patience with weak people.' Then turning to Federica, 'The store room. Now.'

Federica hastily departed as Torquil approached the counter. Greta smiled at him, betraying her desperation and her unhappiness in the way her lips paled and her eyes thawed.

Torquil smiled back tightly. 'Hello, Greta,' he said, looking at her briefly before turning his attention to Harriet. 'Harriet, you look pretty today.'

Harriet swelled with pleasure. 'Awfully kind of you, Mr Jensen,' she replied buoyantly, enjoying the pain it caused

Greta in spite of the fact that she knew she'd have to pay for it later.

'Harriet, I need to start my Christmas shopping. I wonder whether you might be able to help me, when it comes to presents you're a gold medaller.'

'Of course, Mr Jensen, it would be a pleasure,' she replied, sinking into his green eyes and wishing Federica would emerge from the bowels of the store to witness her moment of glory.

'Greta, you're looking a bit pale,' he said, smiling down at her pinched face. 'You must be working too hard.'

'No, no. I am quite well,' she stammered, but her face seemed to melt like an ice cream in summer.

As Torquil and Harriet walked into the crowd of shoppers they parted reverentially, not because of Torquil's status but because of his dazzling beauty.

Greta felt the bile simmer in her stomach and slunk back into the office to lick her wounded pride.

'Fuck off! I'm a lady,' squawked the gypsy in protest.

'You are no lady,' Nigel hissed into the crack in the door, hoping that none of the other customers could hear her. 'Now I will warn you only once more, if you don't come out we're going to have to bash the door down and drag you out.'

'Can't a lady piss in peace?' she shouted. 'I have my rights. A piss is a piss, the same for a duchess as for a tramp. I ain't no duchess, but I'm a lady through and through.'

'Right, that's it. We're coming in.'

'All right, all right,' she said, opening the door. Nigel winced at the stench that followed her. 'Not even allowed to piss in peace,' she squawked as she pushed past him.

The customers grimaced as she waddled through the department, scowling at them angrily. 'I'll bet he lets you piss in peace,' she shrieked to an unsuspecting elderly lady who stood frozen to the ground with disgust. 'This joint smells like the devil's arse!' she added before disappearing into the street. The whole shop seemed to sigh with relief. Only Harriet and Torquil continued to shop oblivious to the commotion.

After a couple of hours of unpacking photograph frames and stacking them in neat piles on the shelves, Federica was pleased to see Harriet's excited face appear in the doorway. 'Darling girl, you're never going to believe it, Torquil Jensen has just been in and spent a whole two hours shopping with me,' she hissed, afraid of being overheard.

'Really!' said Federica, trying to share her excitement.

'He squashed Greta. You should have seen her face. It fell a mile. Silly cow.'

'How wonderful.'

'He is so drop dead handsome. I wish you could have seen him. He's dark and mysterious with the most beautiful green eyes that change to blue depending on what he's wearing and he was wearing a green cashmere sweater today, so they were green, like emeralds. He's so elegant. He exudes wealth and confidence. I can't believe you didn't see him. You simply can't understand.' Federica shrugged her shoulders. 'Anyway, he's bought so many things it's all been taken upstairs and you and I are going to have the honour of wrapping it up.'

'Lucky us!' said Federica sarcastically.

'You'd feel differently if you'd met him,' said Harriet sympathetically, gazing upon the piles of colour-coded frames. 'You know, I wouldn't be at all surprised if Greta sent you down here on purpose because she saw him come into the shop. He'd fancy you, he's got a thing about blondes.'

'I don't think he'd look at me, Harriet. And anyway, I wouldn't want him to. My heart pines for someone else,' she said and sat down on the stool.

'Who?' Harriet asked, leaning back against the doorframe.

'Oh, just someone I've known all my life. It's useless, though, he couldn't be less interested,' she replied and smiled up at her friend in an effort not to reveal the extent of her misery.

'You wouldn't want anyone else if you saw Torquil,' said Harriet, knowing that she would never admire another man as long as she lived. 'If Torquil marries I shall become a nun,' she added with a grin. 'Come on, I think Cinders has suffered enough in the basement.'

Federica didn't have any desire to meet Torquil Jensen. She belonged exclusively to Sam Appleby. As much as she tried to move on and attach her desire to someone else, it ached incessantly for Sam. She loved the mischievous way he grinned, the mop of golden hair that fell over his intelligent eyes, his commanding nature and his confidence. And she missed him all the time.

She spoke to her mother every other day. Helena no longer worried about Federica, who had grown into a sensible young woman, capable of looking after herself. She worried about Hal. He had never been an easy child, not like his sister, but he had always been biddable. Now he was getting into trouble at school, failing exams and acquiring an attitude that questioned everything she did and argued only for the sake of being troublesome. She mourned the loss of the child who used to cling to her and caress her with the adoring eyes of an infatuated lover. Now he scowled at her one moment and loved her the next and she found herself living her life on a permanent roller-coaster without being able to get off. He disappeared with his friends on the weekends and returned sometimes in the early hours of the morning smelling of alcohol and smoke, barely able to drag himself up the stairs and into bed.

Helena despaired. Arthur embraced her with his support and affection and demanded nothing in return. Selflessly he listened to her as she unburdened her tormented thoughts and he gave his advice wisely in spite of the fact that he knew she wouldn't heed a single word of it. She was too involved to be able to see the situation objectively. 'Ignore him, my darling,' Arthur would advise. 'He's living off your attention like a parasite, if the attention runs dry he'll drop off.'

'My son is not some bloody tick!' she'd retort before freezing her face into the expression of a much-misunderstood martyr. But Arthur understood Hal. He had been indulged all his life because Helena had never stopped feeling guilty for taking him away from his father. In Arthur's opinion a guilty mother was a very dangerous thing. Hal needed a firm hand and until he received one he'd push his boundaries as far as they could go. But Helena wouldn't allow her husband to assert his authority and instead of earning her son's respect with severity she tried to win it with leniency.

Federica also listened to her mother's grievances with the patience of a therapist. At the beginning when Federica had just moved up to London, Helena asked her about her new job and flat, but once she had settled in Helena asked less about her life until her curiosity dried up altogether and she spoke of nothing but Hal. If Federica tried to direct the conversation away from her brother Helena would either wind up the conversation or find some way of bringing it back to her son. Hal was no longer her hobby but her life and his demand for attention was all consuming.

Federica's life in London was so far removed from Polperro that she was able to detach herself from the tangle of family politics. At first everything was so new she didn't have time to miss home. Then she spoke to Toby and Julian on the telephone and she suddenly felt a yearning for the sea and the cry of gulls and the fresh salty air and silent nights. She also missed Rasta who she had had to leave with her uncle. When she arrived in London she understood why. The city was no place for a dog like Rasta who thrived on his long country walks and games on the beach. He would decline fast in a place like London, but she missed his company none the less.

At first she found it difficult to sleep in the city for the noise of cars, people and the odd police siren that wailed into the night and turned her blood cold. But after a month she began to find the noise a comfort and the yellow streetlights that flooded into the small bedroom she shared with Hester a trigger of memories long since forgotten. As she familiarized herself with the streets of her new home she began to feel a growing sense of belonging. The city ceased to feel like an overwhelming maze to be feared but a friendly town to be enjoyed. She made new friends and went out almost every night, to the cinema, the theatre or simply to the pub where they'd sit around playing backgammon and talk until closing. But Sam's imaginary presence followed her wherever she went and fought off the men who admired her and longed to have her for themselves.

Then just when she thought that nothing could dilute the ardour she felt for Sam, someone walked into her life to change it for ever.

Chapter 29

'Greta wants us to move all the china to the other side of the department,' Harriet said wearily as Federica entered the department.

'Are you sure? That's a lot of heavy work,' Federica replied, then she noticed the black circles around Harriet's dull eyes. 'Are you all right?'

'I got locked out of my flat last night and ended up walking the streets until dawn.'

'You should have called me,' said Federica.

'I didn't have your number on me, m'darling. I'm fine. Just protect me from Greta, please.' She sighed and smiled weakly. 'Apparently Torquil's coming in today for some more shopping. They delivered all the gifts we wrapped up before the weekend, but he needs a few more. I can't bear it, I look hideous,' she sighed, rubbing her eyes.

'You could never look hideous, Harriet. Greta can look after him,' Federica said, locking her bag under the counter. 'That might put her in a better mood.'

'Some hope,' she moaned.

By mid morning they had moved all the china and were leaning back against the counter exhausted when Mr Jensen entered followed by a group of dark-suited men rubbing their hands together in gestures of deference and answering, 'Yes,

Mr Jensen, of course, Mr Jensen', to everything he said. Harriet and Federica at once stood to attention and smiled politely. 'That's Mr Jensen,' Harriet hissed.

'Don't think I didn't notice,' she hissed back. 'You just have to look at the group of sycophants!' The entourage stopped and looked about the room, commenting in hushed voices on the products and the displays. 'Thank God we did the china before he came in,' said Federica.

'Just in the nick of time,' Harriet replied. 'He'd freak out if he saw the department in a mess.'

Mr Jensen's small eyes missed nothing. He scanned the room in one long scrutinizing sweep. When his gaze rested on the angelic countenance of Federica he pulled himself up and whispered something into the inclined ear of one of his aides. At that moment Greta stalked out of her office.

'I thought I told you two not to stand together gossiping,' she said in exasperation, her accent shaving the words aggressively.

'Good morning, Greta,' said Mr Jensen, appearing behind her as if out of nowhere. 'I don't believe we have met,' he added, turning to Federica. Greta blinked in surprise and drew herself up with self-importance.

'Federica Campione,' Federica replied, extending her hand.

'It is a pleasure to have you here,' he said with a smile, watching her curiously. 'We need sunny faces like yours in the front of the shop.' He chuckled and narrowed his small black eyes. The aides chuckled too. 'Make sure she's always at the front of the shop, Greta.'

Greta nodded enthusiastically. 'Of course, Mr Jensen, I know an asset when I see one,' she gushed.

'Good.' He sniffed, then his expression darkened as he traced his eyes over the newly moved china. 'Why has the department been changed around?' he asked in indignation.

His aides straightened themselves up and folded their arms in front of their pigeon chests in a show of mutual outrage.

'Oh,' gasped Greta, clasping her hands together in horror. 'I can only apologize. Federica is new and did not understand my instructions,' she said without so much as a blink. Federica's cheeks flushed scarlet. Mr Jensen nodded and his aids unfolded their arms.

'Perhaps you'd better make yourself more easily understood next time,' he said firmly. 'I want it all moved back to where it was,' he added, clicking his fingers in the air as if summoning a waiter. Then he turned and led the entourage up the stairs to the furniture department.

'You heard him, do it!' Greta snapped impatiently. 'And, Harriet, if you come into work looking like this again I will send you straight back home – for good. Do you understand?' Harriet nodded. She was too weary to fight. 'Ya! Now hurry, before he comes back.'

Federica watched helplessly as she disappeared into her office. 'I'm speechless,' she breathed.

'You'd better get used to it, m'darling, she does that sort of thing all the time. I've been in trouble so many times because of her shifting the responsibility. She hides behind us. But she takes all the credit when things go well, believe me. Right, back to where we started again. Stupid cow!' she muttered, once again fishing the key to the cabinets out of the drawer.

Federica simmered quietly with fury as she walked about rearranging her department. Harriet was too tired to talk and so Federica wallowed in her own self-pity, wishing she had the strength of character to stand up for herself. When a tall, leather-clad man in a black shiny motorbike helmet stalked into the shop, she pressed the code B button on the telephone in an act of defiance and watched the stairs for Nigel Dalby.

Nigel glided down with as much subtlety as a policeman in a pantomime. Federica caught his eye and nodded towards the man who hovered suspiciously by the door. Nigel approached him, straightened himself up importantly and asked him to remove his helmet. 'I'm afraid we don't permit helmets in the shop,' he explained with self-importance. The man cocked his head to one side in amusement before removing his gloves and then his helmet, shaking out his raven hair and revealing himself to be none other than Torquil Jensen. Nigel spluttered his apologies and visibly shrunk.

Federica sighed heavily as the colour drained from her face. Harriet was right, he was quite the most beautiful man she had ever seen. Nigel withdrew backwards, almost bowing as he went, then scuttled up the stairs to hide while his humiliation subsided in the privacy of his office.

Torquil looked at Federica with green eyes and smirked. 'So you're the shop security, are you?' he said, striding over to her and dropping his helmet onto the counter. 'I'm Torquil Jensen.' He extended his hand. He watched her blush as he traced her features with the same scrutinizing stare as his uncle had done earlier.

'Federica Campione,' she replied hoarsely.

'Italian?'

'Chilean.'

'What a beautiful country,' he exclaimed. 'I travelled there as a young man.' Then he grinned at her brazenly. 'This may sound crass but I'm so completely stunned by your looks, I've forgotten what I came in for.' Federica frowned in discomfort and felt the wings of a butterfly make her stomach quiver. 'You're very pretty,' he continued. 'You must be new. No one's that keen to assist Nigel Dalby.' He laughed, his face creasing into deep lines around his large mouth and surprisingly pale eyes. 'You did him a favour, he thinks he's much more important than he is, those sort of people need to be taken down a peg or two.'

'It was a mistake. I apologize,' she said, thinking of Nigel Dalby's long knuckled fingers tapping his mortification away alone in his office and felt guilty. 'He was only doing his job,' she added in his defence.

'And you were only doing yours,' he said. 'I've just bought a new bike, you must come for a ride sometime,' he added, caressing her with intense eyes. She smiled awkwardly. He folded his arms and leant on the counter. She stepped back as the spicy scent of his skin and the heat of his body invaded her senses with too much intimacy. 'Oh, I know what I came in for. I need something for a young woman,' he said, then thought a moment, rubbing his stubbly chin with his hand. 'A young woman, about your age. A Christmas present. What sort of thing would she like?'

'How well do you know her?' she asked, trying to sound official in spite of his suffocating proximity.

'Not very well. But I want to give her something,' he said casually, grinning at her.

'How much do you want to spend?'

'Money is no object. If you'd been here longer you'd know that. I never look at prices, they only get in the way. So, what do you think you'd like, for example?'

'Well, if you don't know her too well, I'd go for something pretty but not too intimate. Let me see,' she said, casting her eyes about the shop, feeling the shamelessness of his stare burn her face crimson. She saw Harriet hiding behind the glass cabinets displaying the china they had just moved, and wished she'd come to her aid. But Harriet felt too ugly to show herself and cowered lower until even Federica couldn't see her.

'What about one of those china pots, you could buy a plant and present them together?'

'Would you like a plant?' he asked.

'Of course. All women like plants.'

'I like your ideas, give me another one,' he said, without taking his eyes off her.

'A painting?' she suggested, looking up at the patchwork of pictures on the wall.

'I don't know her taste,' he said thoughtfully. 'What about a silver photograph frame or something pretty that she can use?'

'Oh, I know,' she said, leading him through the shop to a locked glass case that contained exquisite ornate silver frames. 'This one's just come in, it's from China. It's so delicate, isn't it? If you don't know her very well, it's perfect.'

'You're a good salesgirl,' he said, taking the frame from her. 'If a man gave this to you, would you like it?'

'Of course. If anyone gave it to me, I'd like it.'

'Good, wrap it up then. That was easy.'

She began to wrap it up with an unsteady hand for his eyes watched her every move with undisguised fascination. 'Would you like to take it now or shall I have it delivered?'

'I'll take it now,' he replied, disarming her with another wide smile.

'Is there anything else you want?'

'I'm not in the mood any more. I'll come back another time, that will also give me an opportunity to see you again,' he said in a low voice. Federica frantically searched for something to say, but nothing came. She stood mutely staring back at him. When he left the department a large vacuum remained into which Federica stared as if she were seeing something that no one else could see. Then she breathed again and realized that she had hardly dared breathe at all while Torquil had been beside her.

The rest of the day passed in an exquisitely somnambulant haze. When she returned to the flat she couldn't recall a single thing that had happened after Torquil Jensen had left, but she remembered every word of their conversation as if she had learnt it all by heart. As she sat enjoying a glass of wine with Hester and Molly, the doorbell rang. Hester answered it to find a delivery boy with two packages for Federica. When Federica saw the size of the second package she began to tremble. It was a large plant in a blue and white china pot, like the one she had recommended to Torquil that morning.

'Who's this all from?' Hester gasped in amazement.

'This will look divine in the flat,' said Molly, taking it from Federica and placing it in the sitting room where she proceeded to unwrap it. 'What's in the other package?'

'I imagine it's a silver photograph frame,' said Federica in amazement.

'How do you know?' Hester asked.

'I just do.'

'Well, come on,' said Molly impatiently, flicking ash into the gas fire. 'It won't open by you staring at it.'

Federica carefully peeled off the paper and pulled out the delicate frame imported from China. 'It's stunning,' Hester gasped in admiration. 'Look, it's got birds carved into it,' she added, running her hand over it in wonder.

'That would look good in the sitting room too,' said Molly, dragging on her cigarette.

But Federica held it tightly. 'I'll put the photograph of Papa in there,' she said firmly. 'It's going beside my bed.'

'Goodie,' Hester exclaimed. 'I can enjoy it too.'

Federica hurried along the corridor to her bedroom and closed the door behind her. She could hear the whisperings of Molly and Hester who were curious to know who had bought her such expensive gifts. But she ignored them and sat on the bed to carefully exchange her father's frame for the new one. She ran a fond finger over his handsome face and noticed how Torquil's dark looks resembled Ramon's. The same raven hair, the same olive skin and the same generous mouth. But their eyes were very different. Ramon's were black and mysterious like the universe, whereas Torquil's were light and shimmering like a shallow green pool. She set the photograph into the frame and placed it on the side table, then sat back and admired it. That was how Hester found her, gazing transfixed into her father's hidden world.

'I don't want to disturb you,' she said, waking her friend from her trance.

'No, no, that's fine.' Federica pulled her eyes away.

'Who is he?' she asked. 'I imagine he's a "he",' she giggled.

'My God, Hester. You should see him. He's the most beautiful man I've ever laid eyes on,' she said emphatically, lying back against the pillows. 'He's tall and dark with the palest green eyes. When he smiles my stomach turns over. I feel I've been hit by a lorry.'

'More like one of Cupid's arrows.' She chuckled, settling onto her own bed. 'Where did you meet him?'

'He's the nephew of the man who owns St John and Smithe. Thankfully, he's not short and bald like his uncle.'

'So, he just came into the shop?'

'Yes, I thought he was a shoplifter because he wore a biker helmet, so I called Nigel Dalby down to check him out, it was really embarrassing.'

'Well, he obviously didn't take offence.'

'No, he was amused.' She smiled, recalling the moment.

'Very amused, I can see,' said Hester, admiring the frame. 'He's smitten too.'

'I think he's smitten by a lot of women.'

'How old is he?'

'Old,' Federica replied and blushed.

'Okay, how old. Fifty?'

'No, more like late thirties.'

'Hmm, that's old,' Hester agreed, but she couldn't hide her admiration.

'But mature, confident, settled,' Federica breathed and bit her lip anxiously.

'You mean, rich and secure. Someone who will look after you and take away all your troubles with one twinkle of an engagement ring.' She laughed.

'No, just more grown up than the boys I usually meet.'

'God, how exciting. I can't believe it,' Hester enthused, clasping her hands together.

'Neither can I.'

'What are you going to do?'

'I don't know.' Federica sighed and a shudder of excitement momentarily debilitated her whole body. 'I don't think I'll get much sleep tonight.'

'Oh, your fickle heart,' Hester laughed, getting up slowly.

'What do you mean?'

'To think you were in love with Sam,' she said, smiling at her friend. 'I was rather hoping he'd make you into a proper member of our family.'

'Oh, really, Hester,' Federica replied dismissively, shaking her head. 'That childhood crush was over long ago.'

'Well, it's certainly over now, isn't it?' she said. Then she shrugged her shoulders in resignation before leaving Federica alone with her thoughts.

The following day Federica arrived at the shop with her cheeks aflame, fearing that everyone would know Torquil had sent her those gifts the night before. But Greta demanded a department meeting and gave them all an angry lecture about how to behave on the shop floor and how not to stand in huddles gossiping when there were customers to be looked after. No one noticed Federica's furtive eyes as they shifted from one face to the next before settling on the carpet where they relaxed their focus and hovered in the space between the floor and the vivid images of Torquil that she caressed secretly in her mind.

When the doors opened at ten Federica received a telephone call. She picked up the receiver with a thumping heart.

'Good morning,' said Torquil in a buoyant voice. 'Did you receive my gifts?'

'Yes,' Federica replied, trying to sound calm. 'You shouldn't have.'

'Of course not. But it gave me pleasure,' he replied, touched by her obvious nervousness.

'Thank you.'

'I know it's a little hasty, but I couldn't help myself. Will you forgive me?'

Federica laughed to cover her embarrassment. 'Of course.'

'I know this is also a bit hasty, but will you allow me to take you out tonight?'

'Oh, I . . .'

'Please don't say no, you'll break my heart,' he pleaded.

'Well . . .'

'It's the only way I can get to know you. I can't keep coming into the shop, can I?'

Federica giggled. 'Okay, that would be lovely,' she agreed, fanning her face with the pad of order forms.

'I'll pick you up at eight at your flat. I've something special planned for you,' he said. 'Wear something warm.'

'Okay,' she replied, curious to know the nature of a surprise that required her to wear 'something warm'.

'I'll see you then,' he added.

Federica put down the telephone and stood staring about her as if the world suddenly looked different. It frightened her.

★

When Greta summoned Federica into her office, she knew her boss had found out about the call and began to apologize, anxious not to lose her job. But Greta silenced her with a single slice of her cold blue eyes. 'It must not happen again. You know all the telephone calls are monitored in this company. It is for your own good that I tell you.'

'I'm sorry,' said Federica.

'If you want to receive a personal call you must tell them to telephone you at lunchtime in the staff quarters. If it is urgent they can call my office and I will pass on a message. If everyone in the company received personal calls no one would be on the floor. Do I make myself clear?'

'Yes, Greta.'

'Good. I don't want to have this conversation again.'

Federica was too afraid of upsetting Harriet to tell her about Torquil. So she went about her day as normal, hiding the churnings of a stomach turned to liquid and the rapid pumping of her heart that gave her twice as much energy as everyone else. By the afternoon she could barely concentrate on even the simplest task and was relieved when she was finally able to calm her nerves in the scented water of a deep aromatherapy bath.

Molly cancelled the drinks she had planned with a couple of friends from university and hovered with her sister by the window to catch a glimpse of the dark stranger who was courting their friend.

Federica had nothing glamorous to wear. Her wardrobe consisted of sensible work suits. So Molly leant her a cream cashmere polo neck to go with black jeans and Hester offered her the new sheepskin coat she had bought in Harvey Nichols. But when the shiny Porsche drew up outside the flat and the immaculately dressed Torquil stepped out in a pair of black suede trousers, which he wore over boots, Molly knew someone would have to take Federica in hand.

'Christ, he's a knock-out,' Molly exclaimed, her mouth agape.

Hester rushed to her sister's side. 'Wow, Fede, is it really him?' she squealed in amazement. 'You lucky thing.'

Federica stalled by the door, trembling. 'I'm so nervous, I feel sick,' she said hoarsely. 'I won't know what to say.'

'Don't be ridiculous,' said Molly sharply. 'Of course you'll know what to say. Just because he's handsome doesn't mean he's different from everyone else. He's probably just as nervous.'

'Enjoy it, Fede,' said Hester encouragingly. 'Let him entertain you, that's what Mummy always says.'

'He's bloody gorgeous,' Molly sighed, lighting a cigarette and wishing he had seen her first. 'Just don't be innocent. He'll be expecting a sophisticate.'

'Oh, God, Molly,' she wailed. 'You're making me even more nervous.'

'Well, if you don't go out now he'll drive off and that'll be that,' Molly added bossily. 'Go on!'

When Federica descended the steps onto the street, her pale face and anxious eyes were illuminated by the incandescence of the street lamps and Torquil felt as if his stomach was floating inside his belly, lifting him off the ground. She walked up to him with the same shy smile that had made his spirits soar the day before. He greeted her with a kiss and smelt the sweet scent of ylang-ylang that she had put into her bath. 'You look beautiful,' he breathed and noticed the colour sting her cheeks with pleasure. Then he opened the door and watched her settle onto the tanned leather seat. As he closed it and walked around to the other side of the car he cast his eyes up to the window where the faces of Molly and Hester were pressed up against the glass and waved. To his amusement the faces disappeared like a couple of apparitions.

'I'm glad you dressed warmly,' he said, turning the key in the ignition and pulling out into the road.

'Where are we going?' she asked.

'Surprise,' he replied and she watched his profile as he grinned with satisfaction.

'You like surprises, don't you?' she said.

'As long as I'm the one doing the surprising. Don't ever think about surprising me. I won't like it.'

'I'll remember that.'

They drove along the Embankment towards Parliament Square. It was a cold, dry night. The sky sparkled above the hazy glow of a city that is never dark and the crescent of the moon floated on the surface of the Thames like the ghost of a sunken ship. Federica could not have hoped for a more romantic night. She opened the window and let the cool air brush away her nervousness. Torquil parked the car and pulled a wicker basket and rug out of the trunk.

'What's that for?' she asked in amusement.

'All part of the surprise,' he said, raising an eyebrow. 'Follow me and you'll find out.' She followed him to a gap in the wall beside the Thames and descended the damp steps towards a pretty red boat that bobbed up and down on the swell. An old skipper waited with the same philosophical patience as the men of the sea that Federica had grown up with in Polperro and she felt a breath of nostalgia. He nodded to her without smiling and extended his rough hand to help her down onto the deck. She accepted his assistance and stepped onto the boat. Torquil climbed up to the front and threw the rug down.

'There, come on up, we're going for a long ride,' he said, watching her smile in delight. He took her hand to steady her. 'It's much more fun over here, we can see where we're going for a start,' he said, moving the picnic basket.

'I can't believe you've organized this for me,' she exclaimed, sitting down.

'I want to impress you,' he replied truthfully. 'Okay, Jack, we're ready to roll,' he shouted to the skipper who tapped his cap and disappeared behind the controls. The engine roared before settling into a gentle rattle and they made their way down the moonlit Thames.

Torquil settled down beside her and opened the basket. 'Let's start with a glass of champagne, shall we?' he said, handing her a crystal glass. 'Have you ever been on the Thames?'

'Only in the car along the Embankment.' She laughed.

'Good. I'm glad this is a first,' he said, pouring the champagne into her glass.

'It's such a stunning night, did you organize that too?'

'I did my best.'

'You did well.'

'I did well finding you,' he said softly, tapping her glass with his. 'Here's to us.'

Federica sipped the champagne and swallowed her reservations. 'I gather you met my uncle,' he said, raising an eyebrow.

'Yes,' she replied carefully, not wishing to comment on the toad-like man who stalked the shop with an inflated self-importance that was both unnecessary and absurd.

'He liked you.'

'Oh?'

'He has very good taste. He's perceptive about people. That quality runs in the family.' Then he looked at her with predatory eyes, admiring her lack of sophistication. 'You're too innocent to have been brought up in London. Were you raised in Chile?'

'Only until I was seven, then I was brought up in Cornwall.'

'From the sublime to the ridiculous,' he chuckled. 'That's why you're different. A bit Latin, a bit Cornish. Something of a mongrel,' he joked. 'I like mongrels,' he added, draining his glass. 'I'm not a mongrel. I hope you like pure-blooded Englishmen.'

'Of course I like Englishmen. I don't know many Latin men. I left when I was young,' she explained.

'And now you're old,' he smirked. 'I'd hazard a guess that you're eighteen,' he said, taking the bottle out of the basket and refilling their glasses.

'You're right,' she replied in surprise. 'Do you know everything?'

'Like I said, I'm a perceptive old devil.' He put on a cockney accent.

Federica laughed. 'Then, I guess you're about thirty-five,' she said and sipped the champagne.

'Wrong, I'm afraid, I'm much older than that. I'm thirty-eight. Far too old for you.'

Federica felt her stomach plummet with disappointment. She wondered what he meant by that and if he really felt he was too old for her, why had he asked her out in the first place?

'Let's have something to eat,' he suggested, pulling out a couple of plates of toast, foie gras and caviar.

The boat moved slowly down the Thames, under bridges which cast ominous shadows over the water, past the Tower of London and on into the darkness. They ate the picnic and opened another bottle of champagne. 'I was brought up by my father and stepmother, my natural mother died when I was a little boy,' Torquil said casually.

'I'm so sorry,' said Federica, feeling the full extent of his loss. Although her father hadn't died he had barely shown much sign of life in the last ten years.

'Oh, I was too small to understand and then Cynthia came along. She's been a good mother to me. You see, she was unable to bear children so she adored me to compensate.

Being an only child I've been spoilt all my life.' He said this with a chuckle, omitting to mention that Cynthia's love was at times claustrophobic and his father's overbearing.

'I think you probably deserve it. You must have suffered terribly,' she said, and squeezed his arm compassionately.

He frowned at her. 'You've suffered, haven't you?' he said gently, tilting his head to one side. 'Do you want to talk about it?'

Federica found herself letting him into her life. Her tongue loosened with the alcohol and the beauty of the surroundings, allowing all the pain to slip out uncensored. She hadn't meant to, but there was something in his eyes and his smile that drew her to him. He seemed to see right through her, slicing away her defences with each piercing gaze and understanding what he saw. 'You poor darling thing,' he said, noticing that she had begun to shiver and putting an arm around her shoulders. 'You need someone to look after you. I grew up with too much love, you've grown up with too little.'

'Not at all,' she said, attempting to blink away the light feeling in her head. 'I've been very lucky.'

'Don't fool yourself, sweetness, everyone needs a mother and a father. If you're lucky like me to have a wonderful stepparent, that can make up for the loss of a natural parent in many ways. But Arthur's obviously not a patch on your father.'

'He certainly isn't!' she exclaimed hotly. 'I can't stand him.'

'Well, it's time you had someone to think about *you* for a change. Your mother didn't think about you when she left Chile, did she? Your father didn't put you first either. You need someone to put *you* first.' He pulled out another rug and wrapped it around her. She suddenly felt emotional but didn't know whether it was because she was talking about her father or because he had said that he was too old for her. She wanted to tell him that he wasn't too old for her, but she didn't have the courage. Silently she opened her heart to him and hoped that he might notice.

'Don't be sad,' he whispered, watching her eyes glitter like the water of the Thames.

She shook her head. 'Oh, I'm not sad,' she replied and smiled wistfully. 'I'm very happy. I'm happy to be here sharing this beautiful night with you. You've been sweet listening to me. Don't get the wrong idea. I've had a magical childhood and I've been very happy. Some people, like you, suffer the death of a parent, sometimes a whole family. I really have nothing to complain about. Papa's not dead, is he?'

'No, he's not dead, just thoughtless,' he said, squeezing her. 'I'm going to make you very happy,' he avowed. He lifted her chin with his hand and wiped away her melancholy with his thumb. 'I've found you now,' he said before kissing her salty lips. She responded with eagerness as his rough face scratched at her skin and his wet lips parted hers to penetrate her innocence and claim it for himself. In those moments of intimacy Federica forgot Sam's tender kisses because she had finally found a man who promised to love her and protect her and erase the scars of abandonment.

Chapter 30

'Fede's in love,' Hester said to her mother who stood at the foot of the Christmas tree directing Sam with a vague wave of her hand.

'No, darling, a little more to the left, there,' she said, 'now let's see if Angus will fly in.'

Sam stepped down from the ladder and looked up at the nest that he had secured firmly onto the top branch. 'Who's she in love with?' he asked, folding the steps away.

'He's so handsome you'll faint,' said Hester. 'He's dark with the palest green eyes you ever saw. Sends her presents all the time. Do you know, Mum, he flew her off to Paris just for the day and bought her bags of clothes. You won't recognize her now. She's so sophisticated.'

Sam flopped onto the sofa, stretching his legs out in front of him and placing his hands behind his head.

'To think she was once in love with *you*,' Hester added with a grin.

'No she wasn't,' Sam replied aggressively. 'At least not since she was a child.'

'Where's Angus. ANGUS!' Ingrid shouted, casting her eyes about the room. 'He was in here a moment ago,' she complained, her agitated fingers playing with the monocle that hung between her large bosoms.

'He's probably flown outside,' Sam said irritably.

'In this cold, I doubt it,' she replied, sweeping into the hall with the skirts of her ethnic dress billowing out behind her like the sails of a ship. 'Molly, have you seen Angus?' she said as Molly wandered past her into the sitting room.

'Yes, he's in the library with Nuno. He's trying to teach him to read.' She sighed, rolling her eyes. 'For God's sake, he's a dove, not a parrot!'

'So, Mol, what's Federica's new boyfriend like?' Sam asked, recalling out of the mists of his memory the innocent evening he had shared with her in the barn and the brief walk they had enjoyed on the hill.

'He's nice,' said Molly, sitting down next to her brother. 'Great tree!' she exclaimed. 'But I don't think Angus is going to like it in there, he's happier in Dad's dressing room.'

'Is that all? Nice?' he persisted curiously, wondering why he felt rattled.

'Well,' said Molly, pushing her auburn hair off her face. 'He's handsome and charming . . . but . . .' She paused, trying to put her thoughts into words. 'He's a little too good to be true,' she said decisively. 'Mind you, Fede looks marvellous. I tell you, Sam, you won't recognize her.'

'She really does,' Hester agreed.

Molly loathed talking about Federica and Torquil. Every time she saw them together she felt a nagging jealousy and hated herself for it.

'Is she happy?' Sam asked somewhat grudgingly.

'She's infatuated,' said Molly tightly.

'Yes, she's happy,' Hester replied. 'I've never seen her so happy. He gives her so much attention. Calls her all the time, takes her out. She's blossoming.'

'He looks like her father,' Molly stated.

'Her father?' Sam exclaimed, appalled. 'How old is he, for God's sake?'

'Thirty-eight,' Molly said, raising her eyebrows at her brother, indicating her disapproval.

'What the hell is she doing with someone so old!' Sam retorted crossly. 'He's twenty years older than she is.'

'Age doesn't matter if they love each other,' Hester argued.

'Yes it does,' Sam interjected. 'She's impressionable.'

'What's the difference? She'll be impressionable with whoever she goes out with,' said Hester.

'I don't like the sound of it at all,' Sam sighed, taking off his glasses and rubbing the bridge of his nose between his finger and thumb.

'Well, you can tell her yourself, she's coming over for drinks tonight,' Molly suggested. 'But she's not bringing Torquil,' she added in disappointment.

Sam marched across the cliffs with Trotsky and Amadeus, his mother's new spaniel, watching the waves wrestle with the rocks below, covering them in white foam before retreating to gain momentum for another lashing. He braced himself against the icy wind, pulling his coat around him tightly and hunching his shoulders in an effort to keep warm. Trotsky strode along behind his feet, using him as a shield against the wind, while Amadeus rushed about in a hurry to sniff everything. He thought about Federica crossly, unable to understand why he cared. The kiss in the barn had been a sweet moment of innocent pleasure. It had meant nothing more than that: a kiss on a rainy night. He hadn't planned on kissing her, it had just happened. Afterwards he had felt guilty for taking advantage of her. It was so obvious that she adored him. Then he had impulsively offered to drive her back to her uncle's house one autumn day and they had walked in that heavenly golden light. He had wanted to kiss her up there overlooking the sea. It had been the most romantic moment of his life. That sky, that colour, those smells and Federica looking innocent and ethereal. He couldn't admit his longing, even to himself. She was so much younger than him. He could have anyone he wanted, but Fede had been too young and out of bounds. He thrust his hands into his pockets and sighed heavily. He had felt guilty for desiring her, so he had avoided her again. A cowardly way to go about things, but it was all he could do. He had managed to convince himself that he felt nothing for her whatsoever. But now she was in love with someone else. He wasn't used to not being the focus of her affections. He hoped the relationship wouldn't last. First relationships often didn't.

'This Torquil Jensen rings a bell,' Toby said as they drove up the lane to the manor.

'You won't have met him,' Federica replied from the back seat.

'We have met him,' Julian insisted, shaking his head. 'But I can't remember when.'

'He's a bit old for you, Fede.'

'He's older but not too old,' Federica replied happily 'Love strikes regardless of age. And we love each other.'

'Please tell me he hasn't deflowered you yet, sweetheart?' Julian asked anxiously. 'I'll kill him if he's laid a finger on you.'

Federica laughed. 'No, not yet,' she replied in amusement, feeling a shudder of excitement at the thought of making love to Torquil for the first time.

'Thank God for that!' Julian sighed.

'Don't let him push you into doing anything you don't want to do. He's a man of experience but you're a child.'

'Darling Toby, I'm not a child any more,' she said. 'I'm eighteen.'

'*So* grown up,' Toby replied sarcastically.

'Just don't do anything stupid. You'll go through lots of boyfriends before you find Mr Right,' said Julian. 'And we want to vet all of them.'

'Well, you can meet Torquil whenever you like,' she said, leaning forward between the seats. 'You'll love him. He's handsome, funny, sophisticated, worldly . . .'

'He must have some faults,' said Toby. 'We all have faults.'

'Not Torquil.' She sighed dreamily. 'He's perfect.'

Toby and Julian locked eyes, but it wasn't the moment to share their wisdom.

When Federica walked into the sitting room at Pickthistle Manor, where her mother, Arthur and Hal were already celebrating Christmas Eve with glasses of champagne and admiring the pretty white dove that sat at the top of the tree observing them, Sam felt as if someone had just thumped him in the stomach. She looked radiant in a pair of black leather trousers and pale blue cashmere sweater that clung to her slim frame, emphasizing the swell of her breasts in the V of the neckline. Her long white hair shone with health and fell about her shoulders, setting off the pale skin of her face and the depth of her tanzanite eyes. She embraced Hester and Molly and remained a while by the door talking with animation. Sam felt his throat constrict and drained his glass of champagne in an effort to loosen it. He watched her without distraction. Molly and Hester were right, she looked different. She looked happy.

Nuno was the first to mention the transformation. '*Cara mia*,' he sighed his approval. 'The duckling has grown into a swan.'

'Pa, she was never a duckling,' said Ingrid in Federica's defence. She brought her cigarette holder up to her scarlet lips and dragged in exasperation, the way she always did when she found her father's comments inappropriate.

'Compared to the swan, my dear, she was a duckling,' he retorted firmly, smiling at Federica.

'Thank you, Nuno,' she laughed. Then her eyes fell on the tortured face of Sam, who still watched her from the sofa. She returned his gaze with a smile, but he didn't smile back. He turned to Toby who was seated beside him as if he were ashamed to have been caught looking.

'It's the new London life,' Helena said. 'Hal's going to go to university, though,' she added, desperately trying to lure her son out of his sulk with compliments. But Hal scowled at his mother. He knew he'd never get into a university and had no desire to go. He had only come to the drinks party because she had begged him to. He didn't like Lucien much, he was too clever, just like his brother Sam, whom he didn't like either. They both made him feel inadequate. He watched his sister in the doorway and resented the attention she was getting; he wasn't used to the spotlight shining on her. But when she sat down next to him his bitterness mollified and he allowed her to coax him out of his mood.

'How's it going at school?' she asked. He shook the black hair that fell over his forehead and looked up at her with their father's dark chocolate eyes.

'All right,' he replied impassively.

'You're frustrated there, aren't you?' she said sympathetically.

'I want to leave as soon as possible.'

'And university is not an option,' she added, noticing the rebellious curl in his mouth when he grinned.

'Right,' he said, glancing across the room at Helena.

'Don't worry. You won't have to go. You can do what you like. Come to London. You'd love London,' she said enthusiastically.

'The minute I leave school I'm out of here. I'm sick of Cornwall.' He scowled. 'I'm sick of living with Mama and

Arthur. It's claustrophobic. I need my space. I don't need anyone looking over my shoulder all the time.'

'It's not for much longer,' she said. 'Then you'll be free.'

Once more she raised her eyes to find them unwittingly lock into Sam's. He got up with the excuse of going to get another bottle of champagne from the kitchen and disappeared out of the room. Federica left Hal to wallow in self-pity and followed him.

'Hi, Sam,' she said, finding him alone patting the dogs. He looked up at her in surprise and his face broke into a small smile.

'Hi, Federica,' he replied casually. 'How are you?'

'I'm well. Do you have anything soft?'

'Soft?'

'To drink.'

'Oh, yes,' he replied, feeling stupid. 'Lemonade, Coca-Cola, orange juice?'

'Orange juice would be nice. Thank you.'

He opened the fridge and pulled out a jug of freshly squeezed juice. He poured it unsteadily into a glass and wondered why after having known her for over ten years she suddenly had the power to make him nervous.

'I gather London is treating you well,' he said, endeavouring to extend the conversation in order keep her in the kitchen. Federica noticed that he was beginning to lose his hair. It was no longer blond but darker and cut very short. He looked older and less glossy than before. He blinked at her from behind his glasses and handed her the drink.

'I really enjoy it,' she replied, leaning back against the worktop.

'I hear from Molly and Hester that you've got a new boyfriend,' he said, trying to look pleased for her, but all he could muster was a tight smile that sat awkwardly on his face.

Federica was barely able to contain her excitement. When she talked about Torquil her eyes sparkled and her skin glowed. Sam felt his stomach churn with resentment.

'Yes. He's lovely,' she said and grinned broadly. 'Molly and Hester have met him.'

'What does he do?'

'He works in property,' she replied. 'He has his own company.'

Sam raised his eyebrows, trying to look impressed. 'Good. I look forward to meeting him,' he lied.

'I never see you these days,' she said, shaking her head regretfully. 'Funny, we all live in the same city and yet, you don't even come around to see your sisters.'

'I know.' He sighed, wishing he had been around more often. 'We move in different worlds.'

'Time goes so fast, doesn't it?' she mused. 'I'll never forget that day you rescued me from the lake.'

'Or the time I kissed you in the barn,' he added and looked at her steadily, silently wondering why on earth he had brought it up.

Federica's cheeks flushed with embarrassment. 'It was nice,' she replied tightly, trying to dissemble. 'It seems eons ago.'

'It was your first kiss,' he said, watching her carefully.

'But not my last,' she retaliated boldly. He lowered his eyes, remembering the dreaded Torquil and stared into the bottom of his glass. 'It was nice of you to initiate me into the world of romance, Sam. I should thank you,' she said coolly, recalling the pain his indifference had caused her and wanting to punish him for it. 'I'd better get back to the sitting room. They'll all wonder what we're doing in here. After all, it wasn't so long ago that I had a crush on you.' She laughed flippantly. 'But we all grow up in the end, don't we?' she said before leaving Sam alone to chew on her words.

But Federica didn't go back into the sitting room. She went into the bathroom and locked the door behind her. She sat on the seat and waited for her heartbeat to slow down and for the colour to drain away from her hot face. She was no longer afraid of Sam, but he had hurt her and she couldn't forgive him for that. He had played with her feelings for amusement and then dropped her once his fun had been had. She was no longer infatuated with him. She felt little more than the sweet afterglow of her first innocent love. But she recognized in his eyes a glimmer of regret, a glint of disappointment. She sensed that her new relationship with Torquil infuriated him and it gave her pleasure. He was too late. She belonged to someone else. He had missed his moment and she hoped he would live to regret it.

Federica soon forgot her brief confrontation with Sam. She returned to London after Christmas and into the all-consuming arms of Torquil. When he told her he was taking her skiing to Switzerland for a long weekend, just the two of them, she knew he was going to make love to her and hastily she booked an appointment with the doctor.

She thought about sex often. When he kissed her she longed for his hands to explore her body and discover it as she had explored it and discovered it as a child. Her limbs ached from wanting him so much, but she needed to be sure that he was going to stay. Her deepest fear was of opening up and giving herself to him only to watch him walk out of her life afterwards, leaving her broken and humiliated. She had to trust him first. But little by little Torquil earned her trust. He was always there for her. He called her when he said he would, he was never late when he arrived to take her out, he was dependable, reliable and most importantly he put her at the centre of his world. When she accepted his invitation to stay in his father's chalet in Switzerland she did so with the intention of letting him in.

Torquil's chalet was nestled into the side of the mountain, surrounded by tall fir trees with a spectacular view down the valley. They stood on the snowy balcony watching the stars glimmer in the clear black sky like cut glass. An incandescent moon lit up the mountains with an almost phosphorescent light, allowing them to see details as if it were day. Torquil took her by the hand and led her into their bedroom where a jubilant fire danced in the grate, fighting off the cold mountain air that entered in through the open window. Then he cupped her face in his hands and kissed her tenderly on the mouth. 'I want you to remember this moment for ever,' he breathed.

'I will.'

'I want it to mean as much to you as it does to me,' he said. Too moved to reply she abandoned herself to her senses, taking pleasure from his caresses and from the warm, wet sensation of his mouth loving hers. She trembled as his hands pulled her shirt out from her trousers and crept up inside, feeling the soft innocence of her skin. He was touched by the knowledge that he was peeling open the petals of an unpicked flower, enabling her to experience physical love for the first time. He traced his fingers over her small breasts, touching her nipples and feeling them swell. He removed her shirt and watched the light of the flickering flames lick her flesh. Then he unbuttoned her trousers and pulled them down so that she stood in her panties, smiling at him shyly.

'You're so beautiful,' he whispered admiringly, tracing with heavy eyes every line and curve of her body. For a moment she floundered with embarrassment, aware of her vulnerability and unsure of what to do. But he seemed to sense her shyness and taking her hands in his he kissed them before leading them to unbutton his shirt and his trousers until he was standing naked and proud before her. He pulled her against him and buried his face in the angle of her neck. Then his fingers ran up the inside of her thigh until they reached the line of her panties. Her legs nearly buckled under her, but he didn't lead her to the bed but insisted she stand as they slid inside to where her longing lay hot and undisguised. She caught her breath as he stroked her with deft fingers, watching the colour rise in her cheeks and her eyelids flutter with pleasure. Then when she had lost herself in his rhythmic touch, riding on the delicious waves of an uncharted sea, he swept her up in his arms and carried her to the bed where she was allowed to give in to the trembling of her legs and lie dazed and brazen for him to cover her body with kisses and the sensuous exploring of his tongue. Finally, gently, he entered her to possess her completely.

Torquil lay back and lit a cigarette. 'I've never seen you smoke,' she said, snuggling up to him.

'Only after sex,' he said, drawing the nicotine into his lungs. 'And only the best.'

'That was lovely, Torquil,' she said and blushed at the recollection of her shamelessness.

He drew her against him with his arm and kissed her damp forehead. '*You* were lovely,' he said emphatically.

'So were you,' she replied and laughed.

'This is only the beginning. I want to take you on a lifetime adventure,' he said, then looked at her steadily with his pale green eyes. 'Once again, I know I'm rushing in. But I know what I want.' Federica blinked at him in bewilderment. 'I want to marry you, Fede.'

Federica sat up in alarm. 'You've only known me a few months,' she protested, wondering what miracle had caused him to love her like he did.

'But you love me?' he asked frowning.

'Yes, I do,' she replied. 'But marriage is for life.'

'And I'm going to love you for life,' he insisted, pulling her down to lie in his arms again. 'Marry me, Fede, and make me the happiest man in the world. I know I'm older than you, but that's just it. I know better what I want and I know what's best for you,' he said, kissing her again. 'You need to be looked after and protected and that's what I'm going to do. Look after you and protect you. You need never worry about anything again. Love cures everything.'

'Yes, it does,' she said, smiling at the intensity of emotion that she felt. 'I love you so much. I'm just scared.' She sighed. 'I watched my parents' marriage disintegrate. I just don't want that to happen to me.'

'It won't, I promise. You won't ever be scared again,' he soothed. 'If you marry me, you'll be happy forever, I promise.'

'If you're sure you want me, then, yes, I'll marry you,' she said and laughed happily. 'Mrs Torquil Jensen. That has a certain ring to it.'

'Nothing like the ring I'm going to buy you,' he said and squeezed her so hard she almost had to fight for air.

Torquil pressed his lips against her forehead before dragging once again on his cigarette. How fortunate he was to have found Federica. Fate had been kind to him. She was perfect in every way. After the choruses of worldly city girls, her innocence enchanted him. Her naïvety empowered him and her beauty and grace bedazzled him. With Federica he felt needed and adored. Aware that she was experiencing love for the first time he was touched and honoured that she had chosen him – an emotion that was new to him. He was her hero. She looked up to him, happy for him to make her decisions for her, content for him to always take the lead. Having sailed through life according to the meticulous coordinates set out by his father he was finally asserting control. His father wouldn't like it. He had always been the dominant presence in his son's life. Like the all-consuming shadow of a powerful oak tree the force of his nature had seemed inescapable. But in the last few years Torquil had been growing up and out of his father's shade. Every small move away he saw as a victory, however minute the step. Now he was taking another, larger pace. Federica was *his* choice. No one could control his heart. It felt good.

When Federica returned to London she rang her mother to tell her the news. 'Mama, I'm getting married,' she said.

Helena sat down. 'You're getting married?' she exclaimed in horror. 'To Torquil?'

'Well, who else would it be?' Federica replied and laughed happily.

'But I haven't even met him,' she protested.

'You will. I'll bring him down this weekend.'

'Sweetie, isn't this all a bit hasty? You've only known him a few months.'

'It's what I want,' she said firmly.

Helena fell silent for a moment. She remembered her own hasty marriage to Ramon and shuddered. 'You're only eighteen. You're a child.'

'No, I'm a woman,' Federica replied with emphasis and smiled to herself.

'Have you told Toby?'

'Not yet,' she explained. 'I wanted to tell you first.'

'Well, call Toby,' she suggested. 'I'm afraid this is all too sudden, I haven't met the man yet so I can't make a comment. Why don't you have a long engagement to give you both time to get to know each other?'

'Torquil wants to marry immediately.'

'Really?'

'Yes. He's so impulsive. Mama, we love each other,' she insisted.

'Your father and I loved each other too.'

'It's got nothing to do with you and Papa. This is me and Torquil, we're two entirely different people. We both know what we want.'

Helena sighed heavily. As if Federica was old enough to know what she wanted?

When Toby heard the news he was devastated and furious. 'Julian and I are going up to London immediately to talk to her,' he told Helena briskly. 'We'll take the early train tomorrow. I know I've met this Torquil before, so has Julian, and although we can't remember where, he certainly left a bad taste in our mouths.'

'Try to talk some sense into her, Toby, she's out of her mind.'

'She won't marry him, don't worry,' he replied.

'She's determined.'

'I know. But she listens to me.'

'Thank God, because she doesn't listen to me any more,' she replied defensively, remembering with the residue of an old bitterness how she always listened to her father. 'Where are you meeting her? Won't she be at work?'

'No. Torquil's made her give up her job. She's languishing in his house in The Little Boltons.'

'Very nice,' said Helena tightly.

'Very,' Toby agreed. 'We're going straight there.'

News travelled fast. Polly was appalled and accidentally knocked one of Jake's model boats onto the floor where it shattered into hundreds of small pieces. When he returned home from work in the evening to find his treasured creation in bits his mouth twitched with rage until he recognized the pain in his wife's eyes, because they tended to droop like a sad dog when she was unhappy.

'Federica's marrying this man,' she said helplessly.

Jake shook his head, 'There are more model boats but only one Federica. I hope she knows what she's doing,' he said quietly.

'She thinks she's marrying her father,' said Polly. 'According to Ingrid, who hears it all from her girls, the man's forty years old and looks just like Ramon.'

'Handsome devil then,' he said.

'Devil being the operative word, I fear,' Polly replied gravely.

Helena was giving herself a manicure when she heard the newsflash on the radio. She wasn't concentrating, half listening and half dreaming herself out of her mundane existence. But the words focused her thoughts into one small point that sent cold panic slicing through her veins with the violence of freshly sharpened knives.

The train that Toby and Julian had taken to London had crashed.

Chapter 31

Cachagua

Estella screamed and sat up in bed, staring into the darkness and panting in terror. Ramon was wrenched back from the hot African jungle into the cold fever of his lover's nightmare. He stretched out his hand and switched on the light. He sat up and drew her into his arms, stroking her damp hair and murmuring words of reassurance. '*Mi amor*, it's a bad dream, nothing but a bad dream,' he said, feeling the thumping of her heartbeat vibrate against his body like a terrified creature desperate to break out. 'I'm here, my love, I'm here.'

'I dreamed of death,' she said, still feeling the icy claws of fear scratching at her skin.

'It was just a dream.'

'It's a premonition,' she replied steadily. 'It's the second time I've had it.'

'*Mi amor*, you're frightened of something, that's all.'

'It will happen a third time,' she said, holding him tightly around his shoulders with trembling arms. 'Then it will happen for real.'

Ramon shook his head and kissed her neck. 'So, who died in your dream?' he asked, indulging her.

'I don't know. I didn't see his face,' she replied, blinking away her tears. 'But I fear it was you.'

'It'll take more than a dream to kill me off,' he joked, but Estella didn't smile.

'Perhaps it was Ramoncito,' she choked. 'I don't know.'

'Look at me,' he said, holding her gently away at arm's length. 'Look into my eyes, Estella.' She stared at him with the hollow eyes of the tormented and watched him smile at her with love. 'No one's going to die. At least, you can't predict a death in a dream. You're anxious about something and it's playing with your subconscious. Perhaps you're worried about my trip to Africa.'

She nodded and sighed as the light in the room dispersed the dark horrors of her dream and slowly brought her mind back to reality. 'Perhaps,' she conceded.

'I'm only going for a few weeks,' he said. 'I haven't been away for a long time.'

'I know. You've been a wonderful father to Ramoncito,' she said and smiled.

'And a good lover to you?' he asked, raising his eyebrows and smirking.

'And a good lover to me,' she repeated.

He cocked his head to one side and frowned. 'You know I'll never leave you,' he said. 'You have no reason to be insecure. I'll always love you.'

'I know. And I will always love you, too.'

When Ramon turned out the light and gathered Estella into his arms she was unable to sleep. Not because she was no longer tired, but because she feared that she might dream of death for the third time, thus making it happen in reality. Her mother had once told her that she had predicted her own mother's death in a dream. Three times she dreamed that her mother lay dying in front of a pink house. As she knew of no pink house she didn't worry and forgot all about it. But a few weeks later her mother died of a heart attack tending to the honeysuckle that grew up the side of their white house. It was sunset and the wall glowed a warm, radiant pink. Estella lay fretting until sleep overcame her. When she awoke at dawn she realized to her relief that she hadn't dreamed at all.

When Ramon had finally divorced Helena, Estella had hoped that he would marry her. This hope she guarded secretly, not even telling her parents. But to her dismay he never mentioned marriage. He was contented the way things were. He was free to come and go without the psychological bind of a contract.

Mariana also hoped he would formalize his relationship with Estella. Over the years she and the mother of her grandson had become firm friends. Slowly the divisions imposed upon them by the nature of their places in the world fell away and they were free to live as equals. Estella included Mariana in the life of her son, calling her regularly in Santiago and enjoying her secret visits when she spent the long summer months in Cachagua. At first Mariana had longed to tell Ignacio about Estella and Ramoncito, but little by little she grew accustomed to her secret and it no longer troubled her.

Ramoncito was now eleven years old. He was dark haired and olive skinned like his parents, with the rich, honey eyes of his mother. He was carefree and independent like Ramon and sensitive like his mother, yet his nature was his alone and given to him by God. He was a child who gave only pleasure. He was contented to listen to his father's rambling stories and collect shells on the beach with his mother. He sat talking to the tombstones with his grandfather and indulged both grandmothers with stories of his adventures with his young friends. He hadn't inherited his father's impatient desire to travel nor his selfish need to satisfy his own longings at the expense of those of the people he loved.

Mariana said that he had been blessed with the best of both parents and she was right. She often saw Federica in the honesty of his smile and in the trusting innocence of his eyes, and she wondered whether Ramon saw it, whether he remembered and she consoled herself that she remembered for him. As long as she was alive, Federica and Hal would never be forgotten.

Ramon loved his son with an intensity with which he had once loved Federica. He still loved his daughter and often, when he was inventing stories for Ramoncito, his heart ached with nostalgia, because Federica had loved his stories too. Then he recalled that painful moment when his own negligence had reared up to throttle him with remorse.

He had seen her. Bicycling down the lane on her way home, her face aglow with happiness and exertion combined, ignorant that the man who passed her in the black Mercedes was her father. He had commanded the driver to stop the car at once. Federica, hearing the car screech to a sudden halt, had braked her bicycle and turned around, squinting into the sun. For a few moments, which seemed painfully long in his memory, he had watched her with longing, fighting the impulse to open the car door and run towards her, to sweep her off her feet like he had always done when she had been a child. She was no longer a little girl. She was still small in stature, small for a thirteen-year-old, but her limbs were long and her face that of a young woman; slim, angular, proud. He had suppressed an inner groan that threatened to break out into a desperate cry. Federica was on his lips and he had had to struggle in order to swallow her name. She had shielded her eyes against the sun with her hand, one foot on the pedal, one on the tarmac. Her hair was long and flowing in the wind. She still had the hair of an angel. *La Angelita*. But he had remembered what Helena had told him. Federica was happy without him. If he had embraced her as he had desired, his embrace would have been full of false promises. Promises of commitment, promises of devotion but above all the promise to prevent Helena from marrying Arthur and he knew he couldn't do that. So, faced with promises he could not fulfil he had sadly asked the chauffeur to drive on. He had owed it to Helena to leave her free to marry Arthur and live in peace with her children.

He had returned to Chile consumed with regret and remorse. If only he had begged her to stay, nothing would have changed. He would still have a relationship with his children. But that wasn't enough of a jolt to open his heart to what he had had and lost, for he had returned into the rose-scented arms of Estella and Ramoncito and once again Federica had retreated into the recesses of his mind where her cries for him could no longer be heard.

Estella told her mother about her nightmares. 'I'm afraid,' she said as her mother lay in the armchair like a fat seal, fanning herself with an Hispanic fan. 'I'm afraid that Ramon's going to die in Africa.'

Maria dabbed her sweating brow with a clean, white *pañuelo* that her mother had made for her and considered her daughter's problem with care. 'You must go and visit Fortuna,' she said after giving the matter some thought.

'To read my future?' Estella replied anxiously. She had often heard people speak about Fortuna for she was the only black person anyone had ever seen. It was said that her father had survived a shipwreck when a cargo carrying slaves had sunk off the coast of Chile. Her mother had been a native Chilean who had taken him in and nursed him back to health. Fortuna lived in a small village up the coast and when she wasn't lying in the sun watching the world pass her by she read people's fortunes for a small fee. How she survived on so little money no one knew, but some said she was supported by an old man whose life she had saved by predicting an earthquake which would have killed him had he not left his house on her instructions.

Estella returned home to sleep on her mother's advice. Ramon was sitting in his study tapping his thoughts into a computer. The evening was calm and melancholic, flooding the coast in a soft, pink light. Estella decided not to tell him about Fortuna, although the books he wrote were filled with mysteries and magic. She feared he might think less of her. Fortune-telling was very much associated with the suspicions of the under-classes. She crept up behind him and wound her arms around his neck. He was pleased to see her and kissed the brown skin on her wrists.

'Let's walk along the beach, I need some air,' he said, leading her out by the hand. They walked through the strange pink light and kissed against the rhythm of the sea. 'I'll miss you when I go tomorrow,' he said.

'I'll miss you too,' she replied and frowned.

'You're not still worrying about your dream, are you?' he asked, kissing her forehead.

'No, no,' she lied. 'I just wish you weren't going.'

'I'll be in Santiago tomorrow night, I have to see my agent in the afternoon. I'll fly out Thursday night. I'll call you from Santiago and I'll call you from the airport.'

'Then I'll just wait,' she sighed.

'Yes. But I'll think of you every minute and if you close your ears to the rest of the world you just might hear me sending you messages of love.' He kissed her again, holding her tightly around her slim waist. Later, when he made love to her in the watery light of the moon that reflected off the sea and shimmered in through the window of their room, he tasted the roses on her skin and smelt the heavy scent of their intimacy and knew he would take them with him across the world and savour them when he was alone.

The following day Estella and Ramoncito waved goodbye to Ramon and watched his car disappear up the hill in a cloud of glittering dust. Ramoncito then skipped off to school with his *mochila* on his back filled with books and a box of sandwiches, which Estella had made him for lunch. He turned to wave at his mother, who stood at the foot of the road, and blew her a kiss. She blew one back and then remained there a while, smiling with tenderness at the unguarded affection of her son which never ceased to amaze her.

She hadn't dreamed about death again. She had floated on the memories of Ramon's lovemaking and had awoken with the radiant complexion of a satisfied woman. But she still felt fearful and because of that icy fear she decided to go with her mother and visit Fortuna.

Pablo Rega watched them dig the grave. It was hot and the earth was hard and dry. He leant on the gravestone of Osvaldo Garcia Segundo and chewed on a piece of long grass while they toiled at the other end of the graveyard. 'It's a good position, that,' he told Osvaldo. 'Overlooking the sea, like you. *Sí*, Señor, overlooking the sea is a prime spot. Imagine being stuffed back there without a view. I'd like to be here, where I can see the sea and the horizon. Gives one a feeling of space, of eternity. I like that. I'd like to be part of nature. What does it feel like, Osvaldo?' He breathed in the scent of the dark green pine trees and waited for a reply, but Osvaldo had probably never been a man of words. 'This place is getting pretty full,' he continued. 'Soon there won't be any more room and they'll have to start digging up old graves like yours. There's a good chance I'll be buried on top of you, then we can talk for eternity.' He chuckled. 'I'd like that, *sí*, Señor, I would.'

Estella and her mother arrived by bus and walked directly to Fortuna's small house, which stood just off the dusty road. There were no flowers or bushes, just dry sandy ground and rubbish, which Fortuna scattered around the house – not to ward off the evil spirits as people suspected but because she was too lazy to throw things into a bin. Her house smelt of rotting food and sour milk and Estella and her mother found themselves having to disguise their grimaces by smiling in order not to offend the old woman. Fortuna sat outside on a large wicker rocking-chair, watching the odd car pass by, humming old Negro spirituals her father had taught her as a child. When she saw Maria she laughed from her belly and enquired after Pablo Rega.

'Still talking to the dead?' she asked. 'Hasn't someone told him that they can't hear him? They don't hang around you know, they fly off into the world of spirits the moment they leave this godforsaken earth.'

Maria ignored her and explained that her daughter had come to have her future read. Fortuna stopped rocking and sat up, her expression sliding into the serious guise of a wise woman conscious of the responsibility that came with her gift.

She asked Estella to sit down and pull the chair up so that they faced one another with their knees almost touching. Maria flopped into another chair and pulled out her Hispanic fan. Fortuna took Estella's trembling hands in her own soft fleshy hands that had never experienced a day's hard labour and pressed the pads of Estella's palms with her thumbs. She pulled her mouth into various strange shapes and closed her eyes, leaving her lashes to flutter about as if she had no control over them. Estella looked at her mother anxiously, but Maria nodded to her to concentrate and fanned herself in agitation.

'You have never been so happy,' Fortuna said and Estella smiled, for it was true, she had never been so happy. 'You have a son who will be a famous writer one day like his father.' Estella blushed and grinned with pride. 'He will channel his pain into poetry that will be read by millions.' Estella's smile disintegrated as the icy claws of fear once more scratched at her heart. Fortuna's eyelids fluttered with more speed. Maria stopped fanning herself and stared at her with her mouth agape. 'I see death,' she said. Estella began to choke. 'I can't see the face, but it's close. Very close.' Fortuna opened her eyes as Estella pulled her hands away and heaved as her throat constricted, leaving barely any room for the air to reach her lungs. Her mother threw herself out of her chair with the agility of a much slimmer woman and thrust her daughter's face down between her knees.

'Breathe, Estella, breathe,' she said as her daughter gasped and spluttered, fighting the fear that strangled her. Fortuna sat back in her chair and watched as mother and daughter struggled against the inevitability of her prediction. Finally, when Estella began to breathe again, her choking was replaced by deep sobs that wracked her entire being.

'I don't want him to die,' she wailed. 'I don't want to lose him, he's my life.' Maria pulled her daughter into her large arms and attempted to comfort her, but there was nothing she could say. Fortuna had spoken.

'Please tell me it is not Ramon,' she begged, but Fortuna shook her head.

'I cannot tell you because I do not know,' she replied. 'His face was not revealed to me. I can do no more.'

'Is there nothing we can do?' Maria asked in desperation.

'Nothing. Fate is stronger than all of us.'

Estella was determined to change the future. She told her mother that Ramon was leaving for Africa the following day and that if she could prevent him going she might save his life. Maria didn't try to stop her. She knew she wouldn't listen. She was too distressed to stay in Cachagua and wait for disaster to strike. She embraced her daughter at the bus station and reassured her that she would look after Ramoncito while she was away. 'God go with you,' she said. 'May He protect you.'

Estella cried all the way to Santiago. She sat with her head leaning against the window, replaying all her most treasured memories of Ramon as if he had died already. She closed her eyes and prayed until her silent prayers formed words on her tongue that she mumbled deliriously without realizing that the other passengers could hear her, but were too polite to ask her to be quiet. When she arrived in Santiago she took a taxi to his apartment. She rang the bell but there was no reply. She stood in the doorway of the apartment block and disintegrated once more into tears. She didn't know what to do or where to go. Perhaps she was too late. What if he was dead in his apartment? She collapsed onto the marble steps and put her head in her hands. When she felt a gentle tap on her shoulders she lifted her eyes expecting to see Ramon, only to be disappointed as the porter stood over her with a sympathetic expression etched onto his smooth brown face.

'Are you all right, Señora?' he asked.

'I'm looking for Ramon Campione,' she muttered.

'Don Ramon?' he said, frowning. 'Who are you?'

'My name is Estella Rega. I am . . .' He cocked his head to one side. 'I am his . . . his . . .'

'His wife?' he said helpfully.

'His . . .'

'If you are his wife I can tell you where he is,' he said kindly, grinning at her crookedly.

'I am his wife,' she said firmly, wiping the tears off her face with a white *pañuelo*.

'He's at a meeting. He left over an hour ago, but I will call you a taxi and he will take you to him.' Estella pulled a grateful smile. 'That's better,' said the porter. 'You're too pretty to be so sad.' Then he watched her climb into the taxi he hailed for her and disappear into the traffic.

★

Ramon stood up. 'I'm off to Africa tomorrow,' he said. 'I'll be away three weeks.'

'That's a short visit for you,' his agent commented, smiling knowingly.

'Well, I don't have much reason to stay away these days.' He chuckled.

'You mean to say that this woman you've been hiding away all these years has captured your heart?'

'You ask too many questions, Vicente.'

'I know I'm right. I can tell from your writing. There's love all over the pages.'

Ramon laughed and picked up his case. 'Then there's even less reason to go away.'

'But you'll go anyway.'

'I always do.'

'Call me when you get back.'

Ramon closed the door behind him and stepped into the lift. He thought about what Vicente had said to him, 'there's love all over the pages', and he smiled to himself as he thought of Estella and Ramoncito. Then he glanced at his reflection in the mirror. He wasn't getting any younger. He was already greying around the temples and, looking at his physique, he wasn't getting any thinner either. He cocked his head to one side and rubbed his chin ponderously. 'I should make an honest woman out of Estella,' he thought, 'I should have married her years ago.'

When he opened the door into the busy street he stopped a moment, stunned to see a woman who looked exactly like Estella on the other side of the road. She was looking to her left and right in confusion with swollen red eyes that darted about like a terrified animal unused to the traffic. He blinked a few times before he realized that she was in fact Estella and he shouted at her. She heard her name and raised her eyes.

She smiled with relief when she saw him and lifted her hand to greet him. 'Ramon!' she cried with happiness, and placing her hand over her mouth she blinked away tears of joy. Then she stepped out into the road.

'Estella, no!' he shouted, but it was too late. The sparks from the truck spat into the air as the wheels screeched to a sudden halt in an attempt to avoid the woman who walked blindly out in front of it. Ramon dropped his case and ran across the road, which shuddered to a halt as drivers leapt out of their cars to see what had happened. When Ramon saw the broken body of Estella lying inert at the foot of the vehicle he threw himself upon her with trembling hands, desperate to find a pulse.

'Talk to me, Estella, talk to me,' he pleaded, pressing his face against hers, whispering into her ear. 'Say something, my love, something. Please don't die.'

But she didn't move. He gazed down at her pale face in shock and noticed that she still had traces of a small smile in the gentle curve of her lips. He placed a finger on them, willing her to breathe. But there was not a breath left in her. There was nothing he could do to bring her back. He lifted her shattered body into his arms and pressed it against his heart, then sobbed loudly from the core of his being as he realized that he had killed her.

'Who was she?' someone asked.

'My wife,' he wailed and rocked back and forth dementedly.

Ramon took the woman he had loved as he had loved none other back to her home in Zapallar. Maria had slipped into a deadly fever when she heard the news and lay in a trance, her ears deafened to the desperate pleas of Pablo Rega who held a candlelight vigil by her bed, silently bargaining with God. Mariana went immediately to their house and embraced them both for she had grown to love their daughter as her own. Only Ramoncito remained dry-eyed and composed. Mariana explained to her grandson that his mother had gone to live with Jesus and that she was looking down on him and loving him from Heaven. But Ramoncito just nodded and put his arms around her in order to give comfort. Mariana was confused. His maturity perturbed her. But she didn't hear the breaking of his heart or the crying out of his soul in mute despair.

As Fortuna had predicted, millions would feel his suffering in the words he would write in the future. But for the moment he was unable to comprehend his own grief or know how to express it.

Ramon arrived shrunken and grey with the body of his beloved Estella. He allowed himself to be comforted in the familiar bosom of his mother and then straightened himself up to be strong for his son. When Maria saw Ramon she blinked out of her trance and told them all of Fortuna's prediction. Ramon shook his head. 'She died instead of me,' he said sadly.

'She died because it was her time,' said Maria. 'That's why Fortuna couldn't see her face.'

When Ignacio Campione knocked on the door of Pablo Rega's house the small party of mourners looked at each other in surprise. He walked in with the stride of a man no longer able to play ignorant.

'I'm sorry, son,' he said, pulling Ramon's large frame into his arms. Ramon blinked at his mother in confusion over Ignacio's shoulder. Mariana shrugged and wiped away her tears. 'You don't really believe I'm that stupid,' he said, patting his son on his back. For once Ramon didn't know what to say. He buried his face in his father's neck and sobbed.

*

Estella was buried on the top of the hill overlooking the sea, in the shade of a tall green pine tree. Pablo Rega later apologized to Osvaldo Garcia Segundo because he would from that moment on speak only to his daughter. Unlike Osvaldo, Estella talked back. He could hear her voice in the rise and fall of the tides and feel her breath in the wind that always smelt of roses.

Ramon looked out over the horizon and reflected on his misguided acts of selfishness that had ruined so many lives. He thought about what he had loved and lost. Then he looked down at his eleven-year-old son. Ramoncito glanced up at him and smiled. In his smile Ramon saw the smile of Federica and the tears of Hal, the frustration of Helena and the unconditional love of Estella and he swallowed his regret as if it were a ball of nails in his throat. He placed his hand on the brave shoulder of his son and vowed that he would make up for his negligence by loving Ramoncito, by being there for him, by changing his ways as Helena had once begged him to.

He threw a single red rose onto the coffin, then walked away a different man.

Chapter 32

Polperro

Helena, Jake and Polly sat helplessly watching the television for news of the crash. A number had been given out for worried relatives, but they were still pulling bodies out of the wreckage and had no news of Toby and Julian. Arthur sped over from the office and Hal was picked up from school. Polly's kitchen vibrated with the resonance of their grief. All Jake's model boats lay in scattered abandon, like matchsticks, over the floors and table as he had thrown them all to the ground in a sudden fit of anger and remorse. Polly tried to reach out to him, to give him her hand, as he spiralled into a dark pit where his stubbornness and prejudice laughed at him mockingly, but he didn't take it. He was too ashamed. Too disgusted that he had allowed his intolerance to obscure the value of life.

Sure that Toby was dead and unable to face the rest of the family, Jake stalked out of the house to walk on the cliffs. He strode across the winter grass and allowed tears of self-loathing to sting his face. The bitter wind caused his eyes to burn but he hurried on blindly as if by walking fast he might leave his despair behind him.

He recalled Toby as a little boy. The times he had taken him out on his boat, the times they had sat in silence watching the seagulls and the shoals of fish just beneath the surface. He remembered how he had laughed when Toby had begged him to return to the water a large trout they had just caught. He had teased him, holding the fish in his hands and waving it about in front of the child's tormented face. He winced at the recollection, like so many other recollections. Toby had always known the value of life. He had known it better than anyone.

Then he remembered the times when father and son had been so close they had both believed that nothing could come between them. Toby had helped him glue together his model boats well into the night. They had told each other stories, they had laughed and they had worked together in the familiar silence of the very intimate. There had been a time when Toby had told him everything.

But Julian had arrived and it had all changed.

Jake sat on a cold rock and looked out onto the rough horizon where the waves collided with each other, drawing foam like blood. He searched his tormented soul to find the root of his prejudice. It wasn't just Toby's homosexuality that had set father against son because feelings of resentment had grown up inside him long before he had known of it. There was something else. Something much more primitive. He recalled the first time Toby had introduced him to Julian. He had noticed their closeness immediately. The way they laughed together like old friends, anticipated the other's thoughts like brothers and enjoyed the comfortable silence of father and son. His jealousy had choked him. When he scrutinized his feelings further he realized that he had never really had a problem with Toby's homosexuality, but it had been easier to blame his resentment on that, rather than admit his jealousy, even to himself. He was suddenly consumed with shame.

Jake was not a religious man but he felt the presence of God in Nature and it was there that he prayed. He prayed that God would forgive him and begged him to preserve both Toby's and Julian's lives so that he could make it up to them.

When he returned home Polly noticed that his expression had changed. Somewhere out there in the wind he had slain the dragon that tormented him. Now he was ready to join the rest of the family in hope.

Helena knew she should be strong for her son, but her misery was all consuming. She sat watching her tears send ripples across the surface of her cup of coffee and allowed the drama to engulf her completely. When Arthur arrived she managed to raise her swollen eyes to indicate that she needed comforting. Arthur put down his briefcase and stood in the centre of the kitchen.

'Right,' he said in a commanding tone, placing his hands on his hips. 'I've spoken to the emergency services on site and so far there's no sign of them. At least we can be thankful that they don't feature among the dead.'

Helena began to wail. Polly clamped her pale lips together in an effort to contain her distress. She had to be strong for the rest of her family.

'Now, there's nothing we can do but wait. I suggest I put a call through every fifteen minutes. Jake, keep the radio on for bulletins. Helena, don't mourn them prematurely, while there's no news there's hope, at least give them that courtesy.'

Helena was stunned. She had never heard her husband speak with such authority. She blinked up at him with admiration.

'We all have to be strong for each other. It's not over until it's over,' he continued and watched his wife straighten up obediently.

'Right, anyone for another cup of tea?' said Polly, filling the kettle.

★

Federica wished she were in Polperro with the rest of her family. She lay on Torquil's large bed in The Little Boltons and stared unblinking out of the window, willing the telephone to ring with good news. She had called Torquil's office and left a message for him with his secretary. She strained her ears for the key in the lock until her senses were so acute that her heart leapt at the smallest sound.

Helena had telephoned her with the terrible news. But while there was no evidence of their deaths there was still hope that they were alive. She had turned on the television and watched the various reports. The train looked like a toy made out of tin that had been carelessly scrunched up by an overbearing child. She had watched the firemen struggle with the bodies of the dead and searched behind them for those of the living. But she couldn't see Toby or Julian in the blur of unfamiliar faces. When it became too much she had turned it off, lain on the bed and waited for news from her mother.

When the telephone finally did ring she picked up the receiver with a trembling hand and was barely able to hear the voice for the squealing of her nerves in her ears. 'Fede, it's Hester.'

Federica's heart plummeted. 'Oh, Hester, hi,' she replied in disappointment.

'I got your number from your mother. I'm so sorry. We're all thinking about you,' she said. 'Molly and I are sitting in the flat praying they're all right.'

'Thank you, Hester,' she mumbled weakly. 'I'm praying too.'

Hester had heard about Federica's engagement to Torquil but felt it wasn't the time to mention it. 'I'll leave the line free now, but we're here if you need us,' she added sympathetically before hanging up.

When the key finally turned in the lock Federica's hearing was too concentrated on the telephone to notice. Torquil found her curled up on the bed in a tight ball. He walked over to her and drew her into his arms where she sobbed against his chest. 'I thought you'd never come,' she choked, wrapping her arms around his neck. 'They might be dead.'

'You don't know they're dead,' he replied. 'What's the latest news?'

'That's the worst, there is no news.'

'Have you been watching the television?'

'I couldn't bear to look. I'm waiting for Mama to call. They keep ringing that family line they give out.'

'Right, that's all we can do for the moment. That and pray,' he said, stroking her hot forehead. 'They're going to be all right, sweetness, I just know they are.'

But Federica felt nothing but doom.

After a while Torquil stood up and paced the room. 'Moping around isn't going to change anything and it's making me feel claustrophobic. Why don't you have a bath, get dressed and we can go out for lunch to take your mind off it.'

'I can't have lunch at a time like this!' she exclaimed in horror.

'It'll be good for you to get out of the house, have some hot soup, it'll make the time go faster.'

'But the telephone?' she stammered.

'I'll divert it to my mobile. Don't worry, when they know something they'll call us wherever we are,' he reassured her.

News travelled fast in Polperro. Ingrid chain-smoked, unable to paint or rise in her usual vague way above her cares. Inigo closed his philosophy books and sat with his wife in front of the fire, pondering on the meaning of death. Nuno shook his head and knocked back a glass of brandy lamenting that it should have been him. 'My time is nigh,' he sighed. 'Those boys had years ahead of them.'

Sam sat in front of his computer at work, longing to call
Federica. Molly had rung up and told him the news. He had
immediately turned on the radio and listened to the details of
the crash, wishing he could comfort her like he had that day
in the bluebells after she had overheard Arthur's marriage
proposal. She had been so young and forlorn then, gazing up
at him with timid eyes, adoring him unconditionally. He
recalled the sweet kisses in the barn and their awkward
confrontation in the kitchen at Christmas and felt her drifting
away from him. He already loathed Torquil Jensen. 'What
sort of a name is that, anyway?' he thought to himself with
resentment. In her confusion Molly had forgotten to tell him
that Federica was engaged to be married. She had only
remembered to give him Federica's new number and ask him
to call her. 'She needs our support,' she had explained.

Sam doodled around the number he had written on the
corner of the *Evening Standard* and debated whether or not
she would be pleased to hear from him. Then he pushed his
reservations aside and dialled the number. He leant back in
his chair and listened to the tone with an accelerated heart.
Finally it ceased and a gravelly male voice responded with
urgency, 'Torquil here.'

Sam's gut twisted with irritation. 'It's Sam Appleby for
Federica,' he stated coldly.

The man indicated his disappointment with a loud sigh.
'She's in the bath, I'm afraid.'

'Oh,' Sam replied impatiently, taking off his glasses and
rubbing the bridge of his nose in agitation.

'Can she call you back later? We'd like to leave the lines
free. I don't know whether you know but . . .'

'I do. Just tell her I called,' he interrupted and hung up.
Angrily he stabbed his letter opener into the front of the
newspaper. He regretted having telephoned at all. 'Torquil
Jensen,' he scowled under his breath, 'what an imbecile.'

'Who was that?' Federica shouted from the bathtub. Torquil chewed the inside of his cheek, deliberating whether or not to tell her. He didn't much like the sound of Sam Appleby. His arrogance grated. Anyway, Federica didn't need any male friends now; she had him. 'Nothing, sweetness, just the office,' he replied with a smirk.

Sam Appleby might have hung up on him but he had just had the last word.

Torquil took Federica out to lunch in a small restaurant around the corner from his house. The waiter, who knew Torquil well, gave them a table by the window and Federica sat staring unhappily out onto the grey pavement. 'Uncle Toby has always been like a father to me,' she said, stirring her spoon about the soup bowl. 'My own father never bothered really, but Uncle Toby always had time for us. I have so many memories of him.' She sighed, not bothering to wipe away a heavy tear that balanced on the end of her eyelashes.

'You're talking in the past, sweetness,' said Torquil, stroking her arm with tenderness. 'I'm sure he's alive, you'll see.'

'Oh, he's dead,' she replied sadly. 'If he were alive we would have heard.'

At that moment Torquil's mobile rang with a loud shriek that jolted the entire restaurant.

'Torquil here,' he answered briskly. 'Ah, Mrs Cooke, it's Torquil Jensen. Any news?'

'Is Federica with you?' Helena asked, ignoring the usual pleasantries.

'I'll pass you over.'

'Fede, sweetie, I'm afraid we still don't know for sure. There are thirty-two dead. Toby and Julian aren't among those, but they're not among the survivors either. They still don't know. They're still looking. We're all trying so hard to be strong. Arthur's been wonderful. He's taken over completely. I didn't think he had it in him.'

'Oh Mama, I'm praying so hard,' she whispered.

'So am I. We all are.'

'I never said goodbye,' she choked, casting her eyes into the quiet street. Suddenly she saw Toby and Julian strolling happily up the pavement. Toby was eating a chocolate bar. She paused in astonishment, blinking furiously in case she was mistaken.

'I know, sweetie, neither did I,' Helena said with a sniff. Then after a moment, when Federica failed to respond she added, 'Fede, are you all right?'

'Mama, they're here!' she exclaimed in amazement.

Torquil turned around and looked out of the window.

'Who is?'

'Uncle Toby and Julian!'

'What?'

'They're walking towards me up the road.'

'Are you sure?'

'Yes!' she replied, getting up and running out through the door. 'Toby! Julian!' she shouted.

Toby smiled jovially as his niece ran towards him. She threw herself into his arms. 'You're alive,' she laughed. 'They're alive!' she shouted into the telephone where Helena was anxiously hanging on at the other end.

'Pass me over now!' she ordered crossly. 'They're alive!' she added, looking at her parents, Arthur and Hal in confusion.

'Helena,' said Toby, grinning into the speaker.

'What the hell happened to you?' she demanded.

'What do you mean?'

'The train crash.'

Toby frowned. 'What train crash?' he asked, perplexed.

'For God's sake!' she gasped. 'Don't tell me you weren't even on it?'

'We took an early train, because Julian had a morning appointment in Soho.'

'I don't believe it!' she exclaimed. 'We thought you were dead. You worried us sick.'

'Christ, I'm sorry.'

'You bloody well better be!' she said in fury. 'God, Toby, we thought you were both dead. We've been out of our minds with worry. I'd even planned the speech I was going to give at the funeral. Goddamn it! I love you!' she whimpered before disintegrating into tears.

Jake took the telephone from her. 'Toby.'

'Dad.' There was a brief pause while Jake searched for the words that only a moment ago had balanced impatiently on the end of his tongue.

Toby glanced at Julian in bafflement.

Finally, Jake settled for something less meaningful. 'Come home soon, son, both of you,' he said stiffly. He wanted to say more, but he couldn't do it over the telephone.

Toby's forehead creased in bewilderment. 'Are you all right, Dad?' he asked.

'You're alive. You're *both* alive. I've never felt better in all my life,' he announced triumphantly and Toby recognized his father's old familiar voice, the voice that had resounded with affection before prejudice had throttled it.

Toby was passed to his mother, then Arthur and finally Hal. When he hung up he shook his head in astonishment.

'You'd better come and join us for lunch,' said Torquil, extending his hand. 'I'm Torquil Jensen. You don't know how much of a pleasure it is to meet you both.'

When Toby and Julian returned to Polperro they received a welcome neither felt they deserved. Most of the town joined Toby's family and the Applebys on the platform and all clapped heartily when they stepped down from the train. Even Inigo had come out in his shabby cashmere coat and felt hat to show his delight that they had arrived home safely. Polly watched with pride as Jake embraced them both, patting them heartily on the back because his throat was too choked with emotion to speak. Toby's vision misted as he hugged his father, a hug that destroyed the invisible wall that had grown up between them. Their eyes silently communicated all that they felt and their tears demonstrated the love that both considered inappropriate to express verbally. Helena watched happily as her family were finally reunited again, but she couldn't help but wonder how their meeting went with Federica and whether they had managed to stall her marriage plans.

As Toby made his way through the crowd of well-wishers to the exit he was surprised to see Joanna Black, the girl he had once kissed at school, standing awkwardly by the door. She smiled at him. He smiled back, puzzled. 'Hello, Joanna,' he said.

'Hello, Toby,' she replied. 'I didn't think you'd remember me.'

'Oh, I do,' he said and chuckled amicably.

'I just wanted to apologize for cutting you dead that time in the grocery shop.'

'Oh, don't worry, that's fine. It was a long time ago.' He shrugged, watching her shuffle uneasily.

'I know, but it wasn't kind.'

'*I* wasn't kind. That was a long time ago too.'

She lowered her eyes and curled a strand of her mousy brown hair behind her ear. 'Well, that's just it,' she said quietly. 'When you kissed me all those years ago . . .'

'Yes?'

'And I ran off in tears.'

'Yes.'

'I was hurt not because you kissed me. I wanted you to,' she said shyly and laughed with embarrassment. 'I was hurt because of the look of disgust on your face as you did it.'

'Oh, I'm so sorry,' he said, shrugging his shoulders again.

'No, don't be, really,' she replied hesitantly. 'I understand now. You didn't like girls, I didn't know it at the time.'

'Why tell me now?' he asked.

'I thought you were dead,' she replied, simply.

'Oh.'

'I've been meaning to tell you for years, but I had never plucked up the courage.'

'Thank you,' he muttered, watching her slide through the door. He followed her out.

'Well, that's all I wanted to say. I've said it now.' She laughed nervously, shuffling her feet in the cold. Then she embraced him. Toby stood rigidly as she sighed heavily. She had never got over that first girlish crush, or the hurried kiss in the playground. 'See you around,' she added before hurrying off.

Toby watched her go and shook his head. 'You know, death does the strangest things to people,' he said to Julian.

Julian grinned. 'People should die more often,' he mused. 'It brings out the best in everyone.'

Death certainly did bring the best out in everyone. Without realizing it each member of Toby's family had changed.

Jake had confronted his jealousy and won. Polly's admiration for her husband had swelled thus uniting them where before his prejudice had divided them. Helena realized more than ever before the value of life and thanked God for Arthur who inflated with joy as she began to hold his hand under the table and smile at him with intimacy, the way she had when they first met. Hal emerged out of himself and began to notice those around him, albeit temporarily.

When Helena finally managed to ask Toby how his meeting had gone with Federica, she realized that it didn't matter if they married. After all, marriage wasn't life threatening.

'I was surprised at how charming he was,' Toby said, tucking into Polly's mushroom risotto. 'He's much older than her, very handsome, clever.'

'Very much the father figure, I think you'll find,' Julian added. 'He couldn't have been nicer.'

'Will he be kind to her?' Polly asked, as Jake filled her glass with wine.

'She's young,' said Jake, 'but she's no fool, Polly.'

'Oh, she knows what she wants, Dad,' Toby reassured him. 'There's no denying that. Anyhow, she's not "little Fede" any more. She's a woman. She's grown up in quite a hurry since she met Torquil. She won't budge on this one, I can tell you.'

'She is vulnerable though, especially with a much older man who can manipulate her,' Arthur interjected.

'Yes, she is vulnerable,' Helena agreed. 'She's impressionable and this is her first love, she should probably play the field a bit.'

'Fede's not up to playing the field,' Hal chuckled, squirting tomato ketchup onto his risotto.

'Well, within reason,' Jake argued.

'Helena's not suggesting she sleep around, Dad, just grow up a bit, gain a little more experience, meet other people. I agree with her. It is a worry her marrying the first man she falls in love with, however charming he may be. After all, marriage is for life,' Toby said.

'It should be,' Helena added wryly.

'It can be.' Arthur grinned, pressing her knee with his. She winked at him coquettishly.

'I think marriage sucks,' Hal interjected. Helena smiled at him and shook her head.

'So, what do we do?' Polly asked, draining her glass. 'Can we really do nothing?'

'Nothing,' said Jake. 'She has to sail her own ship, Polly.'

'Well, when are we going to meet him?' Helena asked.

'They said they might come down this weekend,' said Toby.

'Good,' Jake concluded with a nod. 'Now, no more opinions until we've given the poor lad a chance. Any more of that risotto, Polly?'

When Molly rang Sam to let him know that Toby and Julian were alive she remembered to tell him that Federica was getting married. He nearly choked on his jealousy. 'Don't be ridiculous, she's only just met him.'

'I know. The whole thing is ludicrous,' Molly agreed. 'But she is.'

'She's Hester's age, for God's sake, what does she know about marriage?'

'Nothing. If she knew more about it I don't think she'd leap into it like this. But Mum says he's a substitute for the father she never had.'

'Well, that's it then. Father-figure syndrome,' he said bitterly and his heart plummeted.

'Quite.'

'When's the wedding?'

'In the spring.'

'What, *this* spring?' he exclaimed, taking his glasses off and rubbing his eyes, which suddenly felt tired and uncomfortable.

'Torquil wants to marry as soon as possible. You know he's stopped her working already?'

'No!'

'Yes, he has. She's moved lots of her things into his house.'

'Where does he live?'

'The Little Boltons,' she replied, her voice heavy with resentment.

'Well, she won't have to work, will she? He's undoubtedly rich.'

'Everyone should do something,' she argued. 'She'll become one of those ghastly women who do nothing but shop all day.'

'Not Fede,' said Sam defensively.

'Yes, Fede,' she insisted. 'He'll make her into whatever he wants her to be. She hasn't exactly got the strongest character, has she?'

'She's young.'

'Hester's young and she's got more backbone than Fede.'

'She'd have to with a sister like you,' he snapped coldly.

'What do you mean by that?'

'You're just jealous that Fede's been swept up by someone handsome and rich,' he accused, wondering why he was giving her such a hard time.

'Look, I just called to let you know, not to get into a heavy discussion,' she retorted in exasperation.

'Sorry, Mol. It's just been a trying day,' he apologized, sighing deeply. When he put down the telephone he felt nauseous. Unable to focus on his work he pulled on his jacket and left the office early, not caring what his boss thought. He didn't want to work much longer in the City anyway. The sooner he returned to Polperro the better. He certainly didn't want to be in London if Federica and Torquil were married.

He took the tube to Hyde Park Corner and walked around Hyde Park, kicking the leaves and scowling at the squirrels in fury. When it began to rain he stood in the shelter of one of the stone follies, watching miserably as the grey skies opened around him. He couldn't understand why he minded so much that Federica was getting married. After all, he had had his opportunity and let it go. He had kissed her then left her. He consoled himself that he didn't want to be in a relationship, any relationship. He didn't want to be tied down. If

Federica were free he still wouldn't make a play for her. He just didn't want anyone else to have her. When he walked through the drizzle back to his flat he felt much better. So Federica was marrying Torquil, what of it? There were many more fish in the sea.

For a while Sam managed to convince himself that he no longer cared for Federica, but the moment he came face to face with Torquil Jensen he was unable to pretend any longer. All his instincts screamed out against the marriage, which, in his opinion, was doomed to fail before it had even started. But no one else seemed to see it like he did.

Torquil and Federica arrived at Toby's house on a Friday night. He had insisted they drive down, stopping on the way at small inns and pubs for the odd break and refreshments. As they weaved along the winding lanes, Torquil felt an odd sense of *déjà vu*.

'I know I've been here before,' he stated, staring out in front of him at the winter hedgerows and bare trees, wondering why it all looked so familiar.

'Probably in a past life,' Federica suggested with a shrug. 'We might have been lovers then too.'

'No,' he insisted seriously, 'I really have been here and it's bugging me.'

Federica shook her head and thought nothing more about it. She was barely able to sit still in her excitement to show her fiancé off to the family. When they pulled up outside Toby and Julian's cottage Torquil tooted the horn. Toby appeared and stood jovially in the doorway while Rasta bounded out to greet them with unrestrained enthusiasm.

'Welcome,' Toby said, smiling warmly. Julian appeared behind him to capture the moment on film. It was then that Torquil remembered why he was so sure that he knew this place. He still had that Polaroid of Lucia which Julian had taken. He took a deep breath and stepped out of the Porsche. He hoped their memory of him had faded with the years; if his recollections were correct it hadn't been a very positive introduction.

Jake and Polly were the first to arrive for dinner. Jake was mistrustful of 'townies' and believed that Federica should marry someone from Polperro. 'She's been uprooted enough in her life, what she needs is stability and to be around the people and place that she's used to. Still, he deserves a chance to prove he's qualified to take care of her,' he conceded as they drove up to the house.

Polly agreed with him, and nodded her head thoughtfully. 'I just wish he wasn't so old,' she sighed. 'It's nice when two people can grow up together. He'll be an old man before she's touched middle age, which is a shame.'

When they entered the sitting room, Torquil jumped to his feet and extended his hand warmly. They were both immediately disarmed by the beauty of his face and the charm of his wide smile.

Polly returned his smile with gusto. 'It's such a pleasure to meet you,' she gushed, not immune to the appeal of a handsome young man. Jake was more reserved, though thrown by the perfection of his features, and watched Torquil through narrowed eyes, endeavouring not to be influenced by his looks.

But even Jake was easily conquered when Torquil placed an affectionate hand on Federica's and looked him straight in the eye, stating earnestly, 'I only have one priority, Mr Trebeka, and that is to make Fede as happy and secure as I can.'

Jake's old heart surrendered and he nodded his submission. 'Well, as you can see, Torquil, she has a close and loving family. Don't let her stray too far from her home, that way she can enjoy her new life with you *and* the security that lies in her roots.' Then he added gruffly, 'And please call me Jake.'

When Arthur, Helena and Hal arrived the sitting room was already vibrating with laughter. Hal had lingered by the Porsche, loving the owner even before he had met him. 'Wow, he must be really cool to have a car like this!' he exclaimed, hurrying in to meet him. Helena noticed immediately the physical similarities between Torquil and Ramon, but also the differences – Torquil's face lacked the rugged character of Ramon's; it was too polished and smooth. However, she couldn't help but relinquish her reservations in the glare of such magnificence. He was not only tall and good-looking but his clothes were immaculate, from his cashmere jacket to his well-polished brown shoes. Taking a seat next to Federica on the club fender she winked her approval. Federica beamed with happiness.

Only Arthur's suspicions simmered beneath the surface of his cheerfulness.

Helena was placed next to Torquil at dinner. Looking into her eager eyes he told her how he wanted, more than anything in the world, to make her daughter happy. 'I can see where she gets her beauty from. You and she could almost be sisters,' he said, watching her cheeks ignite with pleasure.

'She's very vulnerable, Torquil, and really too young to marry,' she replied, sipping her wine. 'But you're older and wiser and I have no doubt you will make her very happy. What she needs is security; something a younger man would be incapable of giving her. I have to admit, when I first heard about you I did worry that you'd be too old for her and that the whole thing was being rushed unnecessarily. But, now I know you I can see exactly why she doesn't want to wait. Why should you both wait when you are so sure of the way you feel? Marriage is a gamble however long you've known each other. But I think I'd put money on you two.'

'Torquil, can you give me a spin in your car after dinner?' Hal asked, shouting across the noisy table.

'You bet,' Torquil replied. Then he took the opportunity to give a small speech. 'I just want to say that when I fell in love with Fede, I never anticipated falling in love with the whole of her family, but I have been pleasantly surprised.' He cast his eyes around the table of hot faces and glistening eyes and paused, gazing down at Federica, apparently unafraid to show his emotion. 'I want to thank you all for making me feel so welcome and for Federica, because I know that each of you have had a large part to play in making her what she is today; the woman I love with all my heart.'

Polly stifled her tears with a gulp of wine while Helena grinned at Toby who nodded back his approval.

'You know, Torquil thinks he's been here before,' Federica declared in amusement.

'No, I got it wrong, sweetness,' he replied quickly, 'I had one of those *déjà vus*.'

Julian looked at him and frowned.

'Actually, didn't I say, Toby, that the name Torquil Jensen rang a bell?'

'You can't forget a name like Torquil, can you?' Federica giggled.

'Well, I know I haven't been here before,' Torquil said carefully, 'because if I had I simply wouldn't have left.'

Toby raised his glass with a chuckle. 'Well said, Torquil,' he applauded. 'Welcome to the family.' They all raised their glasses.

Only Arthur hesitated before he too lifted his to toast their guest with the others. He couldn't put his finger on it, but there was something not quite right about Torquil. He was altogether too perfect.

★

The following day Torquil and Federica were invited to lunch at Pickthistle Manor to meet the Applebys. Ingrid approved of Federica's choice immediately because he didn't wince at the sight of the wounded stoat which limped nonchalantly across the hall and he patted the dogs with enthusiasm.

Inigo had locked himself in his study asking to be disturbed only under the unlikely circumstances of a house fire, so Ingrid apologized on his behalf and led their guest into the large sitting room where an open fire danced in the chimney beneath a wistful portrait of Violet, Ingrid's mother, and a dusty mantelpiece clustered with curiosities.

Nuno shook the young man's hand and sniffed at him warily while Hester bounded over excitedly and Molly played hard to get, languishing on the sofa, pretending not to notice him. Sam wandered in grimly and kissed Federica on her cheek before nodding to Torquil with an arrogance that ill-suited him. Torquil disguised his aversion behind a friendly smile and nodded back affably before turning away and talking to Hester.

Sam wasn't fooled. He loathed him immediately.

'I don't trust him,' he hissed to Nuno. 'He's too smooth. There's a portrait of him with all his imperfections hidden away in some attic somewhere, I'm telling you.'

'Ah, a Dorian Grey, perhaps. He's certainly beautiful,' Nuno replied as he watched Ingrid, Hester and Molly turn pink under the brilliance of Torquil's physical perfection.

'God, they're such simpletons,' Sam scorned. 'Why is it that women are so dazzled by looks? It's pathetic.'

Nuno scrutinized his grandson and sniffed knowingly. 'Are you perhaps not a trifle jealous, dear boy?'

Sam shook his head and put his hands in his pockets. 'Certainly not. She's like a sister, I feel protective,' he insisted, smarting at the sight of Federica basking in Torquil's reflected glory.

'Ah,' sighed Nuno with a smile. '"O! beware, my lord, of jealousy, It is the green—ey'd monster which doth mock the meat it feeds on."'

'Shakespeare's *Othello*,' said Sam flatly. 'But I assure you, Nuno, I don't covet Fede for myself. I'm just loath to see her falling into the wrong hands.'

'You can't live people's lives for them, dear boy, they have to suffer their own mistakes and learn. We all do.'

'I know, but it's hard to stand back and watch it happen,' he admitted bleakly.

'Nothing in the world would convince Federica today that Torquil is not all that he seems – if, indeed, he does deceive. Keep your thoughts to yourself. Nothing will come of honesty but bitterness.'

Sam sat through lunch watching Torquil holding forth while the women in the family laughed in admiration at every lame joke he delivered. Once or twice Torquil locked eyes with his aggressor, but it was he who turned away first.

He knows I can see straight through him, Sam thought to himself, *the fool*! Federica noticed Sam's silence and felt her enthusiasm dissipate as if his muted disapproval were sucking her energies dry. After lunch they all decided to go for a walk.

'Are you coming with us, Sam?' Federica asked hopefully.

But Sam shook his head. 'I've got things to do,' he replied. *Better things to do than listen to Torquil's oafish jokes*, he thought sourly, and left the room for Nuno's study.

Nuno's study had the benefit of being situated on a corner of the house. One half looked out onto the garden, the other onto the front. Sam stood by the window watching Torquil play with the dogs, who mobbed around on the grass in front of Molly, Hester and Ingrid.

'I adore dogs, Ingrid,' Torquil was saying, patting their soft heads. 'These two are really special.'

'Dog lovers are good people,' she replied, 'you can always be certain of a person's true nature if he likes dogs.' She wrapped her long cardigan about her body. 'If you're going to walk on the cliffs, I suggest you borrow a coat, Torquil.'

'No thank you, I have one in the car, I'll just go and get it,' he said, leaving the girls to chat among themselves. Sam watched him disappear through the archway and out to where his car was parked on the gravel. He wandered over to the other window. Torquil stalked across the driveway to his Porsche, followed eagerly by Trotsky and Amadeus who sniffed and sprung about his feet. To Sam's surprise Torquil turned on them with impatience.

'Stupid dogs. Piss off,' he growled, shunting Amadeus out of the way with a firm nudge of his shoe. Amadeus shrunk momentarily before believing it to be a game and trotted back for some more. 'Bloody animals!' he continued, opening the boot and pulling out his coat. Trotsky lifted his ears in bewilderment and backed away leaving Amadeus to jump up onto Torquil's neatly pressed corduroy trousers with muddy paws. Torquil was furious. He swore again and smacked the spaniel around the face. 'You do that again and I'll eat you for dinner,' he scowled, before marching back through the arch to where the girls eagerly awaited him.

Sam was left floundering by the window, amazed at what he had just witnessed. He wanted to tell Federica immediately, but who would believe him? He sat down in Nuno's leather chair and watched the fire smoulder in the grate. *Over my dead body will he get Federica up the aisle*, he thought to himself, but he didn't have the first idea how he was going to stop him.

Chapter 33

Everyone loved Torquil. He had swept into Polperro like a victorious conqueror, winning over everyone he met, slaying them all with his straight white teeth and lucid eyes. Only Sam and Arthur remained suspicious, forming a silent resistance, unwilling to be deceived. But no one else seemed able to see beyond the charm. Nuno was too absorbed in the works of Stendahl to look, the women were all too smitten even to try and Federica's family were so deeply enamoured with Torquil's glamour that they didn't give Arthur the opportunity to state his case. There was only one option open to both of them, but Nuno had warned Sam against speaking to Federica. He fretted away in a fever of irritation feeling powerless as Federica buzzed deliriously about the web of a very shrewd spider. But Arthur had less to lose – his stepdaughter had disliked him right from the start.

He managed to find a suitable moment on Sunday, when Torquil was being shown the Cornish coast in Toby's boat, accompanied by Jake, Hal and Julian. Federica hadn't wanted to go, preferring to spend some time with her grandmother in the kitchen, preparing the lunch in order to impress her fiancé. Helena sat in the rocking-chair beneath a canopy of hanging miniature ships, sipping a Bloody Mary and discussing wedding plans, while her mother and daughter sweated about the Aga with steaming pots of vegetables and treacle tart. After a while Federica wandered into the sitting room to find Arthur alone by the fire reading the papers. She pulled a polite smile.

'How's the cooking going?' Arthur asked, folding the newspaper and placing it on the sofa beside him.

Federica hovered by the door, reluctant to embark on a conversation with her stepfather. 'Fine,' she replied impassively.

'I can't imagine you'll ever have to cook at home once you're married,' he said and watched her carefully.

'Oh, I'll still cook, I've cooked all my life.' Then she looked at him quizzically. 'You don't like Torquil, do you?'

Arthur sighed and sat back against the cushions. He shook his head. 'I'm afraid I don't trust him, Fede,' he replied, fixing her with his sharp brown eyes.

She shuffled uncomfortably, then placed a defiant hand on her hip. 'What is there to mistrust?'

'It's too soon, Fede,' he argued. 'You've known him all of a few months, why do you have to marry him right now? What's wrong with spending time together first? That in itself makes me suspicious.'

'We love each other?' she insisted crossly.

'What do you know of love, Fede? You have no experience. He's the first man who's swept you off your feet. He's handsome, rich, charming, what else do you know about him?'

'I don't need to know anything else about him. You and Mama aren't exactly the epitome of the perfect marriage,' she retorted defensively.

He folded his arms and chuckled. 'We have our problems, of course. Marriage isn't a treacle tart, Fede. I'm concerned because I care about you.'

'No you don't, you care about Hal,' she snapped impulsively, then wished the hadn't said it. Not because it wasn't true, but because it was a childish response and she was trying desperately hard to present herself as an adult. 'Anyway,' she continued defiantly, 'try as hard as you like to find fault with him, I promise you, you won't find it. He's perfect. That's what gets up your nose.'

'That's not true,' Arthur replied patiently. He wanted to ask her what Torquil, a sophisticated, urbane man of thirty-eight, would want with a provincial eighteen-year-old of limited experience, but he knew that would hurt her. He simply added that he was concerned by the speed of the romance. 'If Torquil's got nothing to hide what's the harm in waiting a few more months? I'm troubled by his urgency.'

'It's called *love*, Arthur,' she replied sarcastically and rolled her eyes in exasperation. 'Look, I really don't want to discuss this any more. Mama likes him, in fact, everyone likes him but you. The truth is I don't care what you think,' she said and stalked out.

When she returned to the kitchen she decided not to mention it to her mother or grandmother – she didn't want to dwell on negative things. This was the happiest time of her life and she wasn't going to let her interfering stepfather ruin it for her. He had always disliked her, right from the start.

When the men returned, red-faced from the wind and their laughter, Torquil retreated upstairs to change for lunch. Federica rushed about the kitchen with excitement, putting finishing touches with the same enthusiasm she had once reserved for her father. Toby and Julian stood by the fire telling Jake and Helena about the giant crab that had nearly sent Torquil overboard.

'He didn't like the look of it, but give him his due he's a man who can laugh at himself!' Toby chuckled.

Arthur wandered into the drinks room to pour himself something strong. He rattled a cube of ice about his glass in agitation before filling it with whisky. He looked out of the French doors onto the winter garden and felt a bleak foreboding gnaw at his gut. His talk with his stepdaughter had been worse than disastrous. Lunch would be awkward. With a sinking spirit he opened the door and walked grimly onto the terrace. He breathed in the bitter air and watched his breath rise up on the cold as he exhaled. Then to his astonishment he heard a low voice in the window above him. Creeping back against the wall he listened with deliberation as Torquil continued a private conversation on his mobile telephone, leaning out of the window for better reception. '. . . The wedding will be the last time I find myself in this godforsaken backwater . . . She loves the city, believe me, she's too good for these provincial people . . . I'm rescuing her from a life of dogs and crabs, I've caught her just in time too. Poor girl, imagine growing up here, no wonder she's so grateful I'm marrying her . . . Don't start on that again, babe, I've told you, I love her to distraction . . . So, she's not worldly like you, that's why I like her. She's pure and innocent, untouched. I don't want someone else's cast-off . . . Just wait until you meet her, then you'll understand . . . You don't work in that department, you work in the basement and that's where I like you.' He laughed throatily. 'That's where you like to be . . . Look, I'd better go. The sooner we have lunch the sooner we can leave.'

Arthur held his breath for fear of being heard and waited a moment before he dared open the door and slip back inside. He felt physically sick, but worse than his nausea was his anger because he had nowhere to vent it. No one would listen.

Feigning a headache he sat quietly through lunch while Torquil acted the perfect guest, expressing his love of Polperro and the sea, forging a false bond with the family Arthur knew he despised. Watching Federica was like witnessing a car crash in slow motion. There was nothing he could do to prevent it.

While Arthur and Sam smarted in the wake of Torquil's triumphant visit, Federica moved into his luxurious house in The Little Boltons. It was exquisite, decorated by one of the top London designers with rich fabrics and expensive paintings. 'I can't believe I'm going to live here for ever,' she breathed in excitement, throwing herself onto the bed.

'Not only that, but you're going to have my name and then my children. We'll fill this house with the patter of tiny feet,' he said, lying beside her and kissing her forehead lovingly.

'Oh, Torquil. I've never been so happy,' she said, holding his face in her hands. 'You're everything I've ever hoped for.'

'And you're a dream come true, I've been looking for you all my life,' he said, smiling down at her. 'You're so good, Fede. I'm not worthy of you. You're sweet and sensitive. You're like an angel. Pure like white sugar. I don't know what you see in me. I'm full of imperfections.'

She gazed deliriously into his pale eyes and wondered why Arthur mistrusted him; he had the most trustworthy expression she had ever encountered.

Later when she admired the tidy cupboards full of Chanel suits, Ferragamo shoes, Ralph Lauren casual wear, La Perla underwear and Tiffany jewellery, she noticed that everything had been bought for her by Torquil. When she asked him where all her old clothes had gone he told her that he had given them to Mrs Hughes, the housekeeper.

'Her daughter is your age and they have very little money, sweetness. Besides, you're different now you're with me,' he explained, drawing her into his arms. 'You're shedding your old skin along with your old name. You're going to be Mrs Torquil Jensen and I want you to have the very best of everything.'

Although she would like him to have asked her first, she didn't want to appear ungrateful. She replied simply that he was too generous and that she was undeserving of him. His obvious delight and approval allayed her fears and her spirits rose again. She wanted nothing more than to please him. When she admired her new maturity in the mirror she marvelled at the distance she had come since that morning in Viña, now over ten years ago, when she had gazed upon her childish reflection with distaste. After so many disappointments, she deserved Torquil.

She longed to share her news with her father, but she resented the fact that he hadn't communicated in years. In spite of her joy she felt desperately let down. Now she had Torquil she no longer searched for happiness within the glittering splendour of the butterfly box. She didn't need to. The shadows of the past were exchanged for the brightness of her new life. She didn't need her memories any more; she was going to build new ones with Torquil. So she placed the box at the top of a cupboard and closed the door.

Sam had spent the night before Federica's wedding in Nuno's leather chair re-reading Alexandre Dumas' *The Count of Monte Cristo*, the most satisfactory story of revenge ever written. The early birds had awoken him at dawn. He had looked about, bewildered that he had managed to sleep on such a night. He rubbed his weary eyes and gazed out of the window onto a fragile foggy morning. The garden was draped in a tender summer mist like a tent of glittering cobwebs. A frail mist that held in the sheer transience of its nature the promise of a magnificent sunny day.

For Sam it promised nothing but misery.

When Nuno shuffled in at eight he found his grandson staring out of the window in gloom. 'I would like to think it was one of my tomes that has kept you up all night,' he said, glancing down at the heavy book on Sam's knee.

Sam turned around slowly and blinked up at his grand-father. 'I'd like to lock Torquil Jensen in the Chateau D'If,' he groaned.

'Ah!' Nuno sighed knowingly and nodded his head. 'Young Federica's getting married today.'

'Quite,' Sam replied, removing his glasses and cleaning them on his shirt.

'"Love is the wisdom of the fool and the folly of the wise,"' Nuno said and raised a thick eyebrow.

'Nuno, I don't have the patience for this today, but to satisfy the demands of your ego I'll tell you it's William Cook, *Life of Samuel Foote*.'

'*Molto bene, caro*. Even in times of great despair you are able to keep your wits about you and indulge an old man.'

'I'm not in love with Fede, Nuno, I've told you before, I just don't want to see her hurt.' Then he added crossly, 'I don't think I can go to the church, the sight of Torquil Jensen's self-regard might just push me to do something I'll later regret.'

'Dear boy, if you cannot recognize your anger as fuelled by jealousy you're less of a man than I thought you were. If you ask me, you had that gentle creature's admiration for years and you chose to reject it. Now pull yourself together and accept defeat with honour. I suggest a bowl of porridge and a cup of tea, then put on your coat and come along to the church with the rest of us, with good grace. These things are sent to test us and this might be your biggest test yet, I trust you don't want to fail.'

So Sam ate his porridge in silence while the excited chatter of his sisters and mother grated on his nerves and pushed him further into his troubled thoughts. Joey wandered in from the garden with a gigantic toad cupped in his trembling hands, explaining that he had found him drowning in the swimming pool. When Ingrid attempted to take the creature from him the toad leapt into the air with the zeal of an acrobat and proceeded to jump about the kitchen floor, outwitting everyone's efforts to catch him.

'Oh, leave him,' Ingrid sighed wearily, pouring herself another cup of tea. 'He'll find his way back to the pond without our help. I think Mr Toad is quite capable of looking after himself!'

Molly and Hester were to be bridesmaids, or as Molly preferred to put it: 'maids of honour'.

'I wish I were marrying Torquil Jensen instead of walking five steps behind the bride,' Hester sighed enviously. 'I can't believe Fede's luck.'

'Fede of all people!' Molly exclaimed, shaking her head in wonder that a man such as Torquil could fall for someone like Federica, when she was so much more attractive and charismatic. *It should be me*, she thought to herself resentfully.

'Oh wake up!' Sam snapped suddenly, rising from his chair. Molly and Hester both stared at him in confusion. 'Don't either of you have the intelligence to see past his pretty face? It doesn't surprise me that Hester's been fooled, but Mol, I always thought you were more perceptive. Torquil Jensen would be more suited to one of those crass American soap operas. What is it you girls used to watch? *Dallas*? In a language you both understand, he's no Bobby Ewing!' And with that he left the room.

The two sisters blinked at each other in amazement. 'Have I missed something here?' said Molly, putting down her mug.

Hester shrugged her shoulders. 'If you have, Mol, then I certainly have,' she replied, baffled.' 'What has *Dallas* got to do with Fede's wedding?'

'Torquil Jensen might be many things, but he's no JR either.' She sniffed angrily. 'How dare he accuse me of lacking perception. God damn him, he's always believed himself to be cleverer than everyone else.'

'He might be cleverer than Torquil, but Torquil's got all the beauty,' Hester giggled.

'That's obviously what's got under Sam's skin. It's all about hair,' Molly laughed scornfully. 'Sam's losing his and Torquil's got plenty!'

Sam sat stiffly in the pew, ignoring Joey who quietly played with Mr Toad, having finally forced his surrender in the dog bowl. He watched the conceited profile of the groom with silent loathing. Torquil whispered to his best man, their heads inclined together like a couple of conspirators. Unable to bear the torment that sight evoked, he turned his eyes to the vast arrangements of white and yellow flowers and across to the other side of the aisle where Torquil's grand friends sat under ostentatious hats, glancing warily about them at what must have appeared a very parochial scene. Reverend Boyble rushed about importantly, bowing low to the altar every time he passed in front of it. Finally, Torquil's father and step-mother appeared and walked down the aisle with great cere-mony. Sam took one look at Mrs Jensen's hat and thought of the Quangle Wangle Quee. He shook his head at the vulgar-ity of it and caught Nuno's eye. His grandfather smiled wryly and scribbled something down on a bit of paper, then passed it to Lucien, who passed it to Ingrid, who leant across her distracted youngest and handed it to Sam. He opened it and laughed out loud. Nuno had read his thoughts exactly for he had quoted from the same poem by Edward Lear: 'And the Golden Grouse came there, and the Pobble who has no toes and the small Olympian bear, and the Dong with a luminous nose . . . all came and built on the lovely Hat of the Quangle Wangle Quee.'

★

Buff Jensen sat in the pew behind his son. He was a large man with a wide forehead and thinning black hair combed back and set with wax to give the impression that he had more than he did. His eyes were pale and imperious, set in smooth skin unblemished by the usual lines of humour. Buff rarely smiled. He was too aware of his own importance and the need to show it. Torquil turned around and grinned at his father, a grin that betrayed his triumph as well as his genuine pride. Buff had hoped for a better match for his son and relinquishing control was hard for him to accept. But this small battle Torquil had won. Cynthia only saw the pride in her stepson's smile. He was marrying the girl he loved, there was no doubt about that. She had liked his little bride very much. Had she been a stronger character she might have felt competitive, but Federica would make the perfect daughter-in-law – provided one managed to forget where she came from.

After a short pause Federica's family made their way to their seats with less ceremony than the Jensens. Helena wore a pink suit with a pillar-box hat to match and Polly wore red – they obviously hadn't planned their outfits together. When Helena saw the vast expanse of Mrs Jensen's creation she winced with rivalry and wished she had had the courage to wear something bigger. She also caught herself longing for Ramon – Arthur's unimposing presence impressed no one. When Mrs Hammond's hesitant fingers alighted on the keyboard, the idle chat was reduced to an expectant silence as everyone stood up and looked behind them to catch the first glimpse of the bride.

Federica hovered momentarily under the archway at the entrance of the church, before stepping out of the sun into the soft light of the nave. Sam was suddenly gripped with regret. He stood as still as marble, the blood drained from his stunned face, and felt the sharp claws of love tighten about his heart. It was as if the world had frozen around him, only Federica moved slowly towards him with the unearthly countenance of an angel. He barely dared breathe. It was only when Mr Toad escaped Joey's grip and sprung onto the wooden bench behind him before leaping into the aisle that Sam was shaken from his trance and realized to his despair that Federica wasn't walking towards him but away from him. She was walking way beyond his reach and he only had himself to blame. The clouds parted in his memory and he pictured their tender kisses in the barn and her golden face on the hill and he almost choked with misery.

Jake watched with pride as his son led Federica up the aisle and wiped a damp eye at the recollection of his daughter's wedding that he had missed. Helena caught her breath, for Federica floated on the arm of her brother like a princess with diamonds in her hair and a choker of diamonds and pearls about her neck. The ivory dress shimmered in the heavenly light that flooded in through the stained-glass windows and her skin seemed to glow with a translucence not of this world. Helena thought of Ramon until the tears stung her eyes and the memory of him became so strong that she could almost smell him. Arthur squeezed her hand, which wrenched her back to the reality of her dull marriage and the tears flowed more abundantly.

Arthur wanted to cry too – tears of fury and frustration, but he could not, so he sat with grim resignation as his stepdaughter walked past to embrace her destiny.

Ingrid's heart sighed at the beauty of the music and Inigo abandoned himself to the positive vibrations of God's house and took his wife's hand in his as he remembered their own wedding all those years ago.

But Nuno watched Sam. He understood his grandson better than the boy understood himself. He saw the anger in the line of his petulant mouth and the hurt behind his stormy grey eyes and wanted to tell him that everything comes to those who wait.

Sam felt he was watching a public hanging; the sacrifice of the innocent. He watched Torquil with the eyes of a predator, studying his every move, his every blink. There was something sinister in the shine of his shoes, the spotless coat, the starched shirt, the gold watch on the perfect chain, the emerald cufflinks. Not even a strand of hair disobeyed him and strayed over his forehead. Sam watched Federica, tremulous and radiant, in the dress Torquil had chosen for her, the jewels he had given her – only her shy smile was still hers, but Torquil grinned down at her, poised to possess that too.

Julian had returned to his place on the end of a pew after having taken the photographs outside the church. He put his camera under the seat and proceeded to watch the ceremony. After a while his attention was caught by a dark-haired woman seated on the other side of the aisle to him. She was sleek and confident in a tight, duck-egg blue suit with her long brown legs crossed, tapping her manicured fingers along to the music. She sensed she was being watched and glanced at him from under her wide-brimmed hat. When she saw it was Julian, she smiled. 'I still have your shirt,' she mouthed. He shuddered as he suddenly remembered where he had seen Torquil before. Those two painfully self-satisfied people he had taken great trouble to forget now surfaced in his thoughts. But it was Federica's wedding day, neither the time nor the place for negative recollections. Perhaps Torquil had grown up since those days, he certainly hoped so. He watched as the ring was slipped onto Federica's finger and Reverend Boyble declared the happy couple man and wife. She belonged to him now. She had left the cove for the wider sea.

Sam lowered his eyes in defeat and noticed Mr Toad staring up at him expectantly from the stone floor. He bent down and gathered the blinking creature into his hands where he held him steadily. 'It's just you and me now,' he said quietly, shaking his head. Then as he watched Torquil's stepmother walk by he changed his mind and placed the sleepy toad onto her hat and grinned.

He hadn't been able to stop the wedding, but this small act of sabotage gave him a shallow sense of pleasure.

Chapter 34

Sam returned to his meaningless job in the City and Helena to the dry residue of her marriage, but for Federica, life would never be the same again.

As soon as she returned bronzed and happy from her honeymoon, she rang up Harriet and booked in for lunch. Slipping into the waiting Mercedes in a new Gucci trouser suit she told the driver where to go, then sat back and savoured her new affluence. The seats were leather, the dashboard polished wood. Federica had never learnt to drive. Torquil didn't encourage her. He insisted she have a chauffeur and organized a car for her. 'I want you to have the best of everything,' he had explained. 'Because I love and cherish you.' She rolled the window down and watched the sweltering, dusty city from the cool comfort of her car. She felt sophisticated and glamorous and her spirits floated on the sweet air of her expensive perfume. She fingered the large emerald ring that Torquil had given her and smiled to herself with perfectly painted lips. She was Mrs Torquil Jensen. To Federica the sound of that name had a glorious resonance and she whispered it to herself a few times, Mrs Torquil Jensen, Mrs Torquil Jensen. How far she had come from her uncertain beginnings in Polperro.

The honeymoon had been idyllic. They had spent a week in Africa on safari, a week on the coast and the final two weeks in Thailand. They had stayed in the most prestigious hotels, hired the best guides and travelled first class. Federica had been enchanted by everything she saw and Torquil had enjoyed watching her absorb each new experience after experience like a proud father. But most of all she had savoured their quiet moments together as husband and wife, when he had made love to her in the humid heat of the African jungle and in the jasmine-scented rooms of Thailand. There he had taught her to listen to the calling of her own sensuality and to abandon herself to it. To lose herself in the pleasure of his caresses without inhibition or guilt. When she had found it difficult to discard her shyness he had tied her to the four bedposts so that she had no choice but to give in to her senses and ride unrestrained on the waves of his stroking. At first she had been horrified by the idea, he had never suggested anything like that before. But Torquil had laughed at her inexperience and with gentle persuasion she had agreed to playfully experiment as long as it was done with love. She now blushed at such recollections although she was secretly proud of her new worldliness.

The car drew up outside the doors of St John & Smithe. The doorman hurried down the steps to assist her. 'Ah, Mrs Jensen,' he said in surprise. 'Good morning,' he added reverently, tapping his hat with his hand.

'Thank you, Peter,' she replied as he closed the car door behind her. He didn't comment on her return or make a joke about her sudden rise up in the world. He was too polite. Now she was Mrs Torquil Jensen an invisible wall had grown up between them. Federica Campione belonged to the other side.

When Harriet saw Federica she barely recognized her friend. She was the colour of milk chocolate and her white hair had been bleached further by the sun. She looked so elegant that Harriet had to suppress a pang of jealousy. 'Darling girl, you look fantastic. Marriage obviously suits you,' she enthused, embracing her.

'I love it,' Federica replied with relish, clasping her hands together like a child with a new toy. 'I'm deliriously happy.'

'I can't believe you share a bed every night with Torquil. I hate you,' she laughed. Harriet played with the string of pearls about her neck then shook her head and added more seriously, 'If I couldn't have him, m'darling, I'm happy he's with someone I know and love.'

'Please don't become a nun!' Federica said, taking her by the hand. 'You really were very fond of him, weren't you?'

Harriet nodded sadly but smiled in spite of her disappointment. 'Yes, I was,' she admitted. 'I always made it out to be a bit of a joke, but . . .'

'Many a true thing is said in jest,' Federica interrupted.

'Spot on.'

'So, are you able to have a quick lunch?' she asked.

Harriet looked around furtively. 'You'll have to ask. Greta's smarting over your wedding,' she hissed, casting her eyes to the closed door of Greta's office. 'I'm going to love watching this confrontation.'

'No one's going to enjoy it more than me,' Federica grinned, pulling herself up in preparation to returning with interest the unkindness her boss had shown her during her short time as salesgirl. 'Go and tell her I'm here,' she said and watched Harriet stalk purposefully across the floor to Greta's office.

Federica looked around at her old workplace, which was now, in effect, her family business. She felt a deep sense of satisfaction and power and resolved to use every ounce of it to humiliate Greta. However, when Greta appeared Federica lost the will to hurt her. It was too easy and besides she had already won. She suddenly remembered one of Nuno's most favourite philosophies, 'What goes around comes around', vengeance was not hers to take.

Greta swallowed hard and smiled with her mouth, leaving her eyes to betray her discomfort. Her face was grey like a bruised apple revealing her unhappiness in every line. She no longer had the power to intimidate.

'Congratulations, Federica,' Greta said tightly.

'Thank you.'

'I hear from Mr Jensen that your wedding was beautiful.'

'It was,' she said, noticing the effort Greta was making to sound enthusiastic, a characteristic that came as unnaturally to her as benevolence. 'I'd like to take Harriet out to lunch, Greta, you don't mind if she takes more than an hour, do you?'

Greta pursed her pale lips together and shook her head. 'Of course not.' Then she laughed uncomfortably and added, 'You're the boss.'

Federica took Harriet to lunch at Oriels in Sloane Square. They laughed at Federica's meeting with Greta and at the absurdity of her sudden change in status.

'I love it,' admitted Federica. 'I feel like a modern-day Cinderella. You know, he's generous to a fault. I can have anything I want. I used to dream of being rich.'

'So what will you do this afternoon?' Harriet asked.

'I don't know. I'm going to have to discuss this with Torquil. I understand that I can't work in the family shop, that would be absurd, but I'd like to be busy. I'd ideally like to do something with my photography. Julian taught me the basics, perhaps I could do a more advanced course and then make a trade of it.'

'That would be wonderful. You've always wanted to be a photographer,' Harriet enthused.

'Mama said I had to earn money before embarking on that sort of career. Well, now I have more money than I dreamed of, I can do anything I like.' She laughed and grinned at her friend who smiled back enviously.

'Darling girl, you are so lucky.' Harriet sighed. 'But no one deserves it more than you.'

That evening, when Torquil returned from work, they had their first serious discussion.

'Now we're back from our honeymoon, Torquil, I'd like to settle into something. I'd like to work,' Federica said, throwing herself onto the sofa in his study.

Torquil wandered over to the drinks table and poured himself a tumbler of whisky. 'Would you like a drink, a glass of wine, perhaps?' he asked. 'They say a glass of red wine a day makes a lady glow. Not that you're not glowing already.'

She laughed. 'A glass of red would be nice, thank you,' she replied.

He handed it to her then sat down in the armchair, putting one foot up on the stool. 'Why do you want to work, sweetness?'

'Well, I have to do something,' she argued, taking a sip of wine. 'Darling, this is delicious.'

'Part of the wedding present from Arthur,' he said. 'He's got very good taste that stepfather of yours.'

'Only in some things,' she replied dryly. 'In others, believe me, he has no taste at all.'

'You're a rich woman now, Fede, you don't need to work,' he said seriously.

'Well, I'll get bored if I don't do something,' she explained. 'It's not for the money. You're more than generous and I really appreciate that. It's to fill my day with, to have a reason to get up every morning.'

'Isn't loving me good enough reason to get up in the morning?' Torquil chuckled.

'You know what I mean,' she insisted jovially.

'You'll be busy soon with babies,' he said and smiled at her tenderly.

'Perhaps,' she replied, hoping God would preserve her from that for at least a few more years. 'But, say I don't get pregnant, surely you don't want me to languish here doing nothing?'

'Sweetness,' he said firmly, 'you have a beautiful house, beautiful clothes, a husband who loves the ground you walk on, what more do you want?' He frowned at her and she immediately felt guilty wanting more.

'Well,' she mumbled, suddenly feeling an uncomfortable sense of uncertainty turn her stomach over. 'Julian gave me photography lessons when I was younger, if you don't want me to work, perhaps I can do a course?'

'If you have to do something,' he conceded reluctantly, 'a course is the only option. No wife of mine is going to work.'

'Thank you,' she replied brightly, relieved the discussion was nearing a conclusive end.

'But not photography,' he added resolutely.

'Why not?' she argued in confusion.

He was no longer joking but looking at her very seriously. 'I'll get a tutor in to teach you whatever you want.' He looked about the room. 'Literature. Yes, you can take a literature course.'

'Literature?' she replied, crestfallen. 'I'm not at all interested in literature.'

'No, I'd like you to do literature,' he insisted, walking over to his bookshelves and pulling one out. 'I've never read any of these. I'd like you to read them.'

'Torquil,' she protested weakly.

'No, I insist,' he said. 'If you want to do a course, literature is the only acceptable one.'

'All right, I'll study literature,' she replied lamely. She'd rather do that than nothing at all.

'Then that's decided,' he said, draining his glass. 'Now, love of my life, come here and give me a kiss, I'd hate to think we've had a disagreement.'

When Federica sunk into her bath she reflected on their conversation. She felt uneasy. But rather than trying to get to the bottom of her ill-ease she made excuses for her husband's reluctance to let her choose her own course. 'It's because he loves me and wants what's best for me,' she thought to herself as the bubbles began to dissolve with the soap. 'Photography can wait,' she resolved and decided to broach the subject again another time, when she was feeling more secure in her marriage.

Later, when Torquil wrapped her in a large white towel and made love to her, any remaining doubt melted away and all that was left was unconditional devotion and a strong desire to do anything in order to please him.

That night she dressed up and took her first step into what would become an endless round of cocktail parties and dinners. She met new faces, tried desperately to remember them all by name and quickly learnt how to adopt their social chitchat that said much without saying anything at all. Torquil always made sure she was the best-dressed woman in the room and smiled with pride when she was complimented. But he would become incandescent with rage if he felt she flirted with other men and forbade her to dance with anyone else, explaining that it was a humiliation for him watching another man rub himself up against his wife.

So Federica was careful not to step out of line. Instinctively she knew when he was watching her and modified her behaviour. If she saw his face cloud with jealousy she would move over and link her arm through his and stand by his side like a lovely appendage. When her instincts rebelled against his commands she told herself firmly that he was of another generation and altered her conduct accordingly.

'Everyone loves you, Fede,' said Torquil as they sat in the back of the car on their way home from a party. Federica smiled with pleasure. 'I'm so proud of you,' he added, running a hand down her cheek. 'You're beautiful and serene. I must have been told by at least ten people tonight how lucky I am to have found you.'

'Well, I'm lucky to have found you,' she replied, taking his hand in hers and kissing his fingers.

He then looked into her face for a long moment, as if searching her features for something. 'Are you lucky, sweetness?' he said, shaking his head. 'I don't know that you are.'

Federica frowned and laughed off his strange remark. Torquil noticed her anxiety and her effort to cover up. To his surprise it gave him a strange sense of satisfaction. But he was unable to interpret these new feelings or understand why he felt them. He was too insensitive to notice that he was beginning to resent his wife for all the reasons he married her. Her purity was beginning to grate, her perfection to irritate. She made him feel inadequate. He was unable to help himself put her down as if by pulling her off her marble pedestal he might raise himself up.

In an effort to exercise more control Torquil announced that he didn't approve of her friendship with Harriet. 'She's not sophisticated enough for you, sweetness. You're too intelligent to waste your affections on some old Sloane. You've moved on in the world, your friends have to change too. Now I've got someone in mind who I know you'll like,' he said happily. 'Lucia Sarafina.'

Lucia was only too happy to be of service. 'I'll befriend your wife if you make time to see me,' she bargained coquettishly when he telephoned her.

Torquil enjoyed the attention. 'She needs to be around women like you,' he said. 'She's too snow white.'

'I know what you mean,' Lucia agreed, delighted by the thought that his devotion might be waning. 'But she's young. She'll grow up.'

'With your help, *maestra*, I hope she will.'

'Leave it to me, darling. Then I want to be thanked in person, *capisci*?'

'*Capisco*.' He laughed. 'You're wicked.' Then he sighed heavily, a sigh that escaped his throat like a deep groan. 'God, I've missed you.'

'You don't have to,' she whispered. 'You know where to find me.'

'I'll hold that thought,' he replied, 'in the meantime you've got a job to do.'

Federica made a great effort to like Lucia. She had to in order to please her husband. Lucia invited her to Harry's Bar where they were given the best table in the far corner of the restaurant. 'Every man in this room will go straight home after lunch and make love to his wife,' Lucia mused in a smooth Italian accent, as Federica sat down. 'You see they're all looking at me. I make them feel lustful.' She sighed and licked her blood-red lips. 'You probably don't remember meeting me at the wedding. You had to be introduced to so many new people.'

'Of course I remember meeting you,' Federica said diplomatically. 'You're Torquil's closest friend.'

'We go back a long way,' she replied wistfully.

'How did you meet?'

'In Italy. I was living in Rome and Torquil came out for the wedding of a mutual friend. We clicked instantly,' she said, smoothing down the manicured cuticles on her nails with a steady hand, recalling their lovemaking in one of the dark halls of the palazzo.

'When did you move to London?'

'Shortly after,' she replied. 'Ah, the menu. Let's choose now then we can get down to some serious gossip. Bloody Mary please and my guest will have . . .?' She looked at Federica and raised a black eyebrow.

'A Spritzer please,' Federica replied and thanked the waiter graciously.

'You don't know how happy it makes me to see Torquil so full of joy,' Lucia continued.

Federica smiled, 'I'm glad I make him happy,' she replied. 'He's made me happier than I ever thought possible.'

'Oh, he's a unique man,' Lucia agreed. 'I've never met a man so devoted. You're so pure and innocent. That's what he loves about you. Don't ever lose that quality,' she added silk-ily. 'You are very lucky. He's been in love many times before, but never the way he is with you.'

'How do you mean?'

'Well . . .' She deliberated, playing with a black strand of hair that flopped onto her shoulder like the tail of a fat rat. 'He always wanted to marry an innocent. Someone unspoiled, unworldly. Just like you. He dated sophisticates but he wanted his wife to be untouched by anyone else. That is your strength.'

'I see.' Federica nodded, fighting her unease.

Sensing her discomfort Lucia placed a soft hand on hers. 'I don't mean this as a criticism,' she gushed. 'He worships you, darling. He's never met anyone as perfect as you. He adores you. I'm only giving you advice, woman to woman. You have to be smart in this world to keep your man. You have to know what it is that they love about you and then hold onto it.'

'I can't stay young and innocent for ever,' Federica protested meekly.

'Oh, yes you can.' Lucia nodded and winked. The more 'snow white' Federica was the more Torquil would crave the dark sophistication of his Italian lover. 'You can be anything you want to be.'

Federica shrugged and pulled a thin smile. Lucia had left her feeling uncomfortable. She was becoming sick of being told how angelic and perfect she was. No one could live up to that.

'I'd love to be married to a man like Torquil,' Lucia sighed, pushing the salad around her plate dreamily. 'He's so totally in control. I love that. Unbelievably romantic. And so unusual for an Englishman. Italian men take control and it makes women feel very feminine.'

'Yes, although, sometimes, it's nice to be independent,' Federica argued, remembering their discussion about work and inwardly cringing.

'Don't be a little fool, Fede, you have a gem there, enjoy it,' said Lucia seriously. 'Millions of women would kill to leave their jobs, have their chaotic lives organized by a loving man. You don't know how lucky you are.'

'Oh, I do,' she replied quickly. 'It's just a bit overwhelming.'

'It's his way of showing you he loves you. You'll get used to it and then it will be second nature. Remember he has your interests at heart, always. Every choice he makes for you is for your own good. Goodness, he's, what, twenty years older than you?' Federica nodded. 'Twenty years more experience than you. If I were you I'd put my feet up and enjoy the ride.'

Federica took her advice. She stopped seeing Harriet and avoided going into St John & Smithe in case she bumped into her. She studied literature once a week with an old Cambridge don called Dr Lionel Swanborough, who always wore a three-piece suit with a fedora placed crookedly above his thin face. He was at once impressed with Torquil's library but unimpressed by Federica's lack of knowledge.

'I've barely read anything,' she told him. He gave her *Anna Karenina* and insisted she read the entire book in a week. 'Don't worry, my dear girl, once you've turned the first page the other eight hundred and fifty-two will turn by themselves.' He was right. Once she had analyzed *Anna Karenina* she moved on to *Vanity Fair*, *Emma* and *King Lear*. Her eagerness for learning was bred in the boredom of her daily life as Torquil's wife, where she immersed herself in her studies so that she wouldn't notice the world outside her gilded prison and yearn for it.

One grey evening Torquil returned home yet again to his wife's light chatter echoing gaily through the rooms of the house as she attempted to fill the empty hours with long telephone conversations to her mother and Toby. He felt the irritation crawl up his neck in the form of an uncomfortable prickly heat that was becoming as familiar to him as the nagging sense of inadequacy he felt when faced with his wife's natural grace and virtue. His mouth twitched with impatience as he stalked into the sitting room, leaving his briefcase and coat thrown onto a chair in the hall. When Federica saw him standing crossly in the doorway she hastily put down the receiver and swallowed hard as her stomach turned over with anxiety.

'What's wrong?' she asked, hoping it had nothing to do with her. In the brief moment that passed while Torquil chewed on his jealousy Federica frantically cast her mind back to the previous evening in an attempt to remember anything she might have said to anyone that could have roused his anger.

'I'm fed up with coming home to find you on the telephone,' he snapped finally.

Federica breathed out with relief. 'I'm sorry,' she muttered.

But Torquil wasn't satisfied. He walked over to the fire and stood in front of it with his hands on his hips. He shook his head. 'I'm out at work all day, when I come home I want your undivided attention. You have hours to amuse yourself when I'm not here, why do you have to insist on calling your family at the exact moment I walk through the door?'

'I don't do it on purpose,' she protested weakly.

'Perhaps not,' he conceded. Federica stiffened. He often appeared to back down before delivering a harsher blow. 'Sweetness,' he continued carefully, 'I really think you're too old to still be so attached to your mother and uncle. It's about time you devoted your energies to me.'

'What do you mean?' she asked in bewilderment. He sat beside her on the sofa and ran a hand down her hair with tenderness. When she looked into his face his expression had softened and he was smiling at her with affection.

He sighed heavily. 'I'm a jealous old man, my darling,' he explained meekly. 'I'm guilty of loving you too much.'

Federica was disarmed by the sudden change in his tone and felt the colour rise in her cheeks. 'It's okay, Torquil, I understand,' she replied sympathetically.

'I miss you all day, when I come home to find you on the telephone to your mother this anger wells up inside me. I can't control it. I want you all to myself.' Then he chuckled sheepishly. 'Is that so terrible?'

Federica nestled her face against his hand that now stroked her cheek. 'Of course not,' she said and smiled, once more defeated by his charm. 'I won't do it again, I promise.'

He pulled her into his arms and kissed her on her mouth with an intensity that demonstrated his gratitude. 'You're too good to me, little one. No other woman would understand me like you do.'

She laughed and caressed his face with the gentle eyes of an adoring mother. 'No man would understand me like you do, either.'

'We're made for each other,' he breathed. 'You're happy, aren't you, sweetness? I want you to be happy.'

'Of course I am.'

'You enjoy your course?'

'I love it,' she enthused dutifully.

'You see,' he laughed. 'I know what's good for you better than you do.'

Even though Federica did as her husband had asked and made the calls when he was at work, he seemed to know exactly when they were made and for how long they lasted. In his silky manner he managed to persuade her to limit them to once a week. Molly and Hester went the way of Harriet. Although they put up a fiercer fight, Federica let them go in the end. She had to.

'You're too sophisticated now for these provincial people, sweetness,' Torquil said. 'You'll thank me one day.'

At first they journeyed down to Polperro regularly, but little by little their visits became less frequent until they barely went at all.

Federica felt powerless to complain for every time she made plans, Torquil flew her off to Paris or Madrid or Rome.

'Sweetheart, we never see you these days,' Toby lamented one day when Federica managed to call him from the telephone box in Harrods.

'I know, I'm longing to come down to Polperro, and so is Torquil,' she lied, 'he's just travelling so much at the moment, opening new offices abroad, so we spend most weekends out of the country.'

'I know we shouldn't worry, they always say newly-weds disappear into themselves for a while. It obviously means you're happy. You don't need your home like you used to.'

Federica's heart yearned for Polperro. She needed it more than ever, but she was barely able to admit it, even to herself.

'I *am* happy,' she insisted.

'Then we're happy you're happy. If you missed home all the time that would surely mean there was something wrong with your marriage.'

'There's nothing wrong with that, I can assure you. He's so wonderful; I wake up every day hardly able to believe that I am so blessed to be married to someone so gorgeous. I don't deserve him.' Federica laughed.

'Yes you do, sweetheart.'

'I don't. He does everything for me. I don't have a care in the world. Mrs Hughes looks after the house, in fact she gets cross if I so much as move a photo frame. She's a little too territorial, but then I suppose she's looked after him for so long it's hardly surprising. She knows what he likes better than I do.'

'I doubt that. She's not married to him.'

'That's not what she thinks!' she joked. 'But I shouldn't complain. I live in the most beautiful house. Most men don't buy their wives expensive clothes and jewellery. Torquil indulges my every desire, I'm in great danger of turning into a spoilt princess.'

'Fede, nothing could ever turn you into that. You're a sweet girl and he's bloody lucky to have you. It all sounds so perfect!'

'It is. I do miss you all though,' she said softly and Toby noticed the strain in her voice, as if she were suppressing a cry for help. 'I miss Polperro and the sea, walks along the stormy cliffs with Rasta. Oh, I miss Rasta too, how is he?' she asked, attempting to sound cheerful.

'Missing you. We cuddle him a lot to compensate but he still looks at me with those big sad eyes inquiring where you are.'

'Don't, you'll make me miserable,' she wailed. 'Torquil won't let me have a dog in London because he doesn't want dog hair all over the house. Seeing as he's barely here I'm surprised he'd notice. But he's very proud of his house. He's meticulous about everything.'

'I noticed that. He dresses like a duke,' Toby said enthusiastically but he felt a tingling sensation of discomfort creep up his neck.

'Don't talk to me about his clothes.' She sighed melodramatically. 'He gets enraged if Mrs Hughes leaves creases in his shirts or presses his trousers incorrectly. Thank God he doesn't lose his temper like that with his wife. Well, he does when he's jealous but Lucia tells me that's his way of showing me that he loves me, imagine if he wasn't jealous at all, I'd feel very neglected.'

'Don't you cook any more?' Toby asked, remembering how much pleasure she took from looking after him and Julian during the years they all lived together.

'No, I haven't cooked since I got married. Mrs Hughes cooks or we go out. You see, I'm *very* spoilt.'

Toby didn't dare ask whether she still put flowers in vases, scented the sheets with lavender and filled the house with music because he knew the answer and he couldn't bear to hear it.

'As long as he makes you happy,' he conceded finally. But when he put the telephone down he was besieged by new anxieties, unable to reconcile the Torquil they met before the wedding with the Torquil Federica had just described. Something didn't gel.

But Federica was happy – or at least she believed herself to be happy. She loved her husband to distraction and modified her tastes and her desires to suit him without even realizing it. Torquil denied her nothing but her freedom, which, during the occasional moments when his possessiveness threatened to suffocate her, she justified as an expression of his devotion and forgave him. She rarely questioned his motives or his actions. He was her husband, she had chosen him, so she worked through any feelings of frustration because she didn't know any other way. She was determined to make the marriage work. Above all she needed him. He gave her security and love and she willingly sacrificed her freedom for that.

Unable to make the house into a real home, for Mrs Hughes saw to all the domestic needs, Federica began to eat away her boredom. A biscuit here, and piece of cake there, until she was rarely without something in her fingers, making regular trips up to her mouth. Lucia, who believed it impossible to be too rich or too thin, delighted in the swell of her rival's figure and encouraged her with cunning. Torquil, who loathed fat women, watched his wife's changing body with delight; it reflected the gradual surrendering of her independence. Unable to understand it as an outward expression of her inner discontent he felt empowered by it. The ivory goddess was toppling from her pedestal. As her confidence was subtly undermined she grew more needy. Torquil relished his control. She belonged to him. Without intending to be malicious he began to call her 'my Venus' and 'Voluptuosa' while at the same time encouraging her to eat. 'You're not fat, sweetness, you're sensual and I love you like that,' he would say. She believed him because he seemed to desire her more. After all, sex was his way of telling her he loved her.

Within two years Federica had tuned herself to Torquil's pitch without even noticing the gradual relinquishing of her liberty. It was such a steady shift she didn't even realize she was unhappy. In her limited understanding Torquil was the same, sensitive man she had married – just a little harder to please. She didn't buy her own clothes because she knew he liked choosing them for her. She didn't buy him presents because she learned that if he wanted something he would go out and get it himself. She met Lucia for lunch and was soon included in a small circle of women, who, like herself, had nothing else to do all day except lunch, gossip and shop with each other. Yet, Torquil's controlling nature had taught her how to deceive. She learned to splash the soap with water when she was in a hurry after using the bathroom, because she knew Torquil would check it after to make sure she had washed her hands. She learned to ask the chauffeur to wait for her outside Harrods while she sneaked out the other side and wandered up Walton Street just for the sheer pleasure of doing something without being watched. She called her family from public telephones in shops and met Hester once or twice in the ladies' powder room in Harvey Nichols. She managed to justify Torquil's behaviour to her family, using his arguments without realizing like a well-trained parrot.

Then Sam rang her up, out of the blue.

'Hi, Fede, it's Sam.'

'Sam!' she exclaimed in surprise. 'My God, I haven't seen you since I got married.'

'I hear you've barely seen any of us since you got married,' he replied. 'I gather that husband of yours is hiding you away.'

'No, not at all,' she replied breezily. 'I've just been so busy. Time has flown.'

'Two years?'

'Is it really that long?' she gasped.

'So, how are you?' he asked.

'Well. Very well. Actually, you'll be impressed, I've been studying literature with an old Cambridge don,' she said proudly.

'I am impressed. What's his name?'

'Dr Lionel—'

'Swanborough,' he interjected in admiration. 'Lucky you, he's a very learned man. What have you read?'

'Oh, I've studied everything from Zola to García Márquez.'

'In Spanish?'

'Don't be ridiculous. I forgot my Spanish years ago.' She laughed.

'Shame.'

'Isn't it.'

'So, he's treating you well, is he?' he asked, conjuring up the silky face of Torquil Jensen with distaste.

'Enough of me, how are you?' she asked.

'Hating the City. In fact, I'm going home.'

'Home?' she asked in surprise.

'Back to Polperro.'

'To do what?'

'To write.'

'How lovely,' she said, suffering a silent pang of nostalgia as she envisaged those windy cliffs and choppy sea. She hadn't been back since the previous Christmas.

'Yes, Nuno's delighted, he says I can use his study to write in.'

'That's an honour.' She sighed, recalling Pickthistle Manor and the golden days she had spent there. Sam detected the wistful tone in her voice and longed to know how she *really* was.

'Oh yes it is. He never lets anyone into that room.'

'How is old Nuno?'

'Old.'

'That's sad. He's a one-off.'

'He certainly is,' he chuckled. 'God broke the mould when he'd made Nuno.'

'Tell me, why didn't you ever call him Grandpa?' she asked curiously.

'*Nonno* is grandpa in Italian, Nuno just stuck.'

'I've always wondered about that.'

'Well, now you know.'

'I don't see so much of your sisters.'

'I know, so they tell me.'

'Things are hectic.' She sighed, glancing around her tidy sitting room and feeling lonelier than ever.

'I'm ringing up to see if you can make lunch. I'd like to see you before I disappear into the depths of Nuno's study.'

'Oh, I'd love to,' she enthused. 'I really would. Can you make it this week?'

'What about tomorrow?'

'Tomorrow's great.'

'I'll pick you up at your house,' he said. 'Remind me of your address?'

When Sam saw Federica waiting for him on the doorstep he immediately noticed the change in her. She was wearing an elegant summer suit in blue with a short skirt and high heels, revealing a larger body and heavier bust. Her hair, scraped back into a ponytail, betrayed a rounder face cloaked in makeup. To anyone else she would have looked sensual and glamorous, but to Sam she looked like a sad clown smiling bleakly through a thick layer of paint. He felt his heart stagger as she walked towards him. He wanted to wrap her in his arms and take her home to where she belonged. But she kissed him warmly, commented on how wonderful it was to see him again and climbed into the waiting cab.

It wasn't until coffee was served that he gently tried to break through her façade. 'You look so different, Fede, I hardly recognized you standing outside your house,' he said, gazing into her blue eyes that failed to disguise her melancholy.

'You haven't changed,' she replied, once again diverting the conversation away from herself. 'You're still wearing holey shirts and worn-out trousers. Torquil should take you shopping!' She laughed and dropped two sugar lumps into her cup of coffee.

But Sam didn't laugh. 'I'm afraid I have better things to do than worry about the state of my clothes,' he said, allowing the bitterness he felt towards her husband to seep into his words. He checked himself, aware that if he angered her he would lose her trust. 'I'm thrilled you decided to do a literature course,' he said. 'I hope you're also continuing your photography, you always had a passion for that.'

Federica lowered her eyes and stared into her cup. 'Oh, I've sort of lost interest in photography,' she replied quietly.

'How could you have lost interest? I don't believe you, Fede,' he exclaimed, feeling the fury rise in his throat.

'I just don't have time.'

'What on earth do you fill your day with?'

'Oh, lots of things.'

'Like?'

'Well, I have a lot of reading to do . . .' Her voice trailed off. Sam moved his hand across the table and took hers impulsively. She looked up at him in alarm before scanning the room in panic to see if anyone was looking.

'Fede, you're worrying me,' he said seriously, his face suddenly grey and anxious. She frowned. Sam shook his head slowly then continued in a very low voice, penetrating her eyes with the intensity of his stare. 'Please tell me, darling, that it was *your* decision not to take a photography course, that it was *your* decision to study literature, that it is *your* decision not to come down to Polperro, to cut us all out of your life, to dress like that and paint your face like that . . .' His voice cracked. 'Because if your husband is imposing his will onto you, you're in danger of being smothered. I won't stand by and watch your spirit harnessed and controlled.'

Federica stared at him in confusion, suddenly having to confront her fears. She bit her lower lip. Sam watched her, attempting to read her thoughts as she so clearly balanced between confiding in him as she had always done in the past, and throwing up her defences and shutting him out.

There followed a weighty silence. Sam squeezed her hand in encouragement. 'I'm only asking because I care,' he said softly and smiled at her reassuringly. To his disappointment she stiffened then withdrew her hand.

'I love Torquil, Sam,' she said eventually. Then she added 'Anyway, you wouldn't understand.'

'I'll try,' he suggested, but she was already looking away. The connection had been broken. Devastated, he had no choice but to ask for the bill and escort her back to her house. When he tried to reach her once more, on the marble steps of her home, he realized to his despair that he had lost her again. He wondered if he'd ever get another chance.

Federica curled up on the sofa with a packet of chocolate biscuits and a glass of cold milk. She snivelled into a piece of kitchen roll and reflected on her lunch with Sam. How could he possibly understand her situation? What he didn't realize was that it was *her* choice to love Torquil and *her* choice to want to be the best wife she could be to him. He needed her and cherished her. If he was possessive and controlling, it was simply because he cared. She needed him too. Besides, she thought crossly, the dynamic of their relationship had nothing whatsoever to do with Sam. But, while she dried her eyes and delved further into the packet of biscuits, the seed of doubt Sam had dropped was slowly settling into fertile ground.

When Torquil arrived home that evening his face was red and harassed.

'Darling, you look exhausted, let me run you a nice hot bath and bring up a glass of whisky,' Federica suggested, embracing him warmly.

'We need to talk,' he said coldly, pushing her away.

She shuddered and immediately felt consumed with guilt. 'What about?'

'You know exactly what about,' he snapped, stalking into his study to help himself to a drink.

She followed him nervously. 'Lunch with Sam.' She sighed in defeat. There was no use trying to hide anything from Torquil because somehow he was as omniscient as the devil.

'Exactly. Lunch with Sam,' he repeated, clicking his tongue impatiently. He poured whisky into a tumbler and drank it straight. 'Were you going to tell me, or were you just going to wait and see whether or not you got away with it?'

'What's the big deal, Torquil, he's an old friend?' she protested.

'That's not what I asked,' he replied angrily.

Federica swallowed hard, his expression was so remote she barely recognized him. 'Of course I was going to tell you, but you didn't give me a chance.'

'You had all of last night to tell me. He called you yesterday,' he shouted suddenly, slamming his glass down on the table in exasperation. Federica flinched at the severity of his tone. 'You didn't tell me,' he continued in a menacingly soft voice, turning around to face her, 'because your intentions weren't honourable.'

Federica's chin wobbled as she fought against the impulse to cry. For the first time in her marriage she felt consumed with fear. 'I didn't tell you, because I knew you wouldn't let me go,' she said hoarsely. 'And I so wanted to go.'

'So you lied to me?' he argued, scrutinizing her face with narrowed eyes. 'My own wife lied to me?' He shook his head. 'I can't even trust my own wife.'

'I knew you'd say no,' she explained, unable to swallow the moan that choked up from her chest. 'I haven't seen any of my old friends for years. I miss them.'

'Fede, I'm not your gaoler,' he said in a more gentle tone. 'There's always logic behind my requests. Put yourself in my shoes, how would you feel if I had lunch with an old girl-friend and didn't tell you?'

She gulped. 'I'd probably feel jealous.' Torquil always had a winning argument for everything.

'Look, let me explain with an analogy,' he said, sitting down beside her and taking her hand in his. Torquil loved inventing the perfect analogy to illustrate his case. 'Take a porn video,' he began. She frowned at him. 'No, listen. If there's a porn video sitting on the video player it's all too easy to put it in and have a peek, whereas, if you have to go all the way out to a video shop, risk being seen by someone, face the embarrassment of asking for it, paying for it, then sneaking home to watch it, you're less likely to do it. Do you understand?'

'Are you trying to tell me that by having lunch with Sam, I'm in danger of having an affair?'

'Exactly.'

'But, Torquil,' she insisted. 'That's madness. He's like my brother.'

'But he isn't your brother,' he replied sharply.

'I'm as likely to have an affair with him as have an affair with Hal.'

'It's just logic. I don't want my wife having close male friends. It's dangerous, believe me. I've got more experience than you, you're very naïve, little one,' he said, caressing her cheek. 'I love you. I adore you. I don't want to lose you. In fact, I'll do anything not to lose you. Anything at all.'

Federica shivered and waited apprehensively.

'When I said I'd love you for life, I meant it. All these requests of mine might seem strange to you, but they're implemented to safeguard our marriage. It's for you and me,' he explained. He leant over and kissed her. But Federica didn't feel like being kissed, she felt confused. He took her by the hand. 'Come upstairs, I hate fighting with you. Let's make up.'

'Torquil, please,' she objected in a thin voice that was barely audible.

He seemed not to notice her tears. 'I want to show you why you don't need to have male friends. They can't give you what I give you. Come on, little one, convince me that you're not angry with me.'

Reluctantly she allowed him to unbutton her trousers and pull them off. She lay on the bed in her shirt and panties, trying to control her snivelling. He closed the curtains, took the telephone off the hook and put Pink Floyd in the CD player. Then he dimmed the lights. 'Don't cry, my darling, we're making up now,' he soothed, kissing her forehead. 'I'm going to blindfold you,' he added slowly.

'Oh, Torquil, I . . .'

'Shhh,' he whispered, placing his finger over her mouth. He then put it inside her lips and traced it across her gums. Inwardly she recoiled with revulsion. He pulled a silk scarf out of his bedside drawer and tied it over her eyes. She closed her eyes into the blackness, wondering where he was and what he was doing. Finally, she felt him unbutton her shirt and open it, releasing the catch on her bra. As he traced her skin with a long white feather, slid his tongue between the gaps in her toes and derived a perverse pleasure from making love to her with her panties on she felt nothing and stifled a sob.

She wanted to shout at him to make love to her normally. Then suddenly she realized that he had always made love to her without love and her flesh rippled with an icy chill that debilitated her. But Torquil didn't notice, he liked her to be still. It was then that the seed planted earlier by Sam put out tentative roots and began to grow. For the first time in her marriage she allowed herself to doubt. But once she gave into the first doubt she was unable to control the torrent of uncertainty that invaded her thoughts like wafts of black smoke.

Federica got up and began to rummage around in her cupboard. There at the back, in the very corner where Torquil's pedantic hands had failed to find it to throw away with the rest of her past, was the butterfly box. She sat on the floor, placed it on her knee and opened it. With an unsteady hand she re-read all her father's letters, one by one, reclaiming the past in each tender word until her tears formed another layer of unhappiness on the paper. Then she focused her eyes into the empty distance and drew comfort from the memories she found there.

Chapter 35

Autumn 1998

The following two summers passed in a blur of parties, tedious ladies' lunches and endless visits to the gynaecologist because Federica hadn't got pregnant and Torquil was certain there was something wrong with her. As far as the doctor was concerned she was functioning perfectly. 'Give it time, you've only been trying for a few years and you're only twenty-two,' he said kindly. 'Perhaps you're too anxious. Try to relax more.'

Torquil took it as a personal insult to his manhood that Federica hadn't got pregnant immediately. 'A man could scarcely make love to his wife more than I do,' he complained, 'and you're voluptuous enough to be a fertility symbol.'

Federica took offence. Lonely at home in front of the fire, making her way through magazines and Dr Lionel Swanborough's reading lists, she grazed on panettone and chocolate rolls. Torquil took her whenever he had a spare moment, lifting her skirt up and bending her over to inject her with his potency. Each time he withdrew he patted her on her bottom. 'That'll do it, little one,' he'd say confidently as Federica obeyed his instructions and lay on the bed with her feet in the air for half an hour to help the sperm in their struggle against gravity.

Federica desperately wanted a baby, but not for the right reasons. She felt she was too young to be tied down with such a heavy responsibility and yet she longed to please her husband. Each month her bleeding was accompanied by hot tears of frustration and the painful duty of reporting her failure. When she suggested that he go and see a doctor himself he retorted that everything worked perfectly well in that department, the problem lay with her.

As the cold, melancholic winds of October groaned about her Federica sought solace in her books, her chocolate and her memories.

Then Nuno died.

Under such exceptional circumstances Torquil allowed Federica to be chauffeur-driven down to Polperro for the funeral. 'But I want you back by nightfall,' he said. When Federica explained that that just wasn't possible, Polperro was hours away, he grudgingly conceded and allowed her to stay the night.

'I'm going to miss you, little one,' he added, embracing her, 'I need you here with me.'

Federica was devastated that Nuno had died, but her excitement at returning home to Polperro eclipsed her sadness. She longed for that day with such anticipation that she forgot her cautiousness and called her mother and Toby every day from a call box to discuss it. She even managed to avoid sex with Torquil, claiming that she was far too distressed.

The funeral took place in the little church in the village. Those who couldn't fit in spilled out onto the leafy path, pulling their coats and hats about them to keep warm. Ingrid wore a black hat with a heavy veil so no one could see her crying. Inigo helped her down the aisle with a bowed head and red eyes. 'It's you and me now at the top of the pile,' he said gloomily as they sat together in the front pew.

'I don't know about you, darling, but I'm going to reincarnate into a beautiful bird, you'll see,' she replied, placing her monocle into one eye in order to read the service sheet. Inigo pondered on the theories of reincarnation for the rest of the service.

Molly and Hester sat wiping their wet faces while Sam sat staring at the coffin. He thought of his beloved grandfather and his eyes turned to liquid.

Federica arrived late. She had wept tears of frustration as a broken-down lorry had held them in a tight traffic-jam for over half an hour. Sweating, she shuffled down the aisle just as Reverend Boyble took his solemn place in the nave. Federica squashed in beside Toby and Julian who squeezed her arm affectionately, thrilled to see her. Reverend Boyble cleared his throat and waited for Federica to settle.

'No one will ever forget Nuno,' he began. 'He was one of life's originals, a rare ray of light that shone upon us all. We shall miss that light greatly. But now he shines with God. Let us thank God for the life of our dear friend Nuno, who gave each one of us so much.'

Ingrid began to sniff and her shoulders quivered in an effort to control herself. Sam continued to stare at the coffin as if in a trance. Federica turned around and quietly greeted her family who all stared at her as if she were an alien being. How she had changed!

'I know she's unhappy,' Polly whispered to her husband. Jake sighed and nodded. 'She's put on weight. She's not a strongly built girl. It's unhappiness that's done it,' she added, mouthing the same to Helena who sat on Jake's other side. Toby took Federica's hand and she suddenly felt an overwhelming sense of loss. Not just of Nuno but of everyone. She had lost Polperro in the last few years and now she was back she wanted so much to hold onto it. But she knew she couldn't. Torquil wanted her back tomorrow.

Sam walked gravely up to the pulpit to give the address. He had left his cuffs undone and they flapped about his wrists like white doves. Federica watched him. He had lost a lot of hair since she had last seen him. It was now clearly receding at the front and thinning on top. He looked up with a grey face and surveyed the congregation. He didn't need notes because he hadn't prepared what he was going to say. He removed his glasses, took a deep breath as if collecting his emotions and then began in a confident, articulate voice.

'Nuno was my best and most beloved friend,' he began. 'He taught me everything I know and I owe him for everything that I have become.' Then his grey eyes rested on Federica as he quoted from *The Prophet*. '"And let your best be for your friend,"' he said in a slow, almost theatrical voice. '"If he must know the ebb of your tide, let him know its flood also. For what is your friend that you should seek him with hours to kill? Seek him always with hours to live. For it is his to fill your need, but not your emptiness."'

Federica didn't lower her eyes but looked steadily into his. She felt suffocated by a wave of pity and regret. She recalled with nostalgia the moments they had shared in the past. They had been special moments of great tenderness. Then, as she tried to hold onto them they dissolved before her like mist, leaving only the desolation of the present and Sam's grief-stricken face illuminated by the light of God.

'I always sought Nuno with hours to live,' he continued bravely. 'He filled my need for knowledge and my need for wisdom. He also filled my need to understand myself better and taught me not to desire to be understood or admired by others. He was never understood by others and that gave him great freedom, because he was always himself. I shall miss his tedious quoting, his pedantry, his faux Italian accent and his dry, irreverent humour. But most of all I shall miss his wisdom, because without it I am lost. All I have now are the words he taught me in the past, which I shall replay in my memory in my effort to live better.'

Federica listened to his words as they spilled out, without direction, without constraint but from the heart. He spoke at length, holding the sides of the pulpit with his hands, either for effect or for support. He only lifted his eyes from Federica's to gaze down at the coffin as if he were talking to Nuno himself.

When he finished, no one moved or made a sound. All that could be heard was Sam's soft footsteps as he walked slowly back to his seat.

Nuno's coffin was lowered into the ground in the small graveyard outside the church. The family and close friends stood around in the cold and watched his final journey home. Back into the earth where it had all begun. 'How did he die?' Federica whispered to Julian, who stood solemnly beside her.

'Apparently he knew he was going to go,' he replied, leaning down and speaking quietly into her ear. 'It was Tuesday afternoon and he kissed Ingrid goodbye, then Inigo and went into his study and passed away in his leather chair reading Balzac.' Federica raised her eyebrows. 'Ingrid and Inigo just thought he was going off for a siesta, they didn't realize he really meant "*adieu*".'

'Unpredictable to the last,' she replied, catching Sam's hollow eyes blinking sadly behind his glasses. He watched her but didn't see her. 'Sam's taking it very badly,' she added, smiling at him with sympathy.

But his vision had clouded with grief. He couldn't see anything. Then he turned and walked to the waiting cars with his family and everyone made their way back to Pickthistle Manor.

Federica gave Julian and Hal a lift in her chauffeur-driven car. Hal was impressed. Julian was not. 'Why don't you learn to drive, Fede?' he asked.

'I don't need to.'

'Of course you need to, it's a question of independence.' Federica eyed him nervously and nodded towards the chauffeur. Julian raised his eyebrows. She knew that Paul reported everything back to Torquil.

'I think it's really cool to have a chauffeur,' said Hal. 'Swish car too. You married well, Fede.'

Julian looked at Federica and watched her smile at her brother. But he could feel the unease behind her smile because the light in her eyes had grown opaque. He took her hand and squeezed it, but Federica only squeezed it back jovially as if she didn't want her pain to be recognized by anyone.

The atmosphere at Pickthistle Manor was lighter compared with the heaviness that had hung like an invisible miasma in the church. Everyone unburdened their grief with the effect of the wine and Ingrid asked her guests to celebrate Nuno's life, not to mourn it. The sitting room at once filled with smoke and the vapour of alcohol and body heat as it throbbed with the people Nuno had acquired throughout his life. When Lucien brought in a sodden hedgehog he had found in the driveway Ingrid burst into tears, recalling Nuno's aversion to flea-ridden animals, and knocked back half a glass of vodka.

Helena embraced her daughter and complimented her on her designer suit. Then she launched once again into a soliloquy about Hal. 'We're not doing very well at school at the moment,' she said sanctimoniously. 'We're going to fail our A levels. We've got the brains, we just refuse to use them.' She sighed helplessly. 'We're going through a particularly painful time at present. But our heart's in the right place, we're just a little bit misguided.'

Federica's attention drifted, as it always did when her mother obsessed about Hal. She was relieved when Jake intervened and directed the conversation away from his grandson. 'Hal's fine, Helena, your problem is you won't let go,' he said wisely.

'He needs his mother, Dad,' she replied, offended. 'I don't care what any of you say, I'm not going to leave him to flounder when I can pick him up.'

Molly was too affronted by Federica's fickleness even to greet her. She saw her making her way through the crowd in her perfect black suit, her perfect black shoes, her perfect little black bag and perfect black hat and turned her back and walked in the opposite direction. But Hester remained and embraced her friend with the same loyal affection that she had always shown her throughout their childhood. 'You look well,' she said kindly, noticing her larger frame and pallid skin and wondering what had caused it.

'I am well,' she replied.

'How's Torquil?' Hester, asked wondering if Federica would open up to her like she had always done in their secret cave. But she was disappointed.

'He's a dream,' she replied enthusiastically. 'I only wish he were here today. I hate to be parted from him, even for a minute.'

'How nice,' said Hester flatly. 'It's great that you've found your soul mate. I'm still looking for mine.'

'No one, then?'

'No one. It's a desert out there,' she sighed. 'Molly has a penchant for picking up builders,' she added, trying to lighten the conversation. 'She's happiest on a building site.'

'That sounds like Molly. I was lucky Torquil found me so early on. But you're young, you don't need to find someone yet. Enjoy your freedom while you have it.'

'You're right. I'll keep my eyes peeled for a Torquil. He doesn't have any handsome friends by any chance, does he?' They both laughed, but their laughter was uneasy.

'Sam's miserable.' Federica said, watching him talking gravely to his father.

'Oh, he's devastated,' Hester agreed. 'He gave a good address, didn't he?'

'He's so talented.'

'I know. I'm so proud of him.' She sighed. Then she touched Federica on her arm and looked at her imploringly. 'Go and talk to him. He needs cheering up.'

'Sam, I'm so sorry,' said Federica, when Inigo had moved off to seek the quiet sanctuary of his office.

'Federica.' He kissed her. 'I'm glad you could make it. We'd almost forgotten what you looked like.' Federica smiled awkwardly, recalling their last meeting. 'Let's get out of here, I'm feeling claustrophobic,' he suggested. Sam led her down the corridor to Nuno's study. Once inside he closed the door, blocking out the low drone of voices. 'You can see why Nuno liked it so much in here. It's quiet,' he said, sitting down on his grandfather's worn leather chair. Federica sat on the sofa avoiding the holes that revealed the white foam beneath the leather and crossed her legs neatly under her. 'I can still smell him,' he continued. 'This is the only room in the house that literally vibrates with his presence, even now. I come in here and I still feel that he's alive and about to walk in at any moment and catch me reading in the erotica section.'

'Don't tell me Nuno had an erotica section?' she laughed.

'Oh, yes. Nuno was a big fan of erotica,' he replied. 'But not a big fan of the real thing.'

'He must have done it once to have produced Ingrid.'

'Once. Then he put it away for ever.'

'Really!' she exclaimed, lowering her eyes because Sam's had settled on hers and they made her feel uncomfortable. 'He was a wonderfully colourful person,' she sighed, changing the subject. 'I was fortunate to have known him.'

'You were, we all were.' He stood up and started picking up the papers on Nuno's antique desk. 'So how come Torquil let you come down?'

'He wouldn't want to stop me coming to Nuno's funeral,' she replied coolly, hoping he wasn't going to repeat the speech he gave her at lunch.

'You've barely been back since you got married.'

'I know.'

'Still hectic with that time-consuming literature course, I suppose?'

'I do other courses now,' she retorted. 'They take up all my time.'

'Fede,' he said seriously, flopping into Nuno's desk chair and draining his glass. 'You love Polperro, don't tell me you don't miss it?'

'Of course I do, it's just that Torquil has a different sort of life, we do other things.'

'But not to come and visit your family? Family was once everything to you.'

Federica shuffled awkwardly. She didn't appreciate this sudden attack on the way she had chosen to live her life. 'Family *is* everything to me, Sam, but I'm married now,' she said tightly. 'Things change. I really don't want to go into this again.'

'You're married, but you're not happy,' he said, watching her steadily.

Federica stiffened. So she had put on weight, what of it? 'How do you know I'm not happy? You're judging me by your own standards,' she argued. 'I don't want to be sitting down here writing books.'

'You'd like to be sitting down here taking photographs.'

'Oh, really,' she laughed, 'that was a long time ago, like I told you. I adore London, I wouldn't want to live anywhere else.' She watched Sam's tortured face and wondered why he cared.

'You're living in a beautiful shop window. There's nothing behind it, Fede. If I was worried about you two years ago, I'm even more concerned now.'

'For goodness' sake, Sam, this is ridiculous. Why do you care?'

He stood up again and strode over to the window. 'Because you're an old friend,' he said softly, looking out onto the wet garden.

'Because you kissed me once in the barn.'

'Because I kissed you once in the barn,' he repeated with a bitter chuckle. He wanted to add 'and because I let you go when I should have held on to you'.

'I care, Fede, because I've watched you grow up here. You're part of my family. From the moment I dragged you out of the lake to those times when you came and cried on my shoulder, I've been like an older brother to you. I care about you. For God's sake, Federica, look at yourself.' He turned and stared at her with his grey eyes and grey face twisted in anguish. Federica felt her chest constrict and swallowed back her self-pity. 'Darling, you're not yourself. He's changing you. The Fede I know doesn't wear designer suits with matching handbags. The Fede I know doesn't cross her legs like the Queen. The Fede I know doesn't smile from the nose down. She smiles with her eyes, behind her eyes. She's like a lovely swan on the lake, but this husband of hers is pulling her under.'

They both stared at each other not knowing where to go from there. Sam gazed at her forlornly, fighting the impulse to gather her into her arms and kiss her again. Only this time he wouldn't stop, but would go on kissing her for ever.

Federica's skin prickled with an uncomfortable fervour. She looked at him in confusion while the person she was struggled with the person she had become in an agonizing conflict of wills. Finally a fat tear pushed its way through her restraint as she realized that she didn't know who she was any more.

'I'm fine,' she said coldly. 'I'm fine and I'm happy. You're just emotional because your grandfather has died,' she stammered, standing up. 'So am I. I love Torquil and he loves me. I don't think it's right for you to criticize me,' she added defensively before leaving the room.

Sam turned around and stared bleakly out across the lake. The skies were black and dense and a soft drizzle floated on the wind. A few brown leaves swirled about on the paving stones outside the window. Just like Federica, he thought, being tossed about by the will of something far bigger than herself. He remembered the shy, awkward child who had played with Hester in the caves and melted marshmallows on campfires, he hadn't noticed her then. And the inadequate teenager who stammered whenever she spoke to him and blushed with her first tender infatuation, he hadn't noticed her then, either. He couldn't remember exactly when he *had* first noticed her. Perhaps the feeling had crept into his heart without him even noticing, because suddenly his jealousy had been roused, leaving him bewildered at the surprising strength of his emotions.

He had watched helplessly as she had married Torquil. The signs had been there right from the start in large neon letters and yet no one had tried to make her see them. He remembered Nuno's wise words: 'You can teach people knowledge, but wisdom, dear boy, has to be learned through experience.' So far Federica had learned nothing. How much further had she to fall before she gained some self-awareness and inner strength? He sunk into Nuno's leather chair and concentrated on devising a way to help her.

★

Federica returned to the sitting room and attempted to forget about her strange conversation with Sam. She forced a smile and tried her best to listen to what people were saying. But her ears rung with the echo of his words and as much as she made every effort to ignore them she knew in her heart that he was right. She wasn't happy.

The chauffeur drove her to Toby and Julian's cottage where she had arranged to stay the night. Rasta sat by her chair with his ageing white face on her lap, staring up at her with adoring eyes the whole way through dinner. Helena, Arthur and Hal joined them and they talked well into the night. When she slipped beneath the sheets she reflected on the family gathering that had been just like old times. The cottage was the same. The damp scent of the sea that mingled with the smell of rotting autumn had swelled her senses and flooded them with longing for those carefree days of her childhood. They had reminisced, laughing at all the old, well-worn stories that had slipped into family folklore. Even Hal had left his teenage angst back at home and joined in with enthusiasm. Helena was happy because Hal was happy and Federica was happy because she felt herself again.

But no one had failed to notice the change in her and they all worried.

When she left Polperro the following morning she felt a tremendous wave of homesickness. She dreaded returning to London, to the monotonous round of dinners and cocktail parties, ladies' lunches and shopping and shuddered at the thought of Torquil's persistent attempts to impregnate her. She looked down at her crocodile handbag and manicured nails and sighed. What was the point of it all?

Toby watched Federica leave and wondered when he would see her again. As the months rolled into years she was slowly drifting away from them. A small raft barely afloat on the strong undercurrents of a disappointing sea. Her marriage wasn't what she had dreamed of. It wasn't what her family had dreamed for her either. Toby resigned himself to the fact that he was losing her.

'Seeing Fede makes me feel desperately sad,' he said to Helena.

'Oh, she's all right. We all have our ups and downs,' she replied, too concerned with the sorry state of her own marriage to dwell for long on that of her daughter. 'Torquil loves her,' she added, not wanting to sound selfish. 'It'll work itself out.'

'I'm not so sure it will,' he replied bleakly, retreating into the house.

Helena was irritated. All anyone could talk about was Federica. How unhappy she looked. How she had put on weight. How her marriage must be crumbling. From the Applebys to the people who lived in the village, no one had anything else to say. When Arthur decided to add his thoughts to the pile Helena lost her patience. 'For God's sake, Arthur. You don't know what her marriage is like. You never even talk to her. I don't see how you've suddenly managed to penetrate her inner world,' she exclaimed hotly. Arthur's own patience was being slowly ground down by her incessant ill humour. She seemed to thrive on the drama of an argument. If there wasn't a reason to fight she invented one, happier to wallow in misery than try to find a way off her shadowy path of self-destruction.

'Now listen, Helena. Federica might not like me very much for obvious reasons, but I've watched her grow up and I care for her very deeply.'

'So do I,' she retorted. 'She's my daughter, not yours.'

Arthur sighed and narrowed his small brown eyes, resisting the temptation to shout at her. 'I'm only suggesting we do something to help, she's clearly having a hard time. She needs our support,' he said gently.

'What do you want to do? Rush in on a white charger?' she laughed scornfully. 'Fede doesn't want our help. If she did, she would have asked for it. Look, she's top to toe in designer clothes, has more money than King Midas and a husband who clearly worships the ground she walks on. So she looks unhappy; it was Nuno's funeral, if you remember, not exactly a time for celebration.'

'But she never comes down to see us.'

'She doesn't have time.'

'She loves her home, the countryside, the Applebys.'

'She's moved on, Arthur, that's what no one can bear to admit. She's left us all behind. That's fine by me. She's chosen a better life for herself than being stuck down here in bloody obscurity.'

Arthur stared at her in fury. He rarely lost his temper, but this time Helena had gone too far. His face swelled like a ripe tomato. 'Well if you're not happy with your lot, madam, why don't you just leave!' he shouted, throwing his papers onto the floor. Helena gaped at him in surprise. He never raised his voice. 'Go on, put your money where your mouth is, because I'm sick and tired of your hot air!' And with that he left the room.

Chapter 36

'What's this?' Lucia asked, pulling Federica's butterfly box out of her bedside table drawer, where she now kept it hidden beneath her books.

'I don't know,' said Torquil, sitting up in bed and lighting a cigarette.

'How sweet,' she said, opening it. '*Adorabile.*'

'Well, what's in it?'

'Letters.'

'Letters?'

'Mmm.' She sighed, pulling one out. '*Che carina.*'

'Who the fuck are they from?' he asked furiously, grabbing it out of her hand. He opened up the first well-handled epistle and turned it over. His shoulders dropped with relief. 'They're from her father.'

'Sweet,' she said in a patronizing tone. 'You're so possessive.'

'Like I told you, she's my wife, she belongs to me and I adore her.'

'What about me?'

'You don't belong to anyone.' He smirked.

'Torkie!' she breathed huskily, pretending to be hurt.

'All right,' he conceded. 'You belong to me part-time.'

'I don't sleep with anyone else, you know.'

'I know. I'd kill you if you did,' he said and looked at her steadily with impassive green eyes.

'Give me one of those letters, I want to read it,' she said excitedly. She liked it when he was masterful.

'No you can't,' he replied, folding the letter up and putting it back in the box.

'Torkie, come on, don't be a spoil-sport.'

'I said, no. Drop it.' He enjoyed playing Lucia off against his wife.

'Don't speak to me like that, I've just allowed you to ravage my body.' She laughed.

'And you enjoyed every minute of it. When I'm ready I'll take you again.'

'I might not let you,' she goaded.

'I'm stronger than you are. I'll pin you down and fight my way into you. Don't think you can ever prevent me from getting what I want, when I want it.'

'I like it when you sound rough. Like a gangster.' She smiled and stretched like a glossy cat. 'I wish Federica would spend the night away more often.'

'Absolutely not,' he replied. 'The fewer the better. I like her to be where I can see her.'

'You're a jealous husband.'

'She thrives under my guidance. She needs me. She'd be lost without me.'

'Then why the *diavolo* are you sleeping with me?'

Torquil smiled at her indulgently. 'Because, my angel, you work in an entirely different department. Fede's my wife. You're my lover. I love you both in different ways. I wouldn't want to be without either of you. Besides, you and I go back a long, long way. It's hardly an affair. Rather the continuation of an old friendship.'

'How do you know she's not having an affair?' Lucia asked, fixing him with her wide Italian eyes.

Torquil continued to smoke complacently. 'Because I know her every movement, angel.'

'You little spy,' she said, rolling onto her front and running a long nail down his chest. 'Do you spy on me too?'

'That's none of your business.'

'It's sick that you are reduced to spying on your women.'

'It's not spying. You don't seem to understand. I'm looking out for her. She's young and vulnerable.'

'You're spying on her. If she's smart she's sleeping with your informant. That's what I'd do.' She giggled.

'And I'd kill you,' he replied, fixing her with stony eyes. She flinched with a perverse kind of pleasure as she detected the menace in his expression.

'Your little wife is not so little any more.' Lucia grinned and ran a tongue over her thumbnail.

'She's not fat if that's what you're implying.'

'Not fat, just fatter.'

'She's softer to lie on. I like it,' he said. 'Besides, if she were skinny like you I might muddle you both up in the dark.'

'We both have Italian names, I'm surprised you haven't already put your big foot in it.'

'I never lose control. You of all people should know that.'

'Do you love her?' she asked sulkily.

'Yes,' he replied. 'I love her to distraction.'

'Well, it's one very happy marriage then, isn't it?' she stated with sarcasm. 'But I adore you too.' Then she sat up and pouted at him, allowing her long black hair to fall over her breasts, firm like newly whipped egg whites. 'Why didn't you marry me? I'm more beautiful than she is, more intelligent, more street-wise, I'm independent and worldly and I have no doubt that I'm a better lover. So, why didn't you? *Dimmi, perchè non ci siamo mai sposati?*'

Torquil stubbed his cigarette into the ashtray and rolled out of bed. 'For all those reasons, angel,' he replied. 'For all those reasons.'

★

When Federica returned home in the early afternoon, Torquil was waiting for her. He embraced her in his duplicitous arms but she felt nothing but a tingling numbness and saw in front of her eyes those black clouds of doubt. 'Are you all right, little one?' he asked, stroking her hair. 'You look exhausted.'

'It was very sad,' she replied, shaking her head, trying not to look into his eyes.

'I missed you,' he said. 'I could hardly sleep without you.'

Federica smiled tightly. 'I need a hot bath,' she mumbled, pulling away from him.

'And a massage,' he suggested.

'No really, just a bath will do.' She sighed, putting her handbag down and slipping out of her shoes.

'I want to rub away your suffering,' he said and followed her up the stairs. 'I know exactly how to cheer you up.'

Federica shuddered.

Torquil ran her a steaming bath scented with lavender essence and sat talking to her while she washed away the memory of Sam and her nostalgia. He told her he was planning to take her away on a long, hot holiday to Mauritius. 'You're anxious, sweetness, it's no wonder you're having trouble conceiving,' he said.

Federica felt a sense of panic creep up to her throat where it tightened its grip and made it difficult to breathe. 'What you need is a relaxing holiday in the sun. We can make love all day.'

'Yes,' she replied hoarsely, although the idea made her skin prickle with repugnance.

When she declined his offer of a massage and began to get dressed, he insisted that she needed it. 'God, you're tense,' he said, rubbing her shoulders. 'You see?'

'I'm fine, really,' she insisted.

'Lie down.'

'I'm fine, Torquil, please.'

'Little one, I know what's best for you, don't I?' he said, pushing her towards the bed. 'Now, do as you're told and let me massage away all that strain.' Reluctantly she lay naked on her front and closed her eyes because if she opened them she feared she might cry. His strong hands kneaded her skin with lavender oil, rubbing away at the muscles that were taut around her shoulders and neck. The room was warm and she was hot from her bath. Soon his hands got the better of her and she felt her body relax against her will. Her mind cleared of thoughts of Nuno, her family and her conversation with Sam and concentrated on the pleasurable feeling of his fingers on her flesh. She was balancing on that tenuous border between meditation and sleep when her senses were alerted to his sudden shift in position.

He spread her legs in one swift movement and fell on her, probing his way into the centre of her being, jolting her back to consciousness. He rode her hard and selfishly as if he was aware that he was slowly losing control. That little by little she was loving him less. She opened her eyes and fixed them to a point on the wall. Then the strangest thing happened. She mentally withdrew from her body, as if it wasn't happening to her, as if it were someone else lying helpless on the bed. She projected her mind back to Chile, back to Cachagua, to the beach where the sand was warm and soft like Lidia's flour and the sea was hypnotic and soothing, drowning out her discomfort and humiliation.

In the barren months that followed, the butterfly box became her only source of consolation. She opened it to escape her unhappiness, reading her father's letters and floating far away on the memories that were evoked by the magic of the strange, sparkling stones. As Torquil's lovemaking grew more brutal the butterfly box became more vital. It was her lifeline. It was the only thing that sustained her.

★

It was at her lowest ebb that Federica received an anonymous note, delivered by hand through her letterbox like an epistle from Heaven.

> *You shall be free indeed when your days are not without a care nor your nights without a want and a grief,*
> *But rather when these things girdle your life and yet you rise above them naked and unbound.*

She turned the note over in search of a further note explaining whom it was from. But there was nothing. Just a simple piece of white paper with the verse typed onto it. She sat down and read it again. She didn't recognize it. She read it again slowly, thinking very carefully about each word. Whoever had sent it obviously wanted to help her, but remain anonymous at the same time. There was only one person she knew of who would have reason to hide his identity. Her heartbeat quickened and the adrenaline pumped through her veins awakening senses that had grown sluggish with sorrow.

Ramon Campione. It could only be from her father. How typical of him to send an anonymous note. He had never announced himself. He had always just turned up unexpectedly. It had driven her mother mad, but it was his way. Then the content of the note was also very much his style. She remembered his stories, sometimes mystical, often spiritual. The turn of phrase was reminiscent of his own poetry, but above all it was his philosophy. He had always risen so far above every care and grief, risen so high that they had no longer touched him. He had been unaffected by cares even when his own family's cares and needs had driven them away from him. He had let them go. Once he had cared for her. In fact, there had been a time when she had believed his love to be unconditional and everlasting. But she had been disappointed, bitterly disappointed. Perhaps this was a tentative plea for forgiveness. Maybe he was trying to explain himself and his carelessness. But she hadn't seen him for years. Why was he suddenly thinking about her now? Where was he? How come he knew of her unhappiness? Why did he bother?

Later, when she lay in the darkness next to the distant body of her husband, she pondered on the note that she had hidden at the bottom of the butterfly box. Her father cared. He wouldn't have sent the note if he didn't care. She smiled to herself. He knew she was suffering and he wanted to help. The note was a clear instruction. She had to learn how to rise above her problems. The trick was not to let them get her down, to take control. It was all a state of mind. Her unhappiness was because she allowed life's struggles to burden her. For the first time since her marriage she felt a twinge of excitement as she took the initial cautious step in regaining control. She was tired of being a victim, it was time to take a stand. She was going to go on a diet, enrol in a gym and rise above her cares naked and unbound. But most importantly she wasn't alone. Once more she felt the sun on her face and basked in her father's love.

Ramon sat down at his typewriter and began to write. He hadn't attempted to write a book since the death of Estella which was now over three years ago. He had only written poems. Long poems of tormented verse, venting his pain and his regret in each carefully written line. He hadn't left Chile, preferring to stay with his son and near Estella's grave where he would often go to feel close to her, although his reasoning told him that she wasn't in the ground but in the realm of spirit. He had watched with pride as his son had begun to write his feelings down in a diary. Sometimes they would sit on the beach and Ramoncito would read to him the lines he had composed about his mother. They were at first faltering, often clumsy, as he seemed impatient to release a grief that saw no other avenue of escape. But little by little he had refined his style, taken more time and begun to produce poems of great clarity and beauty. Ramon was touched. 'Mama will be so proud of you, Ramoncito,' he'd say, ruffling his hair with his hand.

'How will she know?' the boy would ask.

'Because she can see you, my son,' he would reply, confident that she was with them in spirit. 'Because love has no boundaries.'

It hadn't been easy for either of them. But while Ramoncito was distracted by his school friends and his schoolwork, his father was left alone to wallow in self-pity in the house on the beach where everything reminded him of Estella. Sometimes in the summer, the heavy scent of roses would rise up on the air and waft in through the window to hijack his senses. He would awaken from his dreams believing she was there, lying next to him, ready to caress him with her honey eyes and gentle smile. It was in those tormented moments that he felt the urge to sob like a child, clutch her pillow to his face and breathe in the memories that clung to the linen. So he had turned on the light and written his feelings down. Those poems had saved his sanity. They had also changed his life.

Ramon had learnt, through the intense scrutiny of his emotions, why he had run away all his life. First from his parents, then from Helena, then from his children and finally from Estella. He had run away from love. Love had terrified him. As long as he was on his own, far away from the people who cared about him, he was safe from the suffocating intensity of their love. The responsibility had been too heavy for him to carry. So he had enjoyed their love from a distance, returning every now and then to check it was still there before breaking away again before it overwhelmed him. His intentions had always been good. He had suffered regret when he had watched Helena and the children walk out of his life, when he had travelled to England to find Federica crying in the porch of the church because she missed him, when he had seen her that afternoon on the bicycle, squinting into the sun.

He had suffered terribly because he loved them. But he had also been afraid of his own capacity to love. He had run from that too. But Estella had been different. At first he had run from her like he had run from Helena. But Estella had loved him without wanting to possess him. She had loved him enough to give him his freedom. Her love had been pure and unselfish. Without realizing it he had learnt from her love. It was because of this lesson that he had decided to write a book, not for publication, but for Helena. An allegory with a hidden message. He wanted her to know why he had run from her. He wanted her to learn too from Estella's undemanding love.

Sam sat on the top of the cliff and gazed out onto a sea that never changed, whatever the season. The winter frosts painted the grass-topped cliffs with icy fingers, froze the rivers and streams, yet the sea stayed the same. It could be rough, it could be calm, but it was never dictated to by the seasons. It belonged to itself.

Nuno had belonged to himself. He had never been influenced by anybody. Sam missed him. The house continued to reverberate with his presence and they all still talked about him as if he were alive, retelling stories of the funny things he had said and the odd things he had done. Inigo had given his study to Sam. Sam had been so touched he had wept. His father had patted him firmly on the back and told him that he could do with it whatever he wanted. But Sam had kept it exactly the same. Ingrid was touched that he wanted to keep her father's memory alive in the one room in the house that had truly been his. Sam had cleared the desk, placing all

Nuno's pieces of paper with illegible notes scrawled in his hand across them, into a couple of boxes in order not to throw anything away. Then he had gone through his drawers. It was there that he had come across a yellowing book of Kahlil Gibran's *The Prophet*. It was a book he knew well. Nuno had often quoted from it and had given Sam a copy for his confirmation – indeed he had quoted from it at his funeral. But there was something deeply touching about Nuno's own private copy because he had written down his thoughts and ideas in the margins. However, it was the accompanying letter that inspired him.

It was then that Sam thought of Federica.

The letter was addressed to his wife Violet, Sam's grandmother, and dated 8 May 1935. It was written from Rome. It spoke of his deep love for her and his desire to make her his wife. The marriage was obviously one her parents opposed for she had spiralled into a dark hole of despair from which there seemed no escape. Nuno had seen no other way to console her, being across the waters, so he had sent her his book with notes of encouragement which he had written into the margins alongside the verses he thought would give her strength. Sam was so moved by the letter that he read it more than once. Then he read the verses and Nuno's comments. It had obviously worked for they had married in the end and shared many happy years together.

Sam thought of Federica. If it had helped Violet why not Federica? He sat down at the desk and typed out a verse. He had decided to send it anonymously because he felt there was more chance of her reading it and acting upon it if she didn't know it came from him. After all, he had tried to reach her twice and failed both times. Then he had gone all the way to London on the train to deliver it.

He had stood in wait outside her house under a black umbrella, so that she wouldn't recognize him. Then he had hung around on the pavement for over an hour willing her to return. It had taken him that long to realize that she was already in the house. When he had peered in through the window he had caught a glimpse of her wandering about the rooms in her dressing gown, eating a packet of crisps. It was mid-afternoon. She was most certainly alone. He had resisted the temptation to ring the bell and slipped the letter through the box in the door instead before walking away and returning to Polperro on the late afternoon train.

He had spent the entire journey back to Polperro thinking about her. The image of her wandering through the rooms of her large, elegant house in her dressing gown, eating to assuage her unhappiness, had evoked feelings of both anger and pity. He had wanted to lie in wait for Torquil and hit him over the head, finishing him off for good. But he knew the only way to free her was to teach her how to do it herself. He hoped the letter might inspire her as it had inspired Violet. He dreamed of one day loving her himself, but those dreams were frail clouds on the horizon.

'You know, your wife's going to the gym? She's already lost weight. She only ate a salad last night at the Blights'. Not like her at all,' Lucia said scornfully. '*Poverina*, I'd hate to exercise and diet. Sex is the only pleasant way to stay *in forma*.'

'She's not going to a gym,' Torquil replied loftily. 'She's got a personal trainer. I arranged it for her. It's a good thing too, she needs to lose a bit of weight.'

'Sweet,' she sighed. 'It's all for you, you know.'

'I know. She's been very distracted lately. I can't seem to get through to her. Her silence drives me mad. I don't know what's wrong with her. Perhaps losing some weight will put the smile back onto her face.' He shook his head in order to be rid of his domestic problems and grinned down at his mistress. 'Now how about slipping into that little black ensemble I bought you?'

'Well, you'll have to be quick, I'm meeting Fede for lunch at the Mirabelle.'

'Well, come here then,' he said, holding her against him and running his hand up the backs of her legs.

'Do you still make love to Fede?' she asked as his fingers traced the tops of her lace stockings.

'Of course.'

'No results yet?'

'None.'

'I'm sure *I'm* fertile.'

'I'm sure you are, angel,' he said, spanking her on her naked bottom. 'Ah, you're ready for me.'

'I never wear knickers when you come to visit,' she said and laughed throatily.

But as much as Torquil tried to lose his anxieties in Lucia's succulent flesh, he was unable to stop thinking about his wife. He sensed her detachment and it alarmed him.

Chapter 37

Helena should have recognised her daughter's unhappiness, because she had suffered too and knew marital discontent better than anyone. But Helena had never had the ability to see further than herself and her own needs. She only saw Hal because, unlike Federica, she needed him. He had always been the part of Ramon that she had been able to hold onto. As much as she had tried to convince herself otherwise, she believed she had never stopped loving Ramon.

Arthur was kind and compassionate, doting and generous – everything that a woman should desire in a husband, but she yearned for the magic of those early years with Ramon. They haunted her by night in the form of sensual dreams, which reminded her of that transient paradise, and by day in the form of a constant, nagging regret. The worse she treated Arthur the harder he tried to please her.

At the start of their marriage she had welcomed his affection with gratitude, and she thought she finally had everything she could ever want. But after a while her thoughts had been dragged back across the sea to another life where she believed, at one point, she had truly known happiness. She couldn't help but wish for something else, something more, something better. She seemed always dissatisfied. But Arthur's patience was limitless. He felt he understood his wife. She had been neglected and hurt. She needed attention and understanding not severity. He was sure that given time she would soften and allow herself a piece of happiness. He was certain his love was enough.

The wilder Hal became the tighter Helena held onto him. As a child he had been eager to please, though never as accommodating as his sister. Federica had always been self-sufficient. Like her father, she had been happier in her own company. But Hal had always needed his mother and her unwavering attention and if anything had distracted her from him he had soon found ways of getting her back again. But Helena despaired at his sudden change of character, as if he had been possessed by the spirit of someone else. Someone bent on self-destruction.

Hal was far more complex than his mother believed. Like a clear river Hal's nature was lined with a thick layer of silt accumulated over a long childhood of emotional upheaval. It only needed a bit of agitation for it to churn up and turn the water cloudy. It was his mother's marriage to Arthur and subsequent events that set his heart in turmoil. But the seeds had been sown many years before, as a child, that summer in Cachagua.

At the age of four Hal was painfully aware of his father's obvious affection for Federica. Unable to express his jealousy in anything other than tears and tantrums, Helena had selfishly believed that he sensed the ill ease between his parents and wanted to protect her from Ramon. But Hal longed to be gathered up into the ursine arms of his father and loved like Federica was loved. He felt dejected each time Ramon left the house with his sister and although he had loved his train he had been envious of the attention Federica was given over her butterfly box. When Ramon stayed at the beach house instead of accompanying them to lunch in Zapallar, Hal had taken it, in his own limited way, as a rejection. Ramon barely noticed him and each slight settled into the silt in his character to one day resurface in the form of wretchedness and rebellion. So he had cleaved to his mother like bindweed, suffocating her with his neediness until she could think only of him. Then Helena had failed to tell him that they were leaving Chile for good and promised to give Federica a dog. Hal, unused to being passed over by his mother, took it as a rejection. Desperate not to lose her he clung to her with all his strength, even managing to sleep in her arms at night, exploiting the emptiness Ramon had left and filling it with a need that replenished Helena's longing to be loved.

As he had grown up so had his self-awareness. He felt guilty loving his mother with such intensity and suffered terrible mood swings, adoring her one moment and loathing her the next. He made every effort to hate Arthur because his mother loved him, but he had liked Arthur in spite of himself. Partly because of Arthur's good qualities, but also because his sister hated him and he saw how much her rebellion upset his mother. Hal had always wanted to please Helena so the jealousy bubbled quietly in the pit of his stomach like black tar, to be placated only when he sensed that she didn't love Arthur like she loved him. Her love for her son was as strong as ever. Arthur gave him the attention his father should have given him and Hal found himself responding to his kindness with a thirst that had built up over the years. He embraced him with the same neediness as he embraced his mother. Arthur made time for him, listened to him, bought him gifts, took him out just the two of them – all the things Ramon had done for Federica and what's more, Federica despised him. Arthur belonged exclusively to Hal and his mother. It was Federica's turn to be out in the cold – until Helena had allowed her to live with Toby and Julian.

From that moment on he felt the painful separation from his sister, whom he looked up to and adored. Once more Federica had received special treatment. He suffered silently, unable to communicate his resentment and distress. So he found comfort in the underworld of drink and cigarettes.

At twenty-one Hal was in his final year at Exeter Art school, studying History of Art. But he somehow managed to fall into a group from the university and for the duration of his course, no one knew he wasn't a university undergraduate.

He shared a house with five of his new friends, situated in the middle of a muddy field with no heating and electricity which constantly needed to be activated by slotting money into a meter. There were mice droppings in the kitchen drawers and bags of rubbish by the wall outside which no one could be bothered to move. The house was cold in summer and freezing in winter but they lit the fires and slept in thick jerseys. Hal didn't do any work. He had only agreed to go into further education because he couldn't make up his mind what he wanted to do. As long as he was in education he didn't have to. It gave him three more years to fritter away doing very little.

He smoked because all the other boys smoked and besides, it kept him warm. He drank because it made him forget his worthlessness and his mother, who called him every day to check that he was all right and to dig her clutches in deeper as her husband failed to fulfil her. Alcohol gave him confidence. While the effects lasted he was as charismatic, enigmatic and self-assured as Ramon Campione. During those fleeting hours he even looked like him.

The lows were unbearable. His insecurities would invade the armour the drink had built around him and gnaw at his self-esteem more venomously than before. When the money dried up Helena gave him more, without questioning why he needed it. She didn't ask Arthur, she just gave him what Arthur gave her. When that was no longer enough he seduced Claire Shawton, a mousy girl with a thin, pallid face and long, skinny legs because her father was Shawton Steel and there was no shortage of money in her bank account. Keen to hold on to the dark, impenetrable Hal, Claire gave him money for his drink and his cigarettes, his gambling and his extravagance.

'I'm not an alcoholic,' Hal explained to her when she protested. 'It relaxes me. I'll pay you back, I promise. I'm having trouble getting around the trustees, that's all.' But there were no trustees because there wasn't a trust. Only Helena's blind generosity.

Claire Shawton's uses extended only as far as her bank balance; sexually she couldn't begin to satisfy Hal. He went about his sexual adventures with the same destructiveness with which he confronted everything else in his life. He slept with dozens of girls, promised them devotion and commitment, then dropped them as soon as they wanted a relationship outside the bedroom. Claire knew of his transgressions but instead of closing her cheque book and walking away she gave him more money and received the kisses that followed with pitiful gratitude.

When Hal returned to Cornwall for the holidays Arthur noticed immediately that he was gaunt and pale, unable to sit still or concentrate for very long. He slept most of the day and stayed up watching videos until the early hours of the morning. When Arthur approached Helena on the subject she excused him by saying that he was overtired, studying too hard and needed the holidays to rest.

'Don't hassle him, Arthur, he's very sensitive about it,' she said proprietorially. 'He's got no confidence as it is. Let me deal with this.'

Once again Arthur rolled his eyes and backed off. Helena had been cold and distant in the last few months. She was prone to moods, adoring one moment, aloof the next, but he was used to that. He wasn't used to the consistent ill humour that now seemed to dominate her personality. Like a diminishing candle, her affection for him seemed to be getting noticeably less and less as each day passed. If he didn't do something the flame would go out altogether. But he didn't know what to do. In despair he wondered whether she was seeing someone else.

Helena was seeing someone else. She was seeing Ramon. When she closed her eyes at night and when her mind drifted off by day and finally when she lay in the rough arms of Diego Miranda, she saw the awesome face of Ramon Campione. The only man she believed she had ever loved. She had cried enough bitter tears of remorse to sink one of Diego's ships. She had looked back on her life and recognized her mistakes. Mariana had been right, you often don't know what you have until it is gone.

She knew where Ramon was. But she hadn't heard from him in years. She hadn't even bothered to find him to tell him about his own daughter's wedding. She now wished she had. It would have been a good excuse. Now there was no reason to call him.

Helena hadn't gone out of her way to have an affair. She hadn't even considered it, or desired it. Her heart was somewhere in the past, barely concentrating on the present at all. She had been in the pub in Polperro with Arthur, one cold summer Sunday, when a strange young man with long black hair and deep black eyes had accidentally knocked into her, pouring her glass of red wine all over her pale cashmere sweater. She had lost the little patience she had, not so much with him, but with life and the misery of it all, flinging her arms in the air and swearing furiously.

'I'm so sorry,' he exclaimed, turning to the barman in desperation. The barman handed him a dishcloth and he proceeded to dab at her chest in his confusion. 'I cannot apologize enough,' he said when Helena stared at him in horror.

'Your accent,' she stammered. 'Where are you from?'

'Spain.' She felt her stomach turn over and her head spin with a strange sense of *déjà vu*. He sounded just like Ramon. When she gazed into his eyes she believed they too resembled Ramon's, until in her state of yearning she believed he was Ramon's shadow, split from him by magic, all the way from Chile.

'Diego Miranda,' he declared, extending his hand.

'Helena Cooke,' she replied. 'I used to live in Chile,' she added, forgetting the wet stain on her sweater.

'Really?' he responded politely. 'You must speak Spanish.'

'Yes, I do,' she enthused, her voice hoarse with excitement. 'But I haven't spoken the language for many years.'

'You never forget a language like Spanish.'

'No, I think you're right,' she agreed, drifting on the music in his voice that seemed to call her from the misty shores of the far-distant past. 'What do you do?'

'Shipping.'

'Ah, the Armada.' She laughed.

'Something like that,' he replied indulgently. 'Please let me give you my address so you can send me the bill.'

'Bill?'

'The bill, for the dry cleaning,' he said, frowning at her in amusement.

'Oh, yes, the bill.' She giggled, watching him smile and feeling her stomach turn all over again. 'Do you live in Polperro?'

'No, just passing through.'

'Oh.' She sighed, trying to hide her disappointment. 'Where are you staying?'

'With friends.'

'Sightseeing?'

'Yes.'

'How strange,' she recalled, shaking her head. 'I met Ramon sightseeing too.'

'Who's Ramon?' he asked.

'Another life,' she said, brushing it off and smiling through the memory. 'I took him around the old caves and smuggling haunts. The places you can't find in guidebooks.'

Diego's eyes twinkled with interest. 'Really?' he said, then grinned at her from under his thick Spanish eyes. 'I'm afraid I'm following the map.'

'You mean, your friends aren't showing you around?'

'They don't have time, they work,' he said, watching her mouth curl up at one corner.

'If you want a guide, I could show you some of the places very few people know about. I grew up here, you see,' she explained.

'I would be honoured,' he replied, kissing her hand and bowing.

She gave him a wide, carefree smile before she was distracted by Arthur's insistent waving from the other end of the pub. 'Oh God!' she sighed irritably. 'I completely forgot about him. Don't worry,' she responded to his inquisitive frown, shaking her head. 'Meet me here tomorrow at eleven.' He nodded in understanding and raised an eyebrow, unable to believe his luck. He had noticed her rings and her husband's concern. He was Latin after all.

Diego was surprised by Helena's enthusiasm for an affair and imagined she had had many. She drove him around the coast and allowed him to make love to her on the cliff in the car overlooking the sea. Later she invited him home to her house where she took him to her bed. She enjoyed the firm way he handled her, the confident way he kissed her, the sensual way he caressed her. She closed her eyes and demanded that he speak to her only in Spanish, then she projected her mind across the waters and across the years to a time when Ramon hadn't run off and she hadn't rejected him.

The first time Arthur had trouble turning the tap in the shower he had been surprised. Helena always left it dripping. The second time he was perplexed. The third time his intuition told him that another man had used it. He leant back against the wall to steady himself as his heart plummeted to his feet. In the last few days Helena had been friendlier, happier, she hadn't snapped at him or ignored him. She had embraced him with fondness and quite obviously guilt. He let the hot water pound onto his skin, drowning out the screaming in his head that refused to give him peace to think rationally.

He had believed her detachment to be rooted in her anxiety over her troubled child. Worrying about Hal had become a full-time occupation. He hadn't understood it as a symptom of her waning affection for him. He worshipped her. Sex had never been a problem; they had loved and laughed together in bed even during the difficult times. He was sickened at the thought of her giving herself to another man. He was wounded by her blatant rejection of him in spite of all his efforts to please her.

He wondered who it could possibly be. But Arthur wasn't stupid. He wished he were because it was all too easy and therefore too painful. He had noticed her talking to the dark foreigner in the pub. She had returned to the table crimson-faced and distracted. She had kept looking over at him, watching him, lowering her eyes coyly when he returned her stare. Arthur hadn't liked it, but he had indulged her. There was nothing wrong with a harmless flirt if it made her feel happier, more attractive.

She had left with Arthur in a buoyant mood and talked all the way home in the car. Usually she stared bleakly out of the window responding to his attempts at conversation in monosyllables. But he hadn't suspected anything. He hadn't imagined she could be so devious.

After despair came anger. He thrust the palm of his hand against the wet tiles of the shower room as his lungs filled with fury, causing him to wheeze in torment. He thought of their first kiss, their first touch, their wedding day and their initial marital contentment and felt nothing but hatred and loathing. Then he recalled with precision the many hurtful things she'd said to him, the uncaring manner in which she had treated him and bit his lip with self-loathing. He had taken it all because he loved her. But now he had suffered one humiliation too much.

'I will never forget the face of the Polperro beauty,' Diego said, running his finger down Helena's face, where it lingered on her satisfied lips before following the line of her chin, pulling it towards him and kissing her.

Helena sighed with pleasure. 'When do you leave?' she asked, carelessly revealing the desperate whine in her voice.

'Tomorrow.'

'Tomorrow?' she repeated, the sweat breaking out on her forehead and nose. 'You mean, that's it?'

'You know your problem?' he said, shaking his head at her.

'What?' she replied, pulling away in offence.

'You're too needy.'

'Needy?' she retorted. 'I'm not needy.'

'Yes you are, *mi amor*. You're needy and it's suffocating. You're like an overwhelming octopus. Once in your arms a man feels he can't escape.'

'How dare you,' she snapped, climbing out of the hotel bed.

'Helena, *mi amor*, I'm not criticizing you,' he insisted, smiling in amusement at her sudden change in humour. 'You're a beautiful woman. You're fun, too. I'm sure you break hearts all over Cornwall.'

'But not yours.'

'Helena,' he said indulgently. 'Come here.' She walked sulkily back to the bed where she sat down on the edge and allowed him to caress her hair. 'You're like a fallen angel.

You found me because you were lonely. You're a discontented woman, any man can see that. But don't worry, there will be others.'

'What do you mean, others?' she exclaimed in disgust.

'Other men. Surely, *mi amor*, I'm not the first man you have betrayed your husband with?'

'Well, of course you are. What do you think I am? A whore?'

'Please, don't misunderstand me,' he said quickly, attempting to correct his error.

'I want you to go,' she said icily, suddenly regretting that she had ever met him. Hearing the echoes of Ramon's indifference resound across the years she wondered why she had only remembered the magic.

'Helena.'

'I do. Now!' she continued, getting up and throwing his clothes at him. 'I wanted you because you remind me of someone. But I've been a fool! You're as much of an illusion as he is. I've been dreaming, but I've now woken up.' Diego squinted at her, trying to understand what she was saying. 'Get out!'

'Come on, Helena. Don't be cross,' he cajoled, reluctantly standing up. 'At least let us part as friends.'

'We were never friends in the first place,' she replied. 'We were lovers, but now that is gone, we are nothing.'

'What happened to this "illusion"?'

'He never really existed,' she snapped. 'Just like you.'

'You're too desperate, Helena. You drive men away.'

'Go!'

'It's true. But we made good love,' he said with a smirk, pulling on his shoes. 'You're a desirable woman, Helena Cooke.'

'I don't want to see you ever again!' she shouted after him. The door slammed and he was gone. 'God, what was I thinking?' she exclaimed to herself, sinking into the chair. All that remained was the unmade bed and a heavy sense of self-disgust. She held her head in her hands and heaved with fury. How dare he think she would betray her husband with just anyone? How could she have been so misguided? She thought of Arthur and was suddenly filled with shame. What had she been reduced to? Arthur was guilty only of adoring her. What was the point of clinging onto the shadow of Ramon when Arthur was real and his love absolute? She had made a terrible mistake.

When she arrived back at the house it was dusk. The late summer sun had sunk behind the town making way for a bright harvest moon. She felt weary and defeated. To her surprise she saw the light on in the bedroom, indicating that Arthur was home. Her spirits rose like bubbles, slowly at first but with increasing speed, until she yearned to run to him like a child and apologize for treating him so badly. The thought of Arthur's familiar smell, his cosy embrace and his encouraging smile filled her with remorse. She longed to curl up against him like they had done when they had been newly wed and feel that sense of security, that sense of intimacy and friendship. She wanted to forget Diego Miranda for ever. She wished she had never gone near the pub that day. How close she had come to losing everything for a pitiful infatuation. Why was it that she was constantly chasing dreams?

She put the key in the lock and wriggled it about in frustration. When it wouldn't turn she rang the bell. When Arthur didn't come down she shouted up at the window. Then to her horror the light extinguished in the bedroom, leaving her alone in the empty street, blinking up in fear at the sudden realization that he must know. Somehow he knew. Or he had simply had enough. 'Arthur!' she shouted in panic. 'Arthur!' But the house remained silent and impenetrable. 'Arthur, let me in!' she choked. She shouted until her voice was hoarse, until the cold wall of the house echoed her pleas only to mock her. She sunk to the ground and crumpled into sobs. Arthur's patience had finally snapped.

Arthur watched through the gap in the curtains as his wife finally retreated to her car and drove off into the night. His throat ached from suppressing his emotions and his heart thumped behind his ribcage because he knew that by shutting her out he risked losing the one woman he had ever loved. But he also knew that he couldn't continue being taken for granted. He had been pushed to the limit. She had gone too far. It was time to win back her respect. She needed space to recognize that what she had with him was something precious, something sacred, something to be nurtured, not worn away out of carelessness and complacency.

He slumped on the side of the bed and dropped his head into his hands. For the first time in many years he sobbed.

Hal had drifted away from Federica. She was married now and her life no longer ran parallel to his. So he was surprised when she called him soon after Nuno's funeral and asked him for lunch in London during the university holidays. 'I need to see you, Hal,' she said and her voice sounded different. Hal was relieved to get out of his mother's house. She was crowding him out with her incessant questions and her unspoken demand to be included in his life. She wanted to know every detail about Exeter, who his friends were, whether he had a girlfriend, what he did in the evenings. He found her attention at once gratifying and invasive. It suffocated him.

Arthur watched him prowl around the house like one of the living dead and decided that at last he was growing up and growing away. But he didn't like his pallor or his disquiet.

Hal met Federica in Le Caprice. He noticed that in the space of a couple of months she had lost considerable weight. She noticed how thin and pale he was. 'You look dreadful,

Hal. What on earth is going on?' she asked, ordering a bottle of still water.

'A Bloody Mary for me,' said Hal. 'I'm fine. You look well.'

'Thank you,' she replied. 'I'm getting myself under control,' she added proudly. She had lost almost a whole stone.

'Good for you. This lunch is on you, right?'

'Right.'

'Good, let's order, I'm famished,' he said, opening the menu.

'How's Mama?'

'Fine, I suppose. Annoying as usual,' he muttered.

'Toby and Julian?'

'Why don't you ask them yourself? You never go down and see them.'

'There's been so little time.'

'Sure.'

'Really.'

'I'll have a steak and chips,' he said, closing the menu.

'You don't look as if you eat steak and chips. You look as if you've got an eating disorder.'

'For God's sake, you sound like Mama,' he complained. 'Anyway, what's this lunch for? I can't believe it's just a social.'

'It is a social. I haven't seen you properly in years.'

'Not my fault.'

'No, it's not. But I need your help too.'

'What?' he sighed, rolling his eyes. She had intended to tell him about her father's note, but he was so hostile and aloof she changed her mind.

'I need you to get Abuelita's telephone number from Mama,' she said.

'Why can't you get it yourself?'

'Because I don't want her to know I want it,' she explained. 'All you need to do is look it up in her book, it's sure to be there.'

'Why don't you want her to know? Abuelita is your grandmother.'

'And Papa's mother,' she said. 'Hal, don't be so naïve. Mama hasn't spoken to her in years, literally. She hates Papa. She hated it when he wrote to us.'

'To *you*,' he snapped. 'He never wrote to me.'

'Whatever. It's just better to do it secretly, believe me.'

'It'll cost you.'

'What?'

'Yes, it will,' he said resolutely.

'You're not serious?'

'Of course I am,' he insisted coolly. 'What do I get out of it otherwise?'

'Well, how much then?' she asked.

'One hundred pounds.'

'One hundred pounds?' she gasped. 'You must be joking!'

'I had to take the train, return ticket. Besides, it's a fag. It's the least you can do. It's Torquil's money anyway and he's rolling.'

Federica watched her brother and barely recognized the Hal she had grown up with. She frowned. 'You're strange today. What's the matter with you?' she asked, searching his face for an expression she recognized.

'The money or no telephone number.'

'Address and telephone, Cachagua and Santiago,' she said firmly.

'Okay, done.'

'Good,' she replied, shaking his hand. He dug his knife into the steak.

'I want the money now,' he said, getting up.

'Where are you going?'

'To the men's room. Won't be a minute.' She watched him meander unsteadily through the restaurant and wondered whether their father was keeping an eye on him as well. Then she remembered that Ramon had never written to Hal.

Helena was too ashamed to tell her parents the real reason Arthur had locked her out of the house. She moved back into her old room where she paced the floors in rage.

'Poor Helena,' Polly lamented to her husband. 'She's furious with Arthur.'

'No she's not,' said Jake simply. 'She's furious with herself. She's blown it again.'

Helena wouldn't hear a word said against Arthur. When she called Federica to tell her, she terminated the conversation abruptly by slamming down the telephone because her daughter had immediately blamed her stepfather.

'Oh, Federica,' she sighed impatiently. 'You know nothing about it.'

She had driven round to see Arthur the following morning, beat upon the door and even followed him to work. 'Arthur, I can explain,' she had begged, but he wouldn't listen.

'You've gone too far, Helena,' he had replied flatly. 'You've drained me dry. I don't want you back unless you're willing to change and you can't decide that in a day. Go away and think about it.' Shocked by the apparent stubbing out of his emotions she had limped back home to wail on her mother's shoulder that he no longer loved her.

Only Toby was told the truth. 'I had an affair,' she confessed as they sat on the windy beach, talking over the rush of the surf and the cries of the gulls.

'Oh, Helena,' Toby sighed. 'Who with, for God's sake?'

'A Spaniard.'

'A Spaniard?' he exclaimed, shaking his head at his sister's foolishness.

'A bloody Spaniard,' she retorted, folding her arms in front of her chest and sniffing with self-pity.

'Why?'

'Because he reminded me of Ramon.'

Toby prodded the sand with a stick. 'You're obsessed with a ghost, Helena,' he said gravely.

'I know,' she replied, then more angrily, 'I know *now*, don't I!'

'You always want what you can't have.'

'I don't need you to tell me that,' she snapped defensively. 'I've been an idiot, I'm the first to admit it.'

'Did you ever love Arthur?' he asked. She looked out across the waves to the grey clouds moving swiftly towards them and recalled her husband's fury. 'Well, did you?' he repeated.

'Of course I did. I just didn't recognize it.' Toby frowned. 'It's not the all-consuming love of Ramon,' she explained. 'It's something quieter. I don't think I heard it. I was too busy listening out for the roar. My love for Arthur is more gentle. It's taken me a while, but I hear it now.'

'The roar always subsides before long, then if you're lucky you're left with something much stronger and more lasting,' Toby chuckled, thinking of Julian. 'Arthur's a good man.'

'I realise that now. I can't believe that it took an empty, meaningless affair to wake up and realize how much Arthur means to me. I've treated him so badly. I've been so off-hand with him. He just sat back and let me behave so appallingly. What other man would be so indulgent? I don't deserve him.' Then she looked at her brother with big, sad eyes. 'I've lost him, haven't I?' she said.

Toby put an arm around her shoulders and kissed her head that smelt of salt. 'I don't know, sweetheart. You never seem to learn from your mistakes.'

Chapter 38

Sam watched the rain rattle against the glass windows of Nuno's study. The flames crackled in the fireplace where Nuno had always stoked the logs with the steel poker when he had needed to gather together his thoughts and Trotsky lay on the rug, breathing heavily in his sleep. But Sam felt the cold in his bones and shuddered. He settled his gaze on the leather sofa where Federica had sat and recalled her eyes, opaque with resignation and her unhappy body that took the brunt of too much comfort food. He felt gutted inside. He had lost Nuno, his beloved grandfather and friend, but he had also lost Federica to another, wholly unsuitable man. He sighed hopelessly; he was fooling himself for he had never had her to lose. When he could have had her he hadn't wanted her.

He stood up and paced the room in order to warm up. He pulled his jersey over his icy hands and hunched his shoulders. He hadn't written a word since he had returned home to write. He had toyed with the idea of buying a cottage like Toby and Julian's, a young man of thirty-one shouldn't live at home with his parents, but he didn't have the energy or the incentive to find one. While he was at Pickthistle Manor he didn't have to go out for company, cook his own food, or pay rent or a mortgage. His father was grateful for his company and talked his theories through with him in front of the sitting

room fire where Federica had first toasted marshmallows with
Molly and Hester.

Ingrid floated about the rooms like a spectre in her long
gowns, leaving a trail of smoke behind her and barely noticing
that Sam was there at all. She continued to operate the animal
sanctuary which was so overcrowded that when Sam had
returned home from London he had opened his sweater drawer
to discover a hibernating squirrel curled up in his favourite
cashmere V-neck. When he had confronted her about it she
had smiled happily and replied, 'So that's where Amos is! You
know, darling, I've been looking for him the entire winter.
You won't disturb him until the spring, will you?'

So Sam had borrowed his father's sweaters, which all had
holes in them, either from moths or mice, for he had never
done a day's manual labour in his life and went out so very little
they rarely saw the light of day. When Inigo failed to recognize
the ragged jersey on Sam's back, he patted him firmly on the
shoulder and said, 'Son, if you need money you won't be too
proud to ask, will you?' Sam had replied that he was more than
comfortable. His two younger brothers came home on weekends. Lucien was at Cambridge and Joey in his last year at
school. Molly and Hester came down when they could, as both
now had full-time jobs which gave them very little time off.

Molly always managed to find something snide to say
about Federica while Hester mourned the loss of her friend.
'We were once so close,' she would sigh. 'We told each other
everything.'

'Well, that's what happens when someone lets wealth and
society go to their head,' said Molly unkindly. 'If you and I
were grander, Hester, you can be sure she wouldn't have
dropped us like hot potatoes.'

But Sam knew the truth because he wasn't blinded by jealousy like Molly. He kept his feelings to himself and hid
behind the heavy oak door of Nuno's study.

'Sam's just like Dad,' Molly laughed one weekend when he had only emerged for meals, 'he's growing moody too.'

Sam longed to telephone Federica, but he didn't know what to say and he didn't want her to know that he had written the note. After their conversation at Nuno's funeral he doubted she'd be too happy to hear from him. So, out of frustration at not being able to communicate he decided to write another anonymous note. He opened Nuno's book and sat by the fire, shivering with cold, and endeavoured to find a few lines that would be helpful to her. The lines encircled by Nuno were very different from the ones that would be appropriate for Federica, for Violet had needed encouragement to love whereas Federica needed encouragement to live – to live independently and not according to the will of another. He turned the pages, chewing the end of his pencil in concentration. He could use one of the verses on love, but that would be more apt for himself for he was suffering on the 'threshing-floor' of love because Federica tormented his thoughts and burned holes in his heart. He could use one of the verses on sorrow for that would teach her that joy and sorrow are inseparable, for without one it is impossible to know the other.

Then he came across a verse on freedom and realized that none other was more suitable. He tapped the page triumphantly with the damp end of his pencil and thought: it is within Federica's own power to walk away. Torquil treats her according to how she allows him to treat her. She can always say no and she must say no. He read it out loud to Trotsky who opened his saggy eyes, yawned and stretched before cocking his head to one side and pricking his ears up attentively.

'*For how can a tyrant rule the free and the proud, but for a tyranny in their own freedom and a shame in their own pride? And if it is a care you would cast off, that care has been chosen by you rather than imposed upon you. And if it is a fear you would dispel, the seat of that fear is in your heart and not in the hand of the feared.'*

Sam sat at Nuno's desk in front of his computer and typed it out. Then he spent the next half hour printing it, typing the envelope and sealing it because every action was done with the utmost care as if it were a love letter that contained the secrets of his heart. Excited at the prospect of catching a glimpse of Federica he took the early train the following morning, staring out of the window all the way because he was too distracted to read. He arrived by taxi in time to see her leaving her house and climbing into the awaiting car.

'Follow the Mercedes,' said Sam to the driver, then he sat back and listened to the thumping of his own heart and the cautiously optimistic thoughts that whirred around in his head.

He had been struck immediately by her figure. She had slimmed down a bit and her step had regained that buoyancy it had always had before she married. Her skin was no longer ravaged by strain but glowed with health. He wondered whether his note might have inspired the change. Then his face dropped with gloom; perhaps it was Torquil.

Federica was excited by her new approach to life, though it hadn't been easy. She had had to work hard with her personal trainer to lose the weight and change her diet. It had been demoralizing. She hadn't taken a good look at herself in the mirror for months and when her clothes had no longer fit she had simply asked Torquil to buy her more. She was fatter than she had imagined. She had put on a couple of stone and her skin had suffered because of all the junk food. Suddenly she couldn't hide any more, for John Burly arrived on Mondays, Wednesdays and Fridays to weigh her, measure her and work her until the sweat oozed out of every pore like blood, often making her cry out dispiritedly, 'I can't do it. I'm just made to be fat.'

But he would reply, 'All right, if you want to stay fat, that's fine, you don't need me to stay fat,' until she begged him to continue. She had made sure the fridge was stocked with fruit and vegetables and stuck to the rigorous diet only because every time she hankered after a bag of crisps or a bar of chocolate she remembered Torquil's cruel names and chewed on a carrot instead.

Instead of spending Torquil's money on clothes she paid regular visits to the beautician and began to take pride in her appearance again. As the weight fell off, so her confidence grew. She also derived strength from her father's note that she hid at the bottom of the butterfly box and brought out during the day when Torquil was at work and she could be alone with her thoughts. She was certain her father had been in the country, seen her and sent it. She wished he had approached her but understood why he might have been reticent. She wanted him to know that she didn't blame him and that she still loved him. As the days got increasingly colder in the run-up to Christmas Federica waited for Hal to call her with her grandparents' telephone number, but he never did.

Then Federica took her first tentative step at independence. It was small, but highly significant. She took the car to Sloane Street and bought herself new clothes to replace the ones that were now too big for her. They were still the grey and navy trouser suits that Torquil always chose for her, but the fact that she had gone out and bought them herself gave her a satisfying sense of defiance. She had staged her first rebellion.

To her surprise Torquil didn't notice. To her greater surprise she didn't care. He applauded her on her slimmer shape, embracing her in his overpowering arms and kissing her with adulterous lips. 'Aren't you clever, little one, I'm so proud of you,' he said. 'You're almost back to the Federica I married.'

She should have been thrilled; after all she had slimmed for him. Or had she? Little by little Torquil shifted from the centre of her world.

Now Sam followed Federica to St James's where she stepped out of the car and walked up the street. He waited for her to get half way up the pavement and then leapt out to follow her. She was dressed in a long black coat with black suede boots under a pale grey trouser suit and cream silk shirt. She looked elegant and sophisticated, with her long white hair tied into a neat ponytail that fell down the back of her coat. She wasn't the skinny teenager he had known in Polperro, full of uncertainty and doubt. She was fuller and more womanly, reflecting her growing confidence. His emotions caught in his throat because he loved her better like that. He was consumed with the longing to tell her.

She stopped once or twice to look into shop windows or to glance at her own reflection which still succeeded in surprising her. He walked a hundred yards behind her, his head hidden under his father's felt hat, hands buried in the pockets of his coat covered in dog hair, with a hole gnawed into the elbow by an overzealous mouse, no doubt. He hunched his shoulders and watched her through his glasses that kept steaming up due to the cold and drizzle. He felt like a stalker and blushed in shame, causing his glasses to mist up even more until he could barely see through them.

He followed her up Arlington Street towards the Ritz where he was sure she was meeting someone for lunch. But he was surprised when she walked on past the doormen, who all touched their caps with white-gloved hands, and continued on in the direction of Green Park. He walked faster, dodging the people who spilled out of the tube station, and watched her enter the park. He hid behind the gate as she strolled like a homing pigeon along the path to a bench that stood under the bare winter trees. She sat down, placed her handbag on her knees and stared out across the misty park.

Sam walked along the iron fencing until he stood behind her, about one hundred yards away, and gazed upon the solitary figure who was clearly not waiting for anyone, for she didn't look around in anticipation, or glance at her watch, she just stared in front of her, without moving, lost in thought.

Sam took his hands out of his pockets and held on to the wet iron bars that separated him from the woman he loved. He longed to call out her name. The sound of it on his lips would be a luxury for he never spoke of her to anyone. But he didn't dare. He just stood, with his hands frozen onto the railings, wondering what she was thinking about, content just to be near her. He recognized the lonely slope of her shoulders and the wistful tilt of her head because he knew what it was to be lonely and he understood. Once or twice she scratched her nose or curled a piece of stray hair behind her ear, while he waited for her to get up and move on. But after an hour, when she still hadn't made a move to leave, he decided to return to her house to slip the note through the door.

Reluctantly he left her and walked up the street towards St James's. He suddenly shivered with cold and pushed his hands deep into his pockets again. He strode past her car out of curiosity to find the chauffeur asleep with his head buried into the rolls in his chin. He was dribbling out of the side of his mouth and a long web of saliva extended from his jaw down to his lapel.

Sam seized his moment and pushed the note through the gap in the back window, where Federica had left it slightly open. He watched it fall onto the seat, face up, with the name Federica Campione typed onto the envelope with love.

★

Federica sat and savoured the fact that Torquil didn't know where she was. She enjoyed these private moments alone with her memories. She thought about her inability to conceive and decided that it wouldn't be fair to bring a child into such a troubled marriage. Perhaps it was God's will because He could see the bigger picture. She thought about Christmas and whether Torquil might accompany her down to Polperro to spend it with her family. Every year he had promised, every year he had flown her off to somewhere exotic instead. She had called her mother each time and excused him with such fervour that in the end she had believed her own invented excuses. But inside she had felt desperately let down. She wanted more than anything to go home to Cornwall.

She liked to recall her youth. Her memories comforted her and carried her out of herself and her unhappiness. She remembered the picnics on the beaches when the sand blew into the sandwiches and it was so cold they sat in their Guernsey sweaters shivering in a huddle before Toby would gather them up to hunt for sea urchins and crabs. Julian would collect shells and help them build castles while Helena would sit on the rug talking to her mother, every now and then applauding their efforts absentmindedly. Those had been idyllic days.

She spoke to Toby and Julian, her mother and occasionally Hester, but not as often as in the early days when she had sneaked into Harrods to the payphones. Time and circumstances had come between them like an insurmountable mountain. She made excuses for that too – but if she was honest with herself she knew that it was because Torquil didn't like her family. He thought they were provincial, and he did his best to distance her from them. With determination she could overcome that mountain, but she didn't know whether she had the courage to defy her husband.

Federica was so used to loving Torquil that it had become a habit. At first she had needed him and he had cultivated that need until she had no longer been able to do without him. Then she had lost the ability to think for herself. In the four years of their marriage he had slowly pummelled her into the ground – but from there the only way was up. How auspicious that it had been at the point of utter despair that her father had sent her his secret message, encouraging her to build herself back up again and regain her lost confidence and her lost control. She had been ready to clutch at anything. She couldn't do it alone.

She thought about her father and wondered how she was going to track him down from London. If he had been in the city he would probably have left by now. Ramon never stayed very long in one place. His shadow always caught up with him and urged him on. At one point she felt the heat of someone's eyes burn into the back of her neck. She curled a piece of hair behind her ear self-consciously but didn't dare turn around. She shuffled uneasily on the bench. But there was something familiar about the weight of the stare. Comfortably familiar. She suddenly imagined it might be her father, watching her from the street, not wanting to be seen. With a sudden burst of courage she turned around. With hopeful eyes she searched the crowd of unfamiliar faces through the winter mists, but she didn't recognize a single one. She sighed in disappointment, looked at her watch and decided it was time to make her way back to the car.

She walked down the street, her eyes fixed on the pavement, wondering how she was going to broach the subject of Christmas. When she got back to the car she saw the chauffeur asleep in his own snot and knocked on the window. He jerked back to life, fumbled for the lock and rolled out of his seat to open the door for her. But Federica had already spotted the letter and had opened the door herself. She told him to take her home and with a trembling hand she read the name on the envelope, Federica Campione. It was almost certainly from her father, for he wouldn't know her married name and no one whom she knew would have used Campione. She tore it open and with hungry eyes devoured the words as if they were the word of God. He had been watching her after all.

'For how can a tyrant rule the free and the proud, but for a tyranny in their own freedom and a shame in their own pride? And if it is a care you would cast off, that care has been chosen by you rather than imposed upon you. And if it is a fear you would dispel, the seat of that fear is in your heart and not in the hand of the feared.'

She felt the colour rise in her cheeks until it throbbed with shame. 'Stop the car, I need to get out,' she said suddenly.

'What, now?' exclaimed the chauffeur, glancing at her in the mirror.

'Now,' she repeated.

'Yes, Madam,' he replied in bewilderment. Reluctantly he drew into a quiet street and pulled up at the kerb. Federica threw open the door and staggered out onto the wet pavement. She walked hastily up the road until she found a small café. Dashing inside she took the table in the corner, ordered a cup of tea and stared down at the note in horror. Had she really no pride at all? Was her misery really due to her own weakness and lack of character? Was Torquil, the man she believed she loved, really a tyrant, controlling her every move?

She had wallowed so blindly in misery, feeling sorry for herself, she had never dared believe that her salvation was entirely in her own hands. Obedience had come more naturally to her than rebellion. Now she cringed at her own lack of strength. She was pathetic. She read the lines again and it all suddenly seemed so obvious. Staring into her tea she shone an unforgiving light onto the nature of her marriage. What she saw appalled her. She had allowed Torquil to control every aspect of her life, from the clothes she wore to the people she saw. She recalled with regret how he had cleverly prevented her from going home to Polperro. One by one she remembered each gradual move towards total dictatorship. He hadn't been satisfied with her love; he had wanted her freedom too. Sam had been right. She wished she had had the courage to take his hand when he had reached out to her. Even Arthur had warned her, but she hadn't listened.

She finally returned to the house in the late afternoon. Torquil wasn't home. She opened the fridge and pulled out a bottle of grapefruit juice. Then she walked upstairs and ran a bath. Her body trembled with resolution. She was going to spend Christmas in Polperro whether Torquil liked it or not. In fact, she was going to start standing up for herself. She undressed and slipped into a dressing gown, rehearsing what she was going to say to him. It seemed simple, but she feared her throat would seize up when she confronted him face to face.

Then she panicked that he might have organized something else, recalling his threat to whisk her off to Mauritius and she cringed. There's no reason he would have told her. She had always let him plan everything, she didn't even keep a diary. She had to be prepared so that he couldn't manipulate her. She ran downstairs to his study and began to open all the drawers in his desk. Everything had its own place, even the pencils were neatly lined up, sharpened to the same length, barely used. Finding nothing in his desk drawers she continued the search in the cupboards but once again she found nothing. No plane tickets, nothing. She rushed upstairs into his large walk-in wardrobe where polished shoes were displayed in regimental lines, each pair fitted with mahogany shoe-horns.

Suddenly the search ceased to be for a diary but for something else, as if at once she had grown up and was finally able to see the world outside the cocoon her husband had forged for her. Feverishly her hands searched the pockets of his jackets and the pockets of his trousers, all in perfect rows on wooden hangers. Her heart thumped with anxiety for she was aware that he could turn up at any moment. Her curiosity led her to the drawer in his bedside table where her fingers alighted upon a square pocket book. She picked it up and opened it. It was a leather-bound notebook, which contained handwritten lists of things to be done. Stuck onto the front was a Polaroid of a young woman sitting naked on a chair with her legs spread in shameless abandon, smiling with the knowledge of the power of her allure. Federica's heart froze. She recognised the face and she recognized the occasion. How come it had taken her so long to figure it out?

Federica called Hester. Her friend detected the strange tone in her voice and knew that something dramatic had happened. 'What has he done to you?' she asked.

'I need you now,' Federica pleaded and her eyes filled with tears. 'Will you come and pick me up?'

Hester put down the telephone, grabbed her keys and slammed the door behind her, all without a word to Molly who poked her head out of the steaming bathroom and wondered what on earth was going on.

When Hester arrived at Federica's house she was standing in the doorway in her dressing gown, clutching a plain wooden box. She ran down the steps, fearfully looking about her, and dived into the waiting car.

'You're coming like that?' Hester gasped in amazement.

Federica collapsed into sobs. 'Yes, because this is all I took into my marriage. My box and my trust.'

It was only once she was safely in the flat in Pimlico that Federica's sobs turned into hysterical laughter. Molly and Hester looked at each other anxiously, both recalling Helena's wedding when she had sobbed manically for Sam. When she had calmed down enough to speak she dried her eyes on her dressing gown sleeve and sniffed.

'Are you all right?' Molly asked anxiously.

'Oh, I'm much better,' she replied, controlling herself with difficulty. 'It's just that I forgot to turn off the bath!'

Chapter 39

Torquil returned home to find water pouring down the stairs. Fearing that Federica might be in trouble, he raced up to the bedroom, his feet slipping on the slimy carpet, the blood flooding to his head with anxiety.

'Federica!' he shouted, 'Federica! Are you all right?' He stumbled into the bathroom where the water was cascading over the edges in a final act of defiance. He turned off the taps and thrust his hand to the bottom and pulled out the plug. It gurgled with satisfaction. 'Shit!' he swore, looking at the expensive carpets which would all have to be replaced.

He cast his eyes about for his wife, but all that remained were her clothes neatly folded on the bed. He noticed only one dressing gown hung on the back of the door. He called her name again and proceeded to check the rest of the house. There was no reply, only the empty echo of his own voice as it bounced off the walls. He sat on the edge of the bed and rubbed his chin with his hand.

He was very worried. She had simply disappeared. But there was no indication of a struggle, or a break in, just the overflowing bath. Finally, he picked up the telephone and called the chauffeur.

'Well, Mr Jensen,' Paul replied thoughtfully, 'she goes shopping in St James's for about an hour, then when I'm driving her back, see, she asks me to stop, all of a sudden. Well, as you can imagine, Mr Jensen, I was a bit worried. She looked upset . . . No, I don't know why, Mr Jensen, she just looked pale like. She runs up the pavement and disappears into a caff for about an hour. When I drop her off, see, she's all right. So I go home, Mr Jensen. She said she didn't need me any more.' A short silence followed. 'Mr Jensen?' asked the chauffeur, afraid that he had perhaps made a mistake. 'Mr Jensen? Mrs Jensen didn't need me after that, did she?'

'It's fine, Paul,' Torquil replied, but his voice cracked mid-sentence. He put down the telephone and scratched his bristled jaw line ponderously. Then something caught his eye. The drawer to the bedside table was open a crack where Federica had failed to close it properly. Torquil always noticed details. He opened it to find his pocket book lying upside down, not as he had left it at all. He picked it up and studied it. With a deep groan he eyed the photograph of Lucia, which he had stuck onto the inside cover. Then it all made sense. She had run off in such a state she had forgotten to turn the taps off.

He unstuck the picture and tore it into small pieces before throwing them in the bin in fury. She had completely misunderstood, that photograph had been taken years before. He'd explain it all to her and she'd forgive him. He cast his eyes fretfully about the room to see if she had packed a bag. She hadn't. She hadn't taken anything, not even her underwear. She must have left in her dressing gown. He relaxed his shoulders. She was obviously planning on coming back. After all, how far could she go in a dressing gown?

Federica told Molly and Hester everything, omitting the part about the anonymous notes of poetry, which would remain her secret until she managed to track down her father.

The three friends sat in front of the gas fire with two bottles of cheap red wine, while Kenny Rogers sang 'It's a fine time to leave me, Lucille'.

Molly was fascinated by Federica's unhappy world. She had failed to see past the designer clothes and crocodile handbags.

Hester listened with deep sympathy. 'I knew you were miserable, Fede, I could tell. What are you going to do now?'

'Go home to Polperro and start again,' she said simply.

'You mean, you're going to leave Torquil?' Molly exclaimed, lighting a cigarette.

'Of course she's going to leave Torquil,' Hester said. 'He's a monster. You deserve so much better,' she added, squeezing Federica's arm affectionately.

'Oh, I don't want to look at another man as long as I live,' Federica sniffed. 'I want to be on my own for a while, make my own decisions. I need to work out who I am. I don't think I'm very sure of anything any more.'

When the telephone rang they all froze. Molly and Hester looked at Federica who stared back with fear. 'You answer it, Molly,' she said and her voice thinned with anxiety. She put her thumb to her mouth and bit the skin around her nail. 'You haven't seen me,' she added gravely.

Molly got up from the floor and the wine flushed from her head to her toes, restoring her swiftly back to sobriety. She took a deep breath before picking up the receiver. The shrill tones ceased leaving the room in a silence that hung heavy with anticipation.

'Hello,' Molly responded, trying her best to sound normal. Her shoulders dropped. 'Sam! What the hell are you doing calling me now? We're in crisis, that's why . . . What, now? Oh God! You'll have to sleep in the sitting room, Federica's in with Hester . . . it's a long story, we'll tell you when you arrive . . . Okay, see you in a minute.' She hung up with a smile on her face. 'One more for the party,' she laughed. 'Let's get out another bottle of wine.'

'Sam's missed his flipping train,' Molly announced, skipping through to the kitchen.

'Well, that's typical,' Hester sighed. 'He's in a world of his own these days, ever since Nuno died.'

'Poor Sam,' said Federica. 'He really loved Nuno, didn't he?'

'More than anyone else. More than Mum and Dad, I think,' Molly said, returning with another Bordeaux. 'You see, Nuno spent most of his time with Sam. He never had a son, and being the chauvinist that he was, he probably wished he had. So Sam was a kind of surrogate son for him. Dad gave him Nuno's study to write in. God knows what he's writing. But he spends all day locked away just like Dad. The only person allowed anywhere near him is Trotsky,' she added, opening the bottle.

'He should find a girlfriend,' said Hester. 'He used to have so many girlfriends.'

'That was when he had hair.' Molly laughed unkindly.

'He's not Samson, Mol,' Hester reproved in his defence. 'I think he looks lovely with less hair. He doesn't look pretty any more. He looks rugged and handsome.'

Molly scrunched up her nose in distaste. 'Each to their own, I suppose,' she sniffed, blowing smoke out of her mouth in rings.

'One thing I've learnt from Torquil,' said Federica sadly, 'looks can be deceptive. No one's as beautiful as Torquil, or as selfish. I'd rather a plain outside and a beautiful inside.'

Molly lowered her eyes, ashamed that she fancied him.

*

When Sam arrived at the flat Federica was at once struck by
the rapid deterioration of the young man who had once been
golden-haired and glossy, like a handsome Greek statue. He
shuffled in with his shoulders hunched, shivering with cold.
His face was as grey as it had been at Nuno's funeral and his
eyes betrayed a certain weariness, for his longing had drained
him of all enthusiasm and energy. When he saw her he smiled
sheepishly, though he wanted to run to her and hold her
against him. Federica recalled their awkward conversation at
the funeral and smiled back, indicating that she had forgiven
and forgotten. She stood up to greet him.

He placed his hands on her upper arms. 'Are you all right?'
he asked seriously.

'I'm fine now,' she replied, pulling away and nursing the
bruises he had left on her skin. 'I've left Torquil,' she added,
sitting down again on the carpet in front of the fire.

'You've left Torquil?' he repeated incredulously, turning
away in case she saw the light return to his eyes and the joy
curl his lips into a triumphant grin. 'You've left Torquil?' he
repeated.

'It's over,' she stated.

'We're celebrating with wine,' Molly added with glee.

'I'd say we were commiserating with wine,' said Hester.
'Poor Fede's really been through it.'

'What happened?' he asked, taking off his coat and sitting
on the sofa. He felt very hot. He struggled out of his father's
holey jersey and sat in his blue shirt with the cuffs undone and
hanging loosely on his wrists.

'Oh, it's a long story,' she said, sipping the Bordeaux and
feeling a lot better.

'Mol, hand me a glass,' he said, cheering up. 'Fede, you're
so strong. I'm so proud of you. What you've done is the
most difficult thing in the world. You've done it all by
yourself.'

'Not entirely,' she replied. Sam looked away. 'Let's just say that my eyes have been opened. I suppose I've grown up a bit. I can't believe I've been so blinkered and so weak. I've wasted four years of my life.'

'Nothing is ever wasted, Fede, you've learned a great deal about human nature but above all about yourself,' he said wisely. Then he changed the subject. 'What are you going to do now?'

'I'm going home. Mama and I are going to be a right pair.'

'Yes, we heard about that,' said Hester. 'I'm so sorry.'

'She's a fool,' Federica sighed. They all frowned at her sudden change of attitude, her opinion of her stepfather was well known.

'I thought you despised Arthur?' Molly interjected, flicking ash onto the carpet.

'Let's say I misunderstood him. Everything's much clearer now,' she grinned at Sam. 'I owe him an apology. Someone else I didn't listen to when I should have.'

Sam acknowledged her with a small smile. 'I'll accompany you on the train if you like,' he suggested.

Federica nodded at him gratefully. 'Would you?' She sighed in relief. 'I'd feel so much better. I'm terrified he'll find me and try to drag me back.'

'I'll bloody kill him if he comes anywhere near you,' he said, then chuckled for he didn't want her to know that he really meant it.

That night Federica and Sam barely slept. They sat up drinking and talking long after Hester and Molly had retired to bed. She unburdened her worries and her secrets to him and he listened with sympathy as he had done that day in the bluebells. 'I wish I had had the courage to tell you that time we had lunch,' she said.

'You so nearly did.'

'I know.'

'What frightened you?' he asked gently.

She thought about it for a while, watching the golden flames of the gas fire springing cheerfully in the grate. 'I didn't realise I was unhappy,' she said truthfully and shook her head in disbelief. 'I know it sounds mad, but I couldn't admit it to myself. I believed I loved him.'

'It doesn't sound mad at all.'

'Doesn't it?'

'No,' he said, and took her hand. 'You weren't wrong to love him. He was wrong to abuse your love.'

She grinned at him fondly. 'You understand everything so well.'

'Not everything,' he replied. 'Just you.'

The following morning Federica borrowed clothes from Hester. She was just pulling on a pair of jeans when Molly shrieked from the sitting room. 'Oh God!' she shouted. 'God, God, God.' They all ran to the window. 'No, Fede, not you,' she said, blocking her way. 'He's there! Waiting for you,' she hissed. 'He's seen me looking.'

Federica paced the room. Molly pulled the curtain back and peered out at the handsome man who stood beside his Porsche with his arms crossed miserably in front of him.

'Shit, what am I going to do?' she said nervously, biting her thumb again.

Sam perched on the arm of the sofa. 'I'll book a cab and we'll leave together,' he stated decisively, picking up the telephone. 'It's simple.'

'I don't think I can face him.'

'Of course you can. You had the strength to leave him, didn't you?' he insisted. 'So you can find the strength to tell him it's over.'

'I don't think I can.'

'You can and you will,' he said seriously. 'Or I'll do it for you.'

'You've gone this far, Fede, you can't back out now,' Hester agreed.

'*I* certainly wouldn't want to go home to a sodden carpet and a furious husband,' Molly said. 'However handsome he is.'

Sam rolled his eyes and ordered the cab. 'Just think about what you'd be going back to,' he said carefully. He held his breath as she walked up and down the room, her hands on her hips, deliberating her next move. Then he added simply, 'Fede, do you like the person you are when you're with Torquil?' She looked at him with fearful eyes and shook her head. 'Well, cast her aside then and come with me.' He stood up and took both her hands in his. 'You know you're doing the right thing.'

'But he loves me,' she protested weakly.

Sam squeezed her hands. 'No he doesn't, Fede. He wants to possess you, like his car or his house. If he loved you he'd take pleasure in your freedom, in your growing confidence, in your successes. If he loved you he'd encourage you to make your own path in life. He'd have bought you a camera and paid for you to have lessons rather than buying you ridiculous shoes and handbags, like a doll for him to manipulate. You're not a doll, Fede, you're a person with your own ideas and your own personality. If you go back he'll just sap you dry until you're incapable of a single personal thought. Think about it.'

She stood staring into his eyes knowing that he was right, because she had worked it out herself.

'Okay, let's do it,' she said firmly. 'But when we leave the house I want to talk to him,' she insisted. Then when she noticed Sam's eyebrows rise in objection she added hastily, 'I need to tell him myself. I need to prove to myself that I can do it.'

★

Twenty minutes later when Sam and Federica descended the steps which led onto the pavement, Torquil ran up to her and threw his arms around her. Sam immediately tried to separate them. 'Leave us alone!' Torquil growled. There followed a brief tussle during which Federica managed to wriggle free.

'Go away, Torquil!' she shouted. 'It's over.' Then she noticed his dejected face, his bloodshot eyes and his shoulders, which stooped pitifully.

'I haven't slept all night. I've been so worried,' he explained, raising his palms to the sky. 'You could have let me know where you were. I thought you'd been abducted.'

Federica turned to Sam. 'Wait for me in the cab,' she instructed. With a suspended heart Sam walked away from her. He stood by the car ready to intercede if she needed him, but he hoped she wouldn't need him. She had to learn not to need anyone, not her father, not her husband, not anyone. Once she had mastered that she'd be ready to love properly. He didn't mind how long it took, he'd wait for her.

'That photograph was taken years ago, little one. Didn't you notice it was old?' Torquil argued, reaching out for her. But Federica stepped back, putting her hands up to keep him at a distance. 'Come on, sweetness, I'm not having an affair. I love you. I'm lost without you. We're good together.'

'It's over, Torquil,' she replied, shaking her head.

'Don't be a fool, Federica. You're angry, I understand. Let's just go home and talk this through sensibly. Don't throw what we have away. It's so special,' he implored, casting his eyes over at Sam who stood by protectively.

'Don't call me "little one". I hate it,' she snapped, suddenly empowered by Torquil's vulnerability. 'I'm not coming home.'

Torquil tried to ignore the defiant tone in her voice. 'It's not what you think, damn it!' he snarled, repressing his frustration with gritted teeth. 'So I made a mistake keeping that photograph, are you going to punish me for a little mistake? What's important is that I love you. Love is about forgiveness, goddamnit.'

'Love is about trust,' she replied coldly.

'Then trust me when I tell you I'm not having an affair. Lucia's an old friend, that photograph was a joke.'

'I don't believe you.'

'Do you believe me when I tell you I love you,' he pleaded with her.

'You don't love me, Torquil. You want to possess me, like your car, or your house. I'm like a doll, you dress me, you take me out every now and then to play with me, but you don't love me. If you did you'd let me make my own decisions.' Federica began to feel light in the head with the swelling of her confidence.

Torquil was stunned. She had never spoken like that before. He breathed in through his nose like a seething bull, unable to control his growing anger. 'What are you going to?' he said quietly, narrowing his eyes aggressively. 'A provincial town on the coast? Back to your neurotic mother or your bourgeois grandparents?' Then he nodded in Sam's direction and added cuttingly, 'Or to a family of eccentrics?' Sam suppressed his smile. 'I can give you everything you want.'

Federica straightened herself up boldly. 'What? A few more handbags, a few more pairs of shoes? Please, Torquil, don't patronize me. You're hollow inside and I don't want to be with you any more. We'll communicate through lawyers and don't try to follow me, because, you know what? Sam's family eccentricities are contagious and you wouldn't want to catch them like I have, would you?'

'You'll regret this for the rest of your life. I won't take you back. You'll be sorry,' he shouted as she walked to where Sam waited for her by the open door of the cab. He smiled at her with pride as she climbed in, then he followed her and closed the door behind him. When he looked up at the window to Molly and Hester's flat their happy faces grinned at him from behind the glass. Hester put her thumb up and nodded.

Torquil drove away, the wheels of his Porsche skidding and leaving two black stripes on the tarmac that steamed in fury.

Federica collapsed into the seat, suddenly aware of her trembling hands and legs.

'Any more of those, Gov?' asked the cabbie, who had watched the confrontation with relish. 'That's better than *EastEnders*, that is.'

'To Paddington Station, please,' said Sam, putting his arm around Federica's shoulders.

She allowed him to gather her up as she quietly reflected on the last four years of her life with relief and regret.

Federica returned to much celebrating, because not only was it Christmas, but everyone was delighted to have her back again. Ingrid now admitted that she had thought Torquil a 'ghastly man' while Toby and Julian confessed that they had only remembered where they had seen him when it was too late to do anything about it. 'He was arrogant and self-satisfied then,' they said. 'We really let you down, Fede.'

Helena was delighted that someone else was as miserable as she was and accompanied her daughter on long walks along the cliffs, lamenting Arthur's painful silence. 'I've lost him, Fede. He won't even talk to me,' she whined.

Jake and Polly gathered her up like they had gathered up her mother. Suddenly the family united in the drama. Polly cooked large vegetable lasagnes and bread and butter puddings and all seven of them sat about the table, surrounded by Jake's model boats which now hung suspended from the ceiling so they couldn't be knocked onto the floor by clumsy elbows and hands, drinking large glasses of wine and Polly's elder-flower juice, carrying on four conversations at once.

Federica moved straight back in with Toby and Julian and Rasta, who she'd take out on her long walks with her mother. She helped Toby decorate the rooms for Christmas and Julian took her into town to shop for presents. 'I don't have a bean,' she said, thinking of the mountains of beans she had left in London.

'I do,' said Julian happily, 'and you can have as many as you like.'

She spent as much time at Pickthistle Manor as she did at Toby and Julian's. The squirrel in Sam's sweater drawer had woken up before time, so Ingrid had managed to secure his nest on the top of the Christmas tree, but a family of mice had somehow found their way under Sam's bed so he had to sleep in one of the spare rooms so as not to disturb them. The two families celebrated Christmas with drinks parties and lunch parties that continued long after the festival was over and the New Year had been toasted in with champagne and embraces.

When Sam hugged Federica he kissed her cheek affection-ately and said, 'This will be your year, Fede. You'll see.'

She hoped he was right.

Torquil sent her long letters in an attempt to win her back. He wrote about his deep love for her and his regret that he had ever laid eyes on Lucia. 'Everything I did was for you, because I wanted to protect you. I'm only guilty of caring too much,' he wrote. At first Federica read them, then as they got increasingly repetitive and pitiful she simply destroyed them unopened. However, one line lingered in her thoughts: 'I'm only guilty of caring too much.' Said by the deceiving Torquil it was nothing more than an empty sentence; however, applied to Arthur it was given a whole new meaning.

Federica felt desperately sorry for Arthur, so forgotten amid the destruction of her own marriage. She knew her mother was hard to live with, but she also knew that she desperately cared. After all, she had listened to Helena's soliloquies of remorse during their long walks on the cliffs. It was time to intervene.

When Arthur saw Federica at his door he initially felt sick with disappointment. He had thought it was Helena. But then his surprise turned to amazement. 'What are you doing here?' he asked.

'I've come to apologize, Arthur,' she replied. He remained in the frame of the door with his mouth agape. 'Can I come in?' she asked.

'Of course. Of course,' he stammered, standing aside to let her pass. She walked into the kitchen and took her coat off. 'Please sit down, here, let me take this for you,' he said, draping it over the back of one of the chairs. 'Tea?'

'Yes, please, it's freezing,' she said, rubbing her pink hands together.

'How did you get here?'

'By taxi.'

'Does your mother know you're here?' he asked anxiously.

'No.'

'Good.'

He handed her a cup of tea then sat down opposite her. Federica added milk and watched as it disappeared into the brew.

'I've left Torquil,' she stated simply.

'Right,' Arthur replied with care.

'I should have listened to you.'

'No you shouldn't,' he said quickly, disarmed by her sudden change in attitude. 'It was none of my business.'

'Yes, it was,' she insisted. 'You're my stepfather.'

'Was,' he interjected sadly.

She looked into his anguished eyes and realized that she had never really known him. 'You still are,' she said kindly. 'Mama misses you.'

His face flushed with hope. 'She does?'

'She thinks she's lost you.' Federica watched his small eyes glisten.

'I don't know,' he said, shaking his head and pressing his lips together. 'I just don't know.'

'I'm not coming here to negotiate a peace treaty. I came to apologize because I've treated you badly. You've been wonderful to Mama. I know she can be a nightmare,' she chuckled. 'But you handled her really well.' She looked at him steadily. 'You have to take her back, because no one else would know how to cope with her.'

'She is difficult, but never dull.'

'What attracted you to her in the beginning?' she asked out of curiosity, but unwittingly she unlocked the door to the happy memories that he had wilfully subdued.

He sat back in his chair and smiled. 'I could tell she was difficult. She had had a rough time too, so beneath the frost was a little girl desperate to be loved . . .'

Federica sipped her tea and listened while Arthur related the story of their meeting and their marriage, the good and the bad, until he realized that what he had was worth fighting to keep.

It was late when Arthur drove Federica home. He dropped her off at her uncle's house then hesitated at the wheel, debating whether to drive on to Helena's or to return to his own empty home. He still felt the warmth from his conversation with Federica and smiled inwardly at so many tender recollections. Yet he knew that if a reconciliation was to take place, it had to be on Helena's initiative or the balance of power would weigh in her favour and he'd lose her again. What's more, she had to learn from her mistake and be willing to change. He hoped she hadn't given up on him.

Sam accompanied Federica down to the beach where he'd gather wood for the fires he made and insist on toasting marshmallows just like they had done in the old days. He lent her books to read then discussed them late into the evening beside the happy fire in Nuno's study before driving her home in his father's car. He'd sit in his shirtsleeves on the cliffs as much as in the study because he constantly felt warm inside whether or not there was a fire. As long as he was close to Federica he needed little to exist, just the shared air between them and the knowledge that she was there. Little by little he became as comfortable and as familiar to Federica as Nuno's old chair. She looked forward to their walks and their excursions, to the dinners they had with his parents and the discussions about literature and history. As the weeks tumbled by Federica thought less and less about Torquil and only suffered the occasional nightmare which reminded her in her waking moments of why she had left him.

But she couldn't forget the notes from her father and she knew she wouldn't rest until she found him.

It was a strange telephone call that made up her mind to fly out to Chile. She was just about to leave the house when it rang. She was always reluctant to pick it up in case it was Torquil, but she reassured herself that it couldn't be him, she hadn't heard from him for weeks. Still, her hand trembled when she lifted the receiver. 'Hello,' she said tentatively.

'Hello,' replied a young woman. Federica's shoulders relaxed. 'Am I speaking to Federica Jensen?'

'Federica Campione, yes, I am she,' she answered firmly. 'Whom am I speaking to?'

'My name is Claire Shawton. I'm a friend of Hal's.'

'Oh, hello,' she said in a friendlier tone. 'How can I help you?'

'Well, it's a bit of a delicate subject really,' she began. 'I didn't want to talk to your mother, because I know how Hal feels about his mother.'

'Right,' said Federica, wondering how he did feel about their mother.

'And I couldn't talk to your stepfather either. Hal's funny about him too.'

'Okay.'

'He speaks very highly of you, though,' she said. 'I found your number in his book. No one answered the London number.'

'I see,' she mumbled, trying not to think about Torquil. 'What's up with Hal?'

'He's an alcoholic,' she stated. 'He needs help. He's in a right mess.'

'What?' said Federica, appalled. 'What sort of mess?'

'He misses all his lectures, sleeps all day, drinks all night. He's barely there at all, you know, he's out of it.'

'Are you sure he's an alcoholic?'

'Yes, I am. I know because I've been paying for his drink and his gambling for the last few months.'

'Gambling?'

'You know, fruit machines, poker, horses. I've paid for it all.'

'Why?'

'Because I'm in love with him,' she replied in shame. 'He doesn't have any money and I have lots. But it's got out of hand. He's drinking too much. He's changed.'

'Where is he now?'

'He's here asleep.'

'At this hour?'

'Yes, you see he stays up drinking all night, then he can't get to sleep so he takes sleeping pills, lots of them. Then he can't wake up. It's like he's dead.' She stammered and her voice quivered with emotion. 'I don't know what to do,' she sniffed.

'Oh God!' Federica sighed. 'What can we do?'

'He needs help.'

'I can see that. I'm coming up. But I'll have to bring someone with me,' she said, remembering that she couldn't drive.

Sam was only too happy to drive Federica to Exeter. They talked all the way about the options open to them. But Sam was adamant that the drink was only the symptom of an illness which lay far deeper. 'He drinks to hide from himself,' he said wisely.

'It all leads back to Papa,' Federica sighed. 'I just know it.'

When they found Hal lying asleep on his bed, his face sallow and lifeless, Federica began to shake him violently, fearing that he was dead and not asleep at all. When he woke up his eyes were bloodshot and distant. Not the Hal she knew at all. Sam looked around the room at the squalor he lived in.

Cigarettes were stubbed out on dirty plates which still bore the remains of greasy fry-ups, empty wine glasses and coffee cups lay collecting dust, clothes were strewn around the floor, mildewing from neglect and damp. The room smelt worse than the rabbit hutch that Hester had once had as a child.

'Hal, you're sick,' Federica said kindly.

'Go away and leave me alone!' he cried, thrashing out with his arms. 'I don't need you to come and lecture me.'

'I care about you, Hal. Look at the state you're in. You live like an animal.'

'It's not so bad,' he protested.

'It's terrible. You need help,' she said.

'I'm fine,' he insisted.

'You're an alcoholic,' she stated bluntly.

'I drink occasionally. So does everyone. That hardly qualifies me as an alcoholic,' he said sarcastically.

Then Claire stepped forward out of the shadows. 'I told her everything, Hal,' she said, wiping the tears from her face.

He stared at her a moment, blinking her into focus. Then his face twisted in defeat. 'You bitch,' he spat.

'It's because I love you that I can't stand by and watch you destroy yourself.'

Hal put his head into his hands and wept.

Hal allowed Sam and Federica to take him home. Claire said that she would pack up his things and sort out his room. Federica thanked her gratefully but knew that Hal would probably never want to see her again. He sat in the back of the car shaking with cold and discomfort, his skin an unhealthy pale green colour – he looked as if he already had one foot in the morgue. Federica and Sam decided that they would keep the nature of his illness secret in order not to upset his family. They agreed to say that he had had a nervous breakdown. Federica knew that he needed to get away, start again some-where else, far from Helena's possessive love and the horror of his own demons.

'I'm going to take Hal to Chile,' she told Sam.

'When?' Sam exclaimed in alarm.

'As soon as possible. He needs to leave the country for a while. There's only one person who can help him through this, because he helped me through my trouble too.'

'Who's that?' Sam asked, feeling an invisible hand wrap itself around his throat.

'My father.'

'Your father?'

'Yes, he's at the root of Hal's problem.'

'How did he help you?' he asked, fixing his eyes on the road in front of him and gripping the steering wheel in an effort to control his impulses.

'I wasn't going to tell you, because I feared you might think it ridiculous. But Papa sent me anonymous notes of such lovely poetry. He must have written them himself, after all, he's a poet as well as a novelist.'

'I see,' said Sam tightly. His heart flooded with disappointment, but he couldn't bring himself to dampen her happiness and tell her that the notes had really come from him.

'He's very spiritual and philosophical. His notes just opened my eyes, I suppose, and helped me to see my situation more clearly. I felt I wasn't alone, that he was there helping me. He gave me the strength to leave Torquil. I want to thank him. But I think he could help Hal too.'

'So, how long will you stay?'

'As long as it takes. I've got nothing to keep me here.'

'No,' he said flatly, swallowing his misery in order to brood on it later when he was alone. 'Nothing.'

Chapter 40

Hal wanted to get better. Polly said that was the first step and a very brave step indeed. Helena was appalled when she heard, but Federica was firm. 'He needs a new scene,' she said. 'And so do I.'

Helena insisted that she could nurse him back to health. 'You don't need to take him across the world, for goodness' sake!' she exclaimed, hurt that Hal was ready to leave her and humiliated that she hadn't been able to help him herself.

'We're going to find Papa,' Federica admitted finally. 'I know that Hal's problem goes back to when he was a child in Chile. He needs to talk to him.'

Helena went white with indignation, as if Federica was attacking her personally for leaving Ramon. She sat tight-lipped and furious, smouldering with guilt and jealousy because she wasn't included.

Arthur was so relieved that at last someone had taken responsibility for Hal he bought them their tickets to Santiago.

'Don't thank *me*,' he said to Federica, 'this is to thank *you*. You don't know how grateful I am.'

Federica knew he was discreetly thanking her for more than preserving the health of his stepson. She kissed his fleshy face and whispered, 'Don't forget the good times with Mama, will you. There were many more than bad.'

But Arthur was determined to wait. Sadly he had no choice. If she didn't come back of her own accord, he would have to let her go.

Sam was mortified that Federica was leaving Polperro and hurt that she believed there was no reason to stay. He wanted to shake her, tell her he loved her with his whole heart and his whole being, but he knew that if he did he would ruin any chance he had.

She would come to him when she was ready or not at all. He'd just have to be patient. The day before she left he arrived at Toby and Julian's house to say goodbye. He had bought her a gift, hoping that she'd remember him each time she used it.

'Oh, Sam, you really shouldn't have bought me a present,' she said, taking the package from him. He stood with his hands in his pockets, his moth-eaten jersey barely able to keep out the cold that penetrated right through to his bones. She opened the brown paper to find a Pentax camera. 'My God!' she exclaimed. 'This is a proper camera.'

'It's got a proper zoom lens too,' he said, smiling in order to hide his despair.

'You're so sweet, Sam, thank you,' she replied, kissing him on his taut cheek. He breathed in the scent of her skin that invaded his senses whenever she came close and resisted the impulse to pull her against him and kiss her properly like he had done that night in the barn.

'Don't forget your friend, will you?' he said, suppressing his emotion.

She grinned at him with gratitude. 'You've been such a good friend, Sam. I'm so grateful. If it hadn't been for you, I'd never have got through these last weeks.'

'Well, don't forget that you did it all by yourself,' he said. 'You don't need anyone any more, you're strong on your own.'

Federica frowned at him and thought how like her father he sounded.

Mariana had just come in from a walk along the beach when the telephone rang. She picked it up to hear the crackle of a long-distance call and then the thin voice of a young woman. '*Hola, quìn es?*' she said, putting her hand over her other ear to muffle the sound of Ramoncito who was playing a competitive game of chess with his grandfather.

'It's Federica.'

Mariana caught her breath. 'Fede? Is that you?' she gasped in English.

'Abuelita, it's really me,' she exclaimed, feeling a wave of nostalgia hit her.

'It's been so long! How are you?'

'I'm coming out to Chile tomorrow with Hal. Can we come and stay?'

'Well, of course you can,' she said in excitement. 'I don't believe it. I thought you'd forgotten about us.'

'I never forgot about you, Abuelita. I have so much to tell you, so much . . .' she said, the joy catching in her throat and making it difficult to speak. 'Is Papa with you?' she asked hoarsely.

'He has a house on the beach, between here and Zapallar.'

'Will he be there?'

'Yes,' she said happily. 'Yes he will. He'll be so happy to see you both! I'll send a car to pick you up and bring you down.' Then she added hopefully, 'How long will you be staying?' And Federica couldn't help but laugh for her grandmother hadn't changed at all.

'I don't know,' she replied and then wondered if she'd ever leave.

When Mariana walked out onto the terrace, her old eyes streaming with joy, Ignacio looked up from his chess game.

'What's happened?' he asked, wondering what kind of miracle had the power to make her face glow like that.

Mariana rubbed her hands together, unable to contain her happiness. 'Ramoncito,' she said. 'You're going to meet your half-brother and sister. They're arriving in two days to stay.'

Ramoncito looked at his grandfather whose face crumpled with delight.

'Woman, you sure know how to distract our concentration,' he said and grinned at her. 'I thought they'd forgotten about us,' he added, taking his glasses off and wiping his eyes.

'No, and what's more they have no plans,' she said hopefully.

'Maybe they're coming home,' he said, looking at his wife with tenderness.

'Maybe.' Then she bustled into the cool interior of the house to prepare their rooms. She wanted to do it personally and Gertrude couldn't be trusted to get it right. Gertrude couldn't be trusted to get anything right, but for some reason Ignacio liked her, so she stayed.

'Abuelito?' said Ramoncito, moving his piece across the board. His grandfather put his glasses back on the bridge of his nose and looked at his grandson over the top of them. 'Will I like Hal and Federica?'

'Yes, you will, you'll like them very much. But you have to remember that they were torn from their father when they were very small. They're coming out with a lot of emotional baggage. Be patient and give them time to sort it out. Your father loves you, Ramoncito, and he loved your mother more than he ever loved anyone. Don't forget that.'

The boy nodded and watched his grandfather turn his attention back to the game.

Ramon typed the last line of his book with great satisfaction. It had been cathartic. Estella had shown him that it was possible to love without possessiveness, to love enough to give the other his freedom. Her life had quite literally changed his. In a way he felt she had unwittingly sacrificed herself for his enlightenment. She had set an example and he had learnt from it. He only wished that he had had the inner ability to learn from her while she had been alive. So he aired his feelings of guilt and failure which had clung to his conscience since he had wilfully abandoned his children, in an allegory about three birds: the peacock who demands love's total commitment, the swallow who flies away from love and the third, the phoenix, who brings her unconditional love without asking for anything in return. When the phoenix disappears into the flames the peacock and the swallow have finally learnt how to love without yearning to possess each other. Ramon was pleased with his work. He entitled it *To Love Enough* and dedicated it 'To those I have loved'.

He thought of Federica and Hal. It was too late to try to make up for his negligence in the past and that greatly saddened him. But he had Ramoncito and poured into him the love he had in his heart for three. He sank into an easy chair and in the half-light of his study he read the manuscript from beginning to end. The shutters were closed against the heat of early afternoon but the gentle surge of the sea filtered through with the scent of honeysuckle and jasmine and caressed his soul that still mourned the loss of Estella.

When Ramoncito found him later he was submerged in his memories, his eyes closed and his breathing heavy. Ramoncito couldn't wait to tell him the news; he knew how happy he'd be. So he shook his shoulder gently. 'Wake up, Papa!' he whispered. 'I have good news for you.'

Ramon opened his eyes and pulled himself out of his warm, rose-scented dreams and blinked up at his son.

'Hal and Federica are arriving in two days from England,' he said and watched his father stare at him in bewilderment.

'It's true. Federica telephoned Abuelita this afternoon. I'm finally going to meet my half-brother and sister,' he said and smiled broadly.

Ramon sat up and rubbed his eyes. 'Tell me again,' he said in confusion. 'Federica and Hal are coming here? Are you sure?'

'Yes,' Ramoncito insisted happily.

'And Helena?'

'No, just Federica and Hal.'

'They're going to stay with my parents, right?'

'Yes.'

'My God, I don't deserve this,' he mumbled, standing up and suffering a terrible head spin.

'Yes, you do, Papa,' said Ramoncito. 'Mama was always telling you to go and see them.'

'And I never listened to her.'

'She'd be happy.'

'I know.'

'Have you finished yet?'

'The book?'

'Yes.'

'Yes, I have.'

'Great, let's open a bottle of wine. We have two things to celebrate now,' said Ramoncito joyfully.

But Ramon was anxious. Federica and Hal knew nothing of Estella and Ramoncito.

Hal and Federica boarded the plane for the long journey across the waters to Chile. Neither knew what to expect, but both hoped that somehow the ghosts of the past would be confronted and exorcised. Hal was pale and visibly shaking with discomfort as his body craved the poison that was destroying it. Federica kept forcing him to drink water to flush it all out, fussing over him like an over-protective nurse.

As soon as they boarded the plane he slouched into his chair, closed his fevered eyes and slept.

Federica tried to read but she was unable to concentrate. The events of the last month invaded her thoughts, allowing her no peace. She cast her mind back to Torquil. She had been unhappy right from the start of their marriage, but she had believed she loved him and did everything he asked of her in order to please him. How easy it had been for him to manipulate her and mould her into a submissive pawn. She had taken it all, every humiliation, until she had grown so accustomed to his controlling nature that she had no longer recognized it or realized that it was within her power to withstand it. She had wanted a father figure to look after her and protect her from the world. It was a miracle that she had grown up at all in the stifling air of their marriage where his overbearing personality had stunted her growth, but somehow she had realized that she no longer wanted someone to live for her, but to live herself in the way she wanted.

It sounded simple with hindsight. She should have left earlier. She was appalled at her own lack of character and vowed to herself silently that she would never let anyone treat her like that again. She thought of her father and the notes of poetry he had sent her. It had been due to his support that she had been able to stand back and look at her marriage with detachment. Then there was Sam who had kept her afloat.

When she thought of Sam she smiled inwardly until the smile rested on her lips, curling them up at the corners. She pictured his dishevelled figure, those shabby sweaters he always wore, the dusty shoes that hadn't ever enjoyed the luxury of a lick of polish, his lofty expression and intelligent eyes. He had been a beautiful boy, she recalled wistfully, remembering their first encounter on the lake. He had had thick blond hair that fell over his eyes, pale pink lips that smirked sardonically, luminous skin that glowed with contentment and the charisma of a young man who knows he is much cleverer than everyone else.

So what had happened? Age had stolen his golden hair, experience had humbled him and Nuno's death had robbed him of his contentment. He was more loveable now, less aloof. But Federica didn't allow herself to dwell on her feelings for Sam; she wasn't ready to confront them yet. She pulled the butterfly box out of her bag and turned the focus of her attention to her father and grandparents, reliving all those glorious moments as a child before her mother had taken her away across the sea.

Hal slept most of the way, waking up to eat and go to the bathroom. It was only when they landed in Santiago airport that he sat up and stared out of the window, the view over the Andes mountains strumming within him a familiar chord that caused his throat to tighten and his eyes to well with tears. He swallowed hard, gripping the arm of his seat as the complex jumble of his emotions churned in his stomach.

'We're home, Fede,' he choked, turning to look at her. She nodded, for she too was moved and unable to speak. She blinked away her joy and threaded her hand into his.

Mariana had sent the chauffeur to pick them up and drive them down to Cachagua. He introduced himself as Raul Ferro but didn't speak a word of English and Hal and Federica had forgotten the Spanish they had once spoken fluently. So they communicated with gestures and followed him out to the car. The heat in Santiago was stifling and oppressive but Hal and Federica absorbed it with delight along with the long-forgotten memories. At first they sat in the back in silence, watching the scenery pass by the windows, lost in the dusty halls of their past. Then, when the car left the city and sped up the open road that cut through the arid mountains to the coast, they sat back and looked at one another with different eyes. After years of estrangement they were at once reunited by their shared childhood and their shared longing to reclaim it.

'I was only four when we left, but you know, I remember so much,' said Hal wistfully, wiping his sweating brow with his shirtsleeve. 'I feel better already!'

'I thought it would be strange seeing it all again, but it feels as if I never left,' she sighed, watching the heat shimmering above the road ahead like pools of water.

'I never really felt I belonged to Papa,' said Hal suddenly.

Federica looked at his troubled face and pulled a thin smile of sympathy. 'I know. He ignored you didn't he?' she agreed softly.

'It's odd because I was so small, but I've felt his rejection through the years.'

'You were Mama's golden boy, though.'

'That came with a price, believe me.'

'Pretty suffocating, I know.' Federica shook her head as she remembered her mother's overwhelming neediness and constant discontent.

'She's a deeply unhappy woman,' Hal mused. 'I grew up with the responsibility of making her happy where everyone else had failed. You know, Arthur's given up on her too, just like Papa did. I really thought Arthur could make her happy.'

'Oh, don't give up on Arthur,' she chuckled with a smile.

'What do you mean?' He frowned. 'I thought you hated Arthur.'

'I did. But I never gave him a chance. He's a good man and Mama's lucky to have him.' She noticed the perplexed expression on his face and added, 'I went to see him, Hal. They still love each other.'

'Well, that's good.' Hal sighed. 'She's not all bad. Just very misguided.'

'It's taken a while to get over Papa, but I think she learnt the hard way. "In much wisdom is much grief,"' she quoted wisely.

'You sound like Sam Appleby,' he said.

Federica grinned. 'Do I?'

'Yes, his pomposity is catching. You've obviously been spending too much time with him.' Hal gazed out of the window. 'Why do you suppose Papa deserted us?' he asked tentatively, changing the subject. They had never talked about their father like this before. They'd never dared ask those questions.

Federica lowered her eyes. 'I don't know,' she said, allowing thoughts of Sam Appleby to dissolve into her father's shadow. 'But I'm going to ask him. I need to know and so do you.'

'What makes you think he'll be happy to see us?'

'I just know it,' she replied firmly.

'He could always have come to see us in England but he didn't. So why's he going to be pleased to see us now?'

'I know what you're saying, Hal,' she said carefully. 'Just trust me. I know he regrets the past and I know he still cares.'

Hal rested his eyes on the magnificence that surrounded him, so far from the cold cliffs of Cornwall and felt a deep yearning in his soul. He felt as if an invisible force was filling his spirit with something weightless so that his body felt buoyant and bursting with optimism.

Ramon sat on the terrace of his parents' beach house, looking out across the sea that lay still and gleaming in the late morning light. He had barely slept at all for his mind had itched with guilt and anxiety – how was he going to explain himself to the two children he had abandoned long ago and left to mourn him? How was he going to explain Ramoncito to them – and Estella? Would they understand? How was

Ramoncito going to feel suddenly finding himself having to share his father's devotion when he had grown up with the exclusive right to it? He looked at his watch; they'd be arriving soon. He felt his stomach churn with nerves. He knew he should have gone to pick them up at the airport, but he needed the moral support of his parents.

Mariana had agreed with him. 'Much better that they see us all together at the house, less pressure all round,' she had said.

'Here, son,' said Ignacio, handing him a tumbler of rum. 'You look as though you need it.'

'I don't know what to expect,' he said sheepishly.

'Don't think about it too much,' said Ignacio simply, sitting down opposite Ramon and pulling his panama hat onto his head to protect him from the sun. 'They're coming out to see you because you're their father, not to torment you. Let bygones be bygones and get to know each other again. That's my advice.'

'So much has happened,' said Ramon, staring into his glass. 'Estella, Ramoncito . . .'

'Life goes on. It has many chapters yet it's one book. There's a common thread that runs through each chapter.'

'What's that, Papa?' said Ramon, sighing heavily.

'Love,' said Ignacio bluntly. Ramon frowned at him, but his father just nodded back. 'I'm old and wise, son, I should be after eighty-four years, and I've picked a few things up in my life. That's one of them. Learn something from an old man.' He chuckled. 'Love will unite you all, you'll see.'

'That and forgiveness,' said Ramon, knocking back his glass. 'A large dose of forgiveness.'

As the car drove up the coast Federica and Hal began to reminisce with growing excitement. They recognized the shack where they had always stopped en route to their grandparents' house, where Ramon had always bought them drinks and *empanadas*, where the Chilean children had played football with an empty Coke can under the sycamore trees. They were both struck at how little it had changed in so many years, as if they were driving through a strange void which time was incapable of penetrating.

When they descended the dusty track into Cachagua itself they were both too moved and anxious to speak any more. Hal took Federica's hand, which surprised her for it had always been she who had initiated any demonstrations of affection. She squeezed it, grateful for his support for she was nervous too. The thatched houses were the same, surrounded by verdant trees and bushes, although there were more of them. When the car drew up outside the familiar walls of their grandparents' house they both heard the thumping of their hearts as they beat loudly and in unison.

'I'm scared,' Hal confessed.

'Me too,' Federica replied hoarsely. 'But we're here now, so let's just plunge on in,' she said, trying to make light of their fear.

Ramon heard the engine of the car and then the expectant silence that followed when the ignition was turned off. He heard the doors open and close. He looked across at his parents and Ramoncito, who had all got to their feet and were making their way into the house. Mariana's old legs were slow but she bustled through the sitting room as fast as she could go, her breathing heavy with excitement. Ramoncito didn't understand his father's uneasiness and was caught up in the enthusiasm of his grandparents. He had always wondered what his half-siblings were like, often fantasizing that they lived in Chile so that he could enjoy the fun of having a large family like all his school friends, who often had as many as ten brothers and sisters to play with.

Ignacio turned to his son who hesitated on the terrace, pale-faced and apprehensive. 'Son, it's like diving into the sea, the anticipation is uncomfortable but once you're in the water is warm and pleasant.' He smiled at him in understanding. 'You just have to take the plunge and not think about it.'

Ramon nodded at him and followed his unsteady old frame into the dark interior of the house where it was cool and smelt of tuberose. In his mind he still imagined Federica as he had seen her as a thirteen-year-old child on her bicycle in Cornwall. Hal he remembered less well and that made him feel guiltier than ever.

When Federica and Hal saw their grandmother hurry out of the house to greet them their hearts ceased to beat with anxiety but accelerated with joy. She was much greyer and appeared smaller because the last time they had seen her they had been children. But her smile and her tears were the same expressions of her gentle nature that had clung to their memories for almost two decades and they ran to her and embraced her. She wanted to tell them how tall they were, how beautiful Federica was and how handsome Hal was, but her throat ached with emotion and her lips trembled with regret because she was old and had lost countless precious years of their growing up. So she embraced them again, gesticulating with her shaking hands and expressive face all the things she was unable to put into words.

Ignacio appeared next in the doorway because Ramoncito hung back, suddenly overcome with shyness. He hugged his grandchildren, chuckling with happiness because he also was too moved to speak. Hal remembered him for his shoulder-rides but was barely able to reconcile the ursine man of his childhood with the thin, wizened man who now stood before him.

Then Ramon's large body hesitated in the doorway with his son.

Federica detected the anxiety in his eyes and strode up to him and threw herself into his arms as she had always done as a child. Ramon was stunned at her confident display of affection and wrapped his arms around her with gratitude. He was astonished to see in her features echoes of the young Helena he had fallen in love with on the pier in Polperro. Her hair was white and flowing, her skin translucent and her eyes that same clear blue that had disarmed him in her mother. He held her face in his hands and swallowed his regret. 'You're so grown up,' he choked. 'And you've done all this without me?' he said, pulling her into his arms again.

'Without you, no,' she sniffed, breathing in the familiar scent of him that had carried her through the years and prevented her from ever forgetting him. Ramon looked over Federica's shoulders and saw the grey face of his son who stood staring at him with haunted eyes. He gently disentangled himself from his daughter and walked up to him.

'Hal,' he said, extending his hand. Hal tried to say 'Papa' but all that escaped his throat was a dry rasp. He looked into the face of his father, searching for some sign of affection but all he could see was fear and uncertainty. He swallowed hard. Ramon floundered, not knowing what to do next. He lifted his eyes to his father and remembered the advice he had given him. 'Hal, I'm sorry,' he muttered. The boy's eyes softened and the corners of his mouth twitched with emotion. Ramon took the first step, held out his arms and pulled the trembling young man against him. Hal responded with a moan before his decrepit body shook with sobs. 'I'll make it up to you,' said Ramon. 'I promise.'

Ramoncito watched the scenes of reunion from the doorway and felt excluded. The tears and emotion were alien to him for he hadn't even cried at his own mother's funeral. He watched Federica and Hal with curiosity and listened to them speaking a language that he didn't understand. Federica didn't look anything like Ramon but Hal was uncannily similar, except he looked thin and ill. He wanted to go up and introduce himself but he was aware that he played no part in this family gathering because they were all mourning a parting that had happened before he was born.

Suddenly Ramon remembered Ramoncito. He pulled himself up and turned to face his son who stood anxiously in the shadows. 'Ramoncito,' he said. 'Come and meet your brother and sister.' He said it in Spanish but Hal and Federica understood and blinked at each other in bewilderment. The fifteen-year-old boy emerged into the sunlight. He was tall and athletic with raven-black hair and shiny brown eyes as soft as milk chocolate.

Federica at once recognized Ramon in the languor of his smile and in the poise of his gait, yet his skin was the colour of rich honey and his face was long and gentle, which set him apart from their father.

Hal immediately saw himself reflected in the dark features of Ramoncito and he gathered himself together and strode forward to shake him by the hand. 'I've always wanted a brother,' he said.

When Ramon translated for him, Ramoncito's face broke into a wide smile and he replied in Spanish, 'Me too.'

Federica took him by the hand and kissed him. He blushed to the roots of his glossy hair. Federica smiled at him. Besides their blood, their blushing was something they both had in common.

Chapter 41

Both Hal and Federica remembered their grandparents' large terrace, overlooking the wide sea. The scents of gardenia and eucalyptus transported them back to their childhood – but they were very different people now and the past seemed like another life. They all sat in the sunshine, the heat melting away their apprehensions, but still the atmosphere was awkward. There were so many things they wanted to say to each other and yet no one knew how to start.

Gertrude brought out a tray of *pisco sour* and handed them around, wondering why the place vibrated with such intense joy and sadness all at the same time. For once her scowl was replaced with an expression of curiosity as she eyed the two strangers with suspicion. She was more perplexed when Hal asked for a glass of water.

'I can't believe you're here,' said Mariana happily. 'After all this time, what possessed you?'

Federica sipped the alcoholic drink she'd never been allowed to taste as a child and screwed up her nose. 'This is so sour!' she exclaimed.

'All that lemon,' said Mariana. 'You'll get used to it.'

'After one glass you'll be hooked,' said Ignacio.

'So what made you decide to come now?' asked Ramon.

Federica sighed and glanced at Hal, who sat back in his chair and gulped down his water thirstily.

'Things happen in your life that put everything into perspective,' she said, choosing her words carefully. 'I had an unhappy marriage and Hal, well, Hal's been through a tough time too. We needed to get back to our roots. We needed to see you again. It's not natural to be separated from your family for so long.' She lowered her eyes, not wanting to make her father feel guilty for abandoning them. Mariana glanced at her son and felt uneasy. 'It's wonderful to come out and discover another member of the family,' Federica continued, filling the uncomfortable silence. They all looked at Ramoncito who blushed again and smiled bashfully.

'Have you forgotten all your Spanish?' Mariana asked.

'I'm afraid we have,' said Federica. 'I understand bits but mostly I've forgotten it all.'

'Papa, where is your wife?' Hal asked, draining his glass.

Ramon's face twisted with sadness. 'She's dead,' he replied.

Hal stiffened and mumbled an apology. Mariana commented on the weather and then Ignacio got to his feet.

'Son, why don't you take Federica and Hal for a walk up the beach? You have much to talk about. Then you can come back and we can start all over again.'

Ramon looked relieved and translated for his son. Ramoncito nodded and watched his half-brother and sister stand up and walk into the house with his father.

'For the love of God, that was tense,' Mariana sighed once they had gone.

'Be calm, woman, they just need to thrash it all out together,' said Ignacio. 'How about a game of chess, Ramoncito?' he added to his grandson who looked up at him and smiled.

'Beautiful girl, Abuelito!' he said in admiration.

Ramon didn't want to walk up the beach. 'I want to take you somewhere else,' he said, unlocking his car and climbing in.

'I hear you have a beach house of your own,' said Federica, noticing that his hair had turned completely grey at the temples and the diaphanous skin beneath his eyes sagged from too much melancholy. He looked old.

'Yes, I do, but I'm not taking you there either,' he replied, driving off up the sandy track. 'I'm taking you to meet Estella.'

'Who's Estella?' asked Hal.

'Ramoncito's mother.'

'Oh.' Hal coughed away his embarrassment.

'I want to talk to you somewhere we won't be disturbed,' said Ramon.

The cemetery rested in heavenly stillness on top of the cliff overlooking the sea. It was hot and the smells of the flowers and pine trees scented the air with the serenity of nature. Ramon parked the car and they walked across the shadows, taking care not to trample over the graves of sleeping spirits, to where Estella was buried. 'This is Estella's resting place,' said Ramon, rearranging the flowers he had placed against her tombstone that morning.

'She has a nice view,' said Hal, desperate to make up for his faux pas.

Ramon smiled at him. 'Yes she does.'

'Will you tell us about her, Papa?' Federica asked 'She must have been very beautiful because Ramoncito is tremendously handsome.'

'She was,' he agreed sadly. 'But first I want to start at the beginning. I want to start with you. Federica, Hal and Helena. Let's sit over here,' he suggested, pointing to the grassy slope that led down to the cliffs.

They sat in the sunshine and watched the hypnotic swell of the sea below. Ramon took each child by the hand. 'I ask you both to forgive me,' he said. Hal and Federica didn't know what to say and stared at him in astonishment. 'I ran away from your mother because her love was too intense and I felt claustrophobic. We should have put you both first and tried to work out our problems, but we were both too selfish. I didn't fight for your mother and try to persuade her to stay and she didn't try to change for me. I loved you both but didn't realize what I had lost until it was too late, and then I was too ashamed to face up to it so I just ran away and left you. It was easier to run – after all I had run from love my entire life.' Both Federica and Hal were astounded by his honesty.

He then recounted the moments of their childhood that had touched him and the small details of their characters that he had remembered and taken with him through the years. 'Hal, you used to cling to your mother. I frightened you, I think. You were so sensitive you felt the ill feeling between us and it upset you. You were very small so I used to leave you with Helena and take Federica out with me. I never really knew you. But I'd like to start again and get to know you now,' he said, looking into the troubled eyes of his son and recognizing the torment that lay behind them. 'You're my son, Hal, and nothing is more important than blood. I understand that now. It's taken much unhappiness but I now know what is important.'

'That would be good, Papa,' mumbled Hal, whose ability to express himself had been inhibited by the heat and the alcohol that still contaminated his liver.

Ramon told them about the time he had gone to England to see them and how Helena had protected them from him. How he had seen Federica on her bicycle but driven away following Helena's advice. 'But don't ever blame your mother for that. I was insensitive, popping into your lives when it suited me just to make me feel better. She was right, it wouldn't have done you any good.

'Estella's death taught me the value of life,' he continued solemnly. As much as Federica tried to remember the pretty young maid who had floated through the rooms of the beach house, filling it with the gentle scent of roses, she could not. 'I didn't set out to love Estella. She quenched a physical longing, which then grew into something more urgent, something deeper. When I was with her there was nowhere else I wanted to be. I had never experienced that before. I had spent my life running away from people, yearning to be on my own, not wanting to commit to anyone. Estella was different. She made no demands. She didn't suffocate me with neediness. All she wanted was my affection. So I wrote on the beach instead of travelling the world. I didn't need to go anywhere, for she was my inspiration and I wrote my best work with her. Ramoncito is a living expression of our love. When she died in the road I felt as if my whole world had suddenly imploded. I was consumed with regret. I should have married her but it was more convenient for me to remain single. I should have told her more often I loved her. I should have told you both that I loved you too and made more of an effort to be a part of your lives. But now I can. By coming out here you've both given me a second chance. I'll never have another with Estella.'

'Papa, we forgive you,' Federica whispered, taking his hand in both of hers and squeezing it. 'We're together now and we can get to know each other all over again, can't we, Hal?' Hal nodded. 'If it hadn't been for your poetry I would never have had the strength to leave my husband,' she continued.

'Really?' said Ramon in surprise, wondering which ones she meant. Then she told him about her marriage and how the butterfly box, which contained his letters, had sustained her through unhappy times.

'You didn't know it, Papa, but you were ever-present. You were there when I needed you most,' she said.

Ramon smiled at her but he was aware that Hal said very little.

They sat on the cliff top until the sun grew too intense and they had to retreat beneath the pine trees. They talked about the past, bridging the years that had widened the distance between them, until the rumblings of their stomachs distracted them from their emotions and alerted them to the rapid passing of the day. 'Gertrude will be furious that we're late for lunch,' said Ramon and winked at Hal.

Gertrude was indeed more sour than usual. They had lunch out on the terrace and this time the atmosphere was one of celebration. They reminisced about the past and Federica told them about their life in England, the beauty of Cornwall and the eccentricities of the people who lived there. Hal made a valiant effort to resist the flasks of wine that circled the table, quenching his thirst with endless glasses of water. Weary from the heat and the journey he retreated to his room to sleep a siesta.

Ramon took the opportunity to ask Federica about the state of his health. 'He's very unwell, I'm afraid,' she said.

'He looks terrible, *pobrecito!*' Mariana sighed sympathetically, remembering the little boy who used to love eating ice cream, *manjar blanco* and riding on the shoulders of his grandfather.

'Mind you, he ate enough to sustain an army,' said Ignacio.

'He's deeply unhappy,' Federica admitted. 'He's been slowly destroying himself by drinking too much and leading a useless, decadent life. I thought coming here might take him away from his problems.' Then she looked at her father. 'I hoped you might be able to get through to him. After all, you helped me.'

'I'll try,' he replied sincerely.

'How did Ramon help you, Fede?' Mariana asked curiously, longing to discover that he hadn't completely deserted his children as she had supposed.

'He sent me notes of poetry,' she said and smiled at him tenderly. 'You may think it strange that a few lines of verse can change someone's life, but they really did. I had been so blind to my own situation, they opened my eyes. Knowing Papa was thinking of me gave me the courage to leave Torquil. I knew I wasn't alone.'

Ramon smiled back at her awkwardly. Federica understood it as modesty.

'You dark horse, Ramon,' said Mariana proudly. 'After lunch I would like to show you the family photograph albums, Fede. There are lovely ones of you and Hal as children.'

'And I'd like to get my camera and take photos of all of you. This is a reunion I shall never forget.'

After lunch Federica went into her bedroom. She noticed at once the scent of lavender on her sheets and the large stems of tuberose on the dresser. The shutters were closed, keeping the room cool, but she opened them and let the sunlight tumble into her room, illuminating her memories as she remembered the occasional picture on the wall and the furniture. She opened her suitcase and pulled out her camera. She sat on the bed and drew the lens out of its protective covering, remembering how Julian had taught her to hold it. Then she thought of Sam. She wanted to call him up and tell him how it was all going. But she thought she'd take a few photographs first so that she could tell him she had used his gift.

'Fede, can I come in?'

She turned to see her father standing in the doorway. 'Sure,' she replied. 'I'm just putting together this fabulous camera so I can take some photographs to show everyone back in England.'

'Good idea,' he said, sitting down on the other bed. 'About those notes of poetry,' he began.

'They were inspired,' she enthused happily. 'I'm a different person now.'

'I didn't send them,' he declared.

Federica's face drained of excitement. 'You didn't send them?' she repeated in astonishment.

'No,' he said, shaking his head. 'I didn't want to say it in front of everyone else, I didn't want to embarrass you.'

'Of course you sent them,' she replied in confusion. 'There were two notes, one slipped under my door, the other in the car?'

'Were they signed?'

'No,' she said, narrowing her eyes.

'I haven't been to London for years,' he admitted.

'Truthfully?'

'Truthfully. Listen, when Hal wakes up I'm going to take him to my beach house. There's a book I want him to read. Is that okay with you?'

'Of course it is,' she said unsteadily. 'I can't believe you didn't send me those notes.'

'I'm sorry,' he said, getting up. 'I wish I had.'

'It doesn't matter. The result was the same whoever gave them to me,' she said casually as if it was of little importance.

Once Ramon had left the room she stared down at her camera in bewilderment. Then she felt her stomach plummet as she realized that it could only have been Sam who had sent her the notes. Suddenly it all made sense. He had voiced his concern right from the start. He had confronted her at lunch, then at Nuno's funeral. She hadn't listened. Of course he wasn't going to approach her again, certainly not openly. How obvious it was and yet she had wanted to believe so badly that her father was behind them, she had managed to convince herself. How insensitive of her to give all the credit to Ramon. No wonder Sam had looked so crestfallen.

When Mariana showed her the albums of her childhood and the years that she had missed out, Federica had to force herself to concentrate because all she wanted to think about was Sam. Mariana told her a brief anecdote with each picture in the way old people do who have no concept of time. But Federica was agitated and eyed the telephone. Would it be impertinent to ask to make a call to England? While she half listened to her grandmother's stories she weighed up the chances. When Mariana came across a photograph of Estella, Federica's attention was momentarily diverted while she gazed into the serene face of the woman who had stolen her father's heart. She was beautiful and gentle-looking with the same kind expression and long face as Ramoncito's. She knew instinctively that she would have liked her. The tragedy of her death moved her and reminded her of her own mortality. She had been too young and beautiful to die. She immediately thought of Topahuay and imagined that she must have looked just like Estella. In their deaths Federica recognized the transience of life and the importance to live each moment fully because death could come at any time to steal it away.

Ignacio sat on the terrace talking to Ramoncito and finishing their game of chess. The sun was still hot and occasionally Ignacio would take off his hat and wipe his brow with a white hanky, which he kept in his pocket. Ramoncito would then take the opportunity to let his eyes rest on the beautiful face of his sister when she didn't know that she was being watched. He couldn't wait to tell Pablo and Maria Rega about the sudden arrival of his father's long-lost children. Everything about Ramon fascinated them because he was from another world and yet he had loved their Estella.

When Hal woke up from a long and deep siesta it took him a while to orientate himself. He looked about the room, at the white walls and stark wooden furniture and slowly remembered where he was. His head ached from the heat and his body suffered withdrawals from the alcohol that had nearly destroyed him. He pulled himself up and stumbled into the shower. He let the cool water wash away his exhaustion and any traces of his unhappiness that might have followed him to Chile. When he appeared on the terrace Ramon was waiting to take him to his beach house.

'Is Federica coming?' he asked, when Ramon suggested they go.

'No, just you and me,' Ramon replied. 'I've got something I want you to read.' So Hal followed his father to his car feeling a buoyancy in his step that shamed him, for he was pitifully happy that his father had finally singled him out on his own.

'This was Estella's house,' Ramon explained as they approached. 'I set her up here when she had just had Ramoncito. She loved it by the sea. I love it too.'

'It's charming!' Hal exclaimed, finally finding his voice. 'It's completely charming.' He noticed the abundance of plumbago that crawled up the walls and fell over the roof of the veranda and he noticed the magnificence of the mountains behind. Suddenly he was touched by something that he couldn't understand. 'Does everything here remind you of her?' he asked.

Ramon nodded. 'Everything,' he replied. 'Not a day goes by when I don't think about her at some time or other.'

'I'd like to love like that,' Hal mused wistfully.

'You will one day, I'm sure,' said Ramon. 'You're very young.'

'I know and I have my whole life ahead of me,' he said. 'I've cocked it up so far.'

'There's always time to start again.'

'I want to start again, Papa. And I want to start again here,' he said decisively. 'I can't explain it but I connect with this place.'

'It's in your blood,' Ramon explained.

'Maybe that's what it is,' he agreed. 'In my blood.'

Ramon showed him around the house, grabbed the manuscript he'd written for Helena and a bottle of water and led Hal out onto the beach. They sat down in the waning sunshine and talked, just the two of them, about life and about love. Then Ramon showed him his book. 'I wrote this for your mother and for you and Federica,' he said. Hal took it and flicked through it briefly. 'It's not very long. I'd really like you to read it. No one else has read it yet. I wrote it in English.'

'I'd be honoured,' Hal replied truthfully. 'You really mean that no one's read this yet?'

'No.'

'Why did you write it?'

'Because it was cathartic, because I want Helena to understand where we went wrong.' He hesitated then grinned at Hal. 'Where I went wrong.'

'You've really tortured yourself with this guilt stuff, haven't you?' he said.

Ramon looked at him and laughed. 'Do you think I've overdone it?'

'I don't think you need to flagellate yourself,' he replied and smirked back at him.

'You think I'm flagellating myself, do you?' he said, pushing him playfully on the back.

'A bit. You don't need to feel so ashamed of yourself. Lots of people divorce and leave their children. They survive, don't they? We have, well, just.'

Ramon looked at him with affection and threw his arm around his shoulder. 'You know, for someone who's so unwell you've got quite a mouth on you.'

'I'm glad, I thought I'd lost it.' He chuckled.

'What else did you think you'd lost? Your flippers?'

'You want to swim?' he asked enthusiastically.

'If you'll join me.'

In the magic light of sunset they ran into the golden waters of the icy Pacific. Hal yelped as the cold shot through his body, jolting his senses into focus. Ramon shouted at him to be a man and dive straight in. Following his father's example he dived and felt the water numb his limbs until he was no longer aware of the freezing temperature of the sea. He splashed about, laughing and joking with his father as the gentle waves washed away the turmoil of the last few years. When they finally lay on the sand, drying off in the dying hours of day, Hal knew where he belonged. 'Papa, what if I never go back?' he said, blinking at him with shiny eyes.

'To England?'

'Yes, what if I just don't go back?'

'You'll be where you belong, Hal. Besides, you will have come home,' he said and looked at his son seriously.

'Thank you, Papa,' he breathed, then turned his eyes to the horizon and sighed with contentment. 'I'm home.'

Federica asked Mariana if it would be all right for her to call England. Of course, Mariana was only too happy to lend her the telephone. 'Make as many calls as you like,' she said. 'Your mother will want to know how it's all going.'

But Federica didn't call Helena. She called Sam. The telephone rang for a long while until someone finally picked it up. It was Ingrid. 'Ingrid, it's Federica,' she announced.

'Ah, Fede, darling, how are you?' she asked breezily.

'I'm in Chile,' Federica replied with a suspended heart.

'How lovely.'

'Is Sam about?' she asked.

'No, he's gone,' Ingrid said vaguely.

'Gone?' Federica gasped. 'Gone where?'

'To stay with some old girlfriend, I think.'

'An old girlfriend?'

'Yes, someone he's liked for a very long time. Dear boy, it's about time he started thinking about his future.'

'Yes,' Federica mumbled, but she was barely able to disguise the anxiety in her voice.

'He's not getting any younger,' Ingrid continued, adding to Federica's distress.

'Did he say how long he'd be gone?'

'No, darling, you know Sam! He never lets anyone know his plans.'

'Did he leave a number?'

'No again, darling. Though, I think it's a big house in Scotland if that helps. You know who his friends are better than I. Shall I tell him to call you when he returns?'

'No, it's fine. Just tell him I rang,' she said, swallowing back her disappointment.

Ingrid had just put down the telephone when Sam walked in having taken the dogs out across the cliffs. 'Who was that, Mum?' he asked.

'No one you know, darling,' she said, picking up an orphaned fox cub and stroking its damp fur. 'Someone wanting to know if we had any puppies,' she added, kissing the cub. 'Sadly they're not interested in Little Red, are they, Little Red?' She watched Sam's dejected face and hoped that Federica would realize how much she loved him when she was in danger of losing him. Sam took an apple from the fruit bowl. 'Where are you off to, darling?' she asked, attempting to hide her concern.

'To Nuno's study.'

'You'll lose yourself in there,' she said sympathetically.

'I hope so.'

★

Federica let Hal do most of the talking during supper and retired early to bed. 'You must be so tired, Fede,' said Mariana kindly. 'You have a good sleep and get up whenever you feel like it. You're home now.' Federica went around the table kissing each member of her family with affection. Ramoncito's face burned scarlet once she had placed her lips on his cheek and continued to smoulder like a rekindled coal for the rest of the meal. Hal and Ramon talked with animation, their faces illuminated by the flickering flames of the hurricane lamps. Ignacio caught Mariana's eye and smiled. They understood each other perfectly. Both instinctively felt that Hal would be staying for good, but Federica was distracted, Mariana noticed – it was a woman thing.

Federica had left the shutters open so that the moonlight spilled into her room along with the nocturnal stirrings of the crickets and the sea. She lay in bed watching the shadows slowly creep across the ceiling and thought about Sam. How ironic, she mused, that when she was in England she longed for her father and now that she was in Chile she longed for Sam. She had felt uneasy ever since her conversation with Ingrid. She wondered whom Sam had gone to stay with and found herself suffering an uncomfortable twinge of jealousy deep in the core of her being. She turned over in frustration and lay on her stomach staring out onto the swaying trees and starry sky. She recalled his unshaven face and tormented eyes and wondered whether his silent intervention in her marriage had been inspired by friendship or love. She didn't dare analyze her own feelings for she was afraid of love.

She remembered the long evenings in front of the fire in Nuno's study, discussing literature and poetry, the chilly barbecues on the beach and the brisk walks along the cliff tops. He had been indispensable to her. If he were to fall in love with someone else she'd lose him, and she couldn't bear to lose him. When sleep finally conquered her, dreams persisted in the place of consciousness to torment her. She dreamed of Sam – he was running down the cliff and she was shouting his name, but he didn't hear her and as fast as she ran she couldn't catch up with him. She awoke in the morning as tired as she had been the night before.

The following day Hal sprung out of bed with an energy he didn't know he had. He couldn't remember the last time he had felt so positive about life. He breathed in the scents of his childhood, drawing the air in right to the bottom of his lungs. He had read his father's book, *To Love Enough*, and discovered a powerful story that explained his own path of self-discovery as well as a philosophy on love that would apply to anyone: brothers and sisters, friends, lovers and husband and wife. He had read it well into the early hours of the morning. But he hadn't felt tired. His eyes had continued to scan the lines of prose until the darkness had been burned away by the tender fire of dawn. As he slept his mind had continued to work on the allegory of life and love so that when he awoke he felt his heart had been touched by something magical. Someone, somewhere had given him another chance at life. This time he resolved to live it wisely.

He almost skipped onto the terrace where the sun was dazzling and the smell of toast and coffee so enticing that he inhaled again and reflected on his own good fortune. 'Good morning, everyone,' he said, bending down to kiss his grandmother. 'Where's Papa?'

'He'll be over shortly,' said Mariana. 'We thought it would be nice to have lunch in Zapallar, where you used to eat *locos* at Cesar's, do you remember?"

'Yes, I do,' Hal replied, rubbing his hands together with happiness. 'Very good idea.' He sat down and poured himself a cup of coffee. 'I'm ravenous,' he exclaimed, buttering himself a croissant. Mariana derived enormous pleasure from watching him eat well. The colour had returned to his cheeks, he looked happy and rested. 'Abuelita, I want to learn Spanish,' he said suddenly.

'That can be organized,' she replied, catching eyes with her husband, who put down the paper and began to take an interest in the conversation.

'I'm not going back to England,' he said casually. 'I want to stay here.'

Mariana was unable to hide her delight. She smiled broadly and clasped her hands together. '*Mi amor*, I'm so happy! You belong here,' she said, touching his arm. 'How lovely for Ramoncito to have a brother. What about Federica?' she added.

Hal grinned. 'No, she won't stay,' he said. 'She's in love with someone in England. She just doesn't know it yet.'

It wasn't until the fifth day, when Ramoncito and Hal were deeply engrossed in a game of chess and Ramon and Ignacio were walking along the beach, that Mariana took the opportunity to talk to Federica on her own.

'You've been very distracted in the last few days, Fede,' she said, sitting beside her on the sofa. 'Is it this young man?' she asked.

Federica looked surprised. 'Which young man?' Federica shrugged defensively.

'The one Hal spoke about.'

'How does Hal know?' she exclaimed.

'Perhaps he's been more alert than you think.' Mariana chuckled. 'He's thriving under the Chilean sun,' she added, watching him on the terrace, laughing with Ramoncito as if they had known each other for ever.

'Oh, Abuelita,' Federica sighed in confusion. 'I want to stay here because I so enjoy being with you and Abuelito and it's just wonderful to see Papa again and to have finally put the past behind us. We're friends now. That was all I ever wanted. But . . .'

'But you've grown up, Fede.'

'I've spent the last twenty years yearning for Papa. I'd read his letters when I was unhappy and remember all the strange tales he told me. I clung onto my childhood. I think Torquil was an attempt to find Papa in someone else. Now there's Sam,' she said softly and dropped her shoulders. 'I think I love him.'

'So what's the problem?'

'I think I've hurt him,' she replied gloomily.

'In what way?'

'Well, I adored him as a child. He's seven years older than me, eccentric and clever – there's no one like him in the world, whereas there are hundreds of Torquils. He used to be beautiful, but he's not any more, he's just adorable and lovely. During my marriage to Torquil he wrote me anonymous notes of poetry, which changed my life. He loved me from afar, helped me leave Torquil and supported me once I returned home. I couldn't have done it without him. But I thought the notes were from Papa. I told him so. Then I said . . .' She paused and blushed.

'What did you tell him?' Mariana asked kindly.

Federica squirmed in her chair. 'I told him that I was leaving for Chile, that I didn't know how long I'd be gone because there was nothing in Polperro to make me stay.'

Mariana patted her knee fondly. 'Oh dear,' she sighed. 'I think you'd better go back and tell him how you feel.'

'The thing is, I didn't know how I felt. I didn't dare feel anything for him. I think I said that on purpose, hoping to force him to declare his feelings. But he didn't. He just looked wounded. I can't bear it. I'm such a monster. I realize now that I do care for him. I care very much. What if I'm too late?'

'Why would you be?'

'Because I called his mother,' she said, lowering her eyes, 'she said he had gone away to stay with an old girlfriend and didn't know when he'd be back.'

'Surely you don't believe he could fall in love with someone else so quickly?'

'I don't know. Could he?' Federica asked, eyeing her grandmother hopefully.

'My dear, love isn't something you can turn on and off with a tap. It's not possible. If he loves you he'll be waiting for you. If he doesn't, he won't. And Fede, if he hasn't waited he's not worth the lemon in his *pisco*!'

'What shall I do?'

'Go back to England.'

'But I want to be here with you.'

'Dear girl, Chile isn't the moon. You just call me when you want to come back and I'll arrange your ticket, or Ramon will. This isn't twenty years ago. You're only fifteen hours away.' Then she smiled. 'Perhaps you could bring him with you.'

Federica beamed happily. 'Oh, Abuelita, I hope so,' she enthused and embraced her grandmother. 'Thank you,' she added seriously, looking into Mariana's twinkling eyes.

'No, thank *you*!' replied her grandmother, touching her cheek with a gentle sweep of her old hand. 'This is the way it should be.'

Chapter 42

Polperro

Helena sat on Toby's sofa, sharing a packet of chocolate biscuits with Rasta, smarting after her children's sudden departure to Chile. She munched angrily and imagined their reunion with Ramon and his parents, the beach house in Cachagua and all her memories that lingered there. But by the time she reached the bottom of the packet her thoughts had focused on Arthur and she had barely noticed the digression.

Arthur hadn't made the slightest effort to communicate with her. Not even during the drama with Hal and their subsequent departure. Not a word. She felt desperately isolated and alone. She missed him. She missed his company and his compassion, but what surprised her most was that little by little she began to miss him for the things that she had previously resented: the jolly way he walked, his enthusiasm and brightness, his round girth and his soft doughy hands. Physically he was nothing like Ramon, but her heart yearned for Arthur and she blamed herself entirely for driving him away.

The last few weeks had been painful as she had slowly weaned herself off her delusions. The Ramon in her memory wasn't real. He belonged to a time in the past that had long since dried up and died. She might just as well have been pining for a ghost. All the while she had failed to notice the qualities of the man she had chosen to share her life with, who was real and who needed her. She had been a fool. Like Toby had so wisely said, she never seemed to learn from her mistakes. She was never happy with what she had and only recognized happiness with hindsight. But Arthur had always loved her in spite of her faults. She scrunched up the empty packet and threw it into the fire where it burst into flame and was reduced to ash.

She'd make a new start and this time she'd get it right.

Arthur sat in his office staring out at the blustery street below. It had rained without pause for the last few days, a light drizzle blown about by a vengeful wind. He felt miserable inside, barely able to concentrate on his work, which was unusual as his job had always been an escape from domestic strain. He played about with his pencil, drawing sad faces on his desk notebook. He had told his secretary to take messages; he wasn't in the mood for telephone calls that might require his concentration. All he could think about was Helena. He had hoped she might fight to win him back. Sadly he had misjudged her. He had heard nothing but a screaming silence. Had their marriage really meant so little to her?

He stared at the clock on the wall and watched as the second hand ate its way slowly around the face with methodical regularity. The day had dragged. They had all dragged since the night he had locked Helena out of the house. Her cries still resounded in his ears but he didn't allow himself to feel remorse. He had done the right thing. She hadn't come back so he was now faced with the bleak reality that she wasn't ever going to come back. He had to let her go.

Finally he was able to struggle into his coat and leave the office. He struggled against the wind to his car, then struggled with the traffic to drive home. But most of all he struggled with the impulses that implored him to drop his defences and beg her to come home. Every day was a battle, but so far his determination had won.

It was dark when he arrived home. Gloomily he wondered what he was going to eat that night. He pictured a bowl of cereal or a plate of cheese and biscuits and speculated on the television schedule – there was rarely anything worth watching. Then he noticed the lights on in the house. The cleaner who came twice a week had obviously forgotten to switch them off, which was the least she could do seeing as there was so little work to be done. Helena had needed tidying up after her; Arthur did not. The place was as neat and as dead as a museum. How he longed for his wife's chaos to ruffle the life back into it.

He put his key in the lock and the door. When he stepped inside the aromatic smells from the kitchen reached his nostrils and he recognized at once the familiar whiff of Helena's roast chicken. His breath caught in his throat as his heart accelerated with hope and reserve, in case he should find it a dream and wake disappointed. Without taking his coat off he walked unsteadily up the corridor. He could hear the sound of footsteps and the light clatter of utensils as someone walked about behind the closed door. He dreaded opening it and his trembling fingers hesitated on the handle, aware of the terrible anguish that would follow if he were to discover not his wife but the cleaner, or his daughter or anyone else.

Then he assembled his courage and opened it. When he lifted his eyes he found Helena peering into a steaming saucepan, dressed in a pair of suede trousers and silk shirt protected by her grubby cook's apron. He blinked at her in amazement. She replaced the lid and turned to face him. Her heavily applied mascara could barely conceal her remorse. She smiled at him nervously. But when she recognized the longing in his expression she regained her confidence and walked over to him and drew him into her arms.

Neither spoke. They didn't need to. Arthur pulled her against him and breathed deeply into her softly perfumed neck. They held each other for a long time, appreciating as never before the power of their love. Finally Helena pulled away. She looked into Arthur's shiny eyes and whispered tearfully, 'I'll never behave like that again.'

Arthur stared down at her with intention. 'I know,' he replied gravely, 'because I won't let you.'

Ramon waved as the car carrying Federica to Santiago airport disappeared up the sandy track, leaving behind it a cloud of dust and a cheerful sense of accomplishment. He smiled at her until she was long out of sight and recalled that heartbreaking moment twenty years before when she had waved tearfully goodbye not knowing when she would see him again. But now she was a grown woman she would decide when she would return. He was deeply proud of her and grateful, for they had embraced not only as father and daughter but as friends. He had handed her his manuscript to give to Helena and told her she could read it on the plane. She had embraced her grandparents, Ramoncito and finally Hal. But her tears hadn't been of sorrow but of joy because they had all found each other again and as Mariana said, 'Chile isn't the moon' – it was farewell not goodbye.

Then Ramon drove up to the cemetery to talk to Estella. Ramoncito didn't want to go because he was in the middle of a highly competitive chess game with Hal. 'Tell her I'm with my brother,' he said proudly and Ramon smiled at him and nodded. Chess was a language they both understood.

Ramon parked the car in the shade and walked across the long shadows towards Estella's grave. It was early evening and the rich smells of grass and flowers rose up on the air to mingle with the intangible sense of death that haunted the tranquil cliff top. He paused as he often did at the graves to read the inscriptions chiselled into the stone. One day I'll come up here, he thought, and never go back. The certainty of death didn't frighten him, on the contrary, it gave him a feeling of peace. After all, in an uncertain world it was the only thing one could be sure about.

As he approached the tall green pine tree he saw Pablo Rega sleeping against the headstone with his chin tucked into his chest and his black hat pulled low over his eyes. He greeted him cheerfully with the intention of waking him. But Pablo didn't stir. He remained as still and lifeless as a scarecrow. Then Ramon knew that he had made his final journey and crossed himself. He crouched down and felt the old man's pulse just to be sure. There was no movement in his veins, for his spirit had left his decrepit body and joined those of the people who had gone before him, like Osvaldo Garcia Segundo and, of course, Estella. At that thought Ramon felt an acute twinge of envy. He was aged and alone. His sons would no doubt fall in love just like he had, but Ramon was too old to love again. Estella had tamed his fugitive heart and it would always belong to her.

He would spend the rest of his life living on the memory of love.

Federica watched the Andes mountains simmer below her window as the plane soared into the sky with a rumble that shook her to the bones. She yearned to stay. Like Hal she felt she belonged in Chile, it was in her blood. But she longed for Sam and her longing nearly choked her. She compared the childish infatuation of long ago with the mature love she now felt for him and deduced that her marriage to Torquil had been vital. Without it she would have continued to search for her father in the arms of other men, like Torquil, and she would never have realized that she was a victim of her own making and always had been. Sam had liberated her and she hadn't even thanked him.

When the air hostess came up the aisle with the newspaper Federica took one just to have something to look at, even though she didn't understand the Spanish. She flicked it open and glanced at the first page, relieved to be able to concentrate on something other than her tormented thoughts of Sam. When she saw a photograph of the frozen body of a young Inca girl discovered in the Peruvian Andes she caught her breath and sat up in astonishment.

She turned to the man sitting beside her and asked him if he spoke English. When he replied that he did, she asked him if he would be very kind and translate for her. He was only too happy to engage in conversation with his pretty neighbour and began to read it out loud.

Federica bit her thumbnail as she listened. The mummy was that of a young woman, preserved by the cold conditions of the mountains for five hundred years. She wore a fantastically elaborate cloak made out of the most intricate weave, her hair was still studded with crystals and on her head she still had the remnants of a headdress made of white feathers. It was believed that she had been sacrificed to the Gods. When the man handed her back the paper Federica studied the face of the young girl. She relived the horror of her last moments in the words of her father's story.

'Clasping the box to her breast she was dressed in exquisitely woven wools, her hair plaited and beaded with one hundred shining crystals. Upon her head was placed a large fan of white feathers to carry her into the next world and frighten the demons along the way. Wanchuko was unable to save her.'

After a few attempts to make conversation the man realized that she wasn't going to respond and returned to his book, disappointed. Federica sat staring into the face of Topahuay as if she had seen the Resurrection itself. All these years she had believed the legend in spite of her reasoning that had told her it was a myth. She smiled to herself. Perhaps the butterfly box was magic after all.

Sam woke up early due to the restlessness in his soul and walked across the cliffs with the dogs. He could see the first stirring of spring in the emerging buds that endowed the forest with a vibrancy which seemed to waft through the branches like green smoke. But it did little to lift his heavy spirits. He pulled his coat around his body but the cold came from within and he shivered. He hadn't heard from Federica since she had left the week before and he had the terrible premonition that she might never come back. After all, she had said so herself, there was nothing to keep her here. The potency of those words was in no way diminished by the frequency with which he thought of them and they still managed to debilitate him.

He still hadn't thought of anything to write. It had been years, literally, since he had quit his job in London to make use of his creativity, as Nuno had put it. But his creativity was barren. He had tried once or twice to begin a novel but his mind had drifted to Federica, which had only resulted in the most morose poems about unrequited love and death. So he had picked out books from Nuno's library and instead of writing he had sat in the leather chair and read. Anything rather than surrender his thoughts to the rapacious appetite of his anguish.

Alone on the cliffs in the fragile light of dawn he considered his options if Federica was never to come back. He had to face it. He couldn't allow himself to wallow in self-pity indefinitely. After all, wasn't that what he had taught her by way of the notes? Like a doctor he wasn't too keen on his own medicine. He had to pull himself up, decide on something to write, buy a cottage of his own, perhaps a dog and a pig and crawl out of his self-imposed exile.

★

Federica's journey wouldn't have been as long or arduous if it hadn't been for her feverish impatience that caused her chest to compress with anxiety and her head to ache by the force of her will attempting to change things that it couldn't. The plane was forced to circle Heathrow Airport for twenty minutes before finally landing with a bump. She felt sick from worry as much as from the relentless spiralling of the plane, then hiccuped all the way on the tube to the railway station. It was cold and drizzly, the usual grey skies of London – a cheerless spring. She just managed to catch a train where she sank into a seat by the window and watched the monotonous grey city outside. She closed her eyes for a moment only to open them a few hours later stiff and groggy to find herself passing through the familiar countryside of Cornwall.

As her eyes traced those verdant fields she recalled her long walks with Sam and wondered what she was going to say to him when she saw him. She hoped he'd have returned from Scotland. She knew she'd go out of her mind with frustration if he wasn't at home. Silently she began to rehearse the conversation. 'Sam, there's something I have to tell you . . . no, that's too crass . . . Sam, I love you . . . no, I couldn't, I just couldn't . . . Sam, I realized the notes were from you and came back especially . . . no, no, horrible . . . Sam, I can't believe it's taken me this long to realize that I love you . . . no, I can't, I just can't be so blunt. Oh God!' She sighed, 'I don't know what I'm going to say.'

As the train cut through the Cornish countryside Federica watched the cows grazing in the fields, the charming white houses and small farms and thought how incredibly beautiful it was in spite of the grey skies and rain. She fantasized about living in a small cottage with Sam, perhaps a dog or two, overlooking the sea and she smiled inside. She didn't care for wealth or Bond Street. She didn't care if she never went shopping again. She had certainly had enough handbags and shoes to know just how empty they could be. She yearned to be wrapped in Sam's arms and nothing else mattered.

When the train finally drew up at the station she dragged her suitcase onto the platform and stood in the drizzle. She debated whether to go home to Toby's house, but her impatience drove her to climb into a taxi and head straight for Pickthistle Manor. As the car turned into the driveway her heart pounded in her chest anticipating the disappointment of finding him not there. She looked about for his car but it wasn't parked in its usual place in front of the house. She gulped back her edginess and jumped out of the taxi, instructing him not to wait. If Sam wasn't there she'd call Toby to come and collect her. Besides, it would be nice to see Ingrid. 'Goddamnit,' she murmured, 'I'm fooling myself! If he's not there I just want to be in the house where he's been, sit in Nuno's study where he's sat, feel the echo of his presence in the air and wait.'

She strode into the hall and placed her bag on the marble floor. Then she glanced at herself in the gilt mirror that hung on the wall. She cringed and tried to tidy up her soaking hair and pinch some life into her pale cheeks.

'Sam, is that you?' Ingrid shouted from the landing.

'Ingrid,' said Federica hoarsely. 'It's me, Federica.'

'Fede, darling!' she cried happily, floating down the stairs in a long turquoise dress that reached to the ground. 'We didn't expect you back so soon.'

'Well, I arrived this morning,' she replied, casting her eyes about for Sam.

'You must be exhausted. Poor old you. Do you want a cup of tea or something to warm you up?' she suggested. Then she looked at Federica through her monocle, which enlarged her pale green eye so that it looked like the eye of a monstrous iguana. 'Darling, you're shivering. Really, you don't look very well at all.'

'I'm fine, thank you,' she insisted weakly. 'Is Sam about?' she asked, trying to sound casual.

'He's out with the dogs. He's been out all morning.'

Federica was unable to hide the smile that suddenly opened onto her face like a spring rose. 'Would you mind very much if I went to look for him?'

'You must borrow a coat or you'll die of cold. You won't be any good to Sam if you've died of cold, will you?' she declared, her red lips quivering with delight.

Federica felt the blood rise to her cheeks turning them pink with embarrassment. She followed Ingrid into the cloakroom and took the boots and sheepskin coat she offered her.

'This was Pa's. It's also one of Sam's favourites. If it doesn't keep you warm, Sam will. Try the fox path on the cliff. I imagine he's up there,' she said and watched Federica run outside. In her excitement she forgot to close the door. Ingrid hoped that in her excitement she'd forget to mention Scotland.

Federica ran through the rain not caring how wet she got. The coat made it difficult to run for it was heavy and cumbersome. She searched the cliff top with anxious eyes, scanning the trees and cliffs for any sign of the dogs or their master. 'Sam!' she shouted, but her voice was lost on the wind. 'Saaaam!' She stood helplessly, watching the sea crash against the rocks below and wondered whether he'd be mad enough to venture down to the beach. She recalled her dream and shuddered. Then a movement in the trees made her turn around. She squinted her eyes against the rain and put her hand up to shield her face. First she saw two dogs then the grey figure of Sam in a long coat and hat. He stopped and stared at her. Unsure whether to trust his sight he too squinted and put his hand up to shield his face. 'Sam!' she shouted again.

'Federica?' he replied, and his voice was carried on the wind.

'Sam!' she shouted, walking towards him briskly.

The dogs leapt on her with their tails wagging their entire bodies with enthusiasm and their tongues flopping outside their salivating mouths, breathless and exhausted. She patted their sodden coats, happy that the rain on her face disguised her nervousness.

'Federica!' he called, approaching her. She looked up and blinked at him to clear the rain from her vision. 'When did you get back?' he asked in surprise.

'I—' she began, but the ardour caught in her throat and prevented her from speaking. She looked down at the dogs and patted them again because suddenly she didn't know what to do with herself.

Sam noticed that her hand was shaking. 'Are you all right?' he asked, stepping closer.

She nodded and raised her eyes. She placed her trembling fingers on her lips and swallowed. She wanted to tell him she loved him but all she could do was stare at him mutely while the emotion mounted in her chest.

Sam placed his hand on her arm. 'Did you come back for me?' he asked.

Federica recognized the hope in his voice and she nodded frantically. 'I love you,' she whispered but her voice was swallowed up by the wind. Sam cocked his head. 'I love you,' she repeated, grabbing the lapels of his coat and gazing into his grey eyes with longing. Sam needed no other confirmation of her devotion. He pulled her into his arms and kissed her dripping face. She felt the warmth of his mouth and the rough neglect of his face and closed her eyes so that nothing would distract her from his love.

When Sam made love to Federica in the small room in the attic of the house she realized that she was experiencing for the first time in her life the most intense physical expression of true love. He held her with confidence and gazed into her eyes as if unable to believe that she was really there, reciprocating feelings that he had hidden for so long. Every kiss was a demonstration of his affection, every caress delivered with loving hands. They laughed and talked and then when the weight of their feelings overcame them they cried. So many years of pining prevented Sam from falling asleep. All he could do was watch her soft face while she slept and mentally stroke her until the force of his thoughts penetrated her dreams and she smiled.

Federica opened her eyes onto a different world. She heard the barking of the dogs in the driveway below as the postman threw a couple of Bonios out of his window for them to run after, then made a hasty dash for the porch before beating them back to his car and slamming the door behind him. She heard the tyres on the gravel and then a couple of grating gear-changes as he sped out of the driveway. She stretched luxuriously as her eyes adjusted to the bright sunlight that streamed in through the gap in the curtains, illuminating the unfamiliar walls of a room she had only seen once before, when Molly and Hester had first introduced her to Marmaduke the skunk. Then with a blush she brought her hand up to her face and touched the hot afterglow of love that radiated from her cheeks and she smiled with happiness. She recalled his caresses, his kisses and then the joyous feeling afterwards, as she lay in his arms, that she had finally found love.

She turned to discover a small bunch of early bluebells on the pillow where he had slept, together with a worn brown book. She sat up and brought the flowers to her nose where the scent of spring and the taste of dew made her heart inflate with delight. Then she looked at the book. It was dog-eared and shabby. *The Prophet* by Kahlil Gibran. She opened the cover to discover that it was Nuno's own book with verses encircled in his own unsteady hand and comments written into the margins. She recognized the poetry as the source of the notes Sam had sent her. Then she noticed a bookmark and opened it where indicated. A few lines were highlighted in pencil. She read them carefully, then to fully understand their meaning she read them again.

> Beauty is life when life unveils her holy face.
> But you are life and you are the veil.
> Beauty is eternity gazing at itself in a mirror.
> But you are eternity and you are the mirror.

When Sam entered her room with a tray of breakfast Federica was clutching the bluebells to her nose and reading Nuno's book. She looked up and smiled at him, a smile at once tender and flirtatious. He placed the tray on the dresser and climbed onto the bed beside her. They didn't need to speak for their faces shone with feelings that they could never put into words. He drew her into his arms and knew that this time he would never let her go.

It was a few years before Federica Appleby rediscovered the butterfly box in the back of one of the cupboards in their cottage just outside Polperro.

Sam had successfully published his first book, *Nuno, Brought To Book*, and Federica was pregnant with their second child.

She pulled the box out and brushed the dust off the lid. With a sense of nostalgia grown sweet due to her own happiness and the passing of the years, she leant back against the wall and opened it. She was saddened to see the stones that had once lined the interior lying in a pile on the bottom of the box, exposing the raw wooden walls that once glittered with a magical splendour.

Ponderously, she lifted her eyes to reflect upon the past and saw to her delight a red and orange butterfly alight upon the windowsill. It paused a moment, as if in silent communication, then gently opened its wings, fluttered into the air and disappeared out into the sunshine.

Acknowledgements

I would like to extend my deepest gratitude to my cousin, Anderly Hardy, for her guidance on all Chilean matters and to my husband and family for their advice and support.

Thank you to Suzanne Baboneau and her brilliant team at Simon & Schuster for republishing this book with a beautiful new cover, and to my agent, Sheila Crowley, for her wise counsel.

I would like to thank Gibran National Committee for granting me permission to quote from Kahlil Gibran's *The Prophet*.

Gibran National Committee
PO Box 116–5375
Beirut
Lebanon
Fax (+961 6 1 396921/16)
Email:k.gibran@cyberia.net.lb

Don't miss the brand-new novel by *Sunday Times*
bestselling author Santa Montefiore …

Faced with losing everything, all that matters is …

HERE *and* NOW

Marigold has spent her life taking care of those around her,
juggling family life with the running of the local shop, and being
an all-round leader in her quiet yet welcoming community.
When she finds herself forgetting things, everyone quickly puts it
down to her age. But something about Marigold isn't quite right,
and it's becoming harder for people to ignore.

As Marigold's condition worsens, for the first time in their lives
her family must find ways to care for the woman who has always
cared for them. Desperate to show their support, the local
community come together to celebrate Marigold, and to show
her that losing your memories doesn't matter, when there are
people who will remember them for you …

**Evocative, emotional and full of life, *Here and Now* is
the most moving book you'll read this year – from
Sunday Times bestselling author Santa Montefiore.**

AVAILABLE NOW IN HARDBACK AND EBOOK

**SIMON &
SCHUSTER**

Look out for the *Sunday Times* bestseller from
Santa Montefiore …

The SECRET HOURS

*'Let the wind take me and the soft rain settle me into the
Irish soil from where I came. And may my sins be forgiven …'*

Arethusa Clayton has always been formidable, used to getting her
own way. On her death, she leaves unexpected instructions. Instead
of being buried in America, on the wealthy East Coast where she
and her late husband raised their two children, Arethusa has decreed
that her ashes be scattered in a remote corner of Ireland, on the
hills overlooking the sea.

All Arethusa ever told Faye was that she grew up in a poor farming
family and left Ireland, alone, to start a new life in America as did so
many in those times of hardship and famine. But who were her
family in Ireland and where are they now? What was the real reason
that she turned away from them? And who is the mysterious
benefactor of a significant share of Arethusa's estate?

AVAILABLE NOW IN PAPERBACK AND EBOOK

**SIMON &
SCHUSTER**

booksandthecity.co.uk
the home of female fiction

NEWS & EVENTS | BOOKS | FEATURES | COMPETITIONS

Follow us online to be the first to hear from
your favourite authors

booksandthecity.co.uk

@TeamBATC

Join our mailing list for the latest news, events and
exclusive competitions

Sign up at
booksandthecity.co.uk